IRENE RADFORD
GUARDIAN
OF THE
BALANCE

Merlin's Descendants:

Volume One

IRENE RADFORD
GUARDIAN OF THE BALANCE

Merlin's Descendants:
Volume One

DAW BOOKS, INC.

DONALD A. WOLLHEIM, FOUNDER

375 Hudson Street, New York, NY 10014

ELIZABETH R. WOLLHEIM
SHEILA E. GILBERT
PUBLISHERS

http://www.dawbooks.com

Jacket art by Gordon Crabb.

Map by Michael Gilbert.

DAW Book Collectors No. 1113.

DAW Books are distributed by Penguin Putnam Inc.

Book designed by Stanley S. Drate/Folio Graphics Co. Inc.

First printing, March 1999
1 2 3 4 5 6 7 8 9

DAW TRADEMARK REGISTERED
U.S. PAT. OFF. AND FOREIGN COUNTRIES
—MARCA REGISTRADA
HECHO EN U.S.A.

PRINTED IN THE U.S.A.

Dedication

This book is dedicated to the memory of my father, Edwin Smith Radford, and for my mother, Miriam Bentley Radford. They taught me to believe that I could accomplish anything if only I tried.

And in memory of the original Newynog, a very hungry golden Husky, Mac. She gave me love and companionship above and beyond the call of duty many times over. I still miss you, Puppy.

Map Names

ARTHURIAN ERA:	PRESENT-DAY:
Avalon	Glastonbury
Caerduel	Carlisle
Caerlud	London
Camlann	Cadbury Hill
Deva	Chester
Dun Edin	Edinburgh
Giant's Dance	Stonehenge
The Orcades	Orkney Islands
Saxon Stronghold	Porchester
Venta Belgarum	Winchester

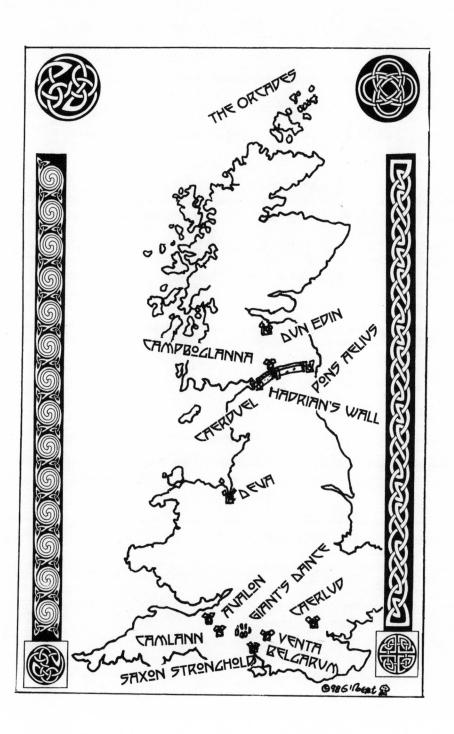

Author's Notes

Any time an author sets about retelling one of the great legends of our culture, she runs into conflicting "facts." Few experts agree on any aspect of the truth behind the myth. I have spent most of my adult life researching King Arthur, Merlin, and Dark Age Britain. My bookshelves overflow with fiction and nonfiction, speculation, and mystical books about these subjects. I'm still not an expert and have had to choose my "facts" to fit my story.

The question of reconciling modern landscapes with ancient documents falls apart with every map. Personal visits to the places listed on the enclosed map helped me get a feel for the lay of the land. There is a sense of continuity in Britain, a sense that if we look hard enough, the past isn't that far out of reach because it is woven into the present and extends into the future. I couldn't have made that wonderful and essential learning trip without all of the research and navigation offered by my husband, as well as his beautiful photographs to record our impressions. Thank you, Tim, for making that trip possible. For twenty-eight years of marriage, love, and partnership, I'll thank him privately.

Where to begin on a book of this depth?

I chose to stick closely to the theories of respected scholar Norma Lorre Goodrich because she offered logical explanations for many of the ideas I believed in my heart. I gleaned bits and pieces from countless other works. And then I let the characters tell their own story.

For this reason Lancelot appears early in the book as a foster brother of the youthful Arthur rather than an adult friend who comes on the scene late. I felt that the bonds of friendship needed to be in place between the two men before Guinevere entered the picture. If you find other discrepancies from your personal view of the legends, please give me the benefit of the doubt and read on. The differences are there for a reason.

The Holy Grail has formed an integral part of the King Arthur legends since the earliest manuscripts. I have made a few references to it but not devoted much time to that particular quest. This is a subject that requires an entire book to itself. Someday. . . .

Thanks need to go to every author who has written on this subject. Besides Dr. Goodrich, I have relied heavily on the works of Stuart Piggot, Geoffry Ashe, R.J. Stewart, and Leslie Alcock, to name just a few of my favorites. There are too many others to list them all. I also need to thank all of the fiction authors who loaned me inspiration and courage to try my own version. Mary Stewart, T.H. White, Marion Zimmer Bradley, Nancy McKenzie, Dafydd ap Hugh, John Jakes and Gil Kane, Sharan Newman, Catherine Christian . . . the list could go on for pages. If your favorite author's name isn't listed here, chalk it up to oversight on my part. The stacks of books are three thick in places, and I couldn't see all of them in one glance.

For the vocabulary I delved into a modern Welsh/English dictionary. Several reference texts actually agree that modern Welsh is close to the dialect spoken in 5th and 6th century Britain—Gaelic with some Latin and Saxon influences. Modern English began as Saxon (Germanic) with an overlay of Norman (French) and now has international influences too numerous to mention. This is the language I speak and had to use to tell my story. Wherever possible I tried to keep the modern words to a minimum and substitute a Welsh word where appropriate.

And wherever possible I have used the oldest place names I could find rather than the Roman or modern names. On the map, I have given you the names used in the book, and on the adjacent page is a listing showing the modern references. Venta Belgarum—Winchester— keeps its Roman name because the town itself grew up around Roman markets and fortifications. Prior to that the people lived atop the nearby fortified hill and only traded on the river. Roman peace and prosperity allowed them to move out of the hill fort and into villas. (Under the Pax Romana the ancient fortifications were demolished.) Caerduel—Carlisle—and Caerlud—London—and other cities, I feel, reverted to the names they had before the Roman conquest until the Saxons dominated the language and political scene.

But don't look for Caer Noddfa on my map or any other. The place exists, but you'll have to find it in your heart, the same way I did.

And then there are the friends who read and reread various drafts of the book. Karen Lewis, Linda Needham, Tim Campbell, Mike Moscoe, and Kim Cook. I can't forget ElizaBeth Gilligan for her tireless search into things magical and demonic and her willingness to share her knowledge. They all offered helpful suggestions as well as arguments for and against various elements of the book. If I failed to put all the pieces together properly, it's my fault, not theirs.

Let's not forget big brother, Ed Radford, either. He gave me the push to write this book when I'd been putting it off for "someday" for about twenty-five years. He reminded me that "someday" never comes and that I should get busy before I ran out of excuses.

Thanks also have to go to my agent, Carol McCleary of the Wilshire Literary Agency. She knows when to push, when to back off, and when to kick me where I most need it. I couldn't have finished this book without her.

Last but certainly not least, I must thank my editor, Sheila E. Gilbert, and her staff. They know what they are doing even when I don't.

I invite you to journey with me through the adventure of a lifetime, back into our distant past. Or is it our future?

Irene Radford
Welches, Oregon

Prologue

KA-THUMP-THM. *Ka-Thump-thm-thm.* The drums echoed Myrddin's heartbeat. Faster and faster the drums beat, calling the college of Druids to Beltane revelries.

Myrddin Emrys stepped into the center of the Giant's Dance. Reverence for the ceremony he was about to preside over tinged the edges of his senses. But something was missing in this time-honored ritual. He watched the revelries taking place all across the broad plain. The huge twin bonfires roared just east of the Heel Stone. The community's livestock had been driven down the processional avenue between the fires to purify them for the coming year.

Woodsmoke, singed hide, and the earthy aroma of livestock bunched together grounded his awareness of his duties. The future and fertility of his community depended upon his proper performance of ritual tonight.

The community danced a serpentine pattern around and between the bonfires. All was in place. Myrddin bent to his task, his ritual knife poised to cut sigils into the dirt—Pridd, the living Goddess.

The four elements, Pridd, Awyr, Tanio, and Dwfr, were present. The omens indicated a season of bounty. He should begin.

Higher and higher the bonfires leaped and danced in imitation of Belenos, the sun. Naked youths broke away from the dance and jumped over the bonfire, defying the growing flames. Red and orange sparks seemed to fly from the bronze torcs encircling their necks. Ale and sacred mead flowed freely among all of the participants. The pattern of life continued in the age-old celebration.

Myrddin downed his third cup of the honey wine, barely tasting the blessing in each swallow. No one should hide from Dana, the

Goddess, tonight by wearing clothing. But he was forced to wear a white robe, woven of the finest virgin wool. He must remain separated from the revelries while presiding over them. Only he among the current generation of Druids had been gifted with prophecy. Only he was commanded to remain separate from the celebration of fertility.

He returned to the solitary ritual the chief Druid must perform.

Ka-Thump-thm. Ka-Thump-thm. The drumbeats called him away from his duties. He deliberately blotted out the images of the annual drunken celebration. He needed concentration to maintain the continuity within the patterns of past, present, and future.

He cut the sigils into the Pridd. Male, female, birth, death, infinity. The same symbols snaked up his arm in vivid tattoos.

Life unfolded in unending patterns of sigils, portents, and choices. Druids interpreted for those who lost sight of their patterns in the midst of the loops and whorls of change. Tonight Myrddin had difficulty finding his own pattern within the sigils he cut into the earth.

Ka-Thump-thm. Ka-Thump-thm-thm.

His concentration wavered as he caught sight of the naked virgins proceeding toward the bonfire through the ritual maze cut into the turf. He needed to join them. Join with them.

To the strongest and bravest of the young men leaping over the bonfires would go the privilege of accepting the gift of virginity from the prettiest maid in the community. Myrddin had never tasted that glorious honor.

The smell of sweat and musky anticipation pulled his concentration away from the sigils.

Tonight the men of the community would scatter their seed among the women. Tomorrow they would scatter different seeds in the freshly plowed fields. Powerful symbolism to entice the blessings of the Goddess.

The wool of his ceremonial robe rasped against his skin. The drums called to him, taunted him with the knowledge his seed would never take root. His gaze lingered on Deirdre, the priestess who led tonight's procession. Sight of her full breasts and gently rounded hips made his palms itch to touch her. A deeper itch grew within him. The mead heated his veins.

He downed another cup of the sacred wine of the Goddess, knowing it would inflame his desire. Yet he needed a degree of alcoholic numbness to proceed with this ritual. Total stupor would make his duties easier, but then the magic would desert him and the symbolism of tonight's ceremonies.

All of Britain needed his sigils, properly and lovingly drawn, to bind together tonight's revelry with tomorrow's planting.

Myrddin turned his back on the sight of Deirdre dancing on the opposite side of the bonfires. Still, the heat of the flames sang in his blood.

Ka-Thump-thm-thm. Ka-Thump-thm-thm. A strong young man prepared to leap over the growing flames of the bonfire. The tempo of the drums built to a driving intensity, inciting the athlete to greater strength and agility.

The drums changed rhythm, creating a new pattern; one Myrddin couldn't interpret. What was different about tonight? Why couldn't he ignore Deirdre's enticing beauty when he had resisted her for most of their adult lives?

Ka-Thump-thm-thump-thm-thm-thm. Faster and faster, the beat echoed in his heart.

His body ached for release. He closed his eyes, begging Lleu for control. Never in his thirty-two summers had the *geas* of celibacy pressed so hard upon him. He couldn't see a pattern in the intensity of his temptation.

Male, female, birth, death, infinity. With the tip of his bronze *athame,* his ritual knife, he traced the lines of the sacred sigils. He concentrated on the embellishments that tied them to Pridd, Awyr, Tanio, and Dwfr. After each straight line, loop, and spiral, he chanted a prayer. The beaten earth surrounding the altar stone of the Giant's Dance became a living tattoo, writhing in the flickering light of bonfires and torches. The living tissue of Dana, the Goddess, parted easily under his sharp blade.

A blast of horns announced the winner of the contest. The last young man to leap the bonfire had bested all other competitors in a triumphant feat. The sleek muscles of his long thighs rippled with power. He raised his arms in victory. His penis rose proudly to meet the challenge before him. He alone would accept the gift of virginity offered by the Queen of the May.

She stepped forward from the array of maiden attendants to meet her champion. Her firm, high breasts brushed against his chest as she stood on tiptoe to kiss his cheek in acceptance of him as her consort tonight.

Myrddin's chest burned beneath his robe as if the virgin pressed her body against him and not the local champion. The Queen of the May trembled in excitement. Moisture slicked her brow and the pale hair between her thighs. The throb in Myrddin's groin intensified. The last rays of the setting sun gave the girl's smooth, dewy skin a lovely blush. Myrddin held his breath lest he gasp aloud at her perfect, ripe beauty.

The fertility of the fields was too important to risk a less than perfect couple performing the symbolic joining of Pridd and Sun, Dana and Belenos.

The serpentine dance of naked couples wound past the bonfires toward the thirty standing stones for the ritual offering. Myrddin completed the sigil for infinity and enclosed them all in three entwined circles of sacrifice, blessing, and continuity.

Ka-Thump-thm-thump-thm. The drums preceded the naked celebrants into the sacred circle of standing stones just as the sun touched the horizon. Myrddin's erection pounded in tempo with the drums. Heat built within him. He couldn't watch. He had to watch. 'Twas his duty to preside over the ceremony.

The processional dance led by Deirdre, lovely Deirdre, entered the circle of standing stones. Myrddin stood beside the altar stone, waiting. He smelled the musk of anticipation on each of the celebrants. Honeysuckle and wild rose perfume drifted around the Queen of the May from her crown of fresh flowers, now slightly askew from her first enthusiastic embrace of her lover. She scooted onto the altar stone with little assistance from her attendants. Eagerly she spread her legs, Pridd ready for the first plowing.

Her mate, now wearing the sun-face mask of Belenos, joined her. Cheers and encouragement from the eager audience drowned out the driving rhythm of the drums.

Deirdre stood beside Myrddin now, living embodiment of the Goddess, blessing this union.

Myrddin closed his eyes in a desperate attempt to keep from pushing the priestess onto the altar stone and driving into her as the drums set the rhythm. *Ka-Thump-thump-thump-thmmmmmmm.*

"Lleu give me strength and understanding," he prayed. He couldn't leave until the couple finished. A bath in the cold waters of the River Avon might help him enforce self-control. But he couldn't leave yet, when he most needed to leave. The chief Druid had to preside and bless the ritual, lest he break the pattern.

Ka-thump-thump-thump. Drums beat. For near an eternity. Horns blared in strident completion.

Myrddin opened his eyes and blinked hard. Sun collapsed upon Pridd, man upon woman, spent and replete. The scent of sex permeated the ever-present smell of woodsmoke and mead. The remaining worshipers of Belenos and Dana paired off into couples ready to complete their own ceremonies of fertility.

One solitary woman remained within the circle of standing stones. Deirdre. The very image of Dana. Lush breasts bursting with life. The dusky nipples tightened from emotions Myrddin didn't need to interpret. She opened her arms in invitation. Her full rounded hips strained forward, eager for his thrust. A dark cloud of hair haloed the delicate features of her face. Another thatch shadowed the secrets between her thighs. A hint of her unique musky scent mingled with the flowers, the smoke, and the heat, whispering to him of joy.

Myrddin gulped and stared at the forbidden treasures that teased his senses. His blood boiled, demanding an escape from too small vessels. "I can't," he said through dry lips.

"On Beltane, the Goddess presides. The Goddess must be obeyed," she said huskily. A slightly drunken giggle followed her pronouncement.

She danced a serpentine pattern around him, winding ever closer. Her hand brushed against his sleeve, exposing the twisting tattoos on his arms. Another circle, closer yet. The tips of her ripe breasts rippled against his back. And then she was in front of him, hips thrust forward, almost touching the proud bulge of his penis, separated by only his thin robe. The scent of spring flowers and freshly plowed Pridd followed her seductive spiral dance.

He reached to grab her, pull her closer yet. She danced away, elusive, demanding, mysterious, exotic.

Ka-Thump-thm-thm-thump-thm-thm. His heart raced faster than the drums.

Too much. The temptation gnawed at his willpower. His golden torc seemed to squeeze the breath from his throat. "Dana, forgive me. I can't!"

The gods had declared him a celibate prophet. All Britons needed his gift to guide them through the turbulent years to come.

He closed his eyes to block out the lusty images that plagued him. Behind his eyelids, Dana/Deirdre continued to dance. Her presence banished all thoughts except his need for her.

"Come with me, Myrddin Emrys. Come," she whispered as she twined her fingers with his own. "I rule tonight, not Lleu. Come, Myrddin Emrys."

"Ah, Deirdre," he murmured. He had pledged obedience to her when she became The Morrigan, high priestess of all Druids. He wanted nothing more than to plunge himself deeply inside her, pounding into her in the same rhythm as the drums, and spilling his seed into her receptive body.

Ka-Thump-thm-thm-thm-thump-thm-thm-thm.

"Come into the faery ring. The faeries will bless us," she whispered huskily, then claimed his mouth in a searing kiss. She smelled of Pridd, clean and fertile. Her mouth tasted of honey mead and yearning.

No man, least of all Myrddin Emrys, could deny The Morrigan, living symbol of the Goddess on Beltane. 'Twas every man's sacred duty to honor her with fertility tonight. He followed her outside the circle of standing stones to the edge of the grassy plateau. Just beyond them, the Great Ditch and Bank marked the perimeter of the sacred site and the boundary of tonight's celebration.

His robe fell to the ground as he stepped into the perfect circle of mushrooms. The faery ring mimicked the huge Giant's Dance in smaller dimensions. *Ka-thump-thump-thm-thm. Thump-thump-thm-thm.* The pulsing intensity built within his erection. *Ka-thump-thump-thump.* The drums guided his hands as he worshiped her body. The intense rhythm drove his thrusts.

So sweet, nearly painful. Deirdre cried out in ecstasy. Myrddin plunged onward, circling, spiraling into harmony with sun, moon, stars, and Life. . . .

The Great Wheel of stars and moon showed the hour almost midnight when Myrddin withdrew from the damp sweetness of Deirdre's body for the third time, exhausted and replete.

"Ye'll not leave me yet?" Deirdre stroked him with knowing fingers.

His flesh responded to her ministrations with a slight quiver. She smiled and continued coaxing him with hands and mouth.

"Later, Deirdre, love. I need a rest." He disengaged himself from her and stepped outside the faery ring of mushrooms. "My priestly duties call. I'll come to your bed when I can, before dawn." He bent over the unbroken faery circle to kiss her one more time.

Ka-Thump. Ka-Thump. The drum slowed as did his heartbeat.

Perhaps the gods, Lleu in particular, had not noticed his lapse. Dana and Belenos reigned during this festival of Life and Tanio.

Deirdre pouted, her big dark eyes luminous with continued desire. She lifted herself onto one elbow. With shoulders thrust back, her full, round breasts rose sharply, nipples erect, enticing. Droplets glimmered in the firelight against the dark thatch between her thighs. Thick, lustrous curls to match the curly mane of hair that fell nearly to her hips.

"Don't leave me yet, Myrddin Emrys!" The Morrigan commanded, clinging to the folds of his robes. "We've barely begun."

Her face blurred and re-formed into the laughing image of Belenos. The sun god had used her to trap Myrddin, a favorite of Lleu, the god of art and music.

"You promised to return 'ere dawn," Deirdre reminded him. "May the gods curse you if you break a promise made inside a faery ring."

Fear overrode Myrddin's lust and carried him away from the faery ring. He strained his long legs beyond comfort, running across the boulder-strewn field toward the ring of standing stones.

"Dana preserve me," he pleaded with every harsh breath. Rough stones bruised his bare feet as he raced over the broken ground. The Giant's Dance loomed ahead. Almost within reach. Wavering flames and shifting shadows masked and blurred directions.

"Belenos tempted me away from my destined path. He is the strongest on this night of his festival. Let him guide me back." With this last prayer, Myrddin leaped through the nearest archway and fell. . . .

"Welcome, Myrddin Emrys. Welcome to the Underworld." The disembodied eagle face of Lleu rose up in the blackness surrounding Myrddin. The predatory gleam of a raptor on the hunt brightened his dark eyes. Behind the god, the roots of the Worldtree tangled in the abyss, reminding Myrddin that the punishment for breaking his geas of celibacy was hanging nine days upon the Tree. Nine days without water or companionship to ease the pain.

"I shouldn't be here. This isn't my time!" The absolute wrongness stabbed into Myrddin's mind and heart. His body seemed to have dissipated in the endless blackness of the abyss. He couldn't find his hands to make emphatic gestures or tear his hair. Only his mind and soul remained, drifting endlessly in—nothing.

The acrid smell of sulfur and the musty smell of rotting wood and leaves told him that some of his senses still lived. He wasn't dead yet. He had a chance to live and return to Deirdre before dawn, as he had promised.

"The gift of prophecy denies you the privilege of laying with a woman. A fair exchange. You broke that geas. You belong to me now." Lleu's melodic voice resounded through the nothingness as he transformed into his manlike form. His long nose and shifting eyes reminded Myrddin of the eagle persona the god assumed at will. Like the Goddess who was Dana, mother of all, as well as Andraste, the warrior queen, Lleu took several forms. Nothing showed of Lleu's other guise, a meek hare that foretold the future. Myrddin knew how and where to stand to divert a running hare. But no man could keep an eagle from relinquishing its focus while its prey remained within sight.

A space of light spread around the god to include Myrddin. Solid ground supported them. Myrddin's body became a wisp of shadows, clothed in his white Druid robe. The tattoos on his arm glowed through the robe, grim reminder of his priesthood and duty to the gods. He'd not solidify or dissipate fully until judged.

The Worldtree stood at the very edge of this temporary reality, half in the light and half in the abyss. Cernunnos, horned god of the Underworld, waited for him within the tangled branches of the Tree.

The smell of sulfur ceased biting his senses but lingered.

"He belongs to me as well." Belenos stepped into the light. " 'Tis my night. I claim a piece of his soul." His radiant visage dripped sheep's blood from the sacrifices offered to him this night. His black eyes opened into a passage into the abyss. He carried the acrid scent of burning blood and rotten wood with him. The smells of death.

A round judgment table and four high-backed chairs appeared in the center of the circle of light. Belenos took a seat in the chair representing East—the position of his rising power. Lleu sat to the West. The Worldtree hovered between them. Cernunnos peeked out from the shadowy branches, patient, knowing that eventually all life passed through his realm.

The Goddess appeared as Dana, draped in flowing robes that outlined Her femininity in maddening secrets, the persona of love and life perpetual. "He also belongs to me. 'Twas at my behest he made himself vulnerable." The voice of all women wove into the tapestry of sound and blinding light emanating from Her.

If She had chosen to be Andraste, the warrior queen clad in golden armor and carrying a flaming sword, Myrddin would have known doom. Dana gave him hope. She chose the position of North for Her throne.

South remained empty. Myrddin wouldn't sit there unless they found him innocent. Only then did he realize his golden torc, the symbol of his manhood and priestly office, didn't encircle his neck.

"I have duties to fulfill and promises to keep," Myrddin protested. "You chose me to make Arthur a king worthy of Britain and the gods. I, and I alone, must provide him with a warband ready to follow his lead. You entrusted his education and training to me. He is still too young to abandon. I must fulfill your tasks."

"Arthur's identity remains secret, as we chose," Belenos said. "Lord Ector and his family protect him and train him as appropriate to his age and status. The other Beltane sons you have placed into similar foster homes thrive as well. Arthur will rise to greatness of his own accord without your interference." The light radiating from Belenos' sun-face nearly blinded Myrddin.

"You can teach him many things," Myrddin challenged the god. "But can you show him how to give many factions common ground? Can you give him the sense of continuity that will insure those rival factions agree on his leadership? You chose me for that task. No other can complete it as I can." He swallowed his fear as the fervor of his mission overtook him. "And what of the college of Druids? Our numbers decrease every year as the Christians grow more numerous. The magic and the prophecy you gave me diminishes as well. The followers of the White Christ will not honor you. I must help fill the empty places in the circle, or the rituals will mean nothing and you will fade into nothingness," Myrddin stated.

"You should have thought of that before you broke your vow of celibacy," Lleu answered. "Celibacy is required of those who are gifted with visions of the future." The South chair began to fade into the mist and shadow of the Underworld.

"A gift imposed upon me before I was old enough to know what it meant or use it properly. Most people don't learn to use their gift until they are adults, have lived a full life, sired or borne children. My gift was imposed upon me before the age of five."

"We have our reasons for keeping you separate from women. Now you must face the consequences of your disobedience," Belenos chortled.

"What of Arthur? You chose him as you chose me for special destinies."

"Your destiny can no longer be fulfilled by you. We must find another." Lleu stood, his eagle's wings grew and his fingers became talons, ready to rip out Myrddin's throat.

Myrddin refused to believe that this was the end of this life. He could still complete any task the gods set for him. Arthur was too important to Britain's future to abandon. One night of passion in honor of the Goddess shouldn't negate a lifetime of faithful work for the gods.

"We must train another to insure the continuance of our kind." Dana bowed her head sadly. "The faeries will help us. If your successor fails, we, the gods, will be forced to abandon your world for another dimension, and so will the faeries. As we speak, the portals between worlds dim and grow weak. Other portals open wider. A balance must be maintained."

"Isn't the propagation of children the way to insure that our way of life, our beliefs, our unity with all life continues through the ages?" Myrddin pleaded with her.

"Our people must face the Christians first." Lleu stood, fists clenched against the table of judgment. " 'Twill take a special child with intense training to survive the strength of their missionaries."

"The Romans massacred all but a handful of us. Can the followers of the White Christ do worse? They are meek. They carry no weapons. They shout peace and love from the hilltops. We should join them, show them the beauty of our ways. Together we would become invincible," Myrddin said, his voice falling into the pattern of song and story.

"Had you honored your geas, protected your gift of prophecy with celibacy, you could have been the bridge between two faiths." Lleu sat down again, once more fully a man.

"I still can—with or without my gift. It is only a tool, not a necessity to my life."

"The Christians respect marriage and fidelity. They do not understand our reverence for the Beltane Festival, and so you have been kept separate from it. They cannot and will not respect and listen to you, an active participant in a ritual they abhor."

"One lapse, in honor of Dana, the one who is all of you *and* all mortal life combined, need not establish a pattern for the rest of my life. For centuries The Merlin and The Morrigan have shared the guidance of Britain, as a couple, joined in purpose in rituals more binding than marriage. I have always considered Deirdre my spouse though I have not lain with her until tonight."

He paused to gather his wits. The gods remained silent, listening, waiting for a better argument.

"I am a bard and a magician. I can help blend the best of our ways with the best of Christianity. Is not their Mary, the mother of Jesus, another manifestation of the Goddess? Is not the respect for all life as their god's creation similar to ours, as well as the cycle of birth, life, death, and rebirth? Do they not invoke Pridd, Awyr, Tanio, and Dwfr in their rituals as do we? The pattern of our joint effort is clear. United, with Arthur leading us, we can drive back the Saxons who threaten Britain and you," he sang as if retelling a great epic. His voice swelled and filled the void with the majesty of his destiny.

Images of glorious battle and victory flitted around the circle of light. Bright banners among the ranks of soldiers depicted all of the gods marching with them.

Dana watched the future unfolding before them and nodded.

"You have the silver tongue of a bard," Belenos laughed, banishing the images.

"And the wisdom of a magician to find and interpret the patterns of life beyond the restriction of time," Lleu added, bringing the visions back.

"And the charm of a diplomat," the Goddess smiled. She plucked the banner bearing her image from the visions flickering about them, gathering it to her breast.

Light filtered into the abyss.

"You chose my destiny before I was born. You chose *me* to make Arthur Ardh Rhi, the High King who will save Britain and both religions," Myrddin pleaded one last time.

"Your arguments have been heard." Lleu's presence grew stronger as the others receded. "For the well-being of Arthur and our people, I forgive this one lapse. We mark your body as a perpetual reminder of your geas against women. We charge you to continue your tutelage of Arthur and those who will form his warband, to raise your successor, and keep your pledge to Deirdre. You promised to return to her before dawn. In your heart you offered love and protection. That oath continues to her child. You must protect the child who will maintain the balance of open and closed portals between dimensions."

"Child? We conceived a child this night?" Myrddin sat heavily in the South chair at the stunning news. "A child to carry my heart and knowledge into the next generation, and the next."

"A child you must protect at all costs. Deirdre cannot survive the birthing." The image of Lleu faded along with the judgment table and the other gods. "On the day the child is born and Deirdre leaves her earthly body, you and your child must go into exile from your college of Druids. But remember . . ." The booming voice that had moments ago filled the abyss receded as the tide. "Next time, we will not forgive. Next time . . ." Lleu's words faded into a breath of wind.

Myrddin fingered the suddenly heavy torc returned to his neck.

"I need the child," Dana whispered into his mind. "The child is why I tempted you. Your descendants form an important part of the pattern of life. Remember your promise in the faery ring."

Chapter 1

"CURYLL!" I jumped up and down in excitement. My friend trudged up the hill toward Da and me. Our summer-long trek through Britain was over. Da and I would spend the cold months with Curyll's foster father, Lord Ector. As we had all eight winters of my life.

Autumn had come early this year. I awoke this morning to find dew had frosted on my blanket. The rags binding my feet barely kept the frost off my toes as we walked the final league to Lord Ector's home outside Deva.

The air smelled of cold, wet, salt.

"Winter chases the wind like a hound on the heels of a hare," I sang, trying very hard to make my voice sound like the wind in the trees. Da did that much better than I.

I didn't want to think about the many hundreds of people who had no shelter or food this winter. Here in the Northwest we were secure from Saxon raiders. Soon I would be warm and safe. Safe from the Saxons and from the Christians who threw rocks at Da and me.

Four huge hunting dogs galloped around my friend Curyll in circles that moved forward and sideways at the same time. As usual, the three brown hounds looked to the larger, shaggy black-and-gray Brenin as their leader. Brenin looked to Curyll for direction.

Joy at finding my friend alive when storm, disease, and Saxon raiders claimed so many, wasn't enough to warm me. I longed for the heat of kitchen fires—any fire, even one of my own making. But Da didn't allow me to show off that trick. My bouncing almost warmed my nearly numb feet while I rubbed my fingers against my hide cloak. I'd missed Curyll terribly this past summer.

Curyll lifted a hand in mute greeting to us. He had another name, one that I could never remember. I didn't want to remember our real names and didn't like my own.

Real names are what parents use when they are angry at you. I'd seen my Da in a rage once. I didn't want to see him that way ever again.

"Another half hour to Lord Ector's stronghold, little Wren. Then we'll be warm," Da said. His deep voice seemed to sing each word. He didn't need the harp he carried in a satchel on his back to make music. But everyone recognized the harp as a symbol that transformed us from beggars to bards.

I had learned eight fun ballads this past summer. One for each year of my life—not quite the nine complex history ballads required to call myself a bard. Four of my songs I could sing all by myself—the other four I needed a little help remembering all the words and to cover the notes I couldn't quite reach. Maybe tonight Da would ask me to sing a solo.

"Blow your nose, Wren." Da handed me a square of almost clean linen. He wasn't angry that my nose ran with the cold or that I had fussed and whined all afternoon.

"The Wind whistles through the heather, telling tales of the cold ocean sharpening its teeth." I chanted a line from another ballad. The tune didn't come out of my raw throat as easily as before.

Clear blue skies sparkled in the afternoon sun. But the weight of clouds building to the West gave me a headache. Damp salt in the air burned the raw patches on my nose. By sunset the storms would come. We would be snug and dry in Lord Ector's fortress before the rain beat the last of the harvest into the ground.

Da folded my small hands in his huge ones and rubbed some feeling into my fingertips. This gesture of love did more to warm me than bright fires.

"May I ride on the back of Brenin, Da?" I asked politely.

"You are much too big, my Wren."

"I rode him last year." I tried very hard not to thrust out my lower lip and screw up my eyes in an ugly face. I used to do that all the time until Da made me look into a still pool so I could see what I looked like. Ugly. Scary. I saw more in the pool than my own scowl. I saw Gwaed, the god of blood, Tanio, the element of fire, and myself grown old and sad. But I didn't tell Da that. I didn't want to scare him.

"Ho, M—Merlin!" Curyll's voice echoed across the moors. I didn't expect my friend to say anything and was surprised at the clarity of his words. Had he practiced speaking with one of his foster brothers? Most likely Lancelot the stinging bee, Curyll's best friend in the world. But if Stinger was busy, then probably Bedewyr, Ceffyl the horse as we called him, or Cai the nearsighted boar had listened politely while Curyll formed each word with time-consuming care. Of all of the boys at Lord Ector's stronghold, Stinger, Boar, and Ceffyl were closest to him in age.

Curyll had used Da's traveling name rather than his real name— that was reserved for the other Druids. We were all birds. Merlin, small falcon. Curyll, a much bigger and fiercer hawk. And I was the little brown Wren, not much to look at, but a very sweet singer—I hoped. The other boys had animal names. They weren't birds. Bards and birds were special.

"Curyll." Da waved to the boy. "Good hunting today." He pressed my back, urging me forward. I ran ahead, eagerly.

Curyll wore hunting leathers. A brace of birds hung from his belt. He'd slung two more across his back on a thong. He smelled of sweat and earth and crushed grass. A bright cap confined his usually tangled hair. The late afternoon sunshine peeking beneath the growing cloud cover picked gold and silver out of the sandstone color. I never tired of watching sunlight dance colors through his hair.

Lord Ector wouldn't let Curyll have lessons because he didn't speak. But Curyll could trounce all of his foster brothers with sword and lance. His big hands seemed just the right size to cradle a fledgling bird without ruffling a feather. And he always treated me with kindness when his foster brothers were too rough with a small girl child who didn't belong to the fortress.

I knew Curyll was as smart as his foster brothers. They tolerated his supposed stupidity because he was the orphaned son of a respected warlord. I loved him for himself.

Curyll greeted me with a hug and picked me up and swung me in a wide circle. Only thirteen, he carried me easily. His back would be almost as good to ride upon as one of the shaggy dogs who stood taller than I did. He smelled better than wet dog fur, too.

"Sit, beasts!" Da said to the dogs. Brenin and the other hounds continued sniffing Da's leather leggings and boots, catching up on all the gossipy scents he'd gathered in the last year. "I said *sit!*" Da fingered his gold torc with his left hand and pointed at Brenin's nose with his right. All four dogs sat and stared obediently at Da.

Curyll and I giggled. No one else, including Curyll, could command the hunting hounds so well.

Our joy at seeing each other couldn't overcome my cold. I sneezed. Messily. But Curyll didn't flinch or drop me in disgust. He shifted his grip on me so that I could wipe my nose once more.

While I mopped my nose and his shoulder, he spoke again. "Ll–Lly–," he stopped, unable to force out the next words.

"Did Llygad have puppies?" I asked, noticing the fifth dog missing from the pack. Llygad belonged to Boar, but she, like the other hounds, looked to Curyll as leader of the pack.

He nodded, smiling that I understood.

I giggled at the prospect of playing with a dozen wiggling bundles of fur.

A deep frown replaced Curyll's grin, and he set me down—not ungently, but with little warmth.

"I didn't mean it, Curyll. I laughed at the puppies, not you. I promise I'll never laugh at you." I spun in a circle on my toes to seal the promise. Circles have no beginning and no end, and neither does a promise. He hugged me again.

"Come." Da herded us toward Lord Ector's caer. Long shadows stretched out from the battlements. "The sun is near to setting and clouds gather. We'd best hurry or miss our supper."

"A–ah–" Curyll halted our progress. He blushed and gulped before making elaborate motions with his hands. He signed the cross of the Christian god, then placed his palms together in front of him as if in prayer.

"Priest?" Da interpreted.

My stomach turned cold. I had thought Lord Ector would protect us from the Christians who threw stones.

Curyll nodded at Da, then made motions as if eating but then stopped and made the signal to halt.

"Has Ector invited a priest to supper and we must stay in the kitchen?" Da's face turned dark with an anger that frightened me. His blue eyes, the same color as the sky at midnight, darkened to the uncertain froth of a storm-ravaged sea. (I'd heard that phrase in one of Da's hero ballads and liked it.)

Curyll hung his head in apology. I edged toward my friend and tried to hide behind him. As I edged around, I noticed he didn't wear his warrior's torc about his neck. A torc was more than a piece of jewelry. The circle of metal was a symbol of manhood and a person's status in the community. Warriors never removed theirs. Curyll had won his last autumn in a tournament. Boar hadn't won his torc until a month later. Stinger and Ceffyl were a year younger, and I didn't know if they had won theirs yet or not.

Da grasped the fat end of his own golden torc in a familiar gesture. His grip seemed to help him master his anger. His temper hadn't sent magic flying from his fingers. He continued, "Why a priest, Curyll? Your foster father has always been faithful to the Goddess and the old ways."

Curyll pointed to his tongue and dropped his gaze to the heather.

"I should have expected this, Curyll. You near the age of manhood and will claim your inheritance soon. Lord Ector must be desperate for you to learn to speak properly. He's invited the priest to exorcise a demon from you."

Exorcise. I didn't like the sound of the ugly Latin word. What would the priest do to Curyll? I hoped it didn't have anything to do with stones.

Da glared at the increasing clouds streaked with the red of sunset as if they were responsible for the priest and Curyll's stutter. Slowly his eyes cleared and brightened. "I have been remiss in allowing your impediment to continue so long. Has the priest arrived yet?"

Curyll shook his head.

"Perhaps we have time. The storm might delay him." Da continued to scan the skies for answers.

I tugged on Da's cloak. "Curyll doesn't have a demon in his tongue. The kitchen cat stole the spirit out of it."

Da lifted one eyebrow at my comment. I loved that gesture and tried to imitate it. I couldn't do more than twist my face in a grimace.

"I told you so last winter, but you didn't believe me," I replied, wanting to stamp my foot in frustration.

Laughter lit Da's eyes. I loved how he looked when he did that.

Their deep blue color invited me to gaze deeper into his soul and trust him.

"Yes, you did tell me that, Wren. Perhaps you are right. I must study the cat."

"I can tell the cat to give it back."

"Can you now? Then we must hurry." Da gestured to Curyll. They each took one of my hands and lifted me high as they ran down the hill laughing.

Merlin clasped his daughter's hand, checking for signs of fever. He hadn't liked the way she had dragged behind him all day. Normally he and Wren chatted and laughed together as they walked through Britain, observing the world. Her childish sense of wonder gave him new perspectives on commonplace events and sights. But today Wren had refused to find delight in an arrowhead of geese flying south. She had complained of the cold instead.

Now she sneezed, and her nose leaked. Her palm remained cool but moist. If she ailed, the sickness hadn't settled yet.

With a sigh of relief he nodded to Curyll and together they swung the little girl above a tussock of grass. She squealed with delight. Another sneeze and a cough followed hard upon the heels of her giggles.

She mustn't be sick. Not now when he thought her grown beyond the dangers of early childhood. He'd almost lost her twice in her first five winters, once to a terrible hacking cough and fever that kept her in bed nearly an entire winter, and once to a terrible wasting sickness that had besieged half of Britain the summer she turned two. Only his skill with medicine had saved her. Wren was so very precious to him, he didn't know how he'd continue without her.

Curyll was special, too, but to protect Wren, Merlin would forsake the boy and all of the other young men he monitored. Wren— Arylwren, a pledge. He'd promised to protect this child at all costs.

She giggled merrily as they set her back down on the ground. Just like her usual cheerful self.

Merlin's heart swelled with love and pride. His worries about her receded into the back of his mind.

They continued downhill another few paces before setting foot on the road. Normally Merlin preferred to keep to the hidden ways over

the hills. He checked on the ancient sacred shrines scattered throughout Britain as he traveled on Ardh Rhi Uther's business—and his own.
But to approach a caer, even one owned by a friend, required some
ceremony and care.

He tugged Wren's hand to the right onto the road rather than
continue across the nearly trackless hills. They should approach formally through the front gate rather than slipping in through the postern like a servant or beggar—or even family.

Curyll shrugged at the change of direction and continued with
them.

One hundred paces farther, the road branched. The left-hand fork
continued North to Deva. The right led up the tor to the fortress that
commanded a view of the surrounding valley.

A bustle of activity upon the point of the crossroad attracted Merlin's attention. Garoth, Lord Ector's second son, directed half a dozen
others in some kind of construction project.

Curious. What kind of shrine could they be erecting at a sacred
crossroad when all that was needed was a clear space for travelers to
leave offerings for safe passage?

"Curse these aging eyes, I can't quite make out what they are
doing!" Merlin moaned.

"You aren't old yet, Da." Wren squeezed his hand. "You just
spend too much time squinting at old scrolls whenever you find them.
Usually in bad light. I told you to light another lamp."

"Always the little mother, Wren." Merlin chuckled. "You look
after me very well. But trust me, I am old enough to lose some of my
keenness. This gray hair tells no lies."

The little girl looked at him skeptically. Sometimes she was just
too wise and observing for her age.

"Curse you, Mihail!" Garoth shouted at a roughly clad laborer.

Mihail dropped to his knees, cradling his left hand. He mumbled
something Merlin could not hear. Garoth slammed his boot into the
man's ribs.

"If you aren't fit to work, why does my father continue to feed
and protect you?" Garoth kicked again. Red rose from his cheekbones
to his forehead. Anger pulled his mouth down and made him narrow
his eyes.

The other men backed away from Garoth and Mihail, revealing
the intricately carved stone crog—a Christian cross—they had been

erecting. It stood on its base tilted to the left and twisted so that it faced half-east rather than due south to the fork in the road.

Merlin froze in his tracks. The crog was a thing of beauty, worked by loving hands. It stood half again as tall as a tall man. A circle joined the four arms and a huge polished green stone had been set into the boss.

"Stop it! Stop it, stop it," Wren cried. She wrenched her hand free of Merlin's grasp and ran to Garoth. Fists beating wildly at his side, she began kicking him with her rag-wrapped feet. Her blows against Garoth's thick boots and leggings must have hurt her more than her victim.

"What is this?" Merlin hurried forward.

Curyll made some inarticulate sounds of warning. Merlin didn't have time or patience to decipher what the boy needed to say.

But he knew a moment of disappointment mixed with fierce pride that his eight-year-old daughter had rushed to rescue the laborer when Curyll, training to be a marchog—a mounted warrior, hung back.

"Oh, it's you," Garoth sneered at Merlin and Curyll. He hardly noticed the girl pounding on him. "Get back to work, all of you!" he shouted to the others who continued to ease distance between themselves and Garoth's anger.

Merlin recognized a few of the laborers as tenants of Lord Ector. The three slighter built among them turned out to be Cai, Ector's youngest son, Lancelot, and Bedewyr, foster boys near Curyll's age.

And all three had the self-confidence to lead other warriors. Curyll wouldn't do it because he could not speak. The situation needed a remedy soon.

"I thought Lord Ector honored the old ways," Merlin said. He fought to keep his face impassive and betray none of the disappointment and . . . and hurt this crog represented.

Almost absently he grabbed Wren by her collar and pulled her back beside him. She continued to fuss and strain to reach Mihail.

"Well, the old ways didn't get us what we need. You'll find your welcome much cooler this year, Merlin—if not out in the cold. Father has a priest coming, and he wants to make sure the man is welcomed." Garoth swung his left foot back in preparation for kicking Mihail again.

The hapless laborer continued to kneel in the road holding his left hand close against his body, supporting it with his right. Pain made his face pale and moist. He sank his teeth into his lower lip to avoid crying out.

In a move too fast and unanticipated for Garoth to counter, Merlin grabbed Garoth's foot, lifting it high enough to threaten the younger man's balance.

Wren neatly inserted herself between Garoth and his intended victim as she cooed soothing noises toward Mihail.

"New religions and old teach us to help the helpless and offer others the kindness we want for ourselves," Merlin said. "Your father never taught you cruelty, Garoth."

"But the creature won't work. He's clumsy and gave up at a crucial moment, ruining the job," Garoth whined. He flailed his arms, trying to keep his balance on one foot. "Let go, you're hurting me!" So like a bully to revert to childish whines of hurt rather than maintain a position of strength.

"Mihail's wrist is broken, Garoth," Merlin said. He assessed the swelling and awkward angle of the hand quickly. He thought he could reset it properly and relieve the man's pain. But Mihail wouldn't work for several weeks. If any of the bones had been crushed, he'd never work with that hand again.

"Then he can't work, and he's useless. I suppose you'll insist we support him while he recovers and drains our resources," Garoth sneered. He seemed to have found his balance on his own.

"You must protect and care for all of your workers as your father swore." Merlin dropped Garoth's foot. "Come, Wren, Curyll. Bring Mihail. I will see about setting those bones."

Curyll gestured to his foster brothers, and they assembled beside him.

Merlin guided Mihail upright with a hand beneath his elbow. The laborer swayed and blanched with the effort of moving.

"You feel no pain." Merlin pressed his left palm against Mihail's eyes, concentrating on the message behind his words. A wave of tiredness swept over him. The moment he withdrew his hand from his patient he lost the aching fatigue.

Mihail straightened and smiled. He nodded his thanks and stepped on the road to follow his rescuers.

Merlin glanced at the others. Cai, Lancelot, and Bedewyr stared at him in awe. Two of the laborers made a fist extending their little and index finger in a ward against the evil eye. Garoth and the rest touched forehead, heart, and each shoulder. The Christian ward against evil.

That chilled Merlin more than mere superstition. Change had reached this remote corner of Britain sooner than he expected, and Curyll wasn't ready to work with the change to become the leader he was destined to be.

Chapter 2

I looked for the cat as soon as we entered the kitchen hut beside Lord Ector's Long Hall. Two steps behind me, Da and Curyll helped the injured worker. Curyll sent Stinger, Ceffyl, and Boar running off in three separate directions for the things Da needed to help Mihail.

A bundle of orange-and-white fur flew past us to the yard before the door slammed shut. A sneeze grabbed hold of me just as I reached for the cat. I missed.

"Poor, motherless little Wren," Lady Glynnis clucked, rushing toward me from where she supervised the salting of the soup. Lord Ector's wife scooped me up in her arms, patting my back as if I were still a babe. She totally ignored Da and the others.

I wriggled and squirmed to get down. Lady Glynnis wouldn't let go.

"We must get you warm, Wren. A hot brick and a cup of my special tonic, I think." She plunked me down on a bench by the fire. Servants scurried out of the way. The warmth made my nose run again. My toes and fingers tingled painfully, too. I coughed the cooking smoke out of my throat.

Da led Mihail to the fire where he had good light. I watched him feel the man's wrist with just the tips of his fingers. Moments later he yanked hard on the injured hand.

Mihail screamed and blanched. He almost passed out. Then his eyes cleared and he smiled. "No pain?"

"The pain is gone for now. It will return, but not as intense," Da replied. He directed one of the kitchen women how to bind the wrist with the splint Boar had brought and the bandages Stinger held. Ceffyl offered a pitcher of ale laced with willow bark. Then Da gave both the woman and Mihail instructions for caring for the injury. Finally Da turned back to Lady Glynnis and me.

"Don't you fuss about Mihail or how he broke his wrist, Wren," Da told me. "*I* will deal with it. Your task is to conquer this cold as soon as possible," he said sternly.

I would have protested, but a chill took hold of my shoulders and I had to fight to keep from trembling all over.

"Now you stay here by the fire, Wren, for as long as it takes to get thoroughly warm. We won't expect you and your Da to sing tonight." Lady Glynnis smoothed grass and twigs out of my tight mass of curly hair. She clucked and shook her head at the perpetual grass stains on my shirt.

I held my breath until the next sneeze passed. Lady Glynnis wouldn't believe I was warm enough to prowl the clusters of outbuildings looking for the elusive cat if I continued to expel demons through my nose. I needed to find the cat before the priest arrived. Cats liked to play hide and seek. They hid, I sought. Sometimes the game went on for days.

Lady Glynnis wrapped a hot brick in flannel and placed it under my feet. I clung to the rough bench as I wriggled my feet flat to absorb as much heat as possible.

"Drink this up." Lady Glynnis handed me a cup of something hot and spicy. "What is your Da thinking? Dragging you from one end of Britain to the other and back again in all weathers and not enough warm clothes to keep the chill off. Not even decent girl-clothes on you. You look like a beggar boy with those barbaric leggings and short shirts that hang only as far as your knees. Children need a home, and a mother to take care of them." She continued to fuss over me, brushing my knotted hair, washing my face, picking burrs off my clothes. 'Twas the same every year when Da and I first arrived for our wintering-in.

Across the room, Da winked at me. Only when Lady Glynnis took a moment away from her sons and fosterlings to notice me did I sense that I missed having a mother. Everything else I needed, including fussing, Da gave me.

Curyll hurried along the passage from the hall and living quarters. The harsh, square lines of Ector's Roman villa had been softened by the cluster of more traditional buildings surrounding it. Unlike many strongholds, covered passageways—some fully enclosed—connected Ector's "rooms."

Curyll handed a thick blanket to his foster mother, his mouth firmly closed. But he wore his torc again. Curious.

"Thank you, Curyll." Lady Glynnis wrapped the length of wool around my shoulders.

I sank into the folds of cloth. Warmth finally penetrated my bones. The soothing drink made me sleepy. I needed to lie down on my bench, but I didn't want to take my feet off the hot brick.

Then I saw a little pink nose and wisp of whisker poking out from beneath a stack of baskets. The wily cat hadn't slipped outside after all. She challenged me to follow her.

"Curyll," Lady Glynnis called as he started to sit next to Da. "You must wash before Father Thomas arrives. I will not have you presented to the priest smelling of dogs and pigeon blood. And take off your torc. You know Father Thomas disapproves of pagan jewelry."

Curyll nodded and rose to his full height, taller than Lord Ector's wife, almost as tall as my Da. He had to walk past me to the passageway. With his back to Lady Glynnis, he patted my head. "Cat," he mouthed the word without uttering a sound. He fingered his torc as if his right to wear it was tied to his ability to speak.

"I promise." I shaped the words with my mouth equally silent. I couldn't turn in a circle while sitting on the bench, so I extended one finger and moved it as if stirring my tonic.

Curyll almost skipped with joy on his way to the baths. A vision of life patterns flickered around the edges of my sight. I knew I'd dream tonight, and perhaps tomorrow it would all make sense.

A flipping tail tip joined the nose and whiskers under the baskets. If I dove across the kitchen as fast as a bird, I might capture the sneaky cat.

"Wren, keep the blanket around your shoulders." Lady Glynnis redraped the heavy wool, pulling it closer around my throat. "Oh, and, Father Merlin, the simnai behind the oven isn't drawing properly. Can you do something before the bread is spoiled?"

I couldn't smell the baking bread, and the extra smoke in the room barely penetrated the clog in my nose.

"Have you cleaned the simnai of birds' nests?" Da raised one eyebrow. His left hand automatically reached for his torc while the fingers of his left hand twisted into a complicated gesture.

"No, I did not!" Hands on hips, Lady Glynnis glared back at him indignantly. "I ordered Lancelot and Bedewyr to do it last week as punishment for stealing apples from the storeroom."

"Well, then that must be the problem." Da's mouth twisted as he fought to suppress a smile. "You didn't include Curyll in the task to supervise and make certain it was done properly." He bowed his head, eyes closed, and mumbled something.

I knew what he was doing and braced myself for the hot, scentless Awyr that swept through the kitchen. The tiny whirlwind circled the room. It flitted into every corner as if seeking an escape and finally found the simnai.

Immediately, much of the smoke cleared away and the fire burned brighter. Da was more gifted with the element Awyr than I. But I controlled Tanio with the ease of a thought.

"Next time, Lady Glynnis, if Curyll is busy elsewhere, I suggest you have one of the older boys, Fallon perhaps, supervise to make sure the job isn't left half done." He didn't mention Garoth.

In the wake of the whirlwind, the cat emerged from her hiding place far enough to wash a dainty paw. The tip of her tail flipped two more times, daring me to try to capture her.

"I'll take Wren to our quarters, Lady Glynnis." Da picked me up, blanket, cup, and all. "The usual place?"

"Of course, Father Merlin." Lady Glynnis fussed with my blanket one more time. "The boys have already set your harp and packs there. We honor a bard with a warm room next to the hall. Not like some of our neighbors." She blew air through her long nose, showing her disgust for those who didn't keep the old ways.

And yet her husband had invited a priest of the new religion to cure Curyll, they erected a Christian crog at the crossroad, and she had ordered my friend to remove his torc.

Da lifted one eyebrow again in question. Lady Glynnis didn't see it because she had stooped to scratch the cat's ears.

Of course, now that I couldn't get to her, the cat emerged from the pile of baskets.

I looked sharply at the cat and then back to Da. He looked at the cat and then back to me, shaking his head. "Later. When you are well." Before I could protest the need for haste, he carried me through the covered passage to the Great Hall. No cat would dare enter the large central chamber of the caer. All of the hunting dogs lazed around the fire pit in the middle of the room, seemingly asleep, but ready to pounce on any prey, especially a presumptuous cat.

"Da, the cat!" I reminded him. "I've got to talk to the cat before supper."

"Don't whine, Wren. Father Thomas won't hurt Curyll, and he doesn't cast stones at unbelievers. We have all winter to cure Curyll. You need to be free of this cold before you try any magic with the cat. She calls herself Helwriaeth, by the way. Remember to call her name properly and she will come."

That night, I succumbed to the fever that often stands behind the left shoulder of a cold. A storm blew in from the Irish Sea, bringing sleet and wind, but no priest. The urgency to cure Curyll left me.

Helwriaeth knew I wasn't strong enough to make demands upon her and perversely settled into my bed with me. She told me a long tale of circling around the outside of the Great Hall to avoid the monstrous dogs. Her very discriminating nose led her to a small crack in the stone foundation—a mousehole from the scent-memory I shared with her—that gave her access to the open space between the walls. From there she managed to find a smoke vent near the rafters filled with the aromas of hundreds of past feasts in the Great Hall. The drop into my room proved easy after that.

"That's a lovely tale, Helwriaeth," I murmured as I stroked her soft fur. "I have a very important job for you. You will be the most special cat in the whole world if you do this job."

Helwriaeth preened and said she was already a very special cat. An important one, too. None of the other kitchen cats could catch as many mice as she.

"Since you have so many mice to play with, you don't need Curyll's tongue, too," I whispered. My breath caught in my chest again, so I held it. My cough might scare Helwriaeth away before she promised to help Curyll.

She sat up, looking offended. Her tail flipped an ominous warning. She hadn't stolen the entire tongue, just the spirit that guided it.

I scratched her ears until her neck sagged. She considered trading the tongue's spirit for a special gift, one worthy of her beauty and her talents as a mouser.

"What kind of gift, Helwriaeth?" I continued scratching her ears until she lay down and purred.

More scratching, she told me, and the right to nap in my bed anytime she chose might be worth giving up the tongue's spirit.

"Promise, Helwriaeth?"

She flipped her tail and thought about it.

"I'll give you an extra bowl of cream after you give back the tongue."

Helwriaeth nudged my hand for more caresses. I stroked her back and scratched her ears.

She purred her acceptance of the bargain.

"Seal the promise, Helwriaeth," I instructed as I traced a neat circle with her tail. She glared at me and retrieved her tail.

"You must seal the promise, or I can't give you the cream."

She drew a circle in the air with the tip of her tail but continued to stare at me. I grabbed her tail and drew a second circle on the blanket.

Satisfied, we both fell asleep.

When I awoke, Helwriaeth still slept, curled up beside me. Curyll and Stinger stood in the curtained doorway. They came as often as Lady Glynnis allowed, sneaking sweets from the kitchen for me and clean-smelling herbs from the stillroom to ease my sore throat. Today, they each brought a squirming puppy. Curyll bent at the waist to show me the bundle of fur secreted under his leather tunic.

Helwriaeth woke up, instantly alert. She hissed and arched her back.

"Oh, my!" I reached to pet the puppy, still cradled in Curyll's arms.

Helwriaeth moved faster than me. She hissed again and batted the shaggy bundle of black fur on the nose. The puppy yelped and hid beneath Curyll's clothing. Stinger laughed and backed away from Helwriaeth and her claws with his puppy. My friends shrugged and retreated from the room, cooing reassurance to the frightened dogs. The indignant cat began her bath with a smug smile, as if she'd done me a favor.

"You didn't give back Curyll's tongue," I scolded.

She left the room in a huff. The angle of her tail told me the presence of the puppy had ruined the opportunity. Besides, Stinger would be jealous of the gift and would want something special, too. That was not part of her bargain. She would let me know what she considered a proper time and place.

At last the day arrived when Lady Glynnis allowed me out of bed. I could smell and taste again. The world looked bright and clean and happy. Frost rimed the edges of the well and bit the exposed noses and fingers of the kitchen lads every time they scooted out for water or wood. But the sky was the deep endless blue that was both so close I could almost touch it and so distant it stretched forever. The sky reminded me of my father's eyes when he smiled at me with love.

Boar and Ceffyl spotted the storm-delayed priest from the watchtower soon after. "Father Thomas comes. He's riding a donkey," Ceffyl shouted to one and all.

"He'll be here about an hour before supper," Boar added, equally as loud. He couldn't see the distance as well as his foster brother, but he could calculate the speed of the donkey.

I had a lot of work to do and a cat to catch. I needed to make sure the priest did not frighten Helwriaeth away forever with his exorcism spell. I also needed to make sure that his spell didn't steal the tongue's spirit from the cat. She had to give it back, or it would not stay.

I had watched the Ladies of Avalon prepare for festivals and magic rites, so I knew how to go about it. First a bath. One had to approach magic clean of body as well as spirit.

Lord Ector's caer had begun as a Roman villa with a hypo . . . hipno . . . a system for heating water and a big pool. I hurried through the ritual cleansing before anyone could haul me back to bed for risking a chill.

Then I assembled my herbs and stole a candle from the stillroom. This was the tricky part. I'd never performed a formal spell before, though I'd seen Da and The Morrigan do it. I knew the general form, but not the substance.

I assembled my tools: flowers from Pridd, Tanio burning, Dwfr in a pristine basin for the vision, and smoke representing Awyr.

As I laid each stalk of dried flowers into the brazier that heated my room—I lit it from the main fire, not from my thoughts since I thought I might need the extra energy Tanio always drained out of me—I said an extra prayer to Dana for guidance. I breathed in the aromatic smoke. It swept away excess thought and sensation, sharpening my senses with simple clarity. Then I gazed into a bowl of clear water. Nothing happened. I breathed deeply again and coughed. I choked and gasped for air, taking in more smoke. It burned inside my barely healed lungs. I tasted green phlegm and coughed again and again. Each time I grabbed a breath, the smoke went deeper into my body and my mind. The room spun around me, bright lights flashed across the smooth surface of the water. Dark clouds creased by lightning blotted all else from my vision.

Abruptly, my sight dimmed and darkened, except around the edges. The water cleared and I saw more than a reflection, less than substance. *Curyll grown older, stronger, more confident, leading armored men into battle. They rode large horses and carried long swords strapped to their backs, the like of which I'd never seen before. Curyll's sword shone through the vision like a star borrowed from the heavens. Power hummed in the air around its jeweled hilt.*

The sharp scent of the smoke turned sour in warning.

Without knowing how I knew, the vision told me that my best friend would receive dire wounds in that battle. I had to go to him, heal him. . . .

I knew an urge to laugh madly, as Da did when he spoke true prophecy. Instead, I coughed again. The vision died. My stomach ached and my back hurt from holding back the racking coughs. Tears ran down my cheeks unchecked. The smoke stabbed my mind and burned in my gut.

I coughed again, trying to rid myself of the foul smoke. I nearly gagged on the taste of burned herbs turned acrid. My body grew weaker. I hadn't the strength to fight the coughs that racked my body.

Da dashed through the curtain separating our room from the other chambers. I was barely aware of his hands as he slapped my back to clear my lungs.

"Cease!" Da cried in an ancient language I did not understand. And yet I knew what he said and why.

The smoke fled the room like a cat exiled by a swift broom. The room remained warm and still.

One last flash of lightning streaked across the basin of water and cleared my vision. Blurred reflections in the water answered my original request. *The orange-and-white cat sat frozen between two barrels of apples in the cellar.* In that moment I knew Helwriaeth had gone to one of her favorite hunting grounds. I knew she had just killed a mouse. And I knew she would remain there. I had called her true name and she awaited my command.

She would return the spirit to Curyll's tongue willingly. But upon my command or another's?

"What were you doing, Wren?" Da's hands made soothing circles on my back as the coughing eased.

"I have to find Helwriaeth, so she doesn't run away forever with Curyll's tongue when the priest comes." Fat tears welled up in my eyes and rolled down my cheeks. I gasped and breathed shallowly, afraid that if I took the great gulps of air I wanted, the coughing would return. My stomach really hurt. My throat burned, crying for water.

A little bit of triumph eased my hurts and exhaustion. I had found Helwriaeth and bound her to my wishes.

"Didn't I tell you to let yourself heal first? Magic takes a lot of strength and training to understand the patterns of past, present, and future. You aren't well enough to formulate the spell properly. And you aren't mature enough to maintain the continuity of the patterns."

"Yes," I sobbed, as much from uncertainty as from the rawness in my throat.

"So why didn't you wait?"

"Because I know Helwriaeth stole the tongue's spirit from Curyll. He isn't possessed by demons. The priest can't cast out demons that aren't there. But he might frighten the cat away forever before she gives the tongue back."

"The cat will not run. This is her place in the world. She might hide for a while, though. We must wait until the priest has failed. That way everyone will know that Curyll belongs to the Goddess, as do you and I. They will know and be grateful."

"Yes, Da." I thought a moment about what he'd said. "Are you angry with me, Da?"

"No, my little Wren. I'm not angry at you. I'm angry with myself for not teaching you how to cast a spell properly before now. You tried to help, the best way you knew how. But you must be careful. Magic is very dangerous. Don't try any spells at all until you have been properly trained and are much stronger. I'd die if you were hurt, or . . . or taken from me because . . . First thing tomorrow I will set you some lessons."

"May I light the fire with my mind?"

"When you are ready to control Tanio once it lights the fuel you provide it and not before."

"Yes, Da." Maybe I should stop playing with Tanio when the coals in the brazier went out in the middle of the night. But I'd still maintain a control on Helwriaeth to keep her close where I could watch her.

Chapter 3

MERLIN left Wren napping on her cot, firmly tucked beneath an extra blanket and the brazier glowing merrily with heat. He fingered the bulbous end of his torc while he mulled over the situation.

"I thought I'd have more time to prepare," he murmured as he made his way to the bathing chamber. Lady Glynnis had ordered the boys to bathe and change to clean clothing before Father Thomas arrived.

He didn't believe for a moment that demons possessed Curyll, nor did he believe Wren's fanciful tale of the cat stealing the boy's tongue. Why, the cat would have to be part demon herself or enchanted by a magician to exhibit that much intelligence.

Merlin stopped in his tracks, one foot poised to take the next step. Could it be?

He and Wren had wintered here with Lord Ector's sprawling household for eight years. Could Wren have attracted the cat as a familiar without his knowledge? He preferred birds himself, and then only temporary relationships. If Wren had formed the intimate bond of a familiar with the cat at so young an age, she possessed a much more powerful gift than he suspected. What was he to do with her?

He'd make that decision later. Right now he had to prepare Curyll for the real cure. "The secret is buried deep within your mind, boy," Merlin said out loud. "Buried along with your ability to lead. I think I can free them both in time. But I need to lay the foundations, and I need this pesky priest out of the way."

The echoes of boys at play within the vast watery chamber confirmed his suspicion of why he hadn't seen any of them for quite some time. He stepped into the bathing chamber, expecting a blast of hot moist air to greet him. The room seemed chilled, barely warmer than the drafty corridors between buildings.

Four naked boys jumped at the same time and swatted at a ball made of an inflated pig's bladder. Water splashed the walls, the walkway around the pool, and Merlin in great quantities as the boys descended into the water. The water level within the square pool seemed diminished. Most of it was elsewhere in the chamber.

And the spray that now dripped from Merlin's beard was cool.

He peered more closely at the boys. Goose bumps rose on their arms and down their backs. Wiry Ceffyl's lips looked pale, almost blue.

But they were energetic boys, and the game was much more important than the temperature of the water or their neatness.

Curyll held the ball aloft. Cai, shorter by half a head, lunged for the prize. Stinger elbowed Curyll in the gut. The taller boy pushed upward and backward away from his assailant. He landed in the water on his back with a mighty splash. Boar flew past him, entering the water face and chest first and compounding the height of the water.

A cold wave drenched Merlin to the knees.

"Enough!" he roared.

The boys froze in place. Almost literally. As soon as they stopped moving, the cold water chilled them. Ceffyl's teeth chattered.

"Sorry, Father Merlin, we were only playing," Stinger apologized.

Boar, Stinger, and Ceffyl hung their heads a little as they tried not to shiver.

Only Curyll stared at his tutor unabashed. There was hope for the boy yet.

"You should apologize to yourselves, not me. Haven't you noticed something wrong?" Merlin asked, raising one eyebrow. He wanted to finger his torc, invoke a little of his listening talent to know what they were thinking. He respected their privacy.

Curyll nodded in reply, still silent. The other boys looked at the water and back to each other.

"We'll get out now," Boar said. "Supper should be almost ready."

"You'll fix the hypocast before you eat." Merlin interrupted the boy's attempt to heave himself out of the water.

"B–but it . . . it's cold!" Ceffyl protested, stuttering almost as badly as Curyll in the cold.

"You'll fix the problem faster with that incentive."

"How?" Stinger asked. He at least had the intelligence to begin looking at the system of pipes that fed hot air through the original villa and hot water to the pool from a central furnace.

Curyll heaved himself free of the water and sprinted from the bathing chamber before Merlin could protest. The boy grabbed a rough linen towel and wrapped it about his middle as he hastened to the narrow staircase that led to the furnace room beneath the central hall of the villa.

Merlin edged closer to the opening and watched as the boy eased around the massive ceramic coal burner. There wasn't room for more than one slender person to squeeze between the furnace and the stone walls. Clay pipes led away from it.

Moments later Curyll climbed the spiral stairs, a puzzled look on his face. "F–fire h–h–ot," he choked out the words.

"We guessed that," Boar sneered. "If the hall got cold, Mother would send someone to fix the hypocast."

"But would Lady Glynnis notice the change in temperature if she remained in the kitchen?" Merlin asked them all.

Boar and Ceffyl grimaced their embarrassment at having missed this detail.

"Ch–check the pipes." Curyll smiled as the words came out a little easier this time. "Ceffyl." He pointed to the place where the hot water entered the pool near the bottom.

Ceffyl glared his protest at Curyll. He was cold enough now to be clutching his arms close to his body and shivering. "Why me? I'll have to dive down there and the water's getting colder. It must be freezing outside by now."

"You—are—b–best diver," Curyll argued.

"You're skinniest and can reach in and see if there's a blockage. We know Curyll is right. Now let's do it." Stinger took up the order Curyll had given.

Merlin smiled to himself. The plan had been Curyll's; the others followed him. He knew what to do and how to delegate authority. Now he just had to learn enough self-confidence to implement his leadership with others—men who weren't his closest friends and confidants. Soon.

The cure would work soon.

"There's a gob of yucky wet hair in the pipe. The women have been here," Ceffyl called as soon as he surfaced from his dive. "The pipe is completely blocked, no heat, no water, nothing coming out of it."

"Clear it," Curyll said.

"He's right. Even if we tell Father about it, he'll order us to do it anyway," Boar said. His look of contempt was deeper than his foster brother's.

"P–p–pipes b–br–br . . ." Curyll trailed off. His face dissolved into an expression of extreme embarrassment.

"Come on, Curyll, spit it out," Stinger encouraged him.

Curyll turned and ran from the room, his throat working as if he tried to contain tears.

"So now what, Merlin? What was Curyll trying to say?" Boar asked.

"Think it through, boys, just as Curyll saw right away. What happens if you block the pipe but keep pouring water into that pipe?"

Stinger screwed up his face a moment, then his eyes opened wide. "They'll burst."

"So?" Merlin pushed him to think. If Curyll failed to develop—more and more he had to take this possibility into consideration—Stinger might prove an adequate substitute. Adequate, not brilliant. Britain needed brilliance right now. Britain might cease to be unless led by a true genius to counter the next wave of Saxon attacks.

"Curse Vortigen!" he said to himself. With the invocation of the Ardh Rhi who had ruled during Merlin's youth, the past and present blended in a confusing mass of images. Vortigen had invited the Saxons to settle in Britain in return for their mercenary services against other Germanic tribes. Now those same Saxons fought for more and more land. Their gods respected blood and valor in battle and little else. Merlin's people had little chance to succeed against their ruthlessness under the current leadership.

Merlin could not grasp a true image of the future. All was confusion.

For the first time in many years he feared he might fail in his destiny.

I watched from a secret alcove in the outer wall around Lord Ector's caer. Father Thomas arrived on his donkey an hour before sunset. An average man of middle height, medium coloring, mild of speech, but determined of step, he didn't look fierce enough to cast out demons. Or mean enough to throw stones. The twinkle in his eyes and the smoothness of his clean-shaven face told me he was younger than I thought a respected priest should be, with a wife and infant son in tow. But a stillness in the core of him invited me to go to him, trust him, and love him.

I'd been beguiled by others with mild manners, only to end up with bruises.

Once he entered the fortress, I followed at a discreet and silent distance. I squinted my eyes and watched him move among the people of Lord Ector's stronghold. As my eyes lost focus, a shimmering light of yellow and orange and healing green pulsed around Father Thomas' head. I held back. The aura surrounding the priest matched my father's in intensity. I'd never met anyone who had as much power in their aura as my Da. Especially not Christian priests.

Lady Glynnis bustled around Father Thomas as she had fussed over me when I first arrived. I couldn't believe she had donned a Roman *stola* over her best tunic. A week ago she had bragged that she honored the old ways and wore only long tunics in the British style. She'd called Da, "Father Merlin." Today she dressed to please the new order. She called the priest "Father," and Da became "friend." She made the priest comfortable in the best chair in the hall and served him mulled wine and sweet cakes herself.

She'd delegated that task to servants when Da and I arrived. A hollowness opened in my middle. Lady Glynnis didn't really love me.

I choked back sudden tears, forcing myself to watch Father Thomas and his family—my new enemies. They stole Lady Glynnis from me.

Da stroked his harp and sang light ballads in the corner. His beautiful voice recited only tunes that would not offend Father Thomas. He wore his formal bard's robes over a long blue tunic; the sleeves of the tunic tied at his wrist, hiding the Druid tattoos that snaked up his forearms. He should have worn a white tunic and displayed his intricate tattoos in reverence.

Lady Glynnis had ordered me to stay in my room and under several blankets so I didn't chill again. But I now knew she was ashamed of me, the ragged bard's daughter who couldn't keep grass stains off her clothes and twigs out of her unruly hair.

I couldn't obey her. Curyll depended upon me. I had made a promise and sealed it in a circle. Father Thomas had enough power to snatch the tongue away from Helwriaeth. Unless the cat voluntarily gave up the tongue's spirit, it would not stay with Curyll. *It would not stay anywhere.*

For Curyll, I had to block Father Thomas' spell.

From the dark shadows of the passage into the sleeping chambers, I watched. Helwriaeth lay in my lap, purring. I needed to keep her close and under control.

"Thank you, Lady Glynnis. Perhaps later," Father Thomas said softly to his hostess as she offered him refreshment. He bowed his head. "I appreciate your hospitality and thank you for the offer. But the sacred Mass we are about to celebrate . . . I must fast beforehand." His Latin rolled off his tongue more musically than I had ever heard that ugly language. His aura grew and sparkled with gold as he spoke. This priest prepared to work magic just like Da and the Ladies of Avalon did.

Father Thomas continued his preparations, sprinkling water from a special flask on the high table while he murmured prayers. A clean length of whitest linen followed the cleansing of the worship space. A silver wine cup for Dwfr, meditative incense for Awyr, candles for Tanio, salt for Pridd, a bronze bell, and finally three heavy scrolls completed his preparations. Then Father Thomas knelt before the altar he had created, head bowed, hands clasped tightly in front of him.

The bell rang in the watchtower then. Not the warning bell of three-times-three sharp clangs, but a long tolling of summons.

All of Lord Ector's household trooped into the hall, as if they had been waiting at the entry for the bell. All three sons and seven fosterlings escorted Curyll, clad only in a clean, white undertunic, to the central fire pit. They stood straight and tall and silent. I saw goose bumps rise on Curyll's arms, but he didn't shiver in the winter-cold room.

The heat had come back, but hadn't had time to penetrate every corner of this room.

Behind the boys came the warriors and other retainers, followed by the servants. They arranged themselves in two straight lines on either side of the fire, running from the dais to the door in order of their rank. They should have stood in a circle to keep the magic from escaping. Da stood apart from the gathering. Only the tenant farmers and their families were missing.

"Let us pray," Father Thomas called them together.

Everyone recited the same words, some in educated Latin, others in rough and halting approximations. But the intent was the same. All sought rapport with the Roman god in the Roman tongue.

Curyll remained mute, his eyes wide. Gently, Father Thomas placed his arm around Curyll's shoulders and drew him close. Reassurance poured out of the priest like water from a pitcher. Curyll relaxed a little. He turned his head slightly toward me and winked.

I smiled at him from my hiding place. He knew where I hid. He would always find me when no other could. His trust that I would not fail him showed in his deliberate squaring of shoulders and lengthening of spine.

Suddenly, his confidence in me seemed misplaced. I had never truly worked magic before. No big or important spells.

I still needed a lot of sleep and had little appetite from the fever. Did I have enough strength to block Father Thomas' spell and protect the tongue?

Helwriaeth continued her silent cat thoughts and didn't encourage me.

The Mass followed no ritual I had ever seen. I had to think too hard when I spoke or listened to Latin to follow the fluid tones of Father Thomas, and yet I understood much of the essence of what happened. Burning incense, not unlike the herbal combination I had used earlier, filled the hall and threatened to choke me again.

Father Thomas chanted secret words to invite his god to attend. He poured salt into Curyll's mouth until he was sick. The caustic properties of salt scoured out the evil spirits. Then the priest doused Curyll with more water from the special vial in a final cleansing. A ritual had to be performed correctly, down to the finest detail, or it didn't work at all.

Father Thomas seemed to have mastered this particular spell. Every moment the power of his aura increased and spread. Like a living cloud, magic swirled about Lord Ector's household, binding them all into the spell of exorcism. Each person in the room added more power to the total until it compounded and increased far beyond the sum of those in attendance. Da's magic never did that. He always kept it close to him, very much his solitary achievement.

Only Da and I—and the cat—remained outside the aura. I huddled over Helwriaeth, murmuring my warding spell. She shrank deeper into my lap, avoiding the cloud of power.

Curyll gagged and twitched uncontrollably, as if truly possessed by demons.

Helwriaeth squirmed, ears up and alert. I should reassure and soothe her, keep her away from the spell. But I couldn't. I sat in awe of the power surrounding Father Thomas—power that he extended to Curyll and the rest of the household.

The cat dug her back claws into my thigh and escaped my embrace in a single leap. The proper time had come. Curyll was restrained, and enough magic filled the air for the tongue's spirit to find its way home, *if properly sent instead of snatched.* Just beyond my enthralled reach she stretched long and slow from front to back. Then she reversed the rippling movement. When each muscle and joint had settled back into its proper place, she sauntered into the center of the ritual, following an undulating path that avoided Father Thomas' pulsing aura. She stropped Curyll's ankles, around and between his legs in a pattern that imitated the sigil for infinity.

"Witch cat!" Lady Glynnis shouted.

Cook screamed and threw her apron over her head. Lord Ector gasped, hand to his throat as if unable to breathe.

Stinger bent and rubbed his fingers together as if he held a treat for the cat. Helwriaeth looked at him with disdain and sauntered away.

I needed to follow and capture her but couldn't seem to make my legs obey me. Tears of failure and frustration streamed down my cheeks.

Boar and Ceffyl threw themselves at Helwriaeth. They sprawled at Curyll's feet, empty-handed.

Da stood from his stool in the corner. A smile played around his mouth as he sought me with his eyes. One eyebrow went up in question.

I shrugged as Helwriaeth led frantic pursuers a merry dance under the high table and around the dais. Finally she landed on Curyll's shoulder, claws digging deeply into his flesh.

"Here, kitty, kitty, kitty," Ceffyl rolled an appeal through his throat in imitation of a purr. Helwriaeth arched her back and hissed at him. Curyll's foster brother backed away, fists clenched at his side.

The room fell silent. Everyone watched the cat and Father Thomas. The priest crossed himself. "Come forth from the body that houses you, oh, demon of the evil one. In the name of the Father, the Son, and the Holy Ghost, come forth and take this cat body, better suited to your kind. Leave this innocent boy and find a new home within Helwriaeth!" He shouted a prayer in the common tongue of our people.

Curyll seemed too dazed to react to the chaos around him.

Helwriaeth looked at the priest and spat her disgust. "Meow-ow-ow," she yowled and finished her part.

I knew the cat gave back Curyll's tongue. The spirit would remain with him forever now.

I thanked Dana for that but regretted that Father Thomas and his god would get the credit.

Helwriaeth leaped from Curyll's shoulder onto the table. She ran the full length of the white tablecloth just ahead of her pursuers. When she reached the corner, she launched herself toward me. I finally got control of my legs and stood to catch her. But she landed short and scampered away toward the kitchen.

Father Thomas bellowed one more prayer, arms extended outward in the symbol of the Christian cross. A wind swirled around the room, stronger and more intense than the light breeze I had called up that morning. Candles and torches died. Incense lay heavy in the air. A flash of bright light. Murmurs and then shouts of fear and bewilderment.

Just as suddenly as it had sprung up, the wind died. The incense dispersed. Silence lay heavy in the room.

"W—will someone l—light the t—torches?" Curyll asked, barely stuttering at all.

Father Thomas stood grinning beside Curyll. He wrapped a strong arm around my friend's shoulders. The look of reverent awe on his face told me he believed in his own miracle.

I followed Helwriaeth to the kitchen, so I could pour her the promised bowl of cream. I placed the treat deep in the storeroom where cook wouldn't find her.

"You must leave this caer now, Helwriaeth. Father Thomas made it look like a demon jumped from Curyll's body into you. He will order you killed. You must leave here and never come back. The Goddess will take care of you if you go to the forest. I'm sorry, Helwriaeth. I'm sorry," I cried and buried my face in her fur.

"Mew." Helwriaeth accepted my apology and told me not to worry about her. She was, after all, a very special cat. She would survive now that she was warned.

I left her with a second bowl of cream and crept back to my room very much afraid of Father Thomas.

From that day forward, I ceased looking for auras of power in people.

Chapter 4

"I don't like changing things around like this," Stinger said. He stood up and started to pace, one hand on his torc in obvious imitation of my father.

I covered my mouth to keep from laughing as he puffed out his chest and tried without success to raise one eyebrow. Stinger was good at details. He had the gestures and the posture, but his facial expression and voice lacked the assurance and maturity of The Merlin. His mock sternness did nothing to diminish the perfection of his face and the grace of his movements. He'd always be the most beautiful man around.

Interesting that Stinger mimicked my father while arguing against him.

"The Merlin has a point. We are older now. We deserve the individuality of different birthdays," Ceffyl argued. He slapped a small daub of brown paint in the middle of a plain white shield.

"But we have always celebrated our births together on Imbolc—even Wren." Stinger continued pacing rather than correcting Ceffyl's inexpert painting of the whitewashed wooden shield for Curyll. We didn't have much time to create another gift for Curyll. Da had announced only yesterday that tonight, the day before the Winter Solstice, we celebrated Curyll's birthday.

"Our birthdays make us special," Stinger continued. "We were all conceived at Beltane and no man can be certain he is our sire even if he claims us! The Merlin has fostered Beltane babies all over the country. That's what holds us together. That's why we're here."

As the only girl in the group and the youngest, I liked the idea of having a birthday all to myself. I'd been forgotten often enough in the bustle of honoring Curyll, Stinger, and Ceffyl at the same time. Only Boar celebrated his birthday on the Spring Equinox, but then he was Lord Ector's son rather than a fosterling.

Da always remembered me with a special treat, a new cloak or sometimes merely a bunch of the first snowdrops gathered in the nearby woods. Once, a green faery kissed my nose on my birthday. He left me with the scent-memory of cedar trees on a bright spring day. But I couldn't tell anyone about that.

"How does The Merlin know on what days each of you was born?" Boar asked. He sat back against the wall, arms folded across his broadening chest. He'd done the hard work of stretching a thick deer hide over the wooden frame of the shield and considered his contribution to the gift finished.

I had whitewashed the whole thing with a special mixture and a few murmured charms of protection. Ceffyl had made the leather hand grip and fastened it to the back. Stinger, with his fine eye for detail, was supposed to paint it with the bear symbol Curyll had adopted. But he paced and shouted instead.

Ceffyl dripped a glob of paint at the bear's rear, making it look as if he trailed shit rather than marching majestically as a revered creature of strength.

"We've got to be more careful with this. It has to be a special gift!" I pushed Ceffyl out of the way and grabbed his paint rag. Luckily I had some whitewash left. I'd mixed rowan and betony into the lime for protection. The paint had a faint greenish tint, but the others wouldn't notice until the shield was held against something very white.

"What we need is an enchantment to help Curyll speak. He talks more now since Father Thomas exorcised the demons, but he still stutters and he's hiding in silence almost as badly as before," Stinger said. All three of the boys stopped to stare at me expectantly.

I stared back at them, eyes as wide and innocent as I could make them. I agreed with them, but there was nothing I could do. Later perhaps, not now.

"Stinger, you've the best eye and control over your brush. You paint the bear. And do it right. Remember, this is for Curyll, so it has to be special. I'm going to talk to Da." I stood up and stalked out of the room as if I really had a purpose.

I almost stumbled over Da and Curyll in our chamber. Curyll sat on my low stool near the door. Da stood in front of him, very still, eyes intent upon my friend. I stopped my headlong dash into the room with a jerk and stood just as still as my father.

He dangled a brightly faceted crystal in front of Curyll, letting it spin on a slender silver chain. Winter sunshine poured in through the tiny window, sending rainbows arcing through the crystal.

"You have nothing to fear, Arthur. No one will laugh at you. When you awaken, you will speak clearly and without hesitation. Do you understand?"

"Y–e–s," Curyll said, very slowly, without repetition.

"Very good, Arthur. You will awaken when I count to three. You will be refreshed as if you had slept well. And you will not stutter. One, two, three." Da snapped his fingers.

Curyll blinked his eyes rapidly and looked around as if he truly had slept.

"Wh–what ha–happened?" he asked.

Da's smile crumbled.

"Nothing, Curyll. You dozed off over your lessons," I said soothingly. "It's nearly time for you to bathe and change your clothes for the fest.

Curyll smiled at me as he nodded. He unfolded his legs and rose from the stool. He'd grown this winter and stood almost as tall as Da. As he passed me, he ruffled my hair affectionately. A small shower of crushed herbs fell to my shoulders. I couldn't keep twigs out of my hair even when I'd been indoors for a month.

"What did I do wrong? The trick should have worked," Da moaned when we were alone again.

"You used his true name, Da." Arthur, the name I disliked and never used. I forgot it again almost as soon as Da spoke it, but whether this was due to my own desire or Da's subtle suggestion I didn't know. "No one uses his real name, and he doesn't answer to it. You should have called him Curyll."

"Aye. But it's too late now. He won't succumb to a trance so easily next time. He barely accepted it this time. I'll have to think of something different."

I had already thought of something but didn't know how to go about doing it.

We gathered at sunset for a small fest. Tomorrow night we would celebrate the Solstice and truly feast and play. But tonight there would be stories and songs and special treats, honeyed nuts, dried fruits stewed in wine, and a haunch of bear that Curyll had brought down in the hunt. All of the men had helped, but Curyll's spear had found the heart. The hunt had been especially prophetic since he'd adopted the bear symbol and this was his fourteenth birthday. Tonight he would be acknowledged a man.

The servants carried in the meat upon a huge platter. They circled the hall three times, deosil, on the path of the sun before setting it on the serving table at the base of the dais.

Curyll and Lord Ector stood shoulder to shoulder—Curyll a little taller—before the platter of meat. They wore their second-best shirts of unbleached linen and long tunics of wool only slightly less coarse and longer than their usual garments. Curyll wore golden brown that precisely matched the bear on his new shield—I'd worked hard to get that color. Lord Ector wore his usual dark green that highlighted the red in his graying hair. Curyll especially looked beautiful tonight—not precisely beautiful as Stinger was, but special, glowing with pride.

I stood between Stinger and Ceffyl at the end of the lower table. Boar and Curyll would sit at the high table tonight, Boar because he was family, Curyll because it was his birthday. My two companions each clasped one of my hands in excitement. Soon they, too, would be allowed to carve the meat as symbol of their manhood. Stinger held the shield at his side, keeping it in the shadows of the table. My heart nearly burst in my chest with emotions I couldn't name. All four of these young men were my friends. But Curyll was special to all of us. I knew deep in my soul that my destiny was entwined with Curyll's.

Curyll reaching for the carving knife. His right to make the first cut tonight.

Stinger raised the shield to be ready to present it to our friend as soon as the ceremony of meat cutting was finished.

Lord Ector stayed Curyll's hand by covering the knife hilt with his own square and hairy fist.

"Lord Ector?" Da asked from the dais.

"He's not a man yet."

"B–but—I—I am four–four–teen," Curyll protested.

"You aren't a man until you can tell me so without hesitation and without stuttering. Until then, you will always be ranked as a commoner or a child." Lord Ector set his chin determinedly.

Lady Glynnis opened her mouth to protest, then clamped it firmly shut. She looked at her hands. Her face turned bright red beneath her fair hair.

"I do protest, Lord Ector," Da said. "Curyll has earned his place in the hunt, in trials of arms, and in his studies."

"Until he can speak, he is not a man." Lord Ector nudged Curyll aside. "Fallon, as my oldest son, I entrust the meat carving to you tonight."

Curyll marched past us, back straight, steps determined. I saw the glitter of tears in his eyes. He shoved Stinger out of the way. The shield clattered to the floor, the only sound in the silent hall.

"Not tonight, Father." Fallon set his ale cup firmly on the table and followed Curyll out the door. Stinger, Boar, and Ceffyl joined him in a unified march. I trailed along behind, plotting furiously in my head.

The winter passed. Curyll barely spoke a dozen words over the next four months.

"I beg of you, Ector, friend, do not send Curyll and Cai to war this year." Da's raised voice broke my concentration. I abandoned my study of Tanio to listen.

Da had forbidden me trying even the tiniest bit of magic since my first near disastrous spell. I now spent my time in endless lessons. I was supposed to spend this first day past the Vernal Equinox contemplating how flames licked sea coal in a brazier. I needed to know the properties of this element in all its forms before I could call it to do my bidding. Differences in color and scent were obvious. But I didn't yet understand why tiny flamelets licked the coal and wore it down slowly rather than long tongues of flame consuming the fuel in large mouthfuls, as they did wood.

Instead, I listened to my elders argue. Much more interesting.

Da often chided me for paying attention to everything but what I should be doing. I had turned nine nearly two months ago at Imbolc and should be past letting my wits flow with every fragment of new thought.

They discussed Curyll. This could be more important than studying Tanio.

"My sons and fosterlings will fight at my side this summer. All of my fosterlings," Lord Ector said. "I cannot deny the orders of the Ardh Rhi. He specifically asked me to bring all of them, trained or no. Cai and Curyll are as fit as Garoth and Fallon, or Lancelot and Bedewyr, who are both a year younger than Cai and Curyll." Lord Ector held up a rolled parchment brought by special messenger that morning.

All of us had seen Ardh Rhi Uther Pendragon's royal emblem of the red dragon rampant on the saddlebags of the courier when he rode through the gates.

"The boys have only just passed their fourteenth birthdays. Their bodies are not yet fully grown," Da argued.

"I fought with Ambrosius Aurelianus and Uther against Vortigen and his Jutish mercenaries when I was twelve!"

I remembered then that the people we called Saxons were actually from a number of tribes. We lumped them all under the same cursed name of the foreign invaders who menaced our shores.

Ector continued bellowing. "I earned my warrior beads that same summer." He shook his head to emphasize the red-brown beads woven into a plait of hair above his left ear. One bead for each life he had taken in battle. "Curyll is more fit and taller than my older sons who have three beads apiece. Cai and Bedewyr won't stay behind if I take Curyll. And I will not leave Lancelot the Stinger behind, as he handles weapons better than most seasoned warriors. The boys follow me into battle this year. They need the experience now, so that they may lead men when they come of age."

"Curyll does not yet speak well enough. He needs another year for confidence."

"Nonsense. When he sinks his sword into the gut of a Saxon, he'll learn confidence. If he doesn't, he'll just have to fight with the men-at-arms instead of on horseback with the marchogs." Lord Ector rubbed his lower back and rotated his shoulders. Then he said more quietly, "I'm getting too old for this."

I crept closer to them through the passage between the sleeping quarters and the hall. The shadows wrapped around me like old friends. I became one with them. To the men in the hall, I was invisible.

This was a trick I'd learned on my own. A trick, not magic. I could observe and listen anytime, anyplace. For a moment I felt a little guilty. Da had caught me yesterday eavesdropping on two servants who kissed and clung together as they made plans to meet in the pantry at midnight.

Last spring I had watched the mating of livestock as part of my education. I presumed this was a first step in preparation for my own Beltane initiation—when the time came. The mystery of human mating still baffled me. I hoped the servants would enlighten me.

"Curiosity is good, if it leads you to ask the proper questions and make the proper observations," Da had said yesterday as he hauled me back to my lessons. "But you, Wren, are just plain nosy. Nothing happens in this caer that you don't spy out, whether you should or not."

I pushed aside the memory and the ensuing guilt of eavesdropping. My senses warned me that this conversation between Da and Lord Ector was important to me and to my dear friend Curyll.

"Give him one more year, Ector, please." Da's eyes burned with emotions too complex for me to read or understand. I smelled the sweat of fear on him from across the room.

"So it is Curyll you plead for. Not my son Cai, or Bedewyr, my brother's son who is a year younger, or Lancelot who mystifies us all with his brilliance with weapons. Curyll, the babe you brought me to foster with only vague hints to an illustrious parentage. Who is Curyll, Myrddin Emrys? Whose bastard is he that you tutor him in policy, religions, and court etiquette when he should be only a common soldier?" A pronounced vein beat angrily in Lord Ector's neck.

I heard a gasp beside me. Only then did I realize Curyll had crept to the same curtained portal to eavesdrop.

Curyll's fists clenched tightly at his sides. Anger darkened his face. His muscles bunched as he prepared to launch himself at his foster father, fists flying.

"Ssh." I held up a finger to my lips. "Listen first."

He didn't move, but his fists remained clenched and ready.

"The boy's destiny is not mine to reveal," Da said. His eyes lost focus a moment and drifted into another world. His left hand touched the fat bulb on his torc. I wondered which spell he was preparing— perhaps he'd invade Ector's mind and make him do as Da wished.

"What have you seen in the stars, Merlin?" Lord Ector grabbed Da's arm, making his sleeve ride up.

I caught a brief glimpse of his Druid tattoos—endless knots winding up his arm with no apparent beginning and no end. The sigils of Male, Female, Birth, Death, and Infinity entwined with the unified knots creating a complex pattern only Da could decipher. Ector saw the tattoos as well and shut his mouth abruptly. No magic burst from Da. Ector listened respectfully.

A hint of mad laughter erupted from Da, a sure sign that what he was about to say carried the weight of true prophecy. Only a hint, not the gales of uncontrollable laughter I had heard him spew forth with true visions of the future. Another trick. "Look at the boy, Ector. Look at his skill on horseback and with weapons. Look at his adeptness with written words and numbers even though you had thought him stupid because he could not speak. Look closely at him and know that there is more in him than just another landless warrior. He must *not* go to war this summer." Da's voice echoed around the hall. His tattoos, symbols of his priesthood, gave him the right to interpret the patterns of past, present, and future. Only a Druid could make sense of the pattern and maintain continuity.

Da merely spoke the truth of what was, not what would be.

I had seen what would be in the bowl of water last winter. I remembered the urge to laugh as the vision grew in the water. But I'd been coughing so hard laughter eluded me.

"I have looked closely at Curyll," Ector said. "I know he can wage war and lead men—if he will but speak. He has had enough practice. Now he needs experience. I intend to give him that experience. He'll need it to win loyalty since you give him no true name. Unless you tell me otherwise, he will be introduced to the Ardh Rhi and the assembled warbands as a bastard of unknowns." Ector seemed to dismiss Da and his vision.

"Then you condemn Curyll to a miserable life and quick death." Da's voice returned to normal, almost sad. "You condemn Britain to decades of endless warfare until the invaders murder everything that is good and true in our land."

This time, to my sensitive ears, his words carried the ring of prophecy. Had he seen the end of the scene that I had glimpsed in the bowl of water?

Curyll turned and stalked to the door, back rigid, knees so stiff he jerked with each step. He held his head high, but I could tell trouble rode his shoulders like a demon poised to work mischief. I watched the archway where he had disappeared for a long moment, wondering at the torment that raged within him. I left the shadows of the corridor to follow.

"Back to your studies, Wren." Da grabbed the back of my gown to restrain me. He'd crept up behind me on soundless feet.

"But Curyll needs me," I protested.

"The boy needs time alone. You can't solve all of his problems for him. Nor can I." Da looked sad at that. "We won't always be here for him. Now back to your contemplation of the fire. Have you learned why the element varies its properties in sea coal?"

I knew that frown on Da's face. If I wanted to avoid his anger, I had to come up with an answer *now*. He might resort to calling me "Arylwren" if I didn't.

What was the difference between sea coal and wood? "Salt," I blurted out the first thing I thought of. "Sea coal bears the salt of the sea."

Da raised one eyebrow but said no word. His blue eyes sparkled with suppressed laughter. I warmed to my subject under his tacit approval.

"I must throw salt onto wood and light it to test my theory," I said. Da always made me prove my guesses.

"And?" Da prompted me.

"Sea salt as well as mined salt. Why are the two different?" My mind wandered down a different track. I didn't want to study, I wanted to cast magic spells so I could help Curyll. But what did he need? Knowledge. Knowledge was gained by observation and study.

I needed to study more than just Tanio to learn about Curyll's family and his future. The right questions asked of the servants with the loosest tongues might help.

"Da, why didn't you use magic to make Lord Ector agree with you?"

"Magic is not the solution to everything. If I had forced Ector's decision, the spell would not have stayed."

"Just like if Father Thomas had forced Helwriaeth to give up Curyll's tongue, it wouldn't have stayed with him. The cat gave it back of her own free will."

"We have discussed this at length, Wren. Now back to your studies and learn why magic must be used only when necessary."

Chapter 5

I found Curyll after sunset in the watchtower. He had made himself scarce about the fortress since he'd left my side before noon. When he skipped supper, I knew I had to find him. Curyll never missed a meal and always consumed more meat and bread than any of his foster brothers. Sometimes he even ate some of mine, if I was incautious enough to let my mind wander and forget to eat as fast as the others.

I'd asked questions all afternoon and learned no more than what Ector had said about Curyll's birth. Druid secrets, guarded by my father, shrouded his past.

For years, Curyll and his foster brothers had tormented the younger children in the caer with tales of Druid punishments for those who trespassed on secrets. I didn't want to be murdered and dismembered, bits and pieces of my body scattered far and wide, because I learned too much too soon. So I ceased my questions and concentrated on an idea.

My friend leaned on the parapet with his face turned into the wind and sleet. This wind was chased by warmth from lands far to the South; so far away, experienced sea men only guessed at their existence. The Awyr hinted at exotic flavors and new life.

"T–this is the l–last storm of the season, Wren," he said without turning to see who disturbed his solitary vigil. "Y–you and M–Merlin will leave soon. Your Da is the only man alive who knows my heritage. If he leaves without telling me, he takes my future with him." His shaggy hair fell to his shoulders. He hadn't cut it to fit under a Roman helm. I wondered what it would look like decorated with warrior beads.

Then I remembered that men must die for him to earn beads. I couldn't dwell on that depressing thought. Saxon deaths shouldn't touch me. They killed innocents as well as warriors.

Death is death, a voice whispered into the back of my mind.

"Perhaps Da and I will stay here in the North this spring. Da will do much to protect you."

"No. Merlin has other work m—more imp–p–portant than me."

We both knew that Da met with many lords and kings on his rounds each summer. He gathered news and gossip, he observed the health of the land and its people. At least once a year he sang at court and reported to the Ardh Rhi in private. I wondered how many of the king's retainers understood that Da was more than just another bard with a quick wit and tongue. Da was a Druid, able to work magic and hold the pattern of the future in his mind while guiding the present toward it. The gift of prophecy gave him the authority of the chief Druid in all of Britain. Uther Pendragon, Ardh Rhi of Britain, trusted him, listened to his advice above all others, and called him friend.

I remained silent, not certain how to ease Curyll's mind or loosen his tongue from the tangles of its own weaving.

For the first time, I heard pain in his voice. Usually I detected only embarrassment or frustration.

"You speak fine now." I couldn't understand why Curyll feared the taint of bastardy, so I dismissed it. The Goddess honored all children regardless of their parents.

I didn't know how the Christians viewed bastards.

"With you as my only audience I do not fear words. You don't laugh at me. There is a stillness about you that gives me confidence. I need more time and practice if I must speak to claim my inheritance. Whatever it may be."

Even if Lord Ector wouldn't let him cut the meat, since his birthday celebration at the Solstice he was considered old enough to go to war, claim land, and take a bride. The last thought chilled me. Lord Ector's oldest sons, Garoth and Fallon, would wed before the end of summer. Both young men boasted they had already fathered children by serving wenches—bastards proudly acknowledged. Another puzzle I didn't understand. Ector also sought brides for Curyll and Boar. Stinger and Ceffyl had parents who would select wives for them.

The wealth, breeding, and alliances of each bride needed careful scrutiny. I wanted Ector to choose me for Curyll more than I wanted to work magic. I claimed only the alliance of my father. We owned nothing but what we could carry.

Only another Druid would value me enough to offer marriage, a plain brown wren, not beautiful enough to be considered valuable for myself alone.

And I was too young. We had celebrated my ninth birthday at *Imbolc,* the lactation of the ewes, nearly two months before. I had to wait at least two years after I became a woman to wed. Any day now I'd begin the cycle into maturity.

"I will have to fight for my claim," Curyll said. "Weapons alone won't bring me warriors. I'll need to earn the trust of men with land to earn a place to call my own and tenants. I will have to have words as well. Men don't trust leaders who can't prove that their ancestors were warriors or landowners."

"Why do people care so much about your unnamed parents? People should judge you for yourself."

"I am bastard born. I have no name, no list of heroic ancestors for bards to sing at victory banquets. No one will follow me. The Christians grow powerful. They sanctify marriage and abhor children born outside that union."

"You might not be a bastard."

"An orphan who has been hidden all his life?" He tried raising one eyebrow like Da and failed. "I will have to seek out the truth myself and then prove myself by feats of arms and feats of words as well."

"Most landowners know only war. Law and justice belong to the strongest," I reminded him. Few lords had Ector's foresight in providing an education for sons and fosterlings. Philosophy and history had little use when fighting for one's life and one's family against ruthless Saxon axes and spears.

"I want more than that, Wren. Law and justice should belong to every man. Honor and loyalty should come from trust, not fear. I want to make a difference in our world. There is change in the wind, change for the better, change I must guide. I sense it. Something big and wonderful and important waits for me; more than just a caer I steal from someone less powerful than I and a warband of desperate men no other lord wants. I sense it in the wind. I know it in my heart."

His words stirred something in my breast. I had seen in a bowl of water what he could become. Perhaps I had been granted that vision in order to guide my friend toward his true destiny.

Law and Justice for all.

"Da says you have a destiny that will live through the ages." As I said the words, a vacancy grew in the back of my neck. I wanted to laugh long and uncontrolled. Dizziness assailed me, just as if I was about to have a vision. I knew that I spoke the truth.

"A destiny I can't claim without a name and stirring words." He bowed his head in resignation.

The dizziness spread, and I knew that only I could lead him to his destiny.

Was it time yet?

The next night Da woke me at midnight and led me outside without a word. I followed without question. Our years on the road, when raiders and outlaws lurked and demons prowled at odd hours, had taught me wariness and instant obedience to my father's wishes.

"Sit beside me, Wren." Da invited me to join him on the ground in the sheltered ell between the Hall and the bath. He fingered his torc, deep in thought. A small fire glowed within a ring of stones before him. He still wouldn't let me light any fires with my mind. I did it when he wasn't looking just to keep in practice.

That kind of magic, like speaking with animals, came easy to me. But true magic, the kind that required a ritual spell frightened me because of the exhaustion I knew must follow.

I crossed my legs and sank down to the damp earth. My bones sighed with relief as I made contact with the Goddess. All winter we'd hidden within walls of stone piled into unnatural barriers. We'd eaten stale food, breathed stale air, and drunk from a well dug into the earth rather than a free spring. How could we be a part of Dana with walls and staleness separating us from the Goddess?

Above us, the last remnants of clouds scudded across the sky. A few stars peeked out at us, tentative, waiting for the last storm to flee.

"Tonight I will show you a different way of looking into Tanio, Wren," Da said quietly.

"I've been looking into fires for nigh on a week." A week of contemplating flames while the household bustled with preparations for the men to go to war and Curyll avoided me. I could tell he really wanted to go with the men, wanted to be one of them.

The Saxons would wait for spring to attack our shores, but Britons couldn't wait. We had to be ready to beat the invaders back at first landing.

But the men couldn't leave until the timing was right. I wouldn't let them. Somehow I had to stall their departure a few more days.

"There is more to Tanio than flames and heat. Tanio is an element Belenos would have kept to himself, but the Goddess gave it to Her people. 'Tis a blessing when captured within a fire ring, an enemy when let loose in a thatched roof or dry forest." Da sang the words as if he composed a new teaching song.

The rhythm of his words swung into harmony with the flying clouds and twinkling stars. I opened my eyes and my heart and stared at the flames.

"Tanio, an element," Da chanted. "One of four. One with four. Pridd supporting us. Awyr sustaining us. Dwfr nourishing us. Tanio heating, blending, binding. . . ."

Hot red, orange, and yellow, leaping high, consuming wood, flickering in the dance of life, reaching ever higher. Blue and white, anchoring, containing, searing, hotter than the rest.

My spirit fell into the flames.

I saw strange sights, frightful sights. . . . I saw more fire upon the earth. Uncontrolled fire and smoke. Gwaed, the god of blood, walked the Pridd, tall and proud. Cernunnos, god of the Underworld, came out of the shadows. I choked on smoke reeking of funeral pyres. My eyes watered. My skin grew oversensitive from the heat. The flames spread outward, thinning briefly.

Into their midst strode Curyll. My friend grown older, taller, stronger. Blood stained his tunic and mail. His helm was dented and his shield missing. He still carried a massive battle sword in his strong left hand—not the long weapon glowing with Power I had seen him wield in another vision. Around him, men fought and cried out. Briton and Saxon clashed together in a life struggle for possession of the land. Land that belonged only to the Goddess.

Curyll bent over, his face hidden in the wreckage of dead and dying. My heart cried out, fearing him wounded or dead. He stood again, a long pole in his right hand. At the end of the shaft of wood fluttered a tattered piece of cloth.

Before my eyes, Curyll raised the battle standard of the Ardh Rhi, Uther Pendragon. A red dragon rampant upon a field of white. Up and up, reaching as high as the flames, Curyll lifted the royal symbol. "To me!" he called. "Rally to me!" No hesitation. No stutter. Around his head flew a halo of many-colored sparks of Life. A great army responded to his cry, gathering around him, following his lead. The army stretched across the field of battle and beyond. Their numbers grew so great the Saxons fell back into the sea; there was no more room for them in Britain.

Men raised new banners to the Pendragon—Ardh Rhi Uther. Women shouted and sang to Uther's champion. My heart swelled with pride for Curyll. My eyes cried because I was not among the throng that surged forward to sing his praises. I, who loved him best in all the world, would not share in his victory.

Sadness sent me plunging back into my body. Once more I sat beside Da on the cold ground in front of a simple stone fire ring. I barely had the strength to sit upright. My head drooped nearly to my knees.

My vision faded with the certainty that Curyll had won—would win—that battle in the name of the Ardh Rhi.

"You convinced Helwriaeth to give back his tongue. But you left the work half-done, Wren. He needs the confidence to use his tongue. You must complete the work, or the spell was for nothing. Each bit of magic left incomplete depletes the value of magic and makes it less effective. You must finish this."

"Yes, Da. I see what he will become. I won't let others keep him from his destiny because he cannot defend his heritage with words. Andraste will fight beside him and make him a hero." I saw the pattern. The Goddess as warrior queen guided Curyll and protected him. His victories would earn him that glorious sword singing with power.

Da chuckled softly in the darkness. "So fierce, my Wren. I almost pity any who oppose Curyll, should I turn you loose on the world."

Chapter 6

"FOLLOW my leader," I called to the laughing children of Lord Ector's household the next day. Free at last from the confines of the fortress, I scrambled atop a fallen oak tree and ran its length to the root ball. My bare feet clung to the crumbling bark. This tree had been an ancient giant among its fellows. Six men linking hands in a circle couldn't span its girth at the base. I counted steps as I ran its length. Nearly three hundred. It had fallen last winter during a fierce storm and had taken several younger trees with it. A broad clearing yawned around the dead giant. Sunlight penetrated to the forest floor here, encouraging new plants and seedling trees to grow.

Da and I had mourned the tree's passing. Today I rejoiced in the life it gave back to the forest. Already young ferns sought to root around it. Insects burrowed for food, and birds gathered twigs and bark for nests.

I inhaled deeply of the intoxicating aromas of damp earth, sprouting green, and warm sunlight. My body seemed about to burst. The forest sang with life, and so did I.

The goddess promised that out of death comes life, manifested in these sights and smells. So did Father Thomas, but in words that drifted far from the ear. I refused to puzzle over the mystery. I needed to run and shout and rejoice in *life* after a winter of being cooped up in the caer. Stale air and smoky fires had no place in today's sunshine.

Behind me I heard Curyll and some of his foster brothers helping the little ones onto the tree trunk. They should have been hunting with the men. But the timing and allotment of horses had been all wrong. I had made certain of that. I didn't have to use magic to divert and misdirect. Lady Glynnis had ordered Boar, Curyll, Stinger, and Ceffyl to watch over us as we played in the forest.

I didn't look back to see who did and who did not manage to keep up with me. I belonged to the forest. I knew places none of the others would think to tread.

False spring had melted the snow and brightened the sunshine. Lady Glynnis rose this morning and ordered a clean sweep of the fortress. New rushes for the floors. Bedding needed airing and laundry hung out-of-doors. Children were a hindrance on such days and I gladly led them in boisterous games away from the industry of the women. Most of the men, including Da, had left early on a last hunt before leaving for war, rather than be commandeered into cleaning. Curyll and his foster brothers agreed that minding the children in the forest was preferable to beating wall hangings or stirring boiling laundry.

"Wait up, Wren," Boar called to me. He didn't like anyone straying beyond his eyes' limited range. He really was a nearsighted boar; bad-tempered and belligerent when crossed. I ignored him.

Curyll should have been the one who directed us all. Maybe today I could break his habit of silence.

Without slowing my pace, I slid gleefully to the ground from the immense height of the trunk near the root ball. Soft moss and ferns cushioned my landing. I laughed out loud and kept running into the depth of the forest.

I knew a place where water sprites played and flower faeries gathered seeds. First I would have to leave the others content to play in the clearing so that they wouldn't disturb the spell I wanted to try.

All winter I had kept magic buried deep within me while I studied the how and why of it. The time had come to allow the elements of my spells full range, out-of-doors where we belonged.

"W—where are you, Wr—Wren?" Curyll stood at the top of the root ball, peering into the darkness of the forest. Beyond the clearing of the fallen giant, the canopy of branches formed a thick ceiling. Little light penetrated to the forest floor.

I giggled to let my friend know I wasn't far off.

"We'd best spread out and search for her," Stinger said sternly. He methodically stripped a heavy broken branch of side twigs and swung it like a club. The Stinger was always ready to fight with whatever weapons came to hand, even if the enemy was only a question.

"It's like she stepped through a door into another world!" Ceffyl gasped. His thick dark hair, newly cropped to fit under his helm, stood out like a ceffyl's bristly mane cut short for war. He looked ready to rear and bolt on his long legs.

"Sh–she's The Merlin's daughter. What do you expect?" Curyll laughed, barely stuttering at all.

I had stepped from sunlight into darkness, from clear vision into secrets. The Otherworld couldn't be more different. Only Curyll would see me, and only if he looked with his heart and not his eyes.

I loosed another little laugh from a different direction. Curyll swung his attention to my hiding place. Ceffyl continued to look where I had been. Stinger and Boar began beating the underbrush with sticks in yet another direction. A grin split Curyll's worried face and he climbed down from the tree trunk, less gracefully than I had.

I trusted him to find me, always.

I stood up and ran again with Curyll in pursuit. My bare feet barely touched the ground, I felt so light and free. I wanted to tear off my gown and fling it away, become one with the elements without the hindrance of clothing. When wind and sun caressed my growing body, I would become one with the Goddess. Only free of coverings could I experience the *gaia,* a sense of unity with all life. Da would understand. Lady Glynnis and the boys wouldn't.

This summer I will run naked and free with the faeries, I promised myself. *This summer when Da and I roam Britain again. I will grow and mature and be ready for Beltane next year, or the year after. Maybe I can arrange for Curyll to be my first partner.*

Soon, within days, I would make the first transition into womanhood. I knew that as well as I knew the answer to Curyll's cure.

The pool I sought shimmered in the sunshine ahead. Ages ago, another forest giant had fallen, its roots weakened by an underground spring. As the tree rotted, water filled the depression. New trees didn't spring up to fill the gap in the canopy because of the swampy ground. So the water continued to fill the clearing. Now the secret lives who inhabited the dark recesses of the forest found it an ideal gathering place.

"Wr–Wren, wh–where are you? Are y–you lost?" Curyll yelled. His booted feet thrashed through the piles of dead leaves left behind by last autumn's fall. Each step stirred a crisp scent left over from previous seasons blending into the new one.

My feet left barely a trace of my passing. Curyll would leave an easy path to follow home. I'd show him how to retrace his steps later. When we finished the spell.

I paused at the edge of the pool still within the darkness of the trees. Awe and silence surrounded me, as if the opening between two trees was really a doorway into the Otherworld. Blending with the stillness, I reached out with my mind and called. . . .

"W–why d–did you run so far a–ahead of the others?" Curyll said, out of breath. "If we g–get sep–separated, we'll be lost. You k–know Merlin warned us to s–stay together."

He'd been running to keep up with me, and the heat of his body reached out to include me. He smelled of sweat and leather and sunshine, healthy and clean. I enfolded myself into his warmth, binding us together to complete a spell. A thrill of something special tickled the base of my spine and spread outward. I pressed a finger to my lips. Then I pointed to the center of the pool. A flutter of bright colors that might have been mayflies danced above the water.

Curyll's eyes opened wide in wonder. He knew, as I did, that no respectable mayfly would hover over a forest pool a week past the Vernal Equinox, false spring or no.

"Faeries?" he mouthed the word without a sound. No sound, no stutter. He fingered his torc, like a protective talisman, just like Da did in the presence of magic.

Don't startle them, I replied with my mind instead of my mouth. Another trick I had learned on my own but not quite perfected. Happily, it worked with Curyll better than anyone else.

He stood hunted-still.

Gradually the fluttering lives gathered around us. Sunlight struck their wings and flashed rainbows, filling the clearing with color. We grinned in delight at the spectacle. Curyll relaxed. The faeries alighted in his hair, on his shoulders and his face. They surrounded us in a halo of bright sparks and laughter.

The faeries never wore clothes. Their tiny naked bodies appeared human except for their brightly colored skin and slightly pointed ears. If I looked very closely, I could see rainbows flickering across their wings.

Curyll twitched his nose where a yellow faery tickled him. I watched him struggle to suppress a sneeze. The faery increased her teasing. Her full breasts jiggled with her laughter. Curyll couldn't hold back any longer. He blasted forth with a mighty explosion of air.

The faeries rose in a chattering and giggling swarm around our heads. Eventually the flighty creatures settled down.

Why have you called us here? a dark green male faery asked. I wondered briefly if Curyll's body was as perfectly formed as this being's.

"Curyll, my dear friend, needs practice speaking," I replied swallowing my curiosity. "The trees have infinite patience and will not laugh at Curyll when he falters. When he has mastered the ability to speak clearly to the trees, will you let him learn to speak to you?"

Every one of the brightly colored beings nodded agreement. Their giggles of mischief tinkled on the wind like a hundred tiny silver bells.

"W–Wren, I–I—can't," Curyll said. He blushed to his ear tips. "They al–already laugh a–at m–me!"

The faeries swarmed in brilliant display of flapping wings and uncontrollable laughter; a full chorus of chiming mirth, much more musical than the heavy church bells the Christians used.

"You can, Curyll. Take your time. Form each word in your head before you wrap your tongue around it. You'll learn quickly enough that faeries laugh at everything, not just you." Another round of musical giggles supported my statement. "When you learn to ignore them, you will be able to ignore people who laugh at nothing as well."

"W–we must g–o ba–ck soon. The others . . ."

"Time means nothing here, my friend. As long as the faeries listen, there is no such thing as time." I settled upon a bed of moss at the side of the pool and waited.

Curyll joined me, shaking his head in wonderment.

"Listen to yourself as you listen to others. Make each word count." I took his hand in both of mine, enjoying the sense of unity his touch gave to me. "We are in gaia, in touch and harmony with every aspect of life. Speak freely without embarrassment or hesitation."

The faeries settled in my lap, beside me, and on various shrubs. Each took up an attitude of intense concentration that quickly shattered as they found mirth in my stillness.

"W–what will this miracle cost me?" Curyll asked, looking at the ground.

"If it works, promise the faeries that you will never forget the Old Gods and will always honor their creatures of forest, field, and spring. Promise the Goddess."

He looked up. A cloud of uncertainty fell over his eyes.

"Promise me."

"I–I promise, Wren. I promise to always honor the Old Gods and all their creatures of forest and field and spring."

"Seal it in a circle, Curyll."

He drew a circle in my palm with his fingertip. I repeated the seal by drawing a circle in the air, a circle big enough to include the faeries. A hint of Tanio tailed my finger as I traced the sigil.

"I. Hope. This. Works," Curyll said, still holding my hand.

"As long as you keep your promise, the faeries will help you speak. As long as they trust you, they will protect you." *Because I can't always be there for you. But I'll try.*

Ceffyl slugged Garoth in the jaw. Garoth reeled back, off-balance. He flailed his arms. Blood trickled from a split in his lower lip. Ceffyl tackled his much larger, and more experienced, foster brother around the waist. His face turned bright red with anger.

Both of their helms tilted as they fell to the ground together.

I hadn't seen what started this fight. Arms practice often disintegrated into brawls. Emotions ran high. My friends and companions turned vicious when they took up sword, ax, or spear. Lord Ector had said 'twas good training for the boys.

"Cease!" Garoth yelled, grabbing the younger boy's neck with a thick forearm.

"Take it back!" Ceffyl choked out the words. He pummeled Garoth's chest with his fists.

I saw Ceffyl prepare his legs for a vicious kick.

Together they rolled in the mud, out of my field of vision.

Lord Ector and the other adults seemed to have disappeared, allowing the boys to settle the dispute themselves.

Siblings and fosterlings gathered in a circle around the grappling youths. They alternately cheered and jeered the wrestlers.

Ceffyl rammed his knee upward. He missed Garoth's groin by a finger's length.

"Get him, Ceffyl!" Fallon yelled. "It's time someone showed my brother he isn't Ardh Rhi of this caer."

Boar, who idolized his brother Garoth, rammed his fist into Fallon's gut.

The oldest of Ector's brood doubled over.

Quickly, the entire throng dissolved into a mass of flying fists, kicking feet, yells of pain, and grunts of satisfaction.

I stepped out of the shadows to get a better view and tripped over two flailing bodies. Before I could catch my balance, I tasted mud and something heavy landed on my back. All the air left my lungs in a whoosh. I couldn't lift my face away from the churned clay of the courtyard. I couldn't breathe.

Every attempt to draw a breath filled my mouth with more mud.

Red-tinged blackness filled my eyes. Strength oozed out of my arms and legs.

Red on black images chased each other across my dimming eyesight. Laughter boiled in my stomach—the mad laughter of prophecy. I needed to stop and see what vision of the future the Goddess offered. Red for fire, black for death . . .

Suddenly, just when I thought the Goddess would show me something important, or claim me once and for all, the weight on my back disappeared. Someone's strong fingers grabbed the back of my dress. I found myself upright, gasping.

"Breathe, Wren." Curyll slapped my back hard. Mud spewed out my mouth. Tears sprang into my eyes.

I gulped a huge mouthful of air.

"Now sit down and stay clear," Curyll ordered. He sounded like an adult giving orders to small children. Or a warrior commanding a battle.

"You've got to stop this, Curyll. They are hurting each other," I gasped as more mud spluttered out of my mouth.

"Give them five more minutes. Then they'll be tired enough to listen to reason." He drew a dirt clod out of my hair.

After a few moments, when the frenzy slowed to a methodical drone, Curyll strode forward. One by one, he separated the combatants.

"Enough!" he commanded in a voice that filled the walled courtyard and echoed against the watchtower.

Everyone, including the watchers, froze in place. The babble ceased. Curyll turned in a full circle, glaring at each person individually. No one questioned him. We waited for him to direct us.

My heart filled with pride. Two days ago, my friend would not have dared command the older boys. After our hours with the faeries, he easily assumed leadership of us all.

"Now tell me, who started this?" Curyll barked, expecting compliance.

No one met his eyes. Ceffyl and Garoth hung their heads slightly. Boar and Fallon looked upward.

Curyll stalked over to them. "You should be ashamed of yourself, Garoth, brawling with a boy half your size."

Garoth said nothing.

"But from the looks of those bruises on your face, Ceffyl held his own against you," Curyll chuckled.

Ceffyl lifted his head and threw back his shoulders.

"Did you start it?" Curyll suddenly grabbed Ceffyl's shirt and dragged him close until they stood nose to nose.

"Y–yes," the slighter boy answered. Fear and confusion shone from his eyes.

"Why? You must have had a good reason to challenge Garoth, who outweighs you by three stone and tops you by a head height."

"He . . . it's personal." Ceffyl met Curyll's gaze and held it.

Curyll jerked his head in a quick nod of acceptance. Then he released Ceffyl and turned toward the rest of his foster brothers and Ector's men at arms.

"And the rest of you? What cause have you to fight your comrades? The rules established by Lord Ector and The Merlin declare that individual disputes must be settled by the individuals and no one else. Have you no respect for rules?"

"In battle, we make our own rules," Fallon said. "When your blood lust gets up, you fight whoever stands in your way." He stepped forward as if to challenge Curyll's authority to impose order.

"This is arms practice, not battle. We are not Saxons who kill indiscriminately. Rules exist for a reason."

"Rules are made by those strong enough to enforce them and broken by any who can get away with it," Garoth argued. He and Fallon stood together, shoulder to shoulder. They presented a solid wall of resistance to Curyll.

"When we ride to battle with the Saxons, we can't afford to fight among ourselves," Curyll reminded them. "We must learn better ways to settle disputes than coming to blows. We must learn to live within the rules."

The watchers drifted apart, some to stand behind Lord Ector's oldest sons; the others to stand behind Curyll. Boar, Stinger, and Ceffyl took positions to Curyll's right and left. The four of them almost massed as much weight as their two opponents.

I stepped up between Stinger and Curyll, suddenly realizing that words counted more than fists and spears right now. As long as Curyll spoke the words.

"Rules and laws are made for the benefit of all," Curyll called loudly so that all within the courtyard could hear. "Without rules, we are little better than a pack of wolves hunting in the night, or Saxons who kill for the love of killing. Rules and laws are intricately woven into our culture. Our civilization. Without them, we have nothing to fight for."

"We fight the Saxons for our lives. Our land," Garoth reminded him.

"We also fight for our right to call ourselves Britons. If our lives and the land are all we care about, we could join the Saxons, let them rule us. We'd have our lives. We'd have the land to feed us. Nothing more. But we are *not* Saxon slaves. Our laws, our rules that guide our daily lives, and the way we honor the Goddess or any god we care to name, make us Britons.

"Together we can beat back the invasion and preserve our way of life. But if we fight each other with no respect for our laws and rules, then we lose our honor, our trust, and the sense of justice that binds us together.

"We must stand together. Die together if necessary. Fighting among ourselves leads to the death of our spirit and the death of Britain!"

Behind me, someone clapped his hands together, slowly, rhythmically. Others joined in the stunning display of approval. Garoth and Fallon stepped back, jaws slightly agape.

I smiled. My heart filled with joy and pride for my special friend.

In the distance I heard my father chuckle. "I guess he is ready to lead men after all," he said to Lord Ector.

"Tonight he cuts the meat. Tomorrow, at dawn, we ride to join Uther's army," Lord Ector replied.

At dawn. At dawn I would say good-bye to Curyll. I'd done all I could to help him. He didn't need me anymore.

Loneliness opened a deep chasm in my chest. I needed to reach out and hold onto Curyll and my friends. They were all preoccupied with each other and making plans for the morrow. No one had time for one plain brown wren lost in a sea of adult males. At dawn I would say good-bye to them and our childhood.

Chapter 7

"WAKE up, Wren, we're here," Merlin said wearily. His neck and shoulders ached from rowing the little boat through the marshes surrounding the islands of Avalon. He'd taken the long and twisted route here to confuse any who might have followed them to the sacred isles rising sharply above water level.

At low tide causeways existed between some of the islands. Treacherous marshes hid the stepping places. He didn't want an enemy to learn the route. So he took a different path each time he came here.

"W–what?" Wren opened her eyes and looked around sleepily. She'd never been a good sailor and usually sought relief from a queasy stomach in sleep.

"Take the rope and lash the bow to the dock, Wren. We have arrived at Avalon. The Morrigan awaits you." The new Morrigan, not his Deirdre. Wren's mother had died in childbirth, as Dana had told him she would. He didn't know the new High Priestess of Britain well. He'd had minimal contact with her over the past nine years.

He heaved a sigh. He missed Deirdre, especially now that Wren approached womanhood and looked so much like her. He missed Deirdre more than any of the others of his kind. Wren's mother had been his friend for many years before he finally succumbed to the inevitable and took her as a lover that one fateful Beltane night. He had no regrets. That one lapse in his lifelong celibacy had given him Wren, a most beautiful and promising daughter. Wren provided wonderful companionship and had proved a discreet confidante. But . . . but some things a man just did not share with his daughter.

And now the time had come to entrust her training to The Morrigan.

Aching emptiness gnawed a hole in his gut. He wouldn't see Wren, or communicate with her for many years to come. Her training would be intense; she needed to sever all ties with her old life in order to complete it.

A part of him hoped she would refuse to stay, that they could continue to be together as they had her entire life.

She needed peace to learn magic and wisdom. His life with Ardh Rhi Uther's army would not be peaceful. She needed the company of women to learn to be a woman. The only women accompanying the men to war would teach her the wrong things about being a woman.

"Dana, let me live long enough to see her again," he whispered a prayer.

"Did you say something, Da?" Wren asked as she tied a competent knot in the rope. She scrambled onto the dock.

On another day, in another time, he'd have teased her about her hasty exit from the boat. Not today. Not when he was about to lose her—no, he wouldn't lose her. They'd just have to endure a separation. The first since her birth.

"I didn't say anything important, Wren. Just that I'll miss you."

"That's important, Da. I still don't see why I have to live here. You could teach me more than the Ladies of Avalon." She set her chin in stubborn mode. She looked so like Deirdre he almost believed her alive again.

"There are many things only The Morrigan can teach you, Wren. Accept it. You will stay here until she determines you ready to go out into the world again." The ache in his gut grew wider with every argument.

Maybe he could keep her with him?

No. He had to let her go. Let her grow.

She glared at him in silence, the worst possible rebuke she could give him. He almost relented and rowed back to the mainland with her rather than endure her silent displeasure.

"Come, Wren. We must find The Morrigan. I am not allowed to remain at the Ladies' enclave after sundown. No man is except on Beltane." He climbed onto the dock. The island rose steeply from a narrow landing area. Groves of apple trees swarmed up the slopes. Sweet blossoms filled the air with an intoxicating perfume. He drank deeply of the scents, relishing the lush greenery.

He remembered the Solstice night the year he turned fourteen.

He had climbed the tor of Avalon along with a dozen other young men, Druids in training. The treacherous and convoluted ritual labyrinth had challenged his ingenuity and his endurance. But he had negotiated the traps and illusions without mishap. Not all of his companions had been successful.

"I wonder if I have time to climb up there and back before sunset?" he said. He could always seek a night's shelter with the Christian hermit on the other side of the island.

Every time he'd climbed the tor he'd been filled with a sense of accomplishment, of completeness. He wished for that again, knowing he'd be incomplete until Wren returned to him. Climbing the tor again wouldn't accomplish anything other than his own fatigue.

Wren shrugged and looked away from the peak of the tor, still not speaking to him. He longed to rush forward and enfold her in his arms. She'd likely push him away in her current mood. He didn't want to part from her with rejection and recriminations. He didn't want to part from her at all.

Three heavily cloaked and hooded figures appeared on the path that wound down the lower slopes of the tor. A fourth figure trailed several paces behind. She threw back the hood of her cloak defiantly, exposing a thick mane of auburn hair.

Merlin raised one eyebrow in question.

Wren edged back toward the boat until she bumped into Merlin's chest. She shrank within her own cloak at sight of the beautiful red-haired girl near her own age.

"You have no reason to be shy, my Wren. You are as beautiful as any woman alive."

She snorted her disbelief of that statement. "What is happening, Da?" she asked, straightening her shoulders and standing away from him. "There is something strange about that girl. . . ."

"Strange? Is it strange that an acolyte of Avalon is very beautiful?" he chuckled.

Wren turned and glared at him again.

Then the lead figure stepped onto the dock. She raised her face and looked into Merlin's eyes.

"My Lady Morrigan." He bowed deeply toward her. She must have had a name before she became High Priestess. No one remembered it now. She embodied the Goddess and thus was known only by her title.

"My Lord Merlin," she replied, inclining her head. He had another name as well but rarely used it.

"I have brought my daughter, as I promised."

"I didn't promise," Wren muttered.

The Morrigan cocked her head. A buttery blonde curl escaped her hood. A decade of care and worry seemed to melt from her face, bringing her seeming age much closer to Wren's than The Merlin's.

"We must beg a favor of you, My Lord Merlin," The Morrigan said, returning her gaze to him. Her blue eyes clouded with regret.

"If it is within my power, My Lady." He inclined his head.

"One of our number has died. Her family has requested her body be returned to them for funeral rites." She swallowed heavily and continued. "We are so few now, I cannot spare another Lady to accompany her on her final journey. Her nephew will meet you on the mainland near the Roman church at the three sacred wells."

"So few?" The last Merlin had known, the number of Ladies diminished each year, but surely a dozen at least remained. They had new acolytes each year. The beautiful redhead studied here. She couldn't be much older than Wren.

"So few. We are but seven and this one leaves us permanently to return to her family." The Morrigan gestured toward the end of the line of those who accompanied her.

The redhead tossed her hair defiantly. She opened her mouth to speak, but the other two women each raised a hand, palm outward gesturing for silence.

"If their numbers are so few, then they can't teach me properly. I'll learn more if I stay with you, Da," Wren said. She stepped back toward the hated boat, a sure sign of her determination to leave.

"Nimuë must leave us. Her father's servants will arrive with their barge when the tide is full and the passage easy." The Morrigan said to Merlin. Then she turned back to Wren. "We can teach you all you need to know, Arylwren. We will delight in helping you explore your talent as well as your destiny." An aura of love and power radiated from her head. The layers of blue and yellow reached out to enfold Wren, almost as if The Morrigan clasped her in a welcoming embrace.

The welcome stopped abruptly at The Merlin's toes.

"Will you stay with us, Wren? Will you grow into your full potential and lead us into a new age?"

Wren took a hesitant step forward. "What can you teach me that my father cannot?"

The Morrigan smiled. Her aura pulsed. Merlin sensed she shared mind images with Wren. He wished he could join in the incredible bond developing between the priestess and his daughter.

"Aye, I'll stay a while. As long as you can teach me." Wren nodded her acceptance as well.

Merlin's heart sank. Wren had committed herself. He had to leave her. No last-minute miracle would let her return with him.

"Father Merlin." The Morrigan touched his arm. A sense of urgency snaked up his skin from the point of contact despite her placid expression. "Dyfrig came looking for you at the full moon."

A cold lump landed in his belly. He tried to isolate it before it froze every muscle and emotion in him. He didn't trust his voice to reply calmly, so he lifted one eyebrow in question. But his left hand stole up to finger his torc before he could control the instinctive gesture.

"He left a message." The Morrigan pulled a scrap of parchment from her pocket.

The Merlin stuffed the roll into his sack without reading it. He guessed the contents. His mother asked for him. For three decades the only contact with his brother had been these brief notes asking him to contact his brother but not to trouble their mother with his presence.

He never contacted his twin brother.

"I entrust your care and education to these good Ladies, Wren," he said, rather too formally. He wanted to crush his daughter to his breast and never let her go, as his mother had not done to him when Blaise, the last Merlin, had claimed him for formal training.

Wren nodded. A fat tear dropped from her eyelashes down her cheek to touch the corner of her mouth.

Tenderly, he wiped it away.

"Come with me now, Wren," The Morrigan invited. "We will rest and sup. Your training begins tomorrow at dawn." She turned to retreat up the tor.

"Good luck. She wasn't able to teach me anything," Nimuë, the redhead, said with a sneer. "I'm glad to leave."

"When you are willing to learn, you may come back. I hope you have at least learned that you must work to discover true knowledge buried deep within you. Information and routines handed to you sit on the surface and fade quickly," The Morrigan replied.

Nimuë sniffed and marched to the end of the dock. She stared at the water as if willing her father's barge to magically appear before her.

"I will take the girl away. Her father can meet her on the mainland," Merlin said. Why had he offered? Something about the girl fascinated him. Not a sexual attraction. He'd never succumb to that again, the experience had cost him much, despite giving him Wren. But the girl had something special, perhaps a true magical talent . . . perhaps . . .

"Da?" Wren's soft voice drew him out of his reverie. "Da, I'll miss you." She threw her arms about his waist and hugged him tight.

"I'll miss you, too, Wren. More than you can know." Tears nearly choked him. He'd be so lonely. . . .

"Promise you will look after Curyll for me, Da. Stinger, Boar, and Ceffyl, too. They may be men, but they still need looking after."

"Yes, Wren, I will look after your friends and do all in my power to keep them safe." He clutched her tight, afraid to say more lest he openly cry.

"Visit me, Da. Visit me often. I don't know what I'll do without you." Wren sobbed. Her tears dampened his tunic.

"I'll come when the time is right. Look for me within the dawn mists, little Wren. Sing sweetly across the water, and I will meet you."

She cried openly now.

"Sing for me when the time is right." Tears streamed down his own cheeks despite his effort to hold them back.

Chapter 8

I was right. The Morrigan and her Ladies couldn't teach me much. My father had given me a bard's education and a deep understanding of the natural world around me. We had performed rituals together at every appropriate occasion. He had taught how to find magic within myself and the world around me.

The Ladies gave me freedom, though, freedom to explore magic and ritual far beyond the limits my father imposed upon me. They gave me an introduction to the womanly arts of spinning, weaving, and sewing.

I never mastered those arts but knew enough to make simple garments and stitch a fine seam in the gaping wound in the hermit's thigh when he slashed it open while chopping wood. Rain had made the ax handle slick, and the old man didn't really have the strength to wield his tool properly. After that, I chopped wood for him as I did for the Ladies.

As I chanted healing and cleansing spells over the ugly gash, the wind whispering through the trees told me that Curyll had suffered a wound as well. I almost abandoned my task to go to him. 'Twas my destiny to heal him, to protect him. How could I do that from the isolation of Avalon?

A faery giggled in my ear and gave me further news. My father stitched the knife slash across Curyll's ribs and bound the wound tightly. He wrapped the bandages about Curyll's chest tight enough that my friend could barely breathe. He certainly couldn't swing a weapon prematurely and reopen the wound. The faeries assured me his hurt was minor. He didn't need me. Yet.

First I must learn the great healing magic. Only The Morrigan could teach me that.

I calmed my heartbeat and waited.

The Ladies did teach me an awareness and appreciation of my maturing body. I learned to welcome the flow of moon blood as a symbol of my femininity and potential fertility.

I didn't expect to participate in Beltane that first year. My womanhood was too new. I stayed in my small round hut alone while the Ladies rowed over to the lake village. In the morning they greeted me as usual, if a little red-eyed from lack of sleep, and nothing more was said of the rituals that had transpired.

The faeries carried more interesting accounts of Beltane. Interspersed with many giggles and a few miniature demonstrations, I learned some of the rituals and excesses of this fertility celebration. My face burned with embarrassment. The secret places on my body heated with longing.

Mostly The Morrigan and her Ladies taught me to be at peace with myself whether alone or in company. I sat for hours contemplating nothing, while I opened myself to the will of the gods.

The Morrigan welcomed people from villages near and far with grace and dignity. She always wore yellow, the same color as her hair. She appeared a ray of sunshine to those in need. We treated their ailments, accepted their offerings, and heard the latest gossip from the outside world.

More and more the chores of healing fell to me, directed by The Morrigan with elegant gestures and gentle words. Of the six Ladies who taught me, four had lived on the Isle of Avalon for fifty years and more. Their eyesight failed, and their hands trembled. So I sewed up wounds, mixed tonics, and applied poultices. For the truly serious ailments, The Morrigan performed great healing rituals. She took me into her hut along with one other, an ancient Lady who could barely see but had a gentle touch with minor magic.

Then I forgot everything that transpired. The Morrigan must have enchanted me. When I awoke from the trance, I ground my teeth and sought information.

The Morrigan's hut was almost empty of furniture and adornment. Any tools she might have used during her ritual had been cleared away before I opened my eyes and my mind.

I found The Morrigan collapsed upon the dirt floor, her patient resting comfortably on her cot.

"What ails you, Lady?" I knelt beside her, feeling for her pulse. I couldn't find the life beat on the inside of her wrist. When I found the great vein in her neck, the shallow and uneven rhythm frightened me.

"A headache only," she whispered. Her voice sounded scratchy and strained.

"She will need sleep," the ancient assistant said. She stumbled up the one step to crawl out the doorway.

I lit a small oil lamp so I could see better.

The Morrigan screamed as the light hit her eyes.

Quickly I doused the lamp and ran to my own hut for my stash of herbs. I prepared a soothing mixture of cleansing herbs to throw on the fire and fed her small sips of an infusion of willow bark until she slept.

Three times that first summer on Avalon I nursed her through the aftermath of a healing spell. "Teach me this magic," I begged her when she recovered the third time. "You are killing yourself by giving too much to others. Please share this burden."

"You will not thank me, Wren. This is something I must do. I am The Morrigan." Her face had lost most of its natural color, and her hair hung limply about her shoulders, pale and lifeless. I knew from experience that a week or more would pass before she regained vitality. Each time she worked a healing, less of her strength returned and she lost weight that she never regained.

"I will be The Morrigan after you. There is no one else to take your place. Please do not do this to yourself anymore. Teach me." Tears sprang to my eyes, and I realized I had come to love this woman. I had come to love Avalon and the Ladies.

I still missed Da and Curyll and the others, but this place had become home, an anchor in my life; something I had never had before.

The Morrigan met my demand for learning with silence.

Then the day came the next winter when two of our Ladies burned with fever and coughed incessantly. I burned special herbs on their hearths. I fed them special tonics and potions. I prayed.

Still the illness persisted, and the women grew weaker by the hour.

I called The Morrigan. She examined each Lady minutely, listening to their breathing through a long tube of seaweed. She felt their pulses at neck and wrist and studied the phlegm they coughed up.

"I can do nothing more for them," she said quietly and left the smoky hut.

"Then teach me how to help them," I demanded, following her to the door of her own shelter.

"I have no more strength, Wren. I have not had that kind of strength since before you came to us. Even the teaching would leave me vulnerable to the sickness that takes our sisters. I would willingly sacrifice myself to show you the secrets. But you are not ready to take my place. When I have passed from this life, Avalon will cease to be. Without Avalon, you cannot do this magic."

"What do you mean? Avalon is merely a place."

"Avalon is a special place. You have experienced the peace and stillness within that follows a ritual at the red spring."

"But Avalon does not work magic. People do. I can do it."

"Not alone."

I raised one eyebrow in question. She looked at me strangely and sighed.

"The great healing magic belongs to women. It must be worked in community. A maiden, a matron, and a crone must work in concert. When I am gone there will be only you and several crones. No more maidens come to us. Why should I kill myself teaching you this magic when you will never be able to use it?"

The world reeled around me. Pieces of a vision flitted before my eyes. Laughter bubbled in my throat.

"I will need it. To save Britain, I will have to heal the Ardh Rhi," I said through numb lips.

"Then you must wait for your father to show you the pieces of the great magic of healing. I cannot." She ducked into her hut without another word.

I dared not follow her. Privacy within our huts must be respected as absolute.

Both of the ailing Ladies left this life in the dark hours just before a rain-soaked dawn. I could not greet the sunrise with joyful song that day. I spent the morning ritual time composing and singing a ballad that celebrated the life of these two gentle women. As I sang, I prepared the winding cloths for their shrouds. Tomorrow at dawn we would commit the bodies to the funeral pyre.

And then only five of us would be left to carry on the legacy of the Ladies of Avalon. As much as I wanted to run to my father and demand the knowledge that would help me heal people, I knew the time was not yet right for me to leave. The pattern of my life was still fragmented.

Three years later, I listened to the wind whispering through the apple trees in early spring. Each rustle of a leaf or creak of bough brought news to me in the slow, simple language of the forest. A language that formed an integral part of the pattern of life.

The scent of apple blossoms lay heavy on Avalon. Bees hummed drowsily in the sunshine. The news brought to me on the breeze flowed slowly through my senses. Nothing to excite the trees or the people they spoke of.

No news of Curyll came to me today. Four years of war against the Saxons had earned him a few scars and many friends. My heart ached more each day I could not share with him.

My training was almost complete. I knew the rituals a priestess must perform. I knew how to conserve my strength to work magic properly and to use my talent sparingly. And I knew when I needed true magic, or if a trick would complete the task. But I had never been allowed to work the great magic of healing—the one bit of knowledge I needed most.

Listening to trees and faeries and animals was neither a trick nor magic, merely a natural part of me that could not be denied.

When the wind and trees finished discussing the latest battle, a minor victory for Ardh Rhi Uther Pendragon over the Saxons, I trudged toward The Morrigan. She had summoned me some time earlier. I was late.

A heaviness in my limbs told me of change in my orderly life. I wasn't ready for it. I needed more time to learn the healing magic.

We lacked only a few weeks to Beltane on my thirteenth summer. I wanted to participate this year, though I wondered if I dared give up my maidenhead before I finally convinced The Morrigan to teach me what I needed to know.

Tall, slim, and elegant in every gesture, The Morrigan sat beneath an apple tree. Some of her vitality and natural color had returned of late. I hadn't seen her work true magic, exhausting magic, in almost a year. She had spread her yellow skirts around her in a graceful circle.

That circle of imitation sunlight set a barrier of space no one dared penetrate. Beside her I knew myself to be merely a short and awkward acolyte who could never get all of the twigs and grass out of her unruly brown hair. My simple gown had permanent grass stains on the skirt.

"Your time in Avalon is over, Arylwren. You depart at dawn with your father," The Morrigan said without polite inquiries about my health and well-being or my studies. My lateness must have disturbed her more than usual for such a breach of manners.

"Why must I leave Avalon now?" The pieces of my life pattern still seemed scattered.

I wondered—fantasized—if Da would take me to Curyll in time for Beltane.

"Your father is much wiser than I, Arylwren. He sees the future. I cannot." The Morrigan looked me straight in the eye. "Father Myrddin, The Merlin, requires that you accompany him on his journeys this summer. You will join him on the mainland at dawn. Ask your questions of him."

"I haven't seen my father in four years. Why this year? Why won't he wait until after Beltane?" Two young men, apprentice bards who lived on one of the nearby islands, had caught my eye this past year. Their blatant virility set my blood steaming and made my skin oversensitive to any touch. The fine linen of my shift rasped across my breasts in an agonizing kind of pleasure. Moisture between my thighs made me squirm every time I thought about those young men jumping the Beltane fires naked, strong, and eager.

If I couldn't have Curyll, either of these bards would satisfy me quite nicely.

Imagining Curyll flying over a Beltane bonfire brought a fierce ache to my unawakened womb. The apprentice bards paled in comparison to my memories of Curyll. In my dreams, I saw him; not the fourteen-year-old boy I had last seen at Lord Ector's fortress, but the man I had glimpsed in a vision. Tall, confident, a warrior of strength and determination.

Consciously, I calmed my pounding heart and heated body lest The Morrigan suspect where my thoughts fled.

"Your father keeps his motives secret, Arylwren. He tells me only that now you have completed your training in the ways of a priestess, you must complete your destiny away from this protected island. Away from the protection our limited numbers can give you." The

Morrigan raised her hand in dismissal. Age lines around her eyes contrasted with her apparently youthful demeanor. Rest and the strengthening tonics I fed her hadn't replenished all of her vitality.

The three remaining Ladies of Avalon were all older than she and growing more feeble each year.

"My destiny? Do you mean marriage?" Marriage would mean never returning to Avalon, not even to check on the Ladies and help them with the daily chores. I didn't want that yet. The Ladies deserved to live out their remaining days here in our home. They needed me to haul wood and water, to wander the fields in search of special plants, to cook and clean for them as well. They had no one else.

"The Goddess claimed you at your naming day. Only She can know for sure what life-quest awaits you. She may have given your father a glimpse of your fate. Ask him tomorrow." The Morrigan flicked her wrist as if to shoo me away.

I wasn't The Merlin's daughter for nothing. I stood my ground. "Who will care for you?"

"We will manage, Wren. A different destiny awaits you."

"My father knows my destiny?"

"Perhaps," The Morrigan sighed. We both knew she wouldn't get rid of me until *I* decided she had nothing more to tell me. Except for that one magical secret.

"Four years ago, the wandering bard known to the world outside Avalon as The Merlin, brought you to me with explicit instructions, Wren. He charged me to make you a priestess in all ways save one. I could not allow you to witness or participate in Beltane. I have kept my promise to your father. Now 'tis up to him to tell you more." The Morrigan stood.

Something in the way she said my father's name intrigued me.

"Are you my mother?" I blurted out the question I had longed to ask for four years. Something about the way Da had looked at her that first day on the docks.

"If I were, your life would have been different, Wren. I'd never have allowed you or your father out of my sight." Without another word she walked back toward her hut, spine straight, head high, and fingers kneading the fabric of her yellow gown into a knot.

I followed her. "Why must I leave now, Lady? Why must I remain a virgin if for no other destiny than to satisfy a husband on a wedding night?"

"Neither the Goddess nor your father told me your destiny, child. My own fate is all too clear. I can no longer teach you or protect you."

"Why? No one comes to this island but those *you* invite."

"I am dying, Wren. By autumn my ashes will return to the earth and my spirit will soar into my next incarnation. There is no one left who can become The Morrigan."

Grief shocked me into momentary silence. I had known she was dying for some time but denied it to myself over and over. This lovely woman had nurtured me as lovingly as a mother. I could no longer imagine life without her.

"I can be the next Morrigan. If I stay here. If I unite with the Goddess this Beltane Festival." I spoke slowly, measuring each word. I glimpsed a piece of the future and knew I could pursue it.

"No, Wren. Your destiny lies elsewhere. Our way of life will die with me. The other Ladies will return to their families. As must you." The Morrigan stopped walking at the doorway to her hut, as small, unadorned, and dark inside as mine. She turned to face me before ducking beneath the low lintel. "Go now, Wren. The afternoon and evening are yours. An hour before dawn I will row you across the lake to the mainland."

"I promised to sing for my father to come for me at dawn when the time is right," I said.

"Very well. A priestess should never break a promise, especially one made out of love." She abruptly ended the conversation by entering her hut. That was the one place I could not, and would not follow.

Chapter 9

SUDDENLY the overpowering scent of apple blossoms that permeated Avalon became cloying. I needed to be above the orchards on the rough slopes of the tor, the central hill rising above our island.

A remote part of me rejoiced that at last I would be able to fulfill my destiny to take care of Curyll on whatever path life took him. A more immediate part of my heart ached that I would leave The Morrigan to die alone.

And she had not taught me the ritual for the healing magic.

I felt empty, drained.

Hastily I walked into the thickest and oldest part of the apple groves—from which the island drew its name—where the trees and underbrush grew so thick, only hedgehogs and rabbits traveled there.

Deep within the thicket lay the beginning of the secret path to the top of the tor.

The Morrigan had dismissed me.

I choked back the loneliness that thickened my throat.

Would I ever have a home again? A place where I belonged and could come and go from whenever *I* chose?

I must move along a different path now, a path that was both familiar and alien.

I wished I could stay with The Morrigan until she passed from this life. Mine should be the task of preparing her shroud and celebrating her life in song when the Ladies committed her to the funeral pyre. *Mine!*

But I knew she wouldn't allow that. I had been dismissed.

A destiny that lies elsewhere, The Morrigan had said. Suddenly I longed for the people who had made my early years special.

Was my destiny to be as celibate as Da? I hoped not.

Da had known a woman. Else I wouldn't be his daughter. Or was I one of those children conceived on Beltane when a woman often mated with many men so that none could truly claim me?

I knew a moment of rebellion in my heart. If the man I called Da wasn't truly my father, had only adopted me upon the death of my mother, did I have an obligation to obey his wishes for my future?

I considered seeking out one of the young men on the nearby isle and grabbing one chance at union with the Goddess. Immediately my heart pounded louder, my skin chafed at the confines of my simple gown. The secret dampness set my feet prancing anxiously. I smelled my own musk and needed to complete the aroma with a man's sweat and need.

" 'Tis selfish," I told myself sternly. "The Goddess, not Da, has decreed my future. I will mate when She decides the time is right."

The Goddess manifested Herself in other ways than sexual union. I knew I must seek Her out on my last day on Avalon.

I had to climb the tor along the ritual labyrinth.

Young men wound their way up this path on the eve of the Summer Solstice. Many tests and traps awaited them along the way. Reaching the top, without faltering or turning back, was part of their quest for manhood. No bard could claim a man's torc unless tested by the tor. Just as a warrior lad could not claim a man's torc until tested by combat in tournament or battle.

Priestesses followed the labyrinth as a test of their worthiness to represent the Goddess—after their first Beltane. I wouldn't share Beltane this year. But I must climb the tor anyway. I knew it. Felt it in my bones and my womb.

The scent of damp earth and new sprouts rose sharply with my footsteps. I wiggled my toes into the Pridd. The aroma of new green life became intoxicating.

As soon as I knew I was alone and out of sight, I cast off my clothing. I must approach the Goddess as myself, unable to hide behind the mask of garments.

Then I stopped at the white spring and sipped some of the mineral-laced water. A short distance away the Christian hermit presided over the red spring. He wasn't about, but he never denied anyone access to the healing waters. Here I sipped a little of the metallic-tasting water before I bathed my hands, face, and feet in a ritual cleansing before mounting the tall hill.

Wood sprites and flower faeries flitted about, enticing me to abandon my quest. I laughed at their joyful antics but never strayed from the looping pathway. They played with sunbeams and shadows diverting my gaze from natural obstacles in my way. I brushed a low-hanging branch, heavy with droplets from last night's rain. Soothing coolness showered down on my heated skin. I shivered in surprise and then delight.

Huge yew trees formed an arch over the obvious path. Their shadows obscured the continuation of the labyrinth. I peered around the trees without shifting my feet off the narrow walkway. A green faery alit on a time-rounded boulder to my right, slightly higher on the slope. He laughed at me and pointed between the trees. I saw only a blue faery within the shadowed arch, not the continuation of the path.

"Are you pointing at him because he is in the opposite direction of the way I must walk?" I asked. The green faery giggled and flitted off, back in the direction I had come, but parallel to my previous steps and climbing slightly higher.

I smiled and followed him. My feet found the narrow places cut deeply into old turf. Barely wider than my own foot, the way was uneven, treacherous to bare toes. But I saw it now. Upward I climbed. A straight path up the side of the tor existed. It was shorter than this one by three or four times the distance. Shortcuts are not the way of ritual or gaining knowledge.

Panting, I reached the rounded peak at last. The scent of cedar filled my head, but I saw no trees. Nothing but sheep-cropped grass, a jumble of man-high boulders, and a splendid view of the marsh and river that made an island of Avalon. Beyond the dark, peaty water, lush farmland and pastures stretched on and on clear to the horizon. If I looked very hard, I could see all the way to the Irish Sea, all the way to . . . Could I see all the way to the Saxon Shore where Curyll nursed a sore head and aching shoulders after the latest battle?

I spun deosil in a circle, glorying in the freedom of the wind refreshing my naked skin, of the birds calling me by name, and the faeries as my constant companions. As I spun, I glimpsed a shining opening. The boulders subtly shifted shape. They became two uprights topped by a low lintel—an ancient barrow where unknown people of forgotten ages buried their dead. Beneath the lintel, a gateway slowly opened into a bright Otherworld.

The green faery darted into the opening, beckoning me to follow. I couldn't move.

Annwn, a male voice whispered in my mind. *You opened the gateway to the land of Faery.*

I looked all around me to see who spoke. A green faery, grown to the size of a tall man, stepped through the portal, from his world to mine. All of him was green: hair, eyes, pointed ears, skin. Like my winged companions he wore no clothes. But he had dropped the wings from his back when he grew.

I studied his maleness, trying not to be obvious about my curiosity. A new heat flushed my skin and tightened my nipples. My breasts grew heavy, and my mind refused to think beyond wondering what he would feel like in my hand, inside of me. . . .

I am Cedar, he said with his mind. He took my hand and led me around the barrow to a spring and pool hidden within a deep forest that hadn't been there before the gateway to Annwn had opened.

You opened the doorway, Wren. You followed the labyrinth correctly and prepared the way for me to cross from my world into yours.

There on the moss, beside a crystal pool, with the scent of cedar flooding my being, I sank to the earth, wondering what I had done. Was I still in my world, or had I wandered into Annwn without realizing it. Did I care?

A dozen winged figures fluttered above me, giggling with the joy of life. Only Cedar remained fully grown.

"Are you the same faery who kissed my nose on my seventh birthday?

He nodded and smiled. Then he touched the tip of my nose with his fingertip. The scent of cedar filled my senses with happy memories of that day.

Rest, friend, Cedar said. *You have earned repose after the arduous climb. By your trials you have done us a great favor.*

"What favor?"

Rest. We will talk when you are ready. For now, enjoy what you have been denied on Beltane.

My winged friends folded their wings and alit on my body. They caressed and tickled my heated skin to new heights of ecstasy while Cedar watched, longing in his green eyes. The faeries fluttered their wings against my breasts until my nipples tightened into pink rosebuds. They tugged upon my earlobes and fanned flower-scented air across my face. The tiny hairs on my face and neck stood up straight, straining for a repeat of the sensuous breath of faeries. Then, my friends moved down into the wisps of soft brown hair that hid my feminine secrets. They giggled and tickled with fluttering wings, tiny bird feathers, and seed tassels from the grass. The scent of cedar intensified and blended with my own feminine humors.

Cedar's hands hovered over me, never quite touching. I longed for him to join his companions in this game of sensuous pleasure. I closed my eyes, half-dreaming.

A niggle of doubt crept into my mind. I shushed it and lay back, receptive to whatever the faeries gave me.

The intensity of the faery caresses increased, grew bolder, larger. My muscles shivered and tightened again and again until I thought I must explode. New delights fluttered up through my being. My body awakened and demanded more until I convulsed in spasms of joy.

I opened my eyes.

Cedar stretched out on the moss beside me. He seemed larger, more human than I remembered. His greenness seemed to fade and flicker darker. His very pronounced maleness drew my gaze.

The other tiny figures fluttered around his head in a myriad of colors.

Heat burned my cheeks. I returned his bold stare, inspecting every inch of his perfect body. Definitely male. Definitely aroused and ready. . . .

You are beautiful, friend Wren. His voice rippled as if many minds spoke the same words through his voice. He smiled at me with full lips that begged me to kiss him.

"Do you speak for all the faeries?"

The tiny winged figures nodded and giggled vigorously. They rose in a flurry of delight, flying intricate patterns that could have been a sigil of power, but not one I knew.

Our numbers decrease, Wren. We need more friends such as you, or we will fade into the Otherworld, unable to come forth.

"My father told me that. I don't know how to help you, other than to be your friend."

Bear a half-caste child for us. A child who will walk both worlds and hold the portals open for us. A child who will mature in your world and be able to bear or sire children to give us new blood and strengthen our numbers. He caressed my neck, drawing me closer to him. My heart raced at his touch. His full lips molded to mine. The other faeries renewed their titillation of my body.

My previous sensual joy deserted me. I stiffened. "This isn't right, Cedar." How could it not be right? I was more than ready for sexual union with a man. Most any man would do.

Cedar was not a man for all the erect power and glory he displayed.

We cannot give you another opportunity, Wren. Transformations are . . . difficult. The gateway opens very rarely for us.

"I'm sorry. I can't do it. I don't know why. I just can't." I rolled over, turning my back on his perfection and my need to draw him and his seed deep within me. My knees drew up to my chest of their own volition.

You are ready.

"Ready to join with a man of my own kind. I'm sorry, Cedar. I'm sorry. I'll do what I can to open the portals for you. But I can't mate with you." I looked back at him, over my shoulder, keeping my knees protectively close to my chest.

That must be enough, Wren. Friend.

My green faery faded and shrank. His color intensified to the deep dark green of a cedar tree in high summer, and his rainbow wings returned. When he was no larger than my finger, he blew me a kiss and smiled. But he didn't giggle. None of my companions did. They flew silently away. A hint of sadness slowed their retreat.

"Come back when you can. Don't abandon me," I pleaded with them.

As long as you are our friend, we will be with you. You have only to look in your heart to find us. He flew in a looping circle to seal the promise.

Exhaustion swept over my body and my spirit. I melted and blended with the land, too spent to know where the moss ended and I began.

Time drifted by me. A sense of unease remained deep in my belly. Had I made the right choice? Bearing a half-faery child wouldn't be so bad. Would it? Would the faeries survive if I didn't call them back? Too late. They said the transformation was too difficult to try again.

I think I slept for a time.

When I opened my eyes again, the forest had disappeared, replaced by the familiar turf and boulders I could see with my mundane senses. The spring and pool remained but much diminished in size. I stretched and sat up, only to discover the image of Dana, the Goddess as fertile Pridd Matron, standing at my feet. Dressed in the blue draperies of the mother of all she radiated a glorious aura of pure white. She stood beside a huge gräal, the cauldron of Life, and stirred the contents with a gnarled wooden staff. Bright strands of Life streamed upward from the gräal as if they were steam. They spread outward, connecting every plant, rock, water droplet, animal, and person. This was the source of the pattern of Life. I needed to reach out to the Life energy, examine it, and understand it once and for all. The many-colored strands of Life as well as its pattern eluded my grasp.

Dana smiled and raised her hand in blessing. The gräal faded into an insubstantial shadow, but the bright energy of Life remained. The Goddess became younger, clothed in white like a virgin bride.

I scrambled to my knees, instantly alert. Mortals were rarely granted true visions while fully awake and unaided by magic. The Goddess and her pantheon of Gods came to us in dreams.

Do not regret your rejection of Cedar, my child. A husband and children will be yours, when the time is right, the Goddess said through my vision. *Your destiny will be shared by many generations to come. Generations fathered by your beloved Curyll. This I promise you and seal.*

Instantly she transformed into an aged grandmother, lines of wisdom and experience creasing her face. She drew a circle in the mist with the tip of her finger. The mist glowed along the path of her gesture. *The faeries know that you are the key to our future. They will stay with you.* Once more she became the mother, nurturer, and guide.

I had seen Dana in all her guises: maiden, matron, and crone. The vision was true and unalterable. Deep in my heart I knew I would share all three phases of life with Dana: maiden, matron, crone. But I would be remembered as a matron.

She faded from my view, a breeze scattering her draperies and image into tendrils of mist.

A chill fog crept up the slopes of the tor from the marsh. I shivered in the new cold, longing for my discarded clothing.

I reached out to hold on to Dana, to reassure myself that this was a true vision and not a dream of wanting. The mist thickened where she had stood. I caught one more brief glimpse of the gräal and the pattern of Life before it, too, became one with the mist.

Keep us alive in your heart and in the hearts of your children. In this way, you will be the mother of us all, the multiple voices of faeries and Goddess called to me as if from a great distance.

Warmth filled me from within and without, protecting me from the weather.

The sun glowed blood red on the horizon. I hadn't much time to retrieve my clothing and meet The Morrigan and her Ladies for one last shared meal. For a time I had been the maiden, The Morrigan was the matron, and the Ladies the crone. The little village on the Isle of Avalon had maintained all three aspects of the Goddess for many generations. That pattern would break when I left at dawn. The community of The Morrigan would die, and Britain would move into a new pattern dominated by some other community.

I must make the most of our final time together, for I'd not see The Morrigan again. The only mother I had known.

At dawn I would stand on the dock and sing for my Da to come for me. We would return to our wandering ways for a time until I moved on to become a mother—the mother of Curyll's children.

Curyll! Da would take me to my true love, my destined husband. The Goddess had promised.

Chapter 10

"GWAED feast on their blood! Cernunnos drag them by their balls into the Underworld!" Nimuë shouted to the midnight wind. Nothing else stirred among the barren hills outside Venta Belgarum, Ardh Rhi Uther's capital. Little starlight penetrated the cloud cover on this night of the dark of the moon. "May every one of them contract a burning rash that eats away at their cocks." She raised a clean knife, blade up, and made symbolic slashes across the night sky.

Tears of frustration blurred her vision and her gestures wobbled. She muttered several foul words she wasn't supposed to know. She knew enough about magic to realize she'd have to repeat the original curse and the gesture. She hoped she wouldn't have to clean the knife again as well.

Four years had passed since she'd left Avalon. Very little magic had gone right for her since.

She'd used a quartet of fertility spells this past Beltane. She'd taken four different lovers in the fields outside her father's ancestral keep. But none of the randy youths had managed to get a child on her. She had even gone down on her hands and knees for them, letting them prove their manhood by using her like an animal. A fortnight later her moon blood flowed freely.

Carradoc of Caer Tair Cigfran, her father, wouldn't allow her to marry until she conceived. He claimed he held to the old tradition. Mostly he invented traditions to suit his convenience. He had reasons to keep Nimuë unmarried and close by his side.

"I'll break your control over me yet, Carradoc," she vowed. This time a faint light of power followed the sigil she carved in the air with her knife. Her hand and arm tingled with the energy of her impromptu spell. She smiled and narrowed her eyes in speculation. "At last something works right."

She continued her clandestine journey across the hills, using a shielded oil lamp to guide her steps. Her legs grew tired from the unaccustomed exercise. She'd rather have worked within the privacy of the women's solar at the palace. But Queen Ygraina's pleasantness invaded the very stones of the palace. Curses needed a different atmosphere.

Eventually she wound down from a hilltop into a hidden copse. The cloud cover thickened and the night grew darker. Nimuë shivered in the sudden chill. Rain would soak the hills again before dawn. She intended to be tucked safely into her bed by then. She yawned and considered retracing her steps.

First she had to finish what she started. The Ladies of Avalon had managed to teach her that much. Nimuë hadn't pried much else out of them in the two years she'd lived on Avalon.

At the bottom of the hill, the trees closed around her. Years ago the sacred spring at the heart of the copse had been kept clear of brush. Neglected and nearly abandoned now, the brush had grown into a small forest. Her lamplight didn't penetrate more than one step ahead of her.

A creaking sound off to the right made her jump. Her heart thudded in her chest, and her skin felt cold and clammy. Then an owl hooted in another direction.

She took a deep breath and forced herself to relax. She didn't really believe in demons. She'd never seen one and certainly hadn't been able to raise one when she'd tried. The spells had fatigued her before she'd half begun, and so she skipped parts of the ritual. But that was the fault of the old hag who'd sold her the spell. The woman wasn't truly a witch, had overcharged the daughter of a lord, and put too many steps in the ritual.

"I'll have her killed next time Carradoc allows me to go home," Nimuë promised herself.

Carefully she edged forward, feeling for the path with her toes. Two dozen small steps later, she sensed the trees opening around her. She'd reached the small clear space around the spring. A little more light penetrated the clouds. Ahead of her the semi-phallic shape of a single sacred stone appeared a darker black against the black backdrop of trees. The top of the stone reached only a little taller than Nimuë.

In daylight a double spiral carved into the surface of the stone showed clearly.

If she made a sacrifice of blood and food here tonight, the gods trapped within the stone should grant her wish for the means to gain her freedom from Carradoc. A husband and child were only a means to that end.

"So you, too, seek power tonight with the old ones," a voice whispered from the direction of the stone.

Nimuë jumped back, hand to her throat. She clenched her fist, extending her little and pointing fingers, a ward against the horned god of the Underworld, in the direction of the voice.

"You need not fear me, sister." Someone moved as if standing up in front of the stone.

"I fear no one." Nimuë straightened her shoulders and stared levelly at the cloaked and hooded figure. Surreptitiously she kept her right hand behind her back still clenched in the ward against the evil eye.

"If you fear no one, then why have you come here on the dark of the moon, on the night of powerful dark magic?"

"I . . . I came to make sacrifices to the powers that truly rule us." Nimuë stalled for time. Curiosity burned within her now that her initial fears had subsided. Something about this figure's educated accent sounded familiar. Surely she'd found another practitioner of the dark arts who resided in Uther's palace.

Wouldn't Archbishop Dyfrig have a fit and fall down in a faint if he found out? She almost giggled at the image of the tall man tumbling onto his scrawny backside while his miter and crosier rolled away from his grasping, clawlike fingers.

The self-righteous prig reminded her too much of The Merlin, another crotchety old man who refused her manipulation.

"Sacrifices are good. Are you prepared to give all to the dark ones who will beg to do your bidding for a taste of your blood?" The figure held up a knife. The lantern light glinted faintly on the keen edge. A small dark stain dripped from the point.

"You . . . you cut yourself!"

"Of course. Demons don't like secondhand blood. And they only respect those who are willing to endure pain. Are you prepared to do this?"

"I . . . I brought this." Nimuë fumbled in her pocket for the stained rag she'd used earlier in the day to soak up her moon blood.

The figure laughed long and loud.

Nimuë looked around her, fearful that someone, some*thing* might hear and come to investigate.

"A sacrifice indeed, my young acolyte. But not enough." The figure grabbed Nimuë with strong fingers and slashed at her inner arm.

At first Nimuë didn't feel anything but the coldness of the sharp blade against her skin. Then a dark line welled up from the invisible cut and hot pain spread rapidly from the finger-length wound up her arm to her shoulder. Her face burned, and her skin felt cold. The darkness whirled around her, confusing her senses.

"Now you can leave real blood for the powers of darkness. Now we can be allies against those who would control us."

"Allies," Nimuë whispered, uncertain if she liked this idea or not. But she knew this person now and smiled at the power that knowledge gave her.

"I will teach you what you need. But no one, *NO ONE,* must ever suspect that we work together. Your death, horrible and painful, will follow if anyone suspects us of conspiring with those who would see Uther Pendragon dead."

"Andraste is drowning Britain," I told Da the day after the Autumnal Equinox.

My knees wobbled and I almost dropped to the soggy verge beside the old Roman road. A fluttering sound inside my head told me more than I wanted to know.

"The Morrigan is dead," Da said. He lifted his face to the dense rain and moaned.

A vast emptiness opened in me as if my soul chased hers into the next world. The Morrigan had indeed died. I barely felt my hot tears in the cold rain that pelted us.

In a few moments, my sense of balance returned, and I knew that The Morrigan had passed into her next incarnation.

The rain had begun in earnest that morning after several weeks of heavy showers followed by annoying drizzle. We hadn't seen the sun in many, many days. Now large drops penetrated our heavily oiled woolen cloaks and stung our unprotected skin. A high wind chilled our wet bodies.

"Come," Da said after several moments of silence. "We must keep moving. Life continues though one of our number has died." He started trudging down the Roman road we usually disdained for more secret pathways.

Everything smelled of mold and damp rot.

I pulled my winter cloak closer around me to combat the chill that ran up and down my spine. The hairs on the back of my neck continued standing on end. Something more than an autumnal rainstorm plagued Britain today.

I searched with all of my senses but saw little beyond the waves of rain and my own grief.

The Morrigan was dead. Avalon was no more. I still had not learned the great healing magic from either Da or The Morrigan.

"Foot rot will infest the sheep with all this rain," Da grumbled beneath his hood that all but covered his face.

His prematurely gray hair and beard were nearly all white now, making him look older than I knew him to be. But his step was still firm, and no traces of the bone fever twisted his knuckles.

Though we'd spent the summer together—a very wet and dismal summer—I still found myself examining him minutely, cherishing every look, every gesture, every curl in his beard. After a joyous reunion last spring we'd fallen into our old routines easily. We had walked nearly the length and breadth of Britain, renewing old acquaintances and making new ones.

But I suspected we'd be separated again before I was ready. My dreams of late had been most specific. I stood on one side of a great chasm. Da stood on the other. Sometimes I tried desperately to jump the gap, or climb down into the bottomless canyon and climb up the other side. Sometimes I turned my back and ignored Da's attempts to reach me. Never did we touch hands before I woke up.

I scanned the puddles that grew into small lakes. Even the Roman road retained ankle-high water in the broken spots.

What few crops grew this summer had been beaten to the ground by the rain and wind. Black fields stretched to the horizon and beyond on our trek north toward Deva and Lord Ector's caer. Why weren't sheep grazing in the sodden pastures? Birds sulked quietly in the trees, their feathers fluffed against the unseasonable cold. Strange smells came to me from the rotten vegetation. I expected to hear carrion crows screeching at us as a meager sign of life amid the devastation. An unnatural silence hung as heavily as the wet air.

This deluge was so fierce and so long-lasting, I hadn't caught sight of a single faery or sprite most of the summer.

The pattern of life unraveled before my eyes. I sensed my separation from Da coming closer, yet I couldn't do anything to prevent it. My throat swelled and made my breathing ragged. The Morrigan was dead. And now I knew I would lose my Da as well.

How? How much time? I asked the wind.

I heard no answer.

Da stopped and sniffed the air, turning his head quickly right and left. His hand burrowed beneath the folds of his cloak to touch his torc. "Fire ruined these crops."

Then I noticed the difference between rotten fields beaten flat and scorched grain burned to the ground, then drenched by rain.

No wonder the faeries had deserted this part of Britain. Fire was bane to them, much like iron.

"Pirates?" I asked. The coast was riddled with inlets for them to beach their boats.

I didn't want to think about murderers lurking behind every shrub and boulder. Shudders ran up and down my spine—from the cold and from my thoughts.

A jumble of mud huts crouched on the horizon. The thatched roofs sagged from burning, then they had rotted in the heavy rains. A few scrawny pigs rooted in the barren mud for absent roots. We hurried forward, alert and wary of lurking predators—humans as well as wolves.

"Irish pirates take what they can throw into their boats and leave quickly," Da said quietly. I could see his thought spinning behind his eyes. "Pirates kill any who stand in their way. But they leave fields, houses, and survivors behind to provide new fodder for the next raid. This is the work of the Saxons and their bloodthirsty gods. They destroy everything in their path to make way for the flood of their relatives who follow them, needing land to settle for themselves."

Saxons!

My heart raced with childhood terrors. I'd seen burned fields and slaughtered villages before. I'd watched from hiding places while tall warriors with clean chins and long drooping mustaches hacked at their victims with axes, dismembering them as they died. All in the name of their god of war. The isolation of Avalon had buried those memories. Saxons had fallen into the category of monsters under the bed to make children behave. Now I faced those monsters for real.

Saxons! They shredded every life pattern of past, present, and future, with their bloody axes.

Da gripped his torc fiercely, eyes closed. A deep grief passed over his face.

"The Saxons have grown bold. They are no longer content to press us from the South and East—the lands ceded to them by Vortigen thirty years ago. Now they raid from the Irish Sea and the Northern inlets as well." Da stared at the destruction that marched to the horizon in all directions.

"But the Ardh Rhi . . . His army . . . Curyll!" Deva, with her Roman fortress, was but two days' walk to the east of us. Lord Ector's home another day beyond. Who would protect Lady Glynnis and her younger children while Lord Ector's warband guarded the Southern coast, fighting more swarms of the invaders?

At our words, one of the pigs stood up. Not a rooting animal. A filthy child. Boy or girl, I couldn't tell. Tangled locks streaked with mud covered the face. A tattered smock, more mud than cloth, clung to a too-thin body. No other garment protected the child from the chill wind and rain. I guessed the child female. I don't know why. She stared at us, eyes too big for her pinched face and her belly distended with hunger. Then she darted into the closest hut in a hunched-over walk, hands nearly touching the ground.

Da pulled a hunk of bread from his pack. The last of our supplies and meant to be our supper. "Come, child, we won't hurt you." He offered it to the wild-eyed child, holding it out before him. Step by step he followed in her footsteps. "I have food for you," he coaxed.

Two eyes reflected a little light in the gloom of the ruined hut. The child peered at us, eyes wide with fear and desperate hunger.

I stilled my mind and body, blending with the landscape. Da did the same.

My eyes separated one shadow from another. The outline of the child's body emerged. Tempted by food. Cautious of the giver.

"Bread, child," Da continued his offer. "We won't hurt you. Come. Eat."

The child shifted her body forward, onto her toes, ready to run. Her hand reached out. Then she dashed forward. Swift as a rabbit, she snatched the bread out of Da's hand and ran past him.

Da moved faster. Druid-trained, he'd anticipated her movements and grabbed the stinking, rotting remnants of her shirt. She strained against the cloth outlining her emaciated body. I'd guessed correctly. Female. Young, just barely budding into puberty.

She screeched and clawed Da's arm, dropping the precious bread rather than be captured. Cloth tore and she ran, forsaking food for freedom.

I dashed after her. She needed help. She needed us. But she was thin and barefoot. I was taller, heavier, and wore my thick winter boots. Her feet slid through the mud at the surface. Mine sank deeper with every step. She disappeared into the ditches and hedges before I had gone three steps.

"We have to catch her," I cried. "She'll die. We have to help her."

Many times in my life, as Da and I tramped the length and breadth of Britain, I'd known hunger and cold. We often slept on the ground with only our cloaks for warmth. I'd always known that the cold and hunger would last only as long as it took us to walk to the next fortress or village. And I'd always had my Da to protect me in the shelter of his arms.

"She is a survivor, Wren. She had the wits to evade the Saxons. She had the instincts to survive a month or more since the raid. Unless her mind heals from the horrors she has witnessed, we cannot get close enough to help her. All we can do is pass news of her to anyone left alive. She is one of the wild ones now." He hung his head in sadness. I saw his lips move in a silent prayer, but I heard no words.

I mimicked his actions, imploring Dana to care for one of her own. The child had gone feral, as wild as the wolves and the deer of the forest. She belonged to the Goddess now.

I had never met any of the wild ones who haunted the forest. But I'd heard legends of them. This girl would become one of them. Villagers would leave offerings for her, supporting her, respecting her need to avoid human contact.

"We have obligations, Wren," Da reminded me. "We must make sure we give the dead proper rest. 'Tis a promise we make to the living and to the Goddess."

"There is no wood for a funeral pyre. It is too wet to light a fire,"

I said through chattering teeth. "We can't honor that promise." I could light a fire very easily, but without fuel, Tanio would not continue to burn. It would resent my lack of a gift of wood or coal or grass; it might not come the next time I called it.

"Then we must bury the dead as the Christians do. Tanio or Pridd, it matters not how they return to the Goddess. 'Tis our respect and prayers that give their deaths meaning." He set the harp down on a stone slab near the well. We'd need her music to send the souls of the dead on their next journey.

First we checked the huts. Burned thatch had covered several of the dead—those more afraid of the Saxons than the fire. Not much was left of them, bits of bone, an arm, a foot. A woman's skull with half a face and burned hair.

A birthmark on her remaining cheek sent a shock recoiling through me. I knew this woman. She had offered me sweet cakes and fresh bread when Da and I came here many years ago. The best bread I had ever tasted—my appetite sharpened because I was hungry. I'd slept in this hut with the children of the household. We'd laughed and told stories long into the night and finally slept in a tangle of arms and legs.

Was the wild girl one of those children who had given me a portion of her meal and her bed?

Deep, racking sobs overtook me. How could Dana let this happen? I *knew* these people!

Shakily I gritted my teeth and set about the task of righting the outflung limbs and closing the woman's one eye that stared at me in reproach.

I prayed her next life was easier than the death she had endured here.

My shoulders heaved with my sobs as I knelt beside the corpse. I knew Death in many forms and had prepared the victims of illness and accident for the pyre. Only when Saxons invaded had I encountered such wanton disregard for the gift of life from the Goddess.

I couldn't even consign these victims to the fire that would liberate their spirits from their bodies.

"Come, Wren. I need help with the digging," Da said from the doorway of the ruined hut. He had found two spades and held them like staffs, one in each hand. His unnaturally pale skin stretched over his facial bones with strain. I scurried to obey before his anger at the

Saxons erupted and found only me as a target. The one time I had seen Da lose control of his temper, he'd shape-changed into an awesome being beyond reason, beyond my love.

Was his anger the cause of the separation I foresaw?

Three more bodies awaited us in the village common. Untouched by the fire, their terrible wounds revealed the viciousness of their murderers. Agony still distorted their faces.

I couldn't look too closely or think about the pain these people had endured before the Goddess mercifully took their spirits. I felt each knife thrust, hatchet slash, and arrow point in my mind.

"Wh . . . where were they, Da?"

"I found two in the field beyond. This one, I fished from the well." He pointed with his foot to a pale, bloated body.

We both gagged. I turned my back so that he wouldn't see my weakness if I lost control of my stomach.

"We'll have to mark the well, so no one drinks the tainted water." He stalked to the stone wall that ringed the water supply. He touched his torc in his habitual manner and worked his fingers in a complicated summoning. A piece of light-colored rock sprang to his hand from some nearby rubble. With the magically charged tool he scratched a warning into the stones. Power burned from his hand, through the markings. For a brief moment the sigil of poison flared, then burned into the wall. By the time the sigil faded, the well would have had many years to sweeten.

I dropped some dried betony into the water to hurry the process.

All that day and into the long twilight we toiled to dig a grave. The mud slid back into the hole almost as fast as we slung it out. At last we returned the dead to the Pridd, marked the grave with a cairn, and sang our prayers.

Occasionally I caught glimpses of the feral girl. A movement in the shadows, or a flash of lighter-colored mud. I hoped she understood our actions and would heal. I dared not hope that she would join us in our grim task.

A chill wind scattered the rain clouds as the moon rose. I looked around for a suitable camp. My stomach recoiled from sleeping anywhere near this village.

"We walk tonight, Wren. Perhaps by morning we will be able to put this behind us."

"I retrieved the bread and cleaned it as best I could," I said. "We'll leave it for the child. She needs it more than we." I looked about one last time for signs of the girl. "I couldn't eat tonight, Da."

He nodded in agreement. We set our feet back on the slippery stones of the Roman road that led to Deva and then on to Lord Ector's fortress.

Chapter 11

THE Merlin curbed his need to run away from the burned village as fast as he could. As much as he wanted to grab Wren and carry her to safety, he knew he had to slow his pace and observe.

Something was terribly wrong in this corner of Britain. Something more wrong than just the passing of The Morrigan. He'd sensed her death the moment it happened, just as he had sensed Deirdre's death nearly fourteen years before. There would never be another Morrigan. Britain must mourn the passing of a way of life as well as the death of a wise and talented woman.

But her death alone would not explain why the Saxons had been allowed to roam freely through this neighborhood.

Where was Ardh Rhi Uther and his army? Every king had pledged warbands to Uther in time of invasion. Uther had made a covenant with the Goddess and with all of the kings to protect Britain with his treasure, his warband, and his life.

"The Ardh Rhi and the land are one," he said, not realizing he had spoken aloud until he heard the words.

"What did you say, Da?" Wren asked. She turned her huge blue eyes up to him. Her cloud of curly dark hair deepened the color of her eyes by contrast. Questions and pain shadowed her face.

"Just questioning all possibilities, Wren," he replied. He had to protect her from the horrible conclusion that nagged at him.

If the Ardh Rhi and the land were one, then both ailed horribly. He had to return to Venta Belgarum immediately. He didn't have time to dally in the North.

Britain was not ready to accept a new Ardh Rhi.

Arthur was not ready to become the next Ardh Rhi. And Arthur must be the next Ardh Rhi. No one else would do.

The Merlin had foreseen the terrible destruction that would engulf Britain if Arthur were not chosen by the client kings to lead them.

"Wren, your eyes are better than mine for fine details. What do
you see in this trampled grass?" he asked, as much to divert her attention away from his chain of logic as to know what information lurked
here.

"Many feet, Da. All going in the same direction, at the same
time." Wren dropped to her knees and searched the broken stalks
with her fingers.

"Human footprints, horses, or sheep?" He, too, lowered himself
into the flattened area. He held his hands flat a hair's breadth above
the grass seeking residual auras. He allowed his eyes to lose focus,
seeking information from all of his senses.

"Not horses, at least not shoed horses," Wren declared. "There
are a few sheep and chicken droppings. The turf is not cut by horse-
shoes."

Merlin sensed much the same with his magic. "A large body of
men with a few sheep and chickens. I think we'd best follow this trail.
Tread carefully and quietly, Wren. We don't know who we will stumble upon. Stay behind me and be prepared to run. Run all the way to
Venta Belgarum if you have to. Do not wait for me, I can take care of
myself. But you must escape, no matter what." He grabbed her shoulders rather fiercely. He needed to hold her close but didn't want to
frighten her with the intensity of his fear for her.

"I will not leave you, Da," she replied with equal determination.
She lifted her chin and set her jaw in a look he knew all too well.

He'd not change her mind easily.

"You will obey me, Wren. If there is trouble, one of us must take
the news to Uther."

"Both of us will run to Venta Belgarum with the news. I won't
leave you behind."

They glared at each other for a long moment. The Merlin looked
away first. Silently he nodded.

Together they followed the trail. Less than one hundred paces off
the Roman road they found a wide clear space outlined by a tumble
of boulders. Merlin knelt by the first of six fire rings. The ashes were
cold and sodden, days old, if not weeks old.

Again he held his hand flat above the ground, seeking information.

Nothing.

"They are long gone." Wren tossed a sheep's thighbone back into the large central fire pit.

"Six campfires, one cooking pit. Sixty men," Merlin guessed. Romans would delegate groups of ten to a fire. Romans were obsessed with order and uniformity. But if Romans had camped here, he'd expect ten fires—one hundred men in a cohort.

But these were not Romans.

"Forty men, I think. No more," Wren replied. She sifted the ashes from the fire pit through her fingers, picking out more bits of charred bone and debris.

"One shipload of Saxons," Merlin said. He tried to keep his tone objective.

"One shipload here." Wren stood up, holding her dirty hands to her sides. "I think we will find many more campsites to have caused as much destruction as we have seen." Her voice sounded flat, as if all emotion had been drained from her.

He felt the same.

As soon as they had confirmation of the number and home base of the Saxons in this area, they must return to Venta Belgarum with all possible speed. Then Merlin must confer with his brother about the future. He dreaded that meeting almost as much as he dreaded the death and destruction he'd find in the next village.

Three days we walked. In all those three days, we found only one rabbit and some roots to fill our bellies. The Saxons had cleared the area of all that lived.

Three days we trudged onward with no sign of living humanity other than a dozen abandoned Saxon campsites. Each one was within an hour's walk of a destroyed village, each one was older than the last. We buried the dead and said our prayers. Each time we dug a grave, I hoped that this was the last time. This time we would restore the pattern of life, death, past, present, and future. Only when the patterns were back in harmony could Britain reforge the covenant with the Goddess.

Oh, yes. I knew Ardh Rhi Uther ailed as badly as did the land. I knew and said nothing to Da. If he hadn't connected the horrible weather and the devastation with the Ardh Rhi's covenant with the Goddess, then he ailed as badly and didn't need more worry.

I asked the spirits of trees and wind for news of the Ardh Rhi. I heard only the passage of Awyr through the branches. None of the creatures of forest or faery whispered news to me.

The faeries continued their absence. I missed their bright colors flitting about my head as they escorted us.

The rain plagued us intermittently until the end of the third day when a brief break in the clouds revealed a glorious sunset across the Deeside estuary. I grabbed the vivid colors and folded them in my memory, praying that this was an omen of better weather and news to come.

Perhaps Uther recovered from his grievous ailment.

The pervasive odor of death and rot gave way to the cleaner scents of salt and fish and seaweed.

Tiredly, we pushed through to the last of the low hills and plunged into the wild sedge grass before a broad sandy beach. A low fogbank hovered just offshore, almost ready to creep inland.

As I walked backward, rejoicing in the glorious red-and-gold pattern of the sunset, I slipped on the loose sand that had drifted over the Roman road. Da grabbed my arm before I scraped my knees against the paving stones. I clung to him, jerking him off-balance. The harp slid across his back and nearly out of its satchel. We both scrambled for balance before the precious instrument crashed and broke.

By the time we righted ourselves, the leaden sea lay only a few paces away, lapping idly onto the shore at low tide. No birds sang. No frogs croaked. Nothing stirred. We crept forward, leery of the silence. Shadows twisted in the dying light, making monsters out of hummocks and turning shrubs into demons.

"Longboats!" I hissed through my teeth. Half-hidden in the fog and estuary grasses, the ugly dragon heads on three bowsprits glared at us. Had the raiders heard our noisy slide on the trade road?

Da and I dove for hiding places. From the thick grasses, I watched the guards crouched in the lee of the hull. The longboats' oars rested upright in their locks, sails furled, clearly beached for a time. No sentries patrolled the exposed deck. The raiders had been here long enough to feel secure.

How far inland had the raiders penetrated? The city of Deva offered rich plunder. I feared for Lady Glynnis and her household in the caer just beyond the city.

I sought signs of encampment and pursuit. Each longboat of this size meant a crew of anywhere from thirty to fifty men.

Three men moved into view from the camp. Big men with long mustaches and heavy helms protecting their faces and skulls. They looked sharply left and right. Each carried a worn shield and un-sheathed ax. The last of the sun glinted off the keen edges of their weapons.

I shuddered and had to clamp my jaw shut to keep my teeth from chattering.

Smoke from a single campfire spiraled upward from the far side of the vessels. The scent of cooking meat and stale ale encircled my senses. I swallowed my hunger. These men offered no hospitality to any but their own.

Silently, I half-stood to spy out the location of the lone fire. How many men guarded the boats? How many more roamed the country-side, butchering, raping, and burning as they went?

Da yanked me back down into cover. He shook his head and pointed back the way we had come.

Inch by inch, we crept backward, on our bellies, seeking the deeper cover of shrubbery.

Stubbornly, the fog held offshore, denying us its shelter.

Dana, preserve us, I thought. *Andraste, save us.*

I began to sweat in the cool autumn air. My heart beat so fast and loud I knew the invaders must hear it over the gentle swish of the waves at low tide.

The Saxons set bare feet onto the stones of the Roman road. Their shaggy heads moved back and forth, seeking the source of the sounds we had made a few moments ago. I flattened myself into the grass. Da did the same.

I drew on my training to make myself as invisible as possible. My heartbeat and breathing slowed to the tempo of growing grass. My thoughts sank into the natural patterns of rock, sea, and fog.

The harp twanged inside the satchel, her strings responding to changes in temperature and moisture.

One of the Saxons lifted his face, alert and wary. The three sepa-rated. They beat the grasses with the butt of their axes. Each man worked his way outward methodically in a widening square.

Memories of the hideous wounds in the corpses I had helped bury sent panic to my feet. I needed to run as fast as I could. The urge to rise up and obey the twitching compulsion nearly overrode good sense.

A cloud of insects flitted around my head. I feared inhaling one of the no-see-ems. A cough or sneeze would betray our position. I heard the tiniest giggle. I looked closer at the circling insects, each a different bright color. Incredibly small, humanlike beings with shimmering wings winked at me in mischief. Cedar flew past my nose, leading the swarm.

'Twas twilight, the time of a faery's greatest power and visibility, when neither sun nor moon ruled and the edges of the Otherworld crept closer to reality.

I stretched my senses to touch the mind of each faery in friendship and thanks. Releasing myself, my mind expanded and merged with my friends. I saw webs of energy connecting all life—even with the Saxons who inflicted death as easily as they breathed. Something new to think about. Later.

I watched myself lying on the ground, facedown, gray cloak merging with the gray-green sedge grass. Beyond me lay Da and the harp, also blending with the surroundings.

The huge Saxons searched closer. They left swaths of trampled grasses and churned sand in their wake. No place to hide there. Nowhere to run.

He needs you, the faeries whispered.

There was only one "He" whom the faeries would speak to me about. Curyll. I had to find him. Soon.

The Saxons kept my body pinned to the ground.

Help me escape from here, please, I begged of my friends.

My othersight swirled as the faeries flew in dizzying circles. I saw them close up, with my mind, and from a distance, with my physical eyes, at the same time. My friends giggled again and invited me to join their fun.

Bare Saxon feet and hairy legs stood two arm's lengths from the shell of flesh and bone I called myself. My physical eyes saw only the lower portion of the man beating at the sedge grass. My mind saw all of him, as well as the cloud of faeries who rose up in a swarm to plague his eyes and nose.

Behind me, Da lay unmoving. His physical form wavered in and out of my physical sight. An invisibility spell surrounded him. I had to rely on stillness and lack of movement to remain hidden.

Every time the Saxon turned to work his way closer to our bodies, the faeries nipped at his legs and face; they invaded his ears and slid between his fingers and toes. *Go back to the fire where it is warm. You see nothing here,* I whispered into his mind as I frolicked with the faeries.

The Saxon swatted at our nuisance between swings of his mighty ax. *Your're hungry. Go eat your supper by the fire,* I reminded him. His next blow touched the hood of my gray cloak, but not me. Each time he turned toward Da and me, the faeries intensified their attacks on him, laughing and giggling at his feeble attempts to dislodge them. When he moved away, the faeries eased their teasing.

After what seemed an age, he got the message and wandered back to the campfire. His compatriots didn't search anywhere near us. The faeries ceased plaguing the invaders and winked out of view.

Silently I thanked them, letting my mind sink back into my body. I sank into *one* body, *one* consciousness with a stomach-wrenching jolt. I fought to keep my stomach from inverting itself at the abrupt shift of viewpoint. Sudden awareness of small aches and pains in my back and arms and legs reminded me of how long I had kept motion-less. I suppressed the urge to stretch and move. Safety lay in stillness.

Finally the fog moved inland. The last of the twilight faded into darkness.

I breathed again in a more natural rhythm.

Da and I remained silently flattened against the Pridd. On the far side of the beach, the odor of food cooking over the open fire drove us mad with hunger. Still we remained, fearful of discovery.

At last, the Saxons settled into their blankets. They posted no pickets. I rose to my knees and listened intently. Nothing stirred. No alarm rose from the campfire.

Da and I drifted inland with the mist. Neither of us spoke until several leagues separated us from the Saxon longboat.

"We must hie to Venta Belgarum, Wren," Da whispered as we hurried along the Roman road.

"We have to see Lady Glynnis—make sure she and the children are safe. We have to find Curyll and Lord Ector," I protested.

"I will summon a vision of Lady Glynnis in the fire tonight. If she is well, we will head due south as fast as we can. As for Lord Ector and his sons? They can't leave the army to patrol this sector without Uther's directive. No British warbands have defended this area for many months. We have to warn the Ardh Rhi that the Saxons infiltrate all his shores, not just the South and East. The army must come. New strategies formed. Battle lines drawn. Our connection to the Goddess reaffirmed."

"Why haven't the warbands come already? Surely word of the raids must have reached the capital by now," I said, nearly breathless at our rapid pace.

But I was pleased we moved so quickly. The faeries might be forgetful, they played pranks, and laughed too much, but they could not lie. Curyll needed me. I would find him with Uther's army.

"I fear that Uther is no longer capable of directing his troops, Wren. The Ardh Rhi's covenant with the Goddess is broken. Why else is the land vulnerable to invasion from foreigners and to alien weather? Uther has either broken every moral and civil law, or he is dying."

He didn't have to remind me that an Ardh Rhi should die in battle. His primary function was to dispense justice and unite the warbands in defense of Britain. The client kings who elected the Ardh Rhi dealt with the everyday governing of their own lands. An Ardh Rhi could not be allowed to outlive his ability to lead men in war.

"But the faeries are still here. They helped us. Not all of the covenant with the Goddess is broken."

"Flighty creatures at best. You are their special friend, so they helped you. I saw naught of them. I haven't been privileged with knowledge of the faery since . . . " He stopped speaking and swallowed deeply.

I knew some old sadness separated Da from the Otherworld. I respected his silence with my own.

"You must not depend upon the faeries too much, Wren. They tempted an old friend of mine to lie with one of their females. They wanted a half-caste child to slip between their world and ours and keep the gateway between worlds open. My friend remained trapped between this world and the Otherworld for more than a decade." Da shook his head sadly. "He was never the same afterward."

I had wanted to tell Da how much the faeries trusted me. Why else would they request I bear them a child? I closed my mouth with a snap.

"Without the direction of the Ardh Rhi, Britain will fall victim to petty squabbles and tribal feuds, making us more vulnerable," Da continued. "Lleu, help us. We have to reach Venta Belgarum before Uther dies and leaves us leaderless."

Chapter 12

VENTA Belgarum sprawled out from the protective wall of the new citadel like a spiderweb. Uther had reoccupied the abandoned Roman town, shoring up crumbling defenses and building new ones. He had chosen to make a stand against Saxon incursion at the closest defensible point to the growing Saxon Shore. The town's population had grown considerably since I'd last been here, five years ago. People gravitated to the Ardh Rhi's protection, swelling the town and straining its resources. On South Hill, outside the riverside town, the old earthwork fortress and ritual maze lay crumbling and abandoned.

Belgaera, home of the Belgae, as we used to call the fortress, had been a trade center on the River Itchen from before the time Roman merchants began the invasion of Britain. Their army finished the invasion. Romans had destroyed the fortress, buried the turf maze, and forced the Belgae to live on the riverbanks.

They'd also done their best to eliminate tribal identity and memory of revered customs.

The trading village of Venta Belgarum was now a city, with a city's false sense of urgency and crowds.

From the river and the land Uther could launch lightning raids and prepare for invasions originating on the Saxon Shore, south and east from here. Why hadn't Uther advanced and destroyed the marauders approaching from the rear?

The war against the Saxon invaders consumed the energy of all Britain. And yet the army had defended only a few square leagues around the capital this campaign season. By rights, they should have gone home if Uther's call to arms proved false.

People bustled along the streets of the city, hawking fresh food, chatting with neighbors, trading livestock. I'd never seen so many people gathered together in one place. Nor smelled anything like it. So many feet churning the mud of the byways, so many slop pots emptied in the gutters, so many unwashed bodies pressed against each other. Was this any better than the devastation I had seen in the North? It didn't smell any sweeter.

We paused at the junction of several streets. In the center of the intersection, a gaggle of women gathered around the well. The only familiar sight I'd seen in this sprawling ugliness. Women always timed their trips to the wells so they'd meet friends and neighbors. The celebration of sharing the life-giving Dwfr of the Goddess became a social event, an enjoyable moment to relieve the hard work of the day, a way of keeping up on local news. Sometimes the gossip at the well provided me more accurate information than listening to men counsel each other.

I scanned the women, hoping for a greeting or a friendly face inviting me to join them. None noticed anything but the gossip they shared. I hadn't had the company of women since leaving the Ladies of Avalon, and I missed them.

Da directed me deeper into the maze of streets, always following the Roman road—the only pathway that wasn't overflowing with mud and debris. Still longing to linger with the women at the well, I didn't follow immediately.

Men bumped against me, never apologizing in their haste. Traders by their clothes and fat purses. I stared at their retreating backs, stunned by their rudeness.

" 'Tis unnatural, Da. How can they honor Dana when they are more concerned with getting where they are going than how they get there?"

"This whole city saddens me, Wren. But the Ardh Rhi keeps his hall and court here. The presence of the army camp swells the numbers who live here. We must report to Uther without delay." The webbing of worry lines deepened as he squinted his eyes and touched his torc. His frown deepened. He looked long and hard into the distance. I wondered if he looked into the past or the future. He hadn't laughed in weeks, mad laughter of prophecy or mundane laughter of joy.

A hand stole into my pocket. "Ungrateful bitch!" cursed a

ragged man who leaned upon a crutch and peered at me with one malevolent eye.

I glared back at him, daring the thief to comment further about the emptiness of my pockets.

Then he spotted the harp upon Da's back. His hand clenched, little and index finger pointed outward—a ward against Cernunnos, the horned god of the Underworld and patron of witchcraft.

"Sorry, Father Bard. Didn't mean no offense." The thief bowed and tugged his forelock in subservience. "But a man's got to eat, can't eat in the city without coin to buy food." He continued bowing and apologizing with every muscle in his decrepit body. Each bow took him another step backward.

"May Dana feed you when the hearts of men ignore our tradition of hospitality and charity." Da nodded his own apology for having nothing to share with the thief.

"Ain't no Goddess ever fed me. Only me—what I could earn or steal. Even the Christian monks only give to the likes of me three times. Then I gots to earn my keep by praying to *their* God. No thanks. I'll take me chances on the street." He turned and hobbled away, his right fist still clenched in the ward against Cernunnos and his followers.

"The Saxons should raze this city so we could start anew," I whispered.

"Hush, Wren. Keep your thoughts to yourself. Who knows which ears listen. You of all people should know how listeners hide while they gather their crop." Da turned and led me to a bulky pile of stone full of unnatural straight lines and sharp corners that could only be the Roman Citadel beside the Roman garrison.

Troopers stood at each of the Citadel gates. Beyond them sprawled a courtyard and more armed men. They appeared more interested in polishing their weapons than using them on the Saxons. No one acknowledged us or questioned our entrance.

"Such laxness does not speak well for the discipline of their superiors," Da said as soon as we were out of earshot. "We aren't even trying to remain unseen."

"Where is the army, Da?" I searched every corner for a glimpse of Curyll and spotted only a few common soldiers.

"Their camp is a league east of here at Cheesefoot Head. We approached from the north. And, yes, they should have marched to meet the enemy many months ago. I fear the kings keep their war-bands close for more sinister reasons than to guard the capital from enemy invasion."

We passed numerous outbuildings, stables, storerooms, and barracks on our way to the central stone tower. A small round structure of carefully dressed stone stood in sharp contrast to the ugly square-ness of the Roman garrison that Uther now called home.

"What is that?" I pointed to the elegant little building. Power emanated from the stones and drew me toward it like lodestone to iron. The building sat astride a well rising from a sacred spring. I hadn't realized I was thirsty, physically and spiritually, until I smelled the clean water. I knew that if I stepped beneath the low lintel into that Power, I would be bathed in beauty and peace.

I knew that if the well were not confined to a building, the power would spread throughout the region. All would be fruitful and peace-ful once more. The crippled thief wouldn't have to steal to eat. Hospi-tality would come from prosperous farms throughout Britain. The Saxons, and their gods, wouldn't be able to land on shores dedicated to the Goddess in all her persona.

" 'Tis the chapel of the White Christ, built by the Romans," Da said simply and turned his back on the pulsing and glowing stones.

The Goddess didn't need buildings to define a place of worship. Her blessing was dispensed to all, not just those who gathered within a chapel to pray.

I remembered Father Thomas at Lord Ector's fortress. He, too, had radiated the same sense of Power. But he'd expanded his magic to include all of the believers present, not contained it within himself. Why the difference?

My simple spell with the cat seemed very weak and childish in comparison to the faith in the one god that clung to the priest and the Roman Chapel in nearly visible layers of magic power. Power that excluded Da and me because we did not believe.

"Ho, Father Merlin!" A tall, dark-haired man stopped us in one of the innumerable corridors of the Citadel. He wore the half mail tunic of a marchog, one of Uther's elite mounted warriors. An immense sword lay sheathed across his back. His hood of mail was thrown back and no helm protected his head, as was appropriate for indoors.

The fact he wore armor inside the Ardh Rhi's caer told me that peace rested uneasily within and without these walls.

The darkness within the marchog's gray-blue eyes beneath his prominent brow made me wonder what secrets lurked there. He carried his bulky muscles and large bones with an aggressive assurance that told me I didn't want to probe deeper for those secrets without permission.

"Lord Carradoc." Da raised his right palm in the Roman greeting of peace.

Startled by the distant gesture when our people habitually met with a kiss of peace, I slipped behind Da. Over his shoulder, I watched the interplay between the two men.

"Up to your old tricks I see, Father Bard. Appearing out of nowhere when we least expect you, with knowledge far beyond the ken of mortals." Lord Carradoc slapped Da heartily on the shoulder.

Da stood unflinching, despite the blow that must have hurt. He captured Lord Carradoc's hand and turned it to read the palm. "What is knowledge but observation and long memory?" he asked. Delicately, he traced the lifeline of the lord's palm.

"And what do you observe in the calluses and creases of a simple warrior's hand?" Carradoc's shoulder muscles tightened as if Da's touch burned and Carradoc must prove his courage with this test of pain.

He stood half a head taller than my tall father. Broader at the shoulder and just as narrow in the hip, he carried himself with the self-assurance of a natural leader. Only a few traces of silver glistened in his black hair, giving evidence of his maturity. His posture reminded me of Curyll, but this man was much older, nearly as old as Da. A seasoned warrior.

A false note rang through his voice and gestures. I could find no specific thing about the man to make me wary. Yet my senses suddenly came alert, looking for danger—or lies.

Few of his class lived to see their third decade complete. He must be very powerful or very lucky.

Would Curyll be wily and strong enough to live to this man's advanced age? Only if I found him soon and helped in whatever task the faeries thought he needed. Perhaps this big man, who stood squarely in our path, could help me find my friend.

Distrust rang in the back of my head. I hesitated to become obligated to Carradoc for anything.

"I see a life that is troubled but long," Da said, still tracing the lines of Carradoc's palm. "A life that endures beyond the grave. You have many triumphs ahead of you, Lord Carradoc. But pain and betrayal follow you every step of the way." Da dropped the lord's hand.

"Superstitious nonsense." Carradoc rubbed his palm against his metal-studded leather tunic as if it truly burned—or were dirty. "The trouble part I believe. Saxons encroaching on all sides, three demanding daughters with tongues so sharp no man will have them, and Uther— I make my own destiny, Father Merlin. Now, let me escort you to your quarters. You must be tired and hungry after your long journey." He gestured us back along the corridor we had just traversed.

"Da," I whispered as I tugged his sleeve. "Ask him about Curyll."

"Ask yourself, Wren." Da drew me from my hiding place behind him.

"Wren? Can this be the little girl I bounced on my knee when first you brought the tot to court, Merlin?" Carradoc's eyes widened. A glint of an emotion I couldn't read brightened his gaze.

"Forgive me, for I have no recollection of meeting you, sir. I must have been very young." I ducked my head away from his penetrating stare.

"I find you well grown and lovely, little Wren. Allow me to escort you to the women's bower. After you have rested, perhaps you will allow me to show you Venta Belgarum. Some of us still honor the Old Gods. The eve of Samhain, three days hence, is occasion for bonfires and dancing and other pleasant diversions. It would please me to escort you through the labyrinth dance." His outstretched arm curved to gather me into an embrace.

One step sideways put me out of reach. "Samhain is more appropriately celebrated with prayers and fasting behind stout doors where the dead and the dwellers of the Otherworlds can't lure us to our doom." I scowled at the lord.

"My daughter will stay by my side, Lord Carradoc. When we have reported to the Ardh Rhi, *I* will escort her to the women's bower where she will be safe from unwanted attention of men." Da placed himself between the warrior and me.

"A virgin, eh? Place her brideprice high, Father Merlin. You'll be a wealthy man by Samhain and a grandfather by the feast of Lleu."

"My daughter's destiny lies elsewhere. My duty is to protect her at all costs." Da continued to stare at Carradoc until the big man squirmed in discomfort.

He forced his gaze away from my father's eyes. Da touched his torc with one hand and captured Lord Carradoc's chin with the other. Then the lord's vision turned glassy and unblinking. His body grew very still, halted in mid-word, mid-gesture.

"Allow us to pass. The Ardh Rhi has need of us," Da said firmly.

Carradoc continued to stare straight ahead, unresponsive.

Da waved a hand before the man's face. Carradoc did not blink or move. His gray-blue eyes glazed over. His mouth froze, half open as if about to speak.

We slid around his big body.

"You must teach me that spell, Da." I stared over my shoulder at the warrior, wondering how long the trance would last. When Da had tried it on Curyll, it lasted only a few moments.

"No spell, Wren. Merely a trick you can teach yourself if you put your mind to it." He tapped his temple and smiled knowingly. "Carradoc only believes himself asleep. He will awaken with no memory of our conversation or his lust for you."

A light snore escaped our recent obstacle.

If he believed himself asleep, then wouldn't he be asleep? I asked myself. No use putting the question to Da. He'd merely tell me to think it through.

"Why did he divert us away from the Ardh Rhi?" I asked instead.

"Why indeed, Wren? We shall soon find out. And perhaps we will also find out why the army remains idle here rather than protecting all of Britain as they should. This way." We turned down another corridor.

"I believe we have found Uther Pendragon's lair," Da said quietly, halting our progress.

Tall double doors marked the end of the passage. Four alert and heavily armed men guarded the portal. Spears snapped as two guards crossed them, blocking our way. Beside them, two more soldiers put hands to sword hilts and stepped forward.

Chapter 13

THE guards' faces told me nothing. The tension in their shoulders and legs revealed determination and pride in their ability to carry out their responsibilities. I believed they would kill or be killed defending the Ardh Rhi.

"Another sleep spell, Da?" I whispered.

"Not yet, Wren. Seek the truth first. Spells are a last resort."

True enough. Magic didn't come easily and always cost us in fatigue, hunger, and sometimes depleted health.

"Halt. No one passes through these doors without leave from the Ardh Rhi," the left-hand guard said in even tones. The two men with swords were so alike in height, coloring, and leather armor studded with bronze, either could have spoken.

"I, The Merlin, Bard of Ardh Rhi Uther, seek audience with my king. You have no right to detain me."

The guards didn't lower their weapons.

"No one may pass," the guard repeated, determination written in every muscle.

"My business with the Ardh Rhi is urgent." Da pressed forward one step.

Neither guard retreated. They both raised their swords a fraction.

A fifth man stepped from the shadows of a cross-corridor behind us. "Your business with Uther Pendragon is only urgent if you brought a healer with you," he said, gesturing the guards to surround us.

I wheeled to face the voice. Instantly I assumed a stance of readiness. I knew how to defend myself with knife and feet, teeth and nails.

Da turned halfway around, keeping the guards and the new man within view.

I'd made a tactical mistake not to do the same. Next time I'd know better.

The two guards with spears continued blocking the door. The two with swords obeyed the newcomer, one in front of Da, and the other in front of me. Both held sword points within a hair's breadth of striking.

"King Leodegran of Carmelide." Da nodded to the newcomer. He didn't bow before the newcomer. A bard was equal in rank to any of the client kings of Uther, the Ardh Rhi. "My daughter Wren learned healing arts from The Morrigan. I have brought her to Uther."

Healing herbs and balances within the body I knew about. The great healing magic was beyond me. Had Da lied to gain access to Uther? Lying was the only crime he'd punished me for as a child.

I looked at my father in a new light. He played with words and tricked people's minds, never lying outright but twisting the truth. No one, not even I, knew for certain his motives, plans, or the extent of his powers. Confusion prevented me from hearing the rest of the words bandied about.

Next thing I knew, King Leodegran took hold of my arm and escorted me past the now respectful guards. His short, wiry stature belied his firm, almost painful grip. Torchlight reflected off his bald head as brightly as the jewels that adorned his fingers. One of them ground into the soft flesh of my upper arm.

Side by side, we entered a large square chamber, dominated by a wide bed in the center. I blinked rapidly, trying to adjust to the dim light cast by a single candle in the far left corner. I dared not step deeper into the room until I knew what, and who, awaited me.

"I don't care if the old fart lives or dies," King Leodegran whispered into my ear. "But I do care who rules as Ardh Rhi. Make certain Uther lives long enough to name me his successor!"

I looked at Da to see if he had heard Leodegran and understood the menace underlying his words. Da seemingly paid no attention to anything but the feeble creature propped up on a bolster in the huge bed. A few limp hairs draped across his skull. His eyes were deep cavities burning with fever. A skeletally thin hand rested atop the embroidered coverlet.

The odor of death assailed my nose as heavy incense burned my eyes. A brazier to the right of the bed added little light but too much smoke.

Objects began to take form as I adjusted to the meager light. A faint line of sunshine crept under the tightly shuttered window near the candle. Beside the waxy flame sat a thin, young man in the dark brown robes of a brotherhood of the White Christ. He read aloud from a precious scroll, twisting the faint writing to catch the light.

At sight of us, the priest snapped his scroll closed. He pressed his back and his chair up against the wall, as if recoiling from evil.

The priest and I stared at each other in silence for a long moment, judging each other.

Da remained behind me. I couldn't see his expression to guess his next move or his wishes for mine.

"The child can be of no use here." The priest sniffed and clutched the cross that hung from a thong around his neck.

I'd seen such talismans before. The wearers held them, prayed to them, depended upon them for protection and guidance. A sprig from a rowan tree served me better.

"You've accomplished little with your prayers, Father John." Leodegran approached the bed where Uther lay, unmoving.

"I do not need a cure for Uther's mortal remains. I seek a cure for his soul. His body cannot enjoy health until his soul is pure," Father John argued. His voice raised and spread from deep inside his chest as if he preached to the entire city.

Leodegran ignored him. "Highness," he whispered. "Highness, I have brought the bard and his daughter."

The limp hand stirred in response. Ardh Rhi Uther turned his head stiffly toward us, as if control of his pain depended upon moving as little as possible.

Beneath the incense and herbs, I smelled death. A demon had found life within Uther and would eat away at his vitals until there was nothing left.

Uther had no son to take up the reins of leadership. The husband of his daughter Blasine or his stepdaughter Morgaine might gain enough prestige from a marriage alliance with the Ardh Rhi to insure election to the position. Could any of the lesser kings hold together the volatile warbands who owed allegiance to one of many client kings rather than to Britain as a whole?

Now I knew why the army hadn't left their camp. The kings kept them close, waiting for Uther to die. Each king knew he'd have to fight all of the other contenders in pitched battle to win the election. The ensuing wars between kings would leave Britain open and vulnerable to invasion.

From the grim frown on Da's face, I knew he had reached the same conclusion.

Suddenly, my father's purpose in roaming the land from one end to the other, year after year, became clear. He sought the next Ardh Rhi. Was Leodegran the right successor, or did I need to stall while Da sought another?

Nimuë grabbed an alder sapling close to the base and braced her feet. With all of the strength in her sore shoulders she pulled, long and steady as her mentor had told her to. The roots gripped the Pridd tenaciously.

"Shit!" she shouted as her grip broke and she landed on her butt in the soft dirt beside the hidden spring. "If I'd wanted hard work, I'd have stayed in Avalon." Even the knowledge of poisons and listening to people's thoughts didn't make up for the sheer hard work of preparing for true magic.

Her mentor had been as close-lipped about those things as the Ladies of Avalon. All they truly wanted of her was a slave to do the dirty work for them.

Wanting to cry, she sucked on the raw skin of her palms. How would she explain this small injury to Carradoc. Or worse, to Brenhines Ygraina?

Ardh Rhi Uther's wife kept close supervision of the ladies entrusted to her.

"All I wanted was a little power to break free of Carradoc." She stuck out her lower lip in a pout that had won the hearts of several suitors—but never Carradoc's permission to marry one of them.

She glared at the double spiral on the single standing stone beside the spring, wondering if the ancient gods could give her the power she needed. The twin motifs seemed to swirl inward, becoming eyes. Accusing eyes.

"Enough!" She broke the spell cast by the carved symbols. "I'll dig out the blasted tree. But that is all. *She* can take care of replanting it in your honor." Nimuë dusted the dirt off the back of her gown. The saffron yellow skirt was ruined. She knew she should have worn an old dark garment for clearing the area around the standing stone and sacred spring. But a somber costume would have provoked questions and watchfulness. She'd never have slipped out of the palace and the city walls dressed as a plain peasant. But everyone expected the flamboyant daughter of Carradoc of Caer Tair Cigfran to prance out to the main army camp in search of her father or other companionship.

She reached for a digging stick and crawled back to the stubborn sapling. She scratched at the dirt listlessly. The tree roots seemed to have crept under and around the standing stone. She tugged again at the trunk, about half the size of her wrist.

Her eyes crossed with the effort. The double spiral seemed to waver and shift, swirling inward again. Nimuë yanked her gaze back to the ground. She watched the cool dark waters of the spring. A reflection of the double spiral rose up from the depths of the little pool. The surface water stilled. The image of twin circles sharpened.

Her vision narrowed, concentrated on the spinning lines of the ancient symbols. They spread, shifted, resolved into a demon face. Square, black, indistinct around the edges, defined by the spinning red eyes.

She continued to stare, fascinated by the reflection.

"Did I raise you from the Netherworld?" she whispered.

You called me to serve you. I cannot obey until I have been fed. I need blood, a harsh voice rasped into the back of her mind.

"Blood," she repeated. "I gave you blood when first I approached here."

Blood to rouse me from my long sleep. I need more blood to live—to do your bidding. I need the blood of the one who will disrupt your plans.

A new image appeared on top of the demon face. A young woman riding a sluggish mare. A mass of unruly dark hair obscured her thin face. Grass and twigs stained the hem of her gown. She sat the horse awkwardly and kept her eyes on the ground.

"Do I know her?" Nimuë searched her memories for a clue to the woman's identity. Where had she seen that hair before?

You will know her. You will deliver her to me and my disciples on Samhain. Once fed with her blood, I will serve you faithfully in your quest for control. We will control.

"Good." Nimuë renewed her efforts to clear the area around the spring. "Only a few days to Samhain. Then I will be free of Carradoc's smothering restricions. I will have a demon to do my bidding. My mentor will have to do her own dirty work from now on."

Even she will not stand against us.

Nimuë dismissed the ugly laughter in the back of her mind as her own.

I flung open the shutters beside the young priest.

"You will kill the king with your pagan demons and heretical methods." Father John stared at me with all the venom of a true fanatic. "I cannot allow you to destroy the Ardh Rhi's soul."

For a moment I was reminded of Father Thomas. But that gentle priest had burned with love and faith in his god, not with hatred. Both priests would command followers. Father John was the more dangerous of the two. Much more dangerous.

A moment of dizziness blurred my vision. Then my eyes and my head cleared. I stood with a firmer balance and clearer mind. My perception of the patterns of life tilted and realigned a little. I knew a fanatic among the Ladies of Avalon. I didn't know the cause of her extreme prejudice, only that she would neither hear nor speak anything good about the Christians and went to great lengths to antagonize the hermit who resided nearby. I wondered briefly if she had caused the old man's hands to slip on the ax handle so that he cut himself so badly. She matched Father John in fervor. Could any of them truly hold a god in their hearts when they excluded others for believing differently?

Fanaticism was about control, not faith. I think I may have been a little guilty myself. In that moment of self-truth, I vowed to mend my ways and look toward tolerance rather than automatic condemnation. The patterns of life seemed brighter and more cohesive with that thought.

Trying and doing aren't always the same thing.

"King Uther needs fresh air and a bath," I replied to the priest. "Only then will my knowledge of healing work. Douse the fire, Da. I will burn my own herbs at the proper time." I glared at the priest as if I had matured far beyond my thirteen summers.

I needed to act with the authority and self-confidence of The Morrigan. My instincts pushed me to come back in the dead of night and work my few spells and mix my medicines in private.

Imagining myself as tall and elegant as The Morrigan, filled with authority and self-confidence, I began planning a ritual for King Uther's cure. Not the great healing magic, but *something*. I wished my unruly hair hadn't escaped its braids into a messy frizz. My hair would always prevent me from appearing mature and elegant. People don't take unkempt children seriously.

"Close out the noxious humors!" Father John clutched his cross tighter and leaned over the ailing Ardh Rhi as if to shield him from a physical enemy. He stared at me, eyes burning with hate.

"Britain needs Uther alive and well, Father John. You can tend to his soul later. Get on with it, girl," Leodegran ordered.

"I—I will need warm water to bathe him, fresh linens, and the brazier cleaned of the incense."

"Uther will die when God ordains and not before!" Father John divided his glare between the smoking brazier and me. "You will rot in hell before I allow you to murder an innocent victim with your vile sacrifices."

"Druids sought to appease the gods with human sacrifice long ago, sir. We have not participated in that ritual for several centuries," Da said quietly. Behind his words I heard intense anger. I busied myself with opening more shutters rather than face Myrddin Emrys in a rage.

"When my people chose to sacrifice to the gods at Beltane, 'twas with the firm conviction that we would live again," Da continued. "We are so certain of our resurrection we accept debts payable into the next life. Is your faith so true, young man?"

"Blasphemy! Only God may choose the time and place of our death. His Son's crucifixion and resurrection ended the need for sacrifice for all time. In Him I believe. I cannot allow you to corrupt my convert, Uther, Ardh Rhi of Britain." Father John backed away from my father, keeping his body between the Ardh Rhi and us.

"You can do nothing to stop The Merlin and his daughter." Leodegran stood beside Father John, waving a long knife beneath the priest's chin "I am in charge here, and I say the girl will heal him. Britain is safer in the hands of The Merlin than in the feeble prayers of the Christians. We need action—not faith." With each word he drove the priest closer to the door.

"I will be back, with Archbishop Dyfrig and Brenhines Ygraina. And others who believe. We will protect King Uther's soul from pagan atrocities." Father John ducked out the door, slamming the wooden panels in his wake.

Da's hands shook. His face looked unnaturally pale. "Not Dyfrig," he whispered. "Anyone but Dyfrig."

I prayed the portal to Annwn, the Otherworld of the Faery would never close as completely or be as heavily guarded as the door to Uther's private chamber.

Right then, Leodegran and my father seemed as dangerous as the priest. I wanted to run from them. Run from responsibility.

I wanted to run to Curyll but didn't know where to find him.

Chapter 14

ALL that long day in Uther's death chamber, I learned about a different kind of power. Politics. I watched Leodegran and Da hold off a frightened brenhines, an angry archbishop, and numerous courtiers and warriors with only words. Words that stung, words that begged or promised, and words that manipulated people and their desires. All in aid of politics.

Da dealt with Brenhines Ygraina; Leodegran spoke with the archbishop. Whenever Dyfrig tried to enter the chamber, Da made himself busy on the opposite side of the room. The two never looked at each other, never spoke.

I pushed aside my curiosity to dwell on the tasks at hand.

By the time I had prepared Uther for my minor spells, exhaustion dragged at my eyelids and added lead to my feet. I couldn't listen anymore to all the words that flew through the partially open doorway.

Servants had willingly brought the things I needed once Leodegran directed them to obey me. After that, I had only to clap my hands or express a wish and my requests appeared almost as if by magic. 'Twas convenient and labor saving, and yet I felt distanced from my work, detached from the person I must heal—and from myself.

In Avalon, we all had to gather, cleanse, and prepare for rituals and spells without help. Now I knew why. If I had drawn the bathwater from a sacred spring, gathered and dried the herbs, and woven the linens, my spells would have permeated every element of the healing. My strength would have been used gradually, a little at each stage. Now I had to spend too much energy in preparing myself and my tools for magic. Would I have enough left for the actual healing?

Political power dissipated my true power. Recognizing that, I knew another moment of truth—two in the same day? My role in life was to work on the fringes, to help people quietly. Any influence I might gain would be subtle, gentle, and, I hoped, longer lasting than the constantly changing politics.

Finally all the extra people left me to my work. Only Da remained. I looked into his anxious face and knew I didn't have enough strength left to perform the simplest magic.

"Now what, Da? How do I cure a man whose body has been eaten away by disease? There isn't enough of him left to cure."

"A cure is impossible, Wren. I stayed away too long. If I had come at the Solstice, perhaps we could have reversed the damage. Now? We can only try to stop the disintegration for a time. Relief from the pain will allow him to eat and gain a little strength. That is all. With luck and the blessings of Dana 'twill be long enough to do what I must do."

"And what is that, Da?"

A quiet knock on the door stopped his answer. Brenhines Ygraina slipped into the room, a basket over her arm filled with some of the herbs I had requested. She stopped at the doorway. I had expected a servant to deliver the last ingredients.

Da raised one eyebrow in query.

"I wish to help you, young Wren," Brenhines Ygraina said. Her blue-gray eyes looked at me honestly, devoid of the mask of politics. "Uther has been my husband these nineteen years. I pray that you may give us a little more time together." She lowered her gaze, keeping it fixed upon the floor so that I couldn't read the grief I knew must fill her. Yet her posture continued to be straight and proud, almost defiant. Determined anyway.

I wished for her poise and beauty. No longer young, she continued to be beautiful and strong in a delicate kind of way. Finely boned features, pale skin and hair, she glowed from within. Her rich gown—without a trace of grass stains—and heavily jeweled cross seemed unnecessary adornments. Like putting jewels upon a rose.

The Morrigan emanated the same kind of regal beauty.

I, with my wild hair and travel-stained clothing, would never command such loveliness. And yet Carradoc had found me attractive. . . .

"Our medicines are not recognized by your Church, lady," Da

warned. "Nor will we offer prayers and readings from your sacred books."

"That does not matter, as long as you save him. Even for a little while. I am not ready to be alone. I love him too much . . ." She begged my father with words and eyes and hands folded together.

Her words had meaning and a power I could not deny. The power of love.

"You, Myrddin Emrys, brought Uther to me once before, when God and my first husband worked very hard to keep us apart. In payment you stole our son. You owe us for that grave misdeed. I cannot hope to see my son again. Bring Uther back to me. For a little time. Please."

"I have no intention of allowing Uther to die just yet, lady." Da moved beside her, taking both her hands in his. "I have never broken a promise to man or woman. This I promise you, Ygraina: Uther will live long enough to see your son restored to you."

"Son?" I gasped. No rumor of Ygraina bearing Uther a son had ever reached my diligent eavesdropping. She had a daughter, Morgaine, by her first husband and had borne Uther another daughter, Blasine. Da knew of a third child. A boy. An heir. Who? Where?

The questions piled up until I thought I would burst unless I asked them. And with the questions came a brief understanding. Da didn't need to search for an heir. He knew where the young man was hidden, free from political corruption and assassination. Free to grow strong and lead men in his own right, not from inherited political power that would evaporate quickly.

I knew of several qualified young men we had met over the years in our wanderings. Any one of Ector's sons and fosterlings—Curyll or Stinger came to mind before nearsighted Boar and Ceffyl. Another lord in Bernicia and one in Dummonia raised herds of boys with similar qualities.

Which one had Da chosen? Uther and Ygraina would not know the young man. They trusted Da to give them *their* son.

I trusted Da to present the best qualified, regardless of heritage. He probably had several candidates to make certain at least one of them survived long enough to become eligible.

Leodegran would not be our next Ardh Rhi. Da and Brenhines Ygraina would see to that. But the client king was ambitious and a power to be reckoned with. He would do his best to prevent an untried boy from usurping political power.

"To work, Wren. We have no time to lose." Da returned to the bed, a half-smile of purpose touching his lips.

"But what do I do? I need a matron and a crone with magic to complete the magic circle. I have never done this before, never witnessed the ritual," I whispered.

"But I have a different magic at my command. I will work the healing. The truth of who brings Uther back to life will remain a secret among us three." He nodded to the brenhines and myself.

"Knowledge of you as the miracle worker will give you much power over the court and the other kings," Ygraina reminded him.

"But will do nothing to protect my daughter. She must be seen as the miracle worker—the heiress to The Morrigan's power. The men who would seek to use her must believe she has value beyond her parentage and her beauty. Thus they will respect her. 'Tis the only way I can be sure she will be safe in this world of war, change, and religious conflict."

He said the words as if he knew he would not be there to protect me and had no plans for me to marry.

I clung to the promise of the Goddess in my vision. *I will have a husband and children by Curyll*—no matter what my Da said or did.

Da's preparations for Uther's cure were simple, and much the same as I had planned myself. We dosed Uther with a potion of herbs brewed in a new cup made of finest pottery. Clay for the cup had come from the living muscle of Dana. Dwfr for the potion was Her lifeblood, and the herbs Her raiment. Tanio to heat and bind the potion was Dana's gift to Her people. The burned herbs became smoke, representing Awyr. By treating Uther with the living Goddess and all four of Her elements, we sought to bring him back into balance with Her.

I prepared the ointment we rubbed into Uther's joints with similar symbols and methods. Dana returned to his aching body with soothing warmth.

And finally a vision of the source of the disease.

I sent new fire into the coal from my mind—a more powerful binding source than from flint and iron. Then I set onto the brazier a copper gräal—the symbol of the cauldron of life the Goddess stirred and nurtured—filled with freshly drawn water from a hillside spring. A secret combination of pungent herbs smoldered in the coals. Smoke drifted into every corner, filling the room with the fragrance of wood and field. Faeries could nourish themselves on that smoke.

Da knelt before the gräal, stirring the contents, murmuring prayers and spells much as the Goddess maintained Her gräal. I should have done this, but without a matron and a crone my magic would be unbalanced. How did he fill the gaps? He bowed his head in meditation to prepare himself for the vision. A simple viewing of friends within the flames of a campfire did not require such careful preparation. He must look deeper into the mysteries of the gods to root out the demon that dwelled within Uther.

I inhaled deeply of the fragrant smoke. My sense of up and down wavered. Colors shifted and burst from every object in the room.

Da placed three drops of Uther's blood into the gräal.

The water in the bowl called to me. But this was to be Da's vision. I closed my eyes lest I see and misinterpret what he needed to know.

Beside me, I heard Da breathing deeply of the smoke and mist from the gräal. At last I opened my eyes to find layers of shadows surrounding him. Not an aura of energy from within, a cloak imposed upon him by the gods. I looked to Ygraina who stood beside the bed. Many-colored layers of light surrounded her. If I looked deep enough into those colored layers, I would know every secret she possessed. Da guarded his secrets too closely with a cloaking aura for me to hope to penetrate it.

I dared not probe Ygraina. She was, after all, my brenhines. Instead I looked to Da and jerked away from him, gasping in fear and surprise. Blackness outlined every shadow layer that surrounded him. The blackness of undeath.

Without wanting to, I looked into the water in the gräal for understanding, drawn there by the compulsion in the smoke and the spell I had prepared for my father. I expected to see visions of Da's past, my mother, the secret sadness he carried after leaving his college of Druids.

The steam rising from the gräal parted before my eyes. Within the still water I saw the sigil for poison glowing with menace upon the limp body of Uther.

No demon ate at his vital organs. Poison! Poison, given to him daily, with his wine, for many months.

A vile crime against Britain and the Goddess. Whoever poisoned the Ardh Rhi poisoned the land.

Such a crime opened the door to the Saxons, civil war, famine, and plague. Whatever earthly power, wealth, and prestige Uther held would waste away and become meaningless.

Christians didn't believe in the covenant with the Goddess. Neither did they believe in murder.

No one who held to the old ways would dare kill the Ardh Rhi, except in single combat after ritual challenge.

Who, then? Who would dare?

I looked deeper into the vision to seek the murderer. *A name,* I pleaded. *Give me a name or a face.* The few remaining Druids would mete out justice.

The sigil grew larger, blinked and brightened to blinding intensity. Before my eyes the symbol shifted and changed into a rare plant, *druidsbane,* creamy white petals cupped around hairy, blood-red centers. Only those initiated into the priesthood of Cernunnos knew the closely guarded secret properties and antidote of this shy forest dweller.

Poison so deadly, the priest had to contain it within a Druid's foot—a pentagram drawn into the Pridd with his athame. Without the powerful sigil cut into the earth with a pristine ritual dagger, the plant would spread its poison into the air for the priest and his attendants to breathe and die.

I had discovered the druidsbane and its cure by accident on one of my solitary forays into the forests surrounding Avalon's marshy lake. My ability to blend into the shadows and observe had saved my life. A priest of the horned god of the Underworld and two of his apprentices gathered the lovely little wildflower with death hidden in its sap and pollen. I watched and listened, learning all I could. I kept to my hiding place long after they moved to another part of the forest. Had they discovered me, the athame that drew the circle of protection would have become the instrument of my death. Only those within the cult of Cernunnos could know the secret poisons and live.

Now I could use that forbidden knowledge to arrest the wasting of Uther's body. But no potion or magic could restore the damage already done.

Clearly Dana had given me the task to help Uther. Justice would have to wait. I didn't know where to look for the culprit.

Please, Dana, don't make us wait too long for justice, I silently prayed. *Don't make us wait too long to bring the guilty one before you. Our covenant with you must be restored before the Saxons kill us all.*

Da stood up, a hand to his head, strange words pushing through his clenched lips. A hint of the mad laughter that preceded prophecy hovered on the edge of the language he uttered. He stumbled slightly as he turned toward the bed. I reached a hand to keep him from falling, but he shook off my touch.

His fumbling footsteps took him in circles and loops toward the window. At last he leaned out and breathed deeply of the clean air.

A breeze cleared the room of the vision smoke and relieved my headache. Da continued to cover his eyes with one hand while pressing his temple with the rigid fingers of the other.

Ygraina stood by the door, her mouth and eyes wide with bewilderment.

"Do you know the antidote, Da?" I whispered.

He whirled to face me, hands braced behind him against the windowsill. The signs of pain on his face faded, replaced by lines of worry and alarm.

"You saw the vision, too?" His words mounted in volume.

I cringed and stepped back. "Yes, Da. I saw the sigil and the nature of the poison."

"If you know the plant, then I presume you know the antidote as well." Anger simmered just below the surface of his eyes, not yet radiating into his muscles. He fingered his torc with his left hand. His right hand clenched into the ward against Cernunnos, little finger and index finger extended, pointing at me.

I hung my head. I could not lie and yet if I admitted to the secret knowledge, would he feel obligated to kill me?

"We will discuss this later, Arylwren. When Uther is safe and I am calm." He turned to look out the window again, his back a broad barrier between us. "Proceed with the antidote. Time is short, but do not hurry the preparation lest you make a mistake and kill him with the cure."

Chapter 15

PREPARE the antidote. I needed a number of ingredients. Dragon teeth and powdered frog saliva I carried in my sach. Milk to contain the dosage and honey to bind the ingredients together I'd find in the kitchen. Certain flowers and minerals I needed, also dyed thread for weaving. I might find them in the women's bower.

"Highness, I need some help preparing your husband's cure," I said.

"Who would poison my husband?" Ygraina asked. She stared into the distance beyond me. Worry lines deepened around her eyes and mouth. For a moment, the image of her face grown very old shadowed her beauty.

My sense of time and place wavered forward and back and then slammed me between the eyes with a headache. I had seen in a vision when I was five myself grown old and sad because I was alone. Now I saw the same fate for Ygraina.

"I don't know who would dare poison the Ardh Rhi or why, Highness." I clutched her elbow to keep her from falling as her knees gave way. Mine weren't much stronger. Sharply, I pinched her arm where I held her, hoping to rouse her from a state of shock. "Will you help me cure him?"

She didn't flinch from my painful grasp. Recognition dawned in her eyes, followed by resolve. Finally she looked at me. "Yes," she said. "What can I do?"

I outlined the list of things I needed and my reluctance to send a servant lest they substitute the wrong ingredient if the right one proved elusive.

I didn't know how to explain in a few words my need to gather everything myself so I would become a part of the cure. I'd milk the cow and harvest the honey, too, if I had time.

"Come. Your father prefers to do everything himself, too." Ygraina took my arm and led me out of Uther's chamber.

"I tell you, Morgaine did not return to her bed until dawn!" exclaimed a young woman to a gaggle of other ladies gathered in the women's bower. "Last night was the dark of the moon, when witchcraft is most powerful. Who knows what evil magic spells she worked! Or which man she worked them upon." She dropped her voice into a supposed whisper, but it carried throughout the large solar. She tossed her freshly washed and lustrous auburn hair over her shoulder with a disdainful flip of her head.

Ygraina stopped short in her drifting progress toward her private chamber. "Nimuë! You know I will not tolerate malicious gossip," the brenhines reprimanded the striking young woman. "If you have a complaint about my daughter's behavior, you will bring it to me in private. Or would you rather I had your father, Lord Carradoc, remove you from court?"

"I understand, Highness." The young woman stood and dipped a brief curtsy to her brenhines, but her head remained high and her face determined. Her haughty expression reminded me of her father—the dark-haired giant who had detained Da and me when we first entered the citadel.

Nimuë's beauty stunned me. Where Ygraina appeared pale and graceful with her fair hair and skin, Nimuë sparkled with color and life. Her bright green gown beneath a gold brocade Roman stola matched and enhanced the color of her eyes. Flawless white skin made her look as if she had just bathed in milk. She stood tall and slim with her shoulders thrown back to emphasize her lush bosom; hips thrust slightly forward in a provocative stance I had seen other girls assume after their Beltane initiations. Her perfume hinted of musk and secrets and pleasure.

Next to her, I knew myself to be small, plain, and dowdy in my homespun gown, splattered with mud. My feet and hands seemed too large for my suddenly clumsy body. I smelled of smoke and the sweat of fear.

"I will speak with you later, Nimuë," Ygraina said, dismissing the young noblewoman. She turned to a hovering maidservant. "Maeve, assist Arylwren with all she requests, no matter how unusual. Treat Lord Merlin's daughter with the same respect you grant my daughters." Then she mounted a winding staircase in the far corner of the high-ceilinged solar. The two maids from our escort trailed in her wake.

Absolute silence descended upon the bower. All gossip ceased. Not even the gentle swish of a needle working through a tapestry whispered in the large room. Seventeen pairs of eyes stared at me with curiosity, suspicion, and malice. I was a stranger here, dressed as a filthy peasant who had suddenly, and without apparent cause, become closer to the brenhines than any of them.

I would find little comfort and no friendship among these women. Nor would they willingly give me any information should I be foolish enough to ask after Lord Ector's foster sons.

Then I remembered that many considered poison a woman's weapon. And if I had spied upon a Druid seeking an elusive plant, any one of these women could have as well.

Nimuë? Was she the same Nimuë who had left Avalon as I arrived? I couldn't remember. Four years and many emotions separated me from that day.

"Do you remember me, Wren?" A young woman with Ygraina's pale hair and features detached herself from the knot of needleworkers by the window. "I'm Blasine, Ygraina's younger daughter. We played together one Solstice when we were both too young to participate in the revelries." She smiled sweetly.

Behind her, Nimuë gasped. Her face turned red with suppressed words. She obviously held sway over many of the ladies in the room, but she could not compete with the young princess for rank. The princess was a year my junior and much the same small stature as myself. She had singled me out for preference.

Nimuë narrowed her eyes and looked down her straight, haughty nose at Blasine.

I clasped Blasine's hand tightly and returned her smile. Now I knew where the lines stood between ranks in the women's bower.

"I remember you and that Solstice festival, Your Highness. 'Twas fun eavesdropping on our elders through a hidden peephole. Do you think anyone ever realized we were there and what we overheard?"

Nimuë gasped and blushed furiously. What did she have to hide? If she was indeed the same Nimuë who had left Avalon four years ago, then she had been too young to participate in that wild Solstice party five years ago. Or was she ever too young for anything?

Nimuë had no way of knowing if Blasine and I had watched her or not when a drunken Solstice revelry became an orgy.

"Oh, yes. What fun we had." Blasine laughed, peering at Nimuë through lowered eyelashes. "We must discuss that scandalous party while you freshen up." She winked at me as we wandered through a side door to the bathing chamber reserved for the women.

I caught a glimpse of Nimuë shredding her embroidery with furious fingers as we left the room.

I wasn't about to tell her that Blasine's nurse had whisked us off to bed before we saw anything truly interesting.

Silence, too, could be a form of power.

Uther's cure seemed ridiculously easy after the trauma of the vision. We forced mundane compounds down Uther's throat, a few drops at a time. Quickly his body purged itself of new toxins. Then we had to bathe him again and change the linens.

A second mixture began neutralizing the more deeply rooted poison. By moonset the Ardh Rhi slept peacefully, healingly.

Da dismissed me with a wave of his hand. I stared at him with longing in my heart and an ache deep in my soul. Prayers for forgiveness sprang to my lips, but I couldn't utter them.

We needed words to heal the breach between us. I had acquired forbidden knowledge. By ancient tradition and law, Da must now kill me rather than allow the knowledge to spread.

Was his love for me stronger than his covenant with the Gods?

No words had passed between us that entire evening and night.

We didn't need words to know that one of us must remain at the Ardh Rhi's side at all times lest he relapse and need a repeat of the antidote. Nor did we need words to know that one of us must taste for poison in the strengthening broth and fortified wine we dribbled into Uther's mouth.

I tiptoed out of the room, silent lest I remind Da that I carried forbidden secrets with me. I had never been so frightened or alone in my life. I had no friends here in Venta Belgarum until I found Curyll among the jumbled masses. Not even the faeries could find me surrounded by straight walls and sharp corners made by men.

The Christian chapel and its aura of blessing called to me. But I feared the power of the place. I wanted only the love of my Da right now, not a confrontation with gods I didn't understand.

Hugging the shadows at every turn, I made my way to the women's bower. I needed a place to rest until dawn when I would relieve my father of his bedside duties. Ygraina had not offered another refuge within the Citadel for me. The women of Uther's castle were all locked up—if not with their husbands, then under the protection of the Ardh Brenhines.

Locking women away made no sense to me. In Avalon, the Goddess was all-powerful and Her priestesses revered as the embodiment of Her. Sexual union was a sacred rite of fulfillment. Raping a woman and defiling the Goddess were the same, the vilest crime a man could commit. Yet here, Ygraina warned me, women were locked away so they would not tempt men to prey upon them.

Puzzled and still leery of who—or what—my father might have sent after me, I passed the dozing guards outside the bower and crept inside.

The solar was empty and silent. The women had placed all of the needlework into baskets. Their spindles and looms rested. Not even a mouse stirred the rushes covering the floor. Such absolute silence seemed unnatural. The hairs on my arms and the back of my neck bristled. Goose bumps climbed my spine.

Samhain was very near. The boundaries between reality and the Otherworld faded with each passing moment. Ghosts and demons could easily have heeded a summons from my father to kidnap me back to their Netherworld.

A single oil lamp on a ledge by the door sent shadows leaping. I cringed away from them. Cautiously I tiptoed toward the large sleeping chamber reserved for servants and ladies of low rank. The widows, unwed sisters, and daughters of kings and lords had separate chambers farther along the corridor.

Pain shot up my foot. A fierce scraping sound, nearly as loud as thunder brought me to an abrupt halt. I had kicked a stool.

Clumsily I hopped and stumbled away from the stool as if it were my enemy. I gritted my teeth and bit my tongue to keep from screaming my fear.

A shadowy, ill-defined figure arose from a dark corner. It held a long object like a sword. I clutched my throat and backed toward the door and escape. My heart pounded in an odd, rapid rhythm. Cold sweat broke out on my brow and chest. What kind of assassin had Cernunnos and Da sent?

"Forgive me if I frightened you," the figure said in a soft feminine voice made husky by weeping. "I thought you might be Nimuë come to condemn me once more."

The owner of the voice smelled of power. I wondered if she had been working magic in her secluded corner. Weak magic, ill formed, and poorly directed by the wispy nature of the scent. But dormant strength seethed around the edges. Was the sword truly only an athame, or perhaps a spindle? Should she ever discover her powers, she could be a magician to rival Da and The Morrigan.

And yourself, a little voice whispered in the back of my mind. *You are a magician, too.*

"I'm Wren, The Merlin's daughter." I stopped dancing around and placed my foot—stubbed toe and all—back on the floor.

"I'm Morgaine. Ygraina's daughter."

I endured a moment of sagging weakness from sheer relief. Father had not yet planned my death. I knew in that moment that I couldn't meekly wait for his decree, I had to confront him and know the truth of his decision.

After I dealt with Uther's weeping stepdaughter who scattered magic about the room indiscriminately. To what purpose?

"Nimuë told the truth," I said. "You don't sleep in your bed in the room you share with her. Do you use these dark nights when the walls between worlds grow thin and weak to summon demons?"

"I might as well, now that she has ruined my reputation," she returned. She smiled slightly with only half her mouth. "But I do not summon demons unless you consider a love charm to be a denizen of the Otherworld. That is the only way I can get a husband and leave this haven of malicious gossip and ugly power struggles."

"Were you weeping because of Nimuë?"

"The lies told by Carradoc's daughter don't touch me. Not anymore," she said. She stepped closer with a firm step and determined chin. "I weep because my *mother*, the Ardh Brenhines, has closed her door to me and to the world. When Uther dies, she becomes the property of the next Ardh Rhi, as do my sister Blasine and I. In times gone by, the next Ardh Rhi would be determined by whom the Ardh Brenhines marries. Mother should rule and I after her. I am no man's property! I am a widow with a son, I should have all the rights and freedoms of a respected matron. But no. I'm an Ardh Brenhines' daughter, still young enough to trade in a profitable alliance, so I am kept a prisoner here."

"Uther will not die tonight, nor tomorrow. His disease wanes for a time. I do not know how long, but you have a reprieve, a few months to find a husband who will protect you."

"I'd rather protect myself. *My* father would have allowed it. I could have joined the Ladies of Avalon. I could have become The Morrigan. But Mother arranged for my father to die in battle while she lay with Uther. Uther didn't even have the decency to slay Gorlois, King of Tintagel, in ritual combat before claiming his wife and titles." Her nostrils flared with anger. A new scent hovered around her, of sulfur and decay.

I backed away from her, uncertain what forces she tapped. I'd never smelled the like in my limited magic repertoire.

"My father could have sent you to Avalon years ago if you asked. You have wasted the opportunity. Avalon is no more. The Morrigan died. The few remaining Ladies have dispersed."

"I know. But your father has the authority to send me to Avalon to start anew. If you ask for me, he will do it. He can deny you nothing."

Except my life.

"You would be the maiden to my matron. We'd need recruit only one of the crones, then the magic would be complete again. No man would rule over women again. I'd see to that."

"There is too much hate in you. You cannot honor the Goddess while you plan revenge against Uther and Ygraina."

She gasped and stepped away from me. "You really are The Merlin's daughter. You read my mind!"

Had I? I didn't think so. I only guessed what actions her emotions would lead her to. Perhaps I could direct her energies elsewhere.

"An entire army of men camps a league east of here. Many of them are ambitious as well as strong and virile. They will welcome the opportunity to gain power and prestige by marriage to Uther's stepdaughter. That is a safer route than confronting the Goddess with hatred in your heart."

"If Uther and my mother haven't found me a husband yet, think you they'll bother now? They dangle me in front of kings and lords who oppose them. But they never agree to the marriage, even after their victim accedes to their demands."

"Those who follow the old ways know that a woman has the final choice and the right of divorce. Fathers may urge a marriage for alliance or wealth, but the daughter says 'aye' or 'nay.' Make your choice, Morgaine. Find a husband to your liking or wait for someone else to choose a man you detest, simply because you didn't choose him."

"Wise words from one so young. Are you really only a child?"

"Nearly fourteen."

"Of an age to marry. Tell me, will you marry the man your father chooses for you?"

"That isn't likely to happen. The Goddess has chosen my destiny already."

A husband and children fathered by Curyll, the Goddess had said.

Strange wording. For the first time I considered the possibility that the father of my children might not be my husband. My fears matched Morgaine's.

Dawn came late the next morning. Between the lateness of the year and the depth of clouds, Belenos, the sun, caught me still sleeping long after my usual rising time.

Da had been sitting with Uther all night while I slept. I must relieve him.

I donned my clothes as I sped through the bower. No one called to stop me as I hurried past the groups of women nibbling daintily at their bread and cheese. I yanked open the door into the main passageway and slammed into the crossed lances of the guards.

These guards kept unwanted men out of the women's bower. They had the authority to hold me until they summoned a suitable escort for me. Before they questioned my purpose, I ducked beneath the lances and ran down the length of the corridor to Uther's chambers. Armed men guarded that doorway, too. Different men from yesterday. They glared at me sternly, awaiting an explanation.

"I am Wren, The Merlin's daughter . . ." I prepared to launch into a lengthy explanation of why they must admit me to Uther's sickroom. The guards apparently already knew it and unbarred the doorway. A third man politely opened it for me.

Inside, all was darkness. Closed shutters barred the weak sunlight. Only a few coals glowed dimly in the brazier. I paused just inside the doorway to let my eyes adjust. When at last I could make out a few shadowy outlines, I stepped forward, one hand extended to keep me from stumbling into something. My toe still hurt from last night's battle with the stool.

"Da?" I whispered

Uther's light snores were the only answer.

"Da?" I asked again a little louder and took another step forward.

Suddenly a snakelike coil tightened against my throat, blocking my breathing. Black stars flashed before my eyes. Demons roared in my ears. I clawed at the constrictions with desperate fingers and nails. My right foot lashed out to sweep away whatever held me.

"Be still, or die this instant!" a raspy voice breathed into my ear.

My fingers stopped their convulsive grasp at the rope I found strangling me and discovered a man's hand holding a knife to my vulnerable great vein. My heart rose into my throat, beating double speed in an irregular rhythm.

Blind panic brought me to absolute immobility. The rope eased just enough for me to breathe shallowly. The stars faded from my limited vision, but my loud pulse continued to compete with the demons roaring in my head. I smelled the fear on me and heard the rapid beating of my heart. Did my assailant as well?

The tip of the knife pressed against my throat. I sensed its wicked sharpness, though it did not draw blood. Yet.

"You spied on my priests. Death is the punishment for carrying forbidden knowledge beyond the Druid Circle," the voice continued.

Had Cernunnos come for me? Had he killed Da, too?

I sought the corners of the big room for signs of my father. The shadows were too deep and unfriendly to tell me anything.

"Cernunnos says you must die. Dana commands you be protected at all costs. Which will it be, Arylwren, daughter of The Merlin? Life or death? Cernunnos or Dana?" The voice lost some of its hoarseness. I recognized my father in the husky whisper.

He offered me a choice. With relief came a flood of love. We walked a narrow path between Cernunnos and the Goddess. The choice was mine.

"The Goddess rules all the spirits of this world as well as the Underworld and the Otherworld. I choose Dana," I said, croaking from the residual panic and constriction on my throat.

"You choose life, but you cannot continue to live with forbidden knowledge. The knowledge must die. A part of you dies with it!"

The knife moved to my right temple. A sharp pain and a sticky wetness flowed down my face. I cried out and reached to pull the knife away from my scalp. The rope around my throat tightened. I couldn't breathe. Pain lanced from the knife wound to my eyes. My knees threatened to collapse, but the strangling rope held me up. The world grew darker. More black stars flashed across my vision. A white tunnel of emptiness beckoned beyond sight. The pain grew more intense. Sharp. Burning. Icy hot.

I screamed.

The blackness of the Netherworld claimed me.

Chapter 16

TOTAL blackness surrounded me. I had no sense of myself. Only the darkness pressing against my mind and my soul. Darkness and guilt. I had done something terribly wrong, and now I must pay.

But what had I done? What cost would Andraste exact?

Panic filled me. I cast about fruitlessly for something, anything. . . .

A glimmer of light grew slowly in the distance. I sighed in relief. I focused on that tiny flicker of light as if it were the essence of my life.

Aching muscles and joints reminded me I had a body after all.

A sense of intense cold penetrated everything but the light. The acrid tang of sulfur dominated the deep darkness. I had to get away. Death awaited me at the source of that odor.

If only I could remember what I had done, I could reach out and know the warmth contained within that light.

After a time the light intensified, taking on a shape. Long. Skinny at the bottom, broad at the top. I willed myself closer to the light and the tiny relief from the growing cold. I would have shivered if I could sense more of my body than a grinding ache and soul-chilling cold.

The light spread upward and outward. Shadows drifted at the core of it.

Help me! I screamed at the shadows with my mind. *Help me remember. I can't atone until I know what I have done.*

The aimless movement stilled a moment, as if something, someone paused to listen.

Please, help me.

An ill-defined dark blob flew out of the light. A dozen hairy limbs reached for me with bright white-and-red pincers. A sickly-sweet odor replaced the sulfur. Poisonous green drool leaked from a gaping, blood-red maw.

A demon!

I ducked, knowing that if any portion of the demon touched my physical or spiritual body, I must stay in this black nothingness for all eternity. Every childhood fear gibbered inside me. I couldn't breathe, couldn't think, and didn't dare remember.

As the demon sped toward me, its body flowed into a new shape—the sigil for poison. Its pincers turned into the white-and-red flowers of a rare forest plant I knew I must never touch, never remember.

The demon reached out those lovely flower pincers. More of the poisonous drool dripped from the tips of the red flower centers. The pristine white petals turned black, crisping at the edge as if burned.

"Da!" I screamed with mind and voice. "Da, save me. Save the Ardh Rhi."

The demon exploded into a thousand shards of black glass. The pieces flew in all directions. Two sharp bits whizzed past me at lightning speed. I ducked again and cowered deep within myself.

The light grew again. The shadows within its heart coalesced into the Worldtree. The massive trunk shot upward. Up and up beyond my limited vision. Up it grew to pierce the darkness above me. Sunlight flooded the darkness.

Warmth returned with the light. And with it a sense of my self and my body.

Da sat in the lower branches of the Worldtree, beckoning me to come to him. He held out his arms in loving welcome. I knew in that moment he had forgiven me.

For what? I couldn't remember. Like a small child, I knew only that I had transgressed and needed forgiveness.

And then my beloved father changed. He grew horns. His long legs shortened and bent. His face twisted and elongated.

Cernunnos, god of the Underworld, beckoned me forward with my father's doting eyes and loving embrace.

"No! no, no, no," I screamed and hid my face. "I won't go with you. It's not my time. I can't go."

"Wren, Wren, wake up." Da shook my shoulder.

Sleep dropped from me like a heavy burden. I had the sense that a great deal of time had passed, and yet my memories of my time in Venta Belgarum blurred together into a confused mass of hurt pride, anxious questions, and aching fatigue.

I did remember Da working a great healing spell to remove the cancerous demon that ate at Uther's innards. I remembered watching the spell and feeling proud that my Da had saved the Ardh Rhi's life.

"You have sat vigil over the Ardh Rhi for a full day and half the night, Wren. You must rest now."

"The demon. . . ?"

"Uther's demon is banished. The danger is over."

"But you must rest, Da. The spell drained all your strength away."

"I have rested while you sat here so diligently. Now you must rest, too, or I will have to find a new spell to heal you as well." He smiled, love radiating out of his face. "Go now. Go to the women's bower and sleep until you wake naturally."

"But the dream . . ."

"Was only a bad dream."

A headache pounded so fiercely in my temples I wondered if the demon that Da and I had rousted from Uther's vital organs had taken up residence in my head. Even the meager moonlight that filtered through the overcast sky threatened to blind me.

I trudged off to my cot in the women's bower. Dreamless sleep grabbed me and held me down until sunshine once more brightened the room.

Samhain dawned bright and clear. I dreaded rising from my soft nest of warm blankets for yet another day of guarding the Ardh Rhi's health. Duty dragged me forth. I refused food and wandered into the corridors of the fortress.

A cold northeast wind swept the skies clean and fanned the bonfires outside the city. An air of expectation hovered inside Uther's fortress. Every cold draft startled the inhabitants and sent them seeking evidence of ghosts and otherworldly spirits. I longed for some of that fresh air to clear the pain from my temples. I hadn't time to slip outside the city and sit quietly on the hillside surrounded by the natural patterns of trees and grass, free running creeks and clean air. Da needed me to take over his vigil.

Giggling children ran through the fortress with innocent abandon. They tugged at hemlines and sleeves from behind unsuspecting adults, then ran away laughing. The adults jumped and gasped. They searched all around them with anxious eyes. Many clasped a cross displayed prominently on their chests and whispered prayers, or they traced the sigil of death backward—as a ward against it—around a corsage of rowan leaves pinned to their left shoulder. Death always sat on the left shoulder.

I watched a large number of them clench their fists in the ward against Cernunnos as I passed. I shuddered, half remembering my nightmare. I clutched the sprig of protective rowan leaves I kept in my sach.

By the time I reached Uther's apartment, the anxious atmosphere these people generated had penetrated my heart. I approached the now open door cautiously. Shadows invited me, and I merged with them as I slipped through the doorway without the guards noticing me. The heavily armed soldiers retained their usual stern expressions. However, a slight relaxation in their postures indicated good news.

I hastened inside the Ardh Rhi's apartment, pausing in the first layer of shadows. Sunlight flooded the sickroom. Ygraina hovered anxiously. Uther paced the room, supported by Da.

The guards hadn't seen me through the shadows, but I couldn't hide from Da.

"Go back to bed, Wren, before you take ill." Da waved me away. "Our vigil is finished. The Ardh Rhi is nearly well again. You will attend the banquet tonight, though, Wren." Satisfaction lighted his eyes and his smile.

"Must I, Da?"

Nimuë and Morgaine would be at the banquet, gorgeous in their best gowns and darting dark looks at me at every opportunity. Next to their exotic plumage I looked more than ever like a plain brown wren. I hadn't the strength or willpower to deal with them tonight. The headache pounded more fiercely.

"Yes, you must attend, Wren. All the court will see how Ardh Rhi Uther honors you. Safety comes with that honor." His tone demanded obedience.

The freedom of the hills beckoned me. I paused in the women's bower only long enough to fetch a cloak. Food didn't appeal to me, but I knew I'd be hungry once the cold, fresh air cleared my head of pain. So I tucked a small round loaf of bread and a hunk of yellow cheese into my sack along with other daily necessities.

As I hastened toward the city gates, I couldn't help but overhear conversations.

"Did you hear? Father John is dying. He gave his life energy to cure Uther. Just like Jesus Christ. We must hasten to the chapel and pray for his soul."

Before I had time to wonder about the nature of Father John's illness, a new conversation filtered through to my thoughts.

"The Merlin and that strange daughter of his stole Father John's life and gave it to Uther. The Druids haven't used that kind of magic in centuries. She must be the new Morrigan," a tall warrior whispered to his lady.

"Uther is the Ardh Rhi. He has to be preserved until a suitable heir is found. It is only right that she use whatever power is necessary," the lady replied, clutching her corsage of rowan leaves.

So I was now The Merlin's strange daughter and the new Morrigan! Perhaps Da's wish that I be respected for my own powers had come to pass. I couldn't think about it while the headache dominated my being. I needed to get out of the noisy Citadel and the noisome city.

The short hours of daylight stretched before me. Time to myself. I had time to find Curyll and clear my aching head.

A chill draft blew around my ankles. The stone walls and sharp corners of the Roman buildings made the seeking wind seem colder—as if it were born in an ancient burial mound and couldn't find its way back. I couldn't dismiss the smell of sulfur and overly sweet demon poison. The hairs on the back of my neck stood on end. I shivered.

Samhain. The sabbat of Cernunnos, god of the Underworld.

The year wound to a close tonight. The doors to the Otherworlds opened wide. No one, magician or mundane, could close them by ritual or accident until dawn.

"I'll be back inside the Citadel before the barrow wights dare think about emerging from their tombs," I promised myself.

Something fluttered against the back of my memory. I tried to grab it, but it died before I could understand. Something about barrow wights and my headache. . . .

Uther's army camped in a great depression surrounded by hills, called Cheesefoot Head since ancient times. The bowl hid the encampment from casual observation and offered protection from the winter winds. The hilltops gave sentries a clear view of the River Itchen and all approaches to the city. Unlit bonfires marked the top of each hill, easy signal devices. Tonight all of the fires would burn for protection from the inhabitants of the Netherworld—the Otherworld men feared most.

No one stopped me, a solitary and plainly dressed woman, from approaching the orderly rows of tents and pavilions. I blended in with the horde of camp followers and idle soldiers that ambled through the muddy "streets" of the camp. The Roman passion for order served me well for once. The straight lines of tents and buildings, marked with numbers and letters painted on posts at each intersection, led me directly to the large pavilion where Lord Ector's banner of a boar surrounded by rowan leaves fluttered from the ridgepole. Ector's son Cai came by his nickname honestly.

Dana and the faeries must have smiled upon me that day. Curyll was just leaving, ducking through the tent flaps, as I approached. For a moment I was blinded by my joy at the sight of him. Then I noticed a new scar on his cheek above his sandy-gold beard and a slight hump and twist to the bridge of his nose.

My heart looked beyond the changes and recognized him at first glance. Taller and broader than I remembered, four years had added grace and maturity to the boy and made him a man. Sunlight danced in his golden hair and beard.

"I'll report back to you at supper, Lord Ector." Curyll saluted his foster father in the Roman manner, and strode away from the pavilion.

I followed hastily. "Curyll!" I called.

He stopped short and turned. A puzzled frown put an intriguing crease between his beard and mustache. I wondered if all that facial hair would tickle or feel like silk against my face—if he kissed me.

"Wren?" His eyes danced with delight as he recognized me. "Wren! Where did you come from?" He reached both arms to enfold me in a bear hug that lifted me free of the earth and swung me in a broad circle. He smelled of horse and sweat and leather. Not so different from my memory of him.

My aching head continued to spin when he stopped whirling. I clung to him for balance, drawing strength from his warmth.

"Oh, Curyll, you are safe and hale," I blurted out. I touched his face and caressed his beard, unable to help myself. His whiskers, as silky as a dog's long fur, tingled against my fingertips. "The faeries said you needed me. I came as quickly as I could, but Uther's illness delayed Da and me. I really worried about you. But you are safe!"

"Slow down, Wren. What is all this about faeries and Uther and your Da?" He laughed, putting me down and ruffling my unruly hair as he had when I was a child. His fingers felt good as they rubbed my tender scalp. "You haven't changed a bit, Wren. You still have grass stains on your skirt and twigs in your hair. Don't ever change." He hugged me again, laughing with joy.

The top of my head barely reached his shoulder. His leather armor, reinforced with bits of metal, added bulk to him. Beside him, I felt like a child, a very muddy and ragged urchin. But my life's pattern looked right for the first time since Da exorcised Uther's demon. Only the habitual pack of dogs hanging about Curyll's heels was missing from the picture.

"I have to talk to you, Curyll. Da and I came across Saxons in the Dee estuary. They've been raiding and pillaging for miles inland. That's when the faeries said you needed me."

"This is serious, Wren. Where is your father? He needs to report to the Ardh Rhi. We have fought only minor skirmishes along the Southern coast this year—just enough to keep us here. We wondered if the Saxons grew tired of feeling the bite of our swords and moved on to weaker prey."

I stared at him, eyes wide and mouth slightly open. "Is there someplace we can talk in private?" I looked askance at the hundreds of men and servitors that made up this army. Most of them seemed to be loitering within an arm's reach of us.

The kings had no right to keep the united warbands in attendance for only minor skirmishes. The men should have gone home to defend their own lands months ago.

But the kings needed their armies close by when Uther died and a new Ardh Rhi was decided by combat. Only they didn't know Uther had a son who could replace him, if he could gather enough support from a majority of the kings. Da had to name the heir soon.

I wondered again which of the young men we knew was truly Uthur's son and which my father would bring forth.

Curyll could be the one. I hoped not. As a respected warrior, he could marry me. The Ardh Rhi needed to marry a princess with political allies.

Curyll grabbed my hand and walked rapidly down an alley lined with middle-sized shelters. Combinations of stone, timber, and sturdy cloth making up the tents created an aura of permanence that bothered me. An army should be mobile, to meet the enemy wherever necessary. A lord brought his warband to the Ardh Rhi only for emergencies that threatened everyone.

"My tent. That is . . ." He stopped short and I nearly bumped into him. "You can't be seen going into my tent alone with me. Brenhines Ygraina is quite strict about her ladies."

"Britain is more important than my reputation."

Without further ado he hauled me in his wake toward an officer's shelter sporting a small banner of a bear. He'd clung to that emblem rather than revert to the hawk of his name.

"No one will disturb us here. I'll leave the door open for your sake, Wren." He pushed inward a wooden door set into a haphazard frame.

"Curyll, where have you been? Oh!" a feminine voice greeted our arrival.

"Morgaine?" Curyll froze in mid-step beside me.

High color spread from his cheekbones to his ears and down into his thick neck. I tore my eyes from his embarrassment to stare at Morgaine. She stood in the center of the small room holding her undertunic in front of her. Above her clasping hands, her naked shoulders and the rounded fullness of her breasts gleamed milky smooth in the flickering light of a single oil lamp. The breeze from the open door fluttered in the folds of her garment, revealing a long leg, naked to the enticing roundness of her bum.

Chapter 17

THE Merlin settled Uther back into his bed for a well deserved nap. The Ardh Rhi had made a remarkable recovery but still lacked essential strength to handle much more than feeding himself and using the chamber pot.

"Sleep now, Highness," he whispered, holding his palm over Uther's eyes.

The Ardh Rhi didn't need help in falling into deep, healing sleep. In moments he snored lightly.

"How long?" Ygraina whispered from her chair beside her husband's bed.

"He will sleep a few hours and then require food and drink again," Merlin replied. He didn't like the waxy color of the brenhines' skin. She needed rest as much as Uther did.

"No. How long will he live?" She brushed a fallen lock of graying hair off of Uther's brow with the touch of a familiar lover.

"Unknown," Merlin shrugged. He envied Uther the love of this gentle woman. Together, they had ruled with strength and a wily hand at politics. Separately, neither one would have succeeded at much. He'd recognized how they completed each other all those long years ago when he cast a glamour on Uther so that he could appear as Gorlois, Ygraina's first husband, and infiltrate her well-guarded caer.

As Uther and Ygraina lay together, conceiving their son, Uther's army had ambushed and slaughtered Gorlois and his warband. Long before Uther left Ygraina's bed, she was a widow.

Merlin's price for his part in the deception was the raising of that son, Arthur. So much depended upon Arthur. The gods knew he was the only one who could hold Britain together long enough to beat off the Saxons.

"You must know something, Myrddin Emrys. You see the future."

"With luck and care and a mild winter, Uther might live to see spring." With Wren around to nurse him, he might surprise them all. She had worked a better cure than Merlin thought possible without the great healing magic.

He almost swelled with pride at his daughter's accomplishments. At the same time he feared for her. Powerful people wanted Uther dead, and she stood between them and the Ardh Rhi.

"No longer?" Panic widened Ygraina's eyes.

"I can promise no more. The poison has eaten away at him for too long."

"And my son. You promised to restore Arthur to me."

"When the time is right."

"I say the time is now!"

Merlin met her gaze in silence. Arthur must be a proven leader of men before Merlin revealed his identity. Otherwise the client kings would reject him, or use his weakness as an excuse to fall into war among themselves.

"Rest, Highness," Merlin ordered Ygraina. "Rest while you can. Your husband will be a demanding patient when he wakes, and until I discover the poisoner, Uther must not be left alone."

"I will rest here." Ygraina settled into her highbacked chair and closed her eyes. "You may go about the business of finding the guilty. Exact whatever revenge you must from this person, but allow me to watch their death."

"I will do what I can, Highness." Merlin backed out of the chamber. He had other chores as well.

Remorse made him more tired than he truly was. He had slept a while during the night while he watched Wren wrestle with her demons. Demons he had planted in her mind.

How could he have done that to his precious daughter?

He hadn't many choices once the nature of the poison was revealed. Whoever had dropped minute doses of druidsbane into Uther's wine must be a powerful magician to have survived the harvesting of the poison. That same magician would be able to read an unguarded mind. Wren had to believe in the cancerous demon rather than the poison for her own protection.

A truly determined assassin might recognize in Wren the one person who could undo the convoluted plot.

Where had Wren gone? He'd best find her and make certain the unknown magician didn't follow her.

If he knew his daughter at all, she would head for the rolling hills south of the city. She'd need fresh air and the renewal she'd find only in solitude.

He hoped he found her before she stumbled upon the sacred spring and its abandoned dolmen. Ten years ago he'd discovered remnants of bloody sacrifices there. Followers of dark powers had perverted the shrine to their own use. The place stank of evil, so he had warded it well and encouraged the forest to retake the place.

Tonight was Samhain. Perhaps he should make a point of renewing the wards to keep any ambitious demons from using the dolmen as a portal into this world tonight.

"I have found a virgin for tonight's festivities." Nimuë licked her lips seductively as she caressed her lover's cheek. "A real screamer. She could raise the dead with her voice."

Hot moisture inflamed the secret place between her legs at the thought of what her lover and his comrades would do to that virgin. That alone would be worth all of the work to get the girl to the ritual site.

"We must have time to work through the entire ritual to satisfy the men," her lover said. "No one must come looking for her prematurely." His voice became husky with desire.

Nimuë smiled to herself. She needed him eager and ready at sundown. Did she have time to slip into a hidden alcove with him right now? The forbidden nature of the tryst heated her as much as the thought of holding him inside herself.

Her knees weakened with her need to join with him. She reached up on tiptoe to kiss the corner of his mouth, brushing the tips of her breasts against his chest. With her free hand she cupped his manhood.

"Not now." Her lover held her shoulders, keeping his elbows rigid and a disappointing distance between them. "You must make certain no one locks the girl away, beyond your reach. She must walk into the ritual site by herself, not under duress or carried there. Can you bewitch her as you have bewitched me?" His hands trembled slightly, but he kept his distance.

Nimuë knew a thrill of power. If she pushed, she'd have him panting and sweating for her, in her, within moments. Later she promised herself. Later when she could take her time and let him know who truly ruled this relationship. He'd never control her again after tonight.

"I have watched her closely for three days now. I know her habits. I will have her ready at the assigned place and time." She almost wished she could substitute her mentor for the screaming virgin. But the demon would know the difference and reject the offering.

"And afterward?" He kissed her neck and pulled her close. His arousal pushed hard against her belly. Only a few layers of clothing separated them.

"If all goes as planned, you won't need to worry about afterward." She forced herself to sound normal, not breathless and wanting. She had to maintain control.

"Just make certain no one suspects either of us in the girl's disappearance. We'll return her in the morning, slightly used but not hurt." He chuckled low in his throat.

If Nimuë worked the ritual correctly, the screaming virgin wouldn't return to Venta Belgarum. She'd be dead, every drop of blood drained from her and fed to Nimuë's demon.

"I know how to keep a secret and appear to be in two places at once," she replied. "You taught me that long ago."

Haven't I kept the secret of my teacher's identity. Haven't I hidden the truth of how and where I found my demon?

I ran away from Curyll and Morgaine. I ran through the straight streets of the army camp, up the hill, past the sentries and bonfires. I ran. I ran until my heart pounded so loud that it drowned out all other sounds. I ran until my lungs ached and my head grew light. All semblance of a pattern in my life evaporated.

At last I collapsed in a heap beside a spring at the bottom of one of the rolling hills. Shrubs and saplings hid the small pool surrounding the spring and me from casual view.

A solitary standing stone guarded the pool. The twin spirals of fertility etched into the surface mocked me.

Curyll loved another. I'd never hold him close or bear his children while beautiful Morgaine captured his heart.

Tears flowed freely down my face. Racking sobs added new pain to my laboring lungs.

Why would Curyll, or any man, look at me after Morgaine had seduced him with her beauty, her wealth, and the promise of royal favor? I hadn't sensed any magic about her today. She didn't need any.

At last I had no more tears to add to the pool. I raised myself up to a sitting position, careful to avoid looking at my face in the watery reflection. I knew I'd see ugly splotches and red-rimmed eyes. Beautiful women like Morgaine seemed to be able to cry and become even lovelier. Men jumped to still their tears with gifts, tenderness, and pretty words.

Not me. My tears angered men and made them avoid me. I tried very hard not to cry. But today I couldn't hold back. A new round of sobs threatened me.

My heart ached for the loss of Curyll. But strangely, my head no longer throbbed, nor did my eyes shy away from the afternoon sunshine.

Without the headache driving me, I could think again. Morgaine and Curyll hadn't announced their betrothal yet. I still had time to work a little seduction of my own. My grief turned to resolve, cold and calculating. Tonight at the banquet Curyll would see me as The Morrigan, graceful and elegant. I would take the time to rest and comb the twigs and moss from my hair. I'd wear a clean gown, too, one suitable to the rank others bestowed upon me. Perhaps Blasine could lend me something more attractive than the plain leaf-green and oak-brown garments I usually wore.

A sturdy stalk of nettle on the other side of the small pool waved to me in the afternoon breeze. He reminded me that my sach was lacking many of the herbs I commonly carried. I should place pots of nettle beneath Uther's sickbed to keep further evils from him.

The fading stalk of wild parsley next to the nettle begged to be added to the herbal pot.

Strange. My sach was empty of parsley, a natural diuretic and one of the ingredients in the standard tonic to relieve a woman's monthly cramps and bloating. I didn't remember preparing a dosage for any of the women in the bower. Had Morgaine stolen some to incite Curyll's lust? Lust, not love. I'd probably given what I had on hand to Uther, to ease his painful swelling after the demon roared out of his body. I had worked so much magic that day I barely remembered any of it—the cancerous demon, the dosage, the spells—

Methodically, I applied myself to harvesting the few medicinal herbs growing around the pool that I could use. The carving on the dolmen enticed my glance. I refused the allure of it. I didn't want it to lead me into a vision of the future. A future devoid of Curyll. That would be a false vision. I would find and implement a new plan to show him where his heart truly belonged. Unlike the double circles, the future was not etched in stone. It could change if one knew what clues to seek out in the vision and avoid them.

Gently, I cut the parsley stalk with my belt knife. My mind reached out to thank the plants for sharing their leaves and late blossoms with me. They accepted my thanks, content they could be of use this season before they retreated back into the earth for the winter.

A feral cat wandered up to the pool for a drink. He stayed to watch me. His orange-and-white fur reminded me of another cat, long ago. I missed Helwriaeth.

"Will you stay with me? I need a friend."

The cat blinked and considered but did not answer. It hunched down and watched me.

In a few moments I had pushed the lingering ache of Morgaine's seduction of Curyll to the back of my mind and lost myself in my tasks. From the spring, I moved uphill again, seeking more seeds, leaves, and mosses.

As usual, I lingered longer than I should have in the rolling hills and high meadows. The cat trailed behind me every step of the way. I was bent over an interesting double-blossomed daisy when a golden-yellow flower faery whispered in my ear.

Look at how long the shadows grow this time of year! He giggled and tickled my nose. His bright orange, brown, and gold wings caught the glow of the descending sun.

"I suppose I have to go back," I sighed. Ghosts and creatures from the Otherworld had never frightened me before. Samhain was just another day in the fascinating calendar of days. Remnants of my nightmare urged me to seek shelter within stone walls and lighted rooms.

I looked about to thank the autumnal spirit for his reminder of the time, but he had disappeared. As had his companions—faeries never traveled alone. Insects, birds, and small field animals had fled as well. The orange-and-white cat blinked at me and retreated without further communication.

An eerie sense of aloneness descended upon me. I had never truly been alone before. Da, the friends we visited, or the Ladies of Avalon had always been no more than a shout away.

I hadn't wandered far. If I left now, I had plenty of time to skirt South Hill and cross the River Itchen at the Roman bridge. Due north offered a more direct route into the city but required fording the river through a tricky marsh. I set my direction east, around the hill that had been home to the old hill fort and the ritual turf maze.

A gentle breeze seemed to guide me in that direction.

Wren! where are you? I heard in my mind more than with my ears Da's shout.

I knew that Da worried about me. His thoughts vibrated out of the distant city, seeking me. I considered the shortcut through the marsh. The wind circled and pushed me back to the east.

I obeyed it and set my course back around the hill toward the Roman bridge, trying to appear as if I didn't care that darkness approached with the lengthening shadows. Barrow wights fed on fear. A fleeing human made herself a target. But I'd be back in the city well before full dark.

Chapter 18

THE shadows lengthened and seemed to grow more substantial, taking on three dimensions. They reached toward me with long tendrils that might have been the fingers of some lost soul seeking to claim my body for its own.

"Nonsense," I said aloud, willing my fearful imagination to rest. "The sun is still above the horizon, and the twilight lingers long this time of year." Hearing my voice speak the words made my reassurance more real than the shadows.

The old fortress and ritual maze stood between me and the bridge over the River Itchen. Should I take the easy path around the hill or the shorter one over the top?

The crumbling earthworks of the fortress and outer walls held many traps for an unwary traveler. Few creatures but demons and lost ghosts would be comfortable within the abandoned hill fort after dark.

I hurried along an overgrown pathway that should lead me around South Hill to East Bridge and a safe crossing of the river. The wind rose to a howl, driving me up the hill. The sun neared the horizon. I tasted chilled salt and sulfur in the air. The gates to the Netherworld creaked open early.

Was someone summoning demons before sunset? Who would be so foolish? Demons set free on Samhain didn't have to obey the spell-caster and return to their own world at dawn.

Over the hill would cut my journey by half a league. My feet sped up the uneven path without me urging them forward.

Voices, loud and rowdy. Smoke. Wavering light. More sulfur greeted my senses as I rounded a curve of the hill. I spotted nine moving creatures. Grotesque, oversized heads, hairy, unclothed bodies, and hunched-over posture branded them as demons.

They blocked my path. Whose magic had summoned them early from the Netherworld?

I didn't think I knew anyone stupid enough, or desperate enough, to try using demons on Samhain. Demons were difficult to control at best. Impossible to contain on this last night of the year.

I bolted off the easy path and up the steep slopes of South Hill toward the ritual labyrinth. If I could walk the entire looping pathway from beginning to end without faltering, I might be able to raise enough power to protect myself from the creatures.

As I reached the first rampart, broken in several places, the demons stepped onto the processional way on a course parallel to mine. The processional way was a kind of labyrinth in itself, twisting and winding around the steepest slope of the hill, filled with traps designed to stop an army, not hinder demons.

I had to reach the center of the labyrinth before the demons reached me. Once they entered the maze, they would grow in power. Unchecked, they might be able to permanently prop open the gateway to the Netherworld.

My heart pounded in my ears. My lungs labored. Cold sweat broke out on my brow, back, and under my arms. Pain stabbed my side. I needed to stop and take deep draughts of air. I couldn't afford the time.

Darkness threatened to overtake me too quickly. Demons controlled this darkness.

Through my side vision, I kept track of the demons as they climbed the hill. Unearthly bobbing lights betrayed their looping passage of switchbacks on the eastern slope.

At last I reached the second rampart. Gulping air in heaving sobs, I scrambled over a small breach in the earthwork wall. The drop into the ditch on the other side was longer than the outside scramble. Brambles and pointed sticks awaited me. I checked over my shoulder for the demons. They were close. Too close. The processional path looped very close to the broken place I had chosen to climb.

No time to think. No time to prepare. I slid and slithered down the wall noisily, keeping my feet out in front of me. The soles of my feet collided with the shaft of one of the pointed stakes. Grateful that I hadn't impaled myself on the stake and ripped great holes in my flesh, I rolled to my knees, seeking my next path.

Among the deep shadows, I spotted the wiggling pink nose of a small creature. Rabbit? Cat? I crawled through a small tunnel in the brambles after the animal. A fully-grown man in armor, carrying weapons, couldn't have navigated that prickly path. Small as I was, thorny vines snagged my gown and plucked at my hair.

I crashed onward until the brambles thinned and the next slope rose before me. Steeper than the outside hill, this last climb held no traps and hindrances. I took two breaths to get my bearings and darted straight toward the jagged silhouette of the fortress.

As the hill leveled, I stumbled over the rotting remains of the town that had once clustered around the protection of the hill fort. Most of the wood had rotted in the centuries since the locals had moved down to the river level. Nearly all of the fortress' stonework now formed the stout walls of Roman-style villas within the city. Enough rubble remained to trip me. My toes burned almost as sharply as my lungs.

The wind pressed me forward.

I counted my steps to the labyrinth. Nine times nine. Sacred number to firm my bond with the Goddess.

A complex pattern of circles within squares, cut into the cropped turf, lay before me. The chalky ground gleamed faintly in the red sunset. I placed my right foot onto the beginning of the path. My foot barely fit between the low ridges of close-cropped grass on either side. I knew that I had to follow the path exactly to the center, then back out to the beginning, just like the labyrinth on Avalon's tor. One wrong step could send me into the arms of Cernunnos or any of his horned servants. Tonight, when the walls between reality and other realms faded and blurred, I needed to be doubly careful.

But the demons had to follow the path, too. They could not cut across the turf of the maze, through the layers of power I built. Once I reached the center, I'd have enough protective magic to safely reverse my path and walk back into the city.

"Please, Dana, guide your handmaiden correctly. Protect me this night from forces that would trick me away from your service." I clutched the two sprigs of rowan tied together with red thread I kept in my sach.

No whisper of wind or giggle of faeries assured me that anyone had heard my prayer.

The sun touched the horizon. Darkness sped across the valleys between the hills. Too soon the half-light would dissolve into full darkness with only a small sliver of a new moon to light my way.

I should have at least another half-hour of twilight. Why was it so dark, so soon?

Magical power enfolded me the moment I placed my left foot on the path, directly in front of my right. I couldn't turn back now if I tried.

The driving wind died. I was on my own.

The path veered sharply right. I teetered, almost lost my balance, one foot and both arms waving wildly. With all of my will, I forced my foot back down onto the path. My senses centered again and I moved onward. I saw torchlight crest the first rampart. I had to hurry.

Strange. Demons shouldn't need fire to light their way. I didn't have time to think the problem through.

The lights crept forward. Deep voices howled.

Nine steps to the next left-hand turn. Nine more steps and I sped along the outermost line of the labyrinth. Only a very thin wall of power separated me from reality. I wasn't sure if the demons could reach through it or not.

Nine more steps and I faced a curving turn to the left. I raised my left foot to step into the turn. The path darkened abruptly, hiding the white chalk that I followed. A lightning jolt of power shoved me backward. My arms flailed. Hastily I set my left foot back where it had been, behind my right.

What had I done wrong?

Begin again, a voice whispered in the back of my head. My father's voice. A memory or instructions?

I couldn't step out of the maze and start over. I had to keep going.

The demons let out a mighty howl of triumph as they spotted me. They ran toward me, ahead of their bobbing lights.

Knowing I had to follow the path correctly, without backtracking or stepping off the chalky line, I closed my eyes and searched for the power that blocked me. Energy pushed back against my seeking hand. A deterrent, not a barricade.

Keeping my eyes closed I stepped forward, this time on my right foot, as I had begun the maze. The energy dissolved. I took another careful step forward.

Six demons approached me. They reached for me with talonlike fingers. They caught the hem of my gown. I yanked it free of their grasp, hearing cloth tear.

The demon screamed his rage at my escape. His voice echoed across the rolling hills, shaking my senses and numbing my ears.

I ran forward, seeking the center with all my senses. I still had three quarters of the maze to traverse.

With a determined screech, another demon ran across the plateau and launched himself through the wall of power. His penis bobbed with each step. Alarm shot through me. Some demons had elongated and engorged genitals, others had no sex. All of them had a lump at the base of their spines—vestigal tails. This one had the normal size and shape of a human.

He landed facedown behind me, inside the labyrinth.

Inside the labyrinth? How? How could he penetrate that far without having walked the pathway first?

He scrambled to his knees, adjusting his face. Not a face. A mask. A hideous mask made to look like a demon. A naked man leered at me and stretched his arms wide. Two long strides across the turf and he captured me within those arms. He held me securely with a warrior's strong muscles.

I must have fainted. When I opened my eyes, a blindingly bright bonfire burned before me.

Dazzled by the flare of fire, I threw my arm up to ward against the glare.

My arm wouldn't move. My shoulders screamed in pain at the movement. I twisted and fought whatever held me in place. The fire flared again, revealing eight naked men in demon masks and deer antlers, in imitation of Cernunnos, dancing around the fire. The face of the horned god of the Underworld seemed outlined in the flames. Magical power shot upward with each new flare of fire.

The ninth man chuckled behind me as he jerked my bound hands upward and tied them to the upright pole that pressed against my back.

Drums throbbed in the distance, matching my rapid heartbeat. I couldn't look away from the naked men. They wore human torcs and their masks—nothing else. Nothing hid their virile arousal. The man who had tied me stepped between the fire and me. He towered over me. His well-muscled shoulders stretched through the uncertain light, seemingly without end.

His penis stood proudly erect, moist and ready.

I shrank away from him. He clasped my jaw within a huge fist and pressed it upward, stretching my neck. Pain shot down my spine.

The drums intensified, filling the center of the moldering fortress with an almost tangible sound until they blotted out thought. The noise and the power came from everywhere and nowhere, beating an odd tempo with no discernible rhythm. A sense of insatiable hunger pulsed with the drum.

More, it demanded. *More.*

More *what?*

I smelled blood and greed. Fear washed over me in waves. My body lost all strength and coordination. Self-defense techniques fled from my mind in the face of the demon-man before me.

Laughing and gloating with his power over me, the tall man grasped the neck of my gown and yanked downward. Cloth tore. Cold night air chilled my skin. My exposed nipples drew into tight balls.

The dancing men circled closer, feeding off of my fear. The ritual they performed was unlike any I knew of. In a bizarre perversion of Beltane where the fertile body was worshiped and enhanced, these creatures inflicted self-mutilation with split switches, small knives, and burning coals. Blood ran down their bodies. In the roaring light of the bonfire, their body tattoos writhed and squirmed into the twisted faces of evil beings.

The paint making those ugly designs faded and ran when mixed with sweat and blood. Vaguely I recognized those men as thrill seekers rather than true disciples.

True priests endured long rituals that embedded their tattoos permanently on their bodies. These men had only painted themselves for the night.

True priests of Cernunnos would have placated the demons, tried to contain them, and reduce the damage they caused. These men incited demons to wreak more havoc.

Virgins willingly gave themselves to Belenos and fertility in the spring. On Samhain Eve, Cernunnos, the trickster, ruled. Women who wandered abroad on this last day of the year were often kidnapped into the Netherworld and raped by demons in a sterile union.

If a child should have the ill luck to be conceived this night, by demon or a human male hosting a demon spirit, he would bear the taint of the Netherworld all his life.

The man who pressed himself against me had genuine tattoos burned into his skin with a hot needle and vivid paint. This man was a priest—not of Cernunnos, with recognizable patterns on his fore-arms like Da—but a priest of some unknown demon/god who de-manded pain and blood and rape.

All of the tattoos on the men circled flat male nipples in reverse spirals, a mockery of the fertility symbol of the Goddess. Slashing arrows and convoluted whorls, which might be demon faces, spread across hard-muscled chests and drew my eye downward toward their flat bellies and anxious erections.

Lust engorged their manhood with each slash of switch and knife, until all of them must seek release within an unwilling woman.

Me.

More! The bonfire flared with the demand. More power, more blood, more uncontrolled lust.

The tall demon-man raked my body from breasts to pelvis with probing hands. His broken fingernails scratched my skin, leaving me raw and sensitive. Behind the mask I saw his eyes widen in glee, then narrow in speculation. I didn't need to see his mouth to visualize his malicious grin.

Da, help me! I screamed in my mind. But Da was in the city, attending Uther's banquet.

Escape must come from my own cunning.

What could I do against nine drunken, lustful men?

My mind and body unfroze at the first touch of his hand in the dark hair between my thighs. He had tied me hastily. My struggles loosened the rope. I lashed at his neck with my fingernails.

He managed to imprison one of my hands within his fist. I darted my free hand into the false pocket of my overgown, hanging loosely from my shoulders. The little eating knife that was belted around my waist came to my fingers readily. I raised the blade and rammed it toward his chest.

He captured my knife hand in his own a hair's breadth from his heart. He laughed wickedly, taunting me to inflict wounds and pain. At the same time he pushed my other hand up and back, painfully twisting my shoulders.

Firelight slithered across his chest, turning his tattoos into demons that dragged my knife into his skin. Demons guided my knife in a long slash diagonally across his chest from left nipple to right rib. Blood drops welled up along the cut, spilling over the straight edges in a growing cascade of fire-touched crimson.

A surface cut only, no lasting damage to muscle or vital organ. But it would leave a scar.

He laughed again and again, head thrown back, shoulders shaking. The pain in my back, shoulders, and neck eased. His laughter drowned out the cries of the other men and the incessant arrhythmic drumbeat.

Then he turned the knife in my hand on me.

I watched, horror stricken, as he forced my hand holding the blade toward my vulnerable throat. Fear fueled my muscles in resistance. Still his strength mastered my feeble attempts to keep the blade away from me.

I screamed. I know I did. But no sound rose above the man's wicked laughter. I raised my knee to slam into his vulnerable genitals. He laughed again and caught my leg with one hand. Then he pushed my knee high into his pelvis and pressed himself closer. I thought he'd crush my ribs with my own knee. My balance tilted.

All trace of my life pattern fled from my mind.

He stopped the blade at the center of my throat, just barely pricking my skin. Suggestive thrusts of his belly mimicked the rape to come. Impatiently he thrust my leg down again. His penis replaced it pressing hard against my lower ribs. Hot, gooey moisture trickled across my belly. I smelled his musk. My stomach turned over in revulsion. I screamed again.

My fear only fueled his lust.

A new figure came into my peripheral vision. I couldn't make out face or form, only a presence watching, waiting.

The new person and I both watched my captor force my knife along my throat, closer and closer to the vulnerable life pulse.

I screamed and tried to slam my knee upward again. My thrust fell short. He was too tall. His weight pressed me off-balance against the pole.

The knife found the tip of my left breast. He circled the nipple with my blade. Hot pain followed the blade's path. He laughed again as my belly muscles quivered with fear.

The sight of his naked flesh so close to my own sent new waves of strength to my limbs.

"If I must die this night, then I take you with me into the Underworld!" I ceased trying to control the knife. My fingers unclenched from the hilt and slid free of his grasp. I raked my fingernails, ragged from picking and digging herbs, across his chest. The clean cut split and tore.

He screamed. The knife fell as he clutched his wound.

I raised my knee in a blow meant to cripple.

A blinding explosion of white light and roaring sound threw me sideways onto the fallen knife.

Chapter 19

ACRID smoke burned the inside of my nose. Angry male voices numbed my ears. Light flashed again and again behind my closed eyelids. I lived.

Cautiously I opened my eyes. I lay on the earth beside the pole, dangerously close to the bonfire. A trickle of blood fed the beaten ground. Mine?

An ache in my side sharpened into cold agony. I couldn't move, barely dared to breathe. My little knife pierced me between the lower two ribs. Dangerous, not lethal.

The chemical flavor of the smoke tasted of those long-ago lessons and experiments with fire. Someone had created the explosion that felled me. Someone trained by Druids who needed a diversion.

I looked around for the source of the blast.

Four armored men fought back-to-back as a team. They wielded heavy, two-handed swords against the revelers. The masked men had grabbed flaming brands from the bonfire. Nothing else stood between them and sharp iron weapons.

The center warrior ducked a thrown torch. The wood knocked his helm askew. Firelight danced upon golden hair.

Curyll! my heart gasped.

Curyll swung his sword in a wide circle, catching one of the revelers in the hamstring. The masked man collapsed screaming into a crippled heap.

I caught a glimpse of Stinger's beautiful profile. The others beside Curyll must be Boar and Ceffyl—one broad and the other wiry. While Curyll and Stinger wielded swords low, Ceffyl kept his high and Boar covered the flank. They fought off my attackers as a team, as they had the last time I'd seen them together on the practice field. Only long years of practice could bring men into such close rapport, sharing tactics without instructions, almost thinking together.

The masked men gave ground, slunk away, cowards now that they faced armed men instead of one small unarmed woman. Curyll and his foster brothers followed them only a short distance beyond the bonfire and the center of the old fortress.

What of the tenth figure who watched from the side? I couldn't raise my voice to alert the four to watch for another.

A log shifted in the fire, sending sparks onto my back. I crawled a few feet away from the blaze, rolling to extinguish the fire. I could light fire with my mind, but only mundane means could extinguish it.

Through a red haze I glimpsed my father battling the big man who had captured me. My father and yet not my father. Glamour shrouded him, making him appear seven feet tall and as broad as a barn. His helm gleamed blue-black. The tattoos on his arms seemingly sprang to life as true vipers. They writhed along his sword adding their venom to the sharp edged blade.

A rage had overcome my father. 'Twas the only time he shape-changed. Instinctively I jerked as far away from him as I could without disturbing my wound. The bonfire blazing at my back seemed safer than my father.

Otherworldly blue flames shot from Da's sword into the other man's torch. Da laughed as the natural fire wielded by my captor exploded with a whoosh and died. The hollow sounds erupting from Da's throat echoed around the roofless building, growing and filling every space with eerie reverberations that began in the Underworld and never ended.

The one other time I'd seen him in a rage this deep, he'd battled a Saxon. With the clarity of hindsight I now knew he'd been protecting me from the raider's fierce ax. But at the age of five I hadn't known this; I'd seen only my father's anger and feared it. He protected me again.

My tears mingled with my blood soaking the ground.

The demon-masked man shifted his grip on the torch shaft to attack with it as a quarterstaff. He countered an overhead blow from Da's sword and ducked to thrust the wood into Da's exposed belly.

Da knocked the torch from his hands with a mighty blow that

moved so fast I could not see it. His opponent ducked the next blow. A third mighty slash knocked the mask aside.

Instantly the tattooed man fled to the shadows. I sensed his footfalls through the earth. He fled downhill along the same route I had climbed. I saw nothing of his face.

Blue fire continued to glow in Da's sword and eyes. He raised his weapon and dashed after his quarry with a shriek bordering on madness.

Boar, Stinger, and Ceffyl retreated from the sight of The Merlin in a rage.

Only Curyll had the courage to grab my father's arm and wrestle the sword from his grasp. "Ho, Merlin. He's gone. Following him would be useless." Curyll continued to hold my father when he would have given chase with no weapon but his anger.

"Look to your daughter, Merlin," Curyll shouted. "She needs your strength and healing now. Revenge won't help her."

Da bent over, hands on his knees, panting for breath and control. Slowly his natural form returned, clad in ordinary linen shirt, leather leggings, and tunic. From his belt hung his everyday dagger—not a mythical sword as tall as he. After endless moments he stood straight and looked Curyll in the eye. "You are right, my boy. When did you become so wise?" Da ground out between his teeth, fighting for calm. Madness still glowed in his eyes.

"What little common sense I have, you beat into me, Father Merlin. Now, look to Wren. My brothers and I will see to the men. Perhaps we can identify them and guess their leader from known associates." Curyll did not flinch from Da's otherworldly gaze. Nor did he release his tight grip on The Merlin's still twitching sword arm.

"Da, how did you find me?" I whispered when he finally knelt at my side.

"I worried about you. I searched for you earlier. Then, when the darkness fell too quickly, too early, I knew something was amiss. Someone worked dark magic this night. Then I heard your scream in my mind. I met Curyll and his comrades on the way here. They already searched for you. It seems you left the army camp in a bit of a rush and you didn't return to the Citadel. Hush now, Wren. Time for questions later." Da touched my wounds with delicate fingers. Politely, he kept his eyes away from my nakedness where my ruined gown gaped open. The circle of blood around my nipple had begun to scab already. I'd not wear tight breast bands for a few weeks though.

"Did he . . . did they rape you, Wren?"

"No, Da. I fought him, but I couldn't hold out much longer." Tears of reaction choked me. but I had to know. "What strange god do these men serve?"

"Hush, Wren. Let me see what damage has been wrought this night."

I groaned out loud when Da touched the knife wound in my side. Warm moisture signaled a new seepage of blood. Blackness filled my vision faster than the blood dripped into the ground.

When I awoke again, tight pressure around my ribs told me Da had bandaged the cut. A heavy cloak covered me. The weight of the wool helped still my shaking limbs. I continued to tremble—from cold or shock?

"Will you need to find her a husband?" Curyll asked.

My eyes refused to open yet. I lay there listening, astonished at the anger behind Curyll's words.

"He . . . they . . . she says not, but I don't know," Da replied.

"I owe Wren much," Curyll said softly. "I'll wed her at dawn if I have to. I would spare her the condemnation that always follows rape. Some will lay the blame on her rather than those perverted—the men weak enough to be controlled by demons."

I heard the iron return to his voice, could see him in my mind, stiff and proud and very angry.

"Bedewyr and I make the same offer if she'll have none of Curyll," Cai said. From our childhood, I knew he shouldered Curyll aside, asserting his superior rights as true son of their mutual foster father.

"As do I," Lancelot added.

Anger at my childhood companions gave me the strength to open my eyes and speak. "I'll have no man as husband who weds me only to save my reputation. The choice of husband is mine, and I'm not asking for volunteers."

"Think, Wren, before you refuse these offers." Da laid a gentle hand on my wound, a not-so-subtle reminder of other hurts my captor intended to inflict.

"The man did not rape me." I leveled my gaze on my father. "I have no need for Curyll or his brothers to sacrifice their precious bachelor status on my behalf." I struggled to sit up. Pain burned straight through to my heart and lungs. I lay back, biting my lip to keep from crying out.

I refused to appear weak and wilting before these proud men.

Da slipped a supportive arm behind my shoulders and gently lifted me to a sitting position. Black stars danced before my eyes, but I didn't lose consciousness again.

"We will discuss this further in the privacy of my quarters, daughter. First we must get you back to the palace and properly dress this wound."

"Excuse me, Father Merlin." Curyll placed a polite hand beneath Da's elbow as he stood. "The sun has fully set. Uther's banquet begins at moonrise. You must attend. Questions will be asked if you don't. You can make excuses for Wren's absence, but not your own."

"If we hurry, I can change and make an appearance by the time Uther dips his knife into the first remove." Da brushed dust from his everyday leather tunic and leggings. "Can you carry her, Curyll? Much as I'd prefer to keep my daughter close to my heart, we will make better time if younger, broader shoulders bear her weight." A look I couldn't decipher passed between them.

"I know a private entrance near the bower, sir," Curyll said. "We won't be seen."

Da raised one eyebrow in question. "That portal is always locked and barred."

"A friend promised me it would be open this night."

I knew his friend could only be Morgaine. Curyll would have made a most reluctant and unsatisfied bridegroom had I accepted his offer of marriage. I needed time to let his love for me grow beyond childhood friendship.

"I promise you, Wren, I will find the man who did this to you," Curyll vowed as he lifted me effortlessly. "I will find him and exact the price of your honor from him."

. "Don't make promises you can't keep, Curyll," I warned him. My voice echoed through the ruins. Demons caught it and echoed it back in ominous portent.

Don't make promises you can't keep, Curyll. I hadn't asked him to seal the promise in a circle.

I shuddered, fighting the flash of vision that crossed my mind.

From the shadows I watched Uther's banquet. A white-and-gray cat crept into my lap. She purred as I stroked her. The rhythm of her rumble calmed my whirling thoughts and kept me focused upon finding my attackers.

I watched Curyll and my father as they watched for signs of guilt among the men in attendance. They looked into the eyes of lords and servants alike. I looked at every man's posture, how they walked, and who might favor a recently inflicted wound.

The hamstrung reveler remained in a dungeon cell. Da had told me that rough questioning of him by Cai, Bedewyr, and Lancelot had proved fruitless. The wounded man had never seen his comrades without masks or wearing identifying clothes. He didn't know who had recruited him. We would have to use other methods to find the men who worshiped pain and degradation.

I also wanted to seek the source of the premature darkness. My wound and Da's stern orders kept me from searching the city, sniffing for dark magic. I hadn't the energy or will to defy him.

From the shadows I watched how conversations ebbed and flowed, how patterns of flirtation and animosity rose as the level of ale in the cask lowered.

Nimuë dominated my field of vision. She flirted outrageously with every man within her orbit. I saw more than one man brush fingers across her breasts in invitation. She batted her eyelashes, smiled her willingness, and promised nothing. Her auburn hair sparkled in the torchlight as if she wore a crown of faeries. But the colors were wrong for my woodland friends. Her father, Lord Carradoc, glowered at Nimuë. He glowered at Ardh Rhi Uther. He glowered at his dinner. The blue warrior beads in his hair looked dull beside Nimuë's vibrant *arial.*

At the high table, Da sat at Uther's right, a place of favor and prestige. The Ardh Rhi appeared more hale and energetic than I thought possible. We had routed the cancerous demon from his vital organs only three days ago. The man should not have recovered enough strength to eat as heartily as he did and sit straight for the duration of the meal without signs of failing.

The wrongness of his restored health and energy dragged my attention away from my vigil of observation. His *arial,* his vigor, must be false, imposed upon him by my father. They would both pay for the illusion later.

Ygraina shared a trencher and wine cup with her husband in her proper place to the king's left. She watched his every bite and sup, making certain she tasted each remove and refill of wine before he did. Her almost greedy reaching for first tastes seemed propelled by a desperation I couldn't understand.

Leodegran and other lords I didn't know sat to Da's right. They ate in silence, as suspiciously watchful of everyone in the room as Da and I were.

Blasine and Morgaine sat beside the queen. Blasine bubbled with good spirits. She laughingly filled the many gaps in the conversation at the table. Morgaine sat in sullen silence, not eating, not talking. She looked frequently to the entrance and bit her lip. Occasionally her glance lingered on Curyll, halfway down the lower table. Then she jerked her gaze back to the door.

Who did she expect to come marching into the banquet hall?

All those favored with seats at the high table wore bright colors and plaids draped Roman style over their equally vivid tunics. All except Da. He wore his white Druid robes, a startling contrast of simplicity; a not-so-subtle reminder of his authority as priest on this night of shadows and demons.

A mixture of Roman and traditional styles garbed the people at the other tables. I noticed those who favored Roman clothing also wore Christian crosses. The others boasted native charms and wards. No one dared be caught without some form of magic charm on Samhain.

The scent of sulfur and salt lingered in my nose. I couldn't tell if it remained with me from the bonfire on South Hill or if someone else had brought the taint of the Netherworld into the banquet hall.

Each time the myriad rushlights and oil lamps threatened to burn low, or wavered in a draft, I stared at them until they flamed anew. Bright fire to ward off the darkness of the horrors I had endured. Men had done more damage to me than any demon had.

Of those at the high table, Morgaine intrigued me most. She had met Curyll and me at the door to the bower. After the first instant of disappointment and surprise, she had washed and bound my wound with quick efficiency. She had known the proper herbs to keep it clean and applied them expertly, if a little roughly. Curyll had demanded secrecy about my wound and how I received it. So far she seemed to have kept her mouth shut. Plots brewed behind her eyes. What would be her price for silence?

Morgaine's latent power hovered near the surface, ready to lash out like a whip to any who crossed her. Did she have enough control over that power to summon demons and cause premature darkness?

I almost left then, rather than watch the man I loved carry on a clandestine affair with the Ardh Rhi's stepdaughter. Almost. The cat dug her claws into my thigh, reminding me that my mission of observation must keep me in my secret alcove watching and waiting for one among them to betray himself.

As the servants cleared the fourth remove from the high table, Uther's face drained of color and vitality. Ygraina and Da consulted each other with their eyes above Uther's head. A brief nod and the High Queen gestured for the banquet to continue without the royal couple.

Visibly drooping, Uther allowed Ygraina and Da to escort him back to his chamber. Two Christian priests followed uninvited, close upon their heels.

A sigh of relief seemed to spread through the chamber. With the Ardh Rhi and Ardh Brenhines gone, the revelers need no longer keep speculation on Uther's health to themselves. No one outside the king's immediate circle of advisers had been told the extent or duration of his illness. Yet they all seemed to know about it.

Everyone could also see that he had beaten the disease that had nearly killed him, but he was not strong yet.

Da returned a few moments later, his harp beneath his arm. Instead of resuming his place of honor on the dais, he wandered into the open center of the horseshoe of tables. He plucked a few sweet notes from the strings, then settled into a catchy rhythm.

The tune he played was familiar to all attending the banquet, one of those simple melodies of five phrases that repeated endlessly with no conclusion. A simple song that stuck in the mind, repeating itself over and over. The kind of tune that lent itself to multiple variations of lyrics.

Da opened his mouth and sang. His words cut the air with a *Glam dicin*, a wicked satire. A proper Glam dicin stripped its victims of honor. Without honor, a warrior could not join a warband, could not perform brave deeds and have his name immortalized by bards in proper song.

Da glanced in my direction, nodding for me to watch and learn. The cat twitched her gray-and-white splotched tail in rhythm with the harp music.

Everyone in the room ceased talking at once, lifting eager ears to the latest juicy gossip contained within Da's song.

Come my friends
and gather now.
Come my friends
I'll tell you all
of hate, greed,
and burning desire.

Come my friends
we'll share a cup.
Come my friends
quiet the pup.
I'll tell of Demon
lust setting all afire.

From the shadows I watched to see who squirmed in discomfort and who was tantalized by the idea of fornicating with denizens of the Netherworld.

Nimuë stood up. A thunderous look crossed her face, and she flounced out of the banquet hall. Righteous indignation or frustration?

Morgaine's face took on new animation. Her eyes shone brightest of any in the room. She licked her lips in eager anticipation.

Chapter 20

I almost fainted at the thought of my beloved Curyll making love to Morgaine. Did a demon possess her aready? Or did she merely anticipate an event she planned and plotted for?

I couldn't know. My weakness sent me back to my bed where I spent a sleepless night. I could not get comfortable in mind or body for many nights thereafter.

Venta Belgarum thrived on secrets. Political secrets, love secrets, religious secrets. I learned most of them over the next few months. By the Winter Solstice I knew which client kings prepared to rebel against Uther. I learned of marriage alliances before the bride and groom were told by their fathers. I knew who made a show of attending Christian mass and wearing a cross but held to older gods in private.

But no one knew who had led the ritual on South Hill that honored pain and degradation.

So I sent my senses sniffing for evidence of dark magic. I suspected that whoever had summoned premature darkness on Samhain might also have incited my attackers. Possibly the same person had lured the cancerous demon to attack King Uther as well.

But every time I tried to puzzle out that mystery, my thoughts skittered in a dozen directions and a headache laid me low for days. Light blinded me. The scent of food nauseated me. All but the faintest of sounds sent waves of pain crashing through my head.

I learned much over the course of the winter. Not enough.

The Vernal Equinox brought warm winds and an early thaw. Desire for revenge glowed like dying embers in my heart, ready to flare into pure flame with the tiniest amount of fuel. The shape of that revenge remained an unformed cloud without direction.

Rumors of Saxon incursions throughout the winter focused my need for vengeance. In my mind the image of my attacker became a blond giant with drooping mustaches, like the foreign invaders.

Curyll led a band of warriors to the Deeside estuary and routed the pirates who raided from there. I'd heard from Morgaine that he had returned to the main army camp but not how he fared.

I asked Da if Curyll's troops had found the wild girl and helped her. He reported back that she had been seen, but remained elusive. The few survivors who crept back to the area left food and warm clothing for her, honoring her as they would the Goddess.

Images of the destroyed villages and the starving feral child haunted my dreams. In my fruitless quest for vengeance I became her during the long hours of sleep I craved. Saxon demons chased her/me endlessly, night after night.

I thought I was more than ready for the conversation that took place in Uther's private sitting room one night shortly after the Equinox.

"The Saxons will raid early this season," Da said to Uther. Ygraina and Leodegran shared a cup of wine with Da and Uther while I strummed the harp by the window. I was never far from Da's side these days.

The gray-and-white cat sat beside me, adding her purr to the music I stroked from the harp strings. The wind smelled of warming earth and fresh green shoots. Time for planting and new life, not for death.

I listened closer to Da's words, no longer lost in my music. This year the army would march to meet the Saxon host. Last year they had merely defended the region around Venta Belgarum against minor raids. With or without Uther riding in the lead, the army would engage the main force of the invaders this campaign season.

I intended to be with the army, searchng for my attacker. On the surface I believed I would find him among the invaders. Deeper in my heart I knew the leader of the demon seekers was one of our own warriors. The city kept too many secrets. On the field of battle men had fewer places to hide their true thoughts and actions.

Curyll would ride to battle and into danger along with every other man camped outside the city.

Determinedly, I pushed my worries away. I had seen visions of his victories. I knew he would survive.

Where he gave his heart remained another secret I could not penetrate. Morgaine told me repeatedly that Curyll loved her. The few times I had seen him, he had welcomed my presence. I knew he cared for me. When and if that caring grew beyond childhood affection, I couldn't tell.

"The Saxon raiders will sail from the North lands at first sign of thaw," Uther said. He'd regained much of his arial. Only a lingering paleness and shortness of breath betrayed his former illness. But Da and I knew that his stamina failed. He appeared at communal meals only because he napped two or three times during the day. When tired, I smelled the sulfur and rot the disease had left behind in his body.

To keep his fractious client kings in docile attendance, Da had suggested to five of them, privately, that he looked to them to hold the union of kingdoms together after Uther's death. I had listened to those conversations and followed the candidates afterward. Each king added warriors to his warband, drawing them away from weaker kings who would not or could not contend for the election to Ardh Rhi. Each of them courted highly placed church officials. One even rode to Caerlud to speak with the archbishop.

But Archbishop Dyfrig of Caerleon, the most powerful and influential churchman in Britain, remained in his diocese all winter.

Da also told Uther that his son lived and had gained almost enough experience to reveal his identity. Uther pressed The Merlin for details. I held my breath so that I wouldn't miss a word.

Da remained enigmatic. The time had not come for the revelation. From the gleam in his eye I knew he planned something dramatic that would capture the imaginations of the people he needed to manipulate.

"We must be ready to meet the Saxons wherever they land," Uther continued. "We must defeat them before they take refuge with their relatives on the Saxon Shore— Curse Vortigen for giving them pieces of our island as payment for mercenary service. My brother, God rest his soul," he crossed himself and bowed his head in memory of Ambrosius Aurelianus, "and I couldn't oust them when we finally slew Vortigen. They are stronger now."

The Ardh Rhi jumped up and circled the room in long, determined strides. His rapid footsteps seemed to keep pace with his thoughts. The shadow of his former warrior vitality flickered around him. He'd been a good war leader in his day, a fitting Ardh Rhi and successor to his older brother Ambrosius. But now. . . ?

"Have the warning beacons been maintained through the winter?" Uther asked, still pacing.

"We keep sentinels on hilltops at one mile intervals," Leodegran reported. "We will know within hours if a dragon ship approaches."

"Hours too late. We must meet them on the shore, before they have time to raid our people!" Some of Uther's former fire shone through the fervor of his words. "Can you scry their first landing, Merlin?"

Da shrugged his shoulders in apology. "I glimpse pieces of the future, what the gods allow me to see. I know only that Saxons come, not where they will land."

"Perhaps we can choose their landing place and force the first battle. A swift victory might keep them from raiding inland." Uther clasped his hands behind his back, keeping his shoulders straight and head high. "I have reports that the Saxons are spreading out from the confines of the Saxon Shore. We must raze those villages and push the settlers back to their deeded lands. The raiders sailing from abroad will then seek to revenge their relatives—but at a battle site of our choosing. Leodegran, inform the lords that the army will march at dawn two days hence."

"And who shall unite the lords and lead this battle, my husband?" Ygraina asked quietly, never looking up from her embroidery. Her skin looked like new parchment, devoid of all color.

"I am Ardh Rhi until I die or am defeated in battle," Uther nearly shouted. "I shall lead a united Britain into battle."

"You are not yet strong enough to sit a warhorse, Highness," Da reminded him.

"I shall ride to battle in a horse-drawn litter if I must. But I shall lead our forces against the invaders."

I plucked a sour twang from the harp. Ygraina's embroidery hoop hit the floor. Cat squeaked a question. The men stared silently at each other, at the floor, anywhere but at Uther.

An Ardh Rhi leading a battle from anywhere but astride his horse or at least a chariot presented an ill omen.

"The Merlin must ride at my side, as healer and adviser. The bevy of priests will follow in their own time. I'll double the dose of those tonics you spoon-feed me five times a day. By the time we actually engage in battle, I shall be strong enough to direct the troops from horseback." Uther continued to pace, restless now and eager to be moving.

But his stride shortened and his steps grew slower. Already he tired.

My fingers plucked a livelier rhythm. I tried to imbue the music and the Ardh Rhi with a sense of hope. My own mood brightened and I could ignore my misgivings as long as I listened to the music.

Soon I would be journeying with Da again. Soon I would be away from the stifling air and smoky buildings of the city. Soon I would feel the Goddess beneath my feet and blend the rhythm of my life to Hers.

Cat mewed her agreement. She wanted to follow me on the hunt. More exciting than mere mice.

I suppressed a laugh and promised Cat I'd secrete her in my pack.

Soon. Two days to replenish all of the herbs Da and I would need to run a field hospital. Cat would help me find them. I wondered if there were enough cobwebs in the entire palace to harvest for bandages. Nothing stanched bleeding like a bandage laced with cobwebs. Who could I recruit to gather more throughout the city?

The court gowns Blasine had given me from her own wardrobe must be left behind—I'd never had the chance to lure Curyll away from Morgaine with their artificial beauty. I would need sturdy woolens, preferably tunics and leggings rather than cumbersome gowns. Would I walk or ride a horse? Da would ride beside the Ardh Rhi. I presumed I would be expected to stay close to him. But I had rarely ridden horses and then uncertainly. The huge beasts didn't frighten me, we just didn't fit. Perhaps the chirurgeons had a place for me with their wagons and medical equipment.

"What of Blasine, husband?" Ygraina retrieved her embroidery, still not looking at Uther. "You must be here to preside over her betrothal ceremony at Beltane. You still have not found a suitable husband for Morgaine either."

Da stared at me, eyes clouded in thought.

"A young man of Ector's is eager to wed Morgaine. I'll listen to his suit tomorrow as well as any other offers. We will have handfastings and weddings for all who wish the night before we leave." Uther dismissed the topic and returned to barking orders to Da and Leodegran.

That young man of Ector's! He could only mean Curyll. My heart sank. The music stopped in my fingers and in my soul.

Uther's other statements ran past me. I barely heard his next comment.

"I presume, Merlin, that now is the proper time to produce my son."

Leodegran dropped his silver goblet. Red wine sprayed his brocaded robe. He took no notice, sitting in stunned silence; his hand curved as if he still held the cup. His eyes narrowed as he closed his gaping jaw with an audible click. Anger radiated from his stiff posture. Plots wove intricate lights in his eyes.

A dangerous man when crossed. I wanted to move away from him as quickly as possible.

"A moment, Highness." Da bowed to Uther, requesting permission to leave the room.

"Summon the rest of my council while you fetch my son." Uther waved his hand again in dismissal.

Da gestured to me to follow him. I settled the harp gently onto my seat in the safe custody of Cat, and slipped out the door behind him. No one seemed to notice my presence or absence now that Uther had found the motivation to do something specific about our enemies and truly name an heir.

Da said not a word to me until he closed the door to his private quarters. "We must talk, Wren."

I didn't state the obvious.

"You cannot accompany me on this journey."

"Why not? We have always been together." Except those four years in Avalon. I had learned much from The Morrigan. I learned more from my travels with Da.

" 'Tis too dangerous. You would be the only woman in an army full of randy men. Need I remind you of what happened last Samhain when you stumbled in a . . . into that . . ."

A chill lodged in my belly and my throat.

"Must I stay in the Citadel with Queen Ygraina and her daughters?" I couldn't go back to Avalon. With The Morrigan dead and the Ladies dispersed, no one remained there except the Christian hermit.

"No!" Da nearly jumped in his agitation. "This city is too dangerous for you alone. The Christians . . . Archbishop Dyfrig will return. . . . You cannot stay here, Wren."

"Then I will return to Lady Glynnis. Surely we can find a suitable escort, Da. Someone you can trust who could ride posthaste to catch up with the army afterward." *Someone like Curyll,* my traitorous mind added. *I could seduce him along the way. Bind him close to me forever.*

"Lady Glynnis has taken the cross. She no longer welcomes me. She will not welcome you." He clutched the bulbous end of his torc. The scowl on his face told me he thought furiously, sorting and discarding options. "I need men I can trust to guard the king. Who can I spare to guard you and the power?"

"What?" What power needed guarding? And Uther? Uther had been ill, certainly. He'd need assistance on the journey. But guarding by other than his own warband?

A new idea tried to birth itself deep in my mind. A headache sprang to life behind my eyes. The thought got lost on the way to consciousness. Maybe it was an old memory; I couldn't puzzle it out and concentrate on Da at the same time. Not with the renewed headache.

Strange, I'd never had headaches before I drove the cancerous demon out of Uther. Now, every time I thought about that arduous night, I was nearly blinded by pain.

"The only way I can protect you, Wren, is to find you a husband. A husband in a postion to help you watch the sacred place." He mumbled the last statement as if talking only to himself. I wasn't certain I'd heard him right, so I concentrated on the important issue.

"I don't want a husband." I didn't think I could bear anyone touching my body after Samhain. No one but Curyll who had kept his distance from me all winter. "My chosen path is to be a bard and healer, wandering through Britain, guarding all of the sacred places, as you do, Da. That is what you raised me to be, trained me to be. And I choose to remain as celibate as you."

He blanched at my statement.

"No, Wren. Your destiny is different from mine. The Goddess chose you before your birth. We must follow the path She opens for you. I see clearly now that along that path is a husband to protect you when I cannot. I have had offers for your hand. In the morning I shall consider them with fresh insight. You will wed the evening before the army marches, as will many other young women in this city."

"Who has offered for me? Whose offer was so demeaning you did not so much as whisper it to me until now?" I clenched my jaw tight lest I scream disobedience to my father and the Goddess.

"I delayed accepting any offer for you until you had healed from your ordeal. Lord Carradoc has asked for your hand. I did not consider him seriously as he is so much older than you. Leodegran asked on behalf of his son, a dissolute young man who would rather drink and gamble than take up his responsibilities as a warrior."

"Leodegran's son suffers from the Roman whore disease." I'd pried the secret from his latest mistress. "Carradoc is indeed too old. His oldest daughter is older than I." Nimuë, the flamboyant redhead who looked upon me as if I were dirt. She sought every opportunity to show me to disadvantage in the bower and among the court.

"I will never marry Lord Carradoc, Da."

"You shall marry the man I choose to protect you, Wren,"

"Have the Christians subverted your faith in the Goddess, Da?" I asked, too angry with him to guard my tongue. "Have you forgotten that the Goddess gives every woman the right to choose her own husband and divorce him if he proves unsatisfactory?"

"We live in a time of change, Wren. My visions falter. My magic diminishes every time a follower of the Goddess accepts baptism. Soon there will be so few believers I won't be able to work spells at all. You must marry now. Neither of us has a choice in this matter."

"You taught me there are always choices."

"We have been robbed of choice by the gods of change and chaos."

You will have a husband, and children by Curyll, the Goddess had promised me. She hadn't promised that Curyll would be my husband, only father my children.

I could see no pattern in my future. In that moment I believed the Goddess had deserted us both. Change and chaos had taken over our lives.

Chapter 21

"I will marry tomorrow," Carradoc said without preamble.

"WHAT!" Nimuë screeched, not caring that her voice sounded like all three of the totem ravens of Caer Tair Cigfran. She whirled to face her father within the small confines of his room in the palace. At home he might be a great lord entitled to many privileges. Here he was just one more warlord attached to one of many kings. So his room was little more than a servant's cubicle. In normal times it might *be* a servant's cubicle.

"Papa, you can't be serious!" Berminia said. Nimuë's younger sister looked to her before responding. As she should. The fat cow had the intelligence of a gnat, the figure of a swine, and the flightiness of a faery. Nimuë controlled all of her sister's decisions before Berminia could do anything truly stupid.

"Why do you need another wife?" Nimuë asked. Her voice still sounded too shrill. She couldn't help it. Ever since she'd lost the demon—sent back to the Netherworld by The Merlin before he fully formed in the bonfire—she couldn't control her temper and didn't particularly care whom she offended. "You've already buried three wives."

"Each of the women I married bore me a daughter. I need a son," Carradoc replied firmly. His eyes hardened.

Nimuë knew that look all too well. The next person to cross him would receive serious injury. She also knew how to channel that murderous rage to do her bidding.

She could manipulate her father to a degree, but he maintained control of her life.

"You have no need of a son. You have me!" She bent over him,

183

pointing to her chest where her gown gaped alluringly to expose most of her breasts.

"I need a son to rule Caer Tair Cigfran after me. Our stronghold has not passed out of our family in more than twenty generations." Carradoc stood from his chair to his full, massive height. He towered over his daughters. And totally ignored what she offered.

When all else failed, sex made Carradoc pliable.

Nimuë straightened her shoulders and thrust out her chest in determination to defy him. As she settled her posture, she tugged at the dangling ties of her shift, making the gap in her clothing larger. He'd never denied her before. Why should he now?

"You don't need a son, you have me." She held her mouth open just a little, as the demon had taught her, exposing her sharp little teeth in an enticingly predatory expression.

"And you have near destroyed my home with your paltry attempts to work magic. Every spell you cast has gone awry. The place reeks of neglect and evil," Carradoc sneered at her. He refused to look at her nearly exposed bosom.

"Papa, I could take over the running of Caer Tair Cigfran. I love it. I'd cherish it and make it the strongest and most beautiful home in all of Britain," Berminia said in her soft wispy voice. But behind the insignificant whispers lay a core of determination Nimuë had never heard from her gross sister.

Nimuë glared at her. Fine time for the cow to start deciding anything.

"You've never stuck to any task other than eating for more than ten heartbeats." Carradoc pointed at Berminia with a shaking finger. His face grew darker in his rage at the defiance from his two eldest daughters. Pale little Marnia had been left at home this court season.

Nimuë decided his anger had reached its optimum point. She needed to twist it now.

"If you truly honored the old ways as you claim, then you'd know that your daughter's *husband* is your only heir. I claim Caer Tair Cigfran as mine, by right of the Goddess. If you do not find me a husband, then I shall find my own and wrest my home from your clutches."

A chuckle in the back of her mind told her the demon had not deserted her entirely.

Carradoc's fist struck her jaw, knocking her backward onto the bed with Berminia.

"I'll marry The Merlin's daughter tomorrow and both of you will witness and accept it. Our son will inherit Caer Tair Cigfran and no one else!"

"Wren?" Nimuë gasped. "You'll marry the sorceress?"

"Priestess. Her father is the sorcerer, not her." Carradoc stalked out of the room. He slammed and locked the door behind him.

"Papa?" Berminia cried. She dashed to the solid door and pounded the wooden panels with her fat, white fists.

"Don't waste your strength, Berminia. He'll let us out when he's ready and not before. I just hope it's in time to set some traps for Wren before the wedding." Nimuë lay back on the bed, plotting furiously.

"Is there no one else willing to wed me?" I knew my eyes were red with weeping and my voice listed toward the dreaded whine. I acknowledged the trait but no longer had the energy to fight the childish response to my father's decree.

"Archbishop Dyfrig holds a great deal of influence over Uther and his court. No Christian man will take you, a priestess of the Goddess. Lord Carradoc has repeated his offer twice and increased his brideprice." Da tried to look me in the eye.

I wouldn't let him. Eye contact was the key to control. Control was the last thing I wanted to give my father in this issue. I wouldn't let him manipulate me as he did others—like wooden counters in a game of strategy. Plans to run away began to tickle my mind. Where could I go?

"What do we care about money?" I shouted, knowing full well that Carradoc listened on the other side of the door to Da's room.

"Money itself is not the issue. His eagerness to wed you is. I need you safe in his stronghold. I have agreed to the marriage. There is nothing left to say."

"There is much to say. I have not agreed to the marriage. Nor will I. Lord Carradoc is nearly as old as you. He has buried three wives already. His eldest daughter is two years older than I. His middle daughter the same age as myself, and the youngest barely a year younger. He doesn't need a wife, he needs to find husbands for his daughters."

"He needs a son. I need you guarding the North."

My mouth opened and closed a few times, soundlessly. I could not argue with these statements. Except why did he need me guarding an already heavily patrolled area along Hadrian's Wall—the great Roman barrier separating Britain from the wild tribes of Gaels and Picts?

"You will meet with your intended husband now and wed him on the morrow," Da said. "Princess Blasine and several other ladies of the court will wed at the same time. You should be honored to be included in the ceremony."

"A Christian ceremony that has no binding on us. I will not make promises to a god I do not believe in."

"The public Christian ceremony is but for show. Carradoc follows the old ways and accepts my blessing under mistletoe at dawn as binding. You will as well. And don't even think about running away, Arylwren. You thrived on the road as long as you were with *me,* a bard and a Druid. On your own, you will be reviled and distrusted. Probably beaten and raped. Homeless women are not protected by either the Christians or the followers of the Goddess these days."

"The women who take religious orders . . ."

"You wouldn't last a day in a house of the sisterhood. I know you, Wren. Poverty you have accepted. Obedience and chastity are not part of your nature." Da almost chuckled. A wry smile tugged at his lips. "That is why you must have a husband."

"Queen Ygraina owes me the life of her husband. She will give me a place in her court. I'd rather wither away in this city than marry Carradoc." Would I really?

"This city is only a little safer than the road for you, Wren. You marry Carradoc tomorrow. You will obey me in this. The Goddess granted me a vision. You are needed in the North." His eyes crossed and glazed. He clutched the end of his torc. His other hand captured my chin and forced me to look at him. "I had hoped it would not come to this, Wren."

Numbness invaded my body and my mind. I couldn't move, couldn't look anywhere but into The Merlin's eyes.

"No." I had to fight the compulsion I knew he wove around me. My voice sounded feeble.

He stared at me harder. The urge to close my eyes and sleep washed over me. I fought the dizziness.

"I won't let you control me with magic, Da. You claim to use it sparingly, only when necessary, but I know you better. You use your magic to manipulate people, to rearrange the patterns of life to suit yourself."

"Do not defy me, Wren." His scowl of concentration deepened.

I tried desperately to turn my back on him. I couldn't move except to obey him. I had to comply though my mind fought to break his spell. I didn't know how; no longer had the will.

Silently I vowed I would never use my magic the way he did. People had to make their own choices. Even if I had to give up my powers entirely, I would not use magic for control, only to clean up the messes he left behind.

What spell could I use to undo the marriage he compelled me toward?

Da threw open the door. Lord Carradoc filled the doorway, his expression blank, as if he hadn't overheard our argument. He couldn't have helped hearing it.

I wanted to rush past him, run into the hills . . . The last time I had done that had ended disastrously. My own fears weighed my limbs as heavily as The Merlin's compulsion.

Carradoc clutched a ragged bunch of spring flowers in his huge hand. His fashionable black-and-silver tunic, belted with fine black leather to match his soft boots, transformed the fierce marchog into a pretty courtier. He wore two dozen blue beads woven into a pair of plaits on the left side of his face amidst his mane of thick black hair as well as into his full beard—warrior beads, one for each life he had taken in battle. The bits of glass matched his gray-blue eyes.

He smelled of lye soap and bruised grass, as if he'd crushed the stems of the flowers he carried rather than pluck them cleanly. I wondered if he would crush me as well.

I turned my back on him, furiously trying to find a way out of this marriage. The thought of joining with this man, any man, dropped stones in my stomach and made my feet itch to run away. Da's compulsion kept me rooted to the floor as firmly as the World-tree.

"Patience and gentleness, Carradoc." Da touched the other man's shoulder in a sympathetic gesture.

"Like a wild mare who must learn to trust before accepting a bridle and a rider," Carradoc said. Pride and lustful humor played around his mouth at his wordplay.

I shuddered and fixed my glance on the unshuttered window. Instead of the busy courtyard of the villa, I saw only blurs of color, as if looking through a pool of water, or my tears.

Carradoc smiled and entered the room, flowers proffered as a token of peace. I didn't believe he offered them out of love.

Da closed the door quietly. I opened my mouth to protest the impropriety of leaving me alone with a man. He wouldn't listen.

"I picked these myself." Carradoc held out the bright bouquet. Daisies for love, asphodel for fertility, butter roses for protecting love, and chicory for removing obstacles, clumsily arranged and tied with a bit of dirty string.

Did he know the message of sincerity the flowers expressed or were they merely an offering he was expected to make to his bride?

My hand shook as I reached to accept the nosegay. I fought the movement. The compulsion continued to strengthen until my fingers wrapped around the flower stems. Da's spell might force me to accept these flowers as a symbol of my acceptance of the man, but I wouldn't touch his hand.

"Your daughters will protest our marriage," I said, hoping he'd withdraw his offer.

His fingers stretched to caress the back of my hand as we transferred possession of the nosegay. I jerked my hand away from him.

"My daughters have no say in this matter. 'Tis between you and me." He touched a curl of my unruly hair that had escaped its braid. The strand coiled around his finger, almost as a caress.

I stared at his finger entwined with my hair. My jaw quivered in uncertainty. He jerked on the strand, pulling me close to him.

I had to obey.

"I'll not hurt you, little Wren." He wrapped my braid around his hand, pinioning me in place. His mouth hovered over mine. I froze as he dropped a long wet kiss on my lips.

I almost gagged. My head barely reached his shoulder. The warmth of his broad chest threatened to suffocate me. The compulsion kept me from wiping my mouth clean of the taste of him with the back of my hand.

"I am honored your Papa chose me to teach you the joy of joining with the Goddess." He kissed me again, ramming his hot tongue deep into my mouth.

I held my breath and closed my eyes—not in passion, but to contain my revulsion. I couldn't fight him. My body refused to obey my orders to break away from Carradoc and run away. Run anywhere as long as it was away from him.

There had to be a way to escape this marriage! But how?

"Come to me without fear, Wren." He drew back a little.

I dragged deep draughts of cleansing air into my lungs as I turned my face into my own shoulder. The compulsion wouldn't let me show him how I wiped my mouth on my gown.

"I see I must go slower and not frighten you. Celebrate the life Dana has given us. Celebrate with me!" He held me tight against his chest while his hands explored my back and bottom.

A small thrill climbed my spine. I ignored it.

Tenderly he brushed my lips with his own, awakening them and me. His strong arms supported me without imprisoning me. He invited me to explore his body as he touched mine.

Confusion tied my stomach in knots and rooted my feet to the ground. Gentleness was the last thing I expected from this fierce warrior.

Slowly he increased the pressure of his caresses, persuading me with sensuous little movements to participate in the kiss. I opened my mouth to protest only to find his tongue teasing mine.

Heat built in my breasts and weakened my knees. As I sagged against him, one of his arms slipped around my waist, supporting my weight, while the other dropped from my hair to my breast. In response to his kneading, my nipples puckered and lifted.

"No." I pushed him away, appalled at my physical reaction to his touch.

"Wren, we will be wed on the morrow." He looked over my shoulder toward Da's bed.

"After we are man and wife, I will do my duty." *If I don't find a way to avoid the marriage.* "Until then I will remain chaste. Please leave me."

"I can wait one more day, Wren. Can you? You know how to find my quarters," he chuckled as he left the room.

As soon as the door closed behind him, I gathered my cloak and boots. I had two chances before I lost all hope.

"Please help me, Morgaine," I pleaded.

"Why?" The dark-haired princess stared at a spider spinning a web between a tall flower stalk and the outside wall of the caer.

I had found her in a sunny corner of her mother's garden. All of the other women flitted about the bower preparing for the hasty weddings. Ygraina and Uther had pushed Blasine's marriage forward. But they had still made no plans for Morgaine.

Relief that Curyll had not yet been named her groom made my resolve firmer.

"Help me break this compulsion because no woman should be forced to marry a man she doesn't want. You know that better than most."

She looked at me then. I couldn't read her eyes or her posture.

"Be grateful your father allows you to marry rather than keep you as a pawn in his games." She returned to her contemplation of the spider.

"My father uses me in this marriage as Uther uses you. He uses magic to force me to marry Lord Carradoc. He uses me to further his own ambitions though he claims to merely protect me."

"Oh?" Morgaine arched a lovely eyebrow, finally interested in my dilemma. "What kind of magic?"

"A compulsion. No matter what I do or say between now and tomorrow I must marry Carradoc. I have no choice. Unless you can help me break the spell."

"I do not acknowledge the Goddess' power over me. I cannot work Her magic."

"You work magic. I've smelled it on you. You are the only one with enough power to break one of my father's spells. Please help me." The reek of sulfur lay faintly on her shoulders, almost like a perfume. Instead of the reek of rotten eggs, this scent was laced with musk. Haunting, Irreverent. Provocative.

"What do I gain by this? If you marry Carradoc, you will no longer interfere with Curyll and me. He will no longer hesitate to marry me if you wed another. Why should I help you?"

I couldn't answer that question.

"You play with magic, without direction, without purpose, so your spells go astray and you accomplish little." I explored the topic cautiously. I sensed that if I gave in to the allure of her dark perfume I'd be lost forever, within her control instead of my father's or Carradoc's. Which was worse? "If you help me, I will teach you what I can." Something twisted inside my brain. Giving Morgaine more power would be dangerous.

"I don't need your worthless little spells," she sneered. "Your Goddess puts too many limitations on magic. Balance you call it. Cowardice. You are too frightened to taste real power. Your father has tried it and fled it. Archbishop Dyfrig won't even contemplate it. I embrace it. No one will control me when I am through."

A cloud passed over the sun. Morgaine's face fell into deep shadow. Blackness encircled her head like an aura. I stepped away from her, frightened.

"Then you won't help me break the compulsion, even to show my father how powerful you have become."

"That's right, little Wren. You will have to endure the same humiliation I went through, married to a drunken brute. In time you will learn to weave the spells that will force your husband to take one chance too many on the battlefield or the hunting field. It matters not where he falls off his horse and breaks his neck, only that he dies before he breaks you completely."

Chapter 22

THE hair on the back of Merlin's neck stood on end. He turned in a slow circle seeking the source of the alarm. Deep guilt burned in his gut. Had he angered the gods by arranging for Wren a marriage that she did not want?

He hated having to compel her obedience. If only he had more time. If only he knew for sure that Arthur was ready. If only . . .

When he faced north, his sense of alarm increased. A familiar itch replaced the standing hair on his neck.

"Dyfrig!" he said on a loud exhale. "Arriving three weeks early. You always had a knack for knowing when you could interfere in my plans." Merlin mastered his urge to run in the opposite direction. "I can't avoid you any longer, so I might as well make use of your influence."

Slowly he wound his way through the sprawling royal palace. He hugged the shadows and found nearly forgotten servants' corridors. All the while he kept careful watch on the milling groups of soldiers and courtiers. All of them gossiped about the upcoming campaign. Little of the information they passed among themselves resembled the real situation—though he found one warrior's idea of confronting the Saxon fleet at Dun Edin in the far North most interesting.

Had the man seen the future as Merlin had? He knew a battle would take place there—the cliff ramparts of Dun Edin were unmistakable in the vision—but not yet. Not until Arthur was Ardh Rhi and wielded a great sword of power.

Merlin escaped the palace and its gossip through a low postern. Six men across the green. He nearly ran across the commons, not bothering to dodge sheep droppings and pecking geese.

"Your Grace," Merlin hailed the archbishop as he dismounted. Dyfrig's entourage unloaded their baggage in front of the guesthouse attached to the largest Christian church in Venta Belgarum.

Dyfrig looked around, startled. His eyes rested on Merlin for a long moment.

Merlin held his brother's gaze for a seeming eternity, hungering for the closeness they had once shared. They studied each other, marking the similarities of face and figure, wondering at the difference. Dyfrig had kept his lustrous black hair and beard. Merlin's had turned gray in a single night almost fifteen years ago at Beltane, after his confrontation with the gods.

Differing experiences had shaped them and sent them on separate paths. They should have walked those paths together.

We should share everything, twin, as we shared our mother's womb. You should be my other half, complete my thoughts and sentences, understand my dreams and ease the nightmares that haunt me in the dark of night.

Dyfrig broke their visual connection. He remained placid and unaffected by meeting his twin brother after many years of separation. He, like Merlin, had kept their close blood ties secret. Out of shame? Or had they both sought to concentrate influence in themselves, fearing their bond of birth and blood would diminish their political power?

"You are dismissed." The churchman waved his attending priests away.

"Your Grace?" one of the aides protested.

"You are dismissed," Dyfrig repeated firmly. His hands shook a little. So he wasn't as unaffected as he pretended.

The five black-robed men backed away from their leader, passing anxious looks among themselves.

"So you have sought me out at last," Dyfrig said. His voice carried no inflection. But the fine muscles beneath his left eye twitched uncontrollably.

"I need your assistance," Merlin ground out between clenched teeth. So much bitterness had built between them over the years. He hated meeting his twin like this. They should confront each other openly or not at all. Decades before they had agreed to avoid airing their differences in public.

"You may not visit our mother. Your presence would only confuse her," Dyfrig said.

"I seek your help on another matter," Merlin admitted, wishing he could approach the issue from a position of strength, not need. Dyfrig would never know how often he did visit their mother.

Dyfrig arched one eyebrow. Merlin tried not to mimic the action, though he was fond of the gesture.

"We must agree on the succession," Merlin said. He needed to control this interview. He'd never succeed if he allowed Dyfrig to dictate to him.

"Uther is dying." Dyfrig bowed his head and crossed himself, looking sad.

"Not yet. My daughter worked a miracle and routed the cancerous demon from him."

"Blasphemy!" Dyfrig crossed himself hastily.

"That accusation depends upon which god you worship."

"I suppose I should accept your magical meddling for the sake of Britain. No other Ardh Rhi could rule as justly or as firmly as Uther."

"Uther has a son. Arthur."

"More of your meddling, Myrddin?" The archbishop did not look surprised.

"Ygraina told you the story."

"The privacy of the confessional does not allow me to answer that."

"Whatever." Merlin waved one hand in dismissal. "Arthur is nearly ready to learn of his heritage. He leads men well. He needs only a solid victory to earn the respect of the kings and lords."

"But?" Again Dyfrig lifted one eyebrow in Merlin's favorite expression.

The similarity of this man's every move began to irk him. In anyone but his twin he'd believe him mocking. Knowing Dyfrig, perhaps it was mockery.

"Arthur needs a great symbol and ceremony to impress the reluctant ones. Five kings at least will withdraw their warbands from any candidate for Ardh Rhi except themselves. They must see for themselves that the gods favor Arthur."

"Only one God needs smile on the next Ardh Rhi. My God. I assume you have found a symbol and arranged for a magical ritual that will impress everyone." Dyfrig did not look impressed.

"Yes."

"You seem to have done it all. What do you need me for?"

"We need to stand united as we preside over the ceremony."

"No."

"Britain needs to see us united in order to stand together against the Saxons. We are a fractious lot and do not tolerate each other easily. The Merlin and the Archbishop united will present a powerful symbol. Combined with the artifact of power . . ."

"No." Silence stretched between them again. Finally Dyfrig spoke again. "I will preside over my own ceremony recognizing Arthur as Ardh Rhi, if he is indeed the best man to succeed his father. When you are baptized, you may stand beside me." Dyfrig pushed past Merlin to mount the three steps to the guesthouse.

"Do not dismiss me so easily, Brother." Merlin captured Dyfrig's arm with one hand, holding him firmly with fingers made strong from years of playing the harp and wielding weapons.

"You dare lay hands on me!" Dyfrig's anger drained his face of color. "I shall never stand on the same dais as you and preside over the same ceremony with you, a heathen. You deserted our mother in her greatest time of need. You persist in defying my authority as head of the church . . ."

"I walk the path of my destiny. You were afraid to walk anywhere but behind our mother's skirts." A cold lump of calculation replaced the aching longing and burning anger that Dyfrig always generated in Merlin.

Dyfrig set his mouth in a determined expression Merlin knew well from seeing his own reflection in other men's eyes.

"Be warned, Dyfrig. I shall make Arthur the next Ardh Rhi, and all of Britain will recognize my power. You shall be left standing in the cold. But because you refuse this gesture of unification, our struggle for peace will be all the harder. Many Britons, Christians and Old Believers alike, will die in the struggle. You and your god will reap no glory in this."

"We shall see, Myrddin. Only when Britain is united behind the cross can it withstand the onslaught of evil from the Saxon invaders. Standing united with you and your kind will diminish the power of Britain bound together by the Church. My God does not need glory. We need prayer and faith to glorify Him. My God shall triumph in the end."

"A thousand years from now, my name shall be linked with Arthur's when the bards sing of his triumphs."

"A thousand years from now neither of us will be alive to care." Dyfrig broke free of Merlin's grasp and retreated majestically into the guesthouse.

Merlin touched his torc. A spell of compulsion sprang to his lips.

Then he remembered when he'd last used this bit of magic. Wren. He'd compelled his daughter to marry a man she loathed.

He couldn't do this again. If he had to do it over, he'd have found another way to persuade Wren to accept Carradoc's protection. But he didn't have time to try another route and he needed Wren in the North guarding Arthur's great symbol of power.

"I hope, brother, that your pride does not bring Britain down because you refuse to stand on the same dais with me."

I fled Morgaine's presence. If I stayed longer, I might begin to think as she did. I couldn't murder anyone, not even Carradoc.

Perhaps I could break the spell myself. Balance. I'd have to balance the strength of the spell with the strength of my love for Curyll. If I married him tonight, before the scheduled wedding with Carradoc, the spell would cease to exist.

I found Curyll drilling his men on horseback. Massive steeds thundered back and forth across an open field, their trencher-sized hooves throwing up clods of earth and grass with each pounding step. The ground vibrated beneath my feet as I watched from the protection of a small grove of alders.

Lancelot rode beside Curyll. For the first time since they had grown up, I had a chance to study the two men side by side. As close as brothers, they were never far from each other. Where Stinger fought best, one on one, Curyll looked at the tactics of the entire battle. Stinger's brilliance with weapons saved Curyll many a hard blow as they fought back to back.

Now they charged and wheeled their horses in unison. Curyll signaled the troop silently. Stinger kept individuals in line with shouted orders.

Stinger was the most beautiful man I had ever encountered, a beauty in no way effeminate. I, like most women, could stare at his profile for hours. But his beauty put him beyond the dreams and desires of ordinary women. On the other hand, Curyll presented a handsome if coarser and more rugged picture. I cherished his humped nose and scar as evidence of his strength. I knew that Morgaine and I were not the only women who lusted after Curyll.

My eyes continually sought Curyll's rugged profile and sandy-gold hair. Lancelot's beautiful face and near perfect proportions seemed almost artificial next to the man I loved.

When the horses had reduced the moist field to a sea of mud, Curyll deigned to notice me. He dismissed his troops and reined in beside me.

"Did you see that, Wren? Not once did they break formation. And the way they pivoted on my command! The Saxons have nothing to match our cavalry." He dismounted and led his horse into the shade of the alders. Steam and dust rose from the beast's black hide as Curyll patted his neck.

Curyll should have ridden a white horse. Every vision of his future had shown me a white horse named . . . Taranis for the god of thunder.

At the sight of me, the black horse rolled his eyes and jerked at the tightly held reins.

I held out my hand for him to show I carried nothing that would hurt him. He settled a little.

Wary of his huge feet and snapping teeth—this was a warhorse, trained to defend his master with the only weapons at his disposal—I grasped the sides of his long face and blew gently into his nostrils. He snuffled a moment, gathering my scent into his limited memory. Only then did he calm down and allow me to stroke him.

"Your magic is strong, Wren. Gwyntmor doesn't like anyone. Not his grooms, not me, no one. But he seems to love you," Curyll laughed.

The horse lifted his tail and let loose a noisy wind but produced nothing substantial.

"Gwyntmor, great wind," I crooned to the now docile horse. I almost wept. A black horse named for a strong wind instead of a white horse called Thunder. If my vision of Curyll on a white horse had been false, then so, too, might my vision of the Goddess be. *A husband and children by Curyll.*

The horse nuzzled my hand as if seeking more pets or a treat.

"I wanted to name him Taranis. But the other name seemed more appropriate." Curyll caressed the horse's cheek lightly. He had to jerk his hand away to avoid a nasty nip.

I scratched behind Gwyntmor's cheeks and reached up—way up—to fondle his twitching ears. He bent his head nearly to the ground to accommodate my small height.

"Maybe I'll have to change his name to Pussy Cat." Curyll tried the same caress and nearly lost a finger to the horse's wicked teeth. "Hey!" He slapped Gwyntmor on the nose in reprimand. "Remember who brings you apples and makes sure the lazy grooms feed you."

Gwyntmor curled his lip at Curyll but didn't snap again. He turned his head into my caress, ignoring his master.

"Is there something you wanted, Wren?" Curyll asked. His eyes followed his men back toward the stables.

"You've heard that the army marches day after tomorrow?" I couldn't look him in the eye. I tried. The Merlin's compulsion forced me to approach the issue of marriage in a roundabout way.

"Of course I've heard. Why do you think I was drilling my men so hard?"

"Da rides beside Ardh Rhi Uther as adviser and healer."

"Good choice on Uther's part. The Merlin is one of the wisest men alive. He'll also be valuable in the hospital after the battle."

"I had thought I would go with Da. I have followed him across the length and breath of Britain all my life."

"The army is no place for a woman, unless she's a pros . . . a camp follow . . . a woman of low reputation."

Like Nimuë, Carradoc's oldest daughter.

"I know about prostitutes, Curyll. I also know that women are forced into that profession because they have no man to protect them and other men see a woman alone as easy prey. Some consider a woman is alone by choice and wants to sell her body to any and all." I grieved for the protection and status women lost with the coming of the Romans and then the Christians.

"Like on Samhain," he said so softly I almost didn't hear him.

I buried my face in the horse's neck rather than look at Curyll. Without a husband, I would soon be a woman alone, unprotected.

I couldn't marry Carradoc.

I had to marry Carradoc.

"I did not choose to become the victim of men playing at invoking demons." Had they only been playing? Memories of the power that rose from the bonfire as they danced and mutilated themselves chilled me. And what of the other figure I had glimpsed off to the side? One of their members at least tried to work magic. "I do not choose to be left alone when the army marches. But I will be."

"What is your father doing about that?" Curyll grabbed my chin and forced me to meet his gaze.

I gulped back sudden tears. "Da has found me a husband. A man I do not love and do not wish to marry." But I would marry him unless I broke the compulsion spell.

"The only wise solution. You must marry someday, Wren. You are old enough and pretty enough to attract any man."

"Didn't you hear me? I said I don't love Carradoc and I find marriage to him repulsive. He's *old* and his daughters dislike me already."

"Lord Carradoc is a fine warrior, well respected, and wealthy. He'll take care of you, Wren."

"There is only one man I wish to marry, Curyll." I tried putting all of my love for him into my eyes.

He dropped my chin and returned his attention to the horse. "Marry Carradoc, Wren. It's a good match." He grabbed the saddle horn, ready to remount.

"What about you, Curyll?"

"Princess Morgaine and I plan to announce our betrothal as soon as I return from battle." He vaulted into the saddle.

"Why Morgaine? She's older than you, a widow with a young son. And I don't think you love her."

"Princess Morgaine is Ygraina's daughter. Uther loves her as one of his own. Marriage to her gives me a name, estates, prestige, things I have no chance of winning on my own. I intend to return from this war a hero and respected warrior, but without Morgaine I will *have* nothing! She chooses a partnership with me rather than be used by Uther in his political games. We can help each other. We need each other."

"What of your dreams, Curyll? Morgaine is selfish and hungry for power." Dark power that would have to be contained. "She will use you in her own games, not help you. You'll never see your ideals of justice and law for everyone if you marry her."

"I'll take my chances."

"Curyll, she dabbles in magic. She doesn't care for balance and limits, only power. She's dangerous." *She'll kill you!* My heart screamed for him to listen. I had no proof. Only innuendo and suggestion. He'd accept nothing but hard evidence.

"I know she has magic, Wren. She won't need it after we help each other."

"Curyll, I think she killed her first husband. She suggested I use her methods to get rid of Carradoc." I hated voicing unfounded suspicions. He left me no choice.

"Wren, I know you are disappointed and jealous. But I won't listen to your made-up tales."

"I have never lied to you, Curyll. And I have never broken a promise."

"Give up, Wren. Marry Carradoc. It's for the best. We were never meant to belong to each other. Your father showed me a different destiny for both of us within his scrying bowl." He kicked his heels into Gwyntmor's sides and galloped back to the stables.

Alone, I let my tears flow.

Chapter 23

I didn't sleep that night. I tried a dozen times to run away. Every escape route led me back to my father's door. No matter how many paths I mapped out and followed meticulously, the compulsion brought me back to The Merlin every time.

The last time I found myself staring at the familiar wooden panels an hour before dawn, I had bathed and dressed in a simple white shift and crown of flowers without realizing it—my wedding attire.

Dawn promised mixed clouds and sunshine. I had wished for rain and wind to match my stormy mood. Da led me to an ancient oak tree deep in the forest. We waited there for Lord Carradoc and his daughters. A dozen bundles of mistletoe hung from the upper branches of the sacred tree. New, delicate green leaves swelled the oak branch tips to nearly bursting.

The scent of damp earth and new green reminded me abruptly of my last day on Avalon. A whiff of cedar on the breeze sent my heart racing and heated my blood. I had refused joining with a faery male then. Unless something drastic occurred, I couldn't refuse the man who came to wed me today.

Before last Samhain I would have selected this very tree for my first Beltane festival or my wedding. Today I dreaded the ritual that I knew would follow the simple ceremony. As soon as I lay with Carradoc, we would be bound together. The promises I would make before the Christian priest this afternoon would seal the bond for the rest of our lives. "Until death do us part." I would not break a promise.

My mind screamed in the agony of dread. My breasts, beneath my almost translucent shift, swelled with anticipation of a husband's touch with an eagerness that heated my face with shame. I had been denied a Beltane initiation for two years. My body wanted this joining even if my mind and heart did not.

The apple blossoms in my crown of flowers reminded me sharply of my training as a priestess of the Goddess. I couldn't be a true priestess until I had joined with a man and borne a child. Today my training would be complete.

Since I could not have Curyll, the man of my choice, Carradoc would have to do. He'd promised he would never hurt me. My faith in promises dwindled rapidly.

The first birds twittered sleepily to warn us of the sun's approach. Da lifted his face to the East and burst into the glorious song of thanksgiving to the Goddess. His deep bass voice sent goose bumps up my arms. Out of long habit, I joined him in the beautiful music of dawn. I could thank the Goddess for the day. But not for the man I would soon wed.

I hoped he wouldn't come. The path to this mistletoe tree twisted and looped back on itself through the dense forest. Many times the way faded into a blur of deer crossings. Maybe he'd get lost along the way.

And if he did fail to meet us, what would I do? I could disguise myself as a boy and join my father's march with the army. Or I could claim protection from Queen Ygraina and remain indoors in the filthy city. I might run away and risk the dangers of wandering as a bard by myself.

None of the options fulfilled me.

"I don't want a new mama. I need a husband!" a female voice wailed from behind a screen of underbrush.

Lord Carradoc burst through the tangle of blackberry vines and ferns, his white tunic and leggings askew and torn from the thorns. He carried Berminia, his middle daughter, over his shoulder. She pounded his back with clenched fists. His thick arm restrained her kicking legs. I held back a chuckle.

"You and your sister will witness this marriage and accept Arylwren, daughter of The Merlin, as my wife." Carradoc swatted Berminia's fat bottom. She was fat all over and must have been a tremendous weight for her father to carry. Her struggles probably increased the burden. Carradoc's breathing showed no sign of strain. Only the small tears in his fine linen tunic indicated his thrashing progress through the thicket. I wondered who had worked the blood-red embroidery at the neck, arms, and hem of the tunic. Beautiful work. Had one of his previous wives made the shirt for him? For a different wedding?

My stomach turned over in dread.

Another loud rustle of underbrush revealed a mutely defiant Ninuë being dragged into the clearing by a warrior I recognized as one of Carradoc's warband—Kalahart, I think. The warrior also carried Carradoc's banner—two black stags butting heads on a field of red.

Marnia, the youngest daughter, a year younger than me, had been left at home in the far North of Britain, almost to Hadrian's Wall. Soon to be my home, far away from the capital, the war, and Da; all that I held familiar and dear. *And Curyll.*

"You have no right to give that girl," Nimuë pointed at me, "power over your daughters and yourself. She deals in dark magic and demons. Morgaine told me so!"

"And so would you, if you had the intelligence to figure out how!" Carradoc returned as he set Berminia down beside her sister. "Now both of you behave, or I'll take a lash to you when we have finished." The blue beads in his beard and hair bounced as he turned his head, mimicking the whip he threatened his daughter with.

Berminia blanched. Nimuë returned his stare, daring him to punish her. A gleam of excitement came into her eyes.

I wondered, and dreaded what she anticipated.

Carradoc "humphed" and turned his back on the witnesses. He stepped up beside me and took my hand. Graciously, he bent over to kiss my palm. "Forgive my tardiness, Wren. I would have this day perfect for you."

I nodded. I couldn't make myself do more. Delays and "what ifs" evaporated. The time had come to make promises that would last a lifetime.

Rituals need to be precise, down to the last detail, in order to be effective. All four elements—Pridd, Awyr, Tanio, and Dwfr—must be represented. The number and arrangement of the witnesses in the proper order must be symbolic.

I repeated the words Da indicated I must. I walked in a circle when directed to seal my promise. I held Carradoc's hand and exchanged rings and flower garlands, more circles. And lastly I raised my face for a kiss of peace from my new husband. The scent of apple blossoms mingled with male humors heightened my awareness of him. I wanted to let my mind wander with the faeries, far away from the proceedings.

Carradoc wouldn't let me remain oblivious. A quick peck on the cheek didn't satisfy him. He lingered, he probed, he caressed, and he enticed until finally, he drew a response from my reluctant lips and body. With his eyes closed he memorized my face and neck with his mouth, then returned to lick my teeth, begging for entrance. I tried to remain stiff and unyielding as his arms enfolded me with warmth. He pressed his mouth harder against mine. I raised my clenched hands to push him away, then found my arms wrapped tightly around his neck.

The compulsion fell away from me like a wave of water retreating with the tide. I was free to run now. Carradoc kept my mind and body firmly imprisoned within his kisses.

One of his large hands cupped my bottom and drew me tight against the evidence of his growing desire. With his superior height he lifted me from the ground and continued his assault upon my mouth. He pressed my entire length against him, as close as two people could be with clothing separating skin from skin.

Dana forgive me, I couldn't help myself. I braced myself against his hips for balance and returned his kiss. My need for him erupted from the very core of my being, almost violently. The sharp tang of his arousal dominated the scents of flowers and earth.

I heard a shuffle of feet somewhere in the distance. A distance that seemingly increased as heat engulfed me from the crown of flowers on my head to the tips of my bare feet. Someone cleared his throat. The kiss continued. On and on.

"Can we leave now?" Nimuë asked in a bored tone.

"Of course, my dear," Da chuckled. "I shall escort you back to the palace."

Out of the corner of my eye I glimpsed Nimuë slipping her hand into the crook of Da's arm. The look she turned on me shot venom. Her attention remained directly on me and totally ignored her father.

Carradoc's fumbling with the neckties of my shift jerked my attention away from Nimuë's resentment. He set me back down on my feet. Grass caressed my soles, reminding me that this union would make me one with the Goddess as well as with this man. My husband.

My previous resentment of Carradoc faded. I couldn't deny his affection—or lust—for me. My heart softened as my body prepared for our union.

A lingering need to control the situation flickered across my mind.

"Not here!" I protested as he slipped the thin shift off my shoulders.

"Where better than here with mistletoe for our bower and the Goddess as the sheet to receive your maiden's blood?" His large hand freed my swollen breasts from their covering. "So full and ripe!" He bent to kiss and suckle each tip until they puckered in delight.

His warrior beads brushed my belly, sending quivers of delight all the way to the back of my throat.

"What if they come back?" I couldn't look over my shoulder to check for privacy. My attention remained on him, studying every flicker of emotion that crossed his face.

The shift fell to the ground. His eyes widened at my exposed belly and legs.

"They won't come back." He licked his lips. I couldn't tell if he fought for control of his actions or exhibited a trace of nervousness. "Even if our families should return, what matter? They will bear witness to the consummation of our union and that the son you give me will be mine!" He knelt before me, trailing nipping little kisses as he moved his mouth to the juncture of my thighs.

I grasped his head for balance as a pleasurable wave of vertigo threatened my senses. Hot moisture rushed to meet his mobile mouth.

"I do like my women with a heavy thatch and full tits." His tongue flicked out and across the most sensitive part of my body.

The world reeled around me and my fingernails dug into his back. My knees no longer supported me. Moss and dried leaves cushioned me as he stretched out my body, hands clasped above my head in one of his giant fists.

"I will teach you all of the delights of Beltane, my Wren. In time I will teach you more than what a dozen uncontrolled youths could manage, though I'd love to watch them try. You are ripe and ready, Dana be praised. The Ladies of Avalon trained you well. I'll have you now." He fumbled with his leggings beneath his tunic.

Before I could gasp at the size of him, he spread my legs and thrust in.

I screamed at the flash of pain.

A gush of moisture softened his hardness. Pressure built upward, through my belly, into my breasts and stifled my brain.

He retreated a fraction, then thrust into me again and again. Sweat covered his brow. I arched to greet him. He released my hands. I wrapped my arms around his neck. He balanced on his elbows.

"I want to watch you as you come!" he gasped as he continued to thrust.

Tingles began at the base of my spine, spreading in wider and wider circles. I moaned in hot pleasure, abandoning myself to the joy that swept over me.

"Yes!" he shouted and claimed my mouth. At last he spasmed and collapsed heavily on top of me.

I feared his ragged breathing would stop his heart.

Slackness replaced the fullness inside me. I squirmed my hips, uncertain what he expected of me now.

"Not yet, Wren. I know you want more, and I'll give it to you in a moment." He heaved off me, rolling to one side. "Sorry I rushed it so. I've waited a long time to have you. I couldn't wait any longer."

He'd lost control and hadn't waited long enough to remove his clothing. Awareness of my power over him dawned. A secret smile spread over my face.

"The next time will be better for both of us. I'll just get a little more comfortable and then we can take our time." He ripped off his tunic, exposing the twisting tattoos on his chest marred by a thin knife scar running from his left nipple to right ribs.

Chapter 24

"SO you recognize me at last, little Wren." Carradoc threw back his head and laughed. "I wondered when you'd put off the prissy virgin act and admit you were disappointed your enthusiastic marchogs came to the 'rescue' last Samhain."

A knot formed in my stomach, twisting and coiling up my spine to my neck and shoulders. Could Carradoc speak the truth? Had I known Samhain revelers awaited me and deliberately lingered past the hour of safety? I had thoroughly enjoyed our first rapid but powerful sex.

To cover my confusion I grabbed my discarded shift and clutched it to my breasts.

What about the premature darkness on Samhain? I hadn't caused that. And the demon worshipers had used it.

"Don't go all meek and embarrassed on me, Wren. Why else would you deliberately walk into that crumbling old hill fort at sunset on Samhain but to delight in ritual rape by demons? You wanted me to fuck you."

I didn't think so.

"I told you and your father that first day you arrived in Venta Belgarum the ritual would take place. You came of your own free will."

Had he mentioned South Hill? I couldn't remember. I'd lost too many of those early days in a haze of magic and exhaustion. And headaches. Another threatened me when I fought too hard for memories.

And what of the unnatural wind that had urged me up the hill?

Certainly I'd looked forward to my first Beltane, a loving symbolic union between the Goddess and Belenos for the benefit of the entire community. It honored women and their role in life.

Carradoc's fake demons debased women. They sought only their own twisted pleasure in another's pain. Their "ritual" honored nothing but evil.

The little bit of affection I had been feeling toward him faded as mist in the sunshine. All traces of the pleasing scents of flowers and cedars and sun-warmed Pridd became masked by the no-longer-desirable acrid odor of a man with the need on him.

"You and your friends were seeking to raise power by enticing demons with blood and pain. I sensed the magic rising. That power was the only thing that allowed you to penetrate the labyrinth. If Da hadn't stopped your ritual, the *things* you raised from the Netherworld would have rampaged out of control. Britain would have been devastated far worse than any Saxon horde could inflict!"

"Don't preach to me, Wren. Maybe some of those young bucks thought they were raising power. Most of us were merely playing."

"The others wore painted markings on their bodies. Perhaps Samhain was a game to them. But you—*you* wear tattoos unlike a priest ordained by any god I know, not even Cernunnos." I pointed at the blue, red, and black markings etched into his skin. "What perverted god do you serve, Carradoc?"

"I wear the tattoos of a warrior, earned in single combat and full battle! As our people wore tattoos for many centuries until the Romans came and made us exchange honorable body art for mere beads." He shook his head, making the blue beads entwined there rattle. "If I serve any god, it is Cuchulainn, the greatest of heros and warriors."

But not a god of rape and demons.

My newly awakened body tried to tell me Carradoc's past didn't matter. He could give me pleasure. He could give me children.

Common sense told me to never trust him. Memory of his vicious smile beneath a demon mask as he guided my hand to inflict the knife wound on himself sent chills through my body.

"Look, Wren, I promised not to hurt you. And I haven't hurt you now, no matter how hastily I took you. You were hot and wet and as eager as any Beltane maid. More than ready. I swear that you are ready again just as I am." He stood up to shed his leggings. "Why hold a grudge?"

We had made binding promises. I could divorce him, here and now. But that wouldn't gain me the protection my father sought for me. Nor would divorce bring Curyll to my side. He and Lancelot left the city yesterday evening on a mission for King Uther.

"Seal in a circle your promise not to hurt me." I gathered my legs under me to run if he would not do as I asked.

"What will you do if I don't? You have no options but to obey me as any proper wife should."

My only option left was to flee to Avalon, alone, without supplies or the protection of a bardic harp on my back. Once there I could exist as the hermit did, alone. I'd spend my days scraping a living from the earth and honoring the Goddess.

Alone.

Could the faeries protect me in open country for several days?

They hadn't blessed this ceremony with their presence.

I knew in that moment that a solitary life away from Curyll and Da and the Ardh Rhi didn't fit my life pattern.

Carradoc might try to hide me away in his caer up North. But he was ambitious and needed to be near the Ardh Rhi in the capital. He needed my connection to The Merlin to gain more political power.

I had heard enough about the coming war to know that the Saxons targeted Dun Edin in the far North. Uther and my father planned to occupy the caer overlooking the vulnerable Firth of Forth before the Saxons could. The center of political activity would be closer to Carradoc's caer than to Venta Belgarum.

My father had secreted something special in the North. He needed me to guard a specific sacred place. My perception of the future swirled to include an artifact of power. A very special artifact.

I would not be hidden and isolated for long.

"Seal your promise in a circle, or I swear I will make your life so miserable you will long for an honorable death in battle. I am a priestess of the Goddess, The Merlin's daughter. I have access to powers beyond the everyday authority belonging to a wife." We stared at each other a long moment, weighing and assessing.

"A circle, huh?" He snatched a stick from the nearby underbrush. Slowly he walked a large circle around me, dragging the stick behind him. When the curving lines joined, he threw the dead branch back into the brush and stepped inside.

"Within this ring, I promise, Arylwren, that I will never hurt you, as long as you remain faithful to me." In one swift movement, his leggings dropped to the ground and he snatched the shift from my hands.

He pulled me close for one long kiss. Then he flipped me over, facedown on the ground, and forcibly lifted my hips to receive him.

"And I'll make certain you are obedient and faithful with your belly full of my sons."

The circle sealed his vow. His thrust spilled his seed inside me and sealed my fate.

"We are in luck," Carradoc chortled, rubbing his hands together. He raked me with his gaze, eyes lingering on the swell of my breasts above the bright blue gown Blasine had given me for the Christian wedding ceremony.

The same color as my father's eyes when he smiled in the sunshine. I didn't want this reminder of Da. His manipulations had gone too far. Did he know that Carradoc had led the Samhain revelers? Did it matter to him as long as I obeyed his orders? My newly revised view of the patterns of past, present, and future flew apart every time I tried to puzzle out my next move.

I had very few choices left.

"How are we in luck?" I idly arranged the heavy folds of the blue brocade and pale green woolen stola draped over it. Better to fuss with my formal attire than touch him in any way. Surely after three times this morning he couldn't be ready for sex again.

The gleam in Carradoc's eyes told me differently.

"Archbishop Dyfrig has returned from Wales. He will preside over the ceremony." Carradoc puffed out his chest, as a gander is wont to do to impress a mate or intimidate a rival.

He behaved more like a randy goat than a proud gander. I ached terribly from his repeated attentions.

A long bath with Blasine and the other brides this afternoon had helped. The hours of preparation for the large Christian ceremony—hours away from Carradoc—helped.

I had let the serving women comb and braid my unruly hair into an intricate style of graceful loops. I had accepted the gift of perfume from Ygraina. But I had rejected the offer of cosmetics. The beautiful woman who looked back at me from the polished metal mirror almost resembled me, cosmetics would have robbed me of any contact with my sense of self.

The look of appreciation in Carradoc's eyes when he met me at the door to the bower confirmed what the mirror had told me. The usually stone-faced guards also looked twice at me and smiled.

I recognized the power of beauty and cowered within at the way women manipulated men with it. Was this any different from what my father did? Or Nimuë and Morgaine?

This was how I had wished to appear for Curyll the night of the Samhain banquet. If I had won his affection that night, I would always doubt its validity. I didn't want Curyll if his heart truly belonged to another. Where did his heart lie?

Curyll and Morgaine would not wed today. Uther had sent him elsewhere with urgent dispatches. I wasn't certain if I rejoiced that Curyll remained free or not. I had cast my lot with Carradoc, for good or ill.

The six other grooms would leave with the united army on the morrow. Carradoc would escort me to his home before joining a second massing of troops in Dun Edin.

For all my soreness and wariness in my husband's presence, there was a new contentment inside me. More than a heightened sensual awareness, more than knowledge that my training as a priestess was now complete. A little effort brought people's thoughts to my mind. I knew their emotions from the colored layers of energy radiating out from their heads. Fire leaped to my command with a snap of my fingers—much easier than before.

Somehow, sex had awakened more magic within me than I thought possible.

But I wouldn't use it, even from my usually shadowed hiding places. Not if it meant I manipulated and used people to my own ends. Better to forsake all of my magic than do what Da did.

I needed to talk to Da about this. I didn't want to see him again. He hadn't met me at the entrance to the women's bower as I expected. Only Carradoc would escort me to the Christian wedding.

I guessed that having disposed of me, Da poured all of his concentration into battle preparations. He had no need to attend this wedding.

"What difference which cleric says the words at our marriage? By every tradition we hold dear, you are my husband by law and by deed." I wanted the ordeal of the ceremony over. I wanted a routine established. I wanted Carradoc gone to war.

"Dyfrig is well loved by the Ardh Rhi and Ygraina and well on his way to being named a saint in his home province. The archbishop's blessing of our marriage is a sign of political favor. After this, Uther has to back me in my bid for the kingship of Gorre—very near the archbishop's home."

He preceded me by two long strides as we made our way to the courtyard outside the round chapel.

"I did not realize Baudemagus of Gorre had died," I said. Da and I had visited the aging but still vital king last year right after I left Avalon. I had liked the old man. He'd always treated me as an adult, not a scruffy child, and laughed with me at the long and rambling stories he told of his youth. I learned more history from him than from the long ballads authorized by the bards. Gruff and independent, Baudemagus didn't play politics. He sent his warband where they were needed, when they were needed. Otherwise he kept them home, protecting his borders from incursions by Saxons, Irish, or other kings.

"The old fart hasn't died yet. But he took his warband home last autumn. He's out of favor with Uther. His crown is ripe for the plucking, and I intend to grab it before it falls to the ground."

Almost as an afterthought, Carradoc grabbed my hand and tucked it into the crook of his arm. For the crowd Carradoc needed to appear attentive and caring. He didn't need to alter his attitude for me, his bride of a few hours.

I was already his possession.

"With the archbishop's blessing and your magical powers of persuasion, Uther won't be able to resist my bid for the crown of Gorre."

"I will not use my magic to influence anyone," I whispered, yanking my hand away from his arm. He recaptured it in both of his. The delicate bones of my wrist protested the fierceness of his grip.

"Don't balk now, Wren. Uriens is handfasting Leodegran's daughter today. And Galathin weds Princess Blasine. Both want Gorre as badly as I do and will use their marriage alliance to get it. I need you and the Christians, even if I don't need their sniveling god."

"No god should be reviled." I stopped short, dragging him to a reluctant halt. "We may not agree with the god, we may have disagreements with the followers. But no god deserves contempt. I will respect this ceremony and the vows I recite as part of it. Will you?"

He glared at me and tried to pull me forward again without answering.

I dug in my heels. "Will you respect this marriage ceremony and the vows required of us?"

"If I have to. I need the power the Christians control at court." He dismissed my objections. "Don't make me forcibly carry you to this wedding, Wren. You'll look a fool. You will make me look a fool." A threat lay behind his words.

I chose a different pattern.

I shook off his possessive grasp of my elbow and strode purposefully toward the dais beside the doorway of the chapel. Carradoc had to lengthen his stride to keep up or look the reluctant groom. We arrived at the dais at the same time, both a little breathless.

Sniggers ran through the crowd at our seeming eagerness. I proudly faced the cleric who mounted the three steps of the raised platform. Carradoc lowered his eyes and hid his resentful expression.

Now recovered from his life-threatening illness, Father John, in his simple brown robe, strode behind the richly clothed archbishop. Gold brocade ornamented Dyfrig's vestments and the high, mitered hat that made him appear taller and more slender than I knew he must be. Layers of pure white and loving blue energy pulsed out from his entire body. Power, vivid and potent. Power akin to my father's. And mine.

I looked closer, expecting to see a face like Father Thomas', the gentle priest who had tried to exorcise the demon from Curyll's tongue.

My father's face and twinkling bright eyes looked back at me, except this man's hair and beard were jet black. Da's hair had turned prematurely white by the time I was born.

Everything I believed turned upside down. Da had betrayed everything he held dear, including me, by living a double life as Christian archbishop and Druid of the Goddess. I couldn't trust him anymore.

I didn't trust my husband.

Curyll had deserted me for another.

I was as alone as if I had retreated to Avalon.

Chapter 25

MERLIN watched Wren march up to the wedding dais with fierce determination. She should approach this marriage with joy.

Tears blurred his vision. She had grown into such a beautiful woman! So much like her mother he ached with longing to hold her.

But he had lost her trust and good will by forcing the marriage. Possibly he had lost her love as well. He hoped not. But she would be safe. That was all that mattered.

He should go now. He had a mission to complete in the North before he joined Uther in Dun Edin.

Before he could take one step out of the shadows toward his horse, he caught sight of Dyfrig mounting the dais. Dyfrig resplendent in gold brocade and mitered hat. He carried the ornamental crosier that marked him a shepherd of his human flock.

Fascinated by his twin's role in today's ceremony, Merlin blinked away the tears that had filled his eyes moments before. He could have followed the same path as his twin. He could have embraced the Christian Church as his mother wished.

Instead of rich clothing and palaces, he had lonely tracks in the wilderness and simple garb and his harp. He also had Wren. She made all of the loneliness and pain worth the struggle.

He and Dyfrig must stand united again, as they had not been since they were five. Representatives of the old faith and the new had to show their willingness to work together to crown Arthur before the rest of Britain would work together to oust the Saxons once and for all. If Dyfrig wouldn't come to the crystal cave willingly . . . Merlin possessed the means to force him. The symbol of unification was much more important than Dyfrig's pride. The symbol of power . . .

Arthur. Soon everything he had worked for would fall into place. As long as Dyfrig cooperated.

With one last sigh and glance of longing toward his daughter, Merlin set off on his solitary destiny.

"Good-bye, Wren," he whispered. "Remember the good times we had together, my beloved daughter."

"Can't you move that nag any faster?" Carradoc reached back from his own tall stallion to grab the reins of the docile mare I rode.

"I am not used to riding. If you'd let me walk, we'd make better time." I tried not to wince as the jostling gait of the horse irritated muscles stretched and bruised by the long ride.

Walking didn't require concentration like riding. If I strode beside Carradoc and his daughters, I'd have the freedom of mind to puzzle out the mystery of my father's absence from the wedding ceremony and the appearance of a *Christian* archbishop wearing his face and form.

Except for the black hair, Archbishop Dyfrig appeared to be the same man as my father. Both wise religious men who counseled the Ardh Rhi. Both reputedly had visions of the future. And both claimed to be the son of a holy sister.

But . . . My mind slid away from the half-formed thought. Da and I had lived separately for four years while I studied in Avalon. Perhaps I didn't know him as well as I thought. Perhaps he rode the political winds in whatever guise pleased his current audience.

Carradoc wanted to do the same. Neither cared for truth and honor, only expedience.

I wasn't likely to get answers while more than half my mind remained fixed on staying upon a horse's back.

"I am a lord and a marchog in contention for the kingdom of Gorre," Carradoc bellowed. "You will not demean my position by walking like a common peasant." His eyes wandered speculatively to the small retinue of servants behind us. From the loudness of his voice, I guessed he didn't really mind who knew of his displeasure with me.

I held tight to the secret I had gleaned from Uther's mind as Leodegran of Carmelide repeated to Uriens the handfast vows for his absent daughter, Guinevere. As soon as the couple married, at the Autumnal Equinox, Uriens would be named king of Gorre. Uther and the other kings had never even considered Carradoc for the title.

"Morgaine says you bewitch animals and men. Can't you do something to the horse to make her gait as smooth as a cloud?" Nimuë smiled at my discomfort. "That nag is so docile a two-year-old could ride it."

My new stepdaughter rode a high-stepping gelding with ease. She made the animal prance and rear, neatly keeping her seat.

My mare shied away from the high-strung animal. I grimaced at the horse's uneven steps.

Berminia didn't bother to hide her giggles. Her fat pony plodded slower than mine.

I yanked the reins away from my husband. A soft springtime mist made the leather slippery, and he lost his hold.

Defiance sat on my left shoulder. I couldn't allow Carradoc to control me.

I slid off the hard saddle into the soft meadow. The scent of burgeoning wildflowers washed by rain caressed my nose, almost masking the odor of wet horse, wet dogs, and tired people. I shuffled my feet a little and drank in the fresh smells of the fields.

"I will walk." I placed one foot forward, ready to begin the next leg of the journey to Carradoc's stronghold east of Caerduel and south of Campboglanna, the large Roman fort on the wall.

"What do you think you are doing?" Carradoc dismounted beside me. The mare shied away from his looming presence.

"I am walking. Both the horse and I will be more comfortable. We will make much better time." As if to emphasize my statement, the mare pranced and rolled her eyes.

"My wife will ride as befitting a noble. I don't care that your humble birth denied you access to mounts until now. You have married landed nobility and therefore you must ride!" He grabbed for my waist and lifted me onto the saddle. The mare sidled away at first contact.

I landed on my bottom amidst a profusion of sweet flowers. My spine vibrated from the jolt. A small pain compared to the chafing between my thighs.

Thank you, Dawnsio, I silently told the horse. I could communicate with animals, just as Nimuë accused. But I didn't do it casually or to no purpose, and I always thanked the creatures for the privilege.

The mare nodded in acknowledgment of the message.

"Get up, woman. You'll learn to control your horse like a lady. I won't have it said I married beneath me." Carradoc grabbed my arm roughly.

"My father's torc is gold, as is a king's. Yours is only bronze," I retorted. The sting of Carradoc's insult burned my cheeks and firmed my determination to remain off that horse. Bards and their families were supposed to be honored equal to kings. My husband considered my father and me peasants, contemptible, barely worthy of his notice. So why had he married me?

Power. Control. Lust. He needed a son.

"The horse does not wish to be ridden, and I do not wish to ride," I said out loud. Carradoc tried again to pull me up. I relaxed until I was a dead weight against his arm, remaining firmly in contact with the Pridd. This was where I belonged, not atop a horse.

"Since you can't control your mount, you will ride with me," Carradoc announced.

I started at him, not certain what to expect.

Technically he hadn't broken his promise not to hurt me. His lovemaking was rough and fast, hardly gentle, but he always made certain my body wanted him. He left me sore, mostly from the frequency of his attentions, but not hurt.

Nimuë laughed out loud. I ignored her. All my attention focused on my husband and the huge black stallion he positioned in front of me.

"Easy, Dyn." Carradoc gentled his restless horse. "Come here, Wren."

Carradoc lifted me high onto the horse's broad back, sitting me sideways behind the saddle. His shield, strapped to the side of his equipage, bounced against my back. The high saddle offered me nothing to grab hold of as Dyn shifted his feet. The stallion's spine rippled, his rigid muscles pounding into my already sore rump.

"Scoot back, Wren, so I can mount." Carradoc grabbed the pommel in preparation for scrambling aboard the big horse.

I looked down, a long way down to the ground. Gingerly I edged toward the horse's tail. Carradoc heaved his weight up. Dyn reared.

I landed flat on my back. The world spun around me. Darkness fluttered across my vision. I tried to breathe. Paralyzing pain stabbed my lungs.

My body cried out for air. Fire on the rampage in my chest blocked each breath.

Panic sat heavily on my throat. I couldn't breathe. The pain was too much. I had to breathe.

Nothing else mattered. I had to get air. It hurt. Dana how it hurt!

Time and time again I tried. Nothing happened but more pain. Red mist clouded my vision. Air. I had to have air.

Between one gasping struggle for air and the next, the pain faded. Not much. Just enough to be aware that I would not suffocate.

Voices penetrated the crimson fog around my mind.

"Now that you've killed her, can we get on with this interminable journey?" Nimuë whined.

"You'd like that, wouldn't you, Daughter? I'd be honor-bound to leave immediately for the war, and I'd have to report my wife's fate to her father." He paused. "The Merlin will kill me. Then all that I own will be yours. Do you know the hideous death meted out for the murder of a priest or priestess? The only worse punishment the Druids deliver is for forbidden knowledge in the wrong hands."

Alarm rang in my head almost as painfully as the shock to my body from the fall. An almost memory of a gibbering demon waving white petal pincers with fuzzy blood red centers circled around my memory, dribbling pain into my head. What in Carradoc's tirade had triggered this reaction?

The headache took my attention away from my bruised lungs. They relaxed a little and air flowed more freely into me.

I didn't stir. I needed to hear more.

"Accidents happen." Nimuë dismissed his statement with a flutter of her long fingers. "The Merlin will be so grief-stricken, he won't be able to hurt you. Everyone knows how he dotes on her. Though I don't know why, she's so ugly."

A green faery buzzed by my head.

Shall we drive the man and his ugly daughters mad? he asked. *You carry his child, you don't need him anymore.*

A child? Already?

The scent of fresh cedar drifted past my nose. I breathed deeply, determined to keep air moving to the vulnerable new life within me.

I carried a child!

I need to hear how much the woman hates me. She is my enemy and I must share a domicile with her, I replied to the faery. *I must protect myself and my child with knowledge.*

Cedar landed on my wrist. I couldn't tell where his companions lighted. They wouldn't be far off.

"Wren is of the old stock. Sturdy. She will give me healthy sons, something your mother and her successors couldn't," Carradoc sneered at his daughter.

"If she lives. You don't need a son. You have me!"

"I have Roman ideals and Christian blindness to contend with at court. You won't be allowed to inherit."

"Then allow me to marry a man who can inherit."

"The only men willing to accept your acid tongue and bitter heart are too weak of will to be of any use."

"A weak man would allow me to rule and would look away at other . . . indiscretions."

A long silence stretched between them.

I wanted to scream, *What indiscretions?*

Instead of replying to his daughter, Carradoc knelt beside me. He lifted my shoulders gently. "She breathes," he announced. "The rest of you continue on. We will follow shortly."

"I will not ride," I whispered. Cedar and his companions fluttered through the flowers and grasses, barely visible. They hadn't gone far, I knew. But they did not like my husband. They had not blessed our marriage.

"You must ride, Wren. If you do not get back on a horse now, you never will."

"If I must, I will make a show of riding through villages. But not now."

"Now or never, Wren. Come on, stand up and face the mare."

"Are you trying to kill your unborn child?"

"We've only been married two days. You couldn't possibly know if you conceived. And I know you were a virgin yesterday at dawn." He grinned broadly.

"You want me to use my magic at every turn. Do you doubt that such powers would tell me the moment a new life started within my body?" My body couldn't know, but the faeries had access to knowledge beyond mortal understanding.

Wild joy and swelling pride replaced the doubt in his eyes.

"Walking will tire you too much."

"Your horses will damage me more. I am used to walking. I need to caress the Pridd and the Goddess with every step," I said, taking off the shoes he insisted I wear.

He lifted me to my feet then, supporting me until my balance steadied. I took stock of my condition. A few bruises, sore ribs and back, nothing broken. I couldn't breathe deeply without stabbing pain, but I breathed.

"I will walk beside you for now." Carradoc clucked to the horses as he gathered their reins in one hand. He kept his free arm around my waist.

"You are a marchog, at home upon a horse. If you walk, you will slow us down."

"Later you will ride in my lap. I shall linger alone with you a while." He kissed me hard, leaving no doubt of his intentions. "We don't need a bed to unite with the Goddess. If you aren't pregnant now, you will be by the time we reach Caer Tair Cigfran."

The Fortress of Three Ravens. Three ravens portended death or disaster.

Before I had a chance to consider the ill omen, he kissed me and drew me back down to the ground.

"How long has your fortress been haunted by three ravens?" I asked as we emerged from the deep forest. We looked across bright sunshine on fallow fields to the shadowed tor topped by a heavily fortified caer. The three ravens in question croaked from perches on the wooden palisade at the second rampart. The weathered thatch of the long hall, just visible beyond the watchtower, looked as black as the ravens' feathers. The timbered walls had also darkened with age to a similar color.

I could almost imagine Cernunnos lounging along the rooftree. Watching. Waiting for the next death.

"The ancients brought the ravens and named it," Carradoc replied. "For as long as my people have held that fortress we have proudly protected the three ravens."

I shuddered slightly at the horrible omen.

Contrasting sharply with the darkness of the fortress, the sun shone brightly against a deep blue sky, warming the earth, readying it for the plow and the fertility festivals of Beltane, barely a month away.

I stood beside Carradoc's horse, grasping Dyn's bridle, as I had through most of the two-week journey north. No faeries flitted through the forest that filled the rolling hills to the south and west of the tor.

"Come, we must show ourselves to the villagers. You will ride, Arylwren." Carradoc held out his hand.

I grasped it, placing my foot atop his, and swung up into his lap, twisting so that my hips nestled into his thighs. The little bit of this trip I had ridden, mostly through villages or requesting hospitality from villas and caers on the route, I had sat here. We must have made a picture of newlywed happiness.

A finger of forest along a slight ridge stretched northward, between the village and us. We climbed the hill slowly, twisting around tumbled boulders taller than the horses. The thickness of the trees muted the sunlight. The shady road beneath the trees smelled damp. A faery flitted past my ear, giggling. I knew a spring must burst forth from the earth nearby. The faeries called it home.

Once free of this dark tangle of trees and rough ground, the road wound into the village and then looped up the processional way on the east side of the tor. A gaggle of lopsided huts came into view as we skirted the next bend. Weeds stretched from the verge toward muddy ruts on the road.

Almost a mile from the base of the hill, the village was closer to the base of the forested hill and the faery haven within the trees than to the protection of the caer. Almost as if it huddled as far away from the lord of Caer Tair Cigfran as it could.

The village huts stretched in a long semicircle facing away from the tor. I imagined the line of houses extending into a complete circle. Remnants of a ritual ditch and bank marked the perimeter of the dwellings. At the center of the circle stood a tall, solitary stone, partially chiseled smooth by men, partially roughened by centuries of changing weather.

Surprised by the proximity of a monolith in Carradoc's village, I looked closer. Tumbled but not broken stones and quite a few standing stones formed a huge circle. The broken and stony ground, suitable for sheep but not plowing, disguised the pattern. Most of the village huts stood where the circle of stones should continue in an unbroken line. The thatched roofs nearly reached the ground, obscuring the walls. The floors must be sunk below ground level, to conserve building materials and provide extra insulation against fierce winter temperatures and winds. Here and there I glimpsed patches of light gray in a back or side wall. One patch per house. Granite gray. The same color as the standing stones.

I laughed out loud. The villagers had incorporated the sacred stones of their ancestors into their homes. They must accept the stones as a part of everyday life, holding the ancient ways in reverence by habit if not design.

This was a place I wanted to call home. Even before I met them, my heart knew and loved these people more than I could ever love the man who called himself my husband.

In small groups, people emerged from the oddly shaped homes. They stood silently, but respectfully, awaiting their lord and his new bride. No better dressed than most of the peasants of this war-torn land, they weren't starving, but disease and a winter of poor food had taken a heavy toll on their health. Men, old before their time, leaned upon staves. Bone fever twisted their joints and curved their spines. Most of the women looked haggard. Young men remained in the fields, tending sheep or preparing the fields for plowing. They kept their backs to the procession on the road.

I saw no young women. None.

A few of the men tugged their forelocks as a sign of respect. None of the others bowed or curtsied.

I waved to them, shyly. One woman looked up. A brief smile touched her lips, then faded rapidly.

Carradoc scowled in extreme displeasure. All of the villagers retreated a step or two, as far away from their lord as they could get and still line the road to witness this parade.

"I told the village elders to break up those standing stones. I need them to improve the fortifications of the long hall and the first rampart," Carradoc grumbled. "They'll obey or feel my whip on their backs."

"You can't punish these people for maintaining the stones of antiquity!" I protested, squirming to get down from Carradoc's horse.

He held me tight against him.

"Bring ten of these people to the Long Hall. Men and women. They'll answer for this disobedience," Carradoc shouted to three men-at-arms who rode with us.

Nimuë licked her lips as if eager for the taste of blood. I had no doubt she'd wield the whip herself if Carradoc allowed any but himself to do the nasty deed. His eyes glittered just as brightly in anticipation.

"There is plenty of rock around to use without desecrating this site," I replied.

"I gave orders . . ."

"You are newly wed. You should be happy and forgiving, not vengeful." I pinched his hand hard where he held me. He loosened his grip enough for me to slide to the ground. I landed with a jolt but remained upright.

"Get back up here, Arylwren."

"No. Not until you promise to leave the stones alone."

"I can't promise . . ."

I thought about forcing his mind to accept my thoughts. I knew how to do it. But I had vowed not to use my magic to manipulate anyone. We had to make our own choices.

Carradoc and I stared at each other, malice and stubbornness growing between us with each heartbeat.

"Forgive me, Lord Carradoc." A slight man of middle years and balding head skittered down the road from the tor. His tunic was slightly less threadbare and patched than the villagers.

A huge wolfhound bounded beside him. The shaggy beast ignored the man, halting in front of Carradoc's horse, pink tongue lolling, ears flopping, slightly perked in curiosity. It looked at me carefully, then approached slowly, nose working.

"Newynog, come," Carradoc ordered, snapping his fingers beside his thigh.

The dog ignored him while it sniffed my hand. It stood nearly as tall as I and probably weighed twice what I did.

I held still, waiting for Newynog's judgment. Dogs didn't usually frighten me. Wolfhounds—war dogs—tended to be fiercely loyal. Until it accepted me as part of Carradoc's pack of humans I could become a victim of those sharp, meat-tearing teeth. Carradoc would have chosen the name Newynog—*hungry*—for a reason.

A wet tongue covered my hand, then my face. I grimaced as little as I wiped the dog's slobber on my sleeve.

"Good girl, Newynog, you know who belongs to me," Carradoc laughed.

Newynog sat at my feet, leaning her impressive weight into me, demanding I scratch her ears.

Carradoc sobered instantly and glared at the dog. "She doesn't accept the touch of anyone, sometimes not even me," he growled, sounding very like a dog.

"I have a way with some animals." I smiled at the dog and petted her lavishly. Mind pictures of dozing beside a bright fire came to me with great clarity. Our arrival had disrupted Newynog's nap. But she didn't mind.

"Diones, what is the meaning of this disobedience." Carradoc pointed toward the standing stones. "I ordered the stones dismantled and broken up for fortifications."

"Yes, Lord." Diones bowed from the waist, nearly pulling out the few hairs that remained on his brow in subservience. "But we've finished the repairs to the Long Hall foundations and the rampart walls."

"In stone?" Carradoc glowered beneath his heavy brows. I sensed disappointment that he wouldn't need to whip someone. Several someones.

"Yes, Lord. Good strong stone, neatly dressed with square corners, mortared together. Double walls filled with rubble between, just like the Roman wall." Diones risked a glance upward.

Both Carradoc and I looked up to the soaring walls of the fortress. Sure enough, the wooden planks seemed to be resting atop several feet of smooth stone. Very like the construction of the Roman wall to the north of us. I was sure the wall was visible from the watchtower on a clear day like today. I wondered if the new breaches in Hadrian's Wall were also visible. Maybe Diones and the others had gone a little farther afield to keep their pilfering of the Roman stones a secret.

"You see, Carradoc, you have been obeyed. You mustn't assume defiance from your people. Unless you wanted to whip someone for your own pleasure," I accused him. Newynog licked my hand. I sensed her agreement with my words.

Carradoc didn't answer me. He just held out his hand for me to climb back onto his horse.

"I'll walk."

"You will ride." He grabbed the neck of my gown and yanked me up onto his saddle.

The villagers all stepped forward as if to aid me, then thought better of it and retreated again. Newynog looked confused. A low rumble erupted from her throat, more a question than a threat. I turned and waved to the villagers, forcing a smile for them, but not for Carradoc. Newynog relaxed a little and paced beside Carradoc's horse on the twisted road up to the fortress.

I thanked Andraste my husband would leave for the battlefront within a few weeks.

Chapter 26

"COME with me," Nimuë ordered her two sisters. "We must reset the wards about the caer." She beckoned Berminia and Marnia to follow her.

"I don't want to," Marnia whined. Scrawny and colorless, she drifted like a ghost of herself back toward the chamber they shared on the south side of the Hall.

"This isn't a matter of want. We NEED to reset the wards if we are to keep Caer Tair Cigfran ours." Nimuë marched toward the north tower of the second rampart.

"But Gran set wards just before she died," Berminia protested. She waddled in Nimuë's wake, munching on a chicken leg.

"And the wards died with Gran. Just as her Gran's did and her Gran's before her. This is something that has to be done with each new generation. I reset the spells before we left for Venta Belgarum last summer. Now that Carradoc has brought another woman into the caer, we need to set them again."

"What difference does Wren make?" Marnia asked. She stayed a few paces behind Nimuë but didn't retreat farther.

"Carradoc's new wife upsets the balance!" Nimuë guessed at the answer. "She has magic and negates the wards." Besides, Nimuë needed to set up the spells to repel Wren from within as well as enemies from without. Carradoc had no right to pass the caer to Wren's son—if indeed she carried one. That would have to be remedied, too—later.

The caer and the magic and the ancient secrets within Caer Tair Cigfran belonged to the women's line. Carradoc was the first man to inherit in more generations than Nimuë could count. The only reason he was able to claim it was because his three sisters had died before they could wed and bear daughters of their own.

Nimuë suspected Carradoc had murdered his sisters. She'd wanted to murder her own often enough. But just because he had warped the line of succession didn't mean he had to continue it. Caer Tair Cigfran was *hers* and no one else's.

"Why do you need us?" Berminia looked avidly at the rabbit Nimuë carried in a basket.

They had stolen the creature from Cook. It should have been part of the evening meal. Nimuë would have preferred a chicken for this task. She had less trouble wringing their necks. But her mentor insisted that true magic required the sacrifice of fur-bearing animals. The demon who still hovered in the back of Nimuë's head agreed.

"I need you, because we three are of Gran's blood. We three are all that's left of her line of powerful women. The three of us will make the magic stronger." One maiden and two women not yet matrons. They needed a crone, and probably a woman who had actually borne a child, not just been initiated into sexual union. But Nimuë didn't have time to search out the other women. She should have performed this ritual at dawn, but she'd overslept and now the sun approached noon. She thought she had to complete this spell before the sun reached its zenith and started down again. That's what Gran had said. Her mentor hadn't specified.

They reached the outer wall of the north tower. The guard who patrolled the rampart had reached the south tower and lingered, flirting with the kitchen girl Nimuë had sent to intercept him.

Slowly she took three deep breaths to calm her anxious nerves. Then she set out the bitter herbs she had collected under the dark of the moon. She hoped she'd gotten the right combination out of the kitchen garden in Venta Belgarum. Her shielded lantern hadn't given her enough light to distinguish one plant from the other.

"Fire, Berminia." She snapped her fingers to gain her sister's wandering attention.

Berminia placed a bundle of kindling around the pile of herbs. She took her time and placed each stick methodically in a tent over the mound of herbs.

"Hurry up! They don't have to be neat. They just have to hold the flame a few moments!"

"Gran said they have to go in order," Marnia reminded Nimuë.

She still sounded petulant and close to tears. She kept looking toward the postern gate that would take her back within the safety of the compound.

"I've studied magic, and you haven't," Nimuë snapped. "Let's get on with it."

Berminia struck flint against iron, sending a spark into the herbs and kindling with her first try. Like a good housewife.

Nimuë bit her lip to keep herself from shouting with jealousy. Tanio never obeyed her so quickly.

"Now for the finish." She took the rabbit from the basket, holding it by the scruff of the neck. It wiggled its little pink nose. Marnia's hesitant expression softened at the sight of the squirming animal. The little twit looked as if she wanted to pet the damn thing, like it was one of the innumerable cats who hung around Wren, including the gray-and-white one that had followed her all the way from Venta Belgarum.

Shuddering with disgust for her sister's softness, Nimuë wrapped her hands around the rabbit's neck, ready to wrench it around in one quick twist.

"What are you doing?" Marnia cried. She held both hands to her mouth and her face turned a sickly shade of green.

"I am going to kill it," Nimuë replied, disgusted with Marnia's squeamishness.

"Cook said you have to slit its throat and drain it of blood," Berminia corrected her sister.

"If I were going to cook it, I would." Nimuë sighed as she explained. "I'm sacrificing it. Therefore, I have to break its neck first." Before she finished speaking, she did the deed. The rabbit's neck bones ground out of place. It screamed and kicked with its hind legs.

Marnia screamed and looked ready to faint. Hand to mouth, nearly blinded by tears, she screamed again and again—sounding strangely like the rabbit—and stumbled toward the gate.

"Oh, for Dana's sake." Berminia grabbed the rabbit away from Nimuë and finished the murder. With a final kick the rabbit ceased its horrible noise and emptied its bowels. The spray hit Nimuë's gown rather than Berminia's. "I'll take it back to Cook," Berminia chuckled. "You'd better bathe and change before Carradoc smells you and asks questions." She turned to follow Marnia.

"Don't you dare!" Nimuë grabbed the rabbit back. She fumbled for her knife.

"You've ruined it," Berminia said disgustedly. "What good is it if we can't eat it?"

"This isn't about food. This is about magic and protection," Nimuë snapped. She finally managed to slash the cutting edge of her blade across the rabbit's neck. A pitiful amount of blood dribbled onto the almost dead fire.

"I told you we should blood it first, while its heart still beats," Berminia said.

Nimuë ignored her. A wall of power rose from the stinking fire. She opened herself to embrace the energy and channel it to the west, her next stop in her circuit around the wall.

Pain, sharp and hot, lanced from her throat to her eyes and then down to her toes. Her joints ached as if she'd broken every bone in her body. Her skin felt aflame. All of her senses shut down.

She knew only pain. She dropped the rabbit, needing both hands to bury her face, to find her balance, to keep from screaming.

Then, as quickly as it had come, the pain retreated.

Cautiously, Nimuë peered through her fingers to see what had assaulted her. Her mentor had said that magic would make her tired and achy. She hadn't warned her of this awful pain, as if demons burned through her.

Then she saw it. A small pile of clean white ashes two steps away.

Wren had already set her own wards around the caer, stronger, more resilient.

Nimuë didn't know how to counter them.

"I'll just have to try something else," she resolved. But first she needed to sleep and bathe in cool water.

In the back of her head, the demon laughed uproariously.

A predawn chill woke me. Outside the central Long Hall of Caer Tair Cigfran a small bird chirped a question. Is it time to get up yet?

Hush, a few moments more, I told the bird with my mind. Just a few moments more, please. Sleep sand kept my eyes glued shut and my mind tended to drift back to quiet slumber. My bladder had other ideas.

Cautiously I pried one eye open. A faint rosy glow around the edges of the shuttered window of our bedchamber hinted that Belenos, the sun, was near to making his morning appearance.

Carradoc heaved himself over in his sleep, muttering something unintelligible. One of his long arms landed on top of my abdomen. My bladder protested the weight. His hand instinctively closed around my hip. My stomach complained about life in general.

Without delicacy or caution I scrambled from the high bed, grabbing a light robe in my hasty trek to the privy. For once Newynog didn't follow me, though she slept at the foot of the bed. She raised one eyelid and moaned as if she sympathized with my distress.

For the fourth morning in a row I retched and heaved for endless moments. My belly ached from the repeated convulsions. Cold sweat ran down my face and between my breasts. Tremors in my hands and knees kept me sprawled on the cold dirt floor of the outdoor necessary shed. My hair hung in limp strands, devoid of its natural curl.

When it was over, I sat up, still weak. Strength and alertness deserted me. Only the chill seeping through my bones seemed real.

"You finished, Wren?" Carradoc asked through the door.

This privy was tucked between the back of the hall, where we lived, and the exterior wall. It was indeed private and reserved for the use of the lord's family. The hole ran deep into the ground before exiting halfway down the steepest portion of the cliff.

"No, I don't know," I replied weakly. Though empty, my insides continued to churn.

He threw open the door anyway. I wanted to scream at him to go away. Instead I snuggled into the warmth of the blanket he dropped around my shoulders.

"By my figures the child will be born around the Winter Solstice." He picked me up and carried me back to our bedroom. "Admirable of you to conceive so readily. I still have the entire campaign season ahead of me."

His priorities revolved around his warband rather than his family. At least his pattern remained consistent, predictable.

"When will you leave?" I sipped at the water and ate the stale bread he handed me. In a few moments, the last remnants of my earlier discomfort departed. How did he know what I needed?

Our life together seemed to alternate between thoughtful concern and open animosity. Nothing in between. Sex had become rare between us. In some ways I missed the unbridled stimulation. At others, like now, I didn't want him to touch me again. Ever.

Newynog seemed in agreement as she wormed her huge head between Carradoc and me. I scratched her ears, welcoming the added warmth her fur gave me.

"I leave tomorrow or the day after. Bad omen if I leave on Beltane."

"Croo-awk, croo-awk," cried one of the three ravens that hung around Carradoc's dark fortress. The enclosure perched atop its hill like a squat spider waiting for prey. Even the labyrinthine processional way on the gentle southern slope resembled a spiderweb. Generations had added to the original hill fort without plan or symmetry. Most of the additions—which should have been conical one and two room huts—reflected the Roman influence of sharp angles and squares. Unnatural. Appropriate hiding places for demons.

I shuddered in memory of my encounter with Carradoc last Samhain. Every time I saw the tattoos on his chest, I remembered his capacity for inflicting pain and terror. Best if he took himself off to war soon and vented his demons on the Saxons.

"I must greet the dawn." Still a little weak-kneed, I struggled to my feet. Sandals, my shift and gown, a hairbrush. What else did I need to make myself presentable enough to walk through the hall and to the palisade gate? I wouldn't greet the day inside. I needed fresh air.

The song of thanksgiving for the day already thrummed in the back of my throat. Magical power lay dormant beneath the song, waiting to be tapped. The wards I had set around the caer answered the harmony that tickled my throat.

"Why get up now? You need your rest. Stay where you are until you feel stronger." He pushed me back onto the bed. Newynog lay her head on the mattress beside me, whining her agreement with Carradoc.

I didn't want to be there. Now that the initial weakness had passed, my mind cleared and my stomach wanted food. "I am a priestess. I will greet the dawn with song and praise and thanks, as I have every day of my life." I reached for my clothes.

Carradoc's face darkened with anger. His fist clenched. A knotted muscle pulsed beneath an old scar on his left shoulder.

"I forbid you to leave this room until you have eaten and bathed!"

"You dare forbid a priestess to perform her rituals?" I glared at him in defiance. "I should have known that anyone who ordered the desecration of standing stones honors no god."

In less than a day he would leave. Out of my life for many months. Maybe forever if he fell victim to a Saxon ax.

No, I mustn't think along those lines. Morgaine had arranged the death of her first husband. I would not do the same, even in my thoughts.

"I honor warriors and heroes. I respect practicality, not placating ritual that serves no purpose. Sing from the window, then. You must take care of yourself. Surely, even a priestess is allowed some variance of ritual to preserve her health during pregnancy."

I didn't know. None of the Ladies of Avalon had been young enough to conceive while I studied there.

"Please, Wren, do not risk the child by rushing outside too soon." Gently he caressed my hair and cheek with one of his big callused hands.

For a moment, I almost trusted that he held my best interests in his heart.

"Very well. Will you join me at the window?" In the month we had been married, he had yet to join me in the morning ritual so dear to all the Druid-trained. I fully expected him to retreat.

Instead he led me to the east-facing opening and threw open the shutters. He draped a solicitous arm about my waist. We left our clothing behind; ready to let the first rays of sunlight caress us without interference.

Pink, orange, and yellow lit the horizon with a joyous glow. At the moment Belenos shot the first fiery arrow into the sky I lifted my voice in song. A new day had come. Yesterday was a memory. Tomorrow a dream yet to come. *Thank you, God of Light and blessed sun, for the day. Thank you, Goddess of Light and bountiful Pridd, for a new day to make right all that I survey.*

Carradoc bellowed the words beside me in a deep voice that filled me with contentment. Though not as polished or melodious as a trained Druid or bard, he sang pleasantly and maintained a harmony against my high tones.

I could make magic of our harmony, beautiful magic. But Carradoc wasn't beautiful. Anger and cruelty shadowed his aura.

If our marriage continued as comfortably as these moments of harmony, I could be content. I did not love this man. Only occasionally did I trust him. It had to be enough.

"A good beginning to Beltane, Wren. When we have broken our fast and you have rested, we will join my people in celebration. There will be dancing and music, feasting and sacrifices. And then when the sun sets, we will guarantee the fertility of the fields with our symbolic joinings." He held me tight, caressing my back and bottom in a suggestive way. Fire warmed my blood as the sun could not deep within these stout walls.

I had proved my fertility. Tonight I would celebrate life with my husband.

"Who will reign as Queen of the May?" I asked. Though we'd been here a month, I did not yet know all of the villagers.

"Marnia, of course. She is the highest ranking virgin of the proper age."

A little chill crawled up my back, replacing the warmth he invoked. Queen of the May should be selected for health, strength, grace, and accomplishment, not rank. The symbolic joining of Dana and Belenos needed to be performed by the most suitable virgin and the strongest, most agile warrior and athlete to ensure bountiful crops and healthy livestock.

Marnia, Carradoc's youngest daughter, was far too skinny for health and fertility and just like her sister, Berminia, she had oily, pimply skin. Another year might give her enough maturity to reflect the best of nature.

"Last year I allowed Marnia to join the festivities. She was probably too young, her breasts hadn't developed at all. No man approached her. This year the men will have no choice." He buried his face in my hair, nuzzling my ear. The stirrings of his manhood against my belly warned me of his next thoughts. For once, I did not respond.

"I shall truly enjoy laying you upon the sigil of fertility in the center of the newly plowed field and taking you in full view of the village." He thrust his hips at me suggestively.

"After I have proved you to be my wife for the benefit of my people, I must spread my seed to as many as I can."

"Beltane symbolizes much more than just sex! It is for honoring the Goddess and celebrating life."

"And sex is the best medium for demonstrating our joy in life and how we honor the Goddess. Remember, you promised me fidelity, sealed in a circle. You are mine, now, and even on Beltane, only I shall have you."

"And does not the promise of fidelity extend to you, my lord and husband?"

"Of course not. If I don't sire at least three bastards tonight, no one will believe me virile enough, strong enough to hold this land. By the same token, if you should ever seek another lover, the people will believe me incapable of satisfying you and therefore incapable of satisfying the Goddess. You will remain faithful, or I will kill you. Most painfully."

Newynog skulked into a corner and whined in distress.

Chapter 27

HEAT drained from my face. Memory of Samhain Eve, nine naked men, Carradoc tying me to a pole, replayed across my mind. He prepared me for ritual rape then. Would tonight be any different except for the number of partners?

The few sips of water and bites of bread I had eaten threatened to rise again.

"At least I don't need to worry about The Merlin stealing my son away. You've been puking your guts up every morning for nigh on a week. He can't claim this child was conceived on Beltane and its parentage in doubt." Carradoc casually dismissed his threat.

"My father steals children?" I clung to this new topic rather than dwell on tonight's unpleasantness. I knew Da had taken the son of the Ardh Rhi and his queen for fosterage away from the court. The child Arthur. The King's son who must succeed him soon.

The other kings must elect an Ardh Rhi. They agreed on so few things, only Uther's son would gain enough neutral votes to attain the crown.

Another mystery to add to my father. My gentle Da seemed a distant dream. The formidable magician known as The Merlin seemed more shadow and contradiction than the man I had known all my life.

Carradoc didn't seem aware of my pause. "Every few years The Merlin appears out of nowhere, claiming that children born around Imbolc belong to the gods because they were conceived at Beltane. I lost one son that way. I'll not lose this one."

My birthday was on Imbolc. Could I be another Beltane child stolen at birth? No, I had inherited much from Da, including music and magic. Things he couldn't give a foster child.

The room spun around me. Carradoc placed a steadying hand on my shoulder.

"Don't let it fret you, Wren. Our son will be safe. And we both know your father always found good places to foster the sons he stole. I'm sure you visited them all on your yearly treks around Britain."

"We visited many families with foster sons." The stone floor chilled my feet and legs all the way to my belly. "One of them might have been your son."

Curyll? Though Carradoc's hair was dark, worn long with a thin plait decorated with blue beads behind each ear, and Curyll wore his fair hair cropped short in the Roman style, the two men were of similar size and build. I couldn't tell if their mouths and jaws were similar. Carradoc's thick beard, also trimmed in gray-blue beads the same color as his eyes, disguised much of his face. They both wielded heavy swords and lances as easily as toys. But Curyll looked to distant horizons with light blue-gray eyes that longed for a different future. Carradoc's deep, darker gray-blue eyes looked no farther than his own satisfaction.

Had I married the birth father of my beloved Curyll? Only my father knew for sure. The chill spread to my heart.

I hated the depth of The Merlin's manipulation of people and events to suit his purposes. I doubted Da paid attention to the will of the gods, or the will of the Ardh Rhi. The will of the people wouldn't touch his reasons for the games he played.

"I am too ill to participate in Beltane this year, Carradoc." I shuddered from cold within and without. "As soon as the Queen of the May has given her virginity to the gods, I must retire."

"You'll stay and please me in all ways, *Wife*. You promised obedience. The circle of the Roman marriage ring on your finger binds you to that promise.

Ka-Thump-thm. Ka-Thump-thm-thm. The drums echoed my heartbeat. Faster and faster the drums called the villagers, nobles, and warriors to the Beltane revelries. Higher and higher the bonfires leaped and danced in imitation of Belenos. Three naked youths jumped and defied the growing flames. Only three young athletes remained out of fifteen who had begun the day with games of football and wrestling.

Ale and sacred mead flowed freely among those in the community who had not gone to war behind Carradoc's banner. The two stags rampant butting heads in battle on the flag flying above the ramparts should have been a stag in rut with a dozen does.

As naked as the rest of my companions, I joined the serpentine dance around the twin bonfires on either side of the central standing stone and the five maidens awaiting the outcome of the athletic contest.

Ka-Thump. Ka-Thump. Ka-Thump. The drums added intensity to the dance with each log added to the fire and each cup of mead swallowed.

I broke free of the dance as we passed the stone for the third time. No Druids remained in our vicinity. Few remained in all of Britain. The ritual of cutting the sigil of fertility into the living soil fell to me, a recently initiated priestess who carried new life within her womb. I should have been honored and joyful at the powerful omen of my role and my pregnancy.

But Carradoc's perversion of the ritual joining of Dana and Belenos, female and male, mother and father, left me empty. Any of the four maidens who waited with Marnia would make a better Queen of the May. They were all healthier and stronger than my stepdaughter. If Marnia conceived a child tonight, I doubted her extremely narrow hips would allow her to carry the child to term. A malformed or stillborn Beltane child portended famine and plague next year.

With that thought in mind, I paid closer attention to the symbols I cut into the earth around the stone with my athame. Male, female, birth, and death enclosed within infinity, enclosed with a circle. I cut birth deeper and bigger than the other marks, praying for the fertility of the fields and the Queen of the May. Death's symbol barely broke the surface of the soil.

They should all have been equal, part of a balanced life pattern. Did my manipulation of the sigils equal my father's manipulation of people and events? Perhaps. But I had to balance my husband's distortions of the ritual.

The bonfire flared, close enough to warm my bare back and thighs. Its brightness stained my sigils red. Though shallow, Death seemed to bleed.

I clutched my arms across my belly, feeling the cold hand of the Netherworld.

The encouraging shouts around the closest bonfire turned into a wild chant. I stood to watch the young men leap the roaring flames.

Carradoc raced toward the burning logs of last year's Yule decorations. Firelight turned his bronze torc blood red. Every household had contributed branches of greenery that had resided inside their homes for a full cycle of seasons. The larger the village, the higher the bonfire. Carradoc's lands had resisted plague and invasion this past year. That made this village more prosperous and larger than most. Only a man of extraordinary strength and courage could jump over the fire.

As lord of these people and a proven warrior he had every right to join the competition. Carradoc had not been among the football players, wrestlers, and stone hurlers earlier today—nearly all of them torcless peasants since the warband had gone ahead to the battlefront. I had expected Carradoc to leave the competition to younger men now that we were married.

My husband had the strength of body to compete. I had no doubt he could clear the flames untouched. But why? He was no longer a bachelor, no longer young. And this year's Queen of the May, the woman destined to receive the seed of the man who leaped the highest and farthest, was his own daughter.

The chant turned into a roar. Carradoc's well-muscled legs pumped hard. He swung his arms and breathed deeply.

One moment he was on the ground, speeding forward, the next he soared through the air, well clear of the climbing bonfire.

Marnia lost all color in her face. She reached for her crown of flowers, her only clothing on this night. Nimuë forcibly restrained her from casting away the symbol of her status.

A tight knot formed in my belly. How could my husband profane this most sacred of rituals?

Carradoc landed heavily in a bone-jarring tumble. He paused while he regained his balance. Then he stood, arms up in triumph as he approached the waiting virgins. He placed a loving arm around the waiting Queen of the May. She shrank away from him, unable to break his hold upon her.

I leaned against the standing stone, gasping for breath. The ancient granite held the lingering warmth of the sun, but chilled rapidly. As rapidly as I. No comfort in knowing how many rituals had been performed within its shadow. Many of them might very well have involved father and daughter. Many of them had included human sacrifice, too. I turned my back on the stone, on the bonfire, on the celebrants, and the sigils I had cut into the living Goddess. I could not sanction this Beltane.

A huge chanting roar signaled another man approaching the bonfire. I watched over my shoulder, praying this man, whoever he might be, surpassed my husband's feat of prowess. Light brown hair flying about the man's face helped me identify him. He had requested the right to join Carradoc's warband just last week. Llandoc by name. Son of a blacksmith. Carradoc had refused him. His heritage was not worthy of elevation to warrior, no matter his strength and skill. He'd never wear a torc.

If my husband had told Llandoc how essential his skills as a smith were to the entire army, and the village, the young man might have been content to remain a craftsman; might never have the angry courage to challenge Carradoc in this competition.

Right now, I encouraged him. He had to surpass his lord in this competition. He had to!

I had to help him. As a priestess, I wasn't supposed to interfere with the selection of tonight's champion. As a priestess, I had to prevent the celebration from falling into further perversion, even if it meant using my magic on others. Regretfully, I summoned the power within me that would help me control this situation—as my father would have.

Pridd, Awyr, Tanio, and Dwfy were present already. I had prepared myself for ritual at the beginning of the evening. Magic resonated throughout the land. Magic that was supposed to be used to invoke the Goddess and ensure fertility. Healthy fertility, not an abomination born of a father and daughter coupling.

The pattern of my life realigned a little. My purpose in life as a priestess was to insure the fertility of the land and the people. My gift of magic should be used to help that end.

I borrowed a little of the power singing through the land and reached into Llandoc's mind. Determination, courage, and anger fueled his straining body. *Don't think. Push more blood into your legs. Let the Goddess propel you. Don't think about it, just jump. Now!*

Praise Dana, he soared high, impossibly high. A trail of sparks flowed from his heels. The flames seemed to pause, perhaps recede. The crowd held their collective breaths.

Carradoc stood with his mouth hanging open. Terrible anger burned in his eyes.

Llandoc landed lightly, evenly, almost as if the Pridd rose up and cradled his descent.

I breathed a sigh of relief.

Marnia rushed forward, arms open to welcome her champion.

Nimuë laughed long and loud as she caressed her father's shoulder. She ran her fingers up and down his arm intimately, seductively.

Carradoc wrapped his arm around her naked body and pulled her into the shadows. Anger still boiled out of his aura. He beckoned the half dozen of his warriors who hadn't left for battle yet. One of them held rope.

My stepdaughter accompanied her father willingly. She glanced around her at the six extra men and smiled. As darkness enfolded them, she looked back over her shoulder and smiled triumphantly at me. *I don't need a husband, I have yours,* she said into my mind.

Carradoc did not return to my bed that night. I left the Beltane festival as soon as I saw Llandoc lift Marnia in his arms and carry her to the freshly cut sigils by the standing stone. She wrapped her arms around his neck in the closest thing to enthusiasm I had seen in the girl.

The cheers and songs of drunken revelry drifted through the unshuttered windows of Caer Tair Cigfran all night. Sleep would have eluded me even in silence. So I sat in a large chair beside the window, fully clothed, a blanket wrapped around me to ward off the chill of my thoughts as well as the night dampness.

A kitchen cat purred in my lap. I stroked her ordinary tabby fur, wishing she wore the orange-and-white coloring of Helwriaeth. This cat did not know her name and didn't care if she had one. Her rumbling contentment provided a counterpoint to the rhythm of merriment outside. A song tempted me to pick up my small harp. But music would have diverted my thoughts. I made do with a hum in the back of my throat, much like the cat's.

At my feet, Newynog, Carradoc's aging and heavily pregnant wolfhound bitch, dozed and snored. She had embraced me as her own the moment I had entered the environs of Caer Tair Cigfran. Previously she had acknowledged only Carradoc as senior to her in authority of the diverse pack of humans. Now she ignored him completely or fled his presence in fear. She had been trained as a war dog and only recently retired to breed more war dogs. Defense of Carradoc should have been her primary objective in life. Her shift in loyalty provided only one of many irritations in my dealing with my husband.

I did not light a fire or candle during my vigil. The flames would have drawn my eyes and induced visions. I didn't need pictures caught in fire to tell me whose arms welcomed my husband. Nor that he and his eldest daughter were familiar partners.

The Lord and the Land are one. This fortress of three ravens carried an appropriate name. The misfortune that followed the omen wrapped the inhabitants in perversion. Carradoc's incest with Nimuë would come back to him in stunted crops, sickly villagers, and crumbling wealth.

The ladies in Ygraina's bower openly discussed Nimuë's promiscuity. Yet no hint of Carradoc's participation entered the conversation. Had they both sought other partners this past winter, or had they been incredibly discreet?

Gossip hadn't connected Curyll with Morgaine either, and I knew they had spent many nights together. In fact I was surprised they hadn't married along with the other seven couples the day before we left the capital.

Life in Caer Tair Cigfran had to change. Carradoc would leave at dawn to join the army. He wouldn't be around to interfere with my life. He'd already entrusted me with the keys to every room in the caer, symbols of my authority to act in his stead.

The dark of the moon neared; a time for purging negativity from our souls and banishing curses. I had the tools—magical and mundane—to bring light and life back into balance here.

I'd begin as soon as he left. Alone if I had to. Some of the villagers might help.

As the bonfires dimmed to glowing embers and the sounds of Beltane faded to sleepy murmurs, I crept back to my bed, still fully clothed. Newynog and the cat joined me, sprawling over the wide mattress, completely filling it.

A few moments later, the door creaked open. Newynog growled a low warning. Cat's fur stood up as her ears twitched.

I stiffened, prepared to reject Carradoc.

"Wren?" Berminia whispered.

"Yes." I sat up hastily, more surprised than alarmed. I had to kick Newynog to make room for my legs to move.

"Can we talk?" Berminia moved into the chamber hesitantly.

I lit a small lamp beside the bed, needing to read her face and posture. I hadn't learned to fully trust my interpretation of the shimmering aura of energy I perceived around every living thing—even without light.

Berminia had donned her clothes as well. She hugged herself and looked at the floor. Her blonde braids hung limp and greasy over the plump shoulder. Her sadness and disappointment filled the room.

I sat up and reached out a tentative hand in mute comfort and empathy.

She lifted her head at my touch but didn't pull away from me. "Will you teach me how to be a priestess?" Determination firmed her jaw.

"Why?" I couldn't think of anything else to say. Possibilities and questions ran through my mind, each vying for dominance.

"I won't be humiliated again at Beltane. I want to go to Avalon where there are no men." Her voice choked but no trace of tears rose in her eyes.

"Avalon is empty now. You'd be totally alone. Besides, men used to go to Avalon for Beltane and other festivals. They climb the ritual labyrinth on the tor several times a year. Priestesses participate fully in Beltane." I stalled.

"But those men respect the priestesses!"

"Who treated you with less respect than they would offer Dana this night?" Every woman represented the Goddess, especially on Beltane.

"No one!" she replied defensively. "At least . . . Toutates the smith, Llandoc's father, joined with me tonight. He offered me marriage. Me, the daughter of the lord! As if I must settle for a mere smith."

"He is a respected craftsman, Berminia," I said. Her indignation wasn't as firm as her father's would be when he heard the offer. If Berminia bothered to tell him. "You are not yet past the age when no one will consider you for a bride. Nimuë is two years older."

"Hmf," she snorted. "You know as well as I that Nimuë isn't

interested in a husband unless he can give her power. She runs this caer like it was her own."

"But she is not your father's wife and never can be." I shuddered at renewed images of Carradoc caressing his daughter's breasts as intimately as he did mine.

"No. She delights in being his forbidden mistress! His plaything in perversion. It's the only way she can control him and make him give her what she wants."

The spoken words had more power to hurt than the mere thought. Everyone must know my humiliation at being married to a man who preferred incest with his beautiful daughter rather than a healthy relationship with his new wife. I'd never deluded myself that I could be as lovely as Nimuë. Tall and faery slim, she glided gracefully through life. My short legs and broadening hips stumped along with too much purpose and determination to be called lovely. But I had hoped . . . Never mind what I hoped. 'Twas time to deal with reality.

"Carradoc gave me the keys to Caer Tair Cigfran," I reminded her, and myself. "Your sister no longer has authority here. Perhaps now she will accept a husband."

"She won't give up her power without a fight. Carradoc is the first man of his line to inherit the caer. It has always passed to the husband of the eldest daughter. Nimuë wants to restore the ways of our grandmother. You need allies. Teach me to be a priestess. We can fight her together," Berminia pleaded.

"I am sorry for the passing of the old ways. But we live in a new era. The kings will enforce Carradoc's right to pass his land and his caer to his son," I said, while I thought frantically for a defense against Nimuë.

Berminia made sense. Part of me withdrew from sharing my knowledge with her. I sensed no magic in her. Nor did I see any dormant power in her aura. She might learn enough to participate in rituals, prepare herbal remedies, and pay proper homage to the gods, the role of an acolyte. But without the ability to manipulate the energies of nature to restore balances upset by humans, she'd never progress beyond the level of a follower. A priestess needed to be a leader.

Perhaps that would be enough for her. Perhaps not. Only time and discipline would reveal her full potential. In the meantime, I had an ally in the changes I must make to this gloomy caer. Together we would restore the pattern of life around here, and in the process perhaps we would restore the balance within Berminia to improve her health and self-confidence.

"I will teach you what I can, Berminia." I stood up and embraced her with a kiss of peace upon her cheek. To my surprise, I tasted salty tears on her face.

"Thank you," she whispered. "When can we start?"

"Tomorrow. After your father leaves for the battlefront."

Newynog thumped her massive tail against the mattress in agreement with me.

"Before Nimuë wakes up and interferes." Berminia giggled. "She'll sleep until noon. She always does after Beltane."

"Wren?" Marnia asked from the still open doorway. "Can we talk?" She didn't sound quite as forlorn as her sister had, but a note of urgency shadowed her request.

I opened my arms to include her in the embrace I shared with Berminia. She came to us in a rush with hugs for both of us.

"Thank you for whatever you did to help Llandoc win. I couldn't have stood it if Papa had been . . . you know." She gulped and bit her lip. She ran her hands through her unbound hair. Sprigs of flowers floated free of the tangles. She had discarded her crown of flowers. A warm shift covered her from neck to toe.

"What makes you think I did anything to help?" If Marnia had sensed the extra "push" I gave her champion, then perhaps she had magic within her. Another ally or potential rival?

"I don't know." She tangled her fingers in her hair again and shrugged. "I just knew you were the only one brave enough to defy Papa. You and Llandoc. But you know this means he can't stay. He'll have to leave before Papa remembers to be angry with him—and me."

"And when will that be?"

"That depends on how much Nimuë lets him hurt her," both girls replied.

My insides threatened to freeze.

"Marnia, will you join us in the morning? Berminia has asked for me to teach her to be a priestess."

"Yes! I'd really like that—even if I don't have any magic." Marnia smiled. For the first time I saw the potential beauty beneath her sallow skin and too thin body. "And Nimuë will be green with envy. She wants to be a priestess, too, but only for the power and magic. Not that she'd work for it. She wants everything given to her."

They told me how their older sister had botched the attempt to break the benevolent wards I'd set around the first rampart. Their story ended in a rash of giggles that didn't quite mask the horror they truly felt.

"I promise you, I do not sacrifice innocents in my magic," I reassured them. "We must rest now. In the morning we will bathe and break our fast. Then we'll begin with some simple herbs. Violets and cedar to start. Betony, I think, and burdock. Hyssop if we can find some." All of those plants cleansed and purified. I had the help I needed to cleanse this fortress.

"Can we stay with you? I don't want to sleep alone." Marnia looked longingly at the wide bed.

The bed I had shared with Carradoc.

I didn't like the idea of my husband returning and finding the three of us together—as if we waited for him.

On the other hand, we were all clothed, and all determined to refuse his attentions. Allies. Newynog and the cat filled any space left over in the bed. Carradoc couldn't defeat all of us. Just as the Saxons could not fight all of Britain united in a common defense.

Was I as strong a leader as Uther? Or would my allies desert me at the first sign of trouble?

Chapter 28

"REMEMBER to keep the gates closed," Carradoc barked as he strode toward his massive stallion. "Strangers are not welcome unless they bear a missive directly from me. These are unsettled times and you are vulnerable to attack and betrayal!" My husband glared at the assembly of retainers gathered around his horse. Dyn carried the weight of Carradoc's weapons easily. Three pack ponies carried his baggage. Five wolfhounds strained at the leads fixed to Dyn's saddle, eager to be on the way. They sensed they had work to do.

I walked behind my husband toward the waiting animals. The keys to the caer, symbols of my authority as lady of the manor and Carradoc's deputy in his absence, jangled on my belt with every step. I didn't reply to him. He nodded abruptly, accepting my silence as agreement with his orders.

Newynog paced at my heels, her massive head nearly touching my shoulder. She made no move to join the other dogs as leader of the pack, her customary place.

Carradoc glowered at the dog. "You're getting too old for battle I guess. Stay home and breed more healthy pups." He patted her head.

Newynog accepted the greeting but didn't lean into it, begging for more, as she did with me. When my husband transferred his hand from the dog's head to my shoulder, Newynog rumbled a warning from the back of her throat.

Carradoc jerked his hand away with a growl very similar to the dog's. "A disloyal hound is a worse enemy than the Saxons." He jerked his knee as if to kick her. The dog's bared teeth made him reconsider. "Keep her close, Wren. You and my son will need her protection. The kings and lords have a pact not to attack each other while serving the Ardh Rhi. But these are troubled times. No one honors their promises anymore."

He turned his attention back to his departure.

His three daughters awaited him on the bottom step of the central dwelling, one step above the gathered retainers. Berminia and Marnia kept their eyes on the ground and their hands neatly folded in front of them. Only Nimuë met his gaze, bold and confident.

I had seen rope burns on her wrists and sensed a few painful bruises on her body—she didn't walk smoothly this bright spring morning. So far, she had been silent, yawning frequently. Her eyelids drooped and a deep frown marred her expression. Carradoc had roused her early to witness his leave-taking.

"Guard my son well, Wren. I'll be back by Samhain, in time to witness my son's birth at the Solstice and acknowledge him my heir," Carradoc said tersely. He reached to gather me in a tight embrace. I stepped back one pace, firmly beyond his reach—lest he wanted to be seen chasing me. Newynog angled her body between us.

He glowered at me, his dark eyebrows marching together to form one long ridge above his face. I stared back at him evenly. Then he turned his heel and strode to his waiting daughters. He kissed and embraced each of them. Nimuë received a longer hug than her sisters and a pat on her rump, but her kiss on the cheek was no more affectionate or intimate than her sisters'.

My husband barked a few orders to the retainers and warriors who accompanied him, mounted his anxious horse, and rode out the gate. The dogs gamboled eagerly at his heels. The ravens croaked a farewell. I didn't.

I heard a collective sigh of relief from one and all. Even the walls and earthwork of the fortress seemed more relaxed without him. My imagination made the rising sun brighter and warmer.

After the emotional stress of Beltane, Carradoc's leave-taking was unremarkable.

His absence infused me with energy. "Come, Berminia, Marnia. We have much to do. Do you have baskets for the plants we must gather? Diones," I addressed the steward, "the simnais smoke, they are full of birds' nests. Please sweep them clean while I'm collecting medicinal herbs."

The steward looked to Nimuë with questions in his eyes. All of the servants and retainers seemed to hold their breath.

"I do not find the simnais or the birds offensive," Nimuë replied, raising one eyebrow as if questioning my sanity. "I do not order them cleaned. Sweeping the ravens' nests clear will drive the patron birds of Caer Tair Cigfran away."

Precisely, I thought.

"You are no longer lady of this household, Daughter." I lifted my chin and looked over the top of her head. Standing two steps above her, I had the slight advantage of height, an illusion I intended to keep. "Your father entrusted the keys to me."

"You have no right to them!" She clutched her skirt tightly, crumpling the fabric in her fist. Her face and voice remained calm and beautiful. "I am eldest. I have always ruled here in my father's absence. You are but newly come." She mounted the steps to stand level with me and very close. Newynog cowered behind me.

If I looked Nimuë in the eye, I'd have to twist my neck to stare up. Instead, I focused on a point just over her left shoulder, seeking to probe her emotions by reading the energy layers around her. A strange shadow faded in and out of my perception. Nothing else leaked out from her tight control. That ability coincided with magical talent. I'd known for a long time she held the potential. Berminia and Marnia had told me she wanted magical power but wasn't willing to work for it.

I had only words to influence people. I reserved my magic for healing people and the land—and cleaning up the messes left by others who were careless with the lives they meddled with.

"I am your father's wife. I carry his heir. That is something you will never be allowed to do."

She reared back as if I had slapped her.

Quietly I said for her ears alone, "Even if you conceived a child by your father, as a priestess of Dana, I could not allow you to carry it to full term. Never forget I know how to keep such an abomination from being born. Some remedies are safe for the mother, some are not."

For the sake of the land and the people, I could not allow her perversions to continue.

Without further words, I stalked into the central hall of the fortress. Berminia and Marnia followed. They almost skipped in delight. When we neared the passageway to the kitchen, they broke out in giggles.

"Did you see her face?" Marnia smothered her laughter with a hand in front of her mouth.

Berminia nodded, mirth threatening to burst from between her clenched teeth.

Abruptly they straightened and stifled their giggles.

Nimuë appeared in the main doorway. She cast a long and ominous shadow. "Beware, Arylwren. I am not some insignificant child to be trifled with!" she declared to one and all within listening distance.

I sensed magical persuasion in her tones. They did not affect me. Several of the servants cringed away from her.

"Perhaps not. How would you proceed with a thorough spring cleaning? I thought every household in the land swept the last remnants of winter from their houses and their hearts on the day after Beltane."

Nimuë gaped a moment too long.

I took advantage of her silence and turned to Hannah, Diones' wife and cook for the fortress. "Let's renew the rushes on the floor of the Hall. I'm sure some of the children have energy to burn. Set them to sweeping and gathering."

"Yes, Mistress." Hannah dipped a curtsy. But she kept her eyes on Nimuë.

With only the briefest pause, I issued orders for scrubbing the fortress from top to bottom while my allies and I gathered the ingredients to purge this place of imbalance.

"We'll all feel better with fresh bedding and less dust clogging our noses. Surely you can't object to that, Nimuë." I smiled brightly to one and all. Then I left before anyone could protest.

The ravens would be the first unhealthy elements to go. But how could I rid the place of Nimuë, a greater source of disruption?

I dismissed Berminia and Marnia early. They tired of the game of seeking out shy plants and carefully plucking them only after offering prayers to the plant and the Goddess for the gift. Their shoes gave them blisters. The hardened soles of my feet welcomed the touch of the Pridd—dirt, stone, grass, and twigs. Newynog offered me quiet companionship more nourishing than the chatter of my stepdaughters—more like my sisters in age.

I hadn't explored here as much as I liked. Carradoc had forbidden me to venture far unescorted. At last I had the freedom and solitude I craved.

Alone with the forest and the dog, I sought one of the many boulders and sat quietly. Newynog plopped at my feet, tongue lolling, nose working, and ears slightly perked.

Gradually the forest returned to the normal activity that our intrusion had disrupted. Birds sang, small animals rustled in the thick underbrush. The breeze caressed my cheek and danced through the upper branches.

I listened. No news drifted to me where the wind played with the treetops. Just the muted conversation of LIFE getting on with the business of life.

Newynog dozed at my feet. Her sides bulged with the pups she carried.

My breathing slowed. My heartbeat quieted. I reached out with my senses and absorbed the timelessness of the land. My mind merged with soil and rock and green and wildlife. The sap rising in the trees was my lifeblood. The subtle shift of the earth was my heartbeat. The wind became my lungs, moving air to all of the places it needed to be.

An awareness of the land crept into me. Without seeing how or why, I knew the contours of the rocky ridgeline that stretched from a nearby forested hill, jutting a raised finger between the tor and the village. The broken upthrust of land kept the trees far apart. Ferns and moss and berry vines filled in the blank places. Tree roots couldn't sink deep enough into the rock soil on many of the steep slopes of the ridge. Sunlight penetrated the shadows beneath the tree branches. Many springs found openings in the steep rise and fall of the crags and ravines. Water centered, pooled. . . .

Suddenly, I knew why I had smelled damp and seen faeries where the road intruded upon the spreading forest. A deep pool lay at the base of a tumble of boulders, fed by a small cascade above and several seeps below. A faery spring.

I hopped off my perch and set my feet on the path to a rendezvous with my friends, the faeries.

They rose from the water, from the brush, from the sun-warmed rocks in a cloud of joyous greeting. They flitted in and out of the sprays of water tumbling down the hillside. They danced upon fern fronds and tickled Newynog's ears. She snapped at them and received a tweak on her tail in reply. She nipped at her tormentors again and then decided they were not worth her dignity to shake away.

I sought a dark green male among the rainbow of beings. They were so tiny, individual features blurred. Five, six—no, eight different shades of green. Half male, half female. At last Cedar settled on my outstretched palm, giggling at the fine game he and his companions played.

Welcome home! he shouted into my mind with glee.

"Thank you," I replied. My heart lifted. This place was indeed home even if I lived in a dark fortress atop a hill in the near distance. I knew that if the trees did not block my way, the walls of Caer Tair Cigfran would be visible from here. The creek that drained the wide pool flowed around the tor, beside the village and then wound its way downhill to join a small river to the northeast of us.

"This place is splendid. Is the water safe for swimming and bathing?" I looked across the pool, sensing great depth.

The shallows only, Cedar replied. His tone indicated that *another* inhabited the depths. One who valued her privacy but held no animosity toward faeries and those whom the faeries named friend. *She guards a treasure that only the Chosen one can retrieve. You may refresh yourself, but do not intrude.*

I drank deeply of the clear water. "Thank you, Lady, for the gift of water."

No formal reply, just a sense that the lady relaxed her guard.

My life's pattern began to shift into place, the place I had been seeking for a long time. I belonged here, now and forever.

Newynog and I settled on a rock shaped perfectly to received my bottom. I dangled my feet in the water and listened to the gossip related by the faeries. A great gathering of men bearing lethal iron to the north and east. Many ships pushing through erratic storms to reach the coast of this island. Great upsets within the balance of power.

Dun Edin, I thought. *The battle rages near Dun Edin.*

"And my friend, Curyll?" I asked out of long habit. I worried that Morgaine might yet find a way to marry him and bind him with her demon-based magic.

He thrives. But anger makes him reckless. The water at my feet showed me an image of my beloved friend riding into the heart of a battle upon a tall black horse, sword flashing swiftly, indiscriminately.

Far behind him, Cai, Bedewyr, and Lancelot raced to catch up to him, protect him. Others I did not know strove to protect the rear. Curyll howled with rage. He ignored a Saxon ax as it sliced at his leg. He swatted the offending attacker away with the edge of his blade as if the man had been an insect. Now he was food for insects.

I shuddered at the carnage the vision showed me. I had no way of knowing if the scene took place now, a few days ago, or sometime in the future.

For once the faeries did not laugh.

"Who has driven him to this terrible rage?"

Himself.

"How can that be?" A tiny part of me hoped that he realized the mistake we had all made in allowing my marriage to Carradoc to take place.

The faeries laughed at this notion.

I sank into a brooding silence, wondering if I dared light a fire and seek more information from the Goddess in a vision.

The faeries silenced and fled. The birds grew quiet. All the tiny rustlings of the forest stilled. *Danger,* the wind sighed and fled as well.

I looked around, carefully, slowly, so as not to alert a predator with my movement. Newynog rose to her feet in one long fluid motion. Deep thunder grumbled in the back of her throat. Her tail stood straight out behind her. She lowered her head and bared her teeth.

"What?" I whispered.

The scent of a dog rose strongly around me. Not Newynog. The smell was different, more feral, and hungrier.

Then I saw them. Five wolves stalked a scent, keeping low, almost on their bellies beneath the ferns and underbrush. Hungry saliva dripped from their long teeth. Red gleamed in their eyes.

Alone, no single wolf was a match for Newynog. Hunting together, they would make my dog and me—both slowed by pregnancy—easy prey.

Chapter 29

MY brain worked furiously. I edged my hand toward a fallen branch. Sturdy oak. A club.

The wolves inched forward.

This way! Cedar flitted past my ear. His voice in my mind broke the unnatural quiet of the forest.

Keeping one eye on the wolves and one on the darting green figure, I saw my friend fly between two man-high boulders. I hadn't investigated there because of the tall bushes in front.

Trust us, all of the faeries commanded.

"Come, Newynog. Slowly." I eased off my seat.

The wolves snarled and moved closer. Newynog's neck fur bristled. She showed her teeth and returned the challenge.

The alpha wolf rose up, bunching his haunches beneath him. I lit the end of my club with fire from my mind and waved it before the wolf's face.

He backed off, snarling.

And then I saw the scars on his neck and flank. Every member of the pack bore some injury. Rejects from healthy packs, they had formed a new grouping, seeking prey wherever they could find it. Humans and domesticated animals with few defenses.

Keeping my makeshift torch between me and the wolves, I touched the first boulder. Cool granite, smooth to the touch.

The alpha wolf risked my fire again. I poked it at him and pressed my back against the tall stone. Newynog kept close at my side. We slid behind a sharp-twigged bush that exploded with new leaves. The sweet scent of the bush contrasted sharply with the acrid tones of hunger, aggression, and fear that filled the clearing.

Quickly. This way, Cedar repeated his summons.

I wedged myself between the two boulders where Cedar had disappeared. The bush pulled at my clothes, tangled in my hair, tried to keep me prisoner against the rock. I ignored the scratches on my skin and the tears in my clothing.

Newynog whined in distress, not certain either of us would be safe.

Sensing our entrapment, the wolves pressed closer.

I pushed deeper into the crevice. Cool air brushed my back. Startled, I nearly fell when my next step took me into open space.

A cave!

"Quickly, Newynog. Come!"

The moment the dog was fully into the cave, I laid my torch across the opening. It blazed in the face of the wolf leader. He leaped back, yelping. The other wolves replied with similar cries of pain.

Newynog and I fled deeper into the cave.

Cedar flitted ahead of us, an eldritch glow surrounding him, lighting our way.

I sensed openings into side caves. Water dripped.

Not there. You must not enter there, Cedar said as I paused before a tall archway. White marble glowed from its own luminescence within. Rainbows arced from the ceiling as Cedar's glow danced past.

"What is in there?" I peered deeper into the vast opening. Tall spires of white extended upward from the floor and pushed down from the ceiling. Some met to become vast pillars. The ceiling seemed to shift and shimmer with the reflections of a myriad of crystals.

Secrets, Cedar replied. *Only the Chosen may reveal them.*

"The 'Chosen'?" That was the second reference Cedar had made to this unknown entity.

The one the Lady chooses to receive the treasure. The one who will save this land.

I took one step into the cave of marvels. I caught a brief glimpse of a long slab of marble positioned like an altar. Atop it Dana's cauldron of life faded in and out of view, as if it tried to emerge from another world.

You are not the Chosen. You may not enter. This time the voice in my head was feminine, commanding, deeper-toned than any faery.

I stepped back, respecting the one who guarded the pool and the cave. Dana would reveal her purpose when she chose.

Follow me quickly or the wolves will pursue, Cedar renewed his commands.

I left the inner cave reluctantly. Newynog crept close to my heels, uncertain, possibly frightened. I clung to her neck fur to keep her close and safe.

The tunnel system of the cave darkened. Only Cedar's green glow bobbing ahead of me at eye height kept me from bumping into walls. We climbed upward. I think we curved to the right as well. The lack of visual landmarks distorted my sense of time and distance. I knew only the chill air, fatigue in my thighs as the path steepened, and the overwhelming smell of damp.

Flashes of false light burst before my eyes occasionally, but they illuminated nothing.

We stumbled sometimes. Mostly the path was smooth, as if cleared by human hands. Finally Cedar paused.

You may use this brand to guide yourself now. He hovered over a torch set into a wall bracket. The oil-soaked rags of the wick had nearly rotted clear of the shaft.

I lit the remnants eagerly, needing to restore my sense of self with the balance of my other senses. The moment fire touched the wick, Cedar disappeared in a snap, like a lantern shutter closing.

The fire blinded me for several moments. Bit by bit, my surroundings came into view. The cave ended in a circular room with too-smooth dirt walls. Stout wooden braces supported the low ceiling. On the far wall, a crude ladder had been cut into rock and soil. Strategically placed rocks in the wall provided the only handholds. Above them, a wooden trapdoor sealed the rough rock ceiling.

I laughed in relief. Cedar had brought me back to the fortress. The trapdoor undoubtedly led to the storage cellar beneath the kitchen hut.

Tension and uncertainty flowed out of me. I sank onto the bottom step, too tired to stand up anymore.

Newynog sat at my feet, pushing her huge head into my lap. I scratched her ears and buried my face in her neck fur. I found myself rhythmically combing the soft underfur free of the coarser guard hairs.

"Well, Newynog, what do we do now? Do we climb up and announce to everyone in the household that a secret escape route exists, or do we go back to the pool and come home the normal way?"

Newynog did not want to climb those steps. Neither did I. "Let's see if the wolves have given up, shall we?" The dog bounded ahead of me, eager to be out of the cave.

The sun set that evening in a glorious display of pink, purple, and blue. I lingered at the fringes of the forest, watching for the first stars to burst forth. Newynog leaned against me affectionately as I paused, her tongue lolling, eyes half closed.

Berminia and Marnia had carried baskets filled with fragrant flowers and greenery back to the fortress earlier. I kept the herbs of purification close by my side. I would be the one to prepare them, ignite them, and use their essence to cleanse my new home. My intimacy with every aspect of the spells would strengthen them.

The presence of the faeries as I harvested the herbs would have added an even greater blessing. But Cedar and his companions did not show themselves again after I safely left the cave.

The wolves had disappeared as well. Not even their scent lingered within the clearing around the pool.

Woodsmoke and the aroma of roast pork greeted my nose this close to home. Without Carradoc waiting for me, Caer Tair Cigfran truly felt like my home. More than Avalon, more than Lord Ector's villa. I hurried forward.

The wonder of my discovery of the pool and the cave still filled me with awe. Curiosity, too. Who was the "Chosen" and what secrets awaited him? I knew the Lady awaited a man. The treasure she guarded could only be borrowed from her by a man.

Was this the secret, sacred place Papa needed me to guard? I laughed a little. The "Lady" didn't need me to protect the pool and cave. She and the faeries had done a remarkable job of it so far.

Diones the steward opened the postern gate near the kitchens for me. He bit his lip anxiously as he scanned the open fields around the fortress for signs of approaching enemies.

I fought the urge to smile at his trepidation. We were too far west for Saxons. Too far inland for Irish pirates. The Picts and Gaels had other concerns north of the Wall at Dun Edin. My newly awakened magical senses would have warned me if other renegades and outlaws approached. Wolves couldn't climb the exterior walls.

"I see that the central simnai is drawing nicely now," I said, pointing to the column of smoke rising from the hearth in the hall.

"Yes, Lady. The men cleared it of soot and bird nests," he mumbled, keeping his eyes on the ground.

"Did something go wrong with the sweeping?" I asked sharply. His aura pulsed with the dark colors of fear.

"Yes, Lady," he whispered.

"What?"

"The ravens, Lady. They were not pleased that we disturbed their nests with new hatchlings." He still didn't look at me.

"I didn't expect them to be happy."

"Yes, Lady."

I tapped my foot, waiting for further explanation. He cleared his throat and shuffled his feet, clinging to the gate as if it would lend him inspiration or protection.

"You'd better tell me, Diones. What went wrong?"

"The stable lad, Peter, fell from the ladder, Lady. One of the birds flew right into his face and knocked him off."

"Is he hurt badly? Why didn't someone come for me?" I hurried into the kitchen. I hadn't known Peter well. But he seemed an intelligent lad, full of dreams and plans for his beloved horses. He and Ceffyl would have talked for hours on ways to improve the breeding stock.

Homesickness for my childhood friends, or my childhood, brought tears to my eyes. The sense of welcome I'd experienced at sight of the caer vanished. I couldn't dwell on my emotions now. I was the lady of the caer. I had serious concerns and responsibilities.

I fumbled for the key to the medicine chest as I opened the door to the stillroom. In my mind, I pictured the flask of boneset, the bundle of willow bark, betony, and other things I would need. My mind began the ritual for meditation in case I needed to work deeply within the lad to right injuries to his internal organs. If necessary, I could bring Marnia and possibly Hannah into the spell to complete the circle of maiden, matron, and crone. I'd have to guess at much of the detail of the ritual. . . . But Marnia was no longer a maiden. Who could I use?

"He's dead, Lady," Diones said softly behind me.

I stopped in the doorway. Intense sadness gripped my throat. My shoulders grew heavy. Waves of weariness flooded me.

"Did he suffer?"

"Only a little, Lady. He cried out and seemed in great pain. He thrashed wildly with a broken leg. Then Lady Nimuë knelt by his side and instantly he quieted. A moment later he passed on." Diones crossed himself in the Christian manner.

I almost wished for the peace the gesture seemed to give him. "May the gods protect and guide his passage," I whispered.

" 'Tis a terrible omen, Lady. The ravens have cursed us for disturbing them," Diones warned me.

"Does the rest of the household fear the ravens?"

"The Lady Nimuë told us we should. No one will sweep the rest of the simnais now for fear of them."

"Fear of the ravens, or fear of the Lady Nimuë?"

Diones refused to look me in the eye.

"Where is the lad?" I asked.

"In the cellar awaiting the funeral pyre at dawn." My heartbeat stuttered. If I had climbed the steps into this very cellar hours ago, would I have arrived home in time to save the boy?

I turned my steps to the adjacent door in the undercroft that gave access to the underground storage. Seven steps down I found a small oil lamp already burning. Three women hovered over the makeshift bier—Peter's sister, mother, and grandmother. A maiden, a mother, and a crone. The three stages of life. The fates who would guide his passage into his next life rather than help me work the great healing magic.

Each of the women made way for me as I approached.

Reverently, I touched Peter's brow, his lips, and his heart. Pain and surprise were fixed into his open eyes and bared teeth. His death had not been easy.

Quickly, I ran my hands down his body, seeking the source of death. Even opening my senses to any residual energies, I found nothing beyond some twisted muscles and one ankle bent out of alignment.

I returned my attention to his face. What had killed him? I couldn't tell without opening him up—a practice forbidden by the Christians but well known to me. I'd helped Da and The Morrigan do it many times.

Again, I touched his brow, lips, and heart. His head rolled slightly beneath my fingertips. I encircled his neck with both hands. The muscles had begun to freeze, but the bones were loose.

Peter had died of a broken neck. The injury should have killed him instantly after the fall, not several minutes later, after he had screamed and moved. A broken neck would have paralyzed him even if he lived a few moments.

But he had not died until after Nimuë had knelt at his side.

Chapter 30

NIMUË donned a new gown dyed willow green to match her eyes. Success rode her shoulders better than the yellow brocade stola she fished from her clothes chest. After a moment's consideration, she folded the stola and laid it atop Marnia's pile of clothing. She didn't need to cower behind the costumes and customs of Rome and the court now. The ravens had responded to her magic.

She'd learned a few things about snapping a neck after the debacle with the rabbit. This time she had used her magic to aid her in twisting Peter's neck swiftly and cleanly. He'd been dead before she removed her hands.

At the moment his life had passed out of his body, she had absorbed tremendous energy from him. She glowed within for hours afterward.

Carradoc no longer controlled her life. She just had to get rid of Wren and her unborn child. Then her life would be orderly, complete. She'd have true power.

Finally she could be herself. The proud granddaughter of a long line of women of power.

She dismissed the faint doubt in her mind that Gran would not be proud of the way she worked the magic. Gran had followed the same simpering plan of balance and harmony that Wren used. Nimuë refused to be limited by fears for anything but her own power. The demon in the back of her head agreed.

You have only interrupted her influence in our caer. Now you must destroy it, the demon whispered.

"How?" Nimuë brushed some nonexistent lint off her left shoulder. She found the demon coveted the gesture, almost as if she caressed it. She thought perhaps the demon was partially formed in this world, stuck halfway between here and the Netherworld. When she had more power, and more knowledge, she'd bring it forth, her servant and her ally.

This is the castle of three *ravens. Why only three?* The demon chuckled.

"Yes indeed, why only three?" Nimuë had an idea. "Attraction. I need a spell for enticement." Death cap mushrooms, walnut, and skullcap.

Another rabbit or, better, a cat, the demon reminded her.

"One of Wren's pets!" Nimuë giggled. "I'll blood it first before I kill it."

Do not forget to close the pentagram.

"I know," she replied petulantly. She'd probably get a blinding headache, but she'd do it the demon's way. It had been right about how to control the ravens. No more shortcuts.

Work the spell widdershins, away from the route of the sun. And hide the evidence.

"Power!" she exclaimed. "I love it." She danced a little jig on her way to Wren's herb closet where she knew she'd find all of the ingredients she needed. For this spell, stolen tools would be better than gathering them herself. Besides, stealing was a lot less work.

No one would hear a word against Nimuë. I had insufficient evidence to accuse her outright. And so I watched and waited, and grieved that she had managed to commit another outrage against the laws of man and the gods and get away with it. Most of all I grieved for Peter and the promises of his life that she had cut short to serve her own quest for power.

That spring the ravens multiplied. I burned my incense. I cast spells of banishment. I invoked the help of the faeries. Nothing moved the ominous black birds. Dozens flocked to roost in the thatch of cottages for miles around the fortress. More arrived daily to plague the farmers. They ate seed as fast as we planted. They tormented the goats and sheep until they ceased giving milk.

I feared we would have to slaughter all of the new lambs and kids to keep them from starving to death.

Even my wards at the caer would not hold against them.

Yet the people of Caer Tair Cigfran did nothing to disturb the horrible birds. They refused even to erect scarecrows in the fields. Many would not light a fire in their hearths lest they disturb a raven's nest in the smoke hole or simnai.

Everyone attached to my new home walked warily, head bowed, feet listless. No one smiled. New gauntness appeared in their faces and their eyes lost luster and joy.

Our winter stores grew thin. We had no new crops to replace them. The men didn't have the will or strength of spirit to hunt.

Children woke each morning screaming. They had dreamed of demons gnawing at their arms and legs.

Humid air pressed us down more heavily each day.

I feared for the health of the baby that grew daily within my womb even as I rejoiced in the twelve pups Newynog presented us. I wanted to sing with her to welcome the tiny, wet squirming morsels of furry life. No tune rose in my throat. I realized I hadn't sung since I had found the faery pool, since the day Peter died of a broken neck.

Only Nimuë thrived. She watched and waited for me to fail miserably as the Lady of the household. I might be a priestess, but I could not protect my people from the ravens.

Her sisters refused to accompany me on my rounds of the forest, preferring to sit silent and sullen with their needlework. Fear clouded their eyes and perfumed their skin with sour musk.

The faeries didn't venture closer to the caer than the pool. Humans could reach their haven only by a long and circuitous path. The trees ceased talking to me in the hot still air. We received no news from the battlefront for two months. I wished I had Da to talk to, no matter how angry he made me. He would have known how to correct the problems that beset me.

Loneliness and Newynog became my only companions. The heat and humidity weighed heavily on my shoulders and stupefied my mind.

I don't know why I hadn't confronted Nimuë with her murder of Peter the stable boy. Deep inside, I think I feared she would do the same to my unborn child and me. I had to rid Caer Tair Cigfran of both Nimuë and the ravens soon.

The morning before the Solstice dawned hot. A nearly full moon had set an hour before. Belenos seemed sullen and weak behind a haze of woodsmoke and humidity. The pattern of life had wandered off its usual path. I had to restore the balances today. Sun and moon and stars swung into the proper positions. The only opposition I faced was myself and my unwillingness to work magic against another person.

For the health of the land and the people, I had to do something.

The villagers had planned no festival for this day. I needed to make sure there was something to celebrate tomorrow. With luck we might be able to plant the fields and get a harvest before the winter storms.

Determined to end the ravens' reign of terror, I shoved Newynog and three cats off my bed so that I could arise and begin my work.

There should have been five cats. The other two must have gone off in search of a mouse or solitude to think their private cat thoughts.

At moonrise tonight, the forces of nature would be strongest, best aligned to assist me.

I threw on a few clothes. They clung to me as if wet. Nothing dried in the hot moist air. I felt as if I slogged through mud as I made my way to the nearest gate, a small postern by the kitchens. As I opened the portal, Belenos swelled fat and red on the horizon. I lifted my voice in song to greet him for the first time since Beltane.

My voice soared high and bright, firmed by resolve. Two moments ago, I hadn't felt this light of heart and comfortable of body. Music had been missing from my life and my soul. No more. I had already begun the business of restoring the balances.

One hundred ravens rose from their perches in a furious squawk. The beat of their wings sounded a thunderous counterpoint to my song. I smiled and wove my melody around the noise.

Nimuë greeted me in the Long Hall with a sour face and squinting eyes. She never rose before noon and rarely retired before midnight— usually closer to dawn. My song must have roused her.

I ignored her sullen looks and fairly danced to my place at the head of the table.

"How dare you disturb the birds?" she said, an angry scowl marring her beautiful face. Her sisters stood behind her, mute and staring meekly at the floor.

"You mean, how dare I disturb you and your unnatural routine," I replied. I tried raising one eyebrow as Da did. Nimuë didn't react to my expression, so I guess I failed to intimidate her with a look. I needed more practice.

"The birds will kill again if you disturb them," Nimuë warned me.

"They didn't kill the first time." I took my chair without further words. Diones scuttled up with a trencher of bread, cheese, and small ale. The bread was dry, the cheese hard, and the ale sour.

"If you can serve the lady of the household no better, then take to the road," I told him. This time I pushed a little venom into my voice. The steward backed up. His mouth hung slightly open. "Fetch me food fit to eat, Diones. Even if you have to defy my husband's daughter to do it."

"There is nothing else, Lady," he said, looking to Nimuë.

She nodded slightly. A small smile of approval touched the corners of her mouth.

"Nonsense, Diones. The food served last night was fine. We are not so starved yet as to go on short rations. Give this to the pigs and bring me fresh food."

"You order a sinful waste of resources during a summer of famine!" Nimuë announced loudly. Her voice was husky with accusation.

"You call it famine because you want it to be so. You'll have to work much harder to order the world to your will, Nimuë. I know how to do that. You don't. Beware what you wish for, you might get it."

"We'll see about that," Nimuë warned as she stalked out of the hall.

After a good meal, I packed more food into a basket, gathered up my favorite gray-and-white cat, and prodded Newynog away from the cool stones by the well. Her partially weaned pups would be fine without her for a day. Six ravens croaked at me from the rim of the well. They didn't fly off as I dipped the bucket into the water.

"Oh, hush, you obnoxious birds," I said, shooing them away. While I sipped from the dipper, two ravens flew to the low fence around the pigsty. Two flapped and sidled along the stonework, out of my reach. The remaining two stood their ground, cocking their heads to stare at me with black and beady eyes.

"Six of you, eh," I said back to them. "Does double three ravens cancel the bad omen of a single three?" The ravens shifted their heads back and forth in puzzlement. "Tell me this, birds, why do you stay where you aren't welcome?"

In asking the question I knew the answer. Someone welcomed them. Nimuë. Her invitation brought them. A lack of welcome elsewhere kept them here.

"If I find you a better home, will you leave?" I didn't need an answer from the birds. I needed to begin my spell so that it climaxed at the moment the sun set and the full moon rose. Timing and balance. Da had drilled those concepts into me every day of our lives together. I didn't seek to manipulate people or control them with this spell. I sought balance, as was my duty.

"Come," I called to the dog as I hoisted the cat to my shoulder.

My preparations were simple but exhausting. I couldn't fast with the baby growing so rapidly within me. So I had to sink deeper into a trance than I liked. Cat helped. She purred in rhythm with my soft song of adoration for the Goddess. Newynog kept watch over us. Her frequent prowls around the pool and into the cave didn't disturb my meditations. Nor did I notice how often she drank from the creek on this hot day.

Sweat poured from my face and between my breasts as I sat by the spring that burbled from a tumble of old boulders. A constant flow even in this hot weather. We hadn't had rain in nearly a month. The heat made me dizzy. I sang long into the afternoon as I gathered plants and woods to burn within a ring of black rocks. I sang as I placed each rock in the ring, dipping it first in the spring.

With each note, each step of my preparations, I missed my Da. He had taught me the how and why. He showed me how to look deep within myself for the source of magic. And he had first introduced me to the joy of the simple moment of truth when Pridd, Awyr, Tanio, and Dwfr united within me to release my spirit.

As the shadows lengthened, I set the last twig of kindling within the fire ring. I looked to the orderly bundles of herbs and woods. A shining aura outlined each. Purple, blue, yellow, and green. Individual now. Later they would blaze hot white as fire transformed them within my spell.

Belenos hung heavily in the leaden sky. I had time to rest and restore myself. Newynog and the cat would wake me in time. I curled up in the cave mouth, letting cool shadows refresh me and the soothing sound of water running free lull me to sleep.

I dreamed of Da.

"Wren, save me. Only you can save me," he called, reaching for my hand. Some terrible force I didn't understand trapped him and kept me from reaching him.

I ran in circles and spirals through a maze of stone-faced warriors. I couldn't find my beloved Da. Mists clouded my vision. Bright tongues of flame drew him deeper and deeper into the heart of the maze where the Worldtree rose up, towering above the walls.

I ran faster. Da reached out a skeletal hand. I lunged to clasp it. His bones turned to dust beneath my fingers as the Worldtree swallowed him. Cernunnos laughed at us both from the first bough. His horned headdress forked and branched until it was indistinguishable from the branches of the Tree. Each place where a tree limb split and narrowed represented a choice. Each choice a new direction, a new fate.

Da lingered, undying within the Worldtree, trapped by his choices.

Or had my chosen paths driven him into the Tree? I beat on the Worldtree, begging for answers, another chance, and one last glimpse of my beloved Da.

Newynog growled. Cat dug her claws into my ankle.

I woke with a start, beating my fists against the ground. My heart pounded with fear. Tears of grief streamed down my face.

Dreams of such strength and clarity portended events to come. Somehow, the spell I was about to invoke would set me on a life path that doomed my father.

How? Why? None of it made sense. My spell was intended to restore the balance here in the North. All I wanted was to send the ravens elsewhere. How could that affect my father? He was off with Uther's army in some distant part of Britain.

A quick splash of cool water on my face banished much of the lingering fear from the dream. I flipped my unbound hair away from my face and bent over the little pool at the base of the spring as I dipped my hands once more. A finger's length from the water, I halted. My reflection looked back at me. My image and yet— something was different. I expected changes from the last time I had paused over a still pool. Marriage and pregnancy do that to women, even after only a few months.

A scar seemed to glow on my left temple. Sharp rays of the setting sun highlighted the raised skin with a red-gold so bright it seemed on fire. Gingerly, I traced the small blemish, not much bigger around than my thumbnail.

A pentagram enclosed within a circle with an angled plant stem lying across the whole.

The sigil for the druidsbane; the herb that had poisoned Uther Pendragon. Memory of the true events of that night in Venta Belgarum slashed across my mind. A cancerous demon didn't eat away at Uther's innards. Poison did. I had prepared the antidote to the secret plant that only priests of Cernunnos knew.

My father had rid me of the forbidden knowledge by magically cutting it out and leaving this scar. Only now, when magic hummed within me, ready to spring forth, was the scar even visible.

Anger against The Merlin boiled within me. He didn't trust me to keep faith with him and the Goddess. He had married me off to Carradoc, knowing my husband's perversions, just to get rid of me. He had left me with no memory of that day and little desire to ever look in a mirror again.

Why didn't he trust me? I was a priestess, fully trained in many Druid secrets. Certainly he could have talked to me, pledged me to silence.

Remnants of my dream stabbed at me. My father. The man who had raised me when logic dictated he foster me to The Morrigan. The man who had been all things to me.

I loved him as I loved no one else in this world. Not even my love for Curyll matched the bonds shared by Da and me.

He didn't trust me. Had never trusted me. I wasn't as important to him as his plans to control all of Britain through his magic and his manipulations.

I was a priestess, duty bound to maintain the balances of life. A great imbalance existed here and now that had to be rectified.

Resolutely, I plunged my hands into the pool, banishing the image of the ugly scar on my temple. If my spell to banish the ravens also banished my father to the undeath of entrapment within the World-tree, so be it.

Chapter 31

MY spell had two parts. First I must banish the attraction for the ravens from the environs of Caer Tair Cigfran. Second and hardest, I must find a new place for the birds to go.

I dropped the first bundle of herbs upon the flames, singing a thanksgiving to them and inviting them to join and enhance the power within me. The smoke climbed through the air in a lazy spiral. I let my mind drift upward on the same pattern. Another song inviting the Goddess to bless the spell followed the smoke. Belenos glinted bright red against the sparks within. Not much time. I had to finish at the moment of the sun's setting and the moon's beginning.

The smoke spread outward, reaching for the caer, village, and fields. My song drifted with it, seeking out hidden corners and dark places. When I sensed that I had permeated the entire area with the seeking, I added a second bundle of mixed plants—dried and newly harvested. Cleansing followed the seeking. With each breath I sent the combined smokes into every nook and cranny, banishing previous spells with fresh air and bright hope.

Resistance rose up to meet me. Nimuë!

She had grown stronger, more complete.

Her will pushed me back into myself. I wanted to draw back into my quiet fire, letting the smoke dissipate before it finished its work.

But a spell left unfinished and ungrounded would backlash with threefold consequences. I had to persevere.

Go back. Go back to the arms of your father, Nimuë's counterspell whispered into my mind. *No one else wants you. No one else can love you.*

"Never!" I shouted aloud. "I'll never return to The Merlin as his daughter. Not after what he did to me." He didn't trust me. He didn't trust anyone but himself. Since he couldn't trust, he had to control and manipulate.

So did Nimuë. I had to balance her quest for power.

Where had she learned so much about magic since her last pitiful attempt to counteract my wards?

A third bundle of herbs intensified the smoke. I willed this last portion of the spell to overcome my rival's resistance and my own. Deeper I pushed the purifying smoke, singing of cleanliness and health and freedom from the weight of fear. Harder I pushed against her spell.

I pushed until I thought my mind would explode. I kept pushing even after my body rebelled with trembling limbs and terrible hunger. I enfolded Newynog and Cat within my arms. They couldn't help me, but I found comfort in their presence.

Then I pushed one more time, a tremendous effort as if birthing a child.

Thunder rolled, lightning flashed. The stupefying humidity gave way to drenching rain. Nimuë's spell washed away along with the last lingering daylight.

The ravens had nothing left to keep them at Caer Tair Cigfran. Now all I needed was a place to send them. A place they could call home forever.

I sent them to the largest concentration of Saxons. Let the birds ruin their homesteads.

The Merlin stood beside Uther's litter on a rise above the battlefield. Dun Edin rose behind them, forbidding with its steep cliffs broken by jagged ravines. A good, defensible position. No enemy could circle around behind them.

The enemy didn't need to. They outnumbered Uther's exhausted forces three to one.

Uther tried to sit up and peer out at the disarray of his troops. He managed to brace himself on one elbow before collapsing.

"Send the cavalry," he croaked. "We have to break through to their leader and capture their standard. It's the only way. We have to kill the leaders." The Ardh Rhi closed his eyes, exhausted from his few words.

Merlin spotted the standard on a knoll across the field and slightly to the left of his position. Then he searched out the Pendragon banner. The red dragon rampant on the field of yellow stood out in the carnage that littered the field.

Arthur, no longer mounted on the vicious black horse, defended the banner. Blood streaked his face and mail. His helmet was dented. He swung his sword with less enthusiasm than he had at the beginning of the day.

Two of the men beside Arthur fell to enemy axes. Arthur's right side—his weak side—lay exposed.

Three Saxons spotted the vulnerability at the same moment. They roared in unison and sprang forward.

"Not Arthur. I won't let you kill my boy!" Merlin screamed. He needed help. What magic could he conjure to stop the attack?

Lightning shot from his hands. The upheld ax of one enemy caught the bolt, exploding in shards of wood and iron and flame. The man dropped to his knees, screaming as he watched his hand become a torch.

None of his comrades rushed to help him. They stepped over him to aim their own weapons at Arthur's battered shield.

Weakness assailed Merlin. He had nothing left—no strength, no will, no magic—to defend his boy or his land.

He bent over, clasping his knees and breathing hard. Darkness encroached upon his vision.

Had all his hard work, his manipulation and planning come to this? Defeat at the hands of the Saxons on the eve of bringing all of the pieces of Arthur's life pattern into place!

"Ah, Wren, I would give my life to hold you in my arms one more time."

What? What could he do? He must do something. He couldn't fail now.

He stood up again. Dizziness rang in his ears. He fought to retain his balance and his consciousness. All day he'd sent spell after spell into the fray. All day the Saxons had poured more and more men into the battle. They were out of reinforcements. But he was out of strength and ideas.

"I won't let those bastards kill you, Arthur!" Merlin grabbed the reins of a white stallion from one of Uther's aides. He mounted in one easy motion and kicked the beast into a gallop.

"If nothing else, I'll drag you off the field before they get you, Arthur."

Halfway across the battlefield the darkness gathered closer around his vision.

He fought to stay conscious.

The darkness intensified. A great roar, as if the ocean tide rushed toward him from the North, came with the roiling cloud.

Cloud? The day had dawned bright, clear, and hot, and stayed that way. If a storm approached, perhaps he could use it. He gathered every last bit of his resources, ready to throw his last great spell where it would do the most work. He sniffed for traces of rain as he whipped the horse to greater speed with the ends of the reins.

His senses remained clear of any trace of coming storm. Then he looked closer at the dark cloud roaring ever closer.

Birds! A massive swarm of black birds fled something perilous with speed and determination.

"Thank Dana! I don't know who sent you or where you are going, but for now you will descend upon my enemies!" he shouted. He stood up in the stirrups and raised his hands for one last spell.

Before he could do more than breathe deeply, the birds tucked their wings and dove. As if propelled by one mind they sought the Saxons. Ten of them landed on each of the two men beleaguering Arthur. Five more flapped their wings in the faces of the war leaders, pecking eyes, digging talons into any exposed skin on hands, arms, legs.

Hardened warriors dropped their weapons and beat at the plague of birds. One by one they fled the field and the birds.

The massive flock of ravens followed without pausing to peck at the free meal of carrion on the field.

Arthur cheered, raising his sword and the Pendragon banner high. Weary Britons rallied to him, picking up his cry of exultation and repeating it until it swelled and filled the air with life and arial. The standard of Uther Pendragon fluttered in the wind that followed the ravens. Arthur clasped it firmly.

Merlin made his way back to Ardh Rhi Uther. A weary smile caressed his face as he dismounted.

"What?" Uther asked sharply. A measure of vitality returned to him.

"Your son has won the day."

"My son and your magic. You will make a fine team, old friend." Uther paused to breathe heavily. "Take me back to camp. I will meet Arthur and name him my heir before the sun sets."

"Yes, old friend. The time has come. Our boy is now a man. A well-respected warrior." Pride invigorated Merlin. "Well done, Arthur. Well done."

"You must summon Archbishop Dyfrig to bless the naming of my heir."

Merlin stopped cold. "Why Dyfrig?" He pushed the question through clenched jaws. "Is not my blessing sufficient? I raised the boy, after all."

"Precisely why Dyfrig must bless the boy. You had the raising of him. You are prejudiced. You must stand beside the archbishop. The kings and lords *must* see you stand together in this."

"If the archbishop agrees."

Then he heard the victory chant on the field below him.

"Merlin, Mer-lin. All hail The Merlin."

"But I didn't do it—" he started to protest. Then he smiled. If the army hailed him as their savior when the battle was nearly lost, then Dyfrig would have to accept his presence at the blessing. And the crowning.

"No one will believe you didn't conjure those blessed birds, old friend. Take the glory while you can." Uther fell back amongst his cushions again. "All glory is fleeting. Take what you can while you can. Time and God will steal it from you just when you start believing in it."

"She's gone!" Berminia cried loudly. Fat tears ran down her plump face.

I watched the drops of water catch on a pimple, split, and make new tracks. My mind and body were too cold, wet, and exhausted to comprehend the source of her distress. I clung to Newynog's neck to keep myself upright. My trek back to the caer through the storm had not been easy. The spell had taken its toll of my strength before the long walk home. I hadn't the strength to light a fire to lead me through the cave to the storage cellar. My only choice had been the long walk. I hoped I hadn't hurt the baby by pushing so hard to drive the spell to conclusion.

I'd had no choice. At a time when choices should have opened up to me, my options seemed very limited indeed.

"Who is gone?" I finally managed to ask. Newynog broke away from my grip to check her pups.

"Nimuë," Marnia wailed behind her sister. "She's run off into the teeth of the storm. We have to go after her."

"Is she truly gone?" A little bit of interest heated my body enough to think. "Did she take her cloak? Which horse did she ride?"

"I don't know," Berminia sniffled.

"Then find out. Ask the stable lads which direction she went. See if she had any bundles or luggage with her." I trudged toward the back of the Long Hall and the privacy of my bedchamber. "I must bathe and eat before I decide how to proceed."

"But the horse may have thrown her. My sister could be dying, and you can't send someone after her until you bathe!" Berminia didn't sound as outraged as she tried to look.

I wondered how much of her loud cries and copious tears were real and how much for the benefit of the servants.

"If you worry so much, you should have sent Diones after her when you first discovered her absence. You don't need my authority to start a search for someone truly missing." I dismissed her protests and closed the door to my room behind me.

"You don't care about my sister. You don't care about anything but that stupid, traitorous dog!" Her words followed me.

Dana help me, I did care. I'd just walked through the storm, miserable and exhausted after banishing my rival. How would it feel to face the same storm with defeat dragging at every step?

"A search will be fruitless and dangerous without more information. Find out which direction she took and when," I said. I had no doubt that Carradoc's daughters heard me.

Food came with the hot water. I ate every scrap Hannah, Diones' wife, had placed on the tray. She lingered nearby, wringing her hands. I knew she had been nurse to all three of Carradoc's daughters. She must be terribly worried about Nimuë, the favorite.

"Forgive me for intruding, Lady," she said as I drank the last of the ale.

"Yes?" I tried not to sound as irritated as I felt.

"It's them birds, Lady."

"What about the ravens?" A spark of curiosity stopped my quest for a warm wrap to throw over my shoulders. Food had helped, but the chill wouldn't go away so quickly.

"The birds flew off when the storm started."

I knew that, but it was nice to have it confirmed.

"Perhaps they won't return and we can get on with our lives," I replied. "As soon as the rain stops, we must plant again. The harvest will be late and small, but something is better than nothing."

"The Lady Nimuë screamed at the thunder and lightning, Lady. She screamed like the lightning burned her. Then she said, 'She'll pay for this. She'll pay in kind. She stole my father. Now I'll steal hers.' "

My dream. My father reaching for my hand. Only I could save him. Only I could prevent Cernunnos from trapping him within the Worldtree for all eternity, never dying, incapable of living.

What would my stepdaughter do to him?

Whatever happened was my fault.

I'd had no choice. Balance must be restored.

Someone pounded on my door. I stared at the planks, unable to think past the noise. I had doomed my father by defying Nimuë.

What else could I have done?

The pounding interrupted my self-defeating circle of thoughts. "Enter," I called. My voice sounded weak and uncertain to my own ears.

Diones stood framed in the doorway. He stared straight ahead, jaw rigid, eyes blazing with anger. "Her horse just came back. Frothing at the mouth and twitching with fear. It lost a shoe. The saddle is still on him, upside down, the girth partially cut with a knife," he recited the list of woes in a monotone.

"She's dead!" Hannah wailed. "My little girl is dead."

They didn't have to say it. They believed me responsible for the death of their lord's daughter.

All that night and all the next day we searched for Nimuë. We searched while the land dried enough to receive seeds. On the second day, I ordered most of the men and women to replant our barren fields. Diones and Hannah and a few others, I left free to continue the search as far afield as they could ride on a sturdy pony.

"Aren't you going to search any farther than that?" Berminia asked as we broke our fast. "My sister is out there, alone and friendless, maybe even dead, and you can't spare the men to search for her!"

"If she's dead, I can't help her," I replied quietly. "If she managed to travel more than a day's ride away, she probably found shelter elsewhere and will return in her own good time. We must start planting today or risk starvation this winter."

"I hate you!" Marnia screamed. She hadn't eaten much of her bread and cheese. She never did. Berminia transferred the leftover food to her own plate and ate it hastily. Guiltily.

"Nothing has gone right since you seduced our father into marrying you," Marnia continued her tirade. "I hate you, and I hope your baby kills you when it's born." She stormed out of the hall in a flood of tears.

Berminia followed her. Neither of them spoke to me again for a long time after that.

We found no trace of Nimuë. The rain had washed away her tracks and all evidence of her passing. The family mourned her as if dead. The villagers carried on with their lives. And I knew in my heart that my husband's daughter lived and made her way to Uther's army and my father. What would she do to him?

Chapter 32

YOUNG Arthur marched wearily beside Merlin. He made the effort to hold his head up and keep his shoulders straight. But Merlin knew he longed for a hot meal, a bath, and his bed. Every soldier in the camp wanted the same things.

"This shouldn't take long, boy," Merlin reassured his charge. "Uther wants to congratulate you on the splendid rally you performed on the battlefield. You are a hero tonight."

"You're the hero. I wouldn't be alive to rally the troops if you hadn't brought those birds from every corner of Britain." Arthur yawned. His jaw cracked audibly. "Sorry." He covered his open mouth with a callused but clean hand. He'd taken time to wash off at least the surface grime and gore.

Merlin held back the flap of Uther's pavilion for Arthur to enter ahead of him. The boy cocked an eyebrow and held back at the gesture of respect. "Get in there," Merlin growled. "You're expected."

Arthur stopped short, just inside the huge tent. Merlin ran into his broad back. Five of Uther's client kings ringed the Ardh Rhi's bed. He tried to back away from the august company.

"I'm just a soldier," he whispered out of the side of his mouth.

"Tonight you are a hero, and much, much more. Keep moving and don't question what is about to occur," Merlin ordered, giving his boy a small push.

"Do as I say, boy," he commanded when Arthur remained immobile.

"I'm not ten years old and your student any longer," Arthur whispered. He braced himself against Merlin's additional prodding.

"No, you are not. But trust me. You are expected and you *will* stand with them and show respect."

"But Uriens held back his warband until he *knew* we would win. I won't bend a knee to him. And Lot sent his warriors where he wanted them to go, not according to the battle plan."

"After tonight, you won't have to bow a knee to either of them. Now get in there and pay your respects to Uther."

Frantically Merlin searched every corner of the pavilion for his twin. Dyfrig hadn't arrived yet. The archbishop wouldn't dare refuse Uther's command to attend him tonight. He knew how important this announcement was.

Without Dyfrig's *joint* blessing with The Merlin, the kings would never agree to the naming of an heir.

"B—but—I—"

"And don't stutter." Merlin gave Arthur one last shove.

Arthur worked hard not to stumble. Within two steps his training took over. He straightened his shoulders and made his way to the Ardh Rhi's side with proper respect but also with a degree of pride and self-assurance.

Merlin smiled. "He'll do. I promised someone important that he'd have a touch of humility. I think I succeeded."

But Dyfrig wasn't here to acknowledge the boy. What good was all the hard work if Britain remained divided?

"My fellow kings," Uther said with more strength than Merlin thought he had left. "This fine young man, this warrior and leader of men, is Arthur. My true-born son and heir."

All five kings raised their voices in a babble of protest. Arthur took one step back from the noise and rejection. Merlin pressed his back again to keep him from retreating.

"Hear them out," he whispered harshly into the boy's ear.

"This untried pup!" Lot screamed. "I'll not have the likes of him as my Ardh Rhi. I'm taking my warband back to the Orcades and my wife tonight!"

"Gorre will not accept him either," Uriens said. He jerked his head toward the exit with a stern look at Leodegran, his father-in-law in all but deed.

Leodegran kept his place holding Uther's right hand. Perhaps the marriage between Uriens and Leodegran's daughter would not take place.

Merlin smiled. Leodegran knew he was too old, fighting the bone disease, to be named Ardh Rhi. Nor was his wastrel son likely to win favor. He had bet on Uriens rising to the position and betrothed his only daughter, Guinevere, to him. But Uriens had not won acclaim on the field of battle. He had not involved himself in court politics. He had not endeared himself to the other kings.

Leodegran wanted to sit next to the throne if not on it.

Merlin had hoped for this development, but feared it as well. His scrying bowl was rimmed in the black and red of death every time he sought a vision of Arthur's marriage to Guinevere.

"Galathin should be here. As Uther's son-in-law, he has a claim to the throne," Pelinore of Somerset said.

"He is sorely wounded and may not live. The Ardh Rhi must be hale to lead us in battle, and versed in law to judge in open court. Galathin is neither of those." Mark of Cornwall dismissed Blasine's husband as a contender.

"Tell us how this young hero is your son," Leodegran prodded Uther.

The Ardh Rhi swallowed deeply, gathering his strength.

Merlin took his left hand, willing his own energy to replenish the Ardh Rhi. Just a little longer. Uther had to hang on, just a little longer.

"Archbishop Dyfrig should hear this," he said quietly. A servant slipped out of the pavilion, presumably to follow up on the summons.

Lot and Uriens lingered by the tent flap. Curiosity or a wavering in their rejection of Arthur?

"No time to wait." Uther's voice came out in a harsh rasp. "Twenty years ago, I lusted after Ygraina, wife of Gorlois, King of Tintagel. Gorlois perceived our growing love for each other and declared himself my enemy. He took Ygraina away from my court and imprisoned her in his caer before she could divorce him." He went on, in choppy and incomplete sentences, to relate how Uther had battled Gorlois and both had withdrawn from the field, neither the victor, neither totally defeated.

"Fearing I'd never see my beloved Ygraina again, I begged my old friend Merlin to bring her to me with magic. . . ." His voice trailed off in a weak whisper.

Merlin took up the story. "I could not whisk Ygraina out of the fastness of Tintagel. So I cast a glamour upon Uther. He approached the heavily guarded causeway and none of Gorlois' men knew him for other than their own lord. In this guise he entered Ygraina's chamber and lay with her."

"I did not know that Gorlois had launched a last desperate attack against my men. I did not know that as I lay in the arms of my beloved, my men slew Gorlois and made his men prisoners," Uther added. Then his strength fell again.

Arthur's face lost all color. "You could have warned me," he said through clenched jaws.

" 'Twas your father's place to inform you. Not mine. I merely serve."

"Like hell you do. You planned the whole thing long ago." Some color returned to Arthur's face, along with some of his determination and confidence.

"Ygraina conceived a child that night. Uther married her the next morning, claiming her by right of war," Merlin finished the story.

Pelinore, a noted Christian, looked about to protest the casual nature of the holy sacrament of matrimony.

"Thus has been our tradition for many generations, left over from when the woman held the land and her husband defended it," Merlin reminded the gathering. "A son was born of that night. I claimed the raising of him as my price for casting the glamour upon my Ardh Rhi."

"Why? The boy needed to learn the art of kingship from his father!" Leodegran protested. He still kept Uther's right hand in his own, as if claiming kinship and therefore a place beside the next Ardh Rhi as well.

"Britain is not united. Uther's kingship was new and fragile. A son might not live beyond his first birthday. Rivals could easily arrange his death. A son raised knowing he would be next Ardh Rhi would not work hard to build his strength as a leader and a warrior. A son raised in the midst of court politics would have his loyalties tugged in dozens of directions. The gods decreed that I should raise the boy ignorant of his heritage so that he must strive hard to become the best he could be.

"I present to you five kings of Britain, Arthur, the warrior you proclaim a hero, an acknowledged leader of warriors. I also give you a man tutored in law, history, and politics."

"I proclaim Arthur the next Pendragon of Britain," Uther wheezed.

"Where is Dyfrig?" Pelinore asked. "We must have his agreement on this. The Church must agree."

"Aye, the Church must agree," Arthur said firmly. "If I must rule, then I will rule a united Britain. The Church as well as the kings must accept me."

Merlin swelled with pride at how his boy stepped into his role as easily as he swung his battle sword and sat his thundering horse.

"I'll never bow to you!" Uriens proclaimed. "You may be a hero, but you aren't a general."

Arthur raised one eyebrow. "Perhaps, perhaps not," he answered. On the outside he appeared calm and aloof, proper traits for a king. But Merlin knew him well. He rotated the fingers of his left hand, touching each in turn to the thumb as if counting. An old trick he used to keep track of his thoughts, his men, and his horses, when something else demanded his attention.

"May I suggest we look at the maps together. I will show you why we almost lost this battle and how and where we must win the next." Arthur inclined his head toward the map table in the back of the pavilion.

"I know why we almost lost this battle, young Arthur," Pelinore growled. "Without looking at the map, tell us what we already know: where will be the next and how will we win it?"

"We must hasten to the River Dubglas and stake out the high ground before the Saxons arrive," he replied. "We must also seek reinforcements from Cymry and Caerlud."

"We can't leave Caerlud undefended," Leodegran protested.

Merlin noted how closely the kings listened. They had already chosen the ford on the Dubglas as one of three potential battle sites.

"I didn't say we'd strip either place of support," Arthur returned with calm determination. "But we need more men. Both Cymry and Caerlud have been holding troops in reserve, unwilling to commit to a united defense of Britain. They must share the cost as well as the benefit of our efforts!"

The kings consulted each other in harsh whispers.

Merlin leaned closer to catch snatches of their conversation. They must respect young Arthur if they listened this long and questioned his suggestions without dismissing him out of hand.

"Father Merlin." The servant who had left to seek Dyfrig tapped his shoulder.

Merlin cursed silently. He needed to hear what was going on.

"Father Merlin, the archbishop sent his apologies." The servant handed Merlin a small scrap of parchment rolled and tied with a bishopric purple strip of cloth.

Merlin wanted to toss the missive into the fire. He knew it would merely admonish him not to visit his mother. In the last thirty years he had six such messages from his brother and no other communication. For the sake of the watching kings and Arthur, he opened the small scroll.

"Archbishop Dyfrig sends his greetings and regrets to all present." Merlin read the words aloud. Moisture clouded Merlin's vision as a cold knot grew in his stomach. Dyfrig would never stand beside him to proclaim Arthur Ardh Rhi. Myrddin Emrys would never stand beside his twin again.

"Archbishop Dyfrig has been called to Canterbury to confer with his brother archbishop and deal with the latest delegation from the Church in Rome."

"Without Dyfrig's blessing . . ." Pelinore said.

"A compromise!" Arthur declared. Then, before the others could interrupt, he plunged ahead. "Until the Church confirms my father's declaration, I will not assume the title of Ardh Rhi. When we have sent the Saxons fleeing into the sea, we will hold an election with *all* of the client kings present. Until then, I am your *Dux Bellorum*—a leader of a *united* army, as in Roman times."

"Agreed," Leodegran said hastily. "We agree on this. Don't we?" His last words came out more of an order than a question.

"Agreed," Merlin added. He'd have to arrange something else to solidify Arthur's claim. But he'd see Arthur named Ardh Rhi before the end of the year with or without Dyfrig.

Chapter 33

ONLY one raven remained at Caer Tair Cigfran. He perched on the well, too old and cranky to fly away. Every time a human approached him, he squawked and protested our presence, as if we were to blame for his age and his aches and pains.

I left him alone, confident that he would die soon from old age.

On the day we planted, the faeries came back. The villagers batted at them as if plagued by a swarm of insects. Cedar and his friends laughed uproariously. I laughed with them. The villagers glared at me. Many made the sign of the cross or a clenched fist with little and index finger extended, certain that I had invited a new plague to replace the old.

But the faeries tired of the game and retreated to the forest and the sacred spring.

The next day, the trees began whispering among themselves. A mighty clash of men with iron weapons. Many deaths. Many important deaths.

Where? I asked.

Somewhere else, they replied.

Who? Is my father well?

Silence.

I asked about Curyll. The trees and wind had no answer.

I worked alongside the villagers, my skirts kilted up, and a broad hat shading my face. The people were still leery of me, but learning to accept me. I worked as hard as they and asked rather than ordered them when I needed help.

Carradoc's daughters remained firmly inside the caer, aloof from the commoners.

Before the end of the week the first refugees arrived at our gates.

Newynog smelled them from the edge of the field we sowed with the last of the seeds. Her puppies barked with mock fierceness in imitation of her alarm, then tumbled into an equally fun wrestling match.

At the first signs of alarm in my great wolfhound, I scanned the horizon with every sense born in me. The shimmering layer of light that surrounded every living thing glowed a little brighter where the road disappeared over the hill to the southwest.

"Someone comes," I called to men and women who paused to look also.

"More than one, I'd guess, by the size of the dust cloud," Llandoc added. Carradoc hadn't ordered his exile for challenging the lord at Beltane, so I allowed him to stay in the village. We needed every strong man available.

Without much conversation, the villagers moved toward the caer. Carradoc had warned us all to be wary of strangers.

No presentiment of danger sat on my left shoulder. I remained a few moments longer, absorbing the warm sunlight, cherishing the sensation of freshly tilled Pridd caressing my bare toes. The scent of the land rose up in heady waves. A few faeries returned and flew loops around my head after the villagers deserted the field.

I stayed as long as they did, knowing there was no danger to me as long as they flew and giggled in my ear.

"Eeep!" the faeries yelped and disappeared in a twinkling of colored lights.

That drove me toward the safety of the fortress walls faster than the news of strangers approaching. Newynog followed close on my heels, herding her offspring in front of her.

I scanned the road from the top of the watchtower alongside a sharp-eyed lad well noted for his far vision but nearly blind with things close at hand. He bore with humble acceptance the jokes about his clumsiness until we needed him. Now he was one of the most valuable retainers I had.

The magical energy surrounding the swarm of people approaching told me their numbers, nearly two dozen, and that they came afoot. The boy reported the same information a heartbeat later.

Two dozen afoot? They could be outlaws, renegades, or a small raiding party working their way inland from the Irish Sea, like the men Da and I had encountered near Deva last autumn.

I dismissed the last possibility. Raiders or outlaws would have to have grown terribly bold to use the road in broad daylight. We'd heard no rumors of raids from other villages and caers. We'd heard nothing. The trees and faeries spoke of a great battle far away, not of burning and looting close at hand.

Refugees, then. With the recognition, I sensed pain.

"Open the gates!" I called down. "Diones, take some men and help carry the wounded. Hannah, we need bandages and herbs. Lots of hot water and wine to cleanse the wounds."

The steward and his wife crossed themselves, looked to each other for guidance, and set about obeying. Many of the villagers stared at me, mouths agape. Except Llandoc. The young smith grinned at me knowingly. He fairly leaped to haul the huge cauldron we used for soap making out of a storage shed. His father raced to the smithy for charcoal to heat the fire beneath the heavy pot.

Berminia and Marnia poked their heads out of their room, one of the former conical huts that had been incorporated into the foundations of the Long Hall. "Is Nimuë returned?" Berminia asked meekly.

"No," I replied.

She ducked back into her room without another word. Marnia lingered a moment longer before retreating as well.

A few of the villagers looked to where Carradoc's daughter had disappeared, then back to me. They drifted back toward the building in silent agreement with the young women that I was the usurper and they the rightful ladies of the caer.

I raised my eyes to the sky in exasperation and wondered if Uther had as many problems with his client kings as I had with my stepdaughters. Da would know how to handle them. But Da was not here and never would be.

I decided to ignore Berminia and Marnia for now. The villagers would have to learn to trust me on their own, without the directive of the girls.

They were my age, but I considered them children.

Llandoc had just finished filling the cauldron from the well when the ragged knot of people arrived at the gate. Leading the group and half-carrying a limping man was a square-built man wearing the brown robes of a Christian priest. Faeries always fled the presence of the followers of the White Christ. The priest's shimmering blue aura reached out to enfold all of his flock. His inner peace, despite the pain and turmoil around him, spoke to me.

"Welcome, Father Thomas," I said as I rushed to help support the man he held up by sheer force of will.

"Do I know you, lass?" He looked at me with puzzlement.

"I used to spend winters with Lord Ector and his family. I was in the hall the night you exorcised a demon from my friend Curyll."

"Ah, the boy with the stutter. How fares he?"

"I don't know. I haven't seen any of the family for many months."

"I'm afraid I don't remember seeing you in the hall, daughter. But that was four or five years ago. You must have been very young."

"I was." My tongue stumbled over the next words I knew I must say. Some Christians would run from me and the help I offered because of who and what I represented. "My father is The Merlin. I did not participate in your ritual."

"Ah, that explains it. I didn't have the privilege of baptizing you. That is why I didn't recognize your spirit. They call you Wren, don't they, short for Arylwren."

"Yes, Father Thomas. I offer you and yours hospitality. But I am not of your faith."

"Not all of these poor refugees follow the Christian way either, Wren. But they are hurt and need a place of safety. The war rages long and hard in other parts of Britain. There are many who need help."

"They are all welcome. I cannot deny them hospitality because of their faith."

"Are you a healer, like your father?"

"Yes. I have tools at my disposal you will not like." But only tools, not the great healing magic. A gap opened in my thoughts. I knew I'd need that magic some day to save Curyll's life. Perhaps I should start experimenting with it now.

"If they help the innocent, your tools come from God, no matter what you call Him."

"Or Her." I smiled, liking this man immensely.

"We have much work to do, Wren. And more people likely to come."

"My father will not like you spending his stores on strangers,"

Berminia said from behind me. "You've changed everything. Nothing is the same. My father doesn't like change, and neither do I."

I had been so caught up in the powerful aura of the priest I hadn't noticed when she left the sanctuary of her room.

Some of the villagers backed away from us. Carradoc's heavy-handed justice affected all of them. If my husband had not left the morning after Beltane, I was certain he would have flogged Llandoc, possibly even killed him, for daring to jump the bonfire and besting the lord's performance.

"Berminia, your father left me in charge of the fortress. I choose to extend hospitality to those in need. I'm sure the healthier ones will work for their keep. We haven't enough hands to plow and plant on our own. Many of our people marched beside the warband. Many of them may not return. Come, Father Thomas, let us begin by cleaning the wounds to see who needs the most help."

Change. Berminia saw change as chaos. Change didn't frighten me. I saw it as the continual evolution of my life pattern.

"My father does not tolerate Christians." Berminia tried again to undermine my authority. A note of desperation had crept into her voice. Her younger sister cowered behind her.

"Your father doesn't believe in anything but himself," I replied. "But he is not here and I am. I choose to tolerate anyone who needs my help. That is the way of the Goddess."

"And the way of Jesu Christus," Father Thomas added, crossing himself.

"You have no right to give orders here." Berminia took a deep breath and plunged on with her defiance. "You murdered Peter the stable boy by magic and then banished my sister to certain death when she tried to stop you. You, Arylwren, are a murderess, and I can prove it."

Chapter 34

"THOSE are very serious accusations," Father Thomas said, looking carefully at Berminia and then back to me.

Berminia smiled brightly in triumph. Marnia continued to cower. I guessed the younger sister was not in full agreement, but didn't dare defy her sister. They had worked in opposition to Nimuë once, and Peter had died as a result. The ravens had taken over the entire region with Nimuë's domination. If I didn't know the forces at work here, I'd be frightened, too.

Nimuë had quoted Morgaine frequently over the past few months. Had she learned something of demon magic from the princess? I suddenly worried that perhaps I hadn't finished my cleansing spell. I began searching Berminia for traces of lingering demonic influence or some kind of mind control from Nimuë.

Had I reveled in the scents of freshly turned Pridd and newly sprouting trees so much that I missed the smell of sulfur and rot?

I saw nothing on the surface and smelled none of the telltale odors of dark magic. I'd have to go deeper with my magic and intrude on the young woman's most private thoughts to discover more. That kind of violation bothered me as much as my father's manipulations had.

"Your logic is faulty, Berminia," I reminded her. Until I had time to sort this out, I had to counter her with mundane means. "You and your younger sister were with me when Peter died."

"But you were working magic that day. You said so. You showed us the magic in the herbs you picked."

"Herbs of cleansing and healing. Peter died of a broken neck."

"That cannot be right, Mistress," Hannah protested. "He spoke after he fell. He did not die until . . . no, I refuse to believe that my Nimuë had anything to do with the death. She sought to soothe and comfort his pain."

I bit my tongue and let the woman work through the sequence of events. She wrung her hands and cried. Most of the villagers crossed themselves repeatedly, mumbling prayers.

If Carradoc did not tolerate Christians, why had so many of his villagers adopted the faith?

Berminia began backing away in confusion. Her face drained of color. The blemishes on her skin stood out redder and angrier than usual.

"We may never know why Peter died," I said. "But by your own testimony, we know that no one here caused his death. The ravens and their ill omens are gone. We have work to do, fields to finish planting, and preparations to make before more people come here for refuge."

"So be it," Father Thomas prayed. Then he leaned closer and whispered, "Arylwren, you must be careful. There are many here who do not like or trust you and your faith."

"There are as many who do not trust you either, Father Thomas."

"But you do, daughter. There is an instinctive good about you. I sensed the same in your father. I regret you do not share my faith, but I will look for God's light wherever I can find it."

"Light. Yes, we both work for the Light."

Morgaine had accused me of cowardice for seeking a balance and adhering to limitations within magic and power. She obviously didn't know what courage I had to summon to say the *right* words rather than take the easy path.

"Father Thomas, our stores are limited and our harvest will be late and small. Many people will go hungry this winter. But what I have I will share with people in need. Bring your refugees that they may find a physical and spiritual sanctuary here."

"Your charity will not go unrewarded, Wren." He bowed his head in prayer.

I raised my voice for all to hear. "And since I have banished the plague of ravens, this fortress is no longer Caer Tair Cigfran."

A loud murmur broke out among my people. Some in happy speculation. Some in fright.

"Henceforth this place shall be Caer Noddfa, the Fortress of Sanctuary."

"There is still one raven," Berminia argued. "The old one that perches on the well, as if guarding it."

"One raven, not three. Not a multitude to plague us. At sunset we will feast with what we can find and honor a new beginning. Caer Noddfa."

Most of the villagers cheered me. Diones and Hannah huddled with Berminia and Marnia. Uncertainty furrowed their brows and stooped their shoulders.

"Your father would approve, Wren." Father Thomas chuckled. He gestured for his flock to seek resting places. I gestured for Hannah to see to their needs. The men drifted back to the fields to finish planting. A few made plans to hunt for tonight's feast.

"Have you seen my father of late?" I asked Father Thomas when the crowd had dissipated enough to give us the illusion of privacy. My anger toward Da still simmered in the back of my mind. My heart needed to hear that my only parent thrived.

"No, I have not seen The Merlin, child. He moves from place to place too rapidly. Sometimes I think he flies faster than rumors. One of the rumors placed him in the far north making a deal with devils. Another rumor declares him the wild man haunting the forests of the South, yet another puts him at Uther's side, never leaving him, even to tend the battle wounded."

"And what of Archbishop Dyfrig?" I asked. I felt that if anyone had noticed Dyfrig's resemblance to The Merlin, Father Thomas would.

"A saintly man, my archbishop. He remains close by King Uther's side when he can, as does your father. The business of keeping Britain safe draws them both away often. I fear the Ardh Rhi ails again." Father Thomas shook his head in regret.

I grieved for Ygraina who would surely lose her beloved husband soon. Would she lose her missing son to the war as well, before she had a chance to get to know him? "Has Uther named an heir?"

Father Thomas shook his head sadly. "The archbishop counsels patience until the *right* heir is found."

That sounded more like my father, waiting for the precise moment he could stage the most dramatic effect.

"I have heard rumors of this candidate and that warrior, but noth-

ing certain. Until Uther dies and the kings must name a new Ardh
Rhi, the matter remains confused. I fear Britain will split rather than
name a new leader."

Nimuë traced the straight streets of the army camp with care. She
wore her dark cloak pulled tight around her demure gown of reddish
brown and the hood pulled low around her face. With each step, she
willed the hundreds of men marching purposefully from place to place
to look in every direction but at her.

Not that she wouldn't love the attention of some of these incredibly strong and handsome young men. She had a different mission
today. A much more important mission.

Rather than ask questions and betray her presence, she opened her
senses and let the demon on her shoulder guide her steps. Whenever
it directed her to turn, right or left, she looked carefully for a telltale.
By the time she had penetrated the camp to the first tents of officers
and minor lords, she saw the faint trace of blue energy lingering on
the muddy street. The eldritch glows almost formed the shape of footprints. She smiled to herself. Now that she knew how and where to
look, The Merlin would never again escape her.

When she had time, she'd seek the telltales for her father so that
she could avoid him. She'd never let him control her again now that
she'd lost Caer Tair Cigfran to Wren. Carradoc had lost his usefulness.

Deep into the ranks of pavilions occupied by major warlords and
kings, the blue footprints disappeared into a rude circular structure
made of twigs. The roof reached no higher than her shoulder. She
recognized it immediately as a smaller and more temporary hut favored by shepherds. Half sunk into the ground, it would keep the
occupant snug, and if it had to be transported, the wall of sticks rolled
into a convenient bundle. The Merlin could construct a new one in a
very short time, wherever his travels took him.

She shuddered at having to step into the primitive dwelling. She
thought she had forsaken this crudeness once and for all when she left
Avalon.

"This is the only way to achieve our goal," the demon reminded
her. Its voice became clearer and louder with every spell she wove
successfully.

She thought she had lost the creature when battling Wren for possession of the caer. But as she used tricks and disguises, compulsions, and illusions to ride through the storm to Dun Edin, the demon had reasserted itself until it was an almost visible, nearly audible presence on her shoulder.

"Will he detect you?" she asked the demon.

"Not unless we want him to."

She rapped her knuckles on the door. It creaked open. Chinks of light filtered through the stick construction revealing a cot, several small traveling chests, a twig table and stool, and piles of scrolls, pots of herbs, surgical tools, unfinished meals, dirty shirts. The place smelled of an oddly pleasing combination of male sweat, astringent herbs, and wine.

"He's not here," she whispered to the demon.

"He will be soon. Step in now. Quickly. Someone comes!" The demon urged her. Its voice sounded close to panic.

"Who?" Nimuë cast out her senses as the demon had taught her. The fine hairs on the back of her neck stood up in awareness of the presence of magic.

"That is not The Merlin," she told the demon as she ducked into the rough shelter. She peered through a small opening between two not-quite-straight sticks. Another figure drifted past, hooded and cloaked as she had been.

"Morgaine!" she and the demon said together.

"She must not know you are here. She covets a demon of her own. She has smelled me and seeks us," the demon almost gibbered in panic.

"She will not give up her search," Nimuë mused.

"Once The Merlin comes, his magic will mask our scent," the demon said.

"And here he comes," Nimuë felt a little thrill at sight of her quarry.

True to the demon's prediction, Morgaine seemed to fade into the shadows. Nimuë knew she was there because she watched with her magic.

"She's pregnant!" Nimuë gasped. "Lot didn't waste any time." She remembered how Morgaine had been bustled out of the women's bower in Venta Belgarum mere hours before the dawn of Carradoc's marriage to Wren. Nimuë had listened to the heated exchange between Ygraina and her daughter. Lot's name had figured prominently in the argument. Morgaine did not want to marry him. She had designs on another. Ygraina—with the backing of several burly soldiers—persuaded her daughter she had no choice.

"I do not think the war leaders know she is here. See how she hides," the demon whispered. It sounded relieved. "Quickly, prepare for The Merlin."

Nimuë dropped her cloak and arranged herself on the bed. She loosened the neck ties of her shift and opened the bodice of her gown a little. Wriggling her shoulders pushed a fair amount of her shoulders and bosom free of clothing. Then she draped her auburn hair in a wide fan against the rough blankets.

The door creaked open. She closed her eyes, feigning sleep.

Remember, appear innocent, lost, helpless. He loves helpless, the demon chuckled in her ear. *As soon as he lays with you, the gods will claim him. We will have our revenge.*

Chapter 35

WAR ravaged the land that summer as Uther's troops engaged the Saxons in battle after battle. People fled in every direction, out of the path of the battles and the purging fires that followed. Refugees poured into our small, remote sanctuary, many of them led there by Father Thomas. He politely looked the other way when I invoked magic for healing. I politely found other places to be when he held mass for the Christians in my home.

Before long, the good priest moved his wife and children from Deva to my caer. The city functioned under a strong Christian influence with many priests. We had none but him.

Cedar and his faery companions flitted hither and thither and yon throughout the neighborhood. They plagued us with tricks and much laughter. But they always left when Father Thomas appeared.

Newynog was my constant shadow whether in the fortress, fields, or forest. She yipped and chased the faeries when they pulled her tail or pestered her ears, but she didn't try to chase them away from me. Each time a new band of refugees came to us, she made certain she stood between the strangers and me until they had proved their trustworthiness to her. The travelers who did not pass my dog's inspection moved on. The ones she accepted I found places for, either as tenants on my land or as freeholders nearby.

My land. My caer. My home. I had found a place for myself in this world. I did the work I had been trained for, in service to any who sought me out.

By summer's end, I no longer associated anything at Caer Noddfa with my husband, not even my baby.

The babe grew big in my belly. I concentrated more and more of my energy in planning for its arrival, securing its future.

In late autumn, six of my husband's warband returned with their horses, their servants, and their wounds. Six warriors returned. Over one hundred had followed Carradoc and Uther into war.

My heart grieved for all the deaths that occurred throughout the entire campaign season. I met the men at the gate with a sorrowful countenance, knowing they carried sad news. How many widows and orphans would I have to comfort tonight?

"My Lady." Kalahart went down on one knee.

I remembered him slightly from my wedding day, a slender man with wispy brown hair and deep brown eyes that reflected back the emotions of the person looking at him, but not his own. He kept his aura tightly contained today, as he had at the wedding ceremony. A sling supported his sword hand and a bloody bandage encircled his brow.

He hadn't been among the half-dozen warriors who journeyed here after the wedding and participated in Carradoc's perverse Beltane. I could welcome him easily.

"What news do you bring from my husband?" I asked.

"Alas, my Lady. Lord Carradoc was carried from the field of battle gravely wounded. He could not have lived. There was great chaos that day. But the Dux Bellorum, Arthur, rallied the troops and defeated the Saxons. Both armies have withdrawn for the winter. Arthur keeps many of his troops at Campboglanna on the Wall. I took my wounds at the battle of Dubglas, and have spent the summer recovering enough to come home. Only we, of the wounded, were well enough to travel. We must return in the spring to rejoin those of the warband who continue with Arthur."

A wave of dizziness engulfed me. Freedom! My heart sang. Carradoc no longer lived to plague me and this land with his perversions.

"Oh, my Lady. My poor, poor, Lady." Hannah rushed to my side, holding me up. "Such terrible news to give you, and in your condition. The poor babe will never know its father." She cried copiously and dabbed her eyes with her apron.

I just stood there, swaying a little, too stunned to know what to do.

"My husband is dead?" I croaked at last. I wanted to probe the other news first—a Dux Bellorum named *Arthur*. Uther's son now led Britain in war, but not as Ardh Rhi. When? How? But to probe for that information now, in the wake of Kalahart's other news, would be unseemly.

I feared that my beloved Curyll had assumed his place as Uther's heir. Da had dozens of other candidates to fill the role. Now that I was free of Carradoc, had land and titles to give him, I could only hope to win Curyll if he remained a simple warrior.

"Lord Carradoc fought bravely, my Lady, with honor," Kalahart said, still kneeling, head bowed.

"But you did not see him die. You did not witness his funeral or scatter his ashes." My insides turned cold. I did not trust the news. The trees and faeries had said nothing of this.

But would they bother? Carradoc was not a man they favored. Curyll was the only man they had spoken of before. Of him, I knew only that he lived.

"Many hundreds of men died that day, my Lady, including Ardh Rhi Uther Pendragon. There were too many dead to sort out and build individual pyres." Kalahart finally stood. His posture and the little bit of his aura that I could see told me that he believed he spoke the truth.

"And did you see my father, The Merlin, at this battle?"

"Yes, Lady. He worked many great miracles. At the last moment, when we thought all lost and the Saxons must surely break through our defenses, The Merlin rode onto the field upon a snow-white stag. A stag wearing twelve points on his antlers, each one tipped in gold as were its hooves." The man's eyes went wide with that statement, the closest thing to an emotion he had shown.

The gathering of villagers and retainers who always met strangers at the gate crossed themselves or made other gestures of reverence. White stags were exotic creatures of myth. To ride one denoted great holiness. The Goddess had surely blessed my father if She allowed him to ride such a rare beast.

Or had he cast a glamour on a white horse to make his tricks appear to be miracles?

"What happened once my father entered the fray?"

"The Saxons shifted the focus of their attack to The Merlin. But suddenly a great black cloud filled the sky and thousands of black birds descended upon the enemy. They pecked at Saxon eyes and tore flesh from their arms. They fouled weapons and hindered movement.

But they did not interfere with any of the Ardh Rhi's army. The Merlin summoned every raven in Britain to come to our aid."

Murmurs rippled through the people who gathered by the gate. We all knew where the ravens had come from. I had sent them from here. Whether my father had summoned the birds or made use of my sending was debatable. Nearly five months had passed since I had cleansed the fortress of all but one aged and cranky raven who refused to leave his perch by the well.

"The Saxon host thrashed at the birds," Kalahart continued, warming to his story. His voice fell into a poetic cadence as if reciting one of the great histories. "Mightily the Saxons fought the birds until they drove them away. In those moments of distraction, my Lord Arthur grabbed the Ardh Rhi's banner and rallied the troops behind him. He turned the tide of battle and won the day."

In my mind I saw again my childhood vision of Curyll waving a banner over his head and shouting "To me! Gather to me!" as a battle raged around him. Was this the battle I had seen? Did Curyll's rallying call help turn the tide for Uther's long lost son?

Who was now acknowledged as Uther's son? I prayed Curyll was still free to come to me now that I was rid of Carradoc.

"We did not know Lord Arthur for Uther's son until later, as the old king lay dying," Kalahart continued. "Now he leads the army as Dux Bellorum. He will not take the position of Ardh Rhi until he has routed the Saxons." Kalahart sagged wearily. He'd journeyed long and far with injuries. His companions were in worse shape than he.

A dozen questions rose to my lips. Most of them about Curyll and Arthur. Were they one and the same? Who had The Merlin chosen to fill the role of Uther's son? But Kalahart's burst of storytelling seemed to have drained him of the last of his energy.

"Diones, see to these men and their needs. We will hear their stories in the Long Hall tonight. We will mourn our dead with feasting and with songs and stories of their honor and courage." As we should.

And then I would be free at last. I would rule this caer on my own, without the lingering legacy of Carradoc or my father or Nimuë. From this day forward, Caer Noddfa would become a haven for all those who sought a peaceful continuation of the natural rhythms of life, as the Goddess or Jesu Christus dictated. I no longer cared what we called the gods we worshiped.

Curyll's dreams of peace and justice vibrated through me, as if I had spoken his words and not my own. Peace, justice, and law could work. Honor, loyalty, and promises have meaning. Order and balance would reign.

"Welcome home to Caer Noddfa, Kalahart. I offer the hospitality of the caer of sanctuary to you and your men. You need not return to the battlefront in the spring. We will find places for all of you here, working for peace and making a refuge for those the war has displaced."

Kalahart cocked his head and raised his eyebrows in question at my words.

The first winter storm of the Solstice season inspired my son to seek the outside world. The day began with unnatural stillness and a great heaviness in the air. Black clouds piled up on the horizon. We bolted and reinforced shutters. I ordered the courtyard cleared of any debris that the wind could fling about.

The stable lads spent hours soothing restless horses. I paced the Long Hall, rubbing my back and breathing deeply, feeling hungry, not wanting to eat, too tired to remain upright, too restless to lay down.

Hannah and Diones supervised the movement of extra food and water from outside storage to the cellar beneath the kitchen. As I watched, needing a diversion from my pacing, I felt the secret trapdoor thrum with power. It invited, nay begged me, to open it and investigate the cave below.

At that moment the nagging pain in my lower back shifted into tremendous cramps across my belly. Thunder shook the fortress to its foundations. A gush of water from my womb came at the same moment the skies opened with a drenching rain. I screamed, unprepared for the sudden change in the intensity of the cramps.

Hannah bustled me back to the privacy of my bedchamber, shouting orders to one and all. She shoved Newynog out of the room and slammed the door. The birthing chair had been moved into the chamber three days ago.

My son was eager and I healthy. We made short work of it. Blessedly soon it was over, and I dozed with my baby suckling hungrily. He clasped my finger fiercely.

"His name is Yvain," I said. Yvain, a young warrior, strong and proud. "See how he treats my finger as if he wielded a sword already?"

And his name derived from neither my father nor my husband.

I dozed then. Dimly, I remember protesting when someone, probably Hannah, removed the baby to his cradle. Then I slept, deeply.

Too deeply.

My dreams carried the scent of portent, sharp and acrid with a clear understanding of the symbols for each of the four elements ringing the images. . . .

I stood in a great cave. The ceiling and walls refracted torchlight from masses of natural crystals. Columns of crystal created a winding passageway through the cave. Clumps of crystal hung from the ceiling. Loose crystals littered the floor. All of it intensified the light and shot rainbows in all directions, filling the natural room with bright colors.

Men crowded into the room, two dozen or more. Armored and armed they huddled together. Rain dampened their heavy winter cloaks. One man threw off his dark winter garb and stepped forward. He wore Druid white. Though he kept the hood of his robe up and his face down, I knew him to be my father, The Merlin.

Another man stepped forward. Tall, confident, determined. My view from the shadows showed only his broad back. The Merlin moved behind a massive block of dressed marble set on the cave floor near the far end, like an altar. Some ancient artisan had chiseled intricate knotwork into every exposed surface. Time had smoothed the carvings, but the protection of the cave had kept them clean and distinct.

The endless loops and whorls followed a life path I couldn't interpret from a distance. I needed to follow the lovely lines with my fingertips and magic to make sense of it. My dream self couldn't approach the altar or the gathering any closer than the shadows within a deep recess.

The gräal, the cauldron of life I had sensed in this cave the last time I had been here, hovered over The Merlin's head, partially in this world, mostly hidden from mundane eyes in another world. Brightly colored strands of life energy drifted upward from the gräal and reached to include every man in the cave.

My dream self remained curiously separate from the pattern. But then, I wasn't truly there.

Atop the altar lay a sword, a huge sword. It looked as if it had been carved of marble, of a single piece with the altar, entwined with the carvings, a part of them and yet apart from them. I knew the sword to be separate from the stone. Magic lingered in the marble encasing the blade like a scabbard.

"We have agreed, whoever among you draws Uther's sword of state from this stone shall be Ardh Rhi," The Merlin intoned in the stirring voice he reserved for prophecy. "So I have seen in a vision. You have all agreed that possession of this ancient artifact denotes kingship."

"Archbishop Dyfrig has agreed to abide by the decision of the sword," The Merlin intoned.

Somehow, I knew that Dyfrig had agreed to those terms without knowing the precise meaning of the ceremony my father had devised.

A warrior king swaggered toward the altar. I recognized his bald head and arrogant walk. Leodegran, the client king who had wanted me to force Uther into naming him Ardh Rhi. Leodegran, who collected alliances like a hoard of treasure. He bent one knee in obeisance to the altar. Then he stood proudly and clasped both hands around the sword hilt. He pulled and strained mightily. Pulsing blue veins stood out in his neck, sweat dripped from his brow, his shoulders strained beneath the folds of his cloak.

After several long moments he sagged and released his grip. Reluctantly he stepped aside. But his eyes scanned the room, calculating.

Ten more men stepped forward, including Cai, Lord Ector's only surviving son, and Uriens, the man destined to marry Leodegran's daughter and become king of Gorre. They all failed. I couldn't find Stinger, Ceffyl, or Curyll in the crowd. If the Boar was there, they wouldn't be far.

The tall man standing in the shadows shared a physique with Curyll and Stinger and several candidates I knew.

At last The Merlin signaled to the tall, patient man who stood apart from the rest. He hesitated.

His aura radiated strength and compassion. I knew in my heart that this man had to become the next Ardh Rhi. My desires and dreams for a future with Curyll no longer mattered. Only he could hold Britain united against the Saxons. Only he could mend the wounds of generations of war.

My dream self gently nudged his mind forward. His thoughts remained closed to me, but I knew he received and understood my persuasion.

He looked around, startled. His face remained shadowed from the hood of his cloak. I urged him again to take his rightful place. He stepped up to the altar and made his obeisance. He threw back his hood, but mail and a tight helmet covered his hair. I sensed his murmured prayer to any god who might be listening.

I reassured him the Goddess listened. The grӓal gleamed brighter, its image grew more solid. The colored strands of life steaming up from the cauldron encircled the next Ardh Rhi more closely.

Then he stood, still keeping his back to me and yanked the sword free with one hand. He held it up, letting torchlight reflect off the blade, drawing all of the light and the life patterns to the sword so that his face remained a shadowy mask.

Stunned silence filled the cave. Then shouts of protest and proclamation echoed around the crystal chamber. All of the turmoil centered on one name.

Arthur.

Leodegran knelt before Arthur, proffering his sword and swearing allegiance. Several of the client kings and warriors followed suit. Uriens stomped out of the crystal cave, shouting defiance.

My dream faded to wisps and tendrils of memory.

Had I witnessed a true event of past or future? I might have merely dreamed of the crystal cave Cedar had forbidden me to enter until the "Chosen" had come to claim his heritage.

I awoke, drenched in sweat, my mind a muddle of unanswerable questions.

A week later I investigated the cave, gaining access through the trapdoor beneath the kitchen cellar. I carried a cat as my only companion. Newynog could not climb down the steep ladder.

No barrier hindered my entrance to the crystal chamber. The cave refracted my torchlight into a thousand rainbows, as I had dreamed. Yet I found no evidence of men intruding on the quiet sanctity of the place. All traces of the grӓal had disappeared from here as well.

The crystals no longer vibrated with power.

The altar stone had crumbled to dust with no hint of intricate carving or a magnificent sword of state.

Chapter 36

"THIS way, Arthur." Merlin beckoned to the rider behind him. They turned off a muddy, narrow track onto a narrower game trail.

"This isn't a road, Merlin," Arthur said. His golden torc glinted in the weak winter sunshine beneath his voluminous cloak. His white horse was the only other trapping of his kingship today. They had left the entourage of warriors and courtiers happily warming their backsides in Caerduel. They both wore old clothes and carried small, ordinary travel weapons that would not draw attention to them.

"How often have I told you that sometimes a straight road leads away from the true path?" Merlin almost laughed as he cocked one eyebrow. A low-hanging branch knocked the laughter out of him. He returned his attention to what lay ahead.

He had sped their passage with magic along the Roman road until they turned off three leagues ago. Now they traveled at mundane speeds while Merlin restored his strength and senses.

He could have used Nimuë's help on the traveling spell. He just didn't have as much strength as he had a year ago. Once he convinced his protégée she didn't have to share his bed in order to share his knowledge, she had proved herself a strong magician and willing helper. But this chore required privacy. Privacy he had to maintain even from his most promising apprentice.

"How much farther?" Arthur's complaint sounded more like an imperial order than a youthful whine. The past months as Dux Bellorum and Ardh Rhi had matured him beyond his years.

"Not far now," Merlin reassured him. How many times had he said the same thing to Wren during the years of their travels?

Wren. She lived so close to this place. He longed to tarry with her, warm his fingers at her fire, and learn every detail of her life since last spring when they had parted with bitter words. She should be a part of today's expedition. But not until they had made peace with each other. He didn't have time for making amends to Wren for all he'd done to her. The configuration of moon and stars, the visions in the fire, and his dreams all said the deed had to be accomplished today before the sun set. It already passed its zenith.

"I see water reflecting sunshine." Arthur pointed straight ahead.

"Our destination. Come." Merlin kicked his horse to move a little faster.

The sacred pool lay at the base of a tumble of boulders, fed by a small cascade from the ridge above. When Merlin had led the kings and contenders to this place at the Solstice, a storm had raged and they had approached from the other side, closer to the crystal cave. Shallows existed on that side of the pool and ice spread out for a considerable distance. This side fell sharply into a considerable depth with ice spreading only two arm's lengths from the shore.

He checked Arthur for traces of recognition.

The boy seemed more interested in keeping the brisk wind from penetrating his cloak and multiple layers of heavy clothing.

Merlin dismounted and dropped the reins. The horse bowed its head, eager to crop the frozen grasses between the pool and the encroaching forest.

"What is this place?" Arthur dismounted as well, but kept his reins in hand.

"You know, boy, that there are ancient forces and beings that wander between this world and others, rarely acknowledging our short and trivial existence."

Arthur's eyes opened wide. "Wren introduced me to some faeries."

"Faeries are not the only beings who call this pool home." With his words Merlin's blood began to hum. His ears throbbed and every sense available to him came alive.

The light shifted and seemed to sparkle. He cast out his senses seeking the source of the change.

"Who?" Arthur whispered. He inclined his head toward the pool. The boy's sharp military eyes had spotted something before The Merlin had.

Curse these aging eyes. I should see everything first.

Beneath the ice a wavering form began to take shape. Merlin caught the impression of long feminine hair, so pale it was almost blue, drifting in the icy water. Above the hair a silvery crown shone in the sunlight. And then he saw a gown of fine white samite sparkling with diamonds floating like tendrils of water weed. The entire figure rose up from the depths of the pool.

"Lady!" he breathed. When he'd been here before, he'd seen only her diamond beringed hand.

"So beautiful," Arthur whispered. "What does she carry?"

Without looking, Merlin knew the Lady clasped the hilt of an elegantly long sword. Gold and silver decorated the hilt. Ancient runes of power ran the length of the blade. The hum in Merlin's blood increased as the sword became clearly visible in the gentle current—more visible than the Lady.

"She just lies there, drifting in the water. Is she alive?" Arthur unclasped his cloak, ready to risk his own life to plunge into the pool and rescue her.

"She lives. But you must make several promises before she will wake and make her purpose clear." Merlin almost held his breath, waiting for the moment of wonder to be undone. He prayed silently that his boy would prove worthy of the Lady's choice.

Arthur swallowed heavily. "What kind of promises?"

"Do you, Arthur, Pendragon of Britain and Dux Bellorum, swear that you will pursue your stated goal of ruling in peace, using justice and law as your guides, with all of your heart, mind, and soul?"

"I so swear." Arthur smiled out of one side of his mouth. He'd made a similar promise at his coronation last week at Imbolc.

"Do you, Arthur, Pendragon of Britain and Dux Bellorum, swear that you will honor all of the gods, and all of the ancient beings, using your mundane and spiritual powers to suppress the forces that threaten Britain, with all of your heart, mind, and soul?"

Arthur remained silent a moment, mulling over the complexities and hidden traps within the question.

"I so swear," he said at last.

"Do you, Arthur, Pendragon of Britain and Dux Bellorum, swear with your heart, mind, and soul that if gifted with this sword of power, you will use it only to preserve the forces of light against the encroaching darkness?" This one was harder. Merlin waited while his charge sorted through each word.

"As I understand the light, I so swear."

Before Merlin could clarify this last promise, the Lady beneath the water stirred. A great ripple of water and power shifted the balances of past, present, and future. Merlin reeled backward. Images flashed before his eyes so quickly he couldn't sort them. Out of the confusing mass of colors and shapes the gräal of life burst into view above the water. The colored strands of light and life spread out to entangle every rock, blade of grass, tree, and creature.

Strands of life encircled Merlin and Arthur, drawing them together and attaching them to every aspect of land. Golden light bathed the Ardh Rhi, binding him to the land and the lives it supported.

The Lady smiled. She thrust the sword up through the ice with a great shattering sound. The strands of light and life engulfed the sword blade, making it a part of the pattern of Arthur and Merlin and all of Britain.

The past became the future and the present embraced them both.

Merlin fought for balance, for understanding, for consciousness.

"I gift this blade, Excalibur, to you, Arthur, Pendragon of Britain!" the Lady proclaimed in a ringing voice that filled the pool and the clearing with the sound of harp melodies and tinkling bells. The music lingered and echoed, becoming a part of the entire pattern.

"I thank you, Lady," Arthur said, sounding very humble and awed. "May I be worthy of your trust." He bowed his head.

The music intensified and Merlin knew he would compose a great ballad tonight based upon that melody, this moment.

"Take it, boy. Grab it now before she withdraws her blessing on you and the sword," Merlin urged. His fingers itched for his harp.

Arthur stepped onto the ice. Miraculously it held his weight. One cautious step, then another. He bent down and clasped the sword hilt almost in a caress.

Immediately the Lady withdrew to the depths of her watery home, leaving Excalibur in Arthur's custody.

Arthur turned in a great circle, arms out in joy, the sword held up proudly. The strands of light and life circled around him in a wondrous weaving. For a moment he seemed to float above the precarious ice.

"Thank you!" he called. The sound reverberated through the forest, taken up by the wind, birdsong, and pulse of life.

The gräal faded into the sunshine.

The humming left Merlin's blood and he suddenly felt— diminished. Less than half the man he had been before.

But Arthur—Arthur fairly glowed. The sun dropped below the level of the treetops around the clearing, yet Arthur still glowed with power and with Life.

"My days draw to a close," Merlin murmured to himself. "I no longer have the kind of power necessary to wield the sword. I no longer have the will to persevere against Britain's enemies as my boy must. The sword came to him none too soon."

"I wish Wren could have been here," Arthur said as he stepped ashore. "I think she needed to be here to share this moment."

"That was not possible," Merlin said sadly. "Come, we must plan the battle that will lift the siege of Carmelide."

"Yes. We must relieve Leodegran and his daughter Guinevere. But I will hate to give Guinevere to Uriens in marriage. Leodegran should not have had to withhold her hand until Uriens swore loyalty to me. I should have won Uriens' support on my own."

"You and that sword will think of something." The blade continued to shimmer with power as Arthur wrapped it in the bedroll at the back of his saddle.

"Night draws near. Where do you propose we seek shelter?" Arthur asked as he mounted the magnificent while stallion.

Merlin immediately thought of Wren, less than an hour's ride away. Then he dismissed the notion. He'd seen in the gräal's pattern that he and his daughter now followed separate destinies.

"I wish things could have been different, Wren," he whispered.

Chapter 37

"WE will have a grand Beltane tonight," I told Marnia the next spring. "The moon will be waxing, nearly full, a good omen."

"That's what you said last year." Marnia pouted. Gradually, over the winter and spring she had begun following me on my missions into the forest and fields for herbs and plants. She still acted as if she resented my presence in her father's stronghold. But I noticed that she was most disapproving in Berminia's presence. When we were alone together, she acted almost as if she enjoyed my company and the lore I taught her.

Cedar and his friends had shyly fluttered around her hands last time we went to the faery pool. I didn't show her the cave and tunnel.

"We did not starve last year." I shrugged my shoulders in reply. I'd done what I could as priestess and as lady of the caer to keep us all safe and fed. The harvest had been larger than I had expected. We had gone hungry a few times, but never for long. The Goddess always provided something.

Sometimes the fresh meat or sacks of grain came from Father Thomas' refugees, but I knew my Goddess had as much of a hand in the provisions as Jesu Christus.

"You didn't have to give away so much of our harvest." Marnia sounded like her older sister with that statement. There was never enough food available to suit Berminia.

"The Goddess returns our deeds, good or bad, threefold." I dismissed the argument. "I will feed Yvain and then we will see what awaits us in the forest. I noticed a cluster of wildflowers just budding last week. Perhaps they are ready to make wreaths and garlands for tonight." I smiled as I lifted my four-month-old son from his basket.

Yvain had straight dark hair like Carradoc, but the brilliant blue eyes of my father. So far he had shown only an easy temperament, smiling at everything and laughing often.

He waved his fists in delight as I offered my breast. He fed eagerly. I never had enough milk for him and had to supplement with a wet nurse from the village. But I gave him what I could, when I could. A deep contentment washed over me. My sense of unity with the Goddess and the universe narrowed to the tiny focus of my son. What more could I want out of life?

Curyll. The voice in my head sounded like Cedar's giggling faery communications. Quite suddenly, I was transported back to the quiet pool on Avalon where I had confronted my sexuality in the form of Cedar grown to man size. The Goddess had promised me children by Curyll and a husband. I'd had a husband. I had one child.

Could I still have a meaningful relationship with my childhood love?

Our party of flower gatherers increased to seven by the time we actually left the caer. We all seemed determined on making a grand Beltane tonight. I suspected the nudity and blatant sexual overtones might be reduced this year. Father Thomas' influence had grown now that Carradoc no longer exerted stern disapproval of everything Christian.

I did what I could to keep the old ways. Showing Marnia the magic within the flowers and herbs we gathered was only a small part of that. Mostly I worked toward balances in the way I settled disputes and apportioned work, food, and land.

Caer Noddfa and its peace balanced the violence of the war-torn land.

By noon, Yvain fussed continually from the sling on my back. I fed him again and changed him. But still he fussed and chewed his fist, needing more nourishment. I couldn't concentrate on my preparations for Beltane. So I handed him to Hannah and sent him back to the caer with most of the women. Newynog whined to follow my son. She knew I'd be safe alone. She wasn't sure my son would be safe without her. Sometimes it seemed the aging wolfhound was as much a mother to Yvain as I was.

I laughed at the dog and patted her ears affectionately. I understood her need to follow the baby. With a bounding leap, she positioned herself beside Hannah and *our* son.

Marnia looked longingly at their retreating backs.

"Go," I shooed her away. "Rest and eat. I must be alone for a while before I cut the sigils into the newly plowed fields."

Marnia ran lightly to catch up with Hannah and the others. Kalahart had offered marriage to her a few weeks ago. At the time Marnia seemed reluctant to accept him. I wouldn't force her into a marriage she didn't want, not after my father had forced my marriage to Carradoc with near disastrous results. Now that Marnia knew the choice was hers, I hoped she would accept Kalahart tonight.

Grateful for the quiet that surrounded me now, I sought the little spring that cascaded into a pool where the faeries gathered. Since midwinter, the Lady who inhabited the watery depths seemed to sleep. I could barely detect her presence. The sword embedded in the altar had passed to the next Ardh Rhi. Was that the treasure she had guarded for the "Chosen?"

Twilight was the time of the faeries' greatest strength. At noon, I had the place to myself. I sank to the ground, listening to the quiet burble of water, letting shafts of sunlight warm my back.

The gentle rhythm of life within the forest slowly penetrated my hectic thoughts. My breathing slowed, my heart quieted until I heard earthworms crawling through the ground beneath me. Plants sent small shoots toward the sun, swelling with sap until they formed buds, ready to burst into bloom. My blood flowed with the sap, upward, reaching for the light of life. I felt rocks shift and crumble in a slow, endless pattern. I knew each particle of every mineral. The Pridd spun its path through the universe. I became a part of the whole, indistinguishable from any one part. Life from light, light into life. . . .

Time passed as it always does. Consciousness returned. I became aware of another being close by. With my eyes still closed, I heard the rhythmic click of teeth chewing and the soft sigh of breath. Cedar buzzed my ear with a bright giggle. I opened my eyes slowly, prepared to meet the Lady or whoever had found this hidden place. The sun had shifted around to midafternoon. It shone brightly against the brilliant white coat of a very large horse drinking from the creek that drained out of the pool. I'd met the horse before in two visions. Instead of spears and shield, he carried saddlebags today. The Dragon Rampant seal of the Ardh Rhi's couriers stood out on the worn leather.

The horse thought of himself as Taranis—the god of Thunder.

'Twas the horse I had heard munching on the grass. His master lounged against the grassy bank, his bare feet dangling in the pool.

"About time you woke up, Wren," he said. A smile creased his face.

"Curyll!" I squealed with delight and launched myself along the water's edge into his arms. I noted that he wore the ordinary bronze torc of a warrior, not the gold of a king. His leather tunic and leggings were travel-stained with dust and sweat. They looked as if he had worn them for many years.

He hugged me tightly, laughing as we rolled in the grass. "You still have twigs in your hair and grass stains on your skirt, my Wren. I'm glad you haven't changed."

I stilled within his embrace. So much had changed in the year since I'd seen him last. Our bitter parting words left a barrier between us.

I withdrew from his arms and stood up, brushing the offending grass and twigs away. "You are welcome to the hospitality of Caer Noddfa, as are all travelers."

"So formal, Wren?" He cocked one eyebrow in imitation of my father's gesture. This time he succeeded.

"The last time we met . . ."

"I was a foolish young man. I'm sorry, Wren. We've both had time to grow up since then. Many times I regretted leaving you." He reached a tentative hand toward me, then withdrew it.

"Many things have happened to both of us since then. We've had to make choices that took us along different life paths. Did you marry Morgaine?"

"No." He turned his back on me, shredding a long stem of grass with agitated fingers. "I have carved a different destiny for myself than to be her pawn. Or your father's."

My heart lifted. He hadn't been ensnared by Morgaine's magic or her need for demons.

He hadn't succumbed to my father's manipulations either.

Another must bear the name Arthur. My Curyll was free—and so was I.

Silence stretched between us. He rose slowly, gathering his boots and whistling for his horse. I couldn't let him leave on a note of sadness again.

"We were friends for a long time before . . . before we chose separate life paths. Are we still friends?"

"Of course, Wren. You are a dear friend, whom I trust above all others." He dropped his boots and grabbed me. We clung to each other for a long moment.

"Thank you for not hating me, Wren."

Words gathered around a lump in my throat and would rise no farther. I hugged him tighter, gathering his scent and the feel of his strong arms about me deeply into my memory.

I looked up at his face, needing to memorize the adult angles and planes to cherish in later years. I traced the hump of his broken nose and the little scar near his hairline with my forefinger. I relearned every inch of his dear countenance.

He stared back at me. Our eyes met for a very long moment. Then slowly he dipped his head and closed his eyes. I rose up on tiptoe to meet his kiss. We lingered and savored the taste of each other until we both ran out of air.

He jerked his head back, staring at me. His hands gripped me tighter, the caress of a man with a woman in his arms.

"Forgive me, Wren, for thinking you the child I once knew. You have grown into a beautiful woman." This time his kiss was longer, deeper, filled with more passion than friendship.

Dana help me, I returned his embrace with all the passion bottled up in me, cherishing every moment. His warmth filled me with a light-headed need to linger beside this sacred spring and pool for as long as the sun shone on the feast of Beltane. The feast of fertility when we all joined with the land to celebrate the eternal bounty of the Goddess.

He held my face with both of his large hands. This time his kiss promised fulfillment. My blood heated and flowed faster, as sap warmed and swelled within a flower.

Pressed against me, Curyll swelled as well.

We sank to our knees, still holding each other. I deepened our next kiss, accepting the inevitable.

"Wren, are you sure you want this?" he whispered, his finger tracing the neckline of my gown.

"How could I not want you, Curyll? I've waited for this moment since I first knew what men and women do together. And today is Beltane." I traced the line of his neatly trimmed beard, lingering on a scar I didn't remember. The hump on the bridge of his nose added interest and character to his face. I kissed it, flicking my tongue over the old break.

We stretched out on the grass. His hand shifted down to cup my breast, kneading it through the intrusive clothing I wore. He bent his knee, pressing between my legs with an exquisite pleasure. His other hand tangled in my hair, drawing me into yet another searing kiss. Heat filled my body, adding weight to my breasts, to my limbs, to my mind.

We rolled again so that I lay upon the grass. He unbuckled his ordinary and worn sword belt and returned to kiss me again before I could miss his comfortable weight against my breasts. Our clothing disappeared in stages. We explored each new exposed area with wondering hands, gentle kisses, and awe-filled gazes.

The earth, the wind, the sun, the cascading water, the trees, and the faeries watched and blended their gentle caresses to our own.

His penis filled my hand wondrously as he swelled even larger. My legs parted beneath his questing hand and then he filled me. Joy exploded within me in bright arrows that sped outward to include my lover. The faeries caught it and hurled it back, amplified a hundred times.

We arched and moved in rhythm with the pulse of life all around us.

Chapter 38

"SO, tell me about Boar, Ceffyl, and Stinger. And Lord Ector. Have you been home? How are Lady Glynnis and the dogs? Did Cook ever find another orange-and-white cat to replace Helwriaeth?" I asked all in a gush.

We rested our backs against a sun-warmed boulder, our toes dangling in the pool. Our passions simmered just below the surface, temporarily sated, ready to spring forth again at the slightest provocation.

"Cai is recovering from a wound to his left leg. He'll always walk with a limp, but is already reordering the schedule and arrangements of the chirurgeon's tent. They will work more efficiently."

We laughed at that and hugged each other with more than mirth. Boar always had to have everything lined up, in order according to size, shape, and usefulness.

"Ceffyl, as you so affectionately call Bedewyr, is head over heels in love with a new shipment of horses from Gaul. He talks of nothing but breeding a better warhorse with the long legs of the new steeds and the sturdiness of our local ponies."

We laughed at that, too, kissing long and passionately when the fit of giggles left us. The faeries picked up a new round of laughter at our hungry need to explore each other again. This time, we took it slowly, learning new pleasure centers and revisiting ones we already knew.

When he filled me this time, I met each thrust eagerly, building the pressure within us until we reached the pinnacle of joy together, then fell over the peak with shouts that echoed around the clearing.

Some time later, Curyll picked up the threads of our conversation without break. "Lord Ector has retired to the caer. He decided Lady

Glynnis' tongue was less sharp than a Saxon ax." He relaxed beside me, once more sated and limp.

"Is he well?" I asked. The comment was meant to be funny, but I knew Lord Ector's dedication to duty. He'd only retire under the direst of circumstances.

"He's just aging faster than he wants to. He has watched too many of his comrades die. The war is fought by a new generation of warriors with new battle tactics." He stared off into the distance. A dreamy quality overtook his expression.

I wondered at his role in the new generation of warriors.

"You don't ask about your father," Curyll said quietly.

"Da and I parted on less than happy terms."

"I wasn't in Venta Belgarum that last day. Uther sent me as messenger to the advance patrols."

"I wondered why you and Morgaine weren't among the couples Archbishop Dyfrig joined in marriage."

"Uther married her off to King Lot of the Orcades. When I got back to the main army, Uther had sent them back to those forbidding islands. Lot rejoined the main army, leaving her to pacify the Picts and Gaels. I haven't seen her since." He shifted uncomfortably.

"I'm sorry."

"Don't be." His words came out stilted. As if he'd rehearsed them over and over. "It wasn't a love match between us. We both sought to gain by the relationship. In some ways we succeeded better on our own."

After a moment of silence—regret?—he pulled me tight against his chest again. "Now tell me why you have joined the faeries in this forest. Is this your refuge—your Caer Noddfa?"

"You didn't know?"

"Know what?"

"The reason Da and I parted with black feelings. I couldn't break Da's compulsion to marry Carradoc. We parted with bitter words and harsh feelings. This forest is part of Carradoc's lands." I pushed myself away from him, a little.

"You *married* Carradoc and didn't divorce him the next day!" He sat up straighter, removing his arm from about my shoulders.

"I made promises I refused to break. But he died last autumn. I govern his caer and his lands in my son's name."

"I can't believe The Merlin forced you to go through with mar-

riage to that man." The physical distance between us remained less
than the emotional distance I sensed he built. "I can't believe you
stayed married to him."

"You told me it was a good match! Da claimed it was for my
protection. There are . . . were things about Carradoc none of us
suspected at the time. I must say, I do not regret his passing."

"I have to go, Wren. I've dallied too long as it is. I'm expected in
Caerduel tonight." He reached for his shirt and leggings.

"That's a long ride. Come back to Caer Noddfa for refreshment
and journey rations for the road."

"I can't. I have to get going." He stamped his feet into his boots.
"Archbishop Dyfrig awaits me. He's a busy man and can't delay too
long. Take care of yourself, Wren." Without another word, or hug in
farewell, he threw himself onto Taranis' back and kicked the horse
into a fast trot.

The vision granted to me by the Goddess two years ago hit me between the eyes like a headache as I watched Curyll ride off through
the woods.

A husband shall be yours and children by Curyll.

I knew, with a certainty born of my talent and awareness of the
unity of the universe, that I had conceived a child by Curyll.

But I had lost him again.

His horse threw up great clods of turf from his feet as he charged
through the underbrush. Curyll ducked low over Taranis' neck, avoiding low limbs from the grasping oak trees. He rode as if a demon
chased him.

Was I the demon who rode his back like guilt?

I lost sight of him among the new leaves and lengthening shadows.
An emptiness opened in my heart.

What had I said? What had I done to drive him away?

Sunset was nearly upon me and I still had a Beltane festival to
preside over. My awareness of the life beginning inside me pushed me
to thank Dana for my fertility. That blessing must guide me through
the rituals. Otherwise I'd spend the night crying.

We had been talking about Morgaine and her husband, Lot of the

Orcades. We had talked of my father and why I had not asked after his welfare.

We had discussed my dead husband last of all. The mention of Carradoc's name had sent Curyll flying for his horse. Did his meeting with Archbishop Dyfrig in Caerduel possess such great urgency?

Dyfrig, my father's duplicate in face and form. Or perhaps Dyfrig and Myrddin Emrys were the same man. The idea didn't surprise me. Nothing The Merlin did surprised me anymore.

I made my way back to the fortress prepared to preside over Beltane as both priestess and Lady. No one would question the paternity of the child I had conceived. This year. Many widows and maidens conceived on Beltane. No one asked them to name the father. Belenos, the sun god, could claim paternity to all of them. My father had taken advantage of the custom to claim the sons born of Beltane unions. Which of them had he chosen to become Arthur Pendragon?

Next year the growing number of Christians in the region might very well bring about changes in how we celebrated the fertility of the earth.

For now, I must hold Curyll's child close beneath my heart.

I sought no partners that night though several offered.

Life returned to our normal routine after Beltane. We planted new fields, we turned the sheep out to graze, we prepared bandages and healing herbs for the refugees we knew must come after the next battle, we repaired winter storm damage to the caer.

Kalahart and Marnia announced their betrothal the morning after Beltane. They gazed at each other lovingly and held hands whenever together. Several others also announced betrothals. Father Thomas frowned sternly as he hastily sanctioned each union. The night of the Summer Solstice would be busy with wedding celebrations.

Imbolc would be busier with births.

I smiled my approval. The fertility of my people reflected the health of the land.

Carradoc came home.

My world turned upside down.

He rode through the gates one afternoon, bellowing orders as if he'd never left.

Most of my people were out in the fields, even the broken remnants of the warband who had returned over the course of the winter.

Only a few retainers with duties about the caer rushed to greet their returned master.

Returned from the grave.

My footsteps were not as fleet as perhaps they should have been. I shifted the weight of Yvain on my hip before moving to greet the man I thought dead.

The hole in my heart that appeared when Curyll left grew bigger.

"I see you did your duty to me. Is it a boy?" Carradoc asked. He kept his hands firmly crossed in front of him rather than reach for his son. An angry scowl crossed his face, as if he expected me to defy him by producing a daughter.

Violence and anger permeated his aura. I wanted to retreat to the safety of the faery spring.

"Carradoc, meet Yvain. Your son was born three days before the Winter Solstice, as you predicted he would be."

Carradoc did not reach for his son. I held my baby closer.

A groom scuttled up, ready to tend Carradoc's horse.

"Make certain he gets good oats after you rub him down," Carradoc said.

The groom nodded silently, looking to me for confirmation that he should use up our precious store of last year's grain. As he turned, Carradoc slammed his fist into the groom's jaw. The man fell to the ground. He cowered, holding his arms up to protect his face and head.

"I said oats, not rough hay! You'll go hungry before my horse does," Carradoc screamed.

Suddenly, I knew I could never let him know that the new child I carried wasn't his. Our lives depended upon it.

And I could not divorce him. I'd have to leave Caer Noddfa. My people depended upon me. Carradoc would ruin them and the land.

"Come, Carradoc, you have ridden far. Eat and bathe, then we will talk of your adventures. Kalahart thought you dead." Dozens of questions flooded my brain.

Curyll must have known that Carradoc lived. He must have known how violent my husband could be.

Had he done me a favor by riding off so quickly without explanation?

I couldn't touch Carradoc, even to escort him into the hall. Yet I must soon take him to my bed. He must never know.

Llandoc chose that moment to emerge from the smithy. Charcoal and sweat darkened his hair and smudged his face. He carried a piece of broken harness, examining it carefully rather than looking where he was going.

"You!" Carradoc bellowed. "How dare you remain within my household?" He strode toward Llandoc with outstretched hands clenching as if strangling the young blacksmith. Carradoc's aura turned black with murderous intent.

Before I could intervene, Carradoc backhanded Llandoc across the face. The younger man staggered. A blank look filled his eyes as he fought for consciousness.

"Don't, Carradoc. He has done nothing to offend you. He's a valuable craftsman." I hung onto my husband's right arm, doing my best to keep him from striking Llandoc again.

"He defied me at Beltane. He stole the Queen of the May from me when none other dared compete against my prowess." Carradoc lifted his arm for another blow with me still clinging to him with one hand, the other supporting Yvain. Hannah took the baby from me with cries of distress. I added the weight of my second hand to stop Carradoc's violence.

"Every man has the right to compete at Beltane!" I protested. "Every man!"

Carradoc stared at me as if I was stupid.

"I am priestess of the Goddess. I proclaimed Llandoc's victory rightful."

"Did he get a child on my daughter?" A deadly calm spread across Carradoc's face. Anger kept his body rigid.

"No he did not. The Goddess did not wish to bless that union."

"You must have had a pitiful harvest if no child was born of the Beltane union," Carradoc sneered.

"We survived. But your union with Marnia would have produced no better results, Carradoc. She is your daughter." I continued to restrain his sword arm as best I could. My heart raced and felt as if it lodged inside my throat.

Suddenly, Carradoc lashed out with his left fist. He knocked Llandoc flat with one blow. Then he kicked the smith in the groin, viciously.

Llandoc screamed and writhed. He curled into a fetal ball, moaning.

"That's to make sure you never again touch my daughters on

Beltane or any other night. You're just a smith, not even a warrior," Carradoc sneered. "Brand him as a renegade, hamstring him, and throw him out," he shouted to whoever listened. Every man in the courtyard looked to me for direction.

I shook my head slightly, praying the men would obey me rather than the warrior who held these lands by right of sword.

By right of sword rather than by Goddess-blessed union with the land. He could inflict any injustice he chose upon us because of his battle prowess. Law, justice, and right had nothing to do with Carradoc.

What had happened to Curyll's dreams of a better world?

What would happen to the peaceful sanctuary I had built?

Carradoc strode into the Long Hall, never looking to see who obeyed him. He expected obedience.

My husband's anger made my belly cramp into a hard knot. Tonight, I had to make certain he believed my next child came from his seed. He'd never let me, Yvain, or my new baby live otherwise.

Chapter 39

"THIS wound still pains you," I said as I rubbed Carradoc's back with a wet cloth and soap. He sat in the bathing tub before the hearth in our bedchamber. Hannah and the other servants had filled it nearly to the rim with hot water. The water seemed to ease the tension along the angry scar that ran from his right shoulder blade to left hip.

That water cooled now, yet my husband lingered.

He'd been struck from behind by a Saxon ax. That much was clear. Battle often dissolved into the chaos of individual duels. Directions became confused. Enemy warriors could approach from any side.

Still, the placement of the wound suggested that Carradoc might have been fleeing the field. A great dishonor he'd never admit even if true.

"Aye, it pains me," he replied succinctly. Usually warriors gloried in retelling how they received their battle scars. I'd heard detailed reports from every member of the warband who had returned. When I'd first married him, Carradoc himself had related tales about many of the other scars on his body. But not this one.

"How did you survive? The chirurgeons must have worked long and hard to keep your life spirit from fleeing your body."

"The Merlin worked some kind of magic on me. He owed me that after I took you off his hands." Carradoc stood at last. He reached for a towel and covered himself modestly. He'd never bothered with clothing within the privacy of our chamber. He was proud of his body and his prowess in bed.

The knot in my belly twisted a little. I had to ignore his insults and seduce him tonight. Any later and he'd know the new baby was not his.

Reluctantly, I took another thick cloth from the bed and began rubbing him dry, taking time to caress and soothe his body.

"Leave off, woman!" He stalked to the opposite side of the room. "I must dress for the feast. My warband celebrates in the Long Hall already. I have to join them."

The sounds of drinking and merry storytelling had been going on for nearly an hour. Almost from the moment Carradoc had returned.

"They will entertain themselves for a good while yet. Surely they will understand why we linger." Swallowing my distaste, I kissed his shoulder and placed my hand on his hip, well away from the wound.

"I said leave off!" He pushed me away so hard I stumbled against the large tub.

"What ails you, Carradoc? You've always been ready to lay with me, at any time of day or night, in private or not. I haven't seen you in over a year. Why delay?"

"I'm tired. The journey from Campboglanna is long and arduous. I left Ardh Rhi Arthur's quarters yesterday at dawn." He mentioned the Roman fortress on Hadrian's Wall northeast of Caerduel where Arthur maintained his headquarters during the campaign season. Half a day's ride at most. "I am not yet sufficiently recovered to join the army this season. I need rest. I need food. You will only drain me of vitality." He dragged on his leggings.

I remembered Curyll's hasty retreat from my arms.

Beauty had never been mine. Yet Carradoc and Curyll had both made me feel desirable, womanly, and then rejected me. What did I do to them?

Not me. I reminded myself. *Them.* Something ails them both.

Perhaps Carradoc knew that Curyll had lain with me at Beltane.

Infidelity didn't bother Carradoc for himself. He set different rules for me, his wife.

But if Carradoc knew what I had done, he would have directed his anger toward me in the courtyard, rather than toward Llandoc. I wouldn't be alive now to question his motives.

"I must join my warband in the feast. I presume you are capable of honoring my return with a proper meal." Carradoc thrust me aside and stalked through the door into the Long Hall.

"You haven't asked after your other daughter, Nimuë," Berminia said flatly after she had formally greeted her father in the Long Hall.

Sitting beside Carradoc, I saw the muscle along his jaw jump. He turned to look at me before replying. I stared straight ahead.

"Where is my eldest daughter?" he asked in a near monotone.

I swallowed my unease at her threat to steal my father as I had stolen hers. Da would teach her balance and limitation. If she had fled to Morgaine, her lessons in magic would have been filled with demon lust and greed for more and more power.

I couldn't tell what Carradoc was thinking or feeling without looking at the layers of magical energy that surrounded him. I preferred not to look at him at all, but I had to give the illusion of a loving wife, ready and eager for the intimacies of the marriage bed.

"Your wife banished my sister along with the ravens that protected your castle, Father." Berminia pointed an accusing finger at me.

Several of the warband and retainers sighed in disgust and boredom. They'd heard every argument Berminia had come up with against me through the long winter.

Carradoc looked sharply at me.

I kept my expressions bland. No one jumped to add other damning evidence to Berminia's statement.

"Explain, Wren." Carradoc's voice sent cold chills of fear up my spine.

He'd never hidden the fact that Nimuë was his favorite, even before I'd discovered his incestuous relationship with her.

"I cleansed the fortress of a pestilence, an excess of ravens. Hundreds of them, not just the original three. Nimuë left with them. I didn't see her go or speak to her, so I don't know why she chose that path. One raven of the original three remains. He belongs here more than we do."

Carradoc nodded. He didn't give vent to anger. But he had to work at it. His jaw clenched until his cheeks turned white above his beard.

"Your wife also opened the gates of your fortress and welcomed Christians. She gave them food and shelter that we couldn't spare. She broke her covenant with the Goddess and deliberately defied you, Da."

"Is this true, Wren?" The edge in Carradoc's tone told me his control of his temper was fraying. I had to walk carefully.

"I did what I had to do. You left no warriors to defend us. We thought you dead, never to return. In order to hold this land for your son, I bound the people to me through trust and mutual concern. In return for hospitality, healing, and shelter, those who fled the aftermath of war have given us food, work, and loyalty. Some have stayed to work my . . . the land." I'd never call it his land again. "Other chose to freehold nearby. All of them, Christian and followers of the old way, owe us. I did what I had to do."

I didn't dare mention that some of the freeholders had Saxon forefathers. They had fled the violence of chaos along with native Britons, and I welcomed their hard work and loyalty.

"You had no right to open the gates to strangers when I had forbidden it."

"You had no right to let me believe you dead while you played war with your comrades."

"I was too grievously wounded to return home." He stood, thrusting back his chair. His fists balled, ready to slam into something. Into me.

"You could have sent a message. My father could have sent a message that you lived. And thrived. Your muscles have not wasted as they would from months bound to a sickbed. You have been well enough to ride and practice with sword and spear for months." I stood, too, facing him.

He raised his fist.

The entire hall stood silent, waiting. No one knew who to side with.

"There will be no more Christians polluting my lands. Berminia, you have too much time to sit and brood. Find yourself a husband tonight or I'll do it for you in the morning." Carradoc grabbed a pitcher full of ale from the closest serving maid and stalked back into our chamber with it. "Nimuë would never have defied me like this." He slammed the door closed. We all heard the bolt slide into place.

Chapter 40

MUCH later that night, I approached the still bolted door to my bedchamber. I had left Yvain with his wet nurse. Newynog whined at my heels. I sent her back to the kitchen. She slunk away, tail between her legs as if I had punished her.

I didn't want an audience for what I had to do.

Quietly, I knocked on the door. Carradoc didn't answer. I couldn't tell if he slept or ignored me. Biting my lip to hold back my fears and my disgust, I used a trick Da had taught me long ago. It didn't come easily to me so I rarely used it. Concentrating with all my being I manipulated the wood and metal pieces of the lock. The bolt slid open from the inside.

I hesitated a moment longer to see if Carradoc protested my entry. No sounds. I slipped into the room, as quiet as the moonlight that shone through the open window.

He sat in the high-backed chair facing the unshuttered window, gazing out on the courtyard. The hunched form of the single raven perched on the well was outlined in the dim light from the quarter moon. The empty ale pitcher lay on its side at his feet. He'd drunk enough to take the edge off his emotions, not enough to make him pliable.

I'd only seen Carradoc drunk twice. The first time, he had been hunting and returned without any meat for the table. He became surly and mean as he drank pitcher after pitcher of wine while swapping improbable tales of previous, glorious chases, with the other unsuccessful hunters. The other time, after our wedding banquet, he became reckless and demanding in his pursuit of personal gratification. My plans would only succeed if he took the latter course tonight.

"You might as well tell me what ails you. I'll find out eventually."
I handed him another full pitcher of ale. He didn't bother pouring it
into a quaiche—a footed mug big enough to satisfy a warrior's
thirst—just drank long and deep direct from the larger vessel.

"You're just like your father. No one keeps secrets from him either," he said bitterly. Another deep swallow.

"I hope that I am less devious in my life than my father." My
own bitterness rose. I was about to commit a very large deception.

"What did you do to Nimuë? Answer me truly, for I'll know if
you lie." The quietness of his demand betrayed his extreme hurt.

I walked a dangerous line. "I sought to reset the balances around
the fortress. She had unnaturally brought thousands of ravens to
plague us. They destroyed crops, attacked children, fouled the water.
Nimuë resisted the magic I used to send the birds elsewhere. But my
disciplines are stronger than her haphazard spellcasting. By the time I
returned here, she was gone, fled into the teeth of a storm."

"A storm you raised with magic."

"A storm that rushed to fill a temporary vacuum."

He stared at me blankly. Even sober, I doubted he'd understand
how the forces of nature found their own balance.

"I banished her spell and did not fill its place with more unnatural
magic. The winds rushed to fill the vacancy."

"Who will fill the vacancy left by her?" He drained the pitcher of
ale in one long quaff followed by a loud belch. "Bring me more," he
ordered.

Much more and he wouldn't be able to perform. For all that I
wanted him muddleheaded and forgetful, I needed him potent.

"You have two other daughters and a son . . ."

"No one can replace Nimuë!"

"Not replace." I bit my tongue to keep my own temper in check.
"No life can be replaced. But your life isn't empty. You should rejoice
in the blessings left to you."

"You sound like one of your bloody Christians. I expected more
from a priestess of the Goddess. Or have you been seduced by some
mewling peacemonger?"

"No one has seduced me." My afternoon with Curyll had been
mutual passion. "I honor all of the gods by celebrating life. I cannot
allow myself to dwell on death and destruction. That is why I opened
our doors to refugees, to heal the wrongs inflicted upon them by

men." I couldn't hold back the anger that crept into my voice. I shouldn't have to defend myself to this man.

"Nimuë could heal me."

"Heal what? What ails you that I, your wife and a priestess with magic, can't deal with?"

"Shut up and bring me more ale."

"Not until you tell me why you reject my presence and sit here brooding when we should all rejoice at your return?" I stood in front of him, hands braced on the arms of his chair, my face inches from his. His breath stank of stale ale and his body of stale sweat. The sweat of fear.

What could induce such deep dread in this formidable warrior? His self-assurance had grown into arrogance long ago.

"Obey me, Wife! I need more ale."

"No, you don't. You need to tell me the truth. You need to resume your life as lord of this fortress and protector of your people." I could have forced the words from him with tricks or magic. But I didn't. I was violating enough of my scruples tonight.

"I grieve for a beloved daughter." He couldn't hold my gaze, stared at his hands limp in his lap.

" 'Tis more than that. You fornicated with Nimuë regularly. Oh yes, I know all about your abominable relationship with your daughter. Don't look away from me in shame. You weren't ashamed to openly seek her on Beltane last year. But I doubt she satisfied you in any way other than a convenient fuck. I can do that."

"No, you can't."

"Why not? I satisfied you well enough to conceive on our wedding day."

"No one can satisfy me ever again."

A glimmer of an idea flashed across my mind. My heart almost leaped with joy at the thought he might prove impotent. I'd never have to endure sex with him again.

Except that I already carried another man's child. If Carradoc ever suspected he wasn't the father, he'd kill us both.

"I am a priestess. I know how to satisfy Belenos, the most demanding lover of all. Surely I'm good enough for you, Carradoc."

He didn't seem to hear the mockery in my voice.

"My wounds cut deeper than the scar shows," he whispered.

"How deep? I have healing magic."

"More than your father?"

I stood up straight, letting my questions show on my face rather than in words. If I spoke, I might give in to the bitterness I felt toward the father who had betrayed me. A man who lied with every breath and mistrusted everyone, including his daughter.

If I dared, I could bring in a maiden and a crone and try the great healing magic on him. But I had yet to make it work completely and each attempt left me drained and vulnerable. I'd have nothing left in me to deal with Carradoc.

"The Merlin tried several of his spells. Nothing worked."

"Have you tried?"

"Yes, I tried. The camp followers are most skilled in their work, too. None of them raised a bit of interest in my . . ." He looked to his lap where his hands continued to hang limply over his equally limp groin.

I took a deep breath and swallowed my disgust. "Camp followers may be skilled, but they do not worship Dana as I do. They do not recreate the union of Pridd Mother and Sun Father that springs forth in fertility."

Before I could think twice about what I must do, I released his belt and raised his tunic. With deft fingers, I unlaced his masculine garments as quickly as I had Curyll's. I had to close my eyes to keep going.

My mouth and hands pretended they enticed Curyll. With the image of his beautiful body firmly in my mind, I proceeded to coax and entice Carradoc with a measure of enthusiasm. It took longer than I thought. A healthy man would have stood proud and long in moments. Eventually I persuaded enough life into him that he clasped my shoulders with something akin to passion. My clothing fell to the floor. Moonlight bathed us with illusory shadows. Cloaked in the mystery of womanhood, I became Dana, the Goddess in all women. This night's work must insure the safety of my unborn child and the well being of my son.

Dana, help me! I pleaded silently. *Give me strength.*

The soft light seemed to invade my being with gentleness. Pity for this once arrogant and powerful man replaced my dislike.

I slithered into his lap, meeting his almost filled flesh. I forced myself not to recoil from his touch. He buried his face in my breasts. I twisted and shifted and groaned with fake passion.

We achieved something akin to joining. Too soon he lay his head against the chair back and released his grasp on me.

"Now I'll get you that ale," I said, retrieving my clothes. "You are healed if you want to be, Carradoc. But I think you know that your perverted love for Nimuë is what preys on you rather than your wounds. Don't come to me again until you are finished with your grief for her and yourself."

I retched up my dinner in the courtyard before I fetched the ale. Three pitchers this time. I didn't want him remembering how weak his performance truly was. Or how despicably deceitful I had become.

"What makes you think you are good enough to offer marriage to my daughter?" Carradoc roared at Kalahart. He stood in front of his chair in the Long Hall. The remnants of his warband lolled on benches on either side of the hearth down the length of the building. They'd all been drinking heavily, but weren't drunk. They had repeated this pattern nearly every night for three months, every night since Carradoc had returned.

All of our routines had turned upside down under Carradoc's glaring disapproval. All of the weddings planned for Solstice night had been postponed until Carradoc could approve each one individually. Then he refused to consider any of them until autumn.

But tonight, Kalahart had come forth to press his suit of Marnia on his own.

"On the battlefield you and I fought as equals, Lord Carradoc," Kalahart replied. The warrior stood straight and proud in the face of his lord's wrath. In the months since recovering from his wounds he had been a valuable aide in the running of this caer. I'd learned to trust and respect the man. My opinion of him rose further.

"You didn't last the campaign, too weak to stand up to the enemy." Carradoc dismissed him.

"I received my wounds in honorable battle, as did you, my Lord. I dispatched my enemy after a hard fight. A worthy opponent."

I sensed more words hovering on his lips. Kalahart wisely refrained from mentioning that Carradoc's back had been to the man who struck him down.

"Kalahart helped defend and protect your family and lands from

outlaws this past winter while you kept your duty to the Ardh Rhi
and Britain," I reminded Carradoc in a quiet whisper. I sat beside
him. Traditionally, I would have helped serve the men and left the
debate to them. But I had earned my place beside the lord through
the long months of creating a safe haven for our people. Hearing
petitions and dispensing justice formed as much a part of governing
as the hard work.

These people were my people now. I had to defend them against
Carradoc's arrogance and sometimes brutal sense of superiority as well
as against outlaws, bad weather, and years of neglect.

"Without Kalahart's knowledge and skills as a warrior, we could
have been overrun and burned out a dozen times," I whispered in his
ear. Carradoc would reject every word I said if I advised him openly.
"Kalahart is worthy of Marnia. Besides, she carries his child from the
Beltane Festival. She wants to marry him. He is strong. Bind him
close to you through this marriage rather than alienate him and send
him to the warband of your enemy. You'll have grandsons to support
Yvain in battle."

Carradoc blustered and choked on the ale he quaffed in increasing
amounts. Boredom, guilt, or frustration?

"No man is worthy of my daughters. . . ."

"And Nimuë ran away to find a husband when you wouldn't give
her one," Marnia interrupted. "Do you want me to run away, too?"

I silently applauded the girl's determination. A year ago she
wouldn't have stood up for herself, let alone faced Carradoc with a
demand and ultimatum. A year ago, none of us had.

Newynog thumped her tail against the rushes in agreement with
Marnia. I touched the dog's head, and she lapped my fingers before
settling at my feet again. She lay between Carradoc and me. My husband took this as a sign the dog favored him once more. I knew the
wolfhound protected me from him. I hadn't shared Carradoc's bed in
three months and Newynog guarded my pallet among the other
women every night.

"You'll have to continue proving your worthiness, but I guess I'll
accept you. The women of the house will give me no peace until I
do!" Carradoc howled with a measure of levity. The men around him
laughed at his joke. They ceased slapping each other on the back and
pounding the floor with their swords too quickly, drowning their
laughter in another round of ale.

Marnia and I breathed a sigh of relief in unison. The look we exchanged confirmed our alliance in domestic matters. For the first time in her life she blossomed with full breasts and pink cheeks.

Berminia still sulked in corners and ate everything in sight, but she'd stopped openly blaming me for everything that could possibly go wrong with her life. Carradoc hadn't upheld his threat to find her a husband.

"Who are these other petitioners cowering at the back of my hall?" Carradoc peered drunkenly at the three men who stood respectfully silent by the door. Their travel-stained scarlet tunics and weary faces told us they had ridden far.

I don't think anyone but myself noticed the fine cut of the cloth and their disciplined posture. They resembled Curyll in their stance. Royal couriers?

We had heard rumors of Arthur's resounding victory at Mount Badon. I'd had confirmation of it from the faeries and the wind whispering in the trees. These men probably brought official word and news of a celebration. I hoped Carradoc and I weren't invited.

"Come forward," Carradoc said through his next mouthful of ale.

The trio stepped forward in unison, faces set in a mask that betrayed no emotions. Their auras remained equally controlled, as if their military discipline stretched to include their most basic emotions.

"Lord Carradoc, I bear greetings from Arthur Pendragon, Ardh Rhi of Britain." The center man saluted Carradoc and proffered a roll of parchment, as if he expected the warlord could read.

My husband passed the missive to me as if it were trivial. I unrolled it and read the neat Latin words while the messenger repeated the same words in British. His voice rang out in tones meant to carry throughout the noisy hall.

The handwriting on the parchment sent chills up my spine. A roaring in my ears replaced the sound of the man's voice. My father had written this invitation.

"We are invited to witness Arthur's wedding, Wren. He broke Uriens of Gorre's siege of Leodegran's fortress and sent him scuttling home with his tail between his legs. None of Uriens' faction dare stand against Arthur now. As a reward for victory, Leodegran broke Uriens' betrothal to Guinevere and now gives his daughter to Arthur.

I always knew the old lecher would land on the side of power, regardless of who ended up as Ardh Rhi!" Carradoc laughed again.

My heart beat double time. At the bottom of the written invitation Da had scrawled a small private message for me. "Please come, Wren. I need you. I miss you. Only you can prevent disaster." He'd signed it with a tiny drawing of a merlin falcon and a singing wren flying together in harmony.

I couldn't go. I had to go. I couldn't trust my father. I wouldn't be content until I knew why he had pushed me to marry a monster like Carradoc, why Bishop Dyfrig wore Da's face, why magic came so much easier to me after I lost my virginity.

Only The Merlin had the answers to my questions.

I might see Curyll again at the royal wedding since he was a royal courier. Did I dare confront my lover?

"We must have new clothing for the wedding," I heard Carradoc announce to all assembled. "There are journey stores to be packed, horses to be readied, gifts for the bride and groom. . . ."

"I can't go," I said flatly. I couldn't leave my home undefended again.

"Of course you must go." Carradoc waved aside my objection.

"The baby . . . 'twill be too dangerous for me to travel." The baby. What if I met the true father of this child? I wasn't certain I could keep my secrets.

"Nonsense. You're healthy and blooming. Showing after only three months."

Closer to four months, but I didn't correct him.

"We'll be back long before your time. If we're delayed, you'll birth the child in Camlann, and receive the Ardh Rhi's blessing and maybe rich gifts, too. This invitation gives me the chance to win back power and prestige after missing the greatest battle of the century because of these cursed wounds. I might win the crown of Gorre yet. Of course we are going. I'll not hear another objection, Wife."

Chapter 41

"ARE we ready?" Nimuë asked the demon. She petted her shoulder. If she looked very carefully, she could see the outline of the creature. Her magic had given him life and strength. Soon she'd be strong enough to bring him fully into this world.

"I am ready," the demon affirmed. "Full night is upon us. The moon is dark. You have our tools. Let us begin."

"Are you certain this will keep Wren from meeting her father?" Nimuë asked. She'd been unable to seduce the aging magician in over a year. But she had delved into his mind numerous times while he slept and learned much more than he would have willingly taught her. She settled for his knowledge rather than his life. Though, if she could manage to banish his spirit to the Netherworld in Wren's presence, she'd be truly happy for the first time in her life.

Then she'd just transplant the half-formed demon into the old man's body and have a fierce lover as well as a magical partner.

The demon didn't like that idea. It wanted a younger, more resilient body; preferably one of Arthur's warrior companions. They agreed, by mutual silence, to discuss the matter fully when Nimuë commanded enough magic to perform the transformation.

"Our work tonight will give us partial revenge," the demon reassured her. "Wren will not be able to resist the traps we set for her."

Nimuë crept into The Merlin's chamber. He slept deeply, aided by the potion she had slipped into his wine. The tools she needed lay where she had left them on the little travel chest. She grabbed the scroll, herbs, crystals, and vials. At the last minute she lit a small lantern from the smoldering coals in the brazier. Why waste her strength calling the element Tanio to bind her spells when she had fire at hand?

The guards at the gate looked right at her without seeing her. That was a spell she had perfected early on. Few knew she lived in Camlann, fewer still saw her walking beside The Merlin, gleaning knowledge from him.

She passed a hand before the eyes of each guard. "Sleep," she commanded each in turn. "Sleep until I return this way." They dropped their heads, eyes closed, knees locked so they remained standing.

The small pedestrian gate beside the massive entrance to the caer opened easily on well-oiled hinges—a chore she had taken care of last night. The hinges were supposed to squeak to alert the guards of anyone sneaking in or out of Camlann.

Nimuë used the demon's night vision to survey the wide processional way. It ran in a dozen loops and twists down the slope of hill.

"There and there and again here and here." The demon highlighted the nine places Nimuë needed to set her spells.

"Nine! I thought you said I only needed three," Nimuë protested. "I'll be so exhausted I won't be able to watch them work when *she* arrives tomorrow."

"Three times three. We need them all. But don't worry. I'll watch to make sure *she* falls victim to the traps." The demon laughed in her ear.

Pouting, Nimuë reluctantly set her steps for the closer target.

"No," the demon almost shouted. "You must begin at the bottom of the hill and work upward."

"But then the pattern will be set widdershins. I only know how to do this deosil, as The Merlin taught me."

"If you do this *his* way, the magic will invite his daughter in. We need to repel her, make it impossible for her to walk through the gate. And she must walk. If she rides, the horse will protect her from the bulk of the magic. She will feel ill, uncomfortable, but will still be able to pass."

"I assure you, Wren will walk. She never mounts a horse unless she has to."

Grimly, Nimuë marched to the bottom of the hill, cutting across the looping road, tripping over obstacles and sliding on her bum on the steepest part. By the time she reached the first target, she was dusty, sweating, and tired. She wanted a drink and a chance to rest before throwing her remaining strength into magic. The demon prodded her with sharp bites on her neck and shoulders. She swatted at it to make it stop. It merely laughed and faded into the Netherworld a little so that she hit herself.

"Damn you! That *hurt*. I need rest."

"You need to work." The demon bit her again.

"All right!" For once the demon's prodding didn't send sexual thrills through her body. Normally she reveled in them because they reminded her of Carradoc's rough enticements.

She laid the herbs and kindling in proper order, sprinkled them with a little water from a clear spring, and set light to the combination from her little lamp. While Pridd, Tanio, and Dwfr merged with Awyr, she read strange sounding words from the scroll. She didn't know the meaning of the syllables she uttered, but the demon did. She guessed that was enough.

Then she moved uphill, to the next target and set it with the second set of phrases on the scroll.

She was about to add fire to the third target when a heavy hand landed on her shoulder.

"Yeek!" She jumped up, searching for an attacker.

"I won't hurt you, Nimuë," The Merlin said from the darkness behind her. "What are you doing?"

"Um—I'm—um—why are you awake?" She fought to keep the panic out of her voice.

"I rarely sleep more than a few hours these days and often wander the city at this hour. I smelled your magic and came to investigate. I appreciate the help you gave me in getting to sleep tonight. That potion is most efficacious. I believe I lingered in slumber an extra hour, perhaps two." He yawned without bothering to hide his mouth behind his hand.

"But what brings you out tonight, Nimuë? The dark of the moon is a dangerous time to wander unescorted."

"I'm setting wards on the city. We don't want strange magicians sneaking into Camlann to disrupt the Ardh Rhi's wedding." She twisted the truth only a little. The Merlin always knew when she lied.

"Commendable idea, my dear, but you need to start at the top and work deosil."

I told you so! Nimuë sneered at the demon.

"I thought to work in a circle, starting and ending at the bottom, the first ward a stranger would encounter."

"Interesting idea. Let me ponder that. Meanwhile, we will finish in the customary order. I'll do the next ward, at the gate and we'll alternate. Shared magic is always stronger." The Merlin picked up her sach of herbs, vials, and kindling and hoisted it to his shoulder. "What scroll is this?" He spread it out, peering at it from the light of the little lantern.

Nimuë sensed his growing dismay at the same time the demon grew heavier on her shoulder. It reached out one insubstantial pincer to grab the rolled parchment out of the old man's hands.

"These spells will not do at all," The Merlin mused. He let the rolled parchment snap closed. "Though I can see why you thought they might. The Arabic writing is confusing if you are not thoroughly grounded in the language. I will set the rest of the wards with the proper Greek words. Go back to bed, Nimuë."

"No!" She fought for an excuse to stay. He'd do it all wrong. He'd negate the first three wards she'd set. "I need to do it. I started it. I must complete it or it will unravel."

"Yes, you are right. But let me whisper the proper spells into your mind as you recite the words."

"I have a better idea." She smiled with all the brilliance and seductive power she could muster. Holding his gaze with her own, she touched his left temple with her fingertips. The spell he wanted her to use embedded in her own memory quicker than thought.

"You do that remarkably well, my dear."

"I learned from the best." She let her fingers shift from quest to caress, lingering near his mouth. "Go back to bed, Myrddin Emrys. You need your rest."

He froze in place, eyes wide. "Don't move, Nimuë. Don't think, don't breathe."

"What . . . ?" she whispered. What could have frightened the most powerful magician in all of Britain?

"A demon hovers around the ward you were about to set. It has been giving you improper directions."

Nimuë almost relaxed. The dismissive words, "Oh, that," wanted to leap from her tongue. She swallowed them.

"A d . . . de . . . demon!" She feigned panic.

"You must not light this ward. Scatter it to the four winds with your foot."

She obeyed.

The demon growled in her ear. Its ferocity frightened her.

The Merlin wove his hands in an intricate pattern, muttering foreign words. The hair on Nimuë's arms stood on end at the eldritch energy that crackled from his fingertips.

"There, the demon fades and retreats." The Merlin sagged visibly.

The demon left Nimuë. She missed its now familiar weight on her shoulder and in her mind. She felt naked, exposed, vulnerable. She wanted to stamp her foot and scream in frustration.

"Let us start this all again, properly, from the beginning. Whoever summoned that demon wants to destroy the Ardh Rhi. I merely want to disrupt the marriage before it ends in disaster. You will help me, won't you, Nimuë? With Wren's assistance, we just might be able to prevent our lovesick Ardh Rhi from plunging us into another disastrous war."

"Of course, I'll help you, Myrddin Emrys. I'll help you do what must be done." Somehow, she'd take his spells and twist them. Somehow. She hoped the demon reemerged from the Netherworld long enough to help her.

We traveled to Camlann slowly. We took nearly a month when a fast rider could do it in a week, less if he had changes of horses arranged ahead of time. Marnia suffered a miscarriage the day before we left. She and Kalahart remained at Caer Noddfa to guard and manage the estates. Berminia offered to care for her younger sister until she recovered. Mostly, she refused to go anywhere with me.

I stalled and delayed as much as possible. Carradoc's returned confidence and joviality made my own self-absorbed sullenness stand out. Even he noticed how I dragged in the mornings and sought our pavilion early each night. My pregnancy showed more each day. I prayed that this baby would be small like her brother. And late.

More than my pregnancy made the journey interminable.

"I dread the future, Carradoc," I explained when he questioned me two days out from the Ardh Rhi's new capital. "Dana does not privilege me with glimpses of the future often, but every vision I have had has been true. Something terrible awaits us in Camlann." Even though my fingers and toes never warmed, I couldn't linger by the fire lest I look too deeply into the flames and see the nature of the disaster. If Carradoc discovered the truth . . .

"Your father always said that the future is not written in stone. Visions are enigmatic so that men can take charge of their destinies and make changes for the better," he replied, polishing his already gleaming sword.

"Only if you make the changes The Merlin wants," I said bitterly. "His need to control people and events overrides the truth of the gods." I paced the pavilion, straightening the bedding, feeding the brazier, checking the water pitcher. All useless activities. But I couldn't sit still, couldn't rest, couldn't stop asking myself questions.

What, or who, was Da trying to control this time? I wouldn't know until I confronted him in the capital. Two days' easy ride. I had two days to find a way to keep him from controlling me ever again.

We approached the refortified hill from the northwest. Romans had pulled down the centuries-old hall and ramparts. Arthur had re-built them. The sun was nearing the horizon when the caer came into view. The setting sun reflected off the newly erected timber walls topping the first rampart, giving them a golden sheen. Stone founda-tions for the timber made the walls soar higher than normal. A second walled rampart separated the Long Hall from the town that sprawled down the slopes of the hill. The huge Long Hall was clearly visible on the crown of the hill, a suitable capital for a British Ardh Rhi. This was the largest hill fort I had encountered on any of my travels throughout Britain.

The broad dirt road had been pounded flat and smooth by hun-dreds of soldiers, pilgrims, and petitioners over the course of the sum-mer. Dust rose with each plodding step of our horses. Carradoc whipped our mounts into a fast trot, pushing aside anyone who stood in our way and leaving the baggage carts to catch up when and how they could. I closed my ears to the curses of those on foot who also trekked toward the capital for the festivities. All my concentration belonged with my horse and staying mounted. A fall now, at this speed, would surely damage the baby and myself beyond repair.

But I knew better than to try to curb my husband's arrogant push to reach the Ardh Rhi before the city gates closed with the sunset. As we neared the Autumnal Equinox, the days shortened rapidly.

The massive gates still gaped open, wide and inviting through a shining arch. My heart lifted in spite of my doubts and questions about the coming meeting. Camlann seemed to reach out to me, beckoning me forward.

We followed the twisted road up the steep slope. I knew that each switchback and bend offered opportunities for defenders to set traps and rain missiles on enemy heads from the top of these very high walls. My heart beat hard as I recognized a ritual maze in the making. Power rose in my blood as I marked each twist upward. But it was new power, raw and untapped, set there recently rather than the ancient forces I had met above Venta Belgarum or on Avalon's tor.

Had my father surrounded Camlann with magic, or had another? The power sang in my blood as if it were my own, not someone else's.

I gathered the power around me in a cloak of protection. The energy fled as fast as I grasped it. I expended some of my own strength to bring the magic back. It dissipated as sand through my fingers. And so it would for any magician or priest who sought the power. Further attempts to control the power would sap all of my energy while denying me access to fundamental strengths.

What enemy plagued the new Ardh Rhi that his defenses had to be magical as well as military?

I set a mental barrier between myself and the traps. For the sake of my baby, I couldn't waste any more strength on it.

"Your father awaits us, Wren," Carradoc announced quite loudly as we ducked beneath the timbered archway of the first rampart.

"Where?" I didn't see any single figure that stood out in the crowd filling the lower plateau of the hill fort.

"Up there, beside the Pendragon."

I followed Carradoc's pointing finger with my eyes above a second timbered wall to the immense hall that filled the crown of the hill. Tree trunks carved with mystical symbols stood on either side of the doorway. The carvings soared above the rooftree in proud proclamation that here resided a king of note, a warrior worthy of the crown. Victory banners fluttered from dozens of flagpoles marking an avenue approach to the hall. Two mounted warriors could ride through that portal without ducking. Standing in the center of the opening, filling it with his personality, stood my tall, slim father in a robe of bright blue. But he couldn't dwarf the man who stood beside him. Curyll's sun-bleached hair gleamed golden-red in the dying light. His torc glowed in a bright echo of the sun on his hair, the same rich gold as my father's torc. A band of imperial purple graced the Roman toga he'd draped over his white tunic and leggings.

My heart leaped to my throat in joy at the first sight of my lover. My father, The Merlin, stood beside him, in a place of honor given only to a valued adviser.

Then I realized the import of Curyll's majestic clothing and golden torc. Arthur Pendragon, Ardh Rhi of Britain, was the father of my child.

Chapter 42

BLACKNESS roared through my ears. My skin turned to ice while fires burned through my blood. The world tilted and I slid downward . . .

Strong arms grasped my waist, preventing me from falling off my horse. I leaned into the man who held me, knowing instinctively that Curyll would cradle and protect me. His familiar scent filled my head and lulled my panic.

"Stand aside and let the poor girl breathe," a woman ordered. Her even voice and authoritative tone grated on my nerves. I almost opened my eyes. But I didn't want to confront Nimuë yet.

"She's merely tired after a long ride. This babe wearies her," Carradoc said. His tone dismissed my faintness as if I did it every day. I'd never fainted in my life and certainly not in his presence. I'd never reveal a weakness to the monster I had married.

Reluctantly, I stirred within Curyll's embrace. I wanted him to go on holding me forever.

Then I remembered why we had come to Camlann and who my childhood friend truly was. My father's marked attention to a boy shunned by his foster family, his careful tutelage of Curyll when others thought him stupid, my own observations of his intelligence and political insight, had told me the truth long ago. I had grasped at his lack of royal trappings and entourage as evidence that Da had chosen another as Ardh Rhi, making Curyll into a royal courier in my mind.

With a sigh of regret, I found my feet and my balance, pushing myself away from Curyll. He sighed also as he dropped his arms to his sides.

"Wren!" My father enveloped me in a hug that threatened my restored breathing. "You came."

I couldn't return his embrace. Part of me wanted to. Part of me remembered all the manipulative things he'd done to bring us all to this situation.

"But what is this, Daughter? Am I truly to be a grandfather at last?" He held me at arm's length surveying my travel-stained gown and muddy boots. His eyes lingered on the growing bulge of my belly.

"Oh, but you're a grandfather already, Merlin." Carradoc slapped his back with comradely enthusiasm. I was getting tired of that over-hearty gesture. "We left my son, Yvain, at home with a wet nurse. He's a bit young to travel so far. A fine healthy boy who promises to grow tall and strong as any warrior in Britain," Carradoc continued proudly, as if he was totally responsible for the boy's being and I had nothing to do with it.

"Yes, you told me last winter that she was expecting. I hadn't received word of the birth, so I assumed she'd lost the child," Da said softly, looking at Carradoc and not me.

A wall of silence grew between us. We both knew why I hadn't bothered to send a messenger to him. He'd thrown me into a marriage I didn't want merely to exert his control over the lives of all he encountered—of all Britain.

"Merlin, dearheart," Nimuë said, her voice soothing, placating, and far too sweet to be real. "Let the girl wash up and rest. We wouldn't want her to lose this child because you need to keep her standing in this windy courtyard too long." Solicitously, my stepdaughter took my arm and led me toward a large circular hut next to the hall, a place of honor reserved for the Ardh Rhi's favorite adviser.

She hadn't greeted her father with any more enthusiasm than I had greeted mine.

Too many conflicting emotions swirled around us. Everyone here had secrets, me most of all. I needed time and privacy to think. More than that, I needed to watch and listen from the shadows, gathering information. The habits of my childhood would serve me well. I knew how to hide in the shadows.

But so did Nimuë and The Merlin.

From the sheltering shadows, I watched a myriad of servants and retainers prepare the Great Hall for a night of feasting after the wedding of Ardh Rhi Arthur Pendragon to the Lady Guinevere. Only hours separated us from the ceremony. A huge round table, open in the center, filled the hall. Sections of it could be removed to make it smaller for Arthur and his Companions to sit in council. Arthur would not preside at the "head" of this table, he would sit on the same level, in a circle of equality with his men. The table had been a wedding gift from King Leodegran. But I doubted the idea of equality originated with him.

For tonight, every one of the one hundred table sections was in place to accommodate the hundreds of wedding guests. Wherever Arthur and his bride sat would become the head of the table. Prestige lay in proximity to him. I wondered where The Merlin would place me. My father certainly would be on Arthur's right, Guinevere on his left.

Rumor said that Morgaine, her husband Lot, and their children would not have the honor of a place near the king. I wondered what this insult would do to Morgaine's bitter personality. But Lot had not honored his promise to keep the Picts from attacking Britain. Twice this past summer Arthur and his companions had ridden out from Campboglanna to defend British settlements near Hadrian's Wall. Lot hadn't sent a warband when requested to aid the Ardh Rhi in his latest conflict with Uriens of Gorre.

Guinevere entered the Long Hall, scattering servants, flowers, and instructions in her wake. She giggled at each fragmented statement.

Her golden-blonde hair was braided and coiled into an intricate design that highlighted her long neck. Her skin was almost as colorless as her hair. She couldn't be more than twelve. Child slim and fragile.

Curyll, you can't do this! My heart ached. *How can you love this pale child after you loved me last Beltane?*

"Flowers! Lots and lots of spring flowers, here and . . . and wherever," Guinevere giggled.

The steward hovering two paces behind her frowned. "Lady, autumn is upon us. Our selection of flowers is limited and the colors dark rather than the delicate pastels you prefer," he said. He looked as if he'd wearied of this conversation hours ago.

"But you know what I mean," she apologized with an endearing pout. "You know how to make it right."

The steward bowed and smiled and set about the half-formed

plans she had hinted at. He flicked his wrist and a dozen servants scurried about.

They all clearly adored the child.

About my height, her braids seemed wispy and as thin as herself. Tendrils of hair broke free of her restraints and flew about in a wispy cloud resembling an aura every time she moved her head. She wore white and gold, the same hues as her skin and hair. Her delicate laugh sent shivers up my spine like the tinkle of faery bells.

If she'd worn a color and sported wings, I might almost believe her one of Cedar's companions. But all of the faeries had remained in the woods near my home. Too many Christians crowded the capital. Too many iron weapons threatened them here.

From another shadowed corner, Curyll—I must remember to call him Arthur—watched Guinevere. A silly grin creased the blank look of enthrallment on his face. I didn't think he knew I stood so near. His eyes never left his child bride.

A prickling on the back of my neck warned me of my father's presence. I neither turned nor spoke, allowing him the illusion of surprise—for half a moment.

"We must stop this marriage, Wren," Da whispered behind me.

"She has bewitched him," I agreed. I didn't flinch or respond to his startling statement as most would. I knew his tricks.

He wanted to creep up and surprise me as he did everyone, to catch them off guard so they would reveal their true thoughts and emotions. More of his manipulation.

"I have had visions of disaster." Disappointment colored his voice. Disappointment at Curyll's choice of bride? Or disappointment that he couldn't startle me?

"A true vision of disaster or a convenient wish because Curyll defied you and chose his own bride?"

I'd heard enough of the story to know that from their first meeting, Curyll would have no other wife than Guinevere, even though she'd been betrothed to Uriens, Arthur's sworn enemy.

My dream of the crystal cave on the night of Yvain's birth had been of the test my father set to settle the dispute of Arthur's right to rule as Ardh Rhi a few months after Uther's death. Uriens had refused to swear loyalty to Arthur and denounced all who supported him, including his future father-in-law. Leodegran had refused to give up Guinevere to Uriens until he swore loyalty to Arthur.

Uriens had besieged Carmelide, demanding an immediate wedding and Leodegran's allegiance. Arthur broke the siege and claimed Guinevere as his victory prize.

I don't know what magic Da used to set the sword in stone in the crystal cave, but I knew it had to be a trick. He wanted Arthur to be Ardh Rhi; therefore the magic would allow only Arthur to free the blade. More of Da's manipulation.

I wondered what kind of mess would develop from his tricks that I would have to clean up.

"I have had a true vision of Britain at war again, Wren. The only way to stop it is to prevent this marriage," Da continued.

I didn't look at him to see if his aura revealed truth. He could probably control that, too.

"We are too late."

"But he doesn't truly love her. He loves you. He has always loved you."

I laughed, taking pains to do it quietly.

"I am married to another, as you ordained. If you wanted me to marry Curyll, you should have arranged it over a year ago when you had the chance. I have made promises to Carradoc, and I do not break my promises." Only once had I broken my oath of fidelity. The fact that I believed Carradoc dead at the time had no bearing. He lived. I had lain with another.

I turned to leave the hall, sick at heart as well as mind.

"The time was not right then. He had to be free to seek the sword. He came to me and said he'd marry you rather than give you to Carradoc."

"An offer born of duty to an old friend. He loved Morgaine then." The memory of scantily clad Morgaine greeting Curyll in his tent froze my thoughts. "Andraste, protect us. Morgaine is his sister!"

"I couldn't stop that affair, but I managed to make certain it ended before either of them knew of their blood relationship. That is all that saved his sanity when he found out. I thank all the gods that no one else knows of it, or his enemies would depose him."

"You knew his heritage long ago. You could have told him, or Uther—he and Ygraina knew of the affair and encouraged it. They thought him a good suitor for Morgaine, a strong stepfather for her son."

"The time was not right. Such knowledge would have warped his development as a worthy leader of men regardless of his heritage. I stopped the affair as soon as I discovered it. Please, Wren, you must help me before he makes another disastrous mistake. He gives his heart too easily and always to the wrong woman. Remind him of his true love—you. This is Curyll, the boy you have loved all your life."

"No. This is Arthur, Ardh Rhi of Britain, and I, too, am the wrong woman for him. He needs this marriage as an alliance as well as because he loves Guinevere. I am married to another. I will not interfere."

"Then you leave me no choice. I must make the girl choose another—before the marriage is consummated and can be broken, as she will certainly choose another afterward when only destruction of the kingdom will break the marriage."

Da's words chilled me. What did he know?

Chapter 43

I sought the side door leading to the kitchens. Maybe I could slip through the chaos unobserved, just one more body in a too crowded room. A man stood firmly in my way. Shadows hid his face. At first I saw only the tall figure, broad shoulders, and slim hips. A trick of the firelight revealed his blue-gray eyes that seemed to penetrate all my disguises and all my secrets. The golden torc about his neck betrayed his identity. But I would know him anywhere now. His scent, his posture, the tilt of his head, were all etched on my memory with a loving hand.

"Whose child do you carry?" he whispered hoarsely.

My heart skipped a beat then pounded furiously.

"I cannot say," I replied. "You forced my husband to return to my side mere weeks after we—we met by the forest pool."

"Cannot say or will not?"

He half smiled, and I almost blurted out the truth to him. I dared tell no one.

"You are The Merlin's daughter. Surely you knew the moment the child was conceived."

"I am a woman. These things take time to prove themselves."

"Put aside the deceptions and half statements, Wren. We are old friends. We meant much to each other before that day we met by chance beside a spring with faeries dancing in the air."

So he had seen Cedar and the others, too. Perhaps the faeries' enjoyment of our coupling had enhanced his pleasure as well as mine.

"You deceived me that day, Your Highness. Why did you wear your old bronze torc rather than the new gold? If I had known . . ."

"I thought you always knew."

I shook my head. "No one ever told me."

"But I saw you in the shadows the night I pulled Uther's sword of state from the stone . . ."

"Not me. My dream self. I dreamed a vision of that night, mere hours after my son's birth. But I was not there, and I saw no faces but my father's. I did not know you in that dream." But I had. I just had refused to see him there, or I would have had to admit he had become someone other than my dear childhood friend.

"I thought you knew my heritage from our childhood, as your father did."

"If I had known, could I have kept the secret from you so long? Why didn't you wear the gold torc?"

"Because I was traveling alone and swiftly to meet with the archbishop. I neither wanted nor could afford the notoriety and the baggage train of the Ardh Rhi on that mission. Besides, I needed to pay my respects to the Lady."

"The Lady who lives at the bottom of the pool. She guarded a great treasure for the 'Chosen.' Are you the 'Chosen'?"

"She gave me a wondrous sword. A different weapon from Uther's sword of state. She named it Excalibur."

"A sword of power."

"You know it?"

"From visions only. I have seen you many times carrying it into battle, riding a great white horse. Taranis."

He chuckled low in his throat.

I wanted to kiss him, hold him tight, weep for all the times we had been apart.

"You still haven't answered my question, Wren," he said gently. "Who sired your child?"

"Carradoc is my husband by law, and by fact. The child will be his."

"But did his seed start the new life that blooms within you?"

"He believes so, and therefore so must I."

"Rumor made him impotent from his wounds."

"Then why did you send him home after he had languished in camp for so many months?"

"He was useless to the army. When I knew he had a home to go to, a son he'd never met, I believed he would heal better with you." All traces of gentle reminiscence faded from him, replaced by stern calculation. "What magic were you forced to perform to make him virile again—make him believe the child is his?"

"The secrets between a man and his wife do not concern you, Your Highness. Carradoc is a fierce warrior. He remains loyal to you, ready to battle your enemies. His warband is strong and growing in numbers. You do not wish to alienate him. That is all you need to know."

"Does he beat you, Wren?" Pain crossed his face and cracked his voice. He reached out to clasp my shoulder.

I shied away from his touch. It would be too easy to turn a casual gesture of friendship into a passionate embrace.

"Promise me, Wren, that if Carradoc causes you trouble, you will send for me, or one of my Companions—Lancelot, Cai, or Bedewyr would be best, they know you. We will all rush to help you."

"I have taken care of myself for a long time in the isolation of the North lands. Your warband will do me no good stationed in Dun Edin, controlling the Picts, watching the coasts for invasion, or receiving diplomats here in Camlann. I must prepare for your wedding, Highness." I curtsied and dashed around him before he could react. I couldn't let him see my tears of regret. If only I had stood up for my rights that long ago spring morning and refused Carradoc as my husband. . . .

Too disturbed by my encounter with Arthur to rest, or think clearly, I continued my mission to gather information. Later I would lay it all out before me and try to find the pattern. Only then could I plan my next move, even if that move was only to endure in silence the weeks of the wedding celebration.

Guinevere, who would become the focus of the women's bower, was occupied with flitting about Camlann with giggles and half-formed ideas for her wedding. The ladies of the court followed in her wake, arranging flowers, finishing gowns, and supervising the feast. I had no gathering of female gossips to tell me about Nimuë and my father.

For all of my stepdaughter's cooing and calling Da "dearheart," Da did not have the possessive air of a man who shared a bed with a much younger woman. I had never known my father to share his bed with any woman, but he must sometimes. All men did.

No one knew for certain who Nimuë was or where she spent the day. Few remembered seeing her striking figure and flaming hair. But most of my informants thought they had seen a woman clothed in black, always in black, hovering behind The Merlin's shoulder.

I slipped into my father's quarters. Carradoc and I had slept here last night with Da, but not Nimuë. I needed to search the room for evidence of her usual presence.

I had never understood how my father could be so obsessed with balanced order and life—patterns that he was compelled to control—and yet he could not maintain the barest resemblance to order in his chamber. Parchments, drying herbs, bottled elixirs, star charts, dirty clothing, and all of the other paraphernalia of living littered the tiny room. Out of old habit, I began sorting the mess, trying to find his bed. I wondered if he bothered to sleep here? Nimuë certainly didn't. She couldn't tolerate anything out of place in her life—especially me. She would have every piece of equipment shelved and labeled, the laundry would be sent out daily for washing and mending, and no dust mote would dare accumulate.

I put my fist through a tear in one of Da's shirts. I had never had time or inclination to sew, mend, spin, or weave, but I had always made certain to find women who could tend to our needs. Da needed a woman to tend him. He needed me.

No, he didn't. Not anymore.

I shook my head and left the room. *Nimuë wants to keep his life in order.* I didn't like that alternative either.

So, if Da did not share a room or a bed with my stepdaughter, where did the woman live? And what was her role in Da's life that he allowed her to call him "dearheart?"

I found where Nimuë did not sleep. I wouldn't allow myself to believe that the relationship was innocent. Neither party did anything without layers of motives piled on top of layers of self-interest.

If I allowed myself to let magic flow freely through me, I would be able to sense Nimuë's lair. I preferred not to stoop to my father's tricks just for information. Mundane means worked just as well. Nimuë had to sleep somewhere, store clothing, use a privy, bathe, and eat. Where?

I started in the bower—a large stone room attached to the hall, with many wide windows. Women needed lots of light to aid their needlework. Bright autumnal sunshine poured in through the unshuttered windows. Beautiful weavings and spindles full of the finest threads I'd ever seen filled the work space. Guinevere and her ladies had set their mark on Camlann quickly.

Arthur was a soldier. He wouldn't provide this luxury for his warband. This was as much a military camp as a home for the Ardh Rhi. Ygraina had retreated to a house of holy sisters after Uther's death a year ago. She had sent word that she would not leave the sanctuary of her new life for her son's wedding. I could not imagine flighty Guinevere presiding here.

I caught a ghostly impression of how she flitted through here, faery slim, beautiful, and full of energy and laughter.

Among the stacks of pallets in the corner, reserved for the unattached ladies, I found one permeated with the scent of heavy incense. I recognized the combination of herbs from my own early lessons in vision seeking. Da always made me pick the leaves and flowers at the peak of summer when they were fat with oils and the essence of life. The heady scents lingered on this pallet.

Properly dried and measured in precise amounts before casting onto the embers of a dying brazier, the smoke from this combination could initiate a vision of loved ones in distant parts.

The scent of those herbs had clung to Nimuë yesterday evening. Who had she sought in a vision? Her father and sisters, or a dear friend—like Morgaine? One of the chests in another corner revealed an entire lady's wardrobe in black. The fine weave of the linen and wool with the rich black embroidery betrayed Nimuë's preference for luxury.

So she studied magic and slept here with the other women. But she didn't spend much time here. Otherwise someone would have remembered her presence and gossiped about her. The number of women who shared this room probably varied constantly with the fluctuations of court life. Guinevere wouldn't sit anywhere long enough to notice a secretive woman slipping in after dark and out again before dawn.

I had an idea where I would find Nimuë and my father. The same place Da would have taken me when I was his pupil.

The woods were a good hour's walk away. A thick copse dominated by an ancient oak crested the next hill over from Camlann. The wedding was due to begin in less than half that time. The Merlin would be back in time for the ceremony. As Arthur's most trusted adviser, he had to witness this political union.

Britain needed The Merlin to bless the union and bind Arthur to the Goddess and the land. The terrible famine and flooding of Uther's last year had proved to us all that the Ardh Rhi and the land are one. Andraste only knew what disaster would plague us if Arthur and his bride were not firmly united in harmony with the gods and the land.

A new thought chilled my heart. No. My father wouldn't deliberately stay away in order to curse the union. Would he?

"Will you stand with me in blessing this marriage?" Dyfrig, Archbisop of Caerleon, asked Myrddin Emrys, The Merlin of Britain.

"No," The Merlin replied. Dyfrig had waylaid him at the outer rampart just before he left the city. Nimuë faded into the background rather than be seen by the archbishop. She had a true talent for this disappearing act. But she faded in physical ways, too, losing weight and color in her face. Soon she would be transparent, half in this world and half in another.

"But you must stand with me," Dyfrig insisted. He clutched his brother's sleeve with clawlike fingers. "If we do not stand united in this issue, political forces that are jealous of Arthur's power and resentful of the curb provided by any Ardh Rhi will tear this land to pieces."

"You have seen the same portent of disaster as I." Merlin confirmed his brother's vision with a sharp nod. He wasn't surprised. Arthur's marriage would become volatile unless he did something.

"Yes. The marriage is right for Arthur, but the union needs our help. Britain is at stake here." Dyfrig wrung his hands together.

Merlin raised one eyebrow at sight of his brother's anxiety.

"You would not stand with me in naming Arthur Uther's heir. Many hundreds of warriors and innocent Britons lost their lives in the upheaval after that night. *I* found a way to unite the kings in their election of Arthur as Ardh Rhi without you. Why should I stand beside you now?"

"Because God has ordained this marriage. I did not stand with you then because I knew that Arthur had to prove himself as a leader as well as a warrior to every last one of the kings. My blessing would not have aided that."

"My Goddess has not blessed this marriage. She gave me the vision of disaster so that I might prevent it." He'd watched Arthur's child bride. She loved another. The proper spell, set into motion, would push Guinevere into objecting to her marriage vows at the last minute.

The Merlin turned to leave the isolated guard post beneath the north watchtower on the outer rampart. Nimuë stood patiently beside the postern gate, almost the same color as the stone and wooden wall. He felt her pulling him away from this confrontation.

Dana help him, he loved her more every day. If only they could fulfill their love as a man and woman . . . Not again. He couldn't risk joining with her as he truly desired.

Dyfrig detained him once more. "*My* God granted me the vision so that I might unite the factions that will tear apart the marriage— and the alliances." The archbishop abandoned wringing his hands and pounded his left fist into his right palm for emphasis.

"When you embrace the Goddess, I will stand beside you, Brother." Merlin turned on his heel and went to Nimuë where he belonged.

Chapter 44

I dressed in the new willow-green gown Hannah had made for the occasion of the Ardh Rhi's wedding. I might not be able to weave and sew very well myself, but my steward's wife delighted in creating fashions. The soft wool, spun very fine from the long-haired sheep of our Northern hills, swished about my ankles in graceful eddies of color. Elegant clothing had never enticed me before. Today I wanted to look and feel a part of this grand celebration—my armor against the raw emotions inside me.

I braided my hair in a dozen different sized plaits, looping them into an intricate style worthy of any Roman matron. Today I would not fade into the shadows, but take my place at the front of the crowd.

Da might absent himself, but I, as a priestess, could bless the union as well as The Merlin and the Christian archbishop who presided. I must. For all of Britain, I must make certain that Arthur was bound to the land. His strength would be our strength. His vision of peace, justice, and law would become our vision.

We gathered outside the western portal of the small church below the Great Hall of Camlann. I wondered that Arthur chose this small military outpost for the wedding. Dyfrig had crowned him in Caerduel, a large town on Hadrian's Wall used by Romans and Britons for centuries. The stone church in Caerduel could hold hundreds of people within its walls. Only the bride and groom's immediate party would fit in this tiny building. So Arthur guided his bride through the streets of Camlann toward the arched doorway with Archbishop Dyfrig standing just inside the building and the rest of us filling the streets and lanes of the hill fortress. Gray streaked the archbishop's hair and beard making him look even more like The Merlin than ever.

And my father was not present to confirm or deny that he and the Christian prelate were one and the same man.

As the daughter of The Merlin and wife of a powerful lord, I pushed forward to the front rank of witnesses. Cai and Bedewyr made a path for me, grinning excitedly that their friend and foster brother had found love. They expected me to feel as they did about a beloved childhood friend and companion rather than a lover marrying another woman.

A bevy of young maidens trailed behind Guinevere in the procession. She wore white and gold again, shining in the afternoon sunshine like a visitor from Annwn, the Otherworld home of faeries. Beside her, Arthur's war-hardened companions appeared dull and grim, firmly anchored in this world. Arthur also wore white and gold, with a band of purple on his toga denoting his status. But he didn't glow like Guinevere or the magnificent sword he wore within a jeweled scabbard—Excalibur, the other kingly artifact he hadn't worn that day by the faery pool. Both Guinevere and the sword showed evidence of Otherworldly origins. I wondered then if the new queen was indeed one of the faeries, or a half-caste able to move between the worlds freely, semi-mortal and able to tap strange magic. If I had mated with Cedar and survived, our child might look like this. . . .

I jerked myself back to this reality. I had one mortal child and carried another. My mortal life suited me fine. I had no need to wish for a half-caste faery child.

Leodegran basked in Guinevere's light. My old friends Lord Ector and Lady Glynnis preened with pride that their foster son had grown into his heritage. Cai and Bedewyr tried hard to look grim and forbidding with hands on their sword hilts. Their role as protectors of the Ardh Rhi was merely ceremonial today. No one wished Arthur or his bride ill. Beside Arthur strode Lancelot, his most trusted friend and companion, a brother in all but shared parents. Tall, and dark, Lancelot was one of the most beautiful men to walk the Earth. But my heart did not quicken at sight of any but Curyll.

At supper last night Lancelot had merely nodded a greeting and not spoken. He stood beside his king equally silent today. He looked into the distance rather than at the happy couple. Some great sadness haunted his perfectly proportioned features.

Then Guinevere's gaze wandered from greeting the crowd to the face of her groom, not lingering anywhere long. Then she looked at

Lancelot. Their eyes met for a brief moment. His features softened and saddened. Then he looked away sharply, new creases of grief showing at his mouth and eyes. A quick shadow of regret also crossed Guinevere's face.

I froze in horror.

Da had seen, or foreseen, the deep love between these two. If they ever slipped and dishonored her marriage vows, there would be trouble. Arthur and Leodegran had enemies within and without the kingdom. Guinevere's adultery could be interpreted as a loss of strength in Arthur and trigger civil war. Jealous client kings looked for excuses to depose any who held authority over them.

Arthur—my friend Curyll—needed my help, not my curses. Frantically, I sought for a way to protect him. Right now, I had to prevent any spell Da might send from reaching its target. Later Arthur and Guinevere needed time together to let their love grow. She cared for him. He was besotted with her. The marriage as well as the political alliance could work. Did I dare interfere with their lives?

I had to prevent a mess before Da created one.

Quickly I drew two sprigs of rowan from my ever present sach. I whispered a little spell into each, a spell that would block outside magic. Da couldn't use a big flashy spell in this case. He needed to be subtle and quiet. The rowan should be enough.

As Arthur and Guinevere passed me in the procession, I slipped one of the sprigs into the flowers in her nosegay. The other went into Lancelot's belt. I was back in place beside Cai and Bedewyr before they knew I'd been gone.

I thought furiously, seeking a solution. If I found a reason to draw Lancelot away from the royal household, the marriage had a chance.

I forced myself to pay attention to the simple wedding ceremony that bonded Arthur to Guinevere, an Ardh Rhi to his Queen. This union had to succeed, for my friend's happiness and the well-being of Britain.

When it was over, and Arthur had gathered his wife into his arms for a passionate kiss, I eased back into the crowd. My husband remained close to the king's companions, a happy grin on his face. Those most closely concerned with the wedding moved into the church for a nuptial mass. I would not partake of this ceremony though I approved of the form. Dyfrig had blessed the union in a way the Goddess would approve. The ritual mass followed many of my own invocations of divine power.

"I see you do not enter the church," a man whispered behind me. His deep voice flowed in melodic patterns. A bard's voice. A familiar voice as beautiful as the man's face.

The child within my womb stirred uneasily. I turned to face him. "Lancelot." I nodded a greeting but kept moving away from the church toward the hall. "You, too, shun the nuptial mass?"

He didn't reply, merely moved beside me, taking my arm as if escorting me.

"Your grip is too firm, almost desperate. Do you need a healer?"

"No healer can cure me."

"Perhaps I can offer refuge." As I had offered refuge to many who had lost sight of the pattern of their lives. "The North Country is troubled with outlaws and wild tribes. We have need of extra warriors. Arthur might consider dispatching you to us."

"The Ardh Rhi has need of my sword here, near the center of Britain."

"My friend Curyll has need of swords and strong men to wield them all over Britain, not just here. Now that the Saxons are beaten back, there is no common cause to bind us together. We are a fractious lot, we Britons. There are also the men who have lost everything in the wars and do not hesitate to take from others in a blind attempt at vengeance. Warriors like you, who are as good with their swords, would ease many of the troubles in the North."

He nodded curtly.

"You speak as if my father's lessons in poetry and legend linger. Such a gift has many uses—especially in maintaining peace."

"Possibly."

"I will ask that you return with Carradoc and me."

"I am grateful, Lady Wren. But your husband is a strong lord, a fierce warrior, and loyal to Arthur. You do not need me."

"But you have need of us. Caer Noddfa has healed many wounded spirits as well as broken lives. I will remind Curyll that Carradoc is but recently recovered from serious wounds. He does not have the gift of words or a golden voice. I will do my best to bring you to Caer Noddfa."

He nodded curtly again and moved off toward his own quarters.

The baby moved again, a fluttering shift in her position like a sigh of regret that Lancelot no longer stood nearby.

Da and Nimuë strolled into the Great Hall moments after I did. She clung to his arm possessively. He leaned his head close to hers, listening intently to her whispered comments. Both wore black, a matching pair.

If they were not lovers yet, they would be soon.

Other wedding guests mingled in the hall, waiting for the bride and groom and their party to return from the nuptial mass. Dyfrig was with Arthur and Guinevere in the church. Da was here in the Hall. Two men wore the same face, both closely tied to Arthur as advisers and spiritual leaders. Which of them held sway at the moment?

I had no reason to mistrust Dyfrig other than the absence of faeries in Camlann. They feared the priests of the Christian Church even though I had learned to work beside some of them.

Very soon the faeries might have to retreat to Annwn forever to make room for the followers of the White Christ and their saints. I would miss the joy and beauty they brought to this world. I would miss their friendship. But I saw no other course of action that would maintain a balance of peace between the old ways and the growing influence of the Christians.

Da patted Nimuë's hand as if to reassure her. Then he removed her grip on his arm and moved to stand directly in front of me. I couldn't politely ignore him or turn my back on him. If I left now, I'd have to leave the wedding feast entirely. Arthur needed me here to counter any further mischief my father and his lover planned.

"You did something to counter my work!" he said, eyes blazing.

I returned his stare with wide eyes that I hoped appeared innocent. "What do you mean?"

He fumed a moment, then swallowed his anger. "You look well, Wren, now that you are rested. Pregnancy agrees with you," he said.

"Your granddaughter is mild-tempered, unlike your grandson who was restless and hungry from the moment he was conceived," I replied. Too many people listened for me to say what was truly in my heart. *Beware of Nimuë. She wishes only harm and mischief.* Nor did I ask if she initiated a spell to disrupt the wedding.

Old hurts remained in my heart. Da and Nimuë made a likely pair.

A whiff of Nimuë's heavy perfume invaded my senses. Cloying, with a hint of sulfur and old wood, it meant to imitate a woman's musk but failed. I immediately jumped backward in my memory to the night I had surprised Morgaine in Ygraina's bower. The princess had been working dark magic that night. Magic that summoned demons from another world to aid her quest for power.

She had worn the same perfume.

I fought the urge to make a horned fist, warding against Cernunnos.

"I should like to watch my grandchildren grow, Wren. May I visit you at Caer Tair Cigfran?" Da's words jerked me back to the current reality.

"We are now Caer Noddfa, a refuge for all who ail in body and spirit. We are a haven in a troubled world, a balance of peace against chaos. Only one cranky old raven resides there now. I banished all of the others, no thanks to your lover."

"Ravens? Did you supply that marvelous omen that sent the Saxons into a panic when it looked as if they would win the battle of Glein River? Except for those birds, we might all be Saxon slaves now."

"I noticed that you took credit for the 'miracle.' "

"I was given credit for it. The birds flocked to the field at the moment I rode to protect the dragon standard and to rally our retreating troops. I thank you, Wren, for your most timely interference."

I nodded my acceptance of his gratitude. I hadn't planned on interfering and manipulating. All I wanted was to rid my home of a plague and restore a balance.

"May I come visit my grandchildren, Wren? Nimuë would like to make the acquaintance of her half brother, too."

"You may come when the Ardh Rhi gives you leave. I cannot deny my husband's home to his eldest daughter or to the king's adviser."

"But you will not invite her or me."

I didn't answer. The uncomfortable silence stretched between us until he returned to stand beside Nimuë.

Off to one side, Morgaine stood by a portly man many years her senior, most likely her husband, King Lot of the Orcades. He looked bored. She took in every movement and word around her avidly, hungrily. She had left her black hair unbound, contrary to custom. It billowed about her face in a tangle of curls that defied gravity and a comb. A white streak began at her forehead and shot back through the length of her mane. She wore rich black-and-silver draperies that floated about her in wispy tendrils, the same as her hair. Her clothing hid her body effectively. No one could tell her figure or her age to look at her. I sensed she had put on weight since our last encounter. She could carry Lot's child and no one would know.

How much of the cloud of black around her was hair and cloth and how much an aura filled with bitterness? She narrowed her eyes in speculation as she stared at my father and me. Then her eyes slid to Lancelot's grim face. A knowing smile played across her mobile mouth. Mischief danced in her eyes.

Here stood a woman who could become a formidable enemy to any who crossed her. More patient and practiced than Nimuë. Where did her loyalty lie these days? Certainly not with the three adolescent boys who stood impatiently by her side. She ignored them totally, including the middle boy, Gwalchmai, her son by her first marriage.

Arthur and his bride returned to the Hall, without Dyfrig. The Ardh Rhi gazed at Guinevere with the total absorption of a man in love, oblivious to the hundreds of people gathering close to wish him well. Guinevere kept her eyes on her shoes. Lancelot stared at the ceiling.

I empathized with the Ardh Rhi's Champion. I hurt deep inside knowing that the man I had loved since childhood had taken another woman as his bride. But I carried his child. I would cherish this baby. Lancelot didn't have that kind of comfort.

Eventually we all settled down to enjoy the feast. Servants brought us the best of the harvest along with a variety of meats and fish. The bounty of the Goddess smiled upon this meal, a sure sign that with a nudge here and there the pattern of life in Britain could remain just as bountiful.

My small sanctuary in the North was just one piece of the pattern, interlocking with many others.

Jugglers, tumblers, and musicians took turns entertaining us. I picked at my food, watching them all warily, waiting for the disaster

I knew must come. From my father and Nimuë, from Morgaine, or Lancelot?

Nimuë sat on Carradoc's left. I on his right. There wasn't room for her next to my father. Morgaine had usurped that place while her husband and their sons sat farther away, separated from the other client kings.

My husband and his daughter spoke frequently in animated whispers. They touched in fond caresses and loving glances. They barely noticed me, and I ignored them. My attention was on my father and the Ardh Rhi.

As the servants cleared the debris of the feast, petitioners came forward. By long tradition Arthur was obligated to show mercy and grant favors on such a great occasion.

A farmer requested help rebuilding the walls dividing his fields. Warriors had knocked them down to clear a battlefield. The farmer lost his two sons in the battle and had no one to help lift the heavy stones.

A minor lord requested a gift of land as dowry for his daughter. Floods had destroyed much of his land during the bad years of Uther's reign.

A merchant wanted license to peddle his wares across the seas in Armorica, the continental peninsula we called Less Britain.

Another farmer demanded justice. His neighbor had seized land from him while he was away defending his lord's caer. The lord had died while absent and no one had assumed his place to decide disputes.

Arthur weighed all of the requests and handed out just settlements. I approved of each decision.

Then a woman stepped forward holding the hand of a small boy. He couldn't have been more than five and had nervously stuffed a fist into his mouth.

"Your Highness." The woman dropped a deep curtsy to the Ardh Rhi. Her accent was shadowed with Roman intonations, as if British were not native to her tongue.

"Lady Claudia." Arthur nodded his head and gestured for her to rise.

"Highness, I seek a boon for my son."

The smoky air hung heavy within the huge building. The room

grew silent, as if the many hundreds of people within sensed the import of what was about to happen.

Lady Claudia plunged ahead with her speech, as if she knew her courage would not last the length of it. "Do you remember, my lord Ardh Rhi, that summer eve five years ago when you carried a message to my lord husband from your father, Ardh Rhi Uther."

"I was too late. Your husband had already left for the field of battle." Arthur narrowed his eyes and clamped his mouth shut.

"You stayed the night. Accepting my hospitality."

Arthur nodded. Guinevere clutched his arm, her knuckles whitening with the fierceness of her grip.

"When my husband returned to our villa, he accepted the child I carried as his own. But he died last summer in your service. Saxons overran our land. I have nothing left to support the child. I beg you, Your Highness, to acknowledge your son and pay for his upbringing."

An excited babble broke out at this unprecedented request. Certainly men had sired bastards before, but requests for support and acknowledgment were conducted in private.

Another woman stepped forward with a toddler in her arms. The little girl was perhaps two. The mother's gown was not so fine as Lady Claudia's and her accent came from the hill country to the west of Camlann.

"I, too, Your Highness, need your help with the raising of your child. She has no dowry and no man has been willing to take me to wife since I bore a bastard child. Your child."

Five more women stepped forward, all with children ranging from the age of eight down to one that looked to be born any moment. I doubted Curyll could have sired the eight-year-old. The Ardh Rhi had been only a child himself then. But any of the others . . .

Guinevere must have thought the same thing. Her white skin took on a ghostly pallor. The thin gold circlet she wore as a crown looked too heavy for her. She opened her mouth to speak, but Arthur touched her hand in mute comfort. She closed her mouth, gulped and blinked rapidly to suppress tears. She looked around as if seeking an avenue of flight.

Nimuë giggled lightly behind her hand. "I told The Merlin this would work. Better than a mere spell."

Carradoc's guffaw nearly drowned out her whisper. Others in the crowd released the tension with more laughter, none of it truly mirthful.

My father looked incredibly pleased with himself.

Lancelot stood, hand on sword, as if he could fight this threat to Arthur's kingship with metal weapons. Cai and Bedewyr drew their weapons as well.

Curyll's eyes met mine, challenging me to come forth as well.

I wanted to run from this hideous scene. I remained seated, my hands clasped tightly in my lap and my mouth firmly closed. If I could not confess our tryst to the father of my child, I certainly could not confess to all those assembled. Carradoc wouldn't let me live long enough to leave the Hall.

"At least the kingdom knows how virile I truly am," Curyll said. A half-smile tugged at the corner of his lips. The same half-smile I knew from long ago. As a boy that expression warned his foster brothers to duck or run. He had a plan.

My tension eased, but I didn't relax, not yet. Not until I knew Arthur would not group me with these other women.

"I will not apologize for my bachelor behavior," Curyll shrugged. "But I vow before God and all these witnesses, that I will be faithful to my new queen from this moment forward." He bent and gently kissed Guinevere on the lips. She remained absolutely still, not returning the kiss.

"What of the children, Your Highness?" Merlin asked. "We cannot put them on a rudderless boat and cast them out to sea. Nor can we push them out into the cold to fend for themselves. All of these women need help."

"I will not have your bastards in my household," Guinevere whispered. I doubt anyone heard her, but the movement of her lips said it all.

"Ladies, do I presume that all of you wish to remain at court, accepting my bounty in the names of your children?"

In unison they nodded. Guinevere started to rise, ready to flee. Arthur's heavy hand on her shoulder kept her in her chair.

"Very well, I will care for your children." He paused and looked each woman in the eye. "They may even call themselves my children if they wish. But if you, the mothers, wish to remain at court, you must in turn give up your children. If you choose to keep your chil-

dren by your side, you will leave my home and withdraw your claim."
Grimness touched his features.

Two of the women clutched their babies tightly. They searched
the room for someone to give them easy answers. No one offered
them.

Nimuë's face turned redder than her hair in barely contained
anger.

I hadn't believed Curyll capable of such cruelty. But this wasn't
Curyll anymore. This was Arthur Pendragon, Ardh Rhi of Britain.

"I will not have your bastards in my household," Guinevere repeated.

"I agree, beloved." Curyll's hand on her shoulder became a light
caress. "I shall establish a royal nursery elsewhere. I can think of no
better governess for these children than the respected daughter of my
chief adviser and the wife of my loyal warrior, Carradoc. Lady Wren
of Caer Noddfa, will you accept the charge of these children in your
home along with a yearly income to help raise and educate them?"

Chapter 45

NIMUË nearly choked on her laughter. Carradoc spluttered his wine all over his new tunic. The laughter in the rest of the hall died a lingering death.

Morgaine's face drained of color to match Guinevere's. I hadn't the time or concentration to worry about her.

"You can't be serious!" Merlin stood so rapidly his chair fell over backward. He stood and faced the Ardh Rhi, the young man he'd fostered, tutored, and loved as much as his own child. "Acknowledging bastard children before you sire any legitimate ones will endanger the succession."

"What am I supposed to do, put them into a rudderless boat and cast them adrift?" Arthur raised one eyebrow in imitation of the gesture my father used so often. The half-smile tugged at his mouth.

"Yes," Nimuë whispered a reply to Arthur's sarcasm. "Do it and alienate your queen once and for all." *Do it and earn condemnation for all time.*

Her thoughts came to me unbidden. I sensed a magic compulsion in her quiet voice. How far did her words—and her thoughts—reach?

Morgaine nodded mutely in agreement. A nudge of her own magic reached out toward Arthur.

Morgaine's and Nimuë's magic seemingly had no effect upon the Ardh Rhi. My sprig of rowan still protected Guinevere.

With pride strengthening his stance, Arthur turned back to face the women who had named him father to their babies.

"I will not condemn these innocent children to the mockery and disrespect I received when no one knew my father," Curyll said with a fierce determination that sent chills up my spine. "These children will be raised with honor, educated as befitting the sons and daughters of royalty."

Guinevere choked out some protest I couldn't hear. Her face was still too pale. She was probably in shock.

"Never fear, beloved." Arthur patted his bride's hand solicitously. "I will not legitimatize the children, nor will they come to court until they are grown. They will have to earn places in my warband or as suitable wives to warriors, as I earned my place before I was elected to be Ardh Rhi, as our children must do as well. As must any man wishing to be the next Ardh Rhi, my son or no. I trust Lord Carradoc and Lady Wren to keep these babes safe and raise them properly."

"Will you visit them, Your Highness?" Guinevere asked through tight lips. Her eyes remained fixed on me. A flare of jealousy brought color to her aura and her face.

"From time to time."

I noticed how careful Arthur was to keep from looking directly at me. Then I wanted to laugh. This was not so much about the children forced upon him as the one I denied him. He would visit my daughter and me when he came to see the other children. He would provide money and tutors for her as well as the others.

All without giving Carradoc reason to suspect the truth.

"We are honored that you entrust us with such a valuable charge, Your Highness." Carradoc stood and bowed formally.

I looked up then and stared at Arthur. He must have felt my gaze on him and turned away from his queen and my father to face me as if he could no longer deny himself that luxury. I stood beside my husband, careful not to touch him, and curtsied, keeping my back stiff and my expression rigidly neutral.

Nimuë was not so polite. "You can't let this happen, Myrddin Emrys!" she shouted. "You have to stop this injustice. *She,*" she pointed at me, "doesn't deserve this. She will corrupt them with magic. She will command their loyalty, not Arthur. There must be another way!"

Without further explanation, she stormed out of the hall as if she were the jealous bride. Morgaine slipped into the shadows and followed her.

Carradoc stared at his retreating daughter. His mouth opened and closed twice to call her back without uttering a sound. Then he turned bleak eyes upon me. Grief for her loss once more ravaged his face, deepening the lines worry and pain had etched there over the years.

A jolt of fear shot down my spine. What if Carradoc decided to replace Nimuë in his affections with my daughter, or worse—one of the children in our charge? Arthur would kill both of us if Carradoc defiled one of these children.

I had no doubts that Carradoc's potency would return when faced with Nimuë in his bed or a fearful, innocent virgin who was forbidden to him.

I'd take him back to my own bed before I let that happen.

"You had no right to interfere, Myrddin Emrys," I shouted at my father later that evening. I couldn't call him "Da." Not anymore. "You have altered the pattern of many, many lives beyond recognition."

"I had to try. But I couldn't alter the pattern of the future in the way I intended." He looked into the distance sadly, as if grieving over a shattered pattern of life—or acknowledging a painful one.

Arthur and Guinevere had retired to their private chamber some hours before. Carradoc had gone in search of Nimuë. He carried a full skin of wine with him. I'd not see him again this night.

"How did you plan to alter the pattern, Myrddin? By making Guinevere so jealous that she would denounce her marriage to Arthur before it was consummated?"

"Yes."

I gasped at his audacity.

"Since you stopped the spell aimed at her so that she would proclaim her love for Lancelot and refuse to take her vows, I had to do something. The pattern is clear. If Guinevere becomes Ardh Brenhines, Britain will fracture into civil war and leave us vulnerable to the Saxons once more."

No man had the right to see the future so clearly.

"How can you be so certain? Visions of the future are always veiled and symbolic. They give us the opportunity to change our own lives, not the right to manipulate other people like puppets. You are The Merlin. You taught me that principle."

"I am different. The gods have singled me out since birth. My destiny was to put Arthur on the throne and keep him there. He is the only warrior strong enough to hold Britain together, to keep the Saxons at bay long enough to prevent them from destroying our gods, our culture, our uniqueness." He hung his head sadly. "My visions have always been clear, precise in detail. It is a gift and a curse. My twin brother renounced this special gift by taking Christian vows. I could not."

"Dyfrig is your twin," I said, acknowledging what I must have known all along. "Your twin not only in blood, but in his role as leader of his faith and spiritual guide to Arthur. At least Arthur hasn't forsaken the old gods completely. He listens to both of you."

"You noticed the resemblance between Dyfrig and me."

"How could I not?"

"My wandering life has kept me skin and bones all my life. Dyfrig travels widely, too, but more comfortably. He has put on some weight these last years. His hair remains black. The gods marked me with prematurely gray hair and beard . . . and in other ways. He was spared. We have met only a few times since I left the house of the sisterhood with my mother's uncle—and then always in argument. We grew apart in more ways than just our faith."

"He does not manipulate and maneuver people to his own whims."

"He is a politician. He does much the same as I."

"I have not witnessed this, and he doesn't upset natural balances by using magic to manipulate people."

"Remain at court for more than a few days and you will see the balances he upsets—temporal power must be balanced as carefully as natural forces. He would have made our Roman father proud."

"You have never spoken of your family." I knew we had Romans in our heritage. The title "Emrys" denoted such. But so close? My own grandfather one of the invaders I had been raised to disdain?

"My mother was a British princess who loved too well if not wisely. She forsook her family for my father and sought Christian baptism. When she was heavily pregnant with Dyfrig and me, Saxons raided our town. My father was killed. Mother hid, witnessing the horrible death of her beloved from a secret passage in the villa. When it was over and she could safely leave, she fled to the holy sisters. After my brother and I were born, she took the vows of her sisterhood. Dyfrig and I were raised among the sisters until we were five. Even by that time, our gift of prophecy was pronounced. Legends grew and many people came to witness the miracles of our glimpses into the future. My mother's uncle, Blaise, came also. He requested the right to train my twin and me to control our gifts, to become powerful magicians in the old faith. Dyfrig hid behind our mother's skirts, too afraid of the old man and his talent to venture forth. I was bolder, eager to learn. I demanded permission to leave the shelter of the sisters."

"Blaise. He was The Merlin before you."

"Yes."

"Does your mother still live?"

"Yes. But she is very old and frail now. She does not accept change well. She never forgave me for deserting her. She clung to my brother and me as living memorials of our father. I learned later that she did not take her final vows to the sisterhood until after I left her care."

"You could have taken me to her after my mother died. I was but an infant, a great deal of trouble for a man alone who wandered the country year after year."

I had a grandmother. My sense of inner balance stretched a little and resettled. I had a family beyond my father and my children. For the first time in my life I had roots going back in time as well as forward. Curiosity about my mother bubbled up. I'd have to seek out answers to many questions. Later. After I dealt with Da and Arthur.

"The care and tutoring of you, my beloved daughter, was a privilege, not a duty. I felt honored to be entrusted with you. Your destiny and mine are closely linked."

"How?"

He looked at me with sad eyes but said nothing.

"I have a right to know. Your manipulations have changed my life. You forced me into a marriage with an unfaithful and violent brute to keep me away from Curyll." A deep hurt within me kept the accusation of incest away from my lips.

I could use it to divorce Carradoc. But what then? I'd have to leave my home and return to my father. Da lived at court now, in close council with Arthur. I couldn't be happy here as long as my lover was married to another. Could I leave the faery pool by the crystal cave, the standing stones and my people in the village?

"You used a magic compulsion on me to make me marry Carradoc. A compulsion that lasted only until the first time we lay together.

Earlier you played with my memories so that I would not remember the druidsbane poisoning Uther or the antidote I prepared and gave him. I am now *gweinyddes* to nearly a dozen babies that Arthur has acknowledged as his bastards because of your manipulations. Arthur is more than Ardh Rhi. He is Curyll. The boy you nurtured, my friend."

Da bit his lip, the only sign of second thoughts he might have.

"This parade of former lovers and their children feels like Nimuë's warped sense of humor, rather than your puppeteering, Myrddin Emrys. I thought better of you. You have never been swayed by a lover before."

"Nimuë is not my lover and never will be. One of the limitations put upon those of us with the gift of prophecy is celibacy."

"But . . . are you truly my father?"

"Yes, Arylwren. I am your father. The gods did not take my slip graciously. They do not forgive easily and marked me as a constant reminder. Raising you to honor the Goddess and carry on our traditions of magic and balance was part of my penitence. I couldn't have given you up if I wanted to. And I didn't want to."

"Your white hair is the mark of the Goddess' disfavor."

"And—I am constantly reminded that if I ever take another lover, there will be no reprieve, no forgiveness, even if my special destiny is not fulfilled. Nimuë is my apprentice, and a very adept one. She will never be my lover."

Thank Dana for that small blessing.

"Your relationship to Nimuë has no bearing on what you did today. You had no right to embarrass Curyll and the entire court with that ludicrous display. I'm certain that at least half of those women have never slept with Arthur. The Curyll I knew eight years ago was too young and sheltered to have fathered the oldest of them."

"I will endure any amount of embarrassment to maintain peace in Britain, Wren," he said through gritted teeth. He grabbed my shoulders and shook me slightly to emphasize his point. "Arthur is the only man who can hold the loyalty of all the small kingdoms. If Guinevere betrays him, as I know she must, Arthur will appear weak, lacking in virility. The memory of famine and flood when Uther lost his strength is still fresh in the minds of all Britons. Arthur will be deposed rather than risk the separation of the king from land."

"There is another way."

"What? Please, Wren, you must help. Just this once, deliberately interfere. Every time you interact with another life, you alter it no matter your intentions. Just this once use your magic to help Britain."

"No magic. Mundane politics. We must keep Lancelot and Guinevere apart until she has a chance to grow into her love for Arthur. Until she has a chance to mature and control her feelings for Lancelot. Convince Arthur to send Lancelot north with me."

"Arthur will never allow Lancelot to leave. He is the King's Champion, his closest friend, and greatest warrior. They have been inseparable since boyhood."

"Arthur will have no choice but to let him go. I will make it a condition of my taking the children."

"What of Carradoc? Won't he see Lancelot's presence as an insult to his prowess as a warrior and potential tutor-in-arms to the boys?"

"Not if Nimuë persuades him. He can deny her nothing." I shuddered at the form the persuasion would take. I'd hoped that perversion had ended forever.

To save Arthur and his marriage I had to allow it, encourage their incestuous union. To save Arthur and his marriage and thus all of Britain, I would reconcile with my stepdaughter and accept Carradoc back into my bed. If I had to.

Chapter 46

DA and Nimuë rode north with us. At a crossroad half a day away from Camlann, Da looked longingly toward the east, then set his horse firmly in the other direction.

"What?" I reined in my placid mare, grateful for the temporary end to the jolting of her spine against my bottom.

"Nothing, Wren." Da stared straight ahead, but he didn't kick his high-strung stallion into moving.

Carradoc and Nimuë kept riding without looking back. The lengthy baggage train and the carts loaded with children ground to a halt behind me.

"It isn't nothing, or you wouldn't have stopped with that ache in your eyes. What lies up the road?"

"A house of holy sisters."

"Your mother. My grandmother."

He bowed his head. The absolute stillness of his mind and body told me more than his words.

"Come." I leaned over and grabbed the reins of his horse, then kneed Dawnsio into a new path. She plodded where I directed. I had promised myself I would grab this moment if it ever came and act on it. Breaking that promise would upset my inner balance and my place in the stream of past, present, and future.

"No, Wren. We can't." Da tried to jerk his reins out of my hands.

"Yes, we can. You won't be happy until you see her again. I won't have my life pattern anchored until I confront my ancestress."

"I'll tell you anything you ask about your mother."

"Fine. Start with your earliest memory of her." I directed the carts to continue. Da and I would catch up later. I doubted Carradoc or Nimuë would notice our absence.

"I'll tell you about your mother only if we continue north without stopping." Da looked anxiously after the others. He tried turning his mount, but I had touched the beast's mind. It would follow me. Da would have to walk to avoid the meeting we both longed for.

I frowned. Da had taught me well. What consequence awaited my meddling?

The road quickly narrowed into a track, little more than a deer trail. Trees crowded the path, making it a dark and twisted tunnel. Few traveled this way. But someone had preceded us. Fresh hoof-prints and horse droppings showed the way.

Less than two Roman miles after the road dissolved and the forest began, we came upon the house. I expected stout Roman walls protecting the gathering of holy sisters from the outside world. The cluster of thatched huts sunk half into the ground looked more like the village below Caer Noddfa than any of the Roman buildings I had seen. A Christian cross thrust upward from the peak of the largest of the conical huts. Nothing else marked this settlement as different from hundreds of other villages.

One lone woman stepped from beneath the low lintel of the first building. She wore a simple white wool gown and a veil over her hair. Inner peace radiated from her aura. Though aged and lined, her gentle face glowed with contentment.

I longed to take her hands and learn from her.

I dismounted and introduced us. At mention of my father's name, she dropped her eyes in sadness. Some of her glow dimmed.

"She will not see you," the woman whispered.

"Then we will leave without disturbing her. Come, Wren." Da turned his horse back the way we had come.

"Please ask my grandmother if she will spare a few moments from her prayers for me." I looked directly into the woman's eyes, putting all of my longing into my gaze.

A tiny smile touched the corner of her mouth. "Of course, my child. I will ask. But do not expect too much." She walked lightly to the hut closest to the large church building. I wondered briefly if she floated or truly walked like an ordinary mortal.

Da stopped his horse, but he remained mounted, back rigidly turned away from the village and me.

"How dare he!" a man shouted from within the hut. The good

sister who had met us withdrew from the doorway in an awkward back step. Her gentle grace evaporated into hasty retreat.

In a flurry of black robes edged in bishopric purple, Dyfrig stormed out of his mother's home. His eyes blazed with volatile emotions.

I cringed from his rage as I would from my father's.

Da's horse reared and pawed the air. The Merlin dismounted easily and whirled to face his twin brother. "How dare *you* keep us from visiting *my* mother?" he returned.

The two men glared at each other a moment in silence. So alike and yet so different.

I stared at them, memorizing the sameness, cherishing the differences.

"You took a vow never to return, never to disturb her. She thought you dead and accepted your absence," Dyfrig ground out between his teeth. "Now she cries, not understanding who you are. How could you disturb her?"

"I return to make peace with my mother and give my daughter the sense of continuity she craves. You disturb our mother's peace with your shouts and your temper," Da returned evenly. A slight tremble in his shoulders told me how hard he worked at controlling his anger.

I wanted to cringe away from them both.

"Pagans, both of you." Dyfrig spat on the ground. "Have you come to accept baptism? That is the only way to make peace with either of us. You promised never to return to this place unless you accepted Jesu Christus as your only Lord."

"You were not so prejudiced a year ago in Venta Belgarum, Uncle." My voice cracked with emotions I didn't dare analyze at the moment. Anger certainly. Disappointment, fear, and distrust. All emotions that shouldn't disrupt a family reunion, though I knew that most families suffered them, my own included.

"How so?" He eyed me with one eyebrow raised in disdain. My father's gesture.

"You presided at my marriage. Eight couples accepted your blessing that day, Christians and followers of other faiths."

He shuddered slightly as he made the sign of the cross. He turned on his heel and stalked toward his mother's hut.

"I thought your Jesu Christus preached forgiveness and extending the hand of charity to all," Da called after him. "I hoped we could reconcile, Brother. I thought you wanted peace between us." He stepped closer to Dyfrig until they stood nose to nose, mirror images of each other.

I reeled a moment, losing contact with my life pattern. Which man was my father? Which man advised Ardh Rhi Arthur?

Which man. . . ?

"When you are baptized. As you promised many years ago," Dyfrig said.

My world righted again. I knew the differences between them now.

"Does my grandmother feel the same as you?" I asked my uncle. "Does she reject me, her only grandchild, and the babe I carry because of your prejudice, Dyfrig?"

He stopped. I saw him swallow several times before turning back to me, carefully avoiding looking at his twin brother.

"My mother is very old. Her mind has never fully healed from the atrocities she witnessed before our birth. She still believes herself a young mother. In her mind, her husband never died. She clings to two dolls, thinking them the twins she bore many years ago. She waits patiently each day for her husband to return from a brief journey to the nearest city." Dyfrig turned his gaze back to my father. Venom nearly shot from his aura. "Her mind snapped when you left here so eagerly to follow the pagan ways she forsook to marry our father. You are to blame for her condition, Myrddin."

"You are to blame for allowing her to remain a prisoner of her own mind! If you had let me see her when I wished to visit many times over the years, I could have helped her return to reality," Da returned with equal malice.

He lied. I could tell by the twitch at the corner of his mouth as well as the black splotches in his aura. He could not have cured her. Perhaps he had tried, secretly, and failed.

"You are both to blame. Both of you and neither of you." I wanted to scream but feared disturbing the old woman's fragile acceptance of life. "No one can force another to find their inner balance. My grandmother has found peace within her own mind. I'll not disturb her, but I would like to see her, kiss her cheek. Please, Archbishop Dyfrig, let me see her?"

"No."

"I am your niece. Your family."

"My twin brother died when we were barely five. The man you brought here today is a stranger to me."

"Neither of you can see beyond your own hurts and selfish pride. Neither of you wants what is best for me or my grandmother!" I said quietly. Placing one hand on each man's chest, I thrust them away and forced a path between them.

I took a deep breath and then another before stepping down into my grandmother's hut.

A frail old woman, wearing her gray hair loose in a youthful fashion, bent over a basket cradle on the floor. She tucked a tiny blanket around two faded, but meticulously clean, rag dolls. Hannah had woven a similar blanket for my own son.

"Have you come to see my babies?" my grandmother asked. "They have just dropped off to sleep, but you may peek if you are quiet. Such good babies, though quite a chore to get them to sleep at the same time. I rarely have time to say my prayers without one of them crying for something." Her smile lit her brilliant blue eyes and smoothed the age lines on her face. She could have lived a mere thirty years—not sixty.

She had been beautiful. Still was.

I touched her shoulder in love and peace as I peered into the basket cradle.

"You will know soon enough the joys and trials of motherhood." My grandmother touched my swollen belly. Joy and wonderment crossed her lined face.

"You have beautiful babies, Lady. You should be proud."

I kissed her soft, pale cheek. Tears choked me. I couldn't speak again.

My grandmother sat on a low stool beside the cradle, crooning a lullaby, the same tune I sang to Yvain.

I left, biting my lower lip to keep it from trembling.

My father and my uncle still glared at each other. I ignored their animosity and picked up Dawnsio's reins. My horse already stood by a stump, a convenient mounting block for me. I heaved my bulk into the saddle, ready to return to my home, my son, my life.

Archbishop Dyfrig turned abruptly away from my father and ducked beneath the lintel of his mother's hut.

"Are you happy now, Wren? You have found your relatives and

been rejected by them," Da whispered. He mounted hastily and kneed the horse into a dangerous gallop.

I tasted tears and let them flow. We must each find our own peace within. We can't force it upon another, I reminded myself. I couldn't force my father and his twin to accept the life path the other had chosen. I couldn't force my grandmother's mind to heal.

I hoped I could rediscover my own inner peace, accepting my relatives as they were rather than what I would have them be.

"You came back!" Nimuë rejoiced at the heavy weight landing on her shoulder. The demon had left her at Camlann less than two weeks ago. During that time her magic had become erratic and her life very bland. Her invisibility spells didn't work. She felt so exposed and vulnerable that she had pressed Merlin to leave Carradoc and Wren to rejoin Arthur at Campboglanna.

But here, in the luxurious Roman fort with its hypocast, thick carpets, and bright lanterns, she could not hide in the shadows. Everyone knew she accompanied The Merlin. Everyone watched her. So she was forced to sit and play at needlework with the Ardh Brenhines and her ladies rather than listen to Merlin and Arthur plan the next campaign.

She reached up to caress the demon, then thought better of it.

"Who?" Guinevere asked, looking up from her haphazard embroidery. The Ardh Brenhines and her ladies watched every move Nimuë made, certain that she brought scandal with every gesture.

Curse the pale child brenhines and her preternatural hearing. If she ever learned to concentrate and remember, she'd be a formidable storehouse of gossip.

We have work to do, the demon whispered faintly.

"Pray excuse me, Highness." Nimuë rose and curtsied. "I must . . . the necessary . . . moon blood . . ." She excused herself and hurried out the door toward the privy. Let them think her cycle a surprise. Let them believe she slept with Merlin every night and expected to become pregnant.

Word of this latest scandal would reach Wren soon enough and bring her grief. The same grief Nimuë had experienced when she learned of Wren's pregnancy.

Once beyond sight and hearing of the ladies she diverted her path to the outside wall.

A fierce wind blew her cloak around her ankles, threatening to trip her, but no one could hear her conversation with the demon above the roar of the approaching storm. The court was used to her solitary walks. Merlin spent too much time closeted with Arthur where she could not join him, glean knowledge from him, or work magic with him.

"What happened to you?" she asked the demon.

I could not stand against The Merlin. He saw me. I had to flee before he banished me completely to the Netherworld. It paused as if gasping for breath, though it had spoken only with its mind. *Do something. Work some magic. . . .* It trailed off weakly.

"Yes. We must work a great deal of magic. We can work mischief here."

Where is here?

"Campboglanna, Arthur's capital in the North."

So far from my home!

Images of the solitary standing stone by the spring outside Venta Belgarum flashed through her mind. The twin circles spiraling inward . . .

"I am your home," Nimuë said. A flash of anger sent her hand to her shoulder to banish the demon once more.

But she needed the demon. Her magic wasn't complete without it.

She concentrated fiercely on one of the torches set against the watchtower. It smoldered, barely sending out wisps of strength.

Shield it from the wind, the demon advised.

Of course. Even Tanio couldn't maintain a flame in this gale.

She stood between the wind and the torch, holding her cloak out in a protective wall. The wind caught the voluminous folds of cloth like a sail and nearly carried her over the wall. She braced herself and gritted her teeth.

Slowly she recited a spell, pronouncing each unknown word with deliberation and control. She had to force the magic from her mind toward the torch.

A few moments more and the torch finally blazed into life.

Ah, the demon sighed in relief. It sounded stronger already.

Nimuë doused the torch with a wave of her hand and moved on

to the next watchtower. She repeated the fire spell. By the time that torch burst into flame, her knees could barely hold her upright.

"I can't do anymore, demon. My magic is nearly as weak as you are. You've been gone for so long. . . ."

Enough for now. Take us back to a warm hearth and a hot brew. I would listen to gossip and find a weakness here. A weakness that I can use to gain more strength.

"A weakness *we* can exploit. I have raised my expectations, demon. Morgaine showed me true power. I still want my revenge upon Wren. But I also see the advantage to manipulating men in government and war. I will have control of Arthur, and Guinevere is his weakness."

Chapter 47

MY father and Nimuë did not linger at Caer Noddfa long. She did not smile the entire three days they remained in my home. Carradoc mostly ignored her. Da remained almost silent after confronting his brother. Restlessness overtook him and he left within a few days. But before he left, he gave me the precious gift of knowledge of my mother, her life and her death.

My pregnancy sapped my strength and my wits. When I carried Yvain, I had had more than enough energy to be both lord and lady of the caer, village, and extended lands. With this child, all I could do was sit by the fire and listen to the gossip that flowed in with each new messenger and refugee. I knew what happened in every corner of Britain. But I did not know what transpired in the hearts of my family.

My daughter was born on a cold and blustery night just after Imbolc. Ice pellets pounded the shutters and the roof. The wind slashed through stout walls to grab hold of unwary hearts and exposed fingers and noses.

Pain ripped through me like a cold knife. My blood rushed to warm the icy slashes, spilled over, and chilled me more.

The caer compound was full of ewes bleating their distress, needing help birthing their numerous fat lambs. I screamed with my own labor pains, needing more help than the stupid sheep. Only the wind and the rain heard me. Only inexperienced Marnia left the sheep long enough to help me into the birthing chair and deliver my daughter. Arthur's daughter.

Carradoc was so pleased with Arthur's favor and the abundance of healthy lambs that he barely noticed my daughter was born three weeks early. She came precisely on time if you counted the days from last Beltane when I lay with Curyll beside a magical pool while faeries danced about us, sharing our passion.

She came into the world reluctantly and protesting. She screamed louder than I did as she wrenched and twisted inside me, tearing the delicate fabric of my womb.

I barely had the strength to return to the bed.

"Ye'll not bear another child after this," Marnia said as she tried in vain to stop my bleeding. White panic showed in her face and her voice. She had only recently discovered that she carried Kalahart's child. She'd miscarried one child already. I saw fear in her eyes. Fear that she, too, would die a bloody and painful death while giving birth.

For her I had to fight back the chill and my need to drift into Annwn, home of the faeries. An immortal home where no one grew old, pain did not exist, children could not be born, so they didn't rip their mothers apart in birthing.

"In the stillroom," I gasped. "The tisane and the poultice I prepared yesterday." I hadn't the strength to say more. Yesterday I had known I would need help stopping the blood.

Yvain had come into the world so easily. Yvain, the son of a man I didn't love. Why did this daughter make so much trouble when I loved her father so dearly?

Marnia dashed out of the overly warm chamber for the required remedies. I knew her pronouncement accurate. I had felt the rupture with the last huge push of a large infant through the birth canal. No more children would fill my damaged womb, even if I took Carradoc back into my bed.

I must have dozed. Voices and the weight of my daughter atop my swollen belly brought me back from a world of cold winds circling until they found a soul that could be pried loose from its body to join them.

"We must send for her father, Papa," Marnia sobbed. "I don't see how she can live. She's lost so much blood."

The weight on my stomach eased. I pried one eye open to see Carradoc lifting the squalling infant.

"No," I protested weakly. "I must nurse her. 'Twill help the bleeding."

Carradoc and Marnia exchanged worried glances. Silently they shrugged their shoulders.

"Give her what comfort you can," Carradoc said. "I'll send Lancelot to Campboglanna for The Merlin."

"No," I protested weakly. No, he must not send Lancelot to face Guinevere at Campboglanna. Or no, he must not send for my father? I didn't know which. He ignored me anyway.

"Heat the poultice until it is just a bit warmer than I am. The tisane, too," I whispered. Chill shook my body. I'd lost a lot of blood. The wind wanted to carry me away. It promised warmth at the end of its cold journey.

I had to stay here, regain my strength before I confronted my father.

The baby seemed overly heavy as I settled her to my breast. She squalled and fretted until she found the nipple and began sucking.

Relief washed over me like a warm wave.

Marnia applied the poultice. She filled me with the distilled herbs, crying the while.

I drifted out of this reality.

Step by step I traced the labyrinth up the tor of Avalon. My body seemed heavy and reluctant. But I knew I must climb the tor, climb to end the pain and weariness of my ordeal. No time to stop at the two springs, red and white, to drink of the sacred waters. To refresh myself in their healing properties.

I needed more than the waters of the Goddess.

I counted the twists and turns that led me up that lonely hill.

Above me, lightning creased the lowering sky. Bright light against fearsome black clouds. Rain poured down, too heavy for the clouds to hold any longer. Winds followed me up the tor, pushing me closer and closer to my destiny. They tore at my thin garment, my hair, and my identity until I did not know if I was the wind or the wind had become me.

Power rose within me with each step up the tor. My fingertips glowed with an eldritch light. I pulled more lightning down from the sky, draping its glow around me. I became a beacon in the bleak landscape. Did I warn of danger or draw strength to me?

With each step, the blackness of the sky grew thicker, lower. With each step I glowed brighter.

The slope slackened. A round plateau opened before me. Standing stones marked a barrow at the top of the tor. Ancient dead had been placed beneath the stones, guarding the entrance to Annwn, the Otherworld.

The last time I had been here there had only been a tumble of ordinary boulders atop the tor.

I faced the shadowed portal of the barrow with curiosity and fear. I regretted leaving this plane. I longed to join Cedar and his companions in theirs. . . .

Gwynn ap Nudd, king of the faeries stood framed by the standing stones. He held out his arms, welcoming me to his kingdom. Cedar and the other faeries hovered behind him; a brilliant array of colored beings, taller than I, achingly beautiful, incredibly graceful, ready to lift into flight on iridescent wings. The hall of Gwynn ap Nudd stretched deep inside the barrow. Golden walls, marble floors, and delicate furniture borrowed light from the sky to give themselves substance. The lintel of the barrow glowed in the flickering lightning, becoming a glittering crown too bright to look at directly.

Sitting on a throne, crowned in light and love, a shadowy, feminine figure beckoned to me. Without knowing her face, I sensed my mother in the Goddess image. Deirdre, my mother who had died in childbed, as I was dying.

She held the gräal of life on her lap. Idly, she played with one strand in particular. She tested its flexibility as if preparing to break it off short.

As I hesitated, my mother faded into an insubstantial wraith. The glitter of the Great Hall of Annwn shimmered with unreality.

Only the gräal remained.

Such were the tricks of the faeries. Cedar had taught me how the Otherfolk misdirected gazes and flashed illusions around us mortals. I fought the need to look at the lesser light that streaked the black sky, lest the faeries change the hall into something more compelling than the mother I had never known.

In that moment I knew that death awaited me. It hovered, like the lightning, waiting for me to cross the threshold. I had to take but one step forward. The Otherfolk, the faeries, would shelter me from death, give me immortality. I need not give them the half-caste child they longed for. They had Guinevere. . . .

With that knowledge came true vision. Gwynn ap Nudd shifted, changed, lost brilliance. Horns replaced his crown. The barrow became the roots of the Worldtree, anchored in the Underworld, soaring upward into reality. The gräal rested in a fork of the trunk of the Tree. The strands of life entwined with the leaves and branches. Cernunnos perched beside the gräal awaiting me.

I peered beyond the horned god, deep into the barrow. A single candle guttered in the impenetrable darkness. Around the candle stood Dana, the Earth Mother, Belenos, the Sun Father, and Lleu, patron of bards and music. Frozen between them stood my father, a younger Myrddin Emrys than the man I knew, with a full head of dark hair, clean-shaven, proud, and self-assured. He waited while the gods decided his fate. And mine.

They seemed frozen in time. Waiting. Waiting for me.

Da's formal white robe hung limply on his thin frame. Dana's thick rope of golden hair, the color of wheat, rested upon her shoulder as if caught in the middle of a broad swish when she turned her head.

The gods had imposed an impossible geas upon a vibrant man who was supposed to be their representative, not their toy. Da had succumbed to the most basic of human needs, one the gods blessed, but forbade to him. If he hadn't honored the Goddess on Beltane, as all of us were commanded to do, as I had with Curyll, I would not have been born.

Da had been returned to the world, on probation. He must fulfill his destiny, he must prepare Arthur to become Ardh Rhi, and he must raise me to maintain a balance between reverence of life and the politics of chaos and change. No one could halt change, only learn to mold it for the better. I had been selected to pass on my knowledge to succeeding generations and become their anchor of continuity. My mother had died before she could assume that role. My grandmother refused to acknowledge her place in the intricate pattern of life. If I chose to enter the Underworld, realm of Cernunnos, I forsook my destiny.

The choice was mine and mine alone.

I turned my back on the tableau spread out before me. That was the past. The future called me. My daughter called me. She needed my nurturing, my training as a priestess. Only she could perpetuate the magic I had inherited from a long line of the faithful.

One long step away from the barrow the vision ended in a shower of sparks. The strand of life within the gräal the Goddess had toyed with remained whole.

Chapter 48

DA'S face swam into view as my heavy eyes finally focused. He'd been crying as he traced magical sigils over my body. The tip of his finger and the potent signs glowed a lot like Gwynn ap Nudd's crown. My heart fluttered in empathy with him. He'd lost everyone he loved in his life as he pursued the destiny ordained for him by the gods, and nearly lost me, too.

He had his reasons for every action he took, but I knew deep in my soul that his love for me never faltered. Forgiveness swelled within my heart.

At the same time I vowed to myself that I would choose my own destiny and teach my children to choose their own as well. I would bind them close to me with love and tolerance. The rift of misunderstanding that stood between Da and me would not happen to my children and me. I would keep them safe, here in the North, away from the machinations of politicians and magicians. I would teach them the ways of the forest, the life of the Goddess, and the cycles of the sun, moon, and earth. I would be mother to them as Da had been both mother and father to me.

The faeries would always be welcome at the sacred pool where I had loved with Curyll on a sultry Beltane afternoon.

I risked a tiny smile at Da and touched his glowing finger with my own. A tingle of strength wandered up my arm from his touch. Not much, but enough to keep my eyes open a few moments longer.

Father Thomas knelt on the stone floor beside my bed. He worked the chain of wooden beads as he counted prayers, mumbling the words and alternately making the sign of the cross on his own shoulders and over mine. I touched his hand the next time it passed over me. He stilled a moment, smiled, and finished the gesture. "The Lord Jesu Christus recognizes you, Wren, even if you do not recognize Him in your pantheon of old gods."

I tried to smile in return, found it exhausting, and had to close my eyes. When I found the strength to view the world again, Curyll stood beside me, opposite Father Thomas and Da. Worry lines turned his mouth down and creased his eyes. He looked as if he hadn't slept in days. And so did Father Thomas and Da.

I loved these three men, each in a different way. They were the ones I wanted to see upon waking as they stood vigil over me. Tears leaked from the corners of my eyes.

Curyll crossed himself with his right hand as the priest recited his next prayer. He slipped a bead from a bright silver chain, similar to Father Thomas' more modest one, through his fingers. He wore a cross on a chain about his neck. His golden torc was missing, set aside in favor of the Christian symbols.

Da still wore his own torc and refrained from crossing himself.

"My baby?" I asked weakly, praying that Carradoc hadn't taken the child and drowned her.

"She sleeps, here beside you." Da directed my hand to circle the tiny bundle.

I sighed in relief and closed my eyes again. Carradoc hadn't discovered my daughter's true paternity. With luck he never would.

"W–will sh–she be all–right?" Curyll stammered, looking twelve years old again, and very uncertain of himself.

My heart stuttered in fear. My tears dried. Arthur had embraced the Christians. Had the blessings of the faeries deserted him? Had they taken the gift of speech with them?

Without the ability to talk and persuade, to dispense firm and fair justice with words, the Ardh Rhi would have to resort to war to bring fractious kings into line. Britain couldn't survive another war so soon. The last time I had meddled, I had upset a delicate balance of avoidance between my father and Dyfrig. If I intervened again, whose balance would I upset?

Hours later, when I awoke a second time to the hungry cries of my daughter, I realized that Carradoc had not been among the men who grieved for me when they thought me dying.

Did he know? Would he divorce me and throw me out—or kill me and my daughter?

Hannah rushed into the dim chamber before I could pursue my fears. "I'll just take the baby to the wet nurse, Lady Wren." She gathered the red-faced bundle into her arms from the cradle beside my bed.

"No, Hannah. I must nurse her. 'Twill help control the bleeding," I said. My voice sounded a harsh whisper against the squalls of my daughter.

"You haven't the strength, Lady. You have to rest and rebuild the blood you lost."

"I will nurse my daughter if I can. And her name is Deirdre." For my mother.

"Sorrowful wanderer. Aye, that she almost was. Those what lose their mothers afore they know them often are. Look at my poor Nimuë. Never did find herself." Hannah nearly had to shout over the baby's cries.

I reached my arms out to take Deirdre. My breasts grew heavier with each cry. They already leaked fluid; my instinctive response to a hungry infant. The slightly sweet, slightly sour smell set my own stomach to rumbling.

"Ye'll not have enough milk to satisfy this one, Lady." Hannah clucked and shook her head as she handed me a very angry Deirdre. "Two wet nurses have been taking turns with her every two hours while you fought with the dark lord for your life."

"Just like her brother, always hungry. I will do what I can to feed my daughter. It's important to her and to me."

"Then I'll fetch you soup. You'll need it." Hannah ambled out of the room, shaking her head and chuckling at the imperious demands of my daughter.

"Hannah?" I asked when she returned with soup and bread and a hunk of aged cheese. "Did Nimuë come with my father?"

"Nay, Lady. Only The Merlin and the Ardh Rhi rode through that storm like they had demons on their tail."

"And Lord Carradoc ?"

"Father Thomas came the next morning, God bless him," Hannah continued as if I hadn't spoken. Her gaze remained fixed on the baby rather than meet mine. "The storm still raged, but he came to offer you the last rites, though I doubt you'd a' taken them."

"The prayers of all three men were more than welcome, Hannah. It matters not which god they prayed to. They were all heard and they called me back from the edge of the Underworld." I looked down at Deirdre rather than face Hannah's scrutiny. The speed and intensity of the baby's feeding had slowed to a sleepy murmur.

"Bless you, Lady, who'd a known you could produce enough milk to satisfy that one after what you've been through." Hannah shook her head at the sight of a very drowsy Deirdre. A huge smile creased Hannah's face as she fussed over my meal.

"It wasn't just the milk she needed. She needed her Mama."

"Maybe so. Maybe so. Now eat up, Lady Wren, or you'll not have enough milk for the next feeding."

I sipped a little of the soup. It slid down my throat, easing the tightness of illness and the tears I'd shed. My stomach growled for more.

Hannah changed the baby and placed her back in the cradle. While her back was to me, I asked the next question that plagued me. "Who took the message to Arthur's headquarters at Campboglanna? Was it Kalahart or Carradoc ?" That would explain his absence.

"Nay, Lady," Hannah replied, looking over her shoulder toward me. "Lord Lancelot summoned the Ardh Rhi and your father. But he took a chill in that wicked storm and stayed at the fortress."

Dana preserve us. What mischief would follow? Lancelot with Guinevere without my father or Curyll to keep them apart?

"Tell Lord Carradoc that we will return to Campboglanna with the others." My mind spun with plans for the journey. Pack ponies, a litter for myself and the children, which warriors to take with us, which to leave. . . .

"Saints preserve us, Lady Wren! You can't travel. Not for months yet. You aren't even out of your deathbed yet."

I let Hannah's protests roll over me. "Inform Lord Carradoc of my plans, Hannah. We leave as soon as arrangements can be made. Where is he anyway?"

"The master and his warriors are training in the courtyard, Lady." Hannah dropped her head rather than tell me that my husband cared little if I lived or died. "He'll be happy to go to Campboglanna in your stead."

"I must go." I had to continue the work of keeping Lancelot and Guinevere apart, even if I had to resort to magic to do it. I owed

Curyll whatever I could do to preserve his marriage. I couldn't let Lancelot and Guinevere upset the fragile peace.

"You can't do this, Wren. You aren't strong enough," Da yelled at me, being a "Da" and not The Merlin for the first time in many years. He threw my clothing back into the clothespress as fast as I folded them into the traveling chest.

Two weeks had passed since I had made my decision to travel to Campboglanna on Hadrian's Wall. No one took me seriously, least of all my Da. I hadn't seen Carradoc at all.

"I can travel to Campboglanna. I must." I sat down hard on the bed, unable to lift another shift or stocking. Cold sweat broke out on my face and back.

"Lie down before you fall down," he said quietly, easing me back against the pillows. "All of Britain is not worth losing you, Wren."

"You're a little late with your concerns, Da. You should have put my interests ahead of Britain two years ago."

"I'm sorry that I had to almost lose you before I realized that you are right, Daughter." Da faced me forthrightly, acknowledging his guilt. "You would be within your rights to divorce Carradoc," he added. "I know how abusive he can be."

"He has not raised a hand to me—yet. I promised 'until death do us part' and sealed the promise in a circle. I keep my promises. Even if he does not keep his."

A long moment of sad silence stretched between us.

"All of Britain is at stake again," I said, breaking the mood. "Neither one of us can let matters follow their own course between Lancelot and Guinevere. We have to do something."

"The path of the future has been ordained for a long time. No matter what we do, the events are in place. I have seen it." He bowed his head.

"I have the gift of vision as well, Myrddin Emrys."

"What have you seen?" He reared his head up sharply. I was reminded of a merlin, the hawk he was named for, suddenly scenting prey on the wind, alert and anxious to spread his wings in flight.

"I have seen that life is a series of choices, dozens of roads branching away in all directions. We alone can choose which path. The future is fluid and changeable. We can still prevent trouble."

"Arthur made his choice. He selected a bride who will betray him."

I couldn't dwell on Arthur's other choice yet. If he had deserted the faeries and the old gods, then his gift of speech would evaporate. I hadn't seen enough of him in the last two weeks to know if his stutter had returned permanently or only his emotions had hindered his speech by my sickbed.

"Guinevere and Lancelot have choices as well. I intend to make certain they make an informed choice. They may be in love. They may have passions, but they can choose restraint—or discretion." I hoped. The faeries only knew if flighty Guinevere could stop giggling long enough to make a serious decision.

"Arthur returned to Campboglanna this morning. He will arrive before you. The Ardh Rhi will discover the truth before you can hide it." Da dipped a cloth in cool water and bathed my face with it. He hadn't taken such tender care of me since I was nine years old.

I think I had more strength and presence of mind then.

"But Curyll doesn't know the temptations that beset Lancelot and Guinevere. They will not flaunt their affair in his face. As long as he doesn't know. . . ."

"I think he does know all about temptations, Wren. He will suspect his wife and best friend of his own sin of loving where he may not. I saw his face when Lancelot first brought the news that you were near death in childbed."

I looked at the door, frantic that Carradoc might overhear.

"If Arthur knows about Lancelot and Guinevere, he will not acknowledge it until forced to," I said in an undertone, for his ears only. "But he doesn't realize the mischief Nimuë or Morgaine will stir up if they suspect. And you aren't there to stop them."

"Nimuë doesn't even know Morgaine. And she would never do anything to harm the Ardh Rhi or his Ardh Brenhines. Why would she?"

"Because she can. Because it is an exercise in wielding power over others." I tried sitting up again. It was obvious to me that Da was as besotted with my stepdaughter as Arthur had been with Guinevere. Neither man would willingly see faults in the women they loved.

Da pushed me back against the pillows with the touch of one

finger. "You won't save anyone if you die trying to get to Campbog-lanna."

"It's only a half-day's ride."

"Three days by easy stages in a litter. That's too far and too long for you, dear Wren. You cannot take Arthur's children to court and you cannot leave them here untended."

"I have a caer full of servants, retainers, and tutors. The children are not untended. Who do you think has been looking after them while I have been stuck in this bed!"

"I have. By Arthur's request. You or I must be in attendance at all times." Magical protection for children who could be assassinated or held hostage by Arthur's enemies.

I knew the dangers that beset the Ardh Rhi. But who would strike innocent children to get to the father?

Morgaine. The warning came from the wind that always haunted this hilltop caer.

"Then you must follow Arthur now, Da. Make certain Guinevere and Lancelot separate. Stand between Nimuë and her mischief. Keep Morgaine at bay."

"My place is with you, Wren. And Nimuë won't do anything but study and practice her spells. She's quite talented, you know."

"And beautiful, and unscrupulous, and power hungry. I have dealt with her on a level you can never imagine. I know her. If you won't go, then send Carradoc. Nimuë will listen to him." She certainly wouldn't listen to me. And I knew she used Da for her own ends.

Chapter 49

MY strength returned slowly. Da divided his time between Caer Noddfa and Arthur at Campboglanna. I slept so much, I found myself wide awake and wandering the fortress at odd hours. When Da was at Caer Noddfa, he paced with me. Gradually we reforged the bonds of love between us. I think Da began to trust me again, and realized his errors.

Tonight I had the Long Hall to myself.

Frosty moonlight filled the courtyard with shadows eerily reminiscent of Annwn, the Otherworld of the faeries I had glimpsed in my vision atop Avalon's tor. We drifted toward the Equinox very slowly, trapped in an unrelenting cold snap. Warm rains or insulating snow couldn't break through the iron-cold temperatures and clear skies.

I shivered and sent my footsteps to pacing the kitchen and the Long Hall rather than the outdoors. I longed for fresh air and the taste of the wind. But not tonight. Not when the moonlight and the chill reminded me so sharply of the Otherworld and death. Restlessness kept me wandering long past sleepiness.

So many of my body's responses were not yet right that I ignored the faint prickling along my spine. Instead of looking for the source of my disquiet, I continued looping through the two connected buildings, seeking . . . seeking something to settle me, restore my strength, ease me back into sleep.

Newynog paced with me. She snorted and whined in uncertainty. The fur on the back of her neck ruffed up and down as she caught scents and dismissed them.

My feet made little shuffling sounds across the clean floor rushes. Mice and cats stalking each other stirred other sounds through the still night air.

A shutter creaked. A thump of something heavy landing.

What? I stopped in my tracks, every sense available to me alerted. The shutter had been *there,* the direction of the children's quarters. Had one of them fallen out of bed?

More likely the older boys were trying to sneak out on some secret escapade. I had done that often enough at their age, frequently in the company of Curyll and his foster brothers.

Just because I had done it didn't mean I condoned it for the children in my charge. The night was too cold for them to wander around out-of-doors.

I crept on tiptoe out the kitchen door with Newynog and a cat in my wake. We sidled over to the separate hut where the children slept. A shutter on the deeply shadowed side between the Long Hall and the conical hut lay half open. I positioned myself beneath the partially opened window and listened.

Soft, sleepy murmurs, rapid footsteps, a deep, *adult* voice whispering.

Without thought of my own flagging strength or the consequences, I dashed through the door into the single chamber with bunks attached to the sides, where the boys slept. The girls had a similar chamber on the other side of the hall. I stopped short just inside the doorway, letting my eyes adjust to the new dimness.

A man stood beside the top right-hand bunk, arm raised. The eerie light glinted off a metal blade.

"No!" I screamed and lunged for him.

I tripped over blankets and linens tangled on the floor, crying out as my nose hit the floor, cushioned by the blankets.

A heavy foot cuffed my ear. A very large, booted foot. I grabbed hold of the ankle and sank my teeth into the man's calf above the thick leather.

"Yieee!" he screamed, lashing downward with a fist.

I rolled aside before he connected with the back of my neck. A whimper and soft lump within the bundle of blankets told me another child, possibly wounded, lay within the suffocating tangles.

"Who goes there?" Kalahart shouted from the ramparts. More footsteps, running toward me.

"Wren!" a child's voice screamed.

I couldn't tell which of my boys.

"Let go of me! Wren, help me!" Brangore sobbed as he awakened.

The man hauled the child out of the bunk, blankets and all. Brangore kicked and thrashed. Newynog worried the assassin's ankles. She couldn't attack him directly without harming the child.

"Shut up, brat, or I'll strangle you where I stand!" The man's harsh voice betrayed his nervousness. He kicked at the dog repeatedly, never connecting, just keeping her at a distance.

Gyron, the four-year-old boy beneath me, scrambled free of the blankets. He huddled against the inner wall sucking his thumb.

Brangore kept struggling silently as the unknown man retreated toward the door with the boy in his arms.

I tried to pull myself up, block his escape. The blankets snagged my feet, and upset my balance again. The intruder slammed into me. He cried out. Brangore screamed. A small thud on the floor. A heavier crash pushed me to my knees.

Hot pain sliced into my back.

Torches, shouts, heavy footsteps.

I opened my eyes to see a dozen warriors crowding into the small room. Kalahart held a weeping Brangore against his shoulder. Newynog licked my face, whining her distress.

All of the boys screamed their fear.

A short, swarthy man lay dead on the floor, eyes open, mouth pursed in surprise.

"Yannos!" Kalahart gasped. One of his own men turned traitor.

I struggled to stand once more; the pain in my back intensified, white-hot. Deep. Blackness crowded my vision. Flaming starbursts erupted behind my closed eyes.

"Easy, Lady. You're hurt. Let me call the women to help you." Alan, one of my guards, pressed me back into the soft blankets.

"What? Who?" I asked through gritted teeth.

"Traitorous assassin," Kalahart said succinctly.

"What?" I turned my head abruptly, regardless of the pain and dizziness. "Who would dare?"

"An enemy of the Ardh Rhi," Kalahart replied. Marnia arrived and relieved him of the sobbing child. The other boys crowded around her and me, babbling and crying. Hannah herded them all back to the kitchen and out of the way.

"I thought him loyal. Who could corrupt him? How?" I asked. My voice trailed off into a weak whisper.

"No fortress and no man is without a vulnerability, Lady." Relieved of the child, Kalahart knelt beside me, inspecting the knife slash on my lower back. My own fingers had discovered blood and torn tissue. I hurt too much for the spine to be affected. "The men will search his quarters and belongings for signs of corruption." He pressed a piece of sheet against my wound.

The sharp pain spread, dulled, but didn't lessen under the pressure.

"How did he die?" I risked looking at the assassin's slack face. Black blood dribbled from his mouth.

"Poison, I think," Kalahart replied. "There's not a mark on him."

"Smell his mouth."

The former warrior shifted to kneel over the stiffening corpse. He bent his nose close to the man's broken and blackened teeth. Kalahart reared his head back sharply in distaste.

"What does it smell like?" I pressed him for information.

"Like worms been eating refuse. Bitter and old."

"Druidsbane," I gasped. What magician had given him druidsbane, the most secret of arcane poisons? A massive dose to kill so instantly. Whoever had poisoned Ardh Rhi Uther with the plant had used a single drop at a time over a period of months, maybe years, to mimic a cancerous demon.

"Look for the vial," I gasped, fighting the pain and my own weakness.

"This?" Kalahart pried a blue-and-black vessel from the corpse's fingers. He held up a scrolled shell, both ends and the slit opening capped and sealed with silver. It hung from a silver chain.

"Dana preserve us. They used one of the Goddess' treasures as a vessel for evil." I breathed slowly and evenly, measuring each word to minimize the pain. No shell that lovely grew in the Northern waters around Britain. It had to be imported from the warm sea around Rome or farther south.

Nearly the length of a man's palm and as thick as two fingers, remnants of the wax seal on the top showed blood red in the torchlight. No trace of the owner's banner or a protective sigil remained.

"Fine quality silver work," Kalahart said quietly.

"The etched design on the silver?"

"Can't read it, Lady. Don't look like Latin, though. I've seen that written often enough to recognize the letters."

"More ancient." The pain was nearly too great to talk. But I had seen enough. The sigils etched into the silver contained the name of the witch who had prepared this poison and probably Uther's as well. The name was as important to the potency of the drug as the plant. The name that the spirits of forest and wind whispered to me in warning.

Morgaine.

Arthur kept Lot's oldest son and heir, Agravain, with him as hostage against the King of the Orcades' good behavior and continued loyalty. We had all heard rumors of wild Gaels and Picts flocking to Lot's banner. The faeries and trees murmured of Morgaine setting up a demonic attraction. The wild tribes had no choice but to follow her.

No one doubted there would be another war. There was always another war, if not with outsiders, then amongst ourselves.

Soon after the Equinox, Lot sailed from his remote islands with a fleet of war galleys and a large invasion force. He gathered allies as he progressed south.

Uriens of Gorre sallied forth from his protected lands with a huge warband—mostly malcontents and outlaws who couldn't find places with the kings loyal to Arthur.

Lot's eldest son Agravain was reported to be Arthur's strongest supporter as well as hostage for his father's good behavior. Lot seemed not to care for the boy's welfare. I knew Morgaine didn't. She didn't care about anything but her own power and vengeance against Arthur for the scattered pattern of her life.

Guinevere returned to Camlann with her ladies, including Nimuë. Da sent Berminia to her older sister, hoping life at court would fill the emptiness in the girl's life that only rich food and bitter accusations seemed to satisfy. Then he and Carradoc raced with the warband to join Arthur and Lancelot on the march to Dun Edin.

So far no scandal had torn holes in Arthur's reputation and leadership. He could lead in war without the gift of speech.

The week before Beltane the wind and the trees began whispering in turbulent unease. "What?" I asked them, alarmed that another assassin invaded my household. I had barely finished recovering from the last one's attack.

Morgaine, the spirits of forest and field answered. The only name they whispered. The only name they feared.

The spring winds told me that Morgaine sought a new balance in her life by borrowing power from the Otherworld.

For hundreds of generations the many worlds maintained a balance of energies, with gods, faeries, and humans flowing freely between the different worlds. Change and progress blocked some portals and opened others. As long as the opening to the dark world of demons was kept sealed, life for all remained in balance.

I envisioned life as the complex knotwork embroidery on the hem and sleeves of my gowns. The chains of the design encircled the dark Otherworld, containing it. Change added to the design without tearing it to shreds. Morgaine's quest for power threatened to break open a wide pathway.

News from an itinerant priest that Morgaine joined her husband on the military campaign shocked me out of my complacency. Morgaine had blocked Lot's every attempt to make peace with Arthur. Morgaine's new son by Lot, Mordred, the same age as my own son Yvain, could inherit all if Agravain and Lot both died in battle. Lot's other son Gaheris was rumored to be more interested in studying the stars than practicing with his weapons. Gwalchmai, Morgaine's other son, avoided rumor and might have disappeared.

The wind told me that Lot and Morgaine reached Dun Edin before Arthur.

I could no longer hide in the shadows, a silent observer. But I couldn't leave the children unprotected. I needed more information.

Perplexed and anxious, I made my way to the sacred pool at dawn that Beltane. I took with me five children ranging in age from my own newborn daughter and fifteen-month-old Yvain, to a two-year-old, thumb-sucking girl and two four-year-olds, a boy and a girl. These were the innocent and believing ones, the ones most likely to be able to see the faeries and not take fright. Brangore filled his days with a need to master weapons and fighting against the assassins he saw in every shadow. The other older children followed his example.

I hadn't seen any of my faery friends since my deathbed vision of the tor at Avalon. Cedar hadn't brought his companions to the caer at all during my recovery. The passage in and out of Annwn had grown narrow.

As I cast offerings into the spring above the sacred pool, in my private celebration of Beltane, I remembered in vivid detail the conception of my daughter one year ago. Those memories brought the faeries to me. They, too, needed to celebrate the glorious union of Dana and Belenos. The Christians and Father Thomas celebrated spring in their own sober, fully clothed fashion.

Cedar greeted me, flying delirious loops and whorls. He tugged at my hair, buzzed my ear, and tickled my nose. His companions—red, yellow, white, blue, and three more shades of green—joined him.

The children laughed and clapped. They chortled with joy, convinced the aerial display was for their entertainment. Yvain spread his arms and flapped them, trying desperately to join the faeries in flight. The others imitated him, dancing around the pool in such wild abandon, I feared they'd fall in.

I gathered the faeries close to me and settled cross-legged on the grass. Gradually the children quieted. Two toddlers laid their heads in my lap and promptly napped. Yvain discovered a caterpillar on a leaf and watched it intently.

Cedar settled on my shoulder. His companions hovered in flight directly in front of me. The white male tickled my curiosity. I held out my hand, palm up. "May I look at you more closely?" I asked him.

He settled on my outstretched palm rather than answer directly. Cedar was the only faery who communicated with me regularly.

The white faery folded his wings and looked at me, head cocked, awaiting my scrutiny. A stray shaft of sunlight backlit his hair and wings. For a moment, gold touched him as if he'd been dusted with the precious metal. The resemblance to Guinevere struck me forcibly.

"Did her mother mate with you?" I asked. I kept an image of the Ardh Brenhines in her white-and-gold wedding gown firmly in my mind.

The white faery smiled, pleased that I had noticed.

The union was not satisfactory, Cedar whispered into my mind. *There will be no offspring from the half-caste child.*

My breath stopped. I let it out of my lungs, long and slow. "If I had mated with you, Cedar, as you requested three years ago, would that child also have been sterile?"

I felt agreement with my thought rather than an actual statement. Guinevere's mother had died in childbed. Many women did. But I somehow knew the woman's fate was determined by the half-caste nature of the infant more than the normal hazards of childbirth.

We did not know then, Cedar said sadly. *We do not mate casually with Others. Our numbers decrease rapidly. More every one of your years. Enough of your time has passed for the children we did sire to mature. They are all sterile.*

I grieved with my little friends. They gave a tremendous amount of joy to this world. Their laughter and pranks taught us not to take ourselves too seriously and thus become victims of our own pride.

But I sensed that the course of change would continue to close the portal to their world even as the doorway to the Christian faith widened. Such was the nature of life. But if Morgaine's power grew, all portals between worlds would have to close permanently, except the one to her dark Otherworld, the home of demons.

I had to do something. I had to protect this world, and all of the other worlds, using every magic and mundane tool available to me.

The toddlers sensed my sadness and woke up crying. Cedar and his companions rose in a flurry of startled flight.

Gently, I soothed them all, faery and mortal. But I couldn't ease the ache in Curyll's heart when he realized that his beloved wife's womb would never quicken.

Did knowledge of her sterility drive Guinevere to seek solace in Lancelot's arms? Dozens of jealous people would exploit the situation if she were ever caught or suspected. Especially while Arthur battled Lot in the North.

"Please, Cedar, you must go to Guinevere. You must watch and discover who plans mischief against her."

We cannot.

"But she is one of your own. You must guide and guard her, as you have watched over me these many years. Curyll, her husband, is the boy you helped cure of stuttering. There is mischief afoot. Only you can help me keep it from getting out of hand."

We cannot. The half-caste child has forsaken her heritage and accepted the Christian sacrament of water.

"Then will you go north to Morgaine? She, too, must be watched. I need to know whom she corrupts and how."

The faeries winked out of this world all at once, in a flash of light brighter than the spring sunshine.

"Cedar, where are you?" I called. "Cedar, come back to me. I need you!"

He did not reply or return. My mind remained as empty of their presence as did the air. I knew in my heart that they had not gone to watch Morgaine. They feared her as much as the trees and the wind did. As much as I feared her secret use of the druidsbane.

Chapter 50

THAT evening, as the villagers finished their athletic competition and their dance around the bonfire—fully clothed—I gathered my herbs and kindling to set my own purifying blaze on the back side of a standing stone farthest from the houses. Carradoc remained with Arthur's army at Dun Edin, so he couldn't order a fertility ritual with the Queen of the May. I chose to put aside that particular ceremony. Maidens and matrons alike would honor the Goddess in private.

When everyone had retreated to their homes, I called Tanio with my mind and set flame into the herbs and branches within a miniature ring of stones.

I had entrusted the children to the care of Newynog, trusting her more than the human guards. Morgaine couldn't corrupt Newynog, old and stiff as she was. At my order she would stay by the children and defend them to the death. Any enemy, human or magical would find her a formidable barrier.

Branches from last winter's Yule log fed my little fire. Fresh flowers and dried herbs filled the smoke with fragrance. My mind drifted upward and outward with the burning essence of the forest.

I sought a vision of Cedar and his companions within the flames. I had to know they were safe. They had to know that I still loved them, that they could return to me and I would not press them to spy for me again. I'd never penetrated Annwn in my spells before. I didn't know for sure if that Otherworld would open to me.

Slowly I cast about me for the proper direction. Avalon and its tor lay south and slightly west of where I sat. The wind begged me to travel north. *Later,* I promised the insistent breeze. I would investigate Morgaine in the North later. Avalon's tor possessed a gateway to the Otherworld. I didn't know any other place to reach my faery friends.

In my mind I once more traced the labyrinth around the tor. Without a physical body on the tor, I could not stop to fortify myself with the healing waters of the red and white springs. Every footstep took a tremendous effort of concentration. I pushed myself upward, through every layer of the labyrinth. The flattened top of the tor came into view, devoid of the barrow. Devoid of gateways. Devoid of my friends.

The wind scattered my smoke and my quest. It circled me and pushed north.

"Is there another gateway in the North?" I asked the rapidly moving air.

Restore the balance. Find the pattern, it replied.

I fed more sticks and herbs into the fire in front of my physical body. Sweat dotted my back and brow. A chill invaded my bones. I had used much of my strength on the first aborted search. But I sensed I had not the time to replenish my body as I replenished the fire.

The smoke returned as flame consumed my offering. I followed it upward and outward. This time I allowed the wind to determine my course and my quest.

North and east. We flew over the sharp hills and steep valleys of the lands north of Hadrian's Wall. The wind didn't pause at the man-made edifice. The wind had no time or concern with such things.

Crags and deep ravines gave way to rolling hills and open plains. I tasted salt water on the wind. I smelled fresh blood on the earth. Gwaed, the god of blood, walked openly.

The wind paused, circled, and stopped abruptly at a different crag. A fortress topped this one. Though I'd never been there before, I recognized Dun Edin from my father's tales of his youth. Ambrosius Aurelianus, the lawfully elected Ardh Rhi, and his younger brother Uther had fought the usurper Vortigen for the crown of Britain at this caer. Vortigen and Ambrosius had both died. Uther lived to become the Pendragon and make my father his chief adviser.

Another battle raged across the plains to the south of the great crag. The wind let me see Arthur astride his great white horse on a rise at the west end of the field. His chain mail was filthy and rent in several places. He held his battered helm in the crook of his arm while he watched the men slash and hack at each other below him. A bitter smile creased his lips but did not light his eyes. His forces prevailed but at great cost.

Lancelot sat astride his black horse on Arthur's right. The Merlin stood on his own two feet to the Ardh Rhi's left. Behind them, a young squire, Agravain, carried the dragon rampant banner.

They were safe for the moment. I sighed and the wind moved on.

A figure in black draperies stood atop the palisade that encircled the fortress. The wind whipped her skirts and sleeves to a frenzy. Combined with her silver-streaked black hair, she resembled a dark storm cloud, filled with too much energy to contain. She raised her arms, a carved staff clutched in her right hand, a dead hawk in her left. She shouted strange words, imploring the forces of Pridd, Awyr, Tanio, and Dwfr to do her bidding.

Lightning crackled around her. The earth shuddered and ripped open between two armies. Searing flames shot upward from the crevice. The tide in the nearby sea swelled into great waves that dashed far inland of their normal course. Winds twisted and spun in tight spirals, sucking up all that they touched. My guiding wind was caught in a mighty vortex.

We spun out of control.

I fought for balance. All of my energy went into separating my wind from Morgaine's control.

While I struggled, the armies paused in their terrible slaughter of each other. Land, wind, fire, and rain had become more terrible enemies. The two sides drew apart, retreated toward their respective bases.

Morgaine, mistress of dark magic, laughed atop her fortress. Her shrill mirth shot arrows of ice into my mind. She was the sorceress who twisted the bright patterns of life to dark destruction.

This is what the faeries feared. The power that fed Morgaine's spells changed the balances between the worlds.

I forced my wind back and away from Morgaine's command.

I wrenched free of my wind as it fell into a violent spiral. My spirit tried to retreat to my physical body. Without the wind, my spirit was stranded at Dun Edin.

Arthur and my father threw up their arms in the next onslaught of storm and sea and unstable earth. They fought the strange forces and fell to the ground in defeat.

I had to stop this.

How? What could I do from a distance? I hadn't time to retreat to my body and then ride two days north and east to confront Morgaine.

"I don't know how to do this!" I cried.

Then all the dominions of the gods will wither and die. Only you can restore the balance she destroys.

I fell back toward my body. Darkness followed me.

Coward! Andraste screamed back at me before I reached my body. The Goddess in Her warrior queen guise rose up before my vision, blocking my quest from proceeding or retreating.

I cringed away from Her anger. My strength failed me. I could sense my body trembling with cold and weakness. If my spirit drifted any longer, I might not have a body to return to.

You have not your father's courage. He always fights for the forces of light against darkness, no matter the consequences. Your weakness will destroy us all. You forsake the destiny assigned to you alone.

"I have not the strength of will or of body." I withdrew in defeat, every part of me screaming that I must do something to save Curyll and my father.

Negating black magic with white magic requires strength of mind and courage. Think of your children and your children's children. You faced death once before with courage. Do it again to save all you hold dear.

"Morgaine will not give up easily. She has planned this for a long time. I am not prepared." I felt my body slipping away. It slid into a formless slump beside the standing stone.

Morgaine upsets the balance that we established long ago. You are the fulcrum of the balance that keeps the old gods alive and props open the gateways between worlds. Only you can restore the balance this woman distorts.

"But why does she do it?" I asked myself more than Andraste. "I have to know 'why' to figure out 'how.' "

Ask her yourself as she stabs you in the heart with a knife made of demon's teeth, as she tried to stab an innocent child in your care.

The image of Andraste shimmered and faded. Below us, The Merlin launched a spell toward Morgaine. He lobbed a bright ball of magic fire into the center of the caer.

Morgaine captured Da's ball of magic with her staff and flung it back into his face.

He collapsed into a boneless heap. The magic fire hovered over his inert form, shooting tendrils of flame in all directions. Da jerked and convulsed as the fire sought fuel and direction.

Andraste bounced back into view, vibrant with color.

See what she does to your father. See and know how she destroys all in her path because she has forsaken life, forsaken all traces of the light The Merlin upholds.

Arthur and his companions retreated from the magic gone awry, unable to help, unwilling to leave The Merlin. The heat of the eldritch fire sent them retreating down the back side of the hill. The fire followed them. Da remained unmoving where he had fallen.

Grief and guilt flooded my being. *Da, don't die!* Tears streamed down my physical face. I ached. My heart pounded loudly in the quiet night. *Curyll! Save yourself. Save my Da.*

I knew he couldn't. Morgaine was too strong.

The image of Andraste exploded into a thousand shards of brightly colored light. *Only you can restore the balance.* Her words faded into a tinny echo that penetrated my soul.

I grabbed for one of the shards of light, clutching it in my astral hand as if it were life itself.

The standing stone that sheltered my fire cracked and crumbled into dust before my eyes. The spiraling winds rushed down from the North to extinguish the last remnants of my spell.

Angrily I forced my body to rouse and shove more fuel into the fire. I shifted my physical self to shelter the blaze from the twisted forces Morgaine had unleashed.

I'm coming, Da. Hold tight, Curyll. Don't let her win.

The renewed flame and smoke boosted my mind upward.

"Andraste, help me. I don't know what to do." I only knew I had to try.

My hand burned. I looked down and discovered I still held the shard of light that had been Andraste. The golden light blazed and stretched, burning with energy and life.

I held the sword of Andraste, astral twin to Arthur's Excalibur. A weapon against Morgaine.

No. Not against her, against her magic. This sword would not strike down a life.

You have done this before. Seek your memory, the Goddess whispered in my ear. This time She flowed through me with the loving embrace of Dana, the Mother of all—who embraced the light. In the battle against darkness I could not kill, only stop Morgaine's unbalanced magic. It had to be enough to allow Curyll to prevail and rescue my Da.

"When, when did I do this before?"

No answer.

When! I demanded of myself. The last time I had tried a major spell was that midsummer night when I banished Nimuë's ravens from Caer Tair Cigfran.

I had restored a balance then. Not much of a spell really. I had removed the unnatural attraction for the ravens. Without the attraction, they were easy to send elsewhere.

The attraction was the source of the imbalance.

What was the source of this imbalance? Morgaine. Something fueled her magic and her need for vengeance. Something not of this world. Something that thrived on the dankness created by fractured patterns.

I sent my mind back to the battle scene. I circled around the crackling figure atop the palisade of Dun Edin. Pridd, Awyr, Tanio, and Dwfr stood ready for her commands. Ready but unwilling.

How did she chain them?

Chains.

She had to be chained to the source of the imbalance.

I shifted my focus, looking beyond physical sight. Afterimages, like auras, surrounded all I surveyed. The edges of the auras were all tinged with black and blood red: the colors of death.

Black-and-red tendrils of power streamed backward from Morgaine. Back to the North. To her home in the Orcades. These were her chains to the Netherworld and her dark power.

I raised the sword of Andraste and struck at the chains. The force of my blow rebounded through my physical and my astral body, nearly shaking me free of the seeking spell.

I gritted my teeth and recovered my perspective. The chains had to be severed at the source, not Morgaine's end. I followed the chains. Swiftly. I hadn't much time. Da hadn't moved. Arthur and his band still fled the magic fire. Both armies were in disarray.

North, the sword of Andraste led me, a beacon in the growing darkness. Awyr, the winds tried to push me back into my body. I resisted, flying around and over the top of them. Walls of Dwfr in the form of pelting rain blocked my way. I dove under them. Tanio became bolts of lightning and sought me from the blackness. I blocked them with the sword. Pridd sent mountain peaks upward to entrap and enfold me. I flew higher.

The chains thickened and merged. I neared the source. I had to strike at the source. Once Morgaine was separated from the source, the elements would no longer obey her. They would retreat to their natural forms. Healing the damage Morgaine had already caused was another matter. I didn't have time or energy to think that far ahead.

North I followed the glowing sword. North to the Orcades, Lot's island kingdom. I crossed the open sea. The islands reared up before me. Stark and beautiful in their austerity. The sea and harsh climate had shaped the land and the people into hardy ramparts. Did I have the strength and tenacity to fight whatever the islands had forged?

You are the fulcrum of balance, Andraste had said. Balance didn't need strength, only shifts and counterweights. An ancient Greek had said, "Give me something to stand on and I could move the world."

He had been speaking of levers, but levers work with balance and counterweights, too. Something to stand on. A lever to overturn the source of Morgaine's dark powers.

I narrowed my focus to the tangled mass that anchored the black-and-red chains of power. I sensed that it lay within a gateway to the Netherworld. A world filled with demons rather than faeries. A world that was dangerous to touch as well as to unleash. As long as this portal remained open, the doorways to other worlds must close. Humans would lose all of their gods, the faeries, and other beings that tied us to the land. The land, the one constant in a world of change. Without the land we would shatter into chaos and never recover.

Gradually my vision sorted out the shadows within shadows wrapped tightly in chains of dark power. My astral self followed them to a windswept plateau above the sea, crowned with an ancient barrow. A small child slept peacefully within the two uprights of the tall stones that marked the gravesite. He rested at the center of power. Salt spray battered the cliff below the plateau, dampening the edges of the child's blanket. His aura was dark with demonic influences. His pattern of life was distorted, asymmetrical, and filled with darkness. A child only a little older than my son Yvain.

Mordred, Morgaine's son by Lot.

But not by Lot. Nothing of the King of the Orcades pulsed within the child's life pattern. He was solely Morgaine's son. What unnatural demon had sired Mordred so that he reflected only his mother's blood and heritage.

Then the truth struck me. Morgaine had been sent away from Uther Pendragon's court to marry Lot of the Orcades. She hadn't been allowed to participate in the public marriage ceremony performed for eight other couples on the eve of the battle. Her marriage had been arranged in more haste than mine because she was already pregnant.

Arthur, her half brother through Queen Ygraina, had been her lover for months before the weddings. Arthur, not Lot, had sired her child.

This unnatural child, born of incestuous love was the link between Morgaine and the demonic Netherworld.

Did Arthur know?

How could I break the bonds between a mother and her baby? How could I use the sword of Andraste to kill an innocent child?

Chapter 51

HE is not innocent! Andraste whispered to me. *He is as unnatural as the child you feared Nimuë would bear her father. He can never be innocent while he guards the gate to the Netherworld. Demons already feed on his heart.*

Not Andraste. She would never countenance the death of a child, a baby, barely two years old, no matter how twisted and dark its heritage. The Goddess, Dana/Andraste in all Her guises, was a mother as I was a mother. The death of a child wounded us all.

Back at Caer Noddfa, my physical body longed to rush away from my tiny fire to guard my own children. In my astral form I resisted the temptation. No matter the danger, I had to remain separate from my body until I finished my battle with the demons at the portal far to the North.

To save Curyll and your Da, you must destroy the demon child, the demon within the gateway spoke to me seductively. It imitated the speech and rhythm of the Goddess, but it could never match the love and protection of the true Goddess.

I would not give it another death to feed upon and make it stronger. There had to be a way to close the gateway to the Netherworld without harming the baby.

Balances and patterns. Fulcrums and levers. The concepts had been pushing me forward all night.

Gently, I slid the astral sword of Andraste beneath the sleeping baby. I used it as a lever, lifting Mordred as he sucked his fist in his sleep. My heart cried out for my own son, Yvain, so like this little boy in size and manners.

Mordred rolled off the blanket onto his tummy. He lay beyond the narrow gateway between the upright stones, still sucking on his fist, still sleeping. With one swift movement, I slashed at the chains of darkness and blood, severing them, cauterizing the ends. The demon screamed. It tried to climb out of the barrow, out of the Netherworld. One of its many black arms reached up and grabbed my wrists. Searing pain within my mind and body almost made me drop the sword, my only weapon against the beast. My body called my spirit back. My mind needed to retreat and nurse the pain.

Two more arms stretched toward the chains, trying to reforge the connection to Morgaine and the unbalanced elements. Yet more arms reached for me, trying to drag my spirit below. The seventh arm clung to the lintel stone that capped the two uprights. This was not Samhain; the demon could not easily move through the gateway. Some tendril of Andraste's control blocked it.

Before it could climb farther into this world, I slashed at it with the sword. The pain of its brand on my wrist made the blow weak. I missed the demon and struck the tall barrow stones that marked the portal. Sparks of eldritch light, forest green, sky blue, sunny yellow, and blinding white flashed from where the blade struck the stones. The demon cowered beneath the light.

I slashed again and again, wildly. I kept the demon at bay more by force of will than skill or strength with the sword.

Close the door, Andraste said. Her voice was stronger, surer. Driving the demon back restored Her vitality.

"How?" I asked whatever god, spirit, or element listened. I was tiring. I'd been soaring through time and space for a long time. My physical body began to crumple and withdraw from life, too long vacant of my spirit.

I looked at the baby again, reminded more strongly of my own little boy. I couldn't leave my son motherless. But I couldn't return to my body until the gate was closed and the demon safely locked away.

Use the sword. Find the barrier that Morgaine cast aside. Close the portal. Now, before it is too late.

I couldn't find the barrier. Nothing resembling a door or a gate, or even a large stone lay within my dimming vision. Nothing to block the barrow entrance. Nothing to stop the demon. Only the child's blanket lay flat on the ground within the opening.

I raised the sword one last time, determined to slay the demon if

I could do nothing else to stop it. Point down, both hands on the hilt, I jabbed deep into the heart of the demon. My hands slipped at the last moment. I lost my balance and loosed the blade. It slid under the blanket and threw it over the demon. It screamed.

I grabbed the sword one last time and plunged it through the blanket.

As I plummeted back into my body, I heard the sword of Andraste shatter. A thousand shards of blinding light pierced my mind.

Pain engulfed me.

Nimuë clamped her hands over her ears. She couldn't tell which was louder, Morgaine's inhuman screech or the frantic gibbering of her demon. Both hurt her extended senses.

"Quiet!" she commanded.

Her demon subsided into softer whimpers.

Morgaine continued to shout her frustrations to the four winds. But even the winds calmed, the seas retreated, the rain eased to an annoying drizzle, and the land stopped heaving.

Nimuë breathed deeply as she assessed the damage wrought by the sorceress on the ramparts of Dun Edin. Strangely the landscape returned to its normal flat plain at the base of the upthrusting crag.

The dead remained strewn about the field of battle. She turned a full circle to find the living. Morgaine's forces huddled at the base of the crag. Ten individuals fell to their knees, crossing themselves repeatedly. They wouldn't last long in Morgaine's camp. Arthur and his mounted companions rallied their troops back at their campsite. Some men from both sides escaped. They ran and ran as far and as fast as they could.

"Where is he?" Nimuë asked the demon. She continued to circle, seeking one personality with her magic and mundane senses.

Wh—wh—who? the demon sobbed.

"Merlin, you idiot. He was standing on that knoll and then Morgaine knocked him flat. Now he's not there."

I—I think he's dead.

"He can't be dead. Wren isn't here to witness his destruction. I won't let him be dead!" Nimuë stamped her foot.

You have no control over his life. You never did.

"Don't be ridiculous. He loves me. He has given me all of his magical knowledge." She used some of it to narrow her vision to the last place she had seen The Merlin, looking for traces of his aura. Bits of blue light faded before her eyes without trace of which direction he had taken.

You stole the knowledge from him while he slept. He doesn't realize that his strength and his spells fail because you have bled him dry. And now I fail as well. The demon fell back into his pitiful sobs.

"Nonsense. Our magic is as strong as ever. We have maintained our anonymity here in the army when I am supposed to be back in Camlann." She doubted anyone in the army camp knew of her presence except Carradoc. She could never hide from her father, even when she wanted to.

Nimuë brushed her shoulder in her usual gesture. The demon did feel smaller, less substantial.

But the portal to the Netherworld is closed. I can't go back, I can't come forth into this world. I'll be this half-formed being for all eternity! The demon's voice dissolved into wails and screeches. *The portal is closed.*

"We showed Morgaine how to open the portal once. She can do it again. We'll help."

Promise?

"I promise. But first we have to find Merlin. All this time cuddling that disgusting old coot will be wasted if his daughter isn't here to see his demise." She cast out her magical senses, seeking the familiar scent of the old man's magic.

Nothing.

Almost as if he had vanished into thin air.

"Where can he be?"

Morgaine won't give him up easily.

"Morgaine has him?" Of course. Who else could have whisked him away without a trace? The Merlin certainly didn't have enough strength left to manage more than the most rudimentary spells.

She won't give him up. She blames him for all of her troubles. Him and Arthur. She seeks to destroy them both.

Riders thundered up from Arthur's camp. A burial detail and the chirurgeons followed the armed escort.

Nimuë willed herself to fade into the heather and bracken. Her reddish-brown gown, the same color as her hair, eased the process.

Her old black gowns, in stark contrast to her hair, presented a greater challenge to her spell.

"Morgaine will give Merlin to me. We are allies. We have been since I first found you at the standing stone," Nimuë said when the men had passed her.

They began the grisly work of cleaning up the battlefield. The warriors kept the looters at bay. A few of Morgaine's men crept out from the protection of the crag to perform the same chores for the men from the Orcades.

The stench of death drove Nimuë back toward her tent at the fringes of Arthur's camp. The demon reached for the rotten smell, thriving on it. She slapped his pincer away from a staring corpse directly in their path.

The demon wrapped his multiple arms tightly around his shriveled body. *She won't give up Merlin until she finishes killing him. That could take weeks. I need her to open the portal now. I need the portal open!* Its pouts sounded strangely like its earlier screeches of distress.

"I'll find a way to bring you forth later. Right now, I think we need to talk to our ally. And if she won't give me Merlin, then I'll destroy her. I know her secrets and how to use them."

But the portal . . . She has to reopen the portal first!

Father Thomas found me huddled in a weeping mass of cold pain at dawn. Dew had settled on my thin white shift. My bare toes ached with chill, feeling as if they would shatter like ice on a pond at the first touch.

I cried as he lifted me. He clucked soothing noises at me and carried me to the caer.

"Send bandages and healing herbs to Dun Edin," I wailed. "Take your holy water and prayer beads. We must stand against the darkness. All of the gods must stand together against the darkness."

"Hush, child. Your nightmares have ceased. Dawn lights the sky again. What made you spend the night out alone in only your shift, weaving pagan magic? You're barely healed from your winter's ordeal."

"You don't understand. . . ."

"I understand more than you think. Now rest quietly for a bit, or you'll not rise again to fight your demons."

A guard stood ready to open the gate of the caer for us. Marnia and Hannah brought hot soup and blankets that had been warmed by the fire. I melted into the comfort they all offered, desperately needing to regain my stability, and yet too afraid to spend the time healing when I should be on the road to Dun Edin to begin the next battle against Morgaine.

Strangely, the sun rose in a cloudless blue sky. The same color blue as Da's eyes. Birds sang a glorious welcome to the new day. The old raven who perched on the well croaked a grumpy greeting to me as we passed him.

Life continued. Demons did not stalk the earth unhindered. Perhaps I had succeeded in closing the gateway to the Underworld. But if Morgaine lived, she would find another way to open the portal. She still had her unnatural son to anchor her power in darkness.

I couldn't rest until Morgaine was separated from Mordred and the little boy protected from her bitter desire for vengeance. Every time she used Mordred, as she had used him last night, she would tie his soul closer to the demons. The voracious beings of another world hungered for human souls. Their world was so dark they had to blacken our light in order to expand and grow.

All life hungered to grow, in body and spirit.

But demon life quests were mutually exclusive of human life patterns. We couldn't both survive in the same world. Morgaine's gateway had to remain closed.

By midmorning I had slept a little and eaten a little more. The day was warm, but I remained chilled. I dressed in my warmest winter gown and prepared to ride.

Arthur's army hadn't had time to return to Campboglanna, not as scattered and decimated as I had seen them to be. I would have to join the Ardh Rhi and my father at Dun Edin. Two days' hard ride if I took the easy route along Hadrian's Wall to Pons Aelius, the large fort near the eastern end of Hadrian's Wall, then north along the coast to Dun Edin. Due north cross-country was half the distance and an almost impossible ride through some of the wildest country in Britain. That route would take longer, if I survived the steep escarpments, rivers in spate, and bandits.

"You cannot ride that far alone, Lady Wren." Kalahart held my horse's bridle, preventing me from riding out the gate.

"Then catch up to me when you can with the pack pony." I jabbed my heels into the horse's flanks. The horse reared and pawed the air. I barely stayed mounted. Riding still didn't come easily to me, but I was almost used to it. I had chosen one of the fractious stallions Carradoc had been training for war. The beast was too young and wild yet for the disciplines of a warrior, but he was fast, with a stone heart that could run for hours without tiring. He'd get me where I needed to be faster than anything else in the stable. If I managed to stay on his back.

"Let her go, son," Father Thomas said with resignation. "A demon rides her soul. She'll not be rid of it until she finishes this quest. I'll pray for you both."

I didn't hear the click of the priest's prayer beads over the pounding hooves of my stallion. I didn't need to watch to know he fingered the chain of beads uneasily.

Newynog's daughter galloped at my horse's heels. My aging companion wouldn't be able to keep up. She already trained her replacement.

I wondered briefly if Kalahart would indeed follow me. Marnia's baby wasn't due for another four months. She'd not likely deliver while he was away. Still, he doted on her, fetched and carried for her, rarely left her side for more than a few moments. They both feared the dangers of another miscarriage.

"If anything happens to Lady Wren, Carradoc will kill me," Kalahart muttered.

"Her husband's vengeance will be less terrible than her father's or the Ardh Rhi's," Father Thomas replied. The last thing I heard as I galloped down the terraced road of the caer was the priest saying, "You'd better go after her, son."

Chapter 52

"TAKING Gwalchmai and Gaheris as hostages won't keep Morgaine from attacking you again," I said to Arthur for the third time. I had found him limping painfully around his pavilion, drinking too much, muttering too much, and accomplishing nothing.

Most of his army and client kings were camped on the plain south of Dun Edin. Arthur had planted his tent and his banner on the slopes of the tor to the east of the fortress crag. From here he could see everything. I'd heard that he spent hours sitting in front of his tent, brooding about the battle he had almost lost.

The tor had become known to one and all as Arthur's Seat.

"L–lot is K–king of the Or–Orcades." He swallowed deeply and regained control of his speech. "He c–commands the troops that f–ought my army. Taking his second son and M–Mor–gaine's son by her first marriage will remind him most emphatically where his loyalty is supposed to lie," Arthur replied through gritted teeth.

"They will still have Mordred," I replied.

"An infant." He shrugged away my words.

I didn't like the waxy color of his skin, or the over-brightness in his eyes.

"Has anyone seen to your wound?" I asked, watching the nature of his limp. I worried about his stutter, too. He must be very upset about something to allow the hesitation back into his words. The Christian cross he wore about his neck shouldn't have anything to do with it. The faeries had only taught him confidence and self-control, not ensorcelled him.

"The m–edics are all too b–usy with the troops." He continued pacing, favoring his right leg. Blood stained his leggings just above his right knee.

"You need help. Take off those leggings and climb up on the table." I swept a long map table clear of debris with a single sweep of my arm.

"No. I'll not have you tend me." He frowned at the maps and letters and meal remnants that now littered the carpet.

"Either I tend you or I take one of the chirurgeons away from the hospital tent."

"Th–three days since the b–battle and the medics still labor over the wounded and dying." He hung his head as if he alone was responsible for the carnage. He'd never put the blame where it belonged—in Morgaine's lap. That was probably why he stuttered now: guilt.

"I can tend the wound as well as any of your battle-hardened sawbones. Maybe better. Take off the leggings and get atop that table while I fetch supplies."

He hesitated.

"I've seen you naked before. Many times since we were small children. Do it, Curyll, or I'll call in your entire medical staff to tend you."

"The men need . . ."

"The men need a healthy general and Ardh Rhi. If the wound has started to rot, you'll lose the leg. Britain will lose her Ardh Rhi. I'll be back in two moments. No more. Be ready."

I gave him five moments. The wound was painful enough to slow him down. When I returned with herbs and bandages and a needle and thread he sat atop the table, his long legs stretched out before him, his undergarment politely covering his mid-region.

"I w–washed and b–ound the wound as soon as I could. Your father taught me that long ago."

"Good. You may have saved the leg. Have you washed and changed the bandage since?"

"Every d–day, morning and night."

"Does it still bleed?" I could see that it did. The sword gash oozed blood and pus its full length from his knee along the outside thigh almost to his hip. Any movement at all opened the scabs and exposed tissue.

"Morgaine commands her husband," I reminded him as I washed the wound once more, this time with a special mixture of herbs and wine that would cleanse deeper than just water on the surface. Then betony to help the tissue knit clean and even. "This will sting a bit.

Morgaine's youngest child, Mordred, is the only one of the four boys who concerns her. You must take the child hostage. Let the others go if you must, but Mordred is the only thing in this world that your sister cares for," I said calmly, trying to divert his attention away from the wound.

"I have d–done many e–evil things in the name of securing p–peace for Britain, but I will not be so cr–uel as to take a baby hostage." He took another gulp of wine and set his face to endure. "I wish your father were here, Wren. He'd know how to numb the pain while he worked." The first unhesitating sentence he'd uttered.

"Where is The Merlin?" I asked, threading the finest needle in my kit with silk thread. Da hadn't been in the hospital tent with the other chirurgeons when I fetched some of the supplies.

"N–no one h–has seen him s–since the earthquake." He was back to stuttering again. Perhaps worry over my father interfered with his speech.

Arthur blanched as I pulled skin and muscle tight over bone with my sewing. I couldn't manage a presentable garment sewn of cloth, but I knew how to make a fine seam of flesh.

I moved to stand in front of him, looking directly into his eyes. Magic couldn't knit flesh. Herbs and the mundane needle and thread worked miracles on their own. I knew another mundane trick that seemed like a miracle.

"Look into my eyes, Curyll. Look deeply into my eyes. See the sacred pool in the glade. See the Lady slumbering in the depths. See the faeries dancing about. Look, look for them," I chanted.

His attention latched onto something far away and long ago.

"Feel the warmth of the sun on your back. See the sunlight on water. It sparkles so brightly. You need to close your eyes. You need to rest. Let the warmth soothe you. Don't fight the light. Ease the muscles in your back. Accept the warm light that lingers on your eyelids."

He obeyed. Leaning back on his arms, letting his head loll loosely on his shoulders.

"See the pain in your wound. Don't open your eyes. You can see it without opening your eyes. Look at the pain. Examine it closely."

Eyes closed, he dropped his head as if seeing the wound with his usual sight organs.

"The pain wants to spread. You can't let it go beyond the wound.

You can't let it possess you. Draw it back within the confines of the wound. Enclose it. Now grasp it with your hand."

He laid his right hand over the wound, slowly clasping it into a fist as if he did indeed capture the living entity of the pain.

"Now lift the pain free of your body. Drop it to the floor."

He lifted his still clenched fist and "looked" at it through his still closed eyes, examining it closely.

"Loosen your hold on the pain, Curyll. Fling it away from you and be free of it."

He dropped his hand to the side of the table and opened his fist. A blissful expression crossed his face and he sighed contentedly.

"You can let go of the hesitation in your speech as well. You are a proven warrior and the Ardh Rhi. You needn't be afraid to speak clearly and calmly."

A smile twitched at his mouth.

I continued with my litany, keeping my voice even, still chanting rhythmically. "Curyll, you know I wouldn't ask this of you if it weren't important. You must take Mordred as hostage from Morgaine and Lot."

"I may be under your spell to contain the pain, Wren, but I'm not gullible enough to let you use the spell to persuade me. Your father learned not to even try it a long time ago. I will not take Morgaine's son into my court."

"Then let me have the raising of him along with the others. Let me raise him with the same good sense as . . ."

"As my other bastards," Arthur finished for me. "Yes, Wren, I know who sired Mordred. Morgaine told me after my wedding to Guinevere, when I gave the other children to you. Only one of the children in your care could possibly be mine, you know which one. Morgaine wanted me to know that Mordred would never come under my control, even if I acknowledged him. Which I can't. No god, pagan or Christian, will countenance an incestuous Ardh Rhi. My client kings would denounce their loyalty to me in a moment."

"But you didn't know Morgaine was your sister—half sister— until after Uther had married her off to Lot."

"Your father's intervention was all that kept Uther from letting me marry her. Apparently The Merlin told him the truth of my birth and raising at that time. I was sent on a useless errand three days' hard ride from Venta Belgarum. Morgaine was given to Lot in a very private ceremony and shipped to the Orcades before I returned."

"Morgaine has been warped by her own bitterness. She was so bent on revenge against all of Britain that she lost control of the natural forces she called to her command. She used her son to prop open the doorway to the demon world. She will warp Mordred even further and ruin all of Britain in the process."

"The answer is still no. I have the older three boys. That will have to be enough to keep Lot and Morgaine in the Orcades licking their wounds."

When I had finished stitching Arthur's wound, I gave him a draught that would make him sleep through the worst of the pain that would attack him within moments of finishing the stitching and bandaging.

Then I went searching for The Merlin. I found Nimuë instead.

"Why aren't you in Camlann with the queen?" I asked without preamble.

"Why aren't you playing nursemaid to Arthur's bastards?" she replied. Her posture alarmed me. There was something strange about the way she hunched one shoulder and dropped the other, but at the same time thrust the lower shoulder forward. Did she have a spinal injury? Or had her perversions twisted her body as it twisted her soul.

"I search for my father." I did my best to ignore her strange posture and my need to heal her. Then I remembered who she was and her sexual preferences with her own father.

"I also search for The Merlin. You needn't bother. If he is able to call out, it is my name that will cross his lips, not yours," she sneered.

"Do you know what happened during the battle?" I ignored her gibes and headed toward the slight rise facing the crag of Dun Edin. I'd seen Da there when Morgaine backlashed his spell and he collapsed.

"I saw the witch on the palisades commanding all the forces of nature to do her bidding." Nimuë kept close upon my heels.

"What happened after the earthquake?" I asked her without pausing in my march toward the battlefield. Strangely the great rent in the earth no longer existed. Either the land had healed itself or the crevice with fire shooting upward was an illusion born of magic, along with the tidal wave and the spiraling winds.

"I . . . I don't know. The force of the quake knocked me to the ground. I passed out." Nimuë looked beyond the horizon rather than at me.

"If you were here, you should have been supporting my father's battle magic, not cowering in some other man's bed." Unkind. I didn't care if I hurt my stepdaughter.

"Arthur wouldn't let me on the battlefield." The old arrogant sneer was back on her face. "He doesn't believe my magic equal to The Merlin's. But it is. I have studied hard these last two years. My power has surpassed yours, and your father's!"

Doubtful. Power she certainly had. Control was a different matter. Power without control was a temper tantrum. Morgaine had just learned that lesson the hard way. Power with control could rule the world—if a magician desired such immense power after studying the true nature of magic with its balances and patterns. Druids studied an entire lifetime to maintain a grip on the powers they wielded. Morgaine had lost the delicate balance of dark and light, real and unreal, all for more power. She'd lost control of the demon that fed her power and nearly lost everything.

Nimuë would follow the same path. Unless Da's guidance contained her voracious need for more. More power, more sex, more beauty. Carradoc's daughter would never be satisfied.

"In my vision, The Merlin collapsed atop that rise." I pointed to the crest of the hill where the dragon rampant battle banner still flew. A large state banner also flew atop the fortress of Dun Edin. Why hadn't Arthur moved there once Lot and Morgaine were routed?

"I couldn't linger long enough after the earthquake to see what happened here," I continued. "I was needed elsewhere. What did Arthur, Lancelot, and Agravain do when Morgaine's control was severed?"

"I told you I don't know. I wasn't here. I wish to all the gods ever named that I had defied Arthur and stood by The Merlin's side." A tear touched Nimuë's eye and slid down her cheek. She loved Myrddin Emrys. Perhaps that love would keep her power controlled and sane. If my father lived long enough to teach her the essence and need for balance and patterns.

"I saw retreat after the earthquake," I mused. "But the men must have surged forward again as soon as the rain and wind subsided. Morgaine's troops were also routed. Someone followed them and took possession of Dun Edin."

"Perhaps they turned and pursued without topping the rise again," Nimuë suggested. For once we were joined on the same quest with the same motives, love for my father.

"If they took possession of the fortress, why hasn't Arthur moved his headquarters there?" I pointed to the Long Hall and support buildings visible above the palisade.

"Morgaine and Lot are still there. They have another day to gather their forces and retreat to the North."

"Arthur is far too generous."

"He is a fool. Morgaine has a hold over him. I would give my soul to know what."

I wasn't about to tell her.

But Mordred wasn't at Dun Edin. The baby was in the care of others, safe in the Orcades where the portal to the demon Netherworld stood. If Morgaine spoke of Mordred's true sire now, her bitter words could be dismissed as the ravings of a defeated woman. Possibly she didn't dare speak while Lot was strong and healthy and still able to beat her, or dismiss her as his wife. Morgaine needed the Orcades with its gateway to the Netherworld. She needed Lot, King of the Orcades. I doubted Lot's warband would follow *her* into battle. They'd follow Lot to the death and beyond if necessary.

"Are there guards that will prevent us from entering the fortress?" I strode purposefully in that direction, not caring what obstacles lay in the way.

"Morgaine's troops are still there. Arthur has treated her with honor, as befitting his sister." Nimuë hastened to keep up with me. Was that relief I read in her face? She had quoted Morgaine as the authority on everything at one time. She had also reviled the princess in public.

The hair on the back of my neck bristled in warning. Nimuë had always worn two faces. Which one was real?

The half-grown wolfhound pup whined as she galloped across the field to catch up with me. She circled me warily, neck fur standing high and teeth bared. I trusted the dog's awareness of danger.

"Arthur shows his sister too much honor considering what she tried to do. Morgaine has no honor, only a quest for more power," I replied, stepping away from Nimuë. I needed to keep her at a distance.

My path put several cairns between us. Soldiers had piled rocks into commemorative towers at special places on the battlefield. Here a beloved commander fell to the enemy. There a duel was fought to a standstill with a worthy opponent. I'd heard of the custom and wondered that men wished to remember anything about the horrible slaughter that took place here. But if they didn't honor the great moments, the nightmare hours would haunt them forever.

"Arthur is so caught up in his quest for honor and justice and law that he ignores reality. I told you he was a fool." Nimuë kept pace with me. But she shied away from coming too close to the dog.

"Maybe he is a fool, maybe not. What is the one thing Morgaine could hold that would coerce the Ardh Rhi to do her bidding?" I asked the dog.

"The life of someone he loves." Nimuë didn't quite sneer, but her thoughts on Arthur's motives were written quite plainly on her face.

"Queen Guinevere is safely in Camlann. Lord Ector and Lady Glynnis have retired to a villa near Deva. I have the children guarded well at Caer Noddfa. Lancelot, Cai, and Bedewyr are accounted for." I'd made certain the Ardh Rhi's closest friends had survived the battle. Many of the other companions had not fared so well. Carradoc had survived, unscathed and hale. I hadn't bothered to seek him out.

"There is only one other person Arthur values so well as to bow to Morgaine's demands," I continued, increasing my pace.

"The Merlin," Nimuë supplied the name.

"And Morgaine will not vacate Dun Edin while she holds Da. He must be a prisoner. He's of no use to her dead."

"How do *I* get him out?"

"*I* will get him out after I see the lay of the land and what chains she uses to hold him. She can't have much magical strength left after the battle. And I know that nothing mundane would keep The Merlin prisoner unless he is incredibly ill."

Chapter 53

MERLIN tried to open his eyes. White fire lanced across his vision and into his head. Perhaps he screamed. His head buzzed with so much sound he couldn't tell what he heard. He pressed his hands against his eyes. The pressure shifted the core of the pain to his temples and along his jaw.

Gradually he became accustomed to the constant presence of the pain and could think beyond surviving from moment to moment. His back ached, his knees twisted oddly, and he couldn't find his feet.

No light penetrated to his vision.

"Am I blind?" The sound of his voice echoed and brought new pain to his head.

"You might as well be, Myrddin Emrys," a harsh voice filled his being.

"Who?" He wished he hadn't spoken. The movement and the noise made him hurt more.

His empty stomach roiled, adding new distress to the ever present, all pervasive pain.

"Don't you know the voice of your doom?" The voice laughed again, wild cackles like ravens gone wild.

Ravens. Three ravens. Cair Tair Cigfran. Was he in the tunnel beneath Wren's home? If he could only find the crystal cave, the Lady might help him, might ease his pain.

"You don't reply, Myrddin. Surely you know who claims your life?"

"Only Dana claims my life and my soul. I have not violated the geas she laid upon me." He whispered this time and his head didn't hurt quite so badly. But his heart ached worse. *Oh, Wren, I would have liked to hold you close to my heart one more time. I would look on my grandchildren and wish them farewell.*

"Your mewling goddess no longer has the strength or will to protect you, Myrddin. I rule here. You will be a long time dying, as I have been a long time seeking you, the source of my pain."

Feminine undertones to the raspiness. Who?

Morgaine! He could think of no other who hated with as much intensity as she. He called up the vision of her as he had seen her last: flowing black-and-silver draperies echoing her black hair with the broad silver streak, an extension of the lightning-streaked black sky above her. She raised her staff and called down all four elements to wreak havoc on both armies. She cared nothing for the lives of her own soldiers, only for the death of the two men she saw as the cause of everything that had gone wrong in her life: Arthur Pendragon and The Merlin of Britain.

"You are the source of your own pain," he whispered. "You must heal yourself. My death will only add to your guilt."

"Guilt is for weaklings. Think about that while my demons feast on your flesh in this stinking, forgotten hole."

"You can never control demons. They feed on your soul more painfully than anything they can do to my flesh." New pain ripped across his gut. He doubled over, clutching his middle. A scream escaped his raw lips.

"Tell me that again in a few hours," Morgaine replied with another cackling laugh.

The pain eased a trifle. Merlin tried straightening his legs to lessen their stiffness. His cold feet encountered a wall. His legs stretched little more than halfway. He pushed, bracing his feet against the rough surface. His back rammed against the opposite wall. Rough rock poked his spine. Dampness soaked his shirt.

She'd stripped him of his robes as well as his freedom.

Chills coursed up and down his spine. This far North, even in spring, the nights could bring heavy frost. He'd not sleep comfortably even if he could stretch beyond this cramped crouch.

He reached out with both his hands. More rock scraped his knuckles. But he couldn't feel a ceiling above him. Shifting carefully to avoid causing any new pain, he brought his knees under him and shifted his buttocks. Cautiously he eased himself upward. Sitting upon his heels, back straight, his hair brushed a metal grate. Fresh night air caressed his face. He breathed deeply, then pushed at the grate with both hands. It did not budge. He heard the rattle of a lock. He braced his knees and levered himself upward again, testing for weakness.

He sent his mind into the lock, willing the tiny inner pieces to shift into an open pattern.

His talent remained locked firmly within his head.

The grate turned to fire, burning his hands to his elbows. He screamed again as he dropped back to the stone floor of his prison.

"My demons control the pit, Myrddin. Escape is impossible," Morgaine said.

Merlin tried turning the fire back on the sender. The pain in his hands stopped any power that might have lingered within him. His magic had withered and diminished of late. Now it seemed totally dead.

"Don't even bother trying magic on me. My demon allies have stripped you of the last vestige of power. They are very thorough."

He huddled into himself, trying to control his whimpers.

"This cannot be the end. I have foreseen a different death! But Andraste help me, I do not see a way out of this."

He closed his eyes, trying to think.

"Nimuë," he whispered. "If you care for me at all, you will devise an escape from this madwoman's clutches." He held her image close, imagining the way she would feel in his arms, the taste of her sweet mouth. "Beloved. Please know that I love you even though we never honored the Goddess together. My only regret is that you never knew how much I adore you."

I didn't have an invisibility spell at my command. After my astral journey and the long ride to Dun Edin, I didn't have much magic left.

Dun Edin commands an open view of approach from all directions. No one could enter the heavily fortified gates unauthorized without magic.

"I wonder if there are hidden postern gates?" I asked Nimuë as we surveyed the crag from its base. I had to keep her close enough to watch her. The dog sniffed at the trail of moisture and refuse where the latrine pit hung over the edge of the cliff. I hauled the dog away from her investigation and kept her close at my side.

"Would you allow a crack in the defenses like a postern?" Nimuë replied.

"No. But I might want a secret escape route if the place was hopelessly besieged." Like my tunnel into the crystal cave and access to the faery pool.

"Tunnels?" Nimuë asked.

"Solid rock." I shook my head doubtfully. No cliff face is perfectly smooth. I espied potential handholds and footholds, all within full view of the guards on the palisades. If I climbed that crag, I would have to do it under cover of darkness when I couldn't see the next safe place to rest a finger or a toe.

"Maybe Arthur knows of a way. He has spent weeks viewing the place from up there." I pointed to the array of colorful tents on the slopes of the tor. Arthur was there now. I could see him on a chair outside the largest pavilion. He should be asleep.

I turned and retreated toward the army camp, letting defeat drag my shoulders down and curve my spine. At least that was the posture I hoped the guards would view. I dug my hands into the dog's neck fur to keep myself from climbing the cliff there and then.

Like the labyrinth on Avalon's tor, I had seen a hidden pathway up. The finger and toeholds would be tricky. Mundane eyes wouldn't be able to find it. Only my recent experience with a labyrinth showed me how and where to look.

"We need help," I said, more to myself than to Nimuë.

"Carradoc?" she asked almost brightly.

"No. He's a strong warrior, but he's blunt and forthright. This calls for cunning and a young, limber body." Like mine. But I needed darkness and privacy. Between now and then I needed rest to replenish my body and my mind for the ordeal to come. Before I rested, I needed information that only High King Arthur Pendragon could give me.

"You found a way to climb the crag!" Nimuë announced much too loudly. "I will climb with you."

I looked hastily up to the palisades. The guards conferred with wild gestures and heads nodding toward us.

"You just told the entire world of our plans. Morgaine will be ready and waiting." I marched ahead of her, too angry to say another word.

"She might kill your father rather than let you rescue him, Lady Wren," Nimuë said. "Then I won't have to. You deprived me of my father, now I take your father from you."

"You conspired with Morgaine to do this!" My entire being, body and soul shook with outrage.

"What if I did? Will you go running to your lover, Arthur, for him to make all things better for you?" Nimuë stood tall and proud. A laughing sneer marred the beauty of her near perfect features and clear, milky skin. Her flame-colored hair glowed in the afternoon light.

The only flaw in her was the tilted posture, one shoulder lower and thrust forward. Her soul was as warped as her spine.

And I hated her with all of the passion I had kept carefully hidden while I maintained a balance of emotions and magical power. I wanted to fly at her with fingernails and teeth, to scar that beautiful face as her spirit was scarred.

"What are you talking about?" I had to force puzzlement on my face rather than the anger that seethed deep within me. I had to pretend that Arthur and I had never loved and conceived a child that Beltane day beside the faery pool.

"You know very well of what I speak." Nimuë remained calm. Her eyes clouded slightly, showing only a little concern that she might be wrong. "I'm certain Carradoc would dearly love to know that he did not sire your second child, your beloved daughter Deirdre. Neither of you will live out the day once he knows."

"I have never given Carradoc reason to believe he isn't the father of both my children. Unlike my husband, I honor my marriage vows." A broken promise upsets the balance of life as much as does a lie. I'd broken the promise of fidelity and must continue to lie to protect myself and my daughter. I'd done enough lying to last a lifetime.

"You never honored anything but your own self-importance," Nimuë continued to rant. "You robbed me of my father's love when you forced him into this marriage. But you never loved him. You deprived me of his love just because you could. Well, now I turn the tables on you, Wren. You'll never get your father out of Morgaine's hands, and you can't go to Arthur for help because I will tell the world of your affair with him. My father will kill you for it, and be justified. A woman's adultery is punishable by death." She trounced off, head high, triumph tingeing her aura yellow.

"No one will believe you, Nimuë," I returned. But she was right. I couldn't go to Arthur, and I had no new plans that would save my father.

Except . . . Every man and fortress has a vulnerability. Morgaine had found one in my caer. Now I must find one in hers.

Darkness fell slowly over Dun Edin. Twilight lingered seemingly forever. I rested alone in Carradoc's tent for as long as I could. Then I crept away before my husband returned for the night. I doubted he'd sleep there alone. If Nimuë didn't accompany him, then one of the camp followers would. The few words I exchanged with him were cordial but terse. He was preoccupied with keeping his warband in order. I was preoccupied with my plans and the need to rest.

When the shadows lengthened to three times my height, I slid over to the kitchen tent and stole bread, cheese, and dried meat. No one saw me. No one would know I took journey provisions. I had picketed my horse with the other high-strung war stallions. A homely but docile pack pony awaited me well away from camp. I'd left the wolfhound pup tied up outside Carradoc's tent. As long as she remained there, no one would look for me elsewhere.

I'd miss her company on the long trek home. But I needed privacy for this adventure. The presence of a wolfhound, even a half-grown one, is difficult to disguise.

Drifting from shadow to shadow, clad in a boy's leggings and shirt I had stolen, I made my way across the flat plain toward the crag of Dun Edin. To the east of the fortress lay the tor, Arthur's Seat. From the heights of the tor Curyll had looked down on every activity within the fortress. From those heights, I had seen another entrance into Morgaine's stronghold. The dog had showed it to me, too. An entrance I didn't think even Morgaine knew about.

Well, she knew about it. But fastidious Morgaine who couldn't stand ordinary dirt on her person, who bathed twice a day, and washed her hands frequently, would never suspect the latrine chute as being an entryway to her fortress. I didn't like the idea of climbing up through the foul and slick matter that clung to the cliff face. Better the honest body soil of humans than the evil visited upon humans by Morgaine's demons.

If the caer of Dun Edin had been atop the tor where a fire glittered outside of Arthur's pavilion, the builders could have dug normal pits in the dirt to contain their waste. The crag was solid rock. No pits. So the latrines were built into the wooden palisade hanging over the open space above the cliff.

"What do you think you are doing, Wren?" Curyll hissed in my ear as I reached for the first handhold on the crag. He didn't stutter or hesitate.

The dog pranced at his heels and jumped at me, eager to participate in any adventure.

"I am doing what you should have done three days ago," I replied.

"You cannot get your father out of there. I sent Stinger and Ceffyl on this same errand two nights ago. They failed. They couldn't get through the opening and had to retreat. They still stink. And curse me for a fool."

"I hope they came back down before Morgaine discovered them."

"I believe so. You still can't go. I can't risk you."

"The opening may have been too small for hardened warriors with overdeveloped shoulders from flinging swords and axes and such around all their lives. But I am Wren, the small songbird who creeps into tiny nest holes—not a large hawk, or a nearsighted boar, or a stinger bee. Even Ceffyl is too large for this. But I'll get through. And get my father out."

"I forbid it, Wren. You are too valuable. You will become The Merlin when your father dies. I can't risk losing you."

"I'll never be The Merlin. Those days are gone. Da is the last. Avalon is deserted except for one old Christian hermit." I couldn't help the sadness that crept through me and into my voice. The old ways were fading but not dead. I would find a way to compromise and keep them alive in more subtle ways, but only after I rescued my father. The last of his kind.

"Give me a boost, Curyll. I can't quite reach the first handhold."

"Didn't you hear me, Wren? I forbid this."

"Then why are you here, if not to give me an assist?" I held up my left foot for him to shove me farther up the cliff than I could reach on my own. I pointedly ignored the first small ledge level with my knee where I had planned to put my foot. The traitorous dog placed her forepaws there and licked my hands.

"You never listen to anyone. I'd hoped you'd listen to me, your oldest friend, your comrade in childhood mischief, your . . ." He cupped his hands about level with my knee.

I placed my foot there and welcomed the boost to a strong hand-hold. The dog tried to follow, but Curyll pushed her away.

"I'll wait here for you, Wren."

"This may take a while. Take a nap. You need the sleep. And take the dog with you. I can't have her whining and howling to follow me." I had no intention of coming back this way. If Da were ill enough to remain confined by Morgaine, he'd need more help than the mundane medics of the army could give him. Help that Arthur and his Christian priests wouldn't know how to give.

Back home I had a maiden from the village who showed signs of a magic talent, and Hannah, a crone who worked magic with her weaving, and myself a full matron. I'd work the great healing magic on my Da no matter the cost to my strength. I'd restore him. We'd be a family again.

I held those thoughts in my heart as I clambered upward, using starlight and my instincts to find the way.

I have smelled better places upon this Earth. Many times during the noisome assent, I had to blank my mind to the gooey matter beneath my fingers. In the interests of sanitation, someone had flushed the mess recently with a bucket of cold water. It dissipated the odor, a little, but chilled the rocks I clung to. My fingers felt like ice. My bare toes, not much warmer.

I'd never be able to wear these clothes again. Thank Dana, I'd put my good woolen gown along with boots and stockings in the saddle-bags on the pack pony.

When I reached the top of the chute, a wooden seat with a hinged lid covered the slimy narrow hole. After I banged my head on the contraption, it opened with a gentle push. The fortress would have been safer if they had padlocked the lid and only given the key to loyal soldiers. Impractical at best.

Curyll had been right. The hole was narrow. Barely large enough to serve its purpose. A full-grown man couldn't ease his way through it. I barely fit my head and shoulders above the rim. Then I had to rock and inch my hips through. Childbearing had broadened them more than I liked to admit.

I grimaced as the privacy door squeaked when I opened it. No one came to investigate, so I crept out, keeping to the shadows at the base of the palisade. Torches atop the spiked, wooden wall cast fitful light toward the center of the fortress and down the outside. I avoided the pools of light that could betray me. Even so I reeked of the latrine and could alert any guard who didn't have a head cold.

Drunken snores wafted out of the adjacent barracks on fumes thick with sour ale and unwashed bodies. They smelled almost as badly as I did. Perhaps they wouldn't notice my presence from smell alone. Fortunately for me, all the men seemed too deeply asleep to require the use of the latrine.

I walked the entire circumference of the fortress, cataloging the position of each building in my mind. Kitchen, pantry, storehouse, more privies, Long Hall, guest quarters, the well next to the kitchen. No stable. Horses required room to move and lots of fodder to eat. They were secured outside the main gate, somewhere along the sloping processional way that led down the crag in a gentle incline.

Where had Morgaine put her prisoner? Guards walked the ledge near the top of the palisade and stood quietly by the main gate, but none of the interior doors were guarded or held a heavy lock.

I circled the fortress again, lingering and listening frequently. The usual night sounds of a fortress met my ears at every turn. I couldn't smell anything but myself. Without all of my senses, I became nervous, eager to finish my chore and be gone.

Then I heard it; the soft moan of a man in severe distress. A fever dream. I followed the rising tide of screams from a man fighting off nightmare demons. In Morgaine's domain, they could be real demons. The guards didn't rush to assist or wake the dreamer. If anything, the men atop the walls seemed to turn their backs on the noise and drift as far away from it, and me, as they could.

The sounds led me to an irregular outcropping of rock, sticking up into the northern perimeter wall. I felt along every inch of the sharp stone for an entry. No door.

The moans faded, drifted off into lighter snores.

Where are you! I screamed in my mind before he quieted and I lost my only clue.

Quiet reigned once more. I wanted to beat the rocks with my fists.

Useless. Carefully I made my way around the rock pile again. This time I stumbled upon a grate set into the stony ground of the fortress. The faint light from torches and stars showed me a deep, dark hole dug out of solid rock. The grate was the only entrance or exit. A complex lock and rusty hinges held it in place.

Simple latches I could lift with my hand to unbolt a door. Locks defied my magic at every turn.

I'd never get him out without help and without alerting the entire compound.

Chapter 54

I couldn't leave him there. I wouldn't leave a dog in there, let alone my father.

Da had a way with locks. They gave up their secrets and opened for him at the touch of his thoughts. I'd never had his talent for manipulating stubborn mechanical devices.

Why hadn't he opened this one?

I didn't like the answer that came to me.

"I'm coming, Da, I'll get you out," I whispered as I searched the immediate area for inspiration.

A ring of bulky keys hung on the wooden palisade wall. Convenient for the guards who fed the prisoner. Convenient for me, too. But careless of them. Morgaine must feel very confident to allow such a breach of security.

Using both hands to keep the keys from jangling, I lifted the ring off its hook. Three keys. They all looked alike.

I tried them all. Of course, only the last one turned in the heavy lock; turned with a scrape and screech I was sure would awaken everyone in the fortress—if my smell hadn't done so already.

No one came to look for the source of the noise. Either they were all too drunk to awaken, or the guards turned a blind eye and ear to all that happened around this awful pit.

The grate resisted my tug. The hinges looked rusted in place. I ripped off my tunic and used it to muffle the hinges. I shivered in the cool night air in only a shirt. No time to give in to my own discomforts. Da must be half frozen.

The hinges resisted three heavy tugs. I tried again. Sweat broke out on my face and neck. My back and shoulders strained beyond endurance. Still I pulled. When the hinges finally released their hold on the grate, I felt muscles tear in my shoulder. I ignored the sharp ache that spread down my back and into my chest.

"Da?" I whispered into the pit. The sound of my voice echoed loud within the stone cavern. I hoped it spread no farther.

A muffled grunt was the only reply.

"How deep are you?" Without a light, I had no way to tell.

A groan and a shuffling of a body against stone.

Desperate for any clue I braced myself against the grate with one hand and reached down with the other. Just at the point I thought to lose my balance and tumble into the pit with Da, my fingers brushed cloth.

Andraste punish you, Morgaine. You didn't even give him enough room to sit up or stand.

A little more searching with my fingertips discovered there might be enough room for me to drop into the pit without landing on Da. I took a deep breath for courage and braced myself on the edge of the hole with both hands. Straining every ounce of strength in my arms and shoulders, despite the ripped muscles, I slowly lowered my feet into the darkness. Every fiber in my back screamed for release. I had to let go and risk the last little drop into nothingness.

My knees buckled slightly as my feet impacted solid stone. My head and shoulders remained above the opening. The drop was shorter than I thought. The hole was even smaller than I feared. Da could neither sit up fully or stretch out his long legs.

Starlight and torches didn't penetrate this shadowed hole. I doubted much sunlight did either. Da had probably been down here the three days and nights since the battle.

Quickly I sought out his form with my hands. His beard was matted, crusted scabs across his cheek. His arms hung limply in my grasp. But I detected no broken bones.

"Da? Wake up, Da." I shook him slightly. He moaned and shied away from my touch.

"It's only me, Da. I'm Wren. Not Morgaine." I projected my image into his mind.

"Wren . . ." he mumbled. "My Wren."

"Yes, Da, it's me. I have to get you out of here. Have you the strength to stand?"

"Wren . . . so like your mother. If only I could see you one more time before I die . . ."

"You aren't going to die yet. I won't let you, Da. Now stand up so I can haul you out of this hellhole. Morgaine's demons must love this place."

I shook him hard. His head lolled about. I slapped his face. His eyes opened and he looked at me. Recognition almost dawned in his consciousness. Then he shut me out of his mind, muttering about delusions and dreams.

"Well, if you won't help me help you, I guess I'll have to do it myself." As I had done everything in this life. Alone. Without help.

The nightmare struggle to get Da out of that hole lasted, seemingly, for hours. The longer it went on, the more noise we made. And the farther away from the prison the guards drifted.

I realized then that Lot's men didn't want any part of Morgaine's dark magic. But they were loyal to their king. They solved their moral dilemma by turning a blind eye to whatever happened to The Merlin. I caught a drift of their thoughts and emotions. They prayed to a number of gods, even the Christian one, that this was indeed a rescue of Morgaine's prisoner. I didn't want to know what tortures Morgaine had inflicted upon Da to turn these hardened warriors against her.

No wonder Morgaine kept the secret of Mordred's birth. She'd never rule the hardy, self-reliant men of the Orcades by herself. She needed Lot to control the men. To keep him, she had to maintain the lie that he had sired her youngest son.

At last Da lay sprawled against the ground and the palisade wall, breathing clean night air. The cool wind revived him a little. Before he could fully awaken and speak aloud, something the guards could no longer ignore, I pulled myself out of the hole. I had to rest a few moments before moving farther. Then I hauled Da up until he almost stood. He couldn't support himself or direct his feet. My shoulder fit neatly under his arm without either of us bending.

We stumbled together halfway around the perimeter of the wall. I wasn't nearly as careful as I had been earlier. The guards circled the ledge above me on the wall, still avoiding wherever I paused to catch my breath and shift my grasp of Da. The smell of my body probably told them where to avoid.

But the two guards at the main gate still stood vigil, alert and uncompromising. They might turn a blind eye to me hauling Da out of his prison cell. They couldn't open the gate for us and remain loyal to Lot.

About twenty paces from the gate, I let Da slide to the ground. I propped him into a sitting position against the wall. My next chore required both hands and all of my concentration.

I didn't have Da's gift for moving tiny lock mechanisms with my mind. But I had my own talent. Tanio and I were kin.

I fished dry moss out of my belt sach. The moss ignited easily into tiny curls of glowing embers. But Tanio needed better fuel than this little tuft of greenery. I concentrated all of my thoughts on that tiny essence of Tanio.

Food, it demanded.

There, I directed it. *The roof of the Long Hall. Thick thatch awaits you.*

Tanio followed the direction of my thoughts. I spun out the threads of my mind, giving Tanio a pathway. It leaped out of the bit of moss, clinging to my thoughts as a spider clings to its web. Two heartbeats later, a tiny glow ignited in the center of the thatched roof.

I breathed on the embers in the moss. Their brothers in the roof sprang higher, bursting into full flame.

The guards looked at the burning roof uneasily. Then they glanced back at the gate and each other questioningly. No one sounded the alarm. The fire burned brighter, spread toward the back of the hall where King Lot and his sorceress queen slept.

"Fire!" both gate guards screamed and ran toward the well.

"Fire!" the guards on the palisade echoed. They ran toward the steps nearest the well.

They left the gate deserted. Quickly, I unbarred the narrow side gate, barely wide enough to admit one full-grown man. The opening was all I needed.

Crowds of villagers jostled us along the processional way as they rushed to aid the garrison within the fortress. Da gasped and wheezed with the effort of staying upright and semi-conscious.

"Get him to the well, bathe his burns," a man clad only in his shirt yelled at me as he hastened by. "Where'd the fire start—in the latrine?" He covered his nose and mouth and coughed.

"Send the healer to the fortress after she treats the man's burns. We're going to need her," called another man.

I nodded, pretending that Da was only the first of many victims of smoke and flame to come. We staggered down the hill unhindered as the townsfolk organized themselves to fight the fire. More than once I heard speculation that Arthur had sent flaming arrows into Dun Edin to insure that Lot and his army vacated it by dawn as agreed.

"Up onto the pony, Da," I ordered as soon as we reached the dozing beast. "We're going home."

"I have no home. I am The Merlin, destined to wander forever homeless," he recited. I'd heard that often enough over the years of our treks across Britain and back again.

"I have a home, Da. I'm taking you there. We'll both be safe there. Morgaine can't touch us there. The faeries and the Lady in the lake will heal you."

But Nimuë could find us if she really wanted to. Morgaine's magic might be dark and evil, but she didn't hide her affinity with demons. Nimuë's magic, disguised as love, was the more dangerous. She'd find Da and destroy him, no matter where I hid him or what magical protections I wrapped around him.

I no longer cared if Nimuë spread tales of Arthur and me sleeping together. If she turned Carradoc against me, he'd never reclaim Caer Noddfa from me. *My* people, villagers, retainers, and warriors wouldn't let him.

I hoped.

If life behaved according to plan, I think I might roll over and die laughing. Just when I thought I had all the pattern pieces arranged perfectly to make my life comfortable and balanced, my pattern smashed into someone else's and flew into disarray. So why did I expect the journey from Dun Edin back across half of Britain with Da to be an easy walk?

I intended to retrace my earlier route, along the North Sea to Hadrian's Wall and then cross-country alongside the abandoned Roman barrier.

Arthur's army spread out around three sides of Dun Edin. The fire within the fortress alerted them. I nearly ran into Arthur himself as he pelted down the hillside from his pavilion to the village that lined the sloping road up to the caer.

I wouldn't linger here or seek help. Da and I both needed the sanctuary of Caer Noddfa to rest and heal. The mundane chirurgeons with the army couldn't help either of us. They knew how to patch up wounds and amputate limbs, but little of true healing. Da might die before they decided to let him return home with me.

By the time I circumvented the host of warriors, Da was so weak he couldn't stay mounted on the pony. The third time he fell off, I slung him across the horse's back. Not the gentlest of rides, but the only way I could keep him in place.

Dawn found us only a few miles from Dun Edin. A stiff north breeze warned of the storm to come. The sky darkened and the air grew heavy. A deafening roar of thunder preceded the pelting rain by about three heartbeats. A new flash of lightning lit the sky on the tail end of the rumbling thunderclap that seemed to go on forever. One roar of thunder merged into the next without pause.

In the momentary brightness, I scanned the deserted beach for signs of shelter. Nothing. Not even a fisherman's lean-to thrown over a boat.

I made a nest for us on the lee side of a dune. Da, the pony, and I huddled together for warmth. The dog would have been welcome now, but not earlier. I didn't truly regret leaving her with Curyll.

Not even I could keep a fire burning in this downpour. At least the rain washed some of the stink from me.

Like most spring storms, this one passed after only an hour or so. The sun burst through the clouds in a dazzling display of bright rainbows. The gray sea, dark dunes, and stunted grasses were all bathed in glorious color. I stared at the arched prisms, mouth open with wonder. The beauty of the bright colors pierced my heart with joy. I needed the moment to go on forever, to blot out my physical discomfort and the vague discontent that had plagued me since . . . since that moment by the forest pool when the faeries and I had helped Curyll learn to speak without stuttering.

I think I knew even then that Curyll and I would drift apart. Our lives took different paths from that day forward. We occupied ourselves with different destinies. Neither of us had completed our tasks.

A song of tribute to the Goddess for the gift of rainbows bubbled in my throat. I couldn't find adequate words to describe my emotions or the beauty of the moment. Only the bright tune burst forth.

Like all moments of happiness, the rainbow faded, leaving me staring into the moist air that blended with the retreating gray clouds on the horizon. My sight flew with the clouds, farther and farther east, beyond the limits of normal vision.

Vaguely, I knew that Dana, through the gift of the rainbow, drew me to something I needed to see. Most of me was still captured within the beauty.

The sight of a dozen dragon boats aggressively greeting the leading edge of the storm that had just passed over me shocked me back to reality. Each boat carried at least fifty men. Dana had shown me the next Saxon invasion. They sought landing places here in the North rather than Porchester on the South coast that Arthur had taken back from the Saxons last year.

"How far away are they?" I asked the wind and sea.

Enough time, they replied.

Enough time to build a fire and feed my ailing father and myself. Then I had to hasten back to Dun Edin and warn Arthur.

"Will you be all right if I leave you here, Da? I have to go back to Dun Edin. I'll leave you food and fresh water and enough driftwood to keep the fire going."

"What did you see in the rainbow, Wren?" he asked weakly. He was awake and sitting up, but he wouldn't last long.

"I had a vision of the next invasion." I looked at the fire, seeing again the dragon boats tossing in the waves.

"Then I must go with you."

"You aren't strong enough. You'll fall off the pony."

"I'll find the strength. Arthur needs me. Though I don't know how much good I'll be at the actual battle. Nimuë will be worried about me, too."

Nimuë again.

"You probably won't believe me if I tell you the truth about my stepdaughter and why she pretends to love you."

"If you mean that Carradoc used her and abused her frequently since her Beltane initiation, she told me everything."

But probably not about her obsession with her father.

"Believe me, Wren, if I had known what kind of man Carradoc truly is, I would never have allowed your marriage to him. You should have divorced him." Remorse drew the lines around his eyes deeper. His gaunt cheeks looked deeper and more heavily shadowed than usual.

"Yesterday, Nimuë accused me of depriving her of her father's love. In turn, she intended to deprive me of you. She'll kill you eventually."

"You misunderstood her, Wren. Her bitterness against Carradoc is deep. She looks to me for protection from him."

I was right. He wouldn't allow himself to believe ill of his young paramour. More than thirty years separated their ages.

The same could be said for my husband and me.

"We have to start moving. The storm will delay those boats, but not for long." I doused the fire and started packing my few supplies. "I think I should . . . um . . . I'll need help getting up, Wren."

"You need help sitting up. But I suppose even The Merlin must answer the call of his body. I'm a healer and a priestess, I've done this before."

He draped a too limp arm around my shoulders and we heaved him upward together. A few stumbling steps took him to a clump of low shrubs.

I turned my back discreetly until the sounds of water hitting the greenery ceased. His movements must have been slow and clumsy. As I turned back to help him mount the pony, I caught a glimpse of his penis. A part of him that I am certain no one had seen since his Beltane festival with my mother.

The gods had marked him for disobeying their geas. A winding tattoo encircled the full length of him. The agony of the process must have lingered for months, possibly years. Every erection would remind him painfully that he must not violate the decree of the gods again. No matter what Nimuë suggested, she would never be Da's lover. No woman would.

How would Nimuë use this knowledge when she found out? I was certain she would discover it eventually. She had a knack for discovering secrets.

Chapter 55

I walked into Dun Edin and found Arthur's troops and companions lining the walls. Lot's men formed an inner ring, their weapons piled symbolically in the center of the compound. Arthur faced Morgaine in the doorway of the ruined Hall. His face was pale and thunderous. He clenched his fists at his sides. I could tell by the set of his shoulders he worked very hard not to raise his dominant left hand and strike his half sister. His closest companions and Lot stood behind them, slightly removed, staring at their boots.

The wolfhound pup strained at a leash clenched in Arthur's other hand. She barked at everything, including my entrance. No one paid her any attention.

Nimuë wept uncontrollably within the shelter of her father's arm. They stood to Morgaine's left, not quite a part of the inner circle but closer to the confrontation than anyone else. I wondered if she only made noise or if she actually produced tears.

"What have you done with The Merlin and his daughter? Where are they?" Arthur shouted. He reached to grab Morgaine by the throat, thought better of the gesture at the last moment, and made a fist instead. He shook it in her face. Anger blotched red on his pale face.

The dog danced and pulled toward me.

"You will never find The Merlin, brother dearest, even if he lies at your feet." Morgaine remained cool and pale; her cloud of dark hair framed her beautiful face, adding a touch of fragility to her profile. A sculpted profile that was too perfect, too controlled, too beautiful to be real.

The dog broke free of Arthur's restraint and leaped for me, trailing the leash. She nearly knocked me over, but I welcomed her unconditional love with open arms. I grabbed her face and ruffled her ears affectionately as I asked her politely to sit and be quiet.

No one turned to see what fascinated the dog. Arthur and Morgaine presented a much more interesting display.

"You don't have to look in the hellhole prison that Morgaine dug out of solid rock beneath the far palisade," I called in reply.

Arthur whirled to face me. Surprise and relief crossed his face. Anger remained in his eyes. "Where have you been?" he asked as he took in the pack pony and our drenched cloaks. And the stink of my clothes.

"Irrelevant." I adopted my father's superior tone. "A fleet of a dozen dragon boats is headed this way." I fondled the dog's ears, letting her lick some of the stink from my hands and face.

"What?" Arthur's emotions exploded in that one word. "I need details!"

I turned to exit the caer the way I had come, leading the pony with my father riding the beast. The dog kept close to my side. I had delivered my message. Now I needed to get my father home. At the faery pool, with the women I had gathered in my sanctuary I could find enough magic to heal him.

"Myrddin!" Nimuë ceased her weeping and flung herself at my father. Her eyes were slightly red-rimmed from being rubbed, but dry.

Carradoc frowned and glared at me. I shrugged in dismissal. Morgaine's malevolent gaze concerned me more. I could see only one question in her eyes: "How?"

Maybe enough of the stink had washed away from me in the storm so she couldn't detect my route into the caer by smell. I smiled slightly, keeping my eyes away from the lines of guards who were supposed to be loyal to her husband and, by inference, to her. I couldn't have done it without their passive cooperation.

"What? Where? When?" Arthur strode toward me in long purposeful steps, his prisoners forgotten.

"Soon, on this coast. I think they will land close to the long sandbar about five miles south of here," I replied.

"How do you know this, Wren?"

"She had a vision from the Goddess," Da replied from behind me. Nimuë still clung to him, but he seemed more alert than he had on the journey back to Dun Edin.

"I can't trust visions and maybes. I need facts!" Arthur roared. "Cai, take a dozen men on fast horses and scout the sandbar. Send messengers back at first sighting, I don't want to alert the raiders with a signal fire. Bedewyr, take your men and scout south of the bar. Lancelot, you and your men scout north." Arthur continued to bark orders.

"What about them?" I pointed to Morgaine.

"My troops are yours to command, Highness." Lot bent one knee in homage to his Ardh Rhi.

"Arm them and deploy them on the road south. You take orders from Cai. Serve me well, Lot, and I may allow you to keep the Orcades. One hint of betrayal and you won't live long enough to see me elevate Agravain to the kingship."

Lot kept his head bowed in submission. Morgaine bristled with indignation. New plots seemed to form behind her eyes. I doubted Agravain would live very long if he did seek election to the crown of the Orcades.

Arthur ignored his half sister. He turned to face his troops. "I want everyone ready to ride before word comes back of the Saxon landing."

"And Morgaine?" I reminded Arthur in a whisper. "Will you leave her unguarded at your back?"

"Carradoc! You have the honor of escorting my sister to her home in the Orcades. I trust you not to be tempted by her beauty or her magic."

I sighed my relief. Carradoc wouldn't be home anytime soon. And he wouldn't be tempted by anyone but his daughter.

"Curyll?" I stopped the Ardh Rhi before he could be further distracted. "Da is ill. I need to take him home to nurse him. May we go now, unhindered?"

Arthur looked from me to Da and back again.

"Of course, Wren. Bring him back to health quickly. I need him. Britain needs him." He clasped my shoulder affectionately.

I let the warmth of his touch fill me, aching to hold him closer. Cherishing what little of him I could have.

I love you.

He made no sign that he heard my thoughts.

"The Merlin is too ill to travel," Nimuë proclaimed loudly. Da had dismounted and clung to her for support. She caressed his filthy hair and beard. "Highness, may I have the privilege of nursing him back to health here. Lady Wren is needed back at the nursery."

Carradoc crowded my back. His anger radiated out in waves of heat. I needed to leave before he sought me as a target for Nimuë's seeming preference for my father. Every step I took away from him, he followed. The dog snarled and bristled her neck fur. I couldn't step farther away from him without being obvious in my avoidance of my lawful husband. He'd find a way to punish me, even if I divorced him on the spot.

"Myrddin Emrys." Arthur walked over to my father, clasping his arm in true affection and concern. "Can you travel, or do you wish to rest here with Nimuë at your side? Wren really is needed back home."

"My days as The Merlin are numbered," Da said. His tired voice rose barely above a whisper. He fingered his torc in the familiar gesture that helped him think. "There is nothing that Wren can do for me that time and Nimuë cannot also cure. I prefer to stay with her." Da had eyes only for Nimuë; eyes that glowed with love.

"But, Da . . ." I wanted to tell him that I thought I knew how to work the great healing magic. I wanted to tell him of Nimuë's betrayal.

Nimuë's eyes and Carradoc's presence stopped my words. They'd find a way to twist my words to their advantage. They'd find a way to steal my secret knowledge. I knew it.

"So be it," Arthur said. "Wren, take a few hours to bathe and rest. Then you must return to the children." *Our daughter.* This time his thoughts broke through to me loud and clear. *Love our daughter, as I am not allowed to. Protect her when I can't.*

Carradoc followed me to my father's large, two-room tent. What happened to the little hut he could dismantle in minutes? He always preferred the circular shelter half-submerged and lashed together in such a way he could roll the stick walls and twig roof into tight bundles and carry them on his back.

The luxury and orderliness of the campaign tent reeked of Nimuë's perfume and presence.

Da and Nimuë followed us out of Dun Edin at a more leisurely pace. I was alone with my husband for the first time in nearly two years.

The servants had not yet arrived with hot water and clean clothes.

"You embarrassed me!" Carradoc shouted as soon as the outer tent flap dropped behind him.

The wolfhound pup growled and strained at her leash outside the tent.

"I saved the king's most trusted councillor. That should bring honor to our house, not shame."

"You rode across half of Britain by yourself, waded through a sewer, and disappeared." He raised his fist.

I stared at his clenched fingers above my head.

"You only seek an excuse to hit someone because Nimuë seduces my father rather than you. You no longer control her life," I said calmly.

Even watching for the blow, bracing for it, I couldn't duck fast enough. His fist caught me above my left ear.

Bells rang inside my head. Stars burst before my eyes. The world swam around me. I had no balance, no sense of anything but the pain exploding in my head.

Sense returned to me as I hit the ground at his feet. The tent wobbled as the wolfhound barked and jumped, trying to break free to protect me. I heard footsteps approaching, perhaps come to investigate the dog's distress.

"You promised never to hurt me!" I levered myself up on one elbow. Gingerly I fingered the sore spot on my temple. The old scar where Da had cut out my memory of druidsbane bled. I'd have a new scar to remind me how men sought to control my life.

"You aren't hurt," Carradoc sneered. " 'Tis my right to teach you proper behavior." He lifted his foot to kick me.

I rolled away.

"You broke your promise. A promise sealed in a circle." All of my anger at him, my pain, and my outrage at his cruelty and his incest boiled up from my stomach.

"Promises are for cowards. No man will question my honor with accusations of cowardice!"

"I divorce you, Carradoc."

He reared back in surprise.

I had said the words calmly. When I had said them three times in his presence our marriage would end.

"You won't end this marriage while I live." Carradoc raised his fist again.

" 'Tis her right," Arthur said as he wrenched Carradoc's wrist behind him and pressed upward. His mouth turned white with the force of his grip. "I will uphold her right by law, Carradoc. And I will break your arm before I let you hit any woman again."

The two men stared at each other for a long moment.

"You have your orders, Carradoc. Leave now with my sister. Guard her well if you wish to return to court."

"This is not finished, Wren. You won't always have your lover or your father to rush to your defense." Carradoc left the tent rapidly. Anger turned his aura black, shot with silver lightning. As black as the demon in the portal to the Netherworld.

He was vulnerable to Morgaine and her demons! I couldn't let him go with her. I couldn't let him stay.

Curyll paced Da's tent while I bathed behind a small privacy screen. He issued orders for meeting the Saxons in a distracted manner. He paid careful attention to orders for my horse and pack, the feeding of my dog, and selecting two men to escort me and remain at Caer Noddfa to protect the children. His anxiety for the safety and well-being of the children consumed him more than the battle that loomed with the Saxons.

Morgaine had struck at him through the children from a distance before. Thwarted, but not defeated, she could easily lash out again. I knew I had to hurry home to protect the children.

But I lingered with Da as long as Arthur allowed. I didn't need a vision from the Goddess to know that this was the last time I would see my father. He had chosen to stay with Nimuë. Nothing I could do would change his mind or his fate.

The music in my life died as I bid him farewell. Someday I would sing songs to his honor. Not yet. My love for him and my grief were too deep to express in aught but tears.

Arthur's anxiety infected me as well. I didn't know which direction danger would strike from, only that he feared it. My journey home was slower and less desperate than my dangerous ride to Dun Edin. The half-trained warhorse carried me well, my escort eased the finding of shelter with coin and the Ardh Rhi's writ.

I rode through the gates of Caer Noddfa at sunset of the third day of travel. Diones and Hannah greeted me and my escort with wary glances and bowed heads.

"The children?" I asked with frantic glances around the courtyard. Three of my charges played with Yvain by the well under the watchful eyes of Newynog and the old raven. My dog didn't jump to greet me or her pup, a sure sign that the children were in graver danger than I.

Hannah looked at me with wide, frightened eyes, then her gaze drifted to the walls and back to the two weary men who had accompanied me.

Extra guards ringed the fortress. I did not know two faces out of five. They wore standard metal-studded leather armor without distinguishing markings. I knew every man, woman, and child who called Caer Noddfa home. I did not know these two. Three more by the stable were equally unfamiliar to me. "Do you know any of the men on guard?" I whispered to my escort.

They shook their heads.

"Who?" I asked Diones in an undertone not meant to be heard beyond him.

"In the Long Hall," he said so quietly I had to strain to hear him.

I dropped my reins, signaling in the same gesture for my escort to accompany me. They owed their lives and their loyalty to Arthur. They bore his royal writ to protect me and the children.

A messenger wearing the royal insignia of the dragon rampant on his tunic feasted alone in my hall. Somehow he and his men had instilled fear in my people.

"Ah, Lady Wren," the man said when he spied me at the end of the hall. He belched and laid down the haunch of venison he chewed. "I bid you good news. Your duties to the royal children are finished. I am charged to take them back to Camlann."

"Oh?" I raised one eyebrow. The gesture came easily to me now, almost as if Da had bequeathed it to me. "Show me the edict from His Highness Arthur Pendragon." I held out my hand for a scroll, knowing it would not bear Arthur's signature.

"The . . . ah . . . Ardh Brenhines ordered me to give you this." He held out a rolled parchment. The royal seal of the Pendragon decorated the bottom along with a second seal showing a Christian cross. The orders were written in Latin; signed by Archbishop Dyfrig and Queen Guinevere.

This was the danger Arthur feared.

"What will the Lord Bishop and Ardh Brenhines do with Arthur's children? Set them adrift in a rudderless boat?"

The messenger flushed a deep red before stammering some incomprehensible phrases.

"I have just left His Highness the Ardh Rhi. He ordered me to keep his children here, safe as only the daughter of The Merlin can keep them safe." I stared the man directly in the eye as I threw the parchment into the fire.

"Lady Wren," Father Thomas protested. He rushed from the doorway to fish the decree from the flames. "This is signed by my Archbishop Dyfrig and the Ardh Brenhines. It bears the royal seal, kept by the archbishop and brenhines during the Ardh Rhi's absence. There can be no question that these orders must be obeyed." The priest who had become my friend had the grace to appear embarrassed.

"I do not recognize the authority of the archbishop," I replied.

"But I must." Father Thomas bowed his head.

"I command the resources of the fortress. I take my orders only from the Goddess and the Ardh Rhi. I have a more recent writ from Arthur, signed in my presence." I held up the smaller scroll my escort handed me. I snapped it open to reveal Arthur's personal seal.

"That's a forgery!" The messenger half stood, hand on the hilt of his dagger.

My escort drew their long battle swords from the sheaths on their backs. They moved in unison, pointing their weapons at the messenger's throat.

He gulped and sheathed his dagger. My guards did not drop theirs.

"You are no longer welcome here, messenger. Be gone now."

"My horse is not rested." He sat down again at the center of the table, in the lord's place of honor.

"Then walk." I strode to him and yanked the chair from beneath his ample buttocks. "And take your men with you. Ardh Rhi Arthur Pendragon must fetch the children himself if he wishes to make other provisions for them. And remind Brenhines Guinevere that she herself refused to have Arthur's bastards at her court."

The messenger scuttled out the doorway.

"Typical!" I exclaimed. "Guinevere can't think a plan through. She acts on a whim and then doesn't remember what she has done."

"True," Father Thomas stared at the original missive. "But my archbishop . . ."

"Dyfrig will do almost anything to discredit me and my father. He would probably find some way to destroy the children and blame The Merlin. He could not know that I would see the Ardh Rhi in Dun Edin and receive more recent orders. He would not believe that I would question orders sealed with the Pendragon."

Without further comment, I stalked into the nursery and gathered all of the little ones tightly in my arms. The pattern of my life shifted and refocused. All the pieces I had been sorting and fussing with, all of my life, fell into place. I hugged each of the children individually and all of them together. They were really my children, no matter who had borne or sired them. They were my legacy to Britain, as I was my father's legacy. I could be The Merlin in my own quiet way, teaching these precious young lives all that I knew. They would carry my father in their hearts and tell the stories long after the rest of us had crumbled to dust.

Chapter 56

TWO years passed swiftly.

For the first time in three or more generations the wars with the Saxons eased. The tribes who lived in Southeast Britain kept within their own borders. Many fled to Less Britain on the continent. An occasional raiding party attempted to gain a foothold on our shores. But Arthur kept patrols and signal beacons on all of the coasts and borders. His rapid deployment of mounted warriors kept the invaders at bay.

Legends grew around Arthur's Companions. Their valor, their strength, their seemingly magical ability to appear out of nowhere in the nick of time to save beleaguered defenders expanded daily in the ballads and history songs.

Caer Noddfa continued to provide sanctuary for those displaced by the wars and those who sought something beyond war to give meaning to their lives. We also became a convenient way station for couriers who crisscrossed the country.

I studied each messenger and refugee carefully before allowing them near the children. Guinevere did not try to remove my charges again. Morgaine sent no assassins that I detected.

As long as they left the children alone, I said nothing to Arthur about Dyfrig's and Guinevere's aborted attempt to steal the children. But I think he knew. He increased the number of warriors within my household. Rumors claimed that he and Guinevere did not live together very often. She remained at Camlann in the South. He rode the length and breadth of Britain, making his headquarters at Camboglanna. He dispensed justice, enforced his laws, and kept a watchful eye on his client kings.

Occasionally the Ardh Rhi returned South for state events. More often he lived in his saddle.

Gradually the concept of peace within Britain became desirable rather than boring.

The children grew and prospered. Deirdre showed signs of inheriting my father's and my talent for magic. Yvain promised to be as talented with horses and weapons as his father. Unlike Carradoc, my son developed a fine sensitivity to animals, knowing their needs and moods, bonding with them and cherishing their complete loyalty with a sense of wonder. He inherited this magic from me but little else.

Arthur visited me and the children when he could. The stuttering boy I had known with dreams bigger than the night sky became a terse and stern Ardh Rhi.

He never showed a preference for Deirdre, but I saw the ache in his eyes as he kissed the top of her head just before he mounted and galloped away.

An entire college of Druids couldn't provide Arthur with enough trained and trusted bards to carry oral messages about the country. So the Ardh Rhi resorted to Roman efficiency and wrote letters and edicts in precise and efficient Latin. Couriers traveled far and wide with Arthur's written words, as potent as his spoken ones.

Carradoc remained one of Arthur's Companions. But by chance or design he always had duties far away from Caer Noddfa. He did not return home during those two years. The Ardh Rhi visited his children at my home at least twice a year, sometimes more often. He always brought treats and treasures for all of the children and me. Many times I sensed a longing in both of us to wrap our arms around each other and never let go.

We kept our distance.

I lost Newynog soon after I returned to Caer Noddfa from Dun Edin. She just curled up by the well one morning and went to sleep. She never woke up. I cried when I discovered her stiffening body. I cried for my dog as I hadn't dared cry for my father.

Newynog's daughter nuzzled me, offering me comfort and companionship few humans knew how to offer me. She easily wormed her way into my life and my heart. We called her Newynog as well for she was always hungry—for adventure as well as food.

Morgaine retreated to the Orcades. Arthur kept Lot close at hand, not a prisoner, but not free to return home and foment rebellion with his wife. Without Lot, Morgaine could not command an army. I guessed that Morgaine still nursed her power back to full strength, seeking a way to open the gateway that I had closed and sealed with Andraste's sword. She'd defeat Arthur only with powerful magic.

We heard nothing of her son Mordred.

Da and Nimuë stayed at Dun Edin for many months, then took up residence near Camlann. I heard little of them or from them until a hot summer day when not a breath of air stirred and the trees kept silence.

A premonition of disaster hung on the horizon.

The Merlin sat beneath an ancient oak tree atop the hill behind Camlann. The limbs spread out over four arm lengths in every direction. Little light penetrated the canopy of fat leaves. Even in this deep shade the humid heat of high summer made his shirt damp and his muscles limp.

He leaned back against the trunk, watching Nimuë through half-closed eyelids. He loved the way the sunlight played with the golden-bronze colors in her gown and in her hair. The colors suited her much better than the black she had worn when she first came to him. His apprentice had truly come into her own these past two years. He doubted he could teach her anything more about magic.

Patience and wisdom, however, still needed a little work.

She thrived in the heat, gliding effortlessly from one tuft of underbrush to the next. She kept up a barrage of questions and comments about the gossip and politics of court life. As he watched a brightly colored butterfly flirt with her hair, she deftly sliced through woody stems with her athame. His athame actually. He'd given his ritual dagger to her at the Solstice. He certainly had little use for it anymore. He hadn't cast a spell or invoked a ritual in two years. Not since . . .

He shied away from the memory of the time he'd been in Morgaine's clutches. Demons still ate at his innards when he ate too much or slept too little. But sleep didn't come easily. Between the increasing pains throughout his body and his troubled memories, he spent most of each night staring at the cracks in the roof of his quarters or pacing the Long Hall. More and more he resorted to Nimuë's potions to get any rest at all. The more he drank them, the more of them he needed.

The drugs probably contributed to his heavy muscles and listless thinking.

"What is this little flower, Myrddin? I've never seen it before. It's beautiful," Nimuë said in a gasp of awe. She turned toward him from her kneeling position about four strides to his left.

He twisted a little to see where she pointed, too enervated to get up and walk four steps, or even crawl that far.

Something about her posture infused him with fear. The jolt loaned him a little strength and drained the lethargy from him. Her spine twisted awkwardly, dropping her left shoulder. He could almost see a formless shadow weighing her down. Suddenly he realized her balance had always been awkward, as if she carried a heavy weight on that side—a weight that got heavier by the day.

The left shoulder where Death perched, ever watchful for the opportunity to strike.

"That flower . . ." he worked his way to his knees for a better view of her spine as well as the plant in question. "Cernunnos protect us!"

"What?" Color drained from Nimuë's face in alarm.

"Move away from that flower very slowly, Nimuë. Don't disturb the leaves or the pollen in the least. 'Tis very poisonous." He swallowed deeply, gulping air as he did.

"What is it?" Her eyes opened wide. She licked her lips, eager for the knowledge within the plant.

"'Tis forbidden that I speak of it." *Druidsbane*, his mind screeched. He had to get her away from here. He had to protect her from the knowledge. He'd found a compromise to allow Wren to live when she learned about this secret poison. Nimuë did not have the special protection of the Goddess like his daughter. If she wormed the information out of him, he'd have to kill her.

Never! He'd die before he allowed himself to harm his love in any way.

"Tell me, Myrddin. You've taught me many forbidden things in the past." She stood slowly and backed away from the wildflower. How had she found it, almost lost between two clumps of ferns? She had to have swept both ferns aside deliberately, as if someone directed her to look there.

The spindly stem seemed to stretch and thicken, as if begging Myrddin to make use of its unique but deadly properties.

Nimuë knelt beside Myrddin. Her skirts flared out from her in a bronze puddle of shimmering light. Her hair shone in shafts of darting sunlight. A trick of the light made her greeny-hazel eyes reflect the same impenetrable depths of bronze iridescence. He had the sense of those eyes swirling inward, drawing him down into their depths, to the bottom of time. . . .

"Tell me what you know, Myrddin," she said softly as she reached gentle fingertips to caress his temple.

He grabbed her left wrist before she touched him. He couldn't let her draw the knowledge of the druidsbane from him by any means, magic or mundane.

Almost playfully he kissed the palm of her hand. Warmth filled him. He'd longed to kiss her so many times over the years, never dared let his emotions cloud his judgment.

But now. . . ?

A tiny arrow of pain pierced his heart. Cold wind whispered through the treetops. The light in the little clearing around the oak tree diminished. A chill made him shudder slightly.

He looked up sharply, trying to discern the message carried on the breeze; the portent of finding druidsbane today. Wren would know. But she wasn't here. He had only himself and a vague stirring in the tattered remnants of his magic.

"What does the wind tell you?" Nimuë left her hand clasped within his. Her heady perfume fogged his perceptions.

He didn't want to think of anything but the lovely woman so close to him.

"Dyfrig," he said. His voice did not tremble. The pain in his heart did not expand and engulf him as he thought it should. Very little emotion registered. "My twin has died. His heart failed him," he whispered. Druidsbane could mimic a heart attack if given in a single large dose.

"Your twin?" Nimuë had the grace not to show her delight in this juicy piece of gossip. "Truly your brother, born of the same womb?"

"Aye. Twins at birth. Our lives paralleled each other as twins, though we rarely spoke and never agreed. Now he is dead."

And you shall die, too.

Where did that voice in the back of his mind come from?

Not Nimuë. He knew every nuance of her inflections and tones.

"You do not grieve for your brother," Nimuë said flatly.

"I do, and yet . . . what is there to grieve? He lived a full life. His passing is no loss to me. And yet . . ."

"Then do not dwell on him, Myrddin. Tell me the secret of the poison plant."

Though Nimuë moved her mouth, shaping the words, the voice was not hers.

She slid her hand free of his grasp and reached once more for his face.

He couldn't allow that.

She'd get the knowledge from him anyway. If not now, then later while he slept. As she had gleaned much information from him. He had to prevent that transference.

He had nothing left to lose but that last bit of forbidden knowledge.

Arthur reigned, bringing justice, peace, and law to Britain.

Wren thrived as mother to a pack of children.

He'd done all that the goddess had asked of him.

"Nimuë, beloved." He kissed her neck, keeping both her hands prisoner within one of his.

"Ah, Myrddin, I've waited and waited for you to do that." She offered her lips to his.

As he tasted her mouth, drinking of her sweetness, he loosened the ties of her gown. Bronze fabric slid free of her shoulders, exposing her smooth, white skin. Just before it slipped free of her breasts, she grasped it with both hands.

"You need not fear this, Myrddin. The gods placed a geas of celibacy upon The Merlin. You no longer make claims to that title. You haven't for two years."

"I know. I fear nothing anymore, my Nimuë. I will have you and know my destiny fulfilled." The clearest vision he had ever experienced flashed before his eyes. He could not outlive his twin. Though they'd lived separately most of their lives, their life patterns were tightly interwoven. Without Dyfrig, Myrddin's pattern unraveled before his eyes.

He knew a moment of surprise that he hadn't seen his Deirdre as a Bean-Nighe washing bloody clothing in the creek on the way here. Surely she must appear to portend his death.

Chapter 57

SOMETHING had gone terribly wrong. What? Where?

Anxiety tied my neck into knots. I walked warily for days. The tension grew in me, like a thunderstorm waiting for the first strike of lightning to release the rain. Newynog slunk beside me, neck fur on end, as wary of me as she was of whatever plagued me. I was impatient with the children, angry with the villagers, and driven to a massive cleaning fit. No one wanted to work in the hot humid air but me. I couldn't tolerate people bustling around me. So I swept the Hall free of old rushes and replaced them without assistance. I climbed a ladder and repaired the thatch myself.

I worked until I could no longer remain upright and awake. The tension within me grew until I thought the weight of it would crush the breath from my chest.

And still I found chores to keep me busy, keep me from thinking. Maybe I didn't want to know what drove me.

I had just woven the last stook of dried grass into the roof, wondering what I would do next, when a royal messenger pelted up the processional way into the caer. His horse's sides heaved and glistened with sweat. It stood, all four legs splayed out, head pulled down by exhaustion.

The bands of tension tightened still more on my chest. I held out my hand for the written missive.

COME. NOW.

Below the two words Arthur's signature sprawled across the parchment, larger, bolder and more commanding than the message. The Pendragon seal seemed almost insignificant beside the signature.

This time I knew the parchment had come from Arthur himself and not his wife or archbishop usurping regent powers.

"What has transpired?" I asked the courier even as I filled my head with travel plans.

"I don't know, Lady, only that His Highness has withdrawn to his chambers and speaks only to Brenhines Guinevere and Lancelot," he replied, breathing almost as heavily as his beleaguered horse.

"Lancelot is at court?" Of course. He and Arthur were inseparable. I prayed that Stinger and Guinevere had buried their passion or kept it discreet.

"Only recently, Lady. He arrived from Dun Edin only hours before I left. He said he'd been summoned by The Merlin in a dream."

"Then I must leave within the hour. You may stay and rest as long as you need to." I dashed to my chamber flinging orders right and left as fast as I could think of them.

Kalahart had Gwynt—the high-strung stallion that had served me well on my last mad dash cross-country two years ago—saddled and an escort ready by the time I emerged with two packs of clothes and journey food. Each of the warriors carried similar provisions. We rode fast, stopping only when the horses were exhausted. Most of the six nights on the road we spent at farmhouses or caers along the way. Twice we slept rough beneath the trees.

At last we rode into Camlann, exhausted, filthy, and hungry. Guinevere and Bedewyr rushed down the steps of the great hall of Camlann to greet me. Grooms came forward to tend my horse before I could dismount.

"What is it, Ceffyl?" I asked of Bedewyr the moment my feet touched ground. I wouldn't address the Ardh Brenhines after she had tried to wrest control of the children from me.

"Your father . . ." His eyes carried the news I'd been dreading for weeks.

My knees wanted to buckle as hot tears stung the back of my eyes.

"Please, you must help my husband. He refuses to speak. He has closed himself in his chamber. Your father was the only one who could help Arthur when . . . when . . ." Guinevere drifted off, looking anxiously from Bedewyr to me. I sensed that she choked off a nervous giggle. The years had cured her of some her flighty ways, but she'd never lose all of them.

Behind the brenhines, within the shadows of the doorway, Nimuë stood wringing her hands, shoulders slumped. Her left shoulder drooped lower than ever. Her neck was thrust forward to compensate for the unaligned shoulder. A crone's hump had begun to form. But I saw the smile of satisfaction that spread across her face and lighted her eyes.

The bands of tension that constricted my breathing and pained my heart burst open and I knew the truth.

"What have you done to my father, Nimuë? Have you found a way to murder him at last?"

"You cannot accuse this good lady of foul play!" Bedewyr called after me.

"Nimuë grieves for The Merlin as much as my husband does, Lady Wren," Guinevere said. She swallowed deeply, as if she put aside the resentment and jealousy that dominated her aura. "Nimuë has been The Merlin's constant companion these two years and more. They were very much in love." Her eyes went soft and dreamy as her mind wandered to more pleasant topics.

Nimuë buried her smile of triumph in her hands. She appeared to be silently weeping. Her shoulders did not tremble as they should if she truly grieved. The colored energy of her aura darted upward in sun-yellow spikes, betraying her. But the others could not see her as I did. They did not know her as I did.

"Please, Lady Wren, do something. Arthur . . ." Guinevere pleaded. Her attention had drifted in and out of the conversation.

"Perhaps you can make sense of the High King's ailment." Bedewyr led me toward the royal quarters at the back of the Great Hall. He jostled Guinevere's shoulder to draw her attention back to the present. Obviously he knew the Ardh Brenhines' shortcomings even if he didn't understand them.

I followed them, keeping a wary eye on Nimuë. Deep cold enveloped my emotions and my throat. I knew I'd not cry until I had confronted Nimuë and heard the truth from her.

Carradoc's daughter ran lightly—despite her twisted back— toward the circular chamber that Da had used the last time I was here. As her hands dropped from her face, no tears marred her beautifully clear skin and eyes.

Arthur barely looked up from his writing desk at my entrance. Lancelot stood by the Roman-style window that had been built into the old timber hall. Cai polished his sword in a corner. Both of the Companions looked grim, almost defeated. Arthur assumed an air of preoccupation with the daily business of governing Britain through fractious and all-too-independent client kings.

"Arthur, beloved," Guinevere whispered. Her gaze did not stray to Lancelot at all.

I hoped they had put aside the flash of passion they had shared three years ago. Guinevere's half-faery heritage kept her attention span short. Perhaps she had found a new object of her affection. Faeries rarely took anything seriously in this world.

Arthur lifted his head. He looked first at his wife, love and devotion filling his gaze as well as his aura. Yet there was also a hint of an old hurt. Then he caught sight of me. He smiled his welcome as he stood and opened his arms to me in greeting.

"I have come, Curyll. As you asked. What has happened?"

"W–Wren."

The others gasped in unison. Was this the first word he had spoken in some time? I concentrated on my oldest and dearest friend. "Speak slowly, Curyll. Think about your words, then speak them one at a time, just like the . . ." I couldn't mention the faeries. The Christian cross hanging around his neck matched the one Guinevere wore. They'd likely discount the value of my friends from the Otherworld. They might dismiss their existence altogether.

"Y–your Da is dead, Wren," he said with less hesitation. "All of B–Britain grieves with you. The d–death of The M–erlin is a gr–great loss to us all." He held me close against his chest. The fierceness of his grip said more than his words.

"How? Why?" I knew when. Confirming it only deepened the icy chill behind my heart.

"A few hours before my husband sent for you. He needed to tell you himself, rather than write such terrible news," Guinevere said. Her expression soured as Arthur continued to hold me close. She had managed to learn to concentrate on one issue at least—her own jealousy.

Lancelot rested a comforting hand on my shoulder. Cai kissed my hand. I sensed their grief for the loss of their tutor and mentor. They expected me to break into tears and uncontrollable grief. I couldn't. Not yet.

I needed answers to many questions. Like why Da had summoned

Stinger to court when we agreed he must be kept away from Guinevere. Nimuë had those answers and no one else.

"How? Who?" I repeated.

"Nimuë brought us the news," Lancelot said stiffly. He turned back to the window, watching the conical hut where my father had lived with Nimuë. He didn't trust my stepdaughter any more than I did.

"How did he die?"

"H—his heart," Arthur stammered.

"He hadn't been well since Morgaine's demons used him as a plaything back at Dun Edin," Cai finished for his king and foster brother.

"Show me his pyre."

"We buried him within the roots of an ancient oak in the copse at the top of the hill. Very near where he died." Guinevere pursed her lips. "He refused baptism time and again. The only way his soul can be redeemed is for him to face Our Lord Jesus whole. We dared not burn him in a pagan ceremony." She almost spat the end of her proclamation.

I doubted she thought up that long statement by herself. Dyfrig had coached her undoubtedly.

"Da would want the honor of a funeral pyre. We believe that the spirit must be liberated from the body so that it can be reincarnated. If you will not give him the honor due him, then I must. Show me his grave."

"Yes." Arthur tightened his hug briefly, then released me. "I—in the m—orning."

"Now! Before Belenos sets on his trapped spirit one more time."

"The copse is a good distance from Camlann, uphill, surrounded by deep forest," Cai said. "We'd best wait for morning. You can sing your greeting to Belenos at the same time."

"I cannot sing until my father's spirit is liberated." I hadn't sung anything in two years. Not since I said farewell to him the last time. Not even a lullaby to my children. "I will go now. I will find the place on my own if I have to. An ancient oak with a new grave beside it at the top of the hill. I will find it." I thought I knew the tree. It had been a favorite of Da's.

"Surely you need to bathe and rest, at least eat something before you go," Guinevere urged. She would think of comfort first.

"I will go now. But a bite to eat on the way would be welcome."

"F–fresh horses, Boar," Arthur cut through their arguments. "W–we ride now."

I didn't really want to mount a horse ever again. The week on the road had taken its toll on my back and thighs. But my restlessness pulled me toward that ancient oak in the center of the forest. Da's spirit was not easy. I could not rest until I had set him free.

Almost, we have almost reached the point of my emergence, the demon chuckled into Nimuë's ear.

"Yes! At last you will come into the daylight and work beside me as an equal partner." Nimuë nearly shouted with glee. She danced around Myrddin's chamber, flinging his clothing into a pile in the center of the room. She'd burn it later. Perhaps she should haul it out to the ancient oak and set fire to the clothing. A further taunt to The Merlin's memory, giving his clothing the funeral pyre he was denied.

Whatever. The demon bounced upon her shoulder.

She winced. His weight twisted her neck and spine painfully. She'd be glad to get him off her back.

No man controlled her now. She wouldn't let the demon move into the position of power vacated by Carradoc and The Merlin.

With a swipe of her arm she cleared the cot of paraphernalia and lay back against the small pillow. Her position forced the demon to shift to her breasts. She could almost imagine him fondling and suckling her like a lover. Now that his body was almost visible, she detected grossly exaggerated male genitalia beneath his pot belly.

"You became quite substantial when we killed The Merlin." She petted the translucent shadow form, pressing it closer to her breasts.

Yes. The Merlin was forbidden to join with a woman. Performing forbidden acts gives me power and substance. His pincer hands nipped her nipples obediently.

A thrill of pain/pleasure leaped through her blood.

"Like the last time I lay with Carradoc. You gained as much weight that night as you did with the death of The Merlin. Perhaps I should seek out my father again." Hot moisture between her thighs reminded her of that night.

She did enjoy sex now that she controlled her partners.

Don't bother. You conceived a forbidden child with that little act of incest. That is what gave me strength. A repeat performance—though pleasurable when you scream with pain—would add nothing to my form.

"Then what must we do? We have waited a long time for this." She sat up, pouting. She needed a diversion. "Wren is here now. I've wanted to watch her wallow in grief for a long, long time."

And you shall. She will go to his grave. She will weep and tear her hair. She is vulnerable. Kill her with the poison plant we discovered.

"You learned its secrets?" Nimuë bounced upright in excitement. She knew quite a bit about poisons, but using one so potent The Merlin was forbidden to speak of it would give the demon its last bit of strength to come forth into the world completely. It could become her most forbidden lover of all!

Chapter 58

RED-GOLD sunlight streamed through the tall trees at a very low angle as we dismounted. Underbrush grew in a wild tangle beneath the trees. Many of the forest giants had been felled for buildings and fortifications. Fallen limbs and smaller trees had been scavenged for firewood. I wasn't used to the open spaces and lightness throughout this tract of trees. It should be dense and dark with a thick canopy of overlapping branches. The ground should be covered with a thick blanket of fallen leaves from years of buildup. Instead, thick underbrush filled the area between remaining trees, flourishing in the additional light. We had to follow a specific winding track through the nearly impenetrable brush, not ride direct to the spot in question.

Much had changed in the years since I'd been here.

I didn't want to dwell on the biggest change. Da was dead. What would I do without him? Even during the years of estrangement, I had known where he was, that he would come to me in an instant if I needed him. He was my connection to the past, the anchor of my identity. I thought I had said my good-byes to him two years ago. I thought I had accepted the inevitability of his death then.

Faced with the reality, I knew I'd never accept his passing. During all those years of wandering Britain in my youth, I needed no home as long as I walked beside my Da.

Tears threatened to choke me as I approached the bright clearing surrounding the old oak tree. Everything was wrong. Very, very wrong.

Arthur took my arm, as if he knew my knees would soon collapse under me. We walked slowly forward. As we neared the tree, I realized I was humming a haunting tune of allurement. Curyll, Boar, Ceffyl, and Stinger hummed it, too. They moved as if bewitched, unable to do aught but seek the source of the song.

I closed my throat on the vibrations that needed to come out, needed to join with the others, completing the harmony. Another feminine voice filled the enticing gaps, perfectly balancing the deeper male tones. Not my voice.

I shook off Arthur's supporting grasp and lengthened my stride. The mottled whorls of old bark on the oak took on reddish tones from the setting sun, as red as Nimuë's hair.

Then I saw her. Naked, hair streaming to her hips, grasping the tree as if she held a lover. Her hips moved back and forth, undulating in the sensuous rhythm of sex. Every line of her perfect body evoked the beauty of the Goddess in glowing fertility and the promise of renewal. She shifted the song upward into soaring glory and joy.

A dark shadow echoed her movements. At first I thought it a trick of the setting sun, then I realized it moved separately from Nimuë, a half measure behind her in a dissonant counterpoint that grated on my nerves.

As her notes climbed ever higher, she let go her embrace of the tree and danced. Her feet pounded the slight rise of newly turned earth, beating it flat. The shadow followed her, still that agonizing half measure behind her. She raised her arms, highlighting her full breasts, exposing her feminine thatch in open invitation, and shook her fists in victory. The shadow moved to expose its huge male genitalia.

Arthur and his foster brothers stood mouths agape, eyes wide, seeing only Nimuë. Sexual longing colored their auras in deep purple. They leaned closer to Nimuë, needing to join her, join with her, yet unable to move their feet.

The demon shadow behind her repelled me.

The twists and whorls of bark on the tree writhed in rhythm with Nimuë's dance. I saw a living face in agony trapped within the tree.

My father's face.

Then the demon turned its swirling red eyes on me. It drew me into the depths of its dark heart. I couldn't move. Couldn't think. Couldn't free my father from Nimuë's not quite fatal entrapment.

"You come at last, Wren," Nimuë said. She paused in her wild dance, panting a little from her exertion. Sweat slicked her ripe body. The fertile glow remained.

I broke free of the demon's gaze by the simple expedient of closing my eyes. It wasn't fully formed in this world yet. Though strong, it still had vulnerabilities.

I motioned the men to remain behind me, still within the shadows of the sunset. I gathered my strength and spells, waiting for the right moment.

Nimuë didn't look at the men. She may not have seen them. "I've waited for this moment for a long time, waited for you to know that I have at last stolen your father from you, as you stole mine from me." Nimuë laughed, flinging her hair off her shoulders. Her full breasts jiggled, already heavier than the last time I had seen her.

"You carry Da's child." She might not even suspect the truth of that herself yet. "The Merlin could only have lain with you once, moments before his death. He was placed under a geas at birth by the gods. Cursed, more like, never to join with a woman. They forgave his one lapse the night I was conceived because his destiny had not yet run full circle. They marked him so that he would never forget. The next time he took a woman, he would die." I recited Da's history as if setting it to a song.

All the while his agonized face within the tree haunted me. He hadn't fully died. The gods had punished him with more than death.

"Yes!" Nimuë threw back her head and laughed long and loud. "So he told me. So he showed me. I found his tattoos remarkably erotic when he succumbed to me at last." Her nipples hardened as if she relived the moment of orgasm when he entered her with his ridged and tattooed penis. Droplets of moisture gathered on the fringe of her thatch.

Beside her, the demon also panted. Its penis elongated and stiffened.

I sensed heat building in the men behind me.

I had to end this soon.

"You seduced him deliberately. How? What persuasion finally broke through his need to continue living?"

"I stripped from him what little magic he had left. Morgaine's demons stole most of his power in that pit in Dun Edin. I stole every bit of knowledge he could give me as well. Then, I convinced him that since he could no longer function as The Merlin, he might as well live like a man. I made him believe that the geas was placed on The Merlin, the sorcerer who saw the future, not on Myrddin Emrys who hadn't had a vision in two years." She breathed deeply and more rapidly, her breasts thrust out and her hips rotated. Heat and the scent of her sex radiated from every pore in her flawless skin.

The demon darkened, taking on more substance than just shadow.

"You killed my father just so you could claim one more forbidden lover. Your father wasn't enough to satisfy you. Who will be next, a Christian priest?" I couldn't keep the sneer out of my voice.

I suspected the demon was already her lover.

"What a delicious idea." Nimuë licked her lips, excited at the prospect. "Almost as tasty as making you watch me dance on your father's grave."

I lashed out with all of my magic and mind. Bright red flames burst from my hands in long ropes of anger and grief.

The demon screamed. Its high-pitched wails hit my ears like knife blades.

"Noooooo!" Nimuë screamed. She tried to grab the black globular body. Heat repulsed her. One long pincer hand snapped onto her fingers and pulled her closer. She yanked herself away from the crumbling pile of ash. Black demon blood and her own red blood caked her hand.

"You've killed him. You murdered him!" she wailed. "He didn't have time to tell me the secrets of the druidsbane. I can't kill you with the poison." She stared at her bloody hand, sobbing. "I'll kill you with my bare hands!" She dashed toward me, fingers extended like claws, eyes wild, teeth bared.

Dribbles of flame trickled out of her fingers. She stopped short, staring at the useless magic spell.

"You've killed my magic," she cried. "There's nothing left. You've taken everything from me." Fat tears poured forth from her eyes. She stuck out her lower lip in a lovely pout. She could always cry without her face mottling in ugly blotches or her eyes turning red. Her nose didn't even run.

She looked pitiful, lost, desirable.

I knew a moment of panic that Arthur and his men might succumb to her wiles yet.

"Enough," Arthur said, stepping forward, drawing his sword. Excaliber glowed in the dying sunlight. Power hummed along the blade.

I heard Lancelot, Cai, and Bedewyr draw their weapons as well.

Nimuë stared at them in surprise. Her tears stopped as quickly as they had begun.

"I–have h–eard enough to accuse you of murder, Nimuë," the High King announced. "Surrender to us now."

"Not just murder, Highness," Cai added. "I accuse her of treason for depriving you of the counsel of the wisest man in Britain."

"No!" Horror erupted on Nimuë's face and in her aura. She tried to unleash another blast of fire. Her fingertips barely smoked. Her body slackened and seemed to shrink back within itself. All trace of her lust banished. "I didn't murder him. The gods took him. Look, he's there, trapped within the tree. It reached out and engulfed him the moment we finished. I didn't murder him!"

"You knew the consequences when you seduced him," I said.

"I sought vengeance. The law allows me vengeance for the loss of my father."

"Your father still lives. Still thrives and draws honor to his name with his battles," Lancelot replied.

"T–take her b–back to Cam–lann. I will p–ass jud–judgment at dawn. We move the court to Campboglanna at noon." Arthur turned his back on Nimuë. "Cov–cover her with a cl–cloak or s–omething."

"You don't dare capture me alive, Arthur Pendragon. For I know the truth of your affair with Morgaine four years ago. I know who truly fathered her youngest son, Mordred. I know that if you bring me to trial, it will be your downfall." Nimuë laughed as she ran sprightly into the thickening shadows of the forest.

"Bitch!" Cai yelled. "I'll kill you before I let you ruin a great man with your lies." He started after her, sword drawn, murder in his eyes.

"Let her go, Cai." Arthur's quiet words echoed through the clearing.

"Curyll, you can't mean it." Bedewyr lunged forward as if to follow his foster brother and the fugitive. Then he stopped short and turned back to face the man he'd known since early childhood. "You can't let her go. She murdered The Merlin, she admitted to an incestuous affair with her father. She has to be brought to justice. By your own laws, we can't allow her to run free."

"Let her go. Consider her banished from Britain. After three days, if she is found within the borders of my kingdom, her life is forfeit, without trial. That is the law." Arthur turned on his heel and returned to the horses. Only the slightest hesitation marred his speech. "W–wren. You will stay by my side."

"I must stand vigil by my father's grave. Even your Christian god would not deny me this."

He nodded curtly and mounted Taranis.

"You shouldn't be alone out here, Wren. I'll stand vigil with you," Cai said.

"As will I," Bedewyr added.

"This is something I must do alone." Grief grew in a great lump in my throat. The emotions I had suppressed for nearly two weeks threatened to engulf me. I couldn't speak.

First I searched out the druidsbane Nimuë had coveted. I found it between two ferns, withered and dying in its short but deadly life span. Its pollen and the oil in its leaves could no longer hurt anyone. The slightest touch of Tanio finished its demise.

Slowly, I gathered what firewood I could find and placed it above the grave Nimuë had trampled. They had buried his body there. But Da's spirit, the part of him that walked the Earth for a brief span, all his hopes and dreams, his plans and schemes for the future, his wisdom and knowledge, and his love for me were indeed trapped within the tree for all time. The gods had captured the essence of him before his body had turned cold. Nothing I could do would release him.

All I could do was honor him with fire and song and tears.

Chapter 59

I returned to Camlann around midnight. Weariness fogged my brain and made pudding of my limbs. I sat stupidly on the back of the horse in the forecourt of the stable trying to figure out how to dismount. I'd have to do that myself. The grooms had gone to bed.

While I stared at the reins hanging limply in my hands, Arthur strode out of the stable. He shook his head at me and clucked as if he were my nurse and I a small child. Without a word, he lifted me from the saddle, cradling me against his chest. We lingered, drawing warmth and comfort from each other for several long moments. Then he set me on a bale of hay and tended the horse.

He still hadn't spoken.

"Why did you wait up for me?" I finally asked. His silence had gone on too long. I worried about his stuttering. He beckoned me to follow him.

Too tired to think for myself, I stumbled after him to the guest-house that had been my father's. I dreaded entering the round hut with stone foundations, wooden walls, and thatched roof. A proper guesthouse close to the quarters of the Ardh Rhi. Nimuë's scent lingered. I caught a strong draught of it from the doorway. She wore a heavy oil-based perfume from Rome laced with ingredients from her foul magic. A thousand years of scrubbing the walls wouldn't remove the traces she had left behind, a constant reminder of what she had cost us all.

Da! My mind screamed at the outrage of my father trapped within the great oak tree. Ironically, mistletoe, the symbol of peace, hung heavy in the branches of the tree. Da would never be at peace.

Arthur motioned for me to enter the hut. All of Nimuë's possessions had been removed. All traces of her had been erased, except her scent. Only my father's clutter remained. I'd never clean up after him again. I brushed a pile of scrolls with delicate fingertips. A tiny sensation of familiar warmth invaded my hand.

I am here, the scrolls, covered in his tiny, precise script, seemed to say.

I moved on to his metal mirrors and pouches of magical powders and healing herbs.

I am here, they repeated.

The warmth spread up my arm, almost reaching my heart. I half smiled, remembering the lessons Da had set for me, studying the properties of Pridd, Awyr, Tanio, and Dwfr.

"You . . . must . . . stay . . . with . . . me," Arthur said from the doorway. The pause between each word went on forever.

"I can't, Curyll. You know that. The children need me. I have responsibilities back home." I sat on the bed, unable to stand any longer. Just thinking about the long journey home wearied me to the point of illness.

"You . . . must help me talk. Only you. Stay."

"You can speak, Curyll, without stuttering, if you choose."

"The . . . the faeries deserted me. I . . . need your help."

"You frightened away the faeries when you allowed Archbishop Dyfrig to baptize you. The Christians don't allow for the existence of any world but this one. The beings who inhabit the Otherworlds, therefore, don't exist. Christians won't see the faeries even when they are right in front of them. Dyfrig should be the one to help you speak." I sighed, resigned that this conversation must proceed to the end before I could sleep. "Where is the archbishop anyway?"

"D . . . dead."

"Dead? When?" A new unease invaded my fatigue and grief. I sat up straighter, more alert than I'd been for hours.

'The . . . the same day as . . . The Merlin."

"No wonder. . . ."

"What?"

"Did they reconcile?"

Arthur shook his head and shrugged his shoulders. "Explain."

I told him of their connection and their separation. I hadn't seen the archbishop since he denied me the right to see my grandmother. I hadn't wanted to see him again. But I wanted the hurt in my father to go away.

"Their lives followed parallel patterns for all of their differences," I added almost as an afterthought. I should tell Grandmother of her sons' deaths. She wouldn't understand. Her sons were two rag dolls who slept peacefully in a basket cradle.

"Da and Dyfrig were both religious leaders, wise councillors and prophets. Both celibate. Both more concerned with the fate of Britain than themselves," I continued my musing aloud for Curyll.

A new thought stopped my rambling words. Balance. Parallels. "One died. So the other must die, too. Da allowed Nimuë to seduce him. He knew what would happen. He chose the time and place of his death." But not the punishment of the gods. He wouldn't have wanted to haunt the oak tree for the rest of eternity, be denied a new life through the miracle of reincarnation.

So you believe.

Where had that thought come from?

"No one—knew they—were brothers." Curyll bowed his head. "I've—lost them—both. Y–our father was my g–guide for twenty-three years. D–Dyfrig gave me w–wise counsel for four, since I be-came k–king. Both advised m–my f–father well, h–his entire reign. Britain—has lost them both."

"No one can help you now, Curyll. You must help yourself."

"I—need you, Wr–Wren. Your p–resence helps me f–find the words."

"What have you been doing for help since you took baptism? You have functioned well for several years now."

"Your—father gave me the words to speak. When—I know what I must say, I can speak."

"You have had years of practice. Surely you know what words to say to keep this kingdom functioning. You have flooded the courts of the client kings with rolls of parchment carrying your words. You dispense justice and settle disputes with wisdom and caring."

"I write the words well. But when I face people, I do not think fast enough. At court I always had your father or Dyfrig."

"You think fast enough to speak right now."

"With you. Only. I can't do this alone."

"You aren't alone. You have Guinevere. You have Cai and Be-dewyr and Lancelot. You have a hundred Companions you trust with your life. Trust them with your words as well."

"None of them are The Merlin. You are."

"No. There will never be another Merlin. I'm sorry, Curyll. I can't stay here." Being near my beloved Curyll every day, working close to him. Sensing his thoughts. Loving him. Never being able to show it. Guinevere's jealous gaze following every move I made. She'd been treacherous once, she could be again given provocation—real or imagined.

"I forbid you to leave. You are The Merlin now. Your place is here."

"My place is training the next generation to uphold your promise of peace and law and justice. They must learn that honor, loyalty, and promises mean something."

His eyes twinkled briefly as I quoted his own words from long ago.

"The next generation and all of the ones after that must retain their connection with the land. Without the land and our intimate ties to the rituals of the season, we can't keep the portals between worlds open. Faeries and gods will disappear. And so will magic."

"Th–the faeries are—are gone already."

"Not entirely. The door to their world is closing, but remains open a crack for those willing to look. You have forgotten how to look. You can't keep me here, Curyll. I know too many of my father's tricks. My presence will only cause you more problems. The Christians tolerated my father because he advised your father well. They will not tolerate me, a pagan priestess with magic, advising you. The memory of Nimuë and Morgaine and their sorcery is too close. Let me go home without forcing me to trick you. Please."

He bowed his head sadly and nodded. "I—saved The—Merlin's torc for you. His grandson should have it." He swallowed back tears. "I wish we could be together, Wren. I need you."

"I wish the same. But we can't be together. Ever."

I pushed him out into the night, closing the door before either of us could reconsider. I sealed it with the heavy bar and with a touch of magic.

A fierce pounding on the door woke me. Late afternoon sunshine filtered through the small, high window.

"Go away," I called. Sleep still dragged my eyelids down. I didn't want to face the day and new problems. I didn't want to think about my father forever trapped within the oak tree.

I am with you always.

"No, you aren't, Da. You are only my memory and my need to see you one more time. I need to tell you I love you one more time," I whispered, choking on my tears.

I know.

"I only had you for eighteen years, Da." Less than that really. Four years away from him on Avalon and then I hadn't seen him the last two years.

"Wren, let me in, please," Berminia pleaded from the other side of the door. "I brought your dinner."

I smelled the new bread and hot soup. My stomach growled in response. I struggled upright, tangled in the covers.

"Wren, please, I need to talk to you."

"Coming," I called back. My voice cracked, hoarse and dry. I'd spent too many hours crying.

At last I stumbled across the small hut on nearly numb legs and unbarred the door. Berminia, Carradoc's middle daughter, pushed the door open with too much force. I ducked away from it just before it knocked me flat.

"Oh, Wren, I'm sorry to disturb you. Maybe I should let you sleep some more."

"Berminia?" Where had her bitter accusations and deep resentment fled? Then I noticed how her gown clung to her full figure. She'd always be round and earthy rather than slim and ethereal like her older sister, but she'd lost a great deal of the excess weight. Her blonde hair shone with the luster of health and cleanliness. But her face showed the biggest difference, clear of blemish, and she genuinely smiled rather than sneering.

"Aye, Wren, 'tis me. I know I don't have the right to ask, but I need your help."

More than just her body had changed. So had her attitude.

"Come in." I took the tray from her, searching for a place to set it and her. Da's clutter filled every flat surface. He might have just walked out the door. . . .

I hadn't the heart to clear it away.

Finally I shrugged and plunked myself and the tray back on the bed.

Berminia looked about and immediately picked up a pile of Da's shirts from the floor and began folding them. Then she settled on a three-legged stool, where I had sat so many times looking up to my father as he paced the room—whatever room we happened to inhabit. He'd talk about ideas and new spells while I devised experiments to prove them.

A new bout of tears threatened to choke me.

"Go ahead and eat, Wren. I know you must be hungry." Berminia waved her hand at the tray. "I can talk while you eat."

I didn't wait for a second invitation. The bread was still warm from the oven. It melted in my mouth and soothed my aching stomach. The soup was too salty but warmed the cold knot of grief surrounding my heart.

"What do you want to talk about?" I asked around another mouthful of bread. The day began to look a little easier to handle with food in my stomach. My grief might be manageable with a full belly. Manageable, never gone very far away.

"Nimuë." Berminia looked at her hands rather than in my eyes.

I froze in mid-chew.

"I heard what my sister did to your father, Wren," she blurted before I had time to think. "I know she is evil. Many times I did her bidding because . . . because I knew she'd make me even uglier if I refused. I've been afraid of her since we were small children. I think she killed Marnia's mother when we were little more than infants, perhaps my mother as well. But she helped me a lot. She is my sister."

The mouthful of bread turned heavy and tasteless in my mouth. I gulped it down anyway. I couldn't think of anything to say. Outrage began to boil within me.

"Wren, my sister made me beautiful with magic. I've found a man who wants to marry me, make me a lady, wants me to have his children. A man I never thought could love me. But he thinks I'm beautiful only because of the magic. Now that Nimuë is gone, the magic will fade. I'll be fat and ugly again. I need you to make me beautiful again."

I glanced past her left ear, searching for oddities within her aura. Only the pale reflection of orange worry and blue caring met my eye.

"Berminia, I can't see any trace of magic glamour about you. What did your sister do?"

"She gave me a potion to drink, and we danced naked about an ancient oak before dawn as the dew fell on us."

The oak tree again. Nimuë must have selected the forest giant long ago for her rituals. It would remain special for all time now because of my father. I had marked it with magic so that woodcutters would leave it alone for as long as it stood upright.

My father's only hope for release was the natural death of the tree. Destruction of the ancient oak would doom Da's spirit to oblivion with no chance of reincarnation for all eternity.

"I know of Nimuë's ritual, Berminia." I dragged my thoughts back to reality. "She draped a temporary illusion about you. But it could only be temporary. You would have to repeat the potion and the ritual every full moon to maintain it. Nimuë didn't make you beautiful, *you* did."

"How? I don't understand. She told me every day, I had to obey her or lose the glamour," Berminia wailed.

"Did you like being your sister's slave?"

"No. I hated it. I lied to her. I told her cats made me sneeze and swell up so I couldn't catch them for her to slaughter. I realized that no one had a right to murder for the sake of magic. Even just the kitchen cats. There are always plenty of those."

"But never another Helwriaeth," I whispered. I had my own affinity for kitchen cats. My heart thawed a little and accepted Berminia for the woman she had become rather than the girl she had been.

"You resisted her evil." I brought the subject back to Berminia and her own brand of beauty. "You started to find good in yourself and others. You thought yourself beautiful because of the initial glamour and so you made yourself beautiful. You no longer needed to eat to compensate for other things lacking in your life. You no longer needed to belittle others to make you feel good about yourself. Little by little you made your own beauty. You found your own balance and inner peace. Look in the mirror, Berminia. No trace of Nimuë taints you."

I handed her one of Da's polished metal disks. She stared at her face a long time.

"Is this a magic mirror?" she asked, touching her face with wondering fingertips.

"No. It's just a mirror. Now tell me, who is the man you wish to please so much?

"Cai," she whispered.

"The Near-sighted Boar?" I asked, giggling.

"He is not!" Berminia protested. Her giggles bubbled up like my forest spring leaping from a jumble of rocks. "Well, maybe a little near-sighted. But when he kisses me, he stands close enough to see me."

"He can be as aggressive and single-minded as a boar," I reminded her. "That's why we called him that as children. I believe Curyll came up with the name."

"Arthur is Curyll, the fierce and cunning hawk. And you call Lancelot 'Stinger' because he is as fast with weapons as a bee with a stinger. Bedewyr you called Ceffyl because he thinks like a horse and talks to them," Berminia sighed. "I wish I'd grown up with you."

I smiled grimly and patted her hand. Carradoc hadn't been as gentle with her as he had with Marnia and Nimuë.

"Marnia's baby is nearly two now. Newynog passed on last summer, but the runt of her last litter has replaced her as my companion. She looks just like her mother." And guarded the children as admirably. I missed her terribly and needed to go home quickly, to hug my dog and my children—Arthur's children, too, but I thought of them all as mine.

"Is she as hungry as Newynog always was?" Berminia's eyes brightened with happier memories.

"Always. We call her Newynog as well. But tell me about Cai. Has he proposed?"

"Yes!"

We giggled together like young girls, reminiscing, cementing a new friendship.

"You'll make a good wife to Cai," I said. "Now we have to find a match for Bedewyr." But I wouldn't be in Camlann long enough to see the plot through. Already I sensed the need to be home, with the children, away from Arthur. Danger to them didn't pull me this time. Danger to myself, if I stayed and revealed my love for my daughter's father. Even my father's ghost couldn't keep me here.

"Promise me, Berminia, if Nimuë contacts you, you must let me know. She carries my father's child. It will have a great deal of magic potential. We can't let that magic be warped by Nimuë's need for vengeance against me." The image of Morgaine's son wedging open the gateway to the Netherworld tied my stomach in knots.

Chapter 60

THE next I heard about Nimuë, she had fled north to the Orcades. Morgaine gave her sanctuary. I did not know how much magic either could command without their demons. Nimuë had to be nearly crippled by the loss. She must have been dependent upon her Netherworld creature for a long time for it to have become so fully formed and for the weight of it to twist her spine.

No hint of rumor leaked out of the windswept islands about the child I knew Nimuë carried.

Before I left Camlann, I had to confront Guinevere. I didn't want to, but for the sake of my children, I had to make sure she would never threaten them again.

The queen had not accompanied Arthur on his journey to Campboglanna. She rarely left Camlann at all. I found her in the storeroom counting barrels of dried fruit—she nibbled at the expensive imported dates more than she counted. For once she wasn't surrounded by a dozen ladies and servants.

I wondered what drove her to seek solitude in this dark undercroft. Normally she was a sun-loving creature who needed to be surrounded by people.

"What do you want?" she asked, annoyed at any interruption.

"We need to talk."

"No, we don't."

"Two years ago, you tried to kidnap my children."

"Bastards." Her eyes lit with malice.

"My children."

"They threaten my husband." She turned back to her counting, using her fingers to tally the first five barrels.

"They are babies!"

"They will be the focus of rebellion against Arthur! Archbishop Dyfrig saw it in a vision." The Ardh Brenhines whirled back to face me. I saw fear in her face and posture. "I can't give Arthur children. He—he must have an heir, someone who can command the loyalty of all the kings."

"Agreed. Only a very strong man can keep them together, keep them from fighting each other over nothing. The Saxons wait for any breach in Arthur's defenses," I added when her eyes began to wander back to the dates. I wondered again why she sought this solitude.

"If Arthur chooses one of his bastards to succeed him, there will be war. The boy will grab the crown before Arthur dies. Alliances will shatter. The Saxons will come again. Dyfrig saw it!" The fear turned to desperation.

She had grown in intelligence and attention span. But how much of Dyfrig's vision did she understand and how much did she parrot?

"Dyfrig's twin brother, my father, saw you betraying Arthur in a similar vision."

"I would never . . ."

"None of the children in my care will betray their king. Remember that the next time you are tempted to work mischief among them."

Dyfrig's vision claimed one of Arthur's bastards would attempt to seize the crown before Arthur's death. Curyll had said that only one of the children in my care could possibly be his. Deirdre.

Arthur's only other bastard was Mordred. Morgaine's son, the child who had propped open the gateway to the demon's Underworld.

I couldn't tell Guinevere about that child. That information must come from Arthur himself.

"Why are you here?" I had to satisfy my curiosity.

"Dyfrig said I had to deny my faerylike longings. I have to learn to live with aloneness and darkness. But I don't like it. I don't like it at all. I want light and laughter and freedom to love where I choose. I don't like the restrictions religions place on me."

"Restrictions have a purpose. Light and laughter are not prohibited by any god I have ever heard of. But loving where you choose when you have already made binding promises to another could be disastrous. Remember that as you laugh and sit in the sunshine."

I had to remember that myself every time Arthur and I came into the same room.

Berminia and Cai married at the Autumnal Equinox that same year. Bedewyr married his lady—not the one Berminia and I thought perfect for him—at the Solstice.

The marriages seemed to symbolize the settling down of the country and the populace. Arthur's Companions could afford the time to create a home and family because the country found peace more fun than constant warfare. The warrior class dissipated into contented men who had families to provide for and years of life to look forward to. The Companions still rode out on quests to dispense the Ardh Rhi's justice and settle violent disputes.

They also became diplomats, keeping the client kings separated over issues that shouldn't flame into war, but easily could.

A few of the Companions departed on a quest for the Holy Grail, the wine vessel Jesu Christus used at his last supper. His godfather, Joseph of Arimathea, reputedly brought the cup to Britain after the crucifixion. Among the Grail's magical powers were eternal life for those privileged to drink from it, and bringing the dead back to life.

The stories sounded very much like the Goddess' gräal of life. But then the Christians held many beliefs in common with pagans, if only they would look before condemning the differences.

Those who sought the Grail endured many trials in their quest. They brought justice to those who had been wronged and they looked deep within themselves, acknowledging their weaknesses and using their strengths. They found inner peace and brought balance back to others. Whichever god controlled the Grail, or the gräal, should smile upon those men. I had been blessed with a vision of the gräal twice. I hope they found their Grail.

Carradoc rode with the Companions less frequently and he never joined one of the Grail hunts. Pragmatic and unashamed of his sins, he would have little patience with the spiritual nature of the quests.

He was one of the oldest Companions. His many battle wounds pained him. Long days in the saddle followed by bashing a few heads didn't suit him any longer.

My unwanted husband came home voluntarily for the first time in years.

We faced each other in the courtyard. A dozen people ceased their chores to watch us. I gestured them away. I wanted privacy for this confrontation. But I wouldn't allow him into my bedchamber until we settled this. Maybe not even then.

"Bitter words passed between us the last time I saw you," he said. No emotion crossed his face.

I nodded, seeking to understand his motives before I committed myself with words.

"You did not complete your threat of divorce."

"You stayed away, I had no reason to finish it." If ever I spoke the words twice more, our marriage would end.

"I would come home again." He stood slightly off balance, favoring his left side.

What could I say? I didn't want him here. But I had never denied sanctuary to any who needed the refuge of Caer Noddfa. He could claim Arthur's justice and force me to admit him to the caer his family had called home for many generations. My family had never claimed a home. We had all of Britain in our care.

But now. . . ? My children needed a home, roots, a sense of continuity. I had had only Da and missed family more with each passing year.

"Will you strike me again when your temper gets the better of you?"

"Not unless you deserve it."

"Who determines if I deserve it?"

He shrugged and looked at his boots.

"What about the children?"

"Children need a heavy hand to guide them."

"Children need love and understanding. Punishment for infractions of the rules shouldn't always be physical."

"If they deserve . . ."

"You must renew your promise not to hurt me or my children. And seal the promise in a circle."

"Promises are . . ."

"For cowards," I finished for him. "So you have said. But promises are also for honor and balance. Will you tarnish your own honor by breaking a promise? Will you upset the balance established by the gods by breaking a promise?"

Grudgingly he drew a circle in the dirt with his boot. "I promise."

"You may stay, Carradoc." I turned on my heel to retreat to the kitchen. "And I didn't deserve your blows the last time. I keep my promises."

"Then why did the Ardh Rhi rush to your rescue if he isn't your lover?" He took two long strides to catch up with me—within easy striking distance. He had already scuffed his circle with his restless feet. I should have been warned by that ill omen.

"Arthur is my friend." I turned back to face him. Carradoc respected courage. I'd not give him power over me by cringing away from him now. "Do you have any idea what true friendship means?"

A moment of silence stretched between us while he strove to understand the concept of such a deep and abiding bond between people.

"Where will I sleep, Wren?"

"In the barn," I called, turning my back on him. I had work to do.

"Not with you, then."

He had my answer. I continued toward the kitchen without looking back.

The children grew. I taught them to respect all of the gods, including the Christian one. Carradoc taught the boys how to wield sword, spear, and ax, mounted and afoot. Yvain, to the despair of his father, found my forays into the forests for healing herbs and roots more fascinating than weapons. He concentrated on my lessons better than his sister, Deirdre. She had the magic talent, he had the knowledge and patience. Together they would make one formidable Merlin. If there were any followers of the old faith left by the time they matured.

Cedar and the faeries came back to my spring in the Northern woods. But only occasionally. They complained of the cold in my world and the difficulty in getting through the portal. I saw them most often in the height of summer, when heat and humidity laid a haze across the horizon and distant objects shimmered as if not really in one world or the other. On those hot, lazy days when my hair sprang into wild curls that refused taming, I could sit on the rocks near the pool and watch my friends cavort through the ferns and brush around me. They always asked why I did not bring my lover back to the spring.

I didn't know how to tell them that Arthur and I could never be lovers again.

When the boys under my care grew old enough and strong enough, they journeyed to court for final training before being admitted into the elite band of Arthur's Companions.

The day came when Yvain must join his foster brothers at court.

"Now you remember to listen to Bedewyr. He knows as much about horses as any man alive," I admonished my son as he carried his saddlebag to his waiting horse.

"Yes, Mother." He smiled at me fondly and kissed my cheek. Grown as tall as his father, he had to bend a long way down to reach me. "Even though I can speak to horses and know what they need, I'll listen to Uncle Ceffyl."

"Do you have your winter cloak?" I looked at the slimness of his pack. He couldn't possibly have enough supplies in there.

"It's high summer, Mother. I won't need a cloak until the snows come."

I glared at him, a word of warning about tricky weather at Campboglanna stalled in my throat.

"Besides, I put the cloak on the pack pony." My tall handsome son laughed lightly.

"Let him be, Mama," Deirdre said, hands on hips, an air of effrontery heavy on her shoulders. "He's fourteen and a man grown. He needs to go out into the world and prove himself, not be cosseted by a doting mother." My daughter sighed heavily, certain she knew more about life than I ever could.

"You will always be my little baby boy, Yvain. I love you. Remember to write. And come home occasionally." I followed him out to the courtyard and his waiting mounts.

Carradoc checked every bit of Yvain's saddle and tack for signs of wear. "You'll have to replace this strap by the time you reach Campboglanna," he said curtly.

"Yes," Yvain replied. He never addressed his father by name or an affectionate "Da." They rarely spoke except brief comments during arms training. Carradoc still clung to the old style of threading his beard and hair with blue warrior beads. Arthur and most of his Companions had adopted the Roman style of short hair and clean-shaven faces. Yvain cropped his hair and meticulously shaved every day in direct defiance of his father.

Carradoc raised his fist as if to cuff the insolence out of Yvain's posture. I caught his gaze, reminding him of his promise. Then he looked at his son, grown nearly as tall as his father, with the promise of strong shoulders and lithe legs. When he filled out, Yvain could retaliate for any hurts Carradoc dished out now.

My husband thought better of his actions. He retreated to the pack pony without further words. Bright red patches splotched his cheeks. Someone would hurt tonight after he expressed his rage.

"Take a long fast ride into the hills, Carradoc," I whispered as I moved to inspect the food supplies on the pack pony. "Burn your anger some way other than hitting someone."

He glared at me, continuing to clench and unclench his fist.

"Deirdre, run and fetch another loaf of journey bread from the kitchen," I instructed my daughter, turning my back on Carradoc.

Bedewyr, who had come to escort my son to Campboglanna, laughed out loud as I rearranged supplies to make room for another loaf. "We Companions have lived rough most of our lives, Wren. The boy will survive. I'll teach him how." He swung up onto his own stallion, eager to be off with his new trainee.

"You just wait until your own son leaves home, Ceffyl. You will fuss more than I." I wanted to cry. My baby had grown up before I was ready.

Yvain mounted in an easy stride. He caressed the horse's neck. Its skin twitched under his touch, and it tossed its head with light nickers and grunts. Yvain responded in kind. He and the horse made a remarkable pair. Even Ceffyl stared in wonder at the sight of them together.

"If my little Arthur is allowed to grow up, his mother and I will be glad to be rid of him," Ceffyl said through gritted teeth. "How can one five-year-old devise more mischief than all five of us at Ector's could?" He shook his head in dismay.

"Like father, like son." At last, a little lightness entered my heart. Continuity. Patterns. Our children continued the weaving of our lives.

"Come, Mama." Deirdre tucked the extra loaf into the pack. She tugged at my hand, drawing me away from the horses. "You promised to show me how to make that poultice to ease winter cough."

"Yes, but . . ."

"Good-bye, Mother." Yvain saluted me with his hand and kneed his horse into a trot.

"Say your farewells to your father, too." I reminded my son.

He nodded curtly in the vague direction of where Carradoc stood. "If he ever hurts you, you send for me," Yvain ordered quietly through clenched teeth. "I'll make sure he never hurts anyone else again."

With a jaunty salute to his sister, Yvain communicated with his horse in some mysterious manner and trotted out the gate. Bedewyr followed.

Carradoc retreated to the training ground, lashing the ground with a short whip. I didn't like the sharp crack the leather made each time he flicked his wrist.

"At last, maybe we can have some peace," Deirdre muttered. "You've been fussing over Yvain for weeks. Now can we get back to normal?"

"What is normal?" I asked around the tears that washed my cheeks. "My little boy is gone."

"Not for good. He's just riding out to meet the next challenge. You always said that we have to meet change head on and mold it rather than let it catch us unawares and create chaos."

I looked at my daughter. "Only thirteen and already wise." Blonde like her father, she had my Da's deep blue eyes and my untamable curls. She stood nose to nose with me now. A few days from now she'd be taller, more elegant, and much more beautiful.

"What were you doing when you were thirteen?" she asked, hands on hips, tossing her braids back over her shoulders. Half of one plait had worked loose into springy coils.

"I spent my thirteenth summer wandering Britain at my father's side." My mind fled back to that long ago time, the last time I had been close to my father. The last time we had shared the wonders of Britain as well as the tribulations of war with the Saxons.

Deirdre looked after the man she called father. Disgust crossed her face. Obviously she couldn't imagine the closeness Da and I had shared.

"And the following spring you married Papa and began reordering life here at Caer Noddfa. I've heard the stories, Mama. I've learned all the songs. It's time to let us grow up and go our own way."

"I know." I swallowed the lump in my throat. "But I'd like to think of you and your brother as the babies I bore. He was so tiny and helpless. But you were big and demanding and stubborn from the moment you were conceived." I ruffled her hair, further disturbing her attempts at restraining her blonde mane. "Don't leave me for a while yet, Deirdre."

"I'm still big—bigger than you anyway—and stubborn and demanding. I'm not likely to leave for a while. Gyron won't be made a Companion for at least another year—more likely two. We'll marry then. And I'll probably stay here since he won't have a permanent home while riding Arthur's Justice Circuit."

"You're far too young to have your entire life organized so completely." Now that I thought about it, she had always organized the children's games. She had patience aplenty with them. But she easily lost interest in the lessons I had to teach her unless she needed one specific piece of information for an immediate purpose.

You live in the now, baby. The past means nothing to you.

"I'm the same age as you when Papa asked for your hand," she retorted to my last statement.

Oh, Dana, was I ever as young as she?

"Gyron has already asked and I've accepted. You can't break our betrothal," she said haughtily.

"Gyron? That young pup! He is certainly not ready to marry yet." I'd raised the boy since he was two and sent him away to learn to become one of Arthur's Companions almost three years ago. I think I cried as much that day as I did today.

"We'll discuss it while you show me the proper way to mix that poultice, Mama. We have to continue to care for the people here, no matter how much we long to ride with our boys."

"Yes, Deirdre. I'm glad I still have you to take care of me."

"It's about time someone took care of you, Mama. You've taken care of all of Britain for too many years."

Quietly she led me to the stillroom where I kept our stash of healing herbs and medical supplies.

Yvain wrote home often. His gossipy letters gave me more information about Arthur than I could pry out of a dozen couriers.

Arthur didn't speak often or very much. But he spoke when necessary. Most of his words and ideas found their way into lengthy missives that traveled the country by courier. Yvain became the favorite and best known of these fast riders. He rode as if he and the horse were two halves of the same being. He continued as courier long after he was ready to be a Companion. He'd rather ride than bash heads.

Deirdre grew into a tall and graceful young woman. She married Gyron by the faery pool on her fifteenth Beltane in an ancient ceremony, both of them barefoot and crowned with flowers. Later that day they recited their vows again before Father Thomas in the village church.

Eventually age crept up on all of us. I became a grandmother one bright spring day the next year, just after my thirty-second birthday. With Deirdre's permission I took her twins, a boy and a girl, to the sacred spring and introduced the newborns to the faeries. Cedar and his friends approved. Apparently the children had been conceived here in the forest just as their mother had been sixteen years before.

And through all these years of peace and growth, the cranky old raven continued to perch on the well and screech at me every time I passed. How long do ravens normally live? As this one continued into his tenth year, and then his fifteenth, I gave up wondering, accepting his presence as part of my home. Perhaps one raven flew off and died and another took its place without me knowing. I talked to it sometimes. It stared back at me with an intensity that reminded me of my father. Father Thomas and his brood crossed themselves and muttered prayers every time they encountered the bird. They tried chasing him away. He always returned, cackling in tones that sounded like my father, too.

Couriers and messengers continued to use Caer Noddfa as a resting place—off normal routes, but I made the stop worth their while with hot meals and clean beds and peace. Through them I learned everything that happened at court. I followed the politics of Britain closely. From time to time I passed along suggestions, I reminded people to respect the land—forest, field, moor, lake, and river—no matter which god they prayed to.

Then the day came that the twins celebrated their fourth birthday. And Arthur rode through the gates of Caer Noddfa with a young

Companion at his side. Curyll at forty-five boasted a few more scars, and more wrinkles around his eyes. Maturity gave him dignity and poise. I found him more handsome than ever.

At forty I should have been beyond physical longing for any man. I wanted Curyll more now than the day we had lain together by the faery pool.

"Wren," he called to me as he dismounted. "Come see who I have brought to meet you." He delved into his deep saddlebags for gifts for his grandchildren, not that he'd ever be allowed to acknowledge them.

I hastened into the courtyard, scanning the face and figure of the tall man who grabbed Arthur's discarded reins. His eyes were a deep, fathomless brown, almost black. In all else, from golden hair to broad shoulders and long legs, he could have been Curyll twenty years ago.

"Mordred, my son, has come to Campboglanna," Arthur announced proudly. "He's to become a Companion next week in a ceremony at Camlann. You will come, Wren. Please say you will."

Chapter 61

PAPA'S tree had grown in both girth and height in the last twenty years. Some of the older branches had died and dropped. Locals gathered them almost as soon as they fell. Legends had grown up around the tree. Legends of sanctity and haunting. No two stories agreed. But the wood shed by the tree was considered valuable and lucky. It was often carved in talismans but never burned. Not even the shavings felt the touch of Tanio.

I looked around the crowd that gathered within the clearing beneath the spread of the oak's boughs. Companions and initiates formed a tightly knit circle. The few remaining retired Companions, like Carradoc, stood behind the current Companions they had sponsored. Arthur and Guinevere stood near the center at the base of the tree. The Ardh Rhi faced east just as the full moon rose. Behind the warriors I stood with the ladies and minor lords, and a few client kings with their retinues. Flowers and bright clothing adorned the spectators. Music drifted through the forest from the harps of a dozen bards. The acceptance of new Companions within Arthur's personal warband, limited to one hundred of the best and most loyal warriors, was always a great occasion.

The Companions were garbed in leather and armor as suited their profession. They held their helmets beneath their left arms. Each raised an unsheathed sword in turn until the naked blades formed a dome over the initiates. Gray hair glinted in the moonlight from the heads of more than half of the Companions. Many of the original band could retire to a more peaceful, less active life after tonight's ceremony. They looked weary and strained.

I watched carefully as my son knelt before the Ardh Rhi, placed his hands between Arthur's, and recited solemn oaths. Like all the others on this night, he ended his recitation: "By all that I hold holy, I pledge my life, my fortune, the strength of my sword, and my honor to Arthur Pendragon, Ardh Rhi of Britain." Then he rose and exchanged a kiss of peace with the man he had just sworn to obey and support with his life and his honor. Guinevere then gave him a coin, struck in the Roman style, bearing Arthur's image, as a token of the Ardh Rhi's protection of the new Companion.

Yvain stepped aside for the next initiate to repeat the process.

Bedewyr's wife jostled Guinevere's elbow as a gentle reminder for her to pass a coin to the young man who stood in front of her. She smiled and gazed into the eyes of each new Companion at the appropriate times. Otherwise her attention wandered around and around the circle of warriors, alighting most often on Lancelot. Each time she glanced his way, her features softened to wistful longing. Then guilt would harden her gaze and she turned her gaze elsewhere, only to return to Lancelot a moment later.

She still wore only white and gold. As the moon bathed her in gentle light, she seemed to shimmer and pale almost to invisibility, like her faery sire.

I couldn't see Lancelot's face. I didn't really need to. His aura broadcast his love for the brenhines. A love that could never be consummated. Guinevere had sworn to me that she would never betray Arthur.

An empathic ache grew around my heart. I, too, must remain separate from the only man I had ever truly loved.

Then it was time for Mordred, the last of the seven initiates, to swear fealty to his Ardh Rhi. A haunting unease drifted through the clearing. Discords found their way into the music from the bardic harps. Shadows writhed across the bark of the old tree as if the face caught in the whorls and crevices contorted into a deeper grimace.

The moon hid behind a cloud, plunging us all into darkness. Murmurs erupted from the crowd. Ladies shivered. Men crossed themselves and made more ancient signs against evil.

Mordred smiled and recited his oath. "By all that I hold sacred, I pledge my life, my fortune, my honor to (mumble, mumble) *the* Pendragon of Britain."

He hadn't pledged himself to Arthur, but to the Pendragon, the Ardh Rhi. If Arthur failed in his duties as arbitrator, dispenser of justice, and war leader, any of the client kings could renounce his treaty with Arthur and declare himself Pendragon. If *all* of the other kings moved to support another candidate, Arthur would be deposed.

Mordred had pledged himself to whoever claimed the title.

Across the circle of witnesses, I saw Morgaine emerge from the shadows. Her black-and-silver gown glittered in the moonlight. She smiled at her son. I saw no hint of teeth, but I smelled the sulfur and rot of the Underworld.

Then she disappeared into the shadows again.

As the moon burst forth from its hiding place, Mordred stood and exchanged his kiss of peace with Arthur. His smile twisted his face into a mockery of the goodwill and trust the kiss symbolized.

Didn't anyone notice the truth behind his manipulation of the oath? Hadn't anyone else seen Morgaine?

Apparently not. The ceremony dissolved into backslapping camaraderie and calls for wine and food. Before I could protest the mockery Mordred had made of this ritual, the entire crowd set off for Camlann, mounted or in carts, to begin the feast at the Round Table. I tried to hold Arthur back, to make him understand. His attention centered on the loving gaze that passed between Lancelot and Guinevere. Then he shifted his shoulders. The cords of his neck stood out as he composed his face into a smile and looked only at his wife.

"Come, my dear, we must join the oth–others before your acres of fl–lower decorations wilt," he said, tucking Guinevere's hand into the crook of his arm. He patted her hand possessively.

Lancelot fell into step behind them, the proper place for the Champion of the Round Table, dedicated to guarding the safety and well-being of both the Ardh Rhi and his brenhines.

"Arthur, did you see Morgaine hiding at the fringes of the crowd?" I stepped between him and his horse when a quick search of the area failed to reveal a trace of Morgaine.

"No, I didn't." Arthur looked around. "Mordred invited her. But she declined. Something about storms and aching bones. Since Lot died and Agravain succeeded to the crown, she hasn't left the islands."

"She was here. I saw her. Why would she hide when she was invited?"

Arthur shrugged and said, "She'll turn up when she's ready."

He didn't fear her at all. The years of peace had lulled him into complacency. My memories of my battle with Morgaine's demons had become more bitter. I still bore the burn scar on my wrist from where the demon had grabbed me. Perhaps my fears had made me imagine her.

Perhaps not.

The children had all grown. Father Thomas and Kalahart managed Caer Noddfa very well. Nothing called me away from Arthur's side this time. I wouldn't abandon him to the plots and manipulations he refused to see.

The feast was just another celebration. Like so many through the years, there was too much food, too much noise, and far too much wine and ale. Yvain behaved like most young men and partook too much of all that was offered. Mordred did not. Of all the Companions, new and experienced, those ready to retire, and those who were still in their prime, only Mordred kept his consumption moderate, his eyes clear, and his thoughts to himself.

After the celebration, I settled into my father's old guesthouse, not caring that I had to share it with Carradoc, Marnia, her husband, Deirdre and Gyron, their four-year-old twins, two servants, and the latest Newynog.

My education and reputation as The Merlin's daughter eased my way into the council chambers of the Ardh Rhi. But nothing I did eased me into Mordred's thoughts.

I fell into old patterns, observing from the shadows, listening, and gathering secrets like a harvest of medicinal herbs. I learned who lied, who could be trusted, who plotted against the existing pattern of political power. Arthur listened to me, nodded, and made his own decisions. But he would hear nothing ill about Mordred.

When Arthur moved his court about the country, I had to decide between staying with him and watching his constant companion, Mordred, or staying in Camlann and watching Guinevere. The Ardh Brenhines rarely traveled anymore. Campboglanna was too cold. Caerlud, the trading town the Romans used as a capital, was too crowded and dirty. Once in a while, she returned to her father's home at Carmelide where her brother Percival now ruled. But mostly Guinevere stayed at Camlann while Arthur roamed the countryside. Lancelot remained with her as Champion and protector.

I decided that Mordred offered the more immediate threat to peace in Britain.

Twenty-five years of riding had made me more comfortable on horseback. Yvain had taught me to communicate with my mount, to move with the beast in cooperation rather than against it. So when Arthur rode out of Camlann for his summer tour of the entire country, I rode next to him. Mordred rode on the other side of him.

Guinevere was right. Caerlud was very noisy, crowded, and dirty. Ships plied the River Thames at every hour of the day and night, loading and unloading, docking and setting sail. Nearly one hundred years after the Romans had sailed away from this bustling port, the town had filled to the brim and spilled over the sides of the walls like a too full quaiche of ale.

Fiercely independent and quarrelsome, the city dwellers barely recognized Arthur's right to govern them. They refused allegiance or obedience to any one king or lord. Arthur entered the city upon invitation only and remained only as long as there remained disputes for him to settle. New disputes cropped up daily, and his invitation to stay was reluctantly extended by a gaggle of proud merchants.

After the dozen men who ruled trading empires had left Arthur's villa at the end of the day's petitions, caps in hand, but heads and shoulders unbowed, Arthur and I relaxed over a cup of wine. We fell into an easy pattern of quiet talk and laughter—just like an old married couple. He broke a long quiet spell by aptly imitating the haughty disdain of Peter the flax trader who had led the committee of merchants. Arthur tilted his head so far back that when he looked down his nose he had to cross his eyes to see. The clipped nasal tones of his dissertation on the failings of the wine, the weather, the crop, the sea captains, and all else so precisely mimicked the flax trader I couldn't help but laugh.

Arthur clutched his sides trying to hold in his own mirth until he swallowed his last gulp of wine. He didn't succeed. The red droplets sprayed out in a shower that looked like blood dribbling down his mouth.

A violent premonition of watching him die with blood streaming from his mouth, sobered my laughter instantly.

"What is it, Wren?" he asked, also calming his explosion of laughter.

"I . . . I saw you die."

"We all die, Wren. We are both getting old. You are a grand-mother after all, though still damned beautiful. I wish I could say that *we* are grandparents. The twins are delightful."

"Curyll. I saw you as you will be when you die." I kept staring into the distance, trying to make sense of the vision.

"I hope I was ancient and decrepit. There is still so much work to do to stabilize the peace and prosperity of Britain. One generation isn't enough. Some of the young ones accept peace as a way of life now, but too many of the older warriors with nothing but time on their hands and drink in their guts fill the heads of our youth with grand stories of glorious deeds and valiant deaths on the battlefield. Too many restless youths chafe at peace. Wild stories of the adventures of Grail quests aren't enough to divert them. They need to burn off their energy by bashing heads and slashing enemies."

"I know," I replied, rather than tell him the vision had shown him no older than he was now. No older . . . no more time.

"Your Highness," a young courier stood in the doorway, a piece of stained and torn parchment clutched in his fist. Dark rings circled his eyes with fatigue. Sweat and dust clung to his face. He swayed ever so slightly.

"What news from Camlann, Segurades?" Arthur stood and took the parchment from the man's hand, opening it before he finished speaking.

"Queen Morgaine has come to court, wanting to visit her sons," the courier said quietly.

I heard the words he didn't say aloud. Morgaine had settled in at Camlann with no intention of leaving.

"The letter is from Lancelot, Wren. Um—Segurades, go rest and eat. And help yourself to a bath," Arthur said to the courier, clearly dismissing him before he said anything further.

"Morgaine whispers half truths and upsets everyone with her in-nuendos," I said, not having to read the letter to know. "What rumors does she spread to undermine your authority now?"

"How did you know?" Arthur asked. He looked at me with a touch of fear. I sensed he wanted to cross himself but was afraid to risk my disapproval. "I guess I shouldn't have to ask that, Wren. You are The Merlin, daughter of The Merlin. You knew all along."

"Yes," I replied.

"Lancelot warns me that Morgaine preaches to Guinevere that

you and I have renewed the affair we had as children. She has little doubt that either or both of your children are mine as well. Guinevere is packing to go home to her brother, permanently."

"We never had an affair, Curyll."

"Only one afternoon by the pool with faeries cavorting about our heads." He looked wistfully into the distance. "But you have always been my friend, Wren. Sometimes my only friend."

"I will always be your friend, Curyll."

He looked at the letter again and frowned. "I have to go back to Camlann. I ride at dawn."

"What else does the letter say, Curyll?"

"Nimuë is with Morgaine. More than eighteen years have passed since I banished your father's murderer. I failed to renew the decree when it expired at seven years because I never thought she'd dare return to Britain. She is safe from my laws." He paused and looked at the parchment again. "They have within their entourage a young warrior-priest who looks too much like your father, but so far Nimuë has not claimed him as her son, or the son of Myrddin Emrys. Cai and Bedewyr are worried."

"I'll tell the others to start packing." I rose to leave. He grabbed my hand to keep me in place.

"Stay with me a while, Wren."

"I don't think that would be wise, Your Highness, considering the messages you just received."

"I need to talk. I can trust you, Wren."

"You need to rest. Our trust of each other hasn't been questioned. Our willpower has. I choose not to put it to the test yet again."

"Hood up, Myrddin, eyes lowered, and hands tucked into your sleeves," Nimuë ordered her son.

"My heritage is as proud as any, Mother. I'll stand straight and bow to no man." The young man stared at her defiantly. He'd done that all too often since Morgaine had taken him into her bed to teach him the joys of sex.

This tall young man was the only person she had been able to control. For most of his life he never questioned her motives or means in achieving power. Perhaps if she had initiated him, rather than delegating that chore to Morgaine, he'd not challenge her now.

"Soon, Myrddin," she placated him. "Soon Mordred will be Ardh Rhi and you his Merlin. But for now we must show the world our Christian guise. Our success lies in never, ever betraying our true mission to any one," she snapped. Her back hurt more than usual after the agonizing journey to Camlann. Morgaine's luxurious barge could only carry them so far before she had to mount a horse. She'd put up with the constant jolting rather than show weakness by arriving in a litter.

If only Lancelot and Guinevere hadn't taken so long to succumb to temptation, she and Morgaine would have implemented their plan years ago, before the bone disease finished the twisting of her spine that the demon had started. Perhaps the dream she had sent Lancelot all those years ago to come to Camlann hadn't been powerful enough.

"We must attack with strength, Mother, not cower behind disguises and prayers." Myrddin paced their small chamber, leaving his hood down and his hands swinging freely.

"Just until Arthur leaves Britain chasing after his errant wife. He'll never return. Then all of Britain is ours." She sat painfully, then eased her back against the piles of cushions she needed. With a sigh of relief, she reclined and swung her feet up. The pain still didn't go away. It merely waned for a time.

She needed another dose of Morgaine's poppy juice. But she also needed her wits about her.

After she had seen the end of Wren and Arthur, she could indulge in all of the drugs necessary. Wren was to blame for the constant pain. If Wren hadn't murdered her demon, she'd have had enough magic to straighten her spine. If Wren hadn't seduced Arthur into banishing her, she'd not have had to put up with the bone-chilling cold and damp of the Orcades for so many years.

"They come," Myrddin said from the doorway.

"Cernunnos take them now! I just got comfortable."

"Lean on me, Mother." Myrddin stretched out his strong young arm to help her rise. Solicitous of her comfort like a good son. He treated her like an old woman.

At least Mordred found her desirable. When all the lights were out and they had only their hands to see with.

"Is Carradoc with Wren?" she asked as she rolled to her side and eased her legs over the side of the bed.

"I don't see my grandfather among the escort," Myrddin said.

Exile had separated the boy as well as Nimuë from Carradoc. At first her father had come to the Orcades often. But then he'd retired back to Caer Tair Cigfran—Nimuë refused to think of her ancestral caer by the noxious name Wren had given it. He'd been eager to share her bed while in Morgaine's court.

Would he still find her desirable? She prayed he would. She had no other weapons of control. Her revenge against Wren would not be complete until Carradoc renounced his wife once and for all and returned to his daughter forever.

Curse these overly modest Christian robes. She couldn't divert men's gazes away from her twisted back and onto her full breasts and slim waist in these clothes.

"Soon, Mother. We can discard these disguises soon," Myrrdin chuckled. He'd read her mind again. He did that too often. She'd had too much poppy juice if she couldn't keep him out of her mind.

I've grown too strong, Mother. I command more magic than you can dream of, and I don't need a demon to give me strength.

Chapter 62

"WHAT do you mean, my wife is fled?" Arthur roared as he stomped into the Long Hall at Camlann.

Morgaine stood proud and tall between Arthur's chair and the always unoccupied seat to his left—the Siege Perilous reserved for the one perfect Companion. Satisfaction beamed from Morgaine's pale white skin. Her clouds of black hair crackled with energy.

I wondered if she dared sit in the unmarked chair. Legend proclaimed that only an honest Companion pure of heart and innocent of sin could sit there without being burned to ash.

She'd never survive that test. As far as I knew, no one had tried the chair.

Behind Morgaine stood Nimuë and a young man who sported the same bright auburn hair and green eyes as Carradoc's eldest daughter. I searched their faces for the resemblance to my father. Tall and slender, the man had a similar build to Myrddin Emrys. His nose and clean-shaven chin could resemble any man. Da had worn a beard for as long as I had known him, disguising the shape of his face. Beyond that I couldn't tell. Their auras revealed nothing.

Nimuë still stood awkwardly with the drooping left shoulder. I checked her quickly for the presence of a demon with every sense I could muster. If she still carried one, she hid it very well. But her spine seemed permanently twisted. The pain must be excruciating.

My healer's sense wanted to gather a crone and a maiden and reach out to straighten her back. As the daughter of the murdered Merlin I refused to aid her in any way.

I slid into my usual silent place behind a massive oak pillar. I draped shadows around me without thinking.

"I told your insipid little wife the truth," Morgaine replied. "The white-and-gold brenhines had no choice but to flee the poison you bring to Britain."

"W–what p–poison?" Arthur struggled to remain calm. I knew him too well to miss the tension in his back and shoulders. Too many people crowded the hall for him to reveal his true emotions. But his speech patterns dissolved.

Morgaine had chosen her stage well.

"The poison of your infidelity with the witch."

Both Arthur and I flinched at the term the Christians used to denounce those who still followed the Goddess. In this case, Morgaine's statement could mean either her or me.

"You. Lie. You m–must leave."

"I have renounced the evils of the old religion and accepted Jesu Christus!" Morgaine spread her arms as if preaching, revealing a large gold cross on a chain around her neck. "I tell the truth so that we may all be cleansed of your sin of adultery."

The people crowding into the hall crossed themselves. No priest was present, though. Why? There was always a priest hanging around somewhere, Gildas the chronicler if no one else.

"Have you taken baptism?" I asked innocently, keeping my voice anonymous within the crowd. Her demons wouldn't be able to use her as a host body once she truly accepted the sacrament.

Morgaine's gaze focused on the direction of my voice, but I kept hidden behind my pillar within my shadows.

"How dare you allow your pet witch, your adulterous witch, to question my faith?" Morgaine screamed in outrage. She clutched her cross with both hands and rolled her eyes skyward. She still hadn't answered my question.

More mumbling and crossings from the crowd.

"You l–lie to gain p–power for you–yourself. You h–harbor the m–m–murderess N–Nimuë. Leave. Now."

"Think again, Arthur!" Morgaine spat her words. "Guinevere has fled with Lancelot, her lover. They sailed yesterday for Armorica, Less Britain, on the continent. Your client kings have been informed that your pet witch has weakened you to the point you can't satisfy your own wife, let alone beget any heirs. You need my son as your heir and me, your sister, to rally the kings to your banner."

"I do n–not n–eed you, Morgaine."

"But you need the Christians. My son and I are Christians. She," Morgaine pointed directly to my hiding place. "She brings death and betrayal with her witchcraft and her pagan gods."

"I ride with my Companions at dawn." Decision returned force to Arthur's words. "We sail from Porchester with the noon tide! You, Morgaine, will be on a ship for the Orcades tonight. And you will take Nimuë with you. I b—banish her again for the crime of murder."

Morgaine smiled knowingly. I knew she'd be back as soon as Arthur's ship disappeared beyond the horizon.

"You can't leave Mordred as your regent while you sail off on this wild goose chase!" I protested loudly when Arthur and I were alone once more. "Mordred is too young." Arthur wouldn't hear the argument that he was also too much under his mother's influence.

"I was younger than Mordred when I became Ardh Rhi." Arthur played with the heavy royal seal of a dragon rampant. He held it in both hands, examining it from all sides.

"You were a proven war leader, tested and honed in battle. Men respected you. Mordred is none of those things. Send for Bedewyr or Cai. Agravain, Gwalchmai, or Gaheris would be better choices if you must choose one of your nephews."

Panic gibbered inside my head like one of Morgaine's demons. My father must have felt like this as he watched his vision of disaster come true, no matter what he did to prevent it. If I had stayed at Camlann to reassure Guinevere that Arthur and I were not lovers, then Mordred would have had a free hand with Arthur—poisoning his thoughts or his body. By going with Arthur and watching Mordred, I had left the door open for Morgaine to preach malicious lies in vulnerable Guinevere's ear.

"Agravain, Gwalchmai, and Gaheris are not my sons." Arthur stared at me, his jaw firm. Every bit of his stubbornness and determination went into his expression.

"Do you plan to tell the world that Mordred is your son? How will you explain that when your crown is already in jeopardy for the lesser sin of adultery? By both you and your brenhines."

"I don't need to explain anything. I need only prove myself in battle once more. I've done it hundreds of times."

"You are twenty years older than when you battled Saxons on a daily basis."

He shrugged as if stiffening joints and tired muscles didn't matter.

"This is Lancelot and Guinevere," I argued. "Lancelot is on his home ground in Armorica. He's waited over twenty years to openly love Guinevere. He won't give her up easily."

"Then we will both die in battle."

"Leaving Britain in the hands of Mordred, Morgaine's son, the only son she raised, the only son she can influence."

"Why must you persist in your persecution of Mordred?" Arthur turned on me, still juggling the great seal in both hands, symbol of his authority, easily recognized.

"Because I saw demons eating at his soul." I held up my demon-scarred wrist. "Because his mother has never ceased undermining your authority." *Because she and Nimuë are allies.* Together they commanded a great deal more cunning and demonic power than either could alone.

"I have promised Mordred the regency in public. He deserves the opportunity to prove himself. My other councillors agree. *They* trust and respect him."

"Then appoint another councillor as co-regent. Protect yourself with an older guiding voice behind Mordred's, someone who can act decisively when—if—Mordred makes a mistake. Maintain a balance of authority, Arthur." I deliberately appealed to his kingship by using his real name. Bonds of affection and nicknames had no place in this argument.

"An older, wiser voice. Yours perhaps, Wren?" He cocked one eyebrow in a mockery of my father's expression.

"No. I have never desired power. I wish only the safety of the kingdom."

"Nevertheless, you are co-regent." He split the seal into two halves, handing me one of them. He must have had it broken earlier, this was not a spontaneous decision. "You are an older, wiser voice who can counteract Morgaine with magic as well as words. That is where you will be needed. Now leave me, I have much to prepare."

"Making me co-regent will only intensify the rumors that I am your mistress. Guinevere will never return to you while I am here."

"That doesn't matter now. A king proves his virility by scattering his seed. When a queen does the same, she proves only the king's weakness. I must defend my honor on the field of battle in order to defend my kingdom."

"Only three of your kings and the Companions ride with you. And the Companions are of two minds. Lancelot is one of their own."

"He betrayed me. Twenty years I have been able to ignore them, pretend I didn't see the love in their eyes, that I didn't suspect she crept into his bed whenever I left Camlann. Twenty years! Why must it all explode now, just when Britain has gotten used to peace?"

Nothing I could say would ease the anguish I sensed in his heart.

"Three kings with their warbands and the Companions will be enough for now. The others will rally to my side when I am victorious. They always wait to side with the winner. The kings won't cause trouble while I'm gone. Others will. I've done what I could to protect Britain by making you co-regent."

"What am I supposed to do if Morgaine and Nimuë come back? If Mordred rescinds your banishment and welcomes his mother with open arms?"

"You can watch them and prevent them from working sorcery. You can counter their whispers and innuendos. Now leave me, please, before I forget that you and I are only friends." He closed his eyes and held his clenched fists firmly at his side.

I wanted desperately to gather him in my arms and hold him there forever. The time was fast approaching when I would hold him one more time as I prepared his dead body for the grave.

We both knew it.

"Be careful, Curyll." I kissed his cheek and fled before tears betrayed me.

"You, too, Wren."

The dust had barely settled behind Arthur and his Companions when Mordred rescinded the edict of banishment for his mother and Nimuë. They returned to Camlann about noon the day after Arthur sailed for the continent. Carradoc rode into the caer with a small warband less than an hour later.

Nimuë must have contacted him *before* this entire mess began for him to arrive in so timely a manner.

At the evening meal, Nimuë introduced the young man who had

hovered beside her as her son Myrddin Emrys, and therefore the proper heir to the title of The Merlin. She had even named him Myrddin Emrys.

I didn't use the title of The Merlin. Others applied it to me. I should be called The Morrigan, but I didn't reside in Avalon's lakeside village aloof from the world, so people forgot that title. I resented this young man who expected to supplant my place as adviser to the Ardh Rhi and leader of any who might still follow the Goddess. He wore an ornate Christian cross as did his mother and all of Morgaine's party.

If he truly believed in Jesu Christus, he couldn't be The Merlin!

None of them managed a straight answer when asked about their baptism.

My protests went unheard. My demands for proof of Myrddin's paternity met with disdain. Nimuë played the poor, misunderstood widow well. Sympathy for her raising the fine, upstanding young man on her own banished their memory of outrage of how she had brought about my father's downfall.

The next day, Morgaine ordered the felling of Da's oak tree.

"You will do no such thing!" I yelled in protest. All of Arthur's remaining councillors were gathered at the Round Table. Only a few Companions had stayed behind, the older men who would defend Camlann but no longer had the vigor to sail off to war. Carradoc sat among them, next to Nimuë. She sat next to Morgaine, with Mordred on the other side of his mother. I had been pushed several places away from my co-regent. Clearly, Morgaine held more sway with Mordred than I.

"You can't stop me, witch!" Morgaine hissed. "The tree embodies all that is evil about you and your damned collection of impotent gods."

I had yet to hear her speak of Christianity as her true faith. All her religious discussions centered only on my Goddess and my witchcraft.

Nimuë remained quiet, patting her father's hand in mute sympathy for my alleged transgressions.

"I can and will keep you from felling a perfectly healthy tree for no reason but to satisfy your personal whim. Or is it Nimuë who desires the destruction of my father's grave within the roots of the tree? The grave of her son's father. The grave of a man we all held to be wise and a great mentor to our Ardh Rhi and his father before him."

Silence sat heavy around the huge table. The old ways were so far off that almost no one present remembered how we honored trees as gifts from the Goddess, to be used only when necessary—akin to asking an animal's forgiveness before hunting it and making certain that meat, hide, sinew, hooves, and bone were all put to good use. We honored the prey we hunted as well as the trees we used.

"My warriors will fell the tree," Morgaine announced.

"Mother." Mordred patted her hand affectionately. "We don't need the tree. The Merlin's influence is dead." He looked at me and smiled knowingly, silently including me in his proclamation.

I looked more closely at the dozen men who sat around the table. All were close companions of Mordred. They drank together, practiced swordplay together, whored together. Age and weariness hadn't kept them home. Loyalty to Mordred had. Every one of them nodded in silent agreement with my co-regent.

"I want the tree down." Morgaine pounded her fist into the table. "I must know that The Merlin's spirit is extinguished forever. As long as the tree stands, he is alive within it!" She stood up so hastily, her heavy chair crashed backward. Then she pounded the table with both fists. Red blotches stained her cheeks.

"Your zealous faith, madam, is appreciated," Myrddin said, bowing his head and crossing himself. He did that too frequently for me to believe in his sincerity—more like a memorized gesture than a true act of faith. "But chopping down a healthy tree is not the answer. We must purify the site and build a church there. A church dedicated to the Holy Virgin Mother, Mary."

I kept my mouth shut. From what I knew of the Mother of Jesus, she resembled the Goddess in every aspect but name. I'd allow a church dedicated to her next to the tree, though Dana, my Goddess, didn't require buildings as the place of worship.

Mordred rushed through the other business of the day. All of it innocuous, not requiring us to affix the royal seal to a document. As soon as I could, I slipped out of Camlann and ran to the nearby forest. I couldn't find Newynog. She was in heat and had her own business to attend to.

An aura of welcome enveloped me the moment I entered the

clearing around the ancient oak. I traced the outline of a face in the whorls of bark.

"Oh, Da, I miss you. You would have persuaded Arthur to appoint a different regent. You foresaw the disaster with Lancelot and Guinevere. What would you have done to prevent it?"

Nothing. 'Tis fated to be.

I looked around for the source of the voice. Only a raven croaked in the tree branches above me.

The same raven that haunted the well back home?

"Not every vision has to come to pass." I reminded myself. "We who have the gift of prophecy are the tools of the gods. Our destiny is to use our visions to help people make choices, weave a better life pattern." But no alternatives came to my mind.

You saw Curyll's death.

"Yes. And I know I can't do anything to prevent it." Morgaine had schemed and maneuvered me to a position devoid of choices.

All you can do is curb Mordred's excesses as long as possible.

"How, Da?" I knew the voice was born of my imagination. But speaking aloud helped me sort through the problems.

Make certain that all of Britain remembers Arthur's dreams. Government must rule through justice and law. Peace can work. Honor and promises are important.

The raven croaked a raucous warning above.

Horses pounded the well-worn track to the clearing.

I hadn't much time. Myrddin could easily damage the tree while building his church. I had to protect it.

I walked a path deosil, along the path of the sun and light, around the base of the tree, scattering herbs and muttering spells of protection. I wound my path into a tight spiral, moving even closer to the trunk. Not much protection. All I could manage for the moment.

Mordred, Morgaine, and Carradoc reined in their horses as I finished the last circuit of the tree and turned to face them.

All three pulled their mounts to a halt so violently, their horses reared. The beasts pawed the air with their iron-shod hooves. An intimidating display. If I hadn't seen Carradoc teach my boys to do the same when engaging an enemy, I might have been frightened.

I should have been.

Myrddin sat his horse just behind them, a silent observer—like a priest at an execution.

None of them wore crosses now. They had no need to impress the Christians at court.

Carradoc jumped off his war stallion and stalked toward me. His mailed fists clenched. Armor! Why would he wear armor this close to the capital?

Then he backhanded me across the face.

"Whore!" he roared and repeated the blow.

Through the roaring pain in my head, I heard Mordred and his mother giggle.

Chapter 63

I fell to the ground, clutching my cheek, too stunned to speak or fight back. The gash inflicted by the metal links of Carradoc's armor bled freely. It burned clear through to my teeth.

I tried to rise. Protest. Ward off his next blow. He struck me again and again, beating me down before I could recover my wits or strength. I tasted blood. More blood on my face. Pain. Sharp. Dull. Spreading. Blades of pain shot through my veins.

The raven swooped down, flying into Carradoc's face. It tried to peck his eyes. Carradoc brushed the bird aside with one mighty sweep of his arm while he kicked my ribs and stomach. The raven staggered away, wings flapping out of rhythm, feathers flying in all directions. Rage distorted Carradoc's face.

"There is no one left to protect you from what you deserve. No one, whore!" Carradoc screamed. "Were you ever faithful to me? You deprived me of a son. You and that piss-poor excuse for an Ardh Rhi betrayed me from the day we were married. Maybe even before. Witches can fake virginity time and again."

"I keep my promises," I whispered.

He didn't listen.

"I keep my promises," I repeated louder.

"Liar!" Carradoc's heavy boot landed in my ribs once again.

"I divorce you, Carradoc." I'd said it once before. One more time and he'd no longer have the right to beat me, or kill me.

"I div . . ."

He hit me again in the jaw, stopping my words. With the last of my strength I kicked out. Carradoc fell over my outstretched foot. He landed atop me, driving his metal-encased fist into my belly.

I retched and curled into a fetal ball. The exposed roots of the tree seemed to cradle me, begin to grow around me. The roots became my father's arms. I could see him through my left eye though it was swollen shut and filled with blood. I shrank into the enfolding protection of the tree—the Worldtree that bonded all of the worlds together.

Through a haze of red I watched Carradoc lift his foot to kick me in the head. *Get it over with!* I no longer had the strength to speak. *Kill me and end this pain.*

"Leave her, Carradoc," Mordred said. "The tree already takes her. The ravens wait in the branches to pluck out her dead eyes. Get her half of the seal. We have to get back to Camlann."

Carradoc hesitated a moment, then lowered his foot. Dimly, I felt him rummaging through the sack at my waist. He'd not find the seal.

Pain engulfed my entire being. All I could do was pray for a quick end. I'd die in Da's arms. Where I belonged. *No,* another voice whispered into my mind. Da's voice? *You belong with Arthur, the man you love. The man you have loved all your life.*

"We have to cut down the tree," Morgaine protested. I think she lifted an ax from her saddlebag. She had it in her hands as she stepped up to the tree.

Part of me trembled, waiting for her killing blow. Another part of me tried to rise up and protect the tree. I hadn't the strength or the will to move and invoke more pain. Crippling pain.

Her first vicious blow sent tremors through the ground. I screamed in new pain, as if the blow had cut into me as well as the tree. The earth trembled and the sky darkened.

Hush, Wren. Let them think you die. Was that the voice of my father or of the raven that still squawked up in the tree? A dozen of its fellows joined the chorus.

"Later, Mother," Mordred said. "We'll let Lady Arylwren die here, too. When her spirit is trapped within the tree, we'll chop it down and be rid of both her and her father forever."

Yes. Let me die here with Da.

Hold on, Wren. Hold on for Curyll.

A stiff wind rattled the upper branches of the oak. Chills swept over me, and I smelled salt heavy in the air. Thunder rolled in the distance. Perhaps I only heard Myrddin galloping away to tell his mother that I died.

"It's going to rain soon. Carradoc, get the damned seal and let's go!" Mordred's horse pranced in an uneasy circle.

"She doesn't have it on her."

"Where could she have hidden it? We searched her room." Mordred looked to the sky. "We'll find it later. I don't want to get wet. It's not fitting for the Ardh Rhi to return to his capital wet and bedraggled." He laughed and reared his horse again, spinning it in place.

Carradoc left me as the first icy drops of rain fell through the canopy of tree branches.

It isn't supposed to end like this! the raven croaked.

Tears mingled with my blood and the rain.

"Mama?"

A quiet voice roused me from pain-wracked nightmares. A dog's warm tongue licked blood and rain from my face. I shivered violently in the cold and wet. The wind, born in the coldest reaches of the Western Sea, blew through the clearing. More rain fell. I shuddered again and wished I hadn't. Every portion of my body ached or bled or both.

"Dana help us. He's nearly killed you," Deirdre sobbed.

A cloak dropped over me. The huge dog whined and stood over me, blocking the rain, adding her own body warmth to me. My chill eased a little. But soon the cloak and the dog were soaked, too.

"Deirdre. Flee, now. He'll kill you," I whispered through broken lips. "Take Newynog. She'll protect you." As she hadn't protected me when I needed her most.

"Not without you, Mama. If I'd known what they would do, I'd have stopped them. Somehow. Oh, Mama, what do I do first?"

"Leave me. I die." Feebly I pushed aside the dog's cleaning tongue.

"No, you won't die. I won't let you."

"Can't save me."

"Yes, I can. I've rigged a litter behind my horse. I'll take you to Avalon."

"The twins. Take twins . . . flee. Faeries . . . pool . . . protect . . . from Carradoc."

"The twins are safe. I sent them to Father Thomas with their nurse. Carradoc won't leave Camlann for a while yet. Dana, help me, I wish Gyron hadn't sailed with Arthur. He'd have stopped Carradoc. Lie still, Mama. I'll bring the horse closer." Her voice faded and wavered. I don't know if she moved away or if I did.

"Carradoc . . . He'll find me . . . Honor questioned."

"That man has no honor. I'm glad he's not my father. He won't look for you anytime soon, though. Mordred has declared Arthur dead, shipwrecked in this storm. Morgaine saw it in a vision, or so she claims. The kings who remained behind have proclaimed Mordred Ardh Rhi. But there are only three of them, Melwas shifts his allegiance with the wind. There aren't enough of them to uphold the election if challenged. Carradoc sits at Mordred's right hand as Champion. That satisfies his honor more than killing you and publicly humiliating me. Why didn't you divorce him years ago?"

"Promises made in a circle."

"Too bad he doesn't believe in promises like you do."

"The seal. Mordred . . . can't rule without it."

"He's tearing the fortress apart looking for your half." Deirdre ran her hands down my arms and legs looking for broken bones. Then down my back. She straightened me gradually, seeking the worst of the hurts.

I think I screamed as she touched my ribs and belly. Blackness for several moments. A burning mission brought me back to semiconsciousness. "I . . . must go back. Can't let him find seal."

"I have it with me, Mama. I sought you in a scrying bowl. I saw you hide it in the mud beside a spring two hundred paces north of this place. Then I saw . . . I saw this." A catch in her voice told me just how badly hurt I was. As if the knife-sharp pain didn't.

"Good girl."

"I also stole Mordred's half. He'll have to wait for a new one to be struck before he can be crowned." She resumed her efficient examination, and gentle washing of my face.

A little coherency returned to me. If my jaw didn't hurt so badly, I could speak better. I couldn't tell if Carradoc had broken it or not. "Mordred needs . . . Excalibur. It must pass . . . to him. Arthur . . . not part from it."

"Unless the sword is at the bottom of the sea with Arthur and the Companions." Deirdre bound my ribs tightly with bandages she had brought with her. I groaned with each movement. Then, miraculously, the pain faded from sharp to dull. I could breathe without fear or the feeling of knives penetrating my lungs.

"Arthur lives," I asserted. I would know when he died. I'd sense it as I had Da's passing. When Curyll died, I wouldn't long survive him. The fact that I still lived meant that he did, too. That had been the only comforting part of my vision.

I think I fainted again. But not for long. Every bone and muscle in my body screamed when Deirdre lifted my shoulders and dragged me to the triangular litter behind the horse. I couldn't suppress a sharp cry.

Newynog whined in distress. She licked and nuzzled me again, all she could do to ease my hurts.

"I'm sorry, Mama. I don't want to hurt you. But we have to leave now. We have to get you to Avalon."

"Avalon . . . deserted." The ache in my jaw sharpened.

"I know. No one will look for us there."

My daughter tried her best to make our journey gentle. Once we were well beyond Camlann, she eased up onto the old Roman road. The litter jostled less moving across the smooth paving stones than through open forest. But on that road we were more exposed to the storm that continued to rage.

"Avalon will flood," I said. I didn't know if Deirdre heard me or not. She kneed the horse into moving faster.

Twenty miles of straight road took us the better part of a night and a day to travel. Deirdre stopped frequently to bind my wounds, feed me a few sips of water, brush my sopping hair out of my eyes. Newynog stayed close, giving me her warmth whenever we stopped. But she couldn't ride in the litter with me. The horse hadn't the strength to drag both of us.

I remember crying out. I remember the fever dreams of ravens pecking out my eyes. Mercifully I passed most of the trip unconscious.

We never made it to Avalon. Spring had been wet. Summer barely acknowledged. Every creek and river filled to overflowing with the constant downpour. Avalon was cut off, the lake village drowning and deserted. We couldn't even get to the tor to climb above the flood. Arthur had built new fortifications up there occupied by Melwas. We couldn't be certain he'd shelter us if we managed to climb to his doorstep.

Resourceful Deirdre found a deserted crofter's cottage. The sagging thatched roof leaked. Wild pigs rooted in the corners. But the hearth drew smoke upward and burned clear. A smidgen of warmth penetrated my dreams.

I awoke to the smells of a potion that reeked of betony. Deirdre bathed my wounds with it. She tore up her own shift to renew the binding on my cracked ribs. Then she forced another noxious potion down my throat.

"Where did you learn to mix that awful brew?" I nearly spat out the thick oily mess. My jaw worked. Carradoc hadn't managed to break it after all.

But my face must be a mosaic of bruises.

" 'Tis your own remedy, Mama. You used it on Yvain and Gyron every time they bashed each other in the head too often."

"I couldn't have. It's too awful."

"Now you know what you put the rest of us through." She chuckled as she forced more of the bitter brew through my teeth.

Willow bark and mullein I recognized. More betony and the oil of a secret plant from the marshes around Avalon. It shouldn't taste that foul. But it did.

It also put me back to sleep.

When I woke again, I found my left arm tightly bound in a splint and five stitches closing a scalp wound. I could barely breathe from the bandages wrapped around my middle. The pain returned like an unwanted relative. Almost bearable for a very short time.

"Time to sit up, Mama. I don't want those ribs to interfere with your breathing."

"Who told Carradoc that he is not your father?" I asked.

"Nimuë," Deirdre replied. "Who else would dare? Morgaine confirmed it with another vision." She clamped her mouth shut on her next sentence.

"What else did they tell him?"

She looked back at me with Da's blue eyes framed by Curyll's blond hair, tangled now into a mass of damp curls. The firm set of her jaw, so very like her father's, told me she wouldn't willingly say more.

But she was my daughter. I knew her too well.

"The one and only time I made love with Arthur, I truly believed Carradoc dead. I did not break my promise of fidelity," I reassured her.

"I know that, Mama. I've known since I was old enough to reckon days and make sense of the stories people tell. Arthur sent Carradoc home quite suddenly after allowing him to linger in the army camp for over a year. I didn't know that Arthur was my father, but I hoped he was. Most any father would be better than Carradoc."

"At least he didn't use you like he did Nimuë and Berminia. He didn't have Beltane festivals to force you. That is one thing you can thank Father Thomas for."

"Nimuë's son was sired by Carradoc, not Grandda." She looked at me frankly, not willing to spare the hurt.

"How do you know?" I tried sitting up straighter, shocked into alertness. I moaned and slid back into my slump against the saddlebags.

"I overheard Nimuë tell Carradoc. She was two months' pregnant when she finally managed to seduce The Merlin. She did it to make the world believe The Merlin sired the child. She was laughing that Grandda couldn't . . . was scarred and impotent."

Heat drained out of my face. Nimuë had seduced a nearly impotent man to delude the world into believing the wrong man sired her child. I had done the same thing.

"I know about your grandfather. The gods marked him for an early transgression. He bore the constant reminder that he must remain celibate the rest of his life."

"Why? Why would the gods demand such a thing of him?"

"In the old days, Druids only learned to prophesy after many years of serious study, of fasting and purification. The gods would take away the gift if the prophet had sex after they had their first vision. From that day forth, they remained celibate." I lay back, resting before I continued the tale. Deirdre forced some soothing water down my throat. And more of the bitter potion.

"Da had his first vision of the future before his fifth birthday." I coughed and needed to sleep again. But I had to finish the story, for my benefit as well as Deirdre's. "Prophecy is a gift and a curse from the gods. After Da lay with my mother one Beltane, the gods decreed that his destiny was not yet fulfilled. They gave him a reprieve, but only so long as he remained celibate."

"You didn't lose your ability to see the future, Mama."

"My life pattern is different from Da's." I provided the anchor of continuity to my descendants. They must remember the lessons taught by Arthur and The Merlin. My work was not yet finished.

A husband and children by Curyll, the Goddess had promised me long ago. Children. Plural.

"I need sleep." And a dream of the next, and last, time I would be with my beloved Curyll. I closed my eye—the left one was still swollen shut—to hide the tears that prickled behind both eyelids. Arthur and Deirdre were my destiny. Arthur must die soon. I had seen it. And so would I.

But I would give birth to one more baby. Arthur's child.

He's not dead yet. There is still so much for us to do, a raven croaked using my father's voice.

Chapter 64

IN another life I might have been content to remain in the cottage, repairing it, living off the land, doling out my simple cures to the locals, playing with Newynog's next batch of puppies when they came.

But I fretted for news of Arthur. Deirdre fretted for the welfare of her twins and her husband.

The wind and the trees whispered of a great battle and many deaths. Where and who didn't matter to them. Arthur lived. I knew nothing else.

Long before I should have ridden, Deirdre, Newynog, and I headed north. I couldn't wait any longer.

"I should not have stayed away so long," I murmured as I gazed up at Caer Noddfa from the edge of the forest. The sight of my familiar home filled me with warmth and longing. I stood beside Deirdre's horse, hanging onto the bridle, much as I had stood beside Carradoc's horse that long ago day when I first came here. Walking was once more easier than riding.

"That's Carradoc's banner," Deirdre pointed to the limp flag hanging from the standard by the front gates. I couldn't see the two stags butting heads within the folds of cloth. I didn't need to, to know that the lord of the caer was in residence.

A smell of death hovered around the caer like an aura of evil. Fear hovered over the village like a miasma of black smoke.

Not a breath of air stirred on this hot summer day.

My vision rocked forward and back, superimposing my first view of the dark and forbidding buildings with the current sight. The concussion played tricks with my memories. I saw the timber fortifications above the stone foundations crumble in waves of smoke and flame. Then I saw them whole and unbreached. My injured eye blurred and refocused at odd moments, so I was never quite certain what I saw or when. Was this reality or a vision of the future, or even the distant past?

As we watched, a squad of soldiers marched five villagers up the twisting processional way to the fortress. The local men and women were bound together by a long rope that looped around their ankles and stretched to the next prisoner. Their hands were lashed to the ends of heavy wooden yokes that pressed down on their shoulders.

"What is he doing?" I started forward, to protest this rough treatment of *my* villagers. My friends.

"No, Mama." Deirdre held me back. "My guess is that he's trying to flush you out by torturing your supporters." She pointed to thick smoke pouring out of the roof of one of the cottages. The one that used the largest standing stone as its eastern wall, the home that Father Thomas had converted into a church.

That was the source of the black aura and smell of death. How many had died because they couldn't tell Carradoc where I hid?

"My babies, the twins!" Deirdre screamed as she realized the significance of the structure that burned. "I have to go to them, help them . . . What can I do besides give you to him?"

"We must wait, Deirdre. I doubt Father Thomas was foolish enough to leave them in the village. Carradoc would have come galloping up the road, with banners flying and swords drawn. They had time to secrete the children elsewhere. Those villagers are in greater danger than the twins."

"My babies, where are they?" She looked around, as if she could see her children hiding in the woods. "I have to go to Carradoc and make him give back my children."

"Walking into Carradoc's trap won't save the children or the villagers. He'll torture and murder them anyway."

"Why? Why does he persecute them?" Fat tears ran down her cheeks. Despair weighed down her shoulders as much as those massive yokes had the villagers'.

"Because he can."

I had said the same thing about Nimuë once. She'd cause mischief whenever and wherever she could. She might very well be at the fortress with her father. Installed as his mistress and consort. I shuddered at the terrible wrongness of it. How many natural and man-made laws did they break every moment they breathed?

Carradoc had said once before that he believed in no god. He acknowledged no authority over him but superior strength.

"Arthur tamed him for a while," I continued my musing out loud. "The Ardh Rhi tamed the entire country, teaching all of us that 'because I can' is no longer a reason to break the law. To treat others as less than human just to prove one is more powerful, or more ruthless than another is not right or honorable. I have to stop Carradoc."

"Arthur isn't here to enforce the law. We don't even know if he is alive." Deirdre shook off her despair. Anger firmed her jaw and straightened her shoulders. A cold cunning came into her eyes. I'd seen the same look in Curyll's eyes as he plotted some new strategy.

"Arthur lives. I know it in my soul." I didn't know if he was victorious.

"Whatever we do, we have to wait for the cover of darkness. We need the darkness to drape shadows around us so we can slip into the fortress," I said.

"There is the tunnel leading from the cellars beneath the Long Hall. It travels underneath the tor. But you never let Yvain and me explore the full length," Deirdre mused.

"The original builders of the fortress used it as an escape route, in the case of siege or overwhelming attack. I found the tunnel entrance many years ago," I added. "We move out at twilight. Until then we rest and bathe at the pool. The faeries might have news."

I doubted Carradoc knew of the tunnel. Otherwise, long ago, he would have cleared the trees between the cave and the fortress so he could watch the entrance from the ramparts.

The spring burbled from the center of a jumble of boulders, cascading down to the small pool as it had always done. Constant as the cycle of sun and moon, the clear water poured forth without variance regardless of the season or weather. Deirdre and I drank deeply. The water tasted sweetly of home. We splashed some of the travel dust from our clothes and ourselves. Then we lay down in beds of bracken ferns.

I felt the Lady stir restlessly within the depths of the pool. The time was coming when Excalibur must be returned to her. She would fully awaken at the moment of Arthur's death, ready to receive the sword back.

I had no vision of whom she would choose to inherit the sword. Certainly not Mordred.

The faeries stayed away. They must have sensed the violence I harbored in my heart. Violence against Carradoc whom I had promised to love, honor, and obey till death do us part.

My body cried for rest. I hadn't had time to properly heal before this long journey. Part of me screamed with guilt. If only I'd left the cottage a day earlier, I could have prevented the pain and terror my villagers endured at the hands of my husband. If only I had defended myself better from Carradoc's beating. If only Newynog hadn't been in heat that day, she would have ripped out Carradoc's throat before he beat me. If only . . .

I heard faint rustling in the undergrowth. The trees whispered among themselves of people milling about the forest, aimless, lost. Branches and leaves drooped as the plant life absorbed the wanderers' sense of loss and grief. My villagers, fleeing Carradoc. The ones still able to get away.

"Come to me," I whispered into the lengthening shadows. "I need your help." With my fingertip, I idly drew sigils of attraction in the forest floor.

One by one, the people drew closer and closer.

As the sun set, a dozen shadowy forms joined us at the edge of the spring. I couldn't see any of the faces in the growing gloom. Deirdre leaped up, startled, then breathed her relief as she recognized people she had known all her life.

"Lady, we need your help," a man whispered. The miller, I knew him by his broad silhouette and the smell of flour that permeated his clothing.

"As I need yours. Do you have lamps or torches?"

Toutates, the blacksmith and grandson of the original smith I had known here, raised a long stick with dry rushes bound on one end. Others in the group did the same.

"Come." I beckoned them to follow me into the crystal cave. "We will light them when we are safely within the tunnel. The guards on the walls might see them through the trees from here."

Silently we slid one by one between two man-high boulders. I had no need of flint and iron. Fire leaped eagerly from my fingertips into the rush torches. My hands itched to release more flames.

More, Tanio whispered to me. *Unleash me,* the element demanded.

Later, I promised.

The tunnel twisted and climbed over a much longer route than a direct walk back to the fortress. The builders had used a partial cave system, dug other parts and shored it up with stone pillars of the same solid granite as the standing stones. I didn't know the tunnel well, had rarely used it after my initial exploration. Keeping the children from getting lost or trapped by cave-ins had been my primary concern.

The crystal cave did not entice us. No vision of the gräal or the marble altar drew me into its depths. None of the others looked twice into that side path when I directed them to move forward.

We climbed over new rock falls, jumped deep puddles that had collected, and stumbled over the broken pathway. Eventually we faced a steep ladder cut unevenly into the wall. Above the last step, a trapdoor blocked our passage into the sunken storage levels of the fortress. With a wave of my hand, I sent the blacksmith, the strongest among us, ahead to lift the trapdoor. I prayed that no one had barred it with heavy barrels of flour or salted mutton.

The big man stood on the fourth step from the top. He grunted loudly and pushed upward with both hands. The cramped space hindered his leverage. He moved up the staircase, pressing his back against the trapdoor. He heaved again. The wooden planks echoed his groan as they shifted a little and sank back into their accustomed position. He flexed his knees and rammed the trapdoor with a mighty effort.

I remembered my first Beltane festival among these people. This blacksmith's uncle, Llandoc, had outjumped Carradoc in the competition to lay with that year's Queen of the May—Marnia, Carradoc's own daughter. Llandoc had been beaten by Carradoc later and banished. The smith's family had many reasons to seek revenge against my husband. Toutates would use all of his strength if necessary to open the trapdoor.

Another determined push cracked the wooden planks. A few more shoves with his huge, callused hands cleared the opening.

I held my breath for several long moments while we all waited to see if the noise of our entry alerted the kitchen staff. No one came to investigate. We left our extinguished torches at the bottom of the stairs, not certain if we'd need them to guide a quick escape.

The open compound around the Great Hall was dark. The only soldiers I saw were the few who patrolled the palisades atop the wooden wall. I couldn't hope they would ignore my rescue attempt if they saw us, as Morgaine's warriors had overlooked me when I spirited my father out of Dun Edin.

A huge round of drunken laughter told us that everyone not on guard duty was in the Long Hall at the feast Carradoc would demand as his due.

Cautiously, I peeked into the hall from the cook's spyhole in the kitchen. The staff needed to know when to serve the next course, replenish the ale, or clear the tables. I needed to know who joined the feast—allies and enemies alike.

Nimuë, of course, sat at her father's left. Sitting, I couldn't tell if her spine twisted as painfully as before or not. Her gown was cut daringly low, exposing most of her breasts. She wore black lavishly embroidered with black demonic sigils. She leaned against Carradoc, laughing, flirtatious, flaunting the place she had always coveted—my place as consort to the lord. No other lover had satisfied her since her first joining at Beltane during her twelfth summer. Nimuë's son by Carradoc sat at her left. He glared at the assemblage with hard eyes that schemed thoughts I could not penetrate. His robe was also embroidered with the black symbols designed to attract denizens of the Netherworld. Neither of them wore the ostentatious crosses they had affected at Camlann.

At Carradoc's right sat Marnia and her husband Kalahart. They picked at their food and stared at their hands. Shame, fear, and outrage colored their auras. Kalahart carried no weapon beyond his table knife. None of my people were armed. Only the soldiers Carradoc had brought with him kept sword and ax at their sides.

In the center, near the fire pit, Father Thomas was lashed to a central pillar. His naked back looked like raw meat. A scarred soldier, whose lips curled up in a constant sneer, dangled a whip from his hands. I remembered the man from Mordred's entourage. He took more delight in blood and pain than food or sex.

Four other villagers huddled in the far corner, still bound to their yokes, awaiting their turn at the lash.

"I ask you again, Priest," Carradoc barked at the limp figure sagging from his bonds. "Where have you hidden the whore and her unnatural child?"

The snap of the whip jerked my gaze back to Father Thomas. That good and gentle man didn't utter a sound, too far gone in his pain to recognize more. My own back burned in empathy with him. I saw his lips move silently in prayer.

"By all the gods, we have to get him out of there!" I whispered harshly.

"We could rush in and take them by surprise," the blacksmith suggested. "They are drunk and won't reach for weapons until we are in and out again."

"No. They are drunk, but they are trained warriors. We don't stand a chance with a direct attack," I replied. I looked at Deirdre for suggestions. Her sire, after all, was one of the greatest military minds of this generation, maybe for five or more generations.

She stared back at me, dazed and bewildered. Her life had been sheltered. She hadn't encountered the terrible slaughter of the Saxons that I had seen. She didn't know how to think when faced with the cruelty of men maddened by power.

"Deirdre, your talent is mind speech," I roused her from whatever thoughts trapped her mind. "Speak to Marnia, she is receptive to you. Tell her to be alert, ready to grab the others and flee at the first sign of trouble."

"What are you going to do, Mama?" she asked.

"I'm not certain yet." I looked around for a weapon or an idea. Deirdre's talent was mind speech. Yvain's talent was communication with animals. Da communicated with the future.

What could I do? My talents were small pieces of many things. But I communicated best with the elements. Pridd, Awyr, Tanio, and Dwfr.

Tanio begged for more fuel than rushlights. I'd used it as a weapon before, to kill a demon and to provide a diversion at Dun Edin. That Long Hall was mostly wood and thatch, and not mine. Caer Noddfa had been rebuilt bit by bit with stone. But the ceilings, floors, and support beams were still wood. And the roof was last year's thatch.

The central hearth burned high and bright, warming even this narrow passageway. The hall itself must be sweltering. And all those soldiers still wore armor, some of it leather, some of it mail. All of it heavy.

I closed my eyes and concentrated on Tanio, inviting its flames to climb higher, seek new fuel elsewhere. In my mind I showed Tanio how to invade the roofing with a single spark, where the ceiling beams were weakening from age and improper curing. This was my home. I knew every niche and cranny that was vulnerable. My home. And I sacrificed it willingly.

"Blacksmith, carry Father Thomas to safety. Deirdre, guide Marnia. Miller, cut the prisoners free from their yokes," I ordered, watching the smoke gather between the roof beams.

Father Thomas had to endure three more strikes from the whip. The soldier who wielded the weapon as if a toy, was growing bored by the lack of response from the priest. Carradoc drank more deeply, frustrated by his torture.

"Dump the priest in the midden and tie up the woman. Strip her first. I want the whip to tickle her tits and her thatch." Carradoc licked his lips and leaned forward.

His soldiers pushed Mary, Father Thomas' young and pretty granddaughter, forward, removing the yoke as they walked. Mary stretched her shoulders and flexed her arms as much as the men allowed. Free at last from the punishingly heavy yoke.

Nimuë leaned forward, nearly falling out of her bodice in anticipation of Carradoc's arousal from inflicting pain.

Marnia's face turned white with dread. She put her hand to her mouth. She darted glances all around like a deer trapped by hunting dogs.

"Please, Tanio, do your work quickly," I pleaded with my mind and whispered voice.

Smoke piled up near the ceiling, too heavy to filter through the smoke hole.

The torturer ripped Mary's bodice the length of her back. He fondled her breasts as he exposed them to the full view of every amoral man in the hall.

"Faster, Tanio. Please, we have to stop this travesty."

The whip cracked. Mary screamed. My heart tore, sharing her agony and humiliation.

Flames crackled. Smoke thickened. I tasted it. My eyes smarted and filled with grit.

A rumble of surprise rose in the Great Hall. Chairs scraped the wooden floor. Voices rose.

Tanio laughed across my mind, thanking me for guidance to new fuel.

I opened my eyes and looked through the spy hole. Confusion reigned. People hurried in circles. Smoke gathered into thick swirls around eyes and noses and mouths.

"Now," I hissed and pushed open the door. I held my breath and covered my nose and mouth with a piece of my skirt.

"Help me!" Mary screamed. "Someone untie me!"

I aimed straight for her. Foreign soldiers and my own people milled around in confusion, blocking my direct pathway. I couldn't distinguish faces in the darkness. For all the fire in the room, not much light penetrated the smoke. Blindly I pushed aside anyone still on their feet. They could find their own way out. The prisoners couldn't.

Someone opened the double doors. Air rushed in, fanning Tanio to new heights. In the momentary brightness, I fought my way to the central pillar. Three slashes of my belt knife freed the sobbing woman from the post. I guided her back the way I had come.

Angry shouts and scuffling feet drew my attention to the dais. Toutates plunged a long dagger into Carradoc's back.

I flinched. Then the miller grabbed the dagger and added his own blow. The rest of my villagers stood in line to murder their lord. I had to stop this. I'd never left an injury untreated. I'd never allowed anyone to die.

Mary lost strength in her knees, nearly dragging me to the overly hot flooring. I had to get her out.

"Carradoc, I divorce you," I shouted for the third and final time and turned my back on him.

Nimuë rushed past me, pulling her son by the hand. She ran crouched over, heaving huge sobs. I still couldn't tell if her back could straighten or not. The young man followed her eagerly. Neither looked at Mary or me. Nor had they paused to help Carradoc. I saw Deirdre, Marnia, and Kalahart duck into the kitchen passage. I followed.

Seconds later a roof beam crashed to the floor, shooting flames and debris in all directions.

Chapter 65

"YOU must flee Mordred's wrath," Father Thomas said weakly. Blood dribbled from his mouth as we laid him facedown on a pallet of soft ferns and old cloaks beside the spring and pool.

I bathed his poor back with fresh water from the enchanted pool.

"Do not waste your strength with words, Father Thomas," I hushed him. "I've sent for your wife and son."

"He's right, Wren," Marnia said. She wrung her hands in worry, but her voice was clear and matter-of-fact. "Morgaine and Nimuë will push Mordred to chase after you. They'll burn this entire forest to flush you out."

"I can't leave you all here to suffer at the hands of another tyrant," I replied. "Carradoc was bad enough. Mordred and his mother will be worse."

"We can fend for ourselves, Wren. Take Deirdre and the twins and flee. Take a boat to Ireland, or find refuge in the mountains of Dyfed," Kalahart urged, touching my shoulder in sympathy and regret. "Many will shelter the daughter of The Merlin. They still remember him in the mountains and secret hollows of Britain. We'll scatter in all directions. Mordred will have too many to follow."

"How many did we lose in the fire? I have to tend the wounded. It will take time for a message to get to Mordred." I continued my grisly task, wishing for some betony, willow bark, and mullein.

"Too many of Mordred's soldiers survived. They ride to Campboglanna to summon their master as we speak," Kalahart said. "Mordred and his mother may have seen the flames from Campboglanna. You have no time, Wren." He lifted me from my crouch beside Father Thomas. He shook my shoulders gently to emphasize his concern.

"I can't leave until you are all safe. I won't leave you . . ."

"Wren," Marnia interrupted. "We can disappear into the forest, into the hills. Mordred won't find anything but a razed fortress and a deserted village. You must flee, though. Take the royal seal he seeks. He needs Arthur's seal. The client kings demand Arthur's seal—not a new one."

"How many did we lose?" I asked again. My stepdaughter and friend made sense. But I had to know the ugly truth of my vengeance against Carradoc. "How many did I kill with that fire?" I couldn't think beyond the cost to my village of Carradoc's anger.

"We think only Carradoc, may demons eat his soul," Kalahart replied. "We haven't had time to count."

Just then, Father Thomas' wife and son bustled into the clearing, sobbing and frightened. The wife gasped and rushed to her husband's side. She crossed herself repeatedly, sobbing loudly through her prayers.

"Go. Wren. With my blessing," Father Thomas gasped. A restless rattle rose from his chest, choking his last breath from him.

"Bury him here." I closed my eyes to control my grief. "Build a church dedicated to him. Make a tomb in the foundations for his grave. Make it a stone church. A big stone church that will last two thousand years."

"Bless you, Lady," the wife said. "Bless you and thank you. But go. Now. Before we have to make a place for you in the tomb as well."

Time rocked me forward and back. I would join my old friend in the tomb soon enough. And Arthur would be placed at my side.

Another pool in a deep forest where faeries played drew me southward. I returned to the haunts of my childhood, near the home of Lord Ector and Lady Glynnis. I and my daughter and my two grandchildren built a circular hut of lashed branches, half-sunk into the ground beside the remains of the fallen log I had danced across so many years ago. We told no one of our coming, not even Berminia who sheltered with Lord Ector and Lady Glynnis while she waited for Cai to return. Deirdre and I lived quietly, gleaning a living from the rich forest. Newynog hunted for us when we needed meat.

My villagers had given us anonymous clothing and staples to feed us for a while. We lived simply, almost happily through the long summer. Then one morning we awoke to a nip in the air and storm clouds gathering in the West. We would have another day of fine weather, perhaps two, before autumn descended upon us in full force.

As long as the weather remained dry, armies could march to battle. Arthur still had a chance to defeat Mordred this campaign season.

Cedar and his companions came to me, one by one, at the pool where we had taught Curyll to speak without a stutter. The doorways between our worlds had nearly closed forever. Only a few faery folk could slip through at a time. Our world was much too cold for them to stay long, even on a warm day.

Other portals to other worlds opened even as the gateway to Annwn closed. But I would miss the faery folk.

Each day, I asked the wind and the trees for news. *Change,* they called back to me. *Change.*

Nothing more. I shivered in fear. Arthur's reign of peace, justice, and rule by law was coming to an end. Who would keep a balance in Britain when he died? What would come next?

Change.

At noon the trees whispered, *He comes.*

"Who," I asked.

The one you wait for.

I hurried to meet Curyll by the pool. He had known where to look when no one else could find me. Perhaps the faeries allowed him and no one else to penetrate to their pool.

He dismounted from his great white stallion wearily and rested his forehead against the saddle. "I owe you an apology, Wren," he said without preamble.

"Curyll, are you well?"

Worry lines cut deeply into the corners of his mouth and eyes. His hair showed more silver than gold and his shoulders sagged with defeat. His great sword, Excalibur, seemed too heavy for him to lift from its jeweled sheath across his back.

"I'm tired. Tired of fighting, tired of stumbling in the dark without guidance, tired of living."

"I'm sorry, Curyll. Did you lose in Armorica?"

"No," he snorted a laugh. "I won the battle but lost everything I

held dear—my wife, my friend. My faith in mankind and my kingdom, too."

"Guinevere?"

"Entered a house of holy sisters. She'll stay there as long as she
lives."

"Lancelot?"

"Wandering in some forest, living as a holy hermit, half mad with
guilt."

"My son Yvain?"

"Waiting with Lord Ector and Lady Glynnis for my return. He's
safe. He's loyal and true. I trust him more than any man living. But
Gyron, Deirdre's husband, is dead. He died honorably in battle. He'll
never see his children grow. . . ." He choked and leaned more heavily
against his horse.

"And you?" I asked him, reaching a tentative hand to brush the
lines of fatigue and worry from his face. "How do you fare, truly?"

"I returned home to find my honored nephew had declared me
dead and usurped my crown. I find my government in chaos, the
great seal missing, and you outlawed with a huge price on your head."

"I have the seal. I've kept it safe for you."

"Keep it safe a while longer. I trust you to know what to do with
it when the time comes."

"What will you do now?"

"I meet Mordred in pitched battle two days hence, at Campboglanna. He holds the fortress and is backed by Uriens' army and a
horde of Picts from the North. I stormed Camlann and won back my
capital. Nimuë and Morgaine poisoned each other rather than face
my justice. I have no idea what happened to Nimuë's son. He was not
among the dead or captured. I have but one more foul nest to clean
out before I can call Britain mine again. Before we are all safe from
the forces of darkness."

Once again the vision of his death shook me to the core. The two
of us lying side by side in a tomb, not quite touching—separated in
death as we had been in life.

"Curyll." I held out my arms to him, needing to hold him close
one more time.

"I'm sorry, Wren. I should have listened to you. I should never
have trusted Mordred." He enfolded me tightly, nearly bruising my
still healing ribs with the fierceness of his grief. "You still have twigs

in your hair and grass stains on your skirt." He tried to chuckle and failed.

I held him just as tightly, pressing his heart close to mine, hearing them beat in unison. Tears burned my eyes. I blinked them back. Curyll needed me strong and confident.

"Of all those I held dear, you are the only one who never broke your promises, Wren. Only you. I should have respected that."

A lump in my throat blocked any reply. I kissed his cheek instead.

"I ask only one more promise from you, Wren."

"Anything within my power. You have only to ask."

"Don't let my dreams die. See that the next generation, and the next, hears the stories of a time when laws and peace and justice worked. Make sure they know that trust and honor and promises mean something. Maybe then, sometime in the future, those ideals will mean something again."

I nodded my acceptance. My tears flowed unchecked. Or were they his?

"Promise me, Wren. Promise by the life of your faeries. Seal it in a circle."

We kissed then, hungrily, desperately, needing to reaffirm the love we had known since early childhood. Together we spun in a circle, locked together, promising each other.

The past and the present became one with the future. My life pattern became complete.

Faeries flew about our heads, widening the circle of promise to include all of the beings of forest and field, of this world and the next.

EPILOGUE

"PROMISE me, Deirdre, promise that your children and grandchildren and all of our descendants will know what Arthur Pendragon stood for," my mother gasped between the racking pains of a difficult childbirth.

"Hush, Mama, save your strength," I said, mopping her fevered brow with a cool cloth. "Rest."

Her eyes drooped momentarily. Then another pain ripped through her swollen belly. She screamed, unable to contain her labor pains.

"Promise me!" She clutched my hand hard enough to crush the bones.

"I promise, Mama. And I will teach all of the descendants of Arthur that justice, peace, and rule by law can work. That honor, loyalty, and promises mean something," I replied.

Mama shouldn't have conceived this late in her life. Forty is too old to bear children. Especially after the mess I made of her insides when she birthed me. She shouldn't have carried the babe to term. It was killing her. But this was Arthur's child, as I am, conceived at their last meeting before the final battle between the Ardh Rhi and his bastard son/nephew, Mordred.

Ever since Mama followed Arthur to that bloody field and watched Mordred run him through with a sword, her will to live died with the only man she had ever loved. That Arthur retained enough strength to then slay Mordred with Excalibur amazed all who witnessed the feat. All except my mother. She had seen their deaths the night before. She knew how it would end. And still she watched.

She tried working the great healing magic. My young daughter is still a maiden, I am a matron, and Mama acted the crone. But she isn't a crone yet. She is still a matron, carrying Arthur's child.

The magic failed. Arthur died in her arms. I think Mama truly died at that moment. Her body continued to live only to bear this new babe.

She claimed Arthur's golden torc for the new babe. Yvain wears grandda's.

We took Arthur back to the new church in the woods. We buried him in the crypt with Father Thomas. Mama made us carve the tomb large enough for two. She would lie beside her king in death when she hadn't been allowed to stand beside him in life.

She ordered me not to give her body to a funeral pyre that would release her spirit to a new life. She needs to lie beside Arthur for eternity.

My brother, Yvain, took Excalibur and threw the legendary sword into the pool beside the church so that no other could use it to claim authority in Britain. It disappeared in a flash of white light. I thought I saw a feminine arm, clothed in white samite, sparkling rings on the fingers, reach through the starburst and clasp the sword. Both the arm and sword sank into the unknown depths of the dark water.

Yvain wanted to throw the Pendragon seal after the sword, but Mama made him keep it for the next Ardh Rhi.

Enough of the client kings who stood against Mordred believed the rumors that Arthur had sired Yvain to elect him Ardh Rhi. He has Cai and Bedewyr, both aged beyond their years and badly wounded in the last battle, as his councillors.

But my brother is a gentle soul. He has not the ruthlessness, the keen-eyed vision to hold this fractured land together. Grandda's torc is too big for him.

The Saxons gather for invasion once again. The client kings squabble and challenge each other.

Change has come to Britain. Very little of it good. And when Mama dies, as she surely must with the birth of this babe, my life will change irrevocably. I will have responsibilities to family, and village, to the land and the gods, that I'm not certain I want. We have begun rebuilding Caer Noddfa. Britain needs a place of sanctuary.

I have not my mother's tenacity, or her wisdom to do aught but offer a refuge. Each of us must find our own inner peace and balance.

"We are also descended from The Merlin," Mama whispered

through parched lips. Her strength waned. She waited through another pain and a great gush of blood to continue. "I have taught you all I know of magic, of the faeries, and the Goddess. Teach this to our children as well. Don't let them lose contact with the land. For the land is the source of our magic."

"Push, Mama. The baby's coming."

"Promise me you will teach them all!" She panted, holding back the effort to bring the child into the world.

"Push, Mama."

"Promise me and seal it in a circle, Deirdre," she said with more strength than I thought she had left in her.

"I promise, Mama." I drew a circle on her distended belly, sealing the baby into the promise as well as my mother and myself. My beloved mother, dying. . . . "Now push out the baby and live to mother him." *Live for us both. I still need you, Mama. Britain still needs you.*

"You are the Pendragon and The Merlin of this family now, Deirdre. Teach Arthur's son well. Teach him where we come from and how to look at the future and change it for the better."

"I promise, Mama. One more push and he will be born."

The baby came then with more blood, protesting his rude entrance into the world. As I held him up for Mama to see, her eyes lit briefly with joy. "Arthur. My Curyll." She smiled and passed into another world.

I hope she flies with her faeries, watching over my shoulder, guiding me through this life.

"I promise, little Arthur. You shall know how to carry on the legacy of the Pendragon and The Merlin. I have faith in you, little brother." I sealed the promise in a circle of blood and tears upon his newborn face.